WINGS OF ICE AND FIRE COLLECTION

G. BAILEY

WINGS OF

ICE AND FIRE

COLLECTION

USA TODAY BESTSELLING AUTHOR

❀ Created with Vellum

Four Dragon Guards. Three Curses. Two Heirs. One Choice...
Forbidden love or the throne of the dragons?

Isola Dragice thought she knew what her future would bring. Only, one earth-shattering moment destroys everything.

When war threatens her home, Isola returns from earth to the world of dragons she knows nothing about, and to Dragca Academy.
When the four most powerful dragon guards in history are ordered to protect her, they didn't expect to be protecting an accident prone princess. One who, accidentally, nearly kills her whole class at Dragca Academy in her first week.

What happens when fire falls for Ice?

18+ **Reverse harem romance**

Book One of Five.

PROLOGUE

Everything inside me screams as I run through the doors of the castle, seeing the dead dragons lining the floors, the view making me sick to my stomach. I try not to look at the spears in their stomachs, the dragonglass that is rare in this world. *Where did they get it?* The more and more bodies I pass, both dragon and guards, the less hope I have that my father is okay. *No, I can't be too late, I can't lose him, too.* The once grand doors to the throne room are smashed into pieces of stone, in a pile on the floor, and only the hinges to the door still hang on the walls. I run straight over, climbing over the rocks and broken stone. The sight in front of me makes me stop, not believing what I'm seeing, but I know it's true.

"Father . . .?" I plead quietly, knowing he won't reply to me. My father is sitting on his throne, a sword through his stomach, and an open-mouthed expression on his face. His blood drips down onto the gold floors of the throne room, and snow falls from the broken ceiling onto his face. There's no ice in here, no sign he even tried to fight before he was killed. He must not have seen it coming; he trusted whoever killed him.

"No," is all I can think to say as I fall to my knees, bending my head and looking down at the ground instead of at the body of my father. *I couldn't stop this, even after he warned me and risked everything.* I hear footsteps in front of me as I watch my tears drip onto the ground, but I don't look up. I know who it is. I know from the way they smell, my dragon whispers to me their name, but I can't even think it.

"Why?" I ask, even as everything clicks into place. I should have known; I should have never trusted him.

"Because the curse has to end. Because he was no good for Dragca. Our city needs a true heir, me. I'm the heir of fire and ice, the one the prophecy speaks of, and it's finally time I took what is mine," he says, and every word seems to cut straight through my heart. *I trusted him.*

"The curse hasn't ended, I'm still here," I whisper to the dragon in front of me, but I know he can hear my words as if I had just spoken them into his ear.

"Not for long, not even for a moment longer, actually. Your dragon guard will only thank me when you are gone. I didn't want to do this to you, not in the end, but you are too powerful. You are of no use to me anymore, not unless you're gone," he says. I look down at the ground as his words run around my head, and I don't know what to do. I feel lost, powerless, and broken in every way possible. There's a piece of the door in front of me that catches my attention, a part with the royal crest on it. The dragon in a circle, a proud, strong dragon. My father's words come back to me, and I know they are all I need to say.

"There's a reason ice dragons hold the throne and have for centuries. There is a reason the royal name Dragice is feared," I say and stand up slowly, wiping my tears away.

"We don't give up, and we bow to no one. I'm Isola Dragice, and you will pay for what you have done," I tell him as I finally meet his now cruel eyes, before calling my dragon and feeling her take over.

1

ISOLA

"Isola!" I hear shouted from the stairs, but I keep my headphones on as I stare at my laptop, and pretend I didn't hear her shout my name for the tenth time. The music blasts around my head as I try to focus on the history paper that is due tomorrow.

"Isola, will you take those things out and listen to me?" Jules shouts at me again, and I pop one of my headphones out as I look up at her. She stands at the end of my bed, her hands on her hips, and her glasses perched on the end of her nose. Her long grey hair is up in a tight bun, and she has an old-style dress that looks like flowers threw up on it. Jules is my house sitter, or babysitter as I like to call her. I don't think I need a babysitter at seventeen, not when I'm eighteen in a while anyway, and can look after myself.

"Both headphones out, I want them both out while you listen to me," she says. I knew this was coming. I pull the headphones out and pause the music on my phone.

"I did try to clean up after the party, I swear," I say, and she raises her eyebrows.

"How many teenagers did you have in here? Ten? A

hundred?" she says, and I shrug my shoulders as I sit up on the bed and cross my legs.

"I don't know, it's all a little fuzzy," I reply honestly. My head is still pounding; it was probably the wine, or maybe the tequila shots. *Who knows?* I look up again as she shakes her head at me, speaking a sentence in Spanish that she knows I can't understand, but I doubt it's nice. I don't think I want to hear what she has to say about the party I threw last night anyway. I look around my simple room, seeing the dressing table, the wardrobe, and the bed I'm sitting on. There isn't much in here that is personal, no photos or anything that means anything to me.

"Miss Jules, looking as beautiful as always," Jace says, in an overly sweet tone as he walks into my bedroom. He walks straight over to Jules and kisses her cheek, making her giggle. Jace is that typical hot guy, with his white-blonde hair and crystal-blue eyes. Even my sixty-year-old house sitter can't be mad at him for long, he can charm just about anyone.

"Don't start with that pouty cute face," she tuts at him, and he widens his arms, pretending to be shocked.

"What face? I always look like this," he says, and she laughs, any anger she had disappearing.

"I'm going to clean up this state of a house, and you should leave, you're going to be late for school. I don't want to have to tell your father that as well, when I tell him about the party," she says, pointing a finger at me, and I have to hold in the urge to laugh. She emails my father all the time about everything I do, but he never responds. He just pays her to keep the house running and to make sure I don't get into too much trouble. If he hasn't had the time to talk to me in the last ten years, I doubt he's going to have the time to email a human he hired. Jules walks out of the room, and Jace leans against the wall, tucking his hands into his pockets. I run my eyes over his tight jeans, his white shirt that has ridden up a little to show his toned stomach, and finally to his handsome face that is smirking at me. *He knows exactly what he does to me.*

"You look too sexy when you do that," I comment, and he grins.

"Isn't that the point? Now come and give your boyfriend a kiss," he teases, and I fake a sigh before getting up and walking over to him. I lean up, brushing my lips against his cold ones, and he smiles, kissing me back just as gently.

"We should go, but I was wondering if you wanted to go to the mountains this weekend and try some flying?" he asks. I blank my expression before walking away from him and towards the mirror hanging on the wall near the door. I smooth my wavy, shoulder-length blonde hair down, and it just bounces back up, ignoring me. My blue eyes stare back at me, bright and crystal-clear. Jace says it's like looking into a mirror when he looks into my eyes, they are so clear. I check out my jeans and tank top, and grab my leather coat from where it hangs on the back of the door before answering Jace.

"I've got a lot of homework to do–" I say, and he shakes his head as he cuts me off.

"Issy, when was the last time you let her out? It's been, what, months?" he asks, and I turn away, walking out through my bedroom door and hearing him sigh behind me.

"Issy, we can't avoid this forever. Not when we have to go back in two weeks," he reminds me, and I stop, leaning my head back against the plain white walls of the corridor.

"I know we have to go back. We have to train to rule a race we know nothing about, just because of who our parents are. Don't you ever want to run away, hide in the human world we have been left in all these years?" I ask, feeling a grumble of anger from my dragon inside my mind. I quickly slam down the barrier between me and my dragon in my head, stopping her from contacting me, no matter how much it hurts me to do so. *I can't let her control me.*

"Issy, we were left here so we would be safe. We are the last ice dragons, and our parents had no choice. Plus . . . being a dragon around humans is a nightmare, you know that," he says, stepping closer to me.

"I don't want to rule; I don't want anything to do with Dragca," I say, looking away.

"I guess it's lucky we have each other, ruling on our own would have been a disaster," he says, stepping in front of me so I can't move and gently kissing my forehead.

"I know. I just don't want to go back to see my father and everything that has to come with it," I say, and he steps back to tilt my head up to look at him.

"You're the heir to the throne of the dragons. You're the princess of Dragca. Your life was never meant to be lived here, with the humans," he says, and I move away from him, not replying because I know he sees it differently than I do. He is the ice prince, and his parents call him every week until they disappeared when he was twelve and he knows they loved him. I haven't spoken to any of my family in ten years, and I have never stepped back into Dragca since then. It's the only thing we disagree on, our future.

"Issy, let's just have a good day, and then, maybe, I could get you that peanut bacon sandwich you love from the deli?" he suggests, running to catch up with me on the stairs.

"Now you're talking," I grin at him as he hooks an arm around my waist, and leans down to whisper in my ear.

"And maybe later, I could do that thing with my tongue that you–" he gets cut off when Jules opens the door in front of us, clearing her throat, and ushering us out as we laugh.

"LITTLE ISSY, are you coming to my party this weekend? I know I'd love to show you my house and–" Michael asks as he stops me outside my English class, but I'm not listening to whatever he is saying. When I hear the bell ring, relief that it's the last class of the day fills me. Learning human things all day isn't fun, especially when you know you won't ever need to know any of it. The only class I love is my study period, where I can go to the library and find a new book to live in. I lift my bag on my shoulder and look around Michael for Jace, not seeing him anywhere. I look down at my arm as Michael steps closer, and he strokes a hand down it, making me shiver, but not in the good way.

"I don't know, I would have to ask Jace and see if he wants to go, but I don't think he likes you. Also, I'm not little, short is a better word," I say plainly, wanting to get as far away from Michael as possible. Michael is a good-looking human with black hair and is covered in tattoos, which I usually find attractive, but my dragon still wants to eat him, so even being friends with him would be a disaster. Plus, Jace would kill him if he saw how Michael was touching my arm. Dragons see their future mates as treasures, precious, and they don't share often.

"He doesn't own you; you could come alone," Michael snaps, clearly not happy I don't want to sneak off to his stupid frat-boy party.

"Why would I do that?" I ask the idiot football player, as I try to move away. I shove his hand off my arm, turning and walking away before he can reply.

"Because you're so much better than him. Come to my party!" he shouts at me, and everyone stops to look at us. They begin whispering, stupid rumours that will spread around the school by tomorrow. I don't even know Michael really, he's just another human I grew up with, and I know he isn't acting like himself. It's the dragon side of me that is attracting him, and every male human in this damn school. That's why I have always stayed close to Jace's side; male dragons have the opposite effect on humans. All the humans are scared of him here, everyone except for Jules. I stand on my tiptoes as I look around, before remembering Jace's last class was sports management on the other side of the building. I walk out of the school, going around the main entrance and see the gym across the field. I walk slowly across it, just thinking he must have had a shower or something after class, and he is running late. I stop dead in my tracks when I pick up an unfamiliar scent in the mixture of human smells. I smell a dragon, a fire dragon that shouldn't be here.

"Let me out," my dragon hisses in my mind. I slam the barrier down again, holding my head when she fights me, making me have to stop running towards the gym.

"Enough, Jace needs me!" I shout at her in my head, and she stops fighting instantly as she realises that I won't let her out and I can't help Jace like this. Overwhelming worry for Jace is the only thing coming from her as I run, and it floods my own emotions, nearly strangling me with panic. I run towards the door, push it open, and run across the small room that leads to the gym. I open the doors and immediately freeze at the sight in front of me, until a loud scream rips from my throat, and I fall to my knees. Even then, I can't believe it, not until the pain threatens to strangle me, not until I can't see anything other than the truth that is lying right in front of me.

"NO!" I scream out, my dragon's roar following my words as her sorrow and shock mixes with mine. In the middle of the room is Jace, a large red dagger sticking out of his heart, his head is fallen to the side, facing me with wide eyes in the dimly-lit room. I can't look away from his eyes, open in shock as blood drips from his mouth and makes a tiny noise as it hits the floor. I force myself to look away from his eyes, only to look at the blood that makes a circle around him, so much blood that pours from the wound. I crawl across the gym floor, tears running from my eyes, and I don't stop, even as my hands get covered in his blood once I get to him. I pull his head onto my lap, stroking a blood-stained finger across his cheek.

"No! Jace, baby, wake up. Please don't do this to me," I plead, my hand shaking against his cheek as he remains still. I know he is dead, my dragon and I both know it, but I can't believe it. Everything in me feels like it's breaking into a million pieces. I hear footsteps behind me, but I can't look away from Jace, as I raise my hand and close his eyes, leaving bloody fingerprints on his eyelids. I take a deep breath, committing to memory the smell of the fire dragon that did this to Jace.

"I vow revenge, I vow to never let this be forgotten. I will always love you," I whisper, my tears falling onto his face as I press my forehead to his, and then scream and scream, until my throat cracks.

"Don't. Let her say goodbye, we have time," I hear a male voice say behind me. I turn and look over my shoulder, the shock from everything just seeming to merge together as I see my father standing at the door. Ten royal guards stand around him, and his ice-blue eyes watch me. There's no sorrow or remorse in my father's eyes, not that I honestly expected anything else from him.

"Time to leave, there is nothing to be done here, Isola," he tells me. I look back at Jace, not wanting to let him go, but knowing my father's suggestion to leave wasn't really a suggestion at all. I have to go; whoever did this to Jace would kill me in a heartbeat.

"Isola, we must leave. Danger is near," my father warns me once more, and I gently rest Jace's body on the floor.

"I love you, and I'm so sorry I wasn't here. That I couldn't save you," I whisper. As I lean down and kiss Jace's cold cheek, another sob escapes me, and I wipe my eyes.

"Give him a true dragon's burial, or I will not leave," I warn my father as I stand up, blood sticking to both my clothes and my hands. I step back, seeing a young guard my age come to stand next to me. I look up into his hazel eyes, the only part of his body that I can see, thanks to the black uniform that covers his head and all of his body. The only other colour is the ice-blue dragon crest over his heart. All the dragon guards wear uniforms like this in the human world, and what I remember of them in Dragca is not much different.

"You have my vow," he says, and something makes me believe him as we stare at each other. I step back, turning and walking over to my father after one last look at Jace. My father stands tall as he holds a hand out for me, like I'm a child that needs his comfort. I ignore his hand and stand in front of him, feeling the dragon guards close ranks around us.

"I am sorry we were late, we didn't know of the threat until it was too late," he says. I don't say a word, I can't. Jace is dead; my dragon mate and the dragon I was meant to marry. We should have run away, not stayed here.

"What will be done now? There are no ice dragons other than you and me," I comment, needing to focus on anything other than the broken feeling in my heart, as the smell of smoke fills the air. The dragon guard will be burning Jace's body, and the thought makes me want to crumble onto the ground.

"Remember that our bodies are just shells for our dragons, that Jacian will be free to fly the night skies, and you will see him again one day," my father offers advice, and I still stand completely silent. I watch tiny red sparks float into the air around the gym, the soul of Jace leaving this world. They disappear slowly; each time they go, it shatters me a little bit. *No words will take away the pain that is crushing my heart.*

2

ISOLA

"Tell me, what happened today? How did Jacian end up dead?" my father asks me in a disappointed tone, as we walk through the forest behind my home and towards the portal to Dragca. I look down at my red coat, wondering which student the guard stole it from as I pull it closer around myself. I look down at my still blood-covered hands, Jace's blood, and I almost trip on a rock as the image of his dead body flashes into my head. *He is really gone.*

"Why don't you tell me why you are here early? Did you know this would happen?" I ask him, knowing it's no coincidence that he turned up early, just as Jace was killed. *My Jace is gone.* As I wipe more tears away, I think about how I won't be able to kiss him again, how I won't be waking up next to him anymore. The boy I grew up with, fell in love with . . . is gone.

"I asked first," he replies, and I turn to look over at him as he walks at my side. My father's white hair is cut short, his white crown sparkles in the sun. He has a black cloak that slides across the ground, with blue embroidered edges and the dragon crest on the chest. He looks every bit the king I remember, but not my father.

"Nothing abnormal happened, it was a normal day," I reply, looking forward again, I feel the portal magic as we draw closer.

"What of Jules?" I ask, after he doesn't reply to me for a long time.

"Who?" he answers with a question, and I shake my head with a low laugh. I was right, he never read a single one of the hundreds of emails, or checked in on me once over the years. I used to pretend that he couldn't come to me because it wasn't safe, and that maybe he was watching me from a distance. Or talking to Jules about me. *I guess I was wrong.*

"The house sitter, the woman you left me with, the one who brought me up?" I ask, trying not to snap at him.

"Oh, we have left a decent amount of human money for her, she is now retired, which I'm sure she is happy about," he waves me off, clearly not caring at all.

"I wish I could have said goodbye," I say quietly.

"She is just a human, they would not care for goodbyes if they knew what you really are, Isola. Plus, we have bigger issues to focus on," he says, stopping the conversation, and I smile tightly. I'm guessing feelings are not something my father cares about.

"Fine. How did you know we were going to be attacked?" I ask him.

"The royal seer had a vision, a dragon death, but I didn't know which one of you or what time it would be. We came as soon as possible," he replies, his tone is so calm, as he talks about his only child possibly dying, or the man she was due to mate with. I look away as tears start slowly falling down my cold cheeks, wiping them on my coat.

"You must not cry anymore, you must be strong as we return to Dragca. Enemies watch us at all times," he scolds me as I continue to cry. A feeling of numbness spreads over me, just holding myself together until I can be alone and let my feelings out. He has a point, I know my life is in danger, and I can't die now. Jace will have died for nothing if I die, too, and no one would remember him like I do.

"You can't tell me how to feel," I snap, feeling my dragon weeping in my mind. She doesn't even try to contact me anymore, just sits quietly, and that is very unlike her. She feels like I do, broken, and I don't put the barrier up between us, letting her emotions mix with my own.

"I am not telling you what to feel, only how to act. You are Isola Dragice. The powerful princess we have waited for," he grabs my arm to stop me walking. "Act like it. Don't shame Jace's memory," he tells me firmly, and all the guards stop to wait for us as we stare at each other. I look into my father's frosty blue eyes, the coldness of them having nothing to do with the ice dragon inside of him. He is just cold-hearted, just like I remember him being. I never had the loving father, and I don't expect that from him now. It still stings that he demands what I do, how I should act, when he knows nothing of me.

"Are we going to the castle?" I ask, changing the subject, and shoving his hand off my arm. He pauses, looking down at me strangely for a second, before turning away.

"No, we are going to Dragca Academy. The castle is not safe enough for you at the moment. The academy is, and you must learn about your world before you take the throne," he says, making me go silent. It was never the plan to go to Dragca Academy; a school full of fire dragons is no place for an ice dragon like me.

"Father, I was meant to take the throne in two weeks, what has changed?" I ask.

"I will explain more when we get to Dragca," he replies, looking around at the dragon guards. I nod in understanding. He doesn't want to tell me when so many of the dragon guard could hear. I pause as I spot the portal, a yellow wall that shimmers in between some tall trees that look like all the others here. Humans cannot see it, and even if they got close, the portal naturally pushes them away. It makes them want to get away from it at all costs, even scaring the weak-minded humans. Some humans with strong minds have made it through the portal, but they can never find a way to return, and life in Dragca as a human isn't easy.

"In formation, the king and princess follow two guards through, and the others behind," a guard next to my father shouts, and we get into a line at his command. The guard in front whispers to the portal, telling it where we need to go. The guards keep their swords at their sides as we each walk towards the barrier. My father steps through in front of me, and I stop, freezing as a memory of when I last went through a portal flitters into my mind.

"YOU HAVE TO LET GO NOW," my father says, as I clutch his hand tightly and force myself to let go. He walks through the portal, and I follow, trying not to jump at the cold feeling. I pull my cloak closer around myself as I walk towards my father where he is speaking with two guards.

"Take her to the house, and then travel a fair distance away before coming back to Dragca," he tells the guards. I look up at the snow falling from the sky, it lands on my nose, and I wipe it away as I wait.

"Go with them, Isola," my father tells me, not even looking my way, as he walks around me and towards the portal.

"Wait! Father, what is going on? Where are you going?"

"I have a world to rule, and you must stay here, stay alive. We will see each other again, Isola, and I will send information with the ice prince," he says, and I run after him only to be caught by a guard and picked up.

"Father, don't leave me like mother, please don't!" I scream, wiggling and trying to get the guard to put me down. My father looks back at me one more time, no compassion or anything loving for me to remember, as he disappears. I realize that not only did I lose my mother that year, but also my father.

"YOUR HIGHNESS?" a guard says, pressing a hand on my

shoulder, and I quickly shake myself out of the memory that haunted me for years, the heartless father who left me here in the human world and acted like I was forgotten. Jace was sent to me a few months later, with boxes of books and information on dragons. He got me to leave my room for the first time in a long time. He made me laugh, and explained that my father only did what he did to keep me safe. I step through the portal, feeling the cold magic push against my body, and then I open my eyes to the home I've not seen since I was eight.

Dragca Academy is right in the middle of the snowy mountains, and the only way to get in is to use a portal or fly. The academy, itself, is a huge castle with three towers, three levels of balconies for dragons to land on. There is a stone path leading to the doors, a side building with a stone battle field outside, which is covered in weapons in metal holders. There is what looks like an arena behind the castle, but I can't tell from here. I spot three other dragons walking around and one flying over the mountains in the distance, but they are only shadows from here. I look up at the stars, knowing it must be late here. Time is opposite on Earth and Dragca, as are the seasons and just about everything you can think of. Dragca has two suns and two moons in the sky. I look around to see the two moons, the large one and the tiny one by its side.

"My King," a woman says, distracting me from staring, and I turn around to see her walking down the steps of the castle. She has a dark-blue cloak on, the royal crest on a silver pin holding the cloak together. She lowers the hood, her long dark-red hair falling around her shoulders. She smiles widely as I try to think why she looks so familiar to me.

"Esmeralda, it is a pleasure to see you. You're as beautiful as I remember," my father says, taking her hand and kissing it, and I mentally roll my eyes when she laughs sweetly at him.

"It has been many years since you married my sister, and yet you are still the charmer," she says, making me remember why she looks so familiar now. She is my step-aunt and the headmaster of Dragca Academy, if I remember right. I remember them being called the ice and fire twins, one born of ice and the other of fire. A rare birth in our world, nearly impossible, and apparently it shocked all of Dragca. I read about them in one of the books my father left, as I was interested in the stepmother I had only met two months before I was sent to Earth. All I remember about her is her long, perfect white hair, and how cruel she was to the maids and dragon guards in the castle. My father married her not long after my mother died because she was the last female ice dragon alive other than me. They soon found out she couldn't have children, making me and Jace the only heirs to the throne left. The only ice dragons left. Now there are three: my father, me, and my stepmother.

"And yet you still look as beautiful as all those years ago. My wife sends her love," he says, and she rests her hand on his arm in an overly affectionate way. I'm pretty sure my stepmother wouldn't like that her sister seems so familiar with her husband. But then, I don't really know anything about them.

"Come in, we have a lot to discuss. Where is Jacian?" she asks, her eyes finally landing on me.

"Dead," I reply, almost robotically, as I stand completely still.

Esmeralda's hand flies to her mouth, "I am so sorry, Isola."

Part of me believes her, but I can't think about it. I look away as we all start walking quietly towards the castle. I blink and do a double take when I see a man standing in the shadows under one of the towers. He's dressed in all black, and I'm sure he is a guard, but for some reason, I can't stop staring at him as he moves closer. He lifts his hand, and I catch a glint of silver before he throws it at us.

"Get down!" I scream, slamming into my father, and we fall to the ground as the dagger lands in the heart of the guard on his right. The guard falls to the ground in front of us, as the other guards form a tight circle around us and pull their swords out. The guards quickly make a circle of fire around them, the heat blasting against my skin.

"Five to the left, two on the right," my father says, sniffing the air.

"When I say the word, run to the doors and get inside," my father tells me. He grabs my chin with his hand when I don't answer, "Do you understand, Isola?" he asks, and I nod despite the shock.

"Now!" he shouts, throwing his hands in the air and shooting ice in every direction except the one I'm running in. Ice and dragonglass, are the only ways to kill a fire dragon easily. Fire cannot kill an ice dragon, that is what makes us different and stronger. Only dragonglass can–and our own ice, not that we would use our ice on ourselves. *That wouldn't be smart.* The fire wall parts when I get close, closing behind me as I run straight to the closed stone doors.

"Duck, princess!" I hear a man shout from my left, and I turn my head to see a man dressed in the all-black guard uniform running at me. He has black hair that's cut short and shaved at the sides, his lip is pierced with a ring, and the man is built like an actual god. *Or like a rock star from Earth.* I'm too busy staring at the guy to stop him when he slams into me, both of us landing on the floor as a dagger flies past us.

"What part of 'duck' do you not understand?" the man asks, rolling us over, so he is on top of me. He looks down at me, placing his hands near my head as he rolls his lip ring between his lips, somehow frowning at me at the same time.

"Get the hell off of me, who do you think you are?" I ask him, watching as he smirks at me.

"Dagan Fire, nice to meet you princess. Now stay down, or I might as well kill you, myself," he says as he jumps off me in a fluid motion, pulling a red dagger out of his belt and throwing it. I roll on to my stomach to see the dagger land in the forehead of one of the attackers, and the body slams to the floor. When I turn back over, Dagan holds a hand out for me.

"You don't have to say thank you," he says as I accept his hand to pull me up.

"I was going to," I reply, and he grins, still holding my hand as we stare at each other.

"I am one of the dragon guard, your kind doesn't say thank you to us. We die for you royals every day. We are just soldiers, and soldiers don't get thanked as they die," he says, giving me a sarcastic smirk as he drops my hand and steps away. I watch him look around, following his gaze to the five dragon guards lying dead, some from my father's ice that is everywhere, and others from dragonglass daggers.

"Now get inside, princess," Dagan demands, pissing me off, and I step closer, looking up at him.

"Dagan Fire, thank you for saving my life, but if you tell me what to do again, we will have a big problem," I tell him, and before he can reply, my father steps next to me. Dagan looks away, his jaw grinding in annoyance.

"Bring the bodies inside, I want to know who dares to attack the king and princess," he tells Dagan, who nods as he steps back and turns around. My father puts his hand on my back as he walks us inside the castle, and I don't look back once.

3

ISOLA

"**M**y office is this way," Esmeralda says, waving a hand towards a corridor in the middle of the entryway we have walked into. There are two staircases on each side that lead to the next level, and everything in here is different shades of gold and brown. The brown wooden floors Are made of the same wood as the staircases. There are gold walls, which are empty of any decoration, and gold chandeliers light up the corridor. *There must be like ten of them in this space alone, talk about overkill.* We walk down the long corridor, until we get to the end where there is a set of double doors.

"Wait outside," my father tells the guards, who each nod their heads in submission, before he walks in the room. I walk in last, shutting the door behind me as I have a look around. There is a giant desk in front of two windows that overlook a field, the arena, and the mountains. There are some chairs, a bookcase, and little else in here.

"Please sit," Esmeralda says, as she takes her seat behind the desk, and my father sits in one of the two chairs in front of it. I sit down in the spare chair, crossing my legs and raising my eyebrow at my father who sighs.

"We are at war; the fire dragon rebellion has raised an army.

Every day, more and more people are siding with them because of the seers," he says, and I lean back in my seat in shock. That was not what I expected him to say to me, not one tiny bit of what he said. I knew a fire dragon killed my mother years ago, setting a dragon hunt on the fire dragons to find out who did it. Everyone loved my mother, she was a good queen who helped the poor and innocent. She made laws that helped them, opened orphanages and even adopted several dragon children, keeping them in the castle and teaching them in her spare time. No one knew why anyone would kill her, and the seers never saw it.

"The seers? Why would more fire dragons side with the rebellion because of the seers?" I ask confused.

"We have the royal seer locked up because she keeps trying to escape, and the whole of the seer village has joined the fire dragon rebellion," he says with an angry growl following his statement. There is a royal seer family, from what I remember reading, who lived in the castle, but I don't remember them as a child. It's likely I never met them.

"Why don't you give her up? Let her go, and maybe the seers–"

"Enough. Do not tell me what to do, Isola. There is far more you do not understand, and we cannot give up the young seer. She is too powerful, and it was her mother that made the prophecy that started the war in the first place," he says, speaking of the prophecy that was made the day I was born. I've heard of it from Jace, but I never listened to what he had to say. I don't believe that everything is destined to be, seers can be wrong.

"If I was to let her go free, and she has a vision as powerful as her mother's, it would just feed their army and make more people side with them," my father sighs.

"No one believes that prophecy, right?" I ask, but my father doesn't look at me. I don't even remember all of it, something about fire falling for ice or something.

"Remind me of it, it's been years since I've heard it," Esmeralda cuts in, looking between us, and I sit back in my seat.

"When fire falls for ice, Dragca will bear the price.
Ice and fire will destroy the curses, but a new curse will be born.
Only ice can stop the fire that spreads . . . .
The fire that will destroy . . . .
The fire that will burn eternal.
Ice must fall for fire, just as fire must fall for ice.
Sides will be chosen with blood, death will show the way through death.
Only fire must win . . . .
The heir of ice and fire must rule . . . ."

My father recites the prophecy, and none of us say a word as we think it over. Seers can be wrong, most of the time they are, but never wrong about everything. Some parts of the prophecy must come true, if not all of it, and none of it makes any sense to me. I assume it means a fire dragon falling for an ice dragon, but I don't see that happening anytime soon. I also don't see how fire must win. It makes no sense.

"Who is the heir of ice and fire?" I ask the only question I can think of.

"No one, they don't exist," my father snaps and then puts a hand on my shoulder.

"You are the only heir of Dragca. I don't have any siblings, and I never had another child," he tells me what I already know, but he looks at me until I nod, relief spreading over his face as he leans back.

"Can't our army stop the fire dragons?" I say, thinking of the large army my father has, full of dragon guards.

"We can't get to them, Isola, but we are looking for a way, and we will destroy the rebellion before you take the throne. I will not hand you a kingdom at war," he says, growls from his dragon following his word. I see frost escaping his fingers and sliding down the arm of the chair. He must be angry to lose control like that. The chair creaks, threatening to snap from the ice.

"What now?" I eventually ask when he has calmed down a little.

"You will stay here, and your uncle will watch over you. He has been appointed the new headmaster of Dragca Academy," he says, shocking me with an uncle I barely remember. I remember Jace telling me about him, how my grandmother adopted him at a young age. That's why he is a fire dragon, and not ice like my mother.

"Uncle? My mother's brother?" I ask, thinking back to the man with fiery red hair I remember as a child.

"Yes, he is a fantastic fighter, a smart dragon, and he will be a good mentor for you," he tells me.

"And Esmeralda?" I ask, looking over at her as she smiles at me.

"I am to return to the castle to protect my sister. The castle isn't safe, and my family needs me," she replies before my father can.

"Why now? Is it because I was meant to take the throne with Jace? When they find out he is dead, and there is no way for me to take the throne without an ice dragon mate–" I start rambling.

"Enough," my father cuts me off.

"But–"

"There is a reason the royal name Dragice is feared, there is a reason ice dragons have held the throne for thousands of years. You are Isola Dragice, and they will bow to you because Dragice dragons bow to no one. They will see you as their true queen, with or without a king, or I will finish them," he says, the promise coming through his words as more ice leaves his hand, until the whole chair is frozen, and his eyes are completely white. He must be close to shifting into his dragon, and the loss of control of his gifts says it all about the anger he is feeling. I want to think he might even be worried about me, my future, but his emotionless expression makes me feel like he is more frightened about losing the throne.

"I understand," I tell him quietly, and his eyes return back to their normal colour.

"I will take you to your room before I leave," Esmeralda tells me, and I nod at her as I stand up.

"Come here," my father opens his arms as he stands as well, and I step into a hug from him. It feels weird to be held by my father, as I can't remember him ever holding me, even as a child. He was always busy, always had many other things he needed to do.

"Be strong, there is so much of both me and your mother inside of you. Don't let death destroy your heart, and we will see each other in six months, for the winter solstice," he whispers to me. I want to agree with him, but you can't destroy something that is already broken, and my heart is too broken to be destroyed. I don't reply to him as I step out of his arms and walk over to the door that Esmeralda opens. The guards move to the side, two of them following us, and the others staying with my father.

"I'm sure your uncle will want to see you first thing in the morning. I will speak to the remaining dragon guards to work out a way for a guard to be with you at all times," she tells me as we get to the right staircase and start walking up. I don't reply to her, I just keep walking silently, wanting to get to my room and shut the door on the world.

"I am sorry for your loss, I know how crushing it is to lose your mate at a young age," she tells me, and I turn my head to look up at her as she continues to talk. I can't think about Jace right now without bursting into tears, which is not something I can do when I need to be strong right now. Jace wouldn't want me to break down.

"Can we talk about something else?" I ask as we pass two girls. One has long ginger hair and the other black with red tips. They both stare at me for way too long—actually stop walking to stare. I try not to let it bother me, I'm used to humans being weird around me growing up. They might not actually know what is different about me, like the dragons here do, but humans aren't stupid, they can sense something.

"I was promised to a fire dragon at ten, and we grew up together, fell in love at fifteen. The day before our mating ceremony, your mother was killed, and he was one of the dragons who fought to protect her. Losing his life doing so," she tells me, not exactly changing the subject, as she is trying to relate to me in some way, but I do feel sorry for her.

"I didn't realise guards died trying to protect my mother, I thought the attacker caught everyone off guard when he snuck into the castle and killed her," I say, remembering the bells going off in the castle that night. It's one of the only things I remember like it was yesterday. My father woke me up, hiding me in the secret passageways with royal guards. I remember him coming back for me hours later, covered in my mother's blood, and he told me she was gone. I screamed at him, ran to my mother's room, and stared at her dead body on the bed for hours before a guard picked me up and took me away.

"Five guards died trying to stop him–I knew them all–they were good men. As much as your mother was a good queen who didn't deserve to die as she did," she says, and we get to the top of the staircase.

"I was glad when your father found the betrayer and killed him for what he did, though I am sorry that many fire dragons were killed to find the attacker," she says, and I agree with her. I can't wait to find out who killed Jace, because I won't stop until I do. I will train and become strong enough to kill the person that took him from me, there isn't any other option.

"This way," she points at one of the three corridors. We walk down to the bottom of it, which stretches into a longer straight passageway with dozens of wooden doors.

"This is yours," Esmeralda says, pointing at the fifth door in the row and walking over, unlocking it with a key that she hands me after opening the door.

"Please try not to lose the key, they are a nightmare to replace," she tells me as I slide the key into my coat pocket and walk into the large bedroom after her. The room is circular in shape, with another door to the left of me, a round bed in the middle, and a small window with a window seat. There's a storage trunk at the end of the bed and a cream rug in front of it.

"The bathroom is through there, and the morning begins at seven am, Monday to Friday. The weekends are yours to study or socialize," she says, walking past me to the door as I stop in the middle of the room.

"The guards will bring your suitcase up, I'm sure," she says and then surprises me as she shuts the door with the guard on the other side. She walks over to me, placing her hands on my shoulders, and keeping eye contact with me.

"Your father will tell you to lay low here, to be safe, and do as you are asked. Don't do that. You need to stand out, so the other dragons don't push you over. You need to make friends, so you are not alone. Most of all, you need to train every hour because this war isn't going to be over when your father wins. They will always want you dead, they will always want a fire dragon on the throne. Be smart, survive this, and get revenge on whoever killed Jacian," she says and steps away, looking nervously at the door and back to me.

"Why tell me this? Why help me?" I ask her.

"Because I was friends with your mother, she was kind to me when I lost everything. I will protect her child because I see so much of her in you, and you are the true heir. Even as young an heir as you are now, you have power. I believe dark times are coming for Dragca, and we need a true ruler," she says and walks out of the room, shutting the door behind her. I walk over to my bed, sitting down and pulling out my phone from my pocket. The battery is low, but I still get to stare at the photos of Jace, with tears running down my face until I pass out.

4

ISOLA

I ce and fire. Fire and ice. It's everywhere, swirling around a girl I cannot see in the middle of it. Four men are standing around her, protecting her I think.

"Fire and ice is your future," a girl's voice says behind me, and I quickly swirl around to see a shadow of a girl walking into the room.

"What?" I ask her.

"Fire and ice. Light and dark. Good and evil. They need each other, like you will need your guards, your four others," she says, her voice echoing around my mind as she repeats the sentence time and time again.

"Jace?" I call instinctively, as I roll over in my bed and open my eyes to the vacant spot next to me. It takes a few seconds of staring at the empty space before the tears start to fall, and I roll over on my back, forgetting the strange dream to the reality that being awake is stranger. I look up at the unfamiliar ceilings, then over to the light that shines through the thin curtains, noticing the overwhelming scent of fire dragons around here. I feel around the bed, finding my phone and trying to turn it on, only to see it's flat. Looking at the room, I highly doubt I'm going to find a plug, much less my charger.

"Princess, your uncle wishes to see you before class, which starts in an hour," a young-sounding guard shouts after banging

on the door. I don't reply as I put my phone on the side and seriously debate not getting out of bed at all.

"I have breakfast for you," he shouts again when I don't
reply. My stomach grumbles before I can even think of rejecting
the idea of food. I don't even remember when I ate last as I
skipped breakfast yesterday, and then with everything that
happened, food was the last thing on my mind.

"One minute," I shout back as I groan and slide out of bed.
Every part of me wants to get back into it and not move, just
sink into the blankets and forget my life. But there's one part, a
part that makes me walk over to the bathroom and stare at
myself in the mirror above the sink. The part that knows no one
will avenge Jace if I get back into that bed. I look in the mirror at
my eyes, watching as the pupil spreads out and turns silver as I
whisper to my dragon.

*"I know you're hurting like me, but I need you now, okay? Talk to
me?"* I ask, waiting for her to respond. She doesn't, I just get
slammed with a whole load of pain from her that takes my
breath away as I lean against the sink. I sigh as my eyes turn
back to the normal blue, and I pick up the brand-new brush off
the counter and sort my hair out. Once I'm done, I brush my
teeth with the new toothbrush I find and come out of the bathroom, stopping in my tracks at the sight of the guard placing a
bundle of clothes on my bed. He turns at the noise, looking at
me with a small smile. The guard appears to be my age. He has
short, wavy brown hair, and hazel eyes with a touch of red in
them, like most fire dragons have. The redder, the more powerful
they are, but the bloodlines have apparently been diluted over
the years, so most dragons only have dots of red or little specks.
I remember Jace telling me that, but at the time I didn't care or
want to know about Dragca and its inhabitants. But I still
remember everything Jace said to me.

"I'm Thorne Riverle, one of your personal guards. Here is the
uniform you need to wear today and some breakfast, princess,"
he says, bowing low and straightening back up as I look him

over. He is dressed in a uniform of tight black leather and is bare
of weapons, which is odd for a dragon guard. The black trousers
show off his impressive thighs, and the shirt is fitted, with a dip
that puts his defined chest on display. A cloak is tied at his neck
with a silver clip of the royal crest. I clear my throat when I
realize how long I've just spent staring at him without speaking.
He must think I'm an idiot.

"It's Issy, or Isola. I don't mind which you call me, but not
'princess' please, that's just weird," I say, making him chuckle a
little. It's a damn sexy chuckle, too.

"Okay, Issy, I will wait outside to escort you to your uncle,"
he tells me, bowing once more before walking out of my room
and shutting the door. As I watch him leave, I spot the suitcase
by the door. I run over, pull it into the middle of the room and
open it up. There's a bundle of clothes that someone has
chucked in, a lot of it sexy lingerie. The idea of a guard looking
at my underwear makes me cringe. There are two dresses, but
mainly leggings and shirts. I keep searching for my Kindle or
iPod, not finding either.

"Damn it," I grumble, knowing that my phone is flat, and
there is no way for me to read now. I was halfway through a
damn good book before I had to stop reading to do that
annoying thing called sleep. I toss all the clothes back in,
deciding I will have to ask the guards about charging my phone,
so I can use the Kindle app or something. I walk over and pick
up the leather top and trousers and black cloak that is folded on
my bed.

"Dear god, it's like Harry Potter dressed in leather," I mutter
to myself. I put the clothes on, feeling them stick to my body like
another layer of skin and then pull the cloak around my shoulders. I look at the food, knowing I should eat, but I don't want
to. I don't know why, whether it's nerves or the image of Jace
with the dagger through his stomach running through my mind,
but pancakes and orange juice have never looked so horrible. I
walk to the door, pulling it open and see Thorne waiting to the

side. His eyes widen, then slowly make their way down my body before he seems to snap out of it. He quickly straightens and averts his eyes, though my cheeks still burn with embarrassment.

"The clothes suit you," he says as I shut the door and walk with him down the corridor. I don't reply as three girls pass us, all whispering as they look at me, and I just stare back. They don't even try to hide the fact they are talking about me, which I'm not sure whether to respect or hate. We walk past them, straight to the stairs in the middle of this corridor and go down.

"What is with all this leather?" I ask, feeling uncomfortable about how tight it is. I look over at him, noticing the leather outfits of the guards aren't too different from my own, but theirs covers from the neck down their arms, while mine has cold shoulder cutouts.

"It's magic-blessed leather made by the tree spirits," he says plainly, like I should know this, but I've never heard of them.

"Tree spirits?" I ask as we walk past another group of people who also stare and whisper. It's getting annoying now, but I don't know what exactly to say to them. I'm not like them, not really. Fire and ice couldn't be more different. I guess I never expected to be alone to deal with the fire dragons and their hate for my kind. I thought I'd have Jace at my side.

"Each tree has a spirit, that's who you speak to when you ask a portal to take you somewhere. They also make leather, which is blessed so that when you shift, it doesn't rip the clothes and they appear when you shift back. No one sees the tree spirits, they don't appear for dragons or humans anymore, but they will weave leather as gifts for the king," he explains. I've never heard of these tree spirits, but then, I never went to school in Dragca until now. Tree spirits aren't something you get taught about in human high school. I kinda wish it was, I doubt math is useful to me now.

"What do they look like?" I ask curiously.

"Pretty little dolls, with green hair and green skin. They are about the size of your hand, and known for causing mischief," he tells me.

"Sounds cute," I comment.

"Well, light tree spirits are, dark ones have blue hair, blue skin and are said to be a little less cute," he tells me as we move around a big group of students that are engrossed in conversation and don't even notice us.

"What do dark spirits do?" I ask.

"They are tree spirits as well, but they are born when a tree dies. No one knows much about them, to be honest. Most people don't even believe they exist," he says with an almost sad tone as we get to the door of the same office I was in last night. Three guards are standing motionless outside, until they see me and bow.

"I will wait for you here and take you to class," Thorne says with a formal bow as a guard knocks on the door and then opens it for me. I walk in, hearing the door shut behind me as I look at the back of my uncle, who stands looking out the window. He has a grey suit on, his dark-red hair with grey tips is a stark contrast. He waves a hand, beckoning me over.

"Do you remember my name? You were so young when I saw you last, Isola," he says; despite his words coming across as gentle, there's a touch of a snarl in his tone.

"No," I reply as he turns to look at me. His dark-red eyes lock with mine, but although I know he must be powerful, I am not frightened. He walks straight over to me, and I stand still as he moves around me in a circle, examining me.

"You look so much like my sister, it's like going back in time to when we were teenagers," he says, moving a hand to touch me before suddenly changing his mind, lowering his hand.

"I don't have any photos of her, only memories that I'm not sure are even real," I say.

"My name is Louis Pendragon, the last of the Pendragons, as you have the royal name, and I never had a child," he says, with no emotion in his tone. "You should get to your class, I only wished to look at you," he adds, walking away to sit down in his chair. I give him a confused look at being excused so quickly, but turn around, walking towards the door.

"One more thing, Isola," he says, stopping me when I get to the door.

"This is not the human world, nor do we play by their rules. I suggest you get your dragon on your side, otherwise you will be powerless to survive here," he comments.

"How did you know?" I ask, stunned.

"Leave, Isola," he commands, looking down at the paperwork in front of him, and he picks up a pen to start writing something.

"Goodbye, *uncle*," I say, making him flinch a little, and I walk out of the room.

5

ISOLA

"**D**id everything go well?" Thorne asks when I step outside the office. The guards shut the door behind me, moving back into their motionless stance.

"I actually have no idea," I mutter. I don't want to think about my complicated uncle and his strange ability to know that I'm not in control of my dragon, which I should be at my age. No one should know that, it's impossible, and I can't help but think about how he knew. My dragon is inside my mind, speaking only to me.

"Err, okay. So, this is the way to all of the classes, except for a few out buildings where training fights are held," he says, pointing to the left staircase as we walk back to the entrance hall. There are a few students walking around, carrying books, and wearing their hoods up, so I can't see their faces.

"To the right, are all the dorms, study rooms, and the library," he comments.

"Wait, there's a library?" I ask, grabbing his arm, and he looks at me strangely.

"Yes," he says slowly.

"That's the best damn thing I've heard all day," I say cheerily, and walk up the staircase with Thorne hurrying to catch up. At the top is a circle corridor, lined with lockers and classroom doors in between them.

"Lockers? Not what I expected," I tell Thorne, who reaches into his cloak and hands me another key, this one is small and blue. He pulls out a chain from his other pocket, hooking the key on.

"Hand me your room key, Issy?" he asks, holding out a hand. I feel around my cloak pocket until I find it, and hand it to him. He slides the key onto the chain and holds it out for me.

"Thanks," I say, taking it off him.

"It's just easier to have them on a small chain, it's nothing," he smiles and looks around.

"Yours is number one hundred, nice and easy to remember," he says, nodding his head to the left, and I walk just behind him. I stop when I see a guy leaning against the wall; even through all of the students, we just seem to lock eyes with each other. Thorne stops, walking back to my side, and looking at where I'm staring.

"That's the kind of dragon you want to stay away from, Issy," Thorne tells me, my eyes still locked on the almost black ones staring at me from across the hallway. I trail my eyes over his messy black hair, the long tips that brush over his forehead. I look down at his muscular arms crossed against his large chest before raising my eyes back to his. He is dressed in all leather, covered in tattoos, and I get the feeling Thorne is right.

"What's his name?" I ask Thorne.

"Elias Fire," Thorne grumbles, as Elias gets a cigarette out of his pocket and lights it up. He puts it in his mouth, sucking in slowly as he watches me like I watch him. His lips pull up in a sinful smirk before blowing the smoke out and walking away.

"I mean it when I say stay away from him; Elias Fire is nothing but dangerous. A killer that is dripping with dirty blood," Thorne sneers, and I have to agree with him. Elias looks just like everything any normal girl should avoid, and yet, I can't help but stare at him as he walks away.

"Is Dagan Fire his brother?" I ask Thorne, who is watching Elias like I am, but my question makes him glance down at me. He looks furious, his eyes turning slightly black in the corner as his dragon threatens to take over.

"The Fire brothers are not guys you want to make friends with, Isola," he says and walks away, fists held tightly at his sides. I jog a little to catch up with him, and he stops at a door.

"This is yours, I will wait outside each class," he says coldly. I nod, sliding the key chain into my pocket, and walk to the door. I open it and walk in, seeing five other students sitting down, all of them at the front, and they all stare at me with wide eyes. I don't see the teacher in the small room, which is full of dark-brown benches and has a whiteboard at the front, with a desk in front of it. I walk through the students, seeing an empty desk with two seats right at the back, and sit down in it. For the next ten minutes, students rush in, and all pause to stare at me. I try to just ignore it, focusing on the empty whiteboard instead. No one sits next to me, which I'm thankful for.

"Morning, class, good to see most of you are awake today," a woman laughs as she walks into the room with a massive pile of books nearly touching her chin, and slams them down on her desk. She smooths her blonde hair, which is pulled into a ponytail that highlights her dark-red tips. Pushing her glasses up, she smiles brightly when she sees me.

"We have a new student, Isola, right?" she asks me, and I nod.

"Right, well, Isola, this is history of Dragca. You're lucky that we just started learning the history of the royal family," she grins, "I'm sure you will pass this class easily," she winks.

"Sure, the *princess* will get everything right," a guy near the front says sarcastically. He has light-red hair, and his brown eyes glare at me before turning back to the teacher.

"Just for that comment, you can hand out the books, Rye," the teacher snaps at him, and he slides out of his seat and grabs a few books.

"For Isola's benefit, I will introduce myself, I am Miss Claire," the teacher starts off, picking up a whiteboard pen, and walking over to the whiteboard. Rye drops a book on my desk, still glaring at me, before he walks back to his seat.

"Can anyone tell me the name of the very first king of Dragca?" she asks, looking at me, but I don't have a clue. I probably should have read some of the books my father left with us on Earth, like Jace did. A sharp pain lances through me as I picture him, sitting on my bed, reading the books. I remember him laughing when I said I didn't want to know anything about some old dead people. Looking back, I was innocent and stupid, I should have listened to Jace.

"Icahn Dragice was the first king; he took the throne after the war of fire and ice. Many ice dragons were killed, as well as fire dragons, but it was Icahn who created peace," a girl two desks in front of me says.

"Very good. Yes, Icahn Dragice was the only one of his family that wanted peace, and he was awarded the throne because of his actions. Up until then, a fight to the death between siblings was the only way to win the throne. Please open your books to page fifty-one," Miss Claire says as she starts writing on the board. I flip my book open to the page she wanted, and there are three paragraphs and a drawing of a large blue dragon, covered in ice. I don't know if that's what I look like when I shift, but I remember Jace's dragon, and he was a little smaller than the one in this drawing.

"As we all know, there are two different forms of dragons, ice and fire. Ice dragons have kept the throne for many years because fire dragons have a natural weakness to ice. If we are in contact with dragon ice for too long, it can kill us," she says with a pointed look over at Rye. "Maybe some of you should remember that before annoying the only ice dragon here," she adds, making me chuckle and like her instantly. A few students give me a nervous look, and the whispering starts up again.

"Now, read your book, pages 51 to 91 please. I'm going to

test you on it in an hour," she comments, and I start reading. The first page is mainly full of information on Icahn; how he grew up and that his cousins were the ones that started the war. When they were killed, Icahn was the next in line, but the war meant no one was on the fire throne at the time. I turn the page over, and there's a drawing. It is a depiction of Icahn, holding a staff, with an orb on the top and a dragon curled around it. He has long white hair, braided at the sides, and he is huge, built like a giant. I read the next few pages, but no one talks about the staff, and I flip back, staring down at it. Maybe it's just my dragon side and her fascination with collecting shiny things, but I can't stop staring. I skip to the end of the book, hoping to find an index, but instead, there's another passage that I read in shock.

Icahn's first wife was known to be beautiful, but many never realised that it was her strength that made Icahn love her. During a fight on the battlefield, a dragon guard ran away when he was needed most, leaving Icahn alone to fight many fire dragons. Icahn was on the verge of defeat when his wife threw herself in front of him, taking a sword through the heart as she killed the other dragons with her ice. Her last words are the curse on the dragon guard, the curse that was sealed with royal blood.

I turn the page to find the curse written in fancy writing on its own, little fire and ice dragons painted at the sides around it.

"I curse the dragon guard and all its blood, to die for the royal throne and whoever sits upon it.
To desert the throne is to be killed. Either by fate or the throne.
One day, the curse will break due to the final promise.
If a dragon guard ever falls for a royal dragon, then they will lose their dragon in return.
This curse is final and unbreakable on my death.
The dragon guard will pay, and the curse will collect.
Ice will rule, and the dragon guard will protect."

I STOP READING when Miss Claire claps and begins talking, but I think over and over about the curse, a horrible curse, all because one dragon guard ran in a war. A curse that my father uses to control his dragon guard army, and ensure they do everything he demands. No wonder they hate us, the royals who control them but can never set them free. We can't even love them, nor can they love us, or the price would be their dragons. *A fate worse than death.*

6

ISOLA

"How was your first class?" Thorne asks as I walk to him after leaving history. I slide the two textbooks under my arms before I answer.

"Good and bad," I say, thinking that I liked the teacher, but when she said I have to study all these books to catch up the two months I'm behind, that wasn't so great. I love reading, but not this kind of reading. One book is just about the farming lands and what we grow. I need to know every type of edible plant, as well as the unusable ones, grown in Dragca in time for a test in a month.

"Here, hand me those," he says, and I laugh a little.

"Just because I'm a girl, doesn't mean I need a man to hold stuff for me. I can carry them, Thorne, but thanks," I say, squeezing around a couple of students to look at the locker numbers. I'm at eighty, so I keep walking until I find mine. Opening it up, I slide all my books in before slamming it shut again. I will have to remember to get them out, but I'm not carrying them around all day.

"What's next?" I ask Thorne.

"Lunch, and then two hours in geometry," he says and points

down the stairs. *Food.* Food sounds better than it did a few hours ago.

"So how did you get here? Land a job as the dragon guard escorting me around?" I ask Thorne as I expected an older guard. Admittedly though, I don't know much about dragon guards.

"My family is close to the throne, so they thought it would be smart to have me near you. I've also passed a lot of assignments," he tells me as we get down the stairs and follow the students walking down the corridor by the door.

"Assignments?" I ask him.

"We are given tasks to train us, both here and on Earth. You may be born a dragon guard and live to the curse's rules, but it doesn't mean you instantly become a good fighter," he tells me and holds a door open for me. I walk into the large lunch room that has circle tables and what looks like a buffet towards the front, with a kitchen behind it. The tables are mostly full, and it's noisy as dragons walk around, everyone giving me hostile looks.

"Help yourself, I'm just going to check on something. I won't be far from you," he tells me and walks out of the room before I can reply to him. I turn away and walk across to the buffet. I am picking up a tray when someone bumps into me.

"Watch it," a deep voice snaps, and I turn to see Dagan Fire staring down at me. His eyes are slightly black on the edges, but they quickly snap back to a deep-blue colour.

"Oh, it's the moody guard," I reply blankly, and turn back around.

"Is that the princess?" I hear another male voice ask, and I turn to see a guy about our age watching me. He has a short, tidy black beard, curly black hair and tanned skin. He is dressed in the all-leather uniform, and I can see two swords crossed on his back. His green eyes watch me curiously, just as I watch him. *What is with this place and all the dragons being hot?* Even thinking of any of them as attractive sends waves of pain through me, and my own dragon stirs in my mind as I picture Jace. I quickly turn around when I realize I've been staring at them for way too long. *God, everyone is going to think I'm mad.*

"I told you, Korbin, she is as crazy as they come," Dagan says, chuckling. I take a deep breath, trying not to react to the idiots.

"And stunning, you said she was stunning," Korbin replies, his voice low and deep.

"Well, she is stunning, but the crazy ones always are," Dagan replies, and I slam my tray down on the side before turning to face them.

"I am standing right here, don't talk about me like I'm not," I snap as they both look at me, and then at each other, before they start laughing.

"Little princess, you don't have the throne yet, and I won't listen to a word you say. So, if I want to talk about you, I will," Korbin finally says with a shrug. *You know, after they both stop laughing.*

"She won't inherit the throne anyway, not since her precious little prince was killed," Dagan says, "Such a shame about that," he tuts. I lock my eyes with him as anger flows through me, both me and my dragon. I let my dragon out, feeling my eyes glaze over as my hands start to freeze everything near us. Dagan and Korbin take a step back as snow begins to fall from my hands, and I don't move as I try to calm myself down.

"Kill them?" my dragon whispers in my mind; her sadness and anger are overwhelming and make me take a deep gasp. Unfortunately, she uses that as an opportunity to completely take over, shooting ice out of my hands in giant waves, and then spreading across the floor as I fall. I don't hear or see a thing as my dragon pushes against my mind, trying to make me shift and allow her to act on her anger. Her pain is clouding her judgement, making her view everything as a threat and want to destroy all she sees.

"Listen to me, dragon, this is not the way. They didn't hurt Jace, and you could kill them," I manage to grind out in my head, begging

her to listen. She doesn't stop, but she lets me speak to her, lowering the barrier between us a tad.

"We need to work together to get revenge on the real dragon that did this to us, that hurt Jace. Killing these guards won't do that," I beg her, feeling my arms warm up and bones begin to move as the shift starts to happen.

"Please, no," I beg her once more, and she whines in my head, a whine that transforms into a roar that fills my ears as she pulls back.

"Revenge, we have to get revenge," she whispers to me, and for the first time in years, we are in complete agreement. I blink my eyes open, looking up at icicles hanging from the ceiling. My breath comes out in cold white puffs as I struggle to sit up. All around me is a thick wall of ice; I can't see anything, and no one can get to me. I lift myself up, trying not to slip on the ice on the floor as I walk to the ice wall and place my hand on it. I punch my hand through the ice, cutting my knuckles a little. I punch a hole next to it and then another one, until there's a big enough gap for me to climb through. The sight in front of me causes me to forget the cuts stinging my knuckles as I stop and stare in shock. All the students are frozen; the whole room looks like they tried to run away from me, but didn't get far. *Dragon ice can kill fire dragons if they are exposed to it for too long, shit.* I run over to Dagan and Korbin, who are frozen in place with their eyes completely black, as if they tried to call their dragons before this happened.

"Naughty princess, tut, tut," I hear a deep, throaty voice say, and I move around Dagan to see Elias Fire walking towards me, burning footsteps in the ice as he goes. He has a leather jacket on and a cigarette in his hand which he drops on the floor, crushing it with his boot.

"I didn't mean to–" I start to try and explain, and he grins at me, lifts his hand and places a finger against his lips. I step back as he swings his arms out, and fire shoots out of them in the shape of a dragon as he stands still. He burns away the ice, never harming the fireproof students, who fall off their chairs or collapse to the ground. The doors bang open behind Elias, just as his fire passes them, and there my uncle stands. He has a strained expression on his face, and his hands firmly planted on his hips.

"My office, now," my uncle demands as he walks further into the room with Thorne at his side, and watches Elias put the rest of the fire out. Dagan falls to the ground when he is free of the ice, with Korbin following moments later.

"This is your fault," Dagan snaps, glaring up at me.

"Dagan, Korbin, Elias, Thorne, and Isola, get to my office. Everyone else to the medical bay to be checked over," my uncle shouts as Elias lowers his hands. I look around at the students on the floor, wiping ice off of themselves and struggling to stand up. The hostile glares they gave me when I first walked in here are replaced with pure hate now. *Best first day ever.*

"Such a naughty little *princess*, aren't you?" Elias taunts with a low chuckle, before turning and walking straight back out.

7
ISOLA

"**Y**ou froze the entire room! A goddamn room full of fire dragons . . . who you nearly killed, Isola!" my uncle shouts, while I look down at the floor. It was an accident, but I doubt telling him that will make a difference at the moment. He has been shouting at me for the last twenty minutes, and nothing I've tried to say has made even a little difference. If anything, my trying to speak a word just annoys him more.

"All because I called you stunning," Dagan says in a cocky tone, speaking for the first time. Both my uncle and I turn to glare at him. That was not all that he said, and the ass knows it. He holds his hands up, "Well, you are."

"Congratulations, Dagan, you and your friends have a new job. You are not leaving this school for the rest of the year," my uncle says clapping. "You can forget that assignment in Florida."

"What new job?" Korbin asks, moving away from the door he was silently leaning against.

"Watching my niece, the goddamn princess, who is meant to be able to control her powers," he stops to glare at me again before continuing his rant, "and making sure she doesn't freeze everyone . . . again."

"No," Korbin says firmly, making my uncle laugh coldly. I look over to see Elias and Thorne just staring at me, one of them on each side of the room, and neither are listening to my uncle.

"Also, if I catch one of you calling her stunning, flirting, or breaking any of the rules, I will personally kick you out, and none of you will stay in Dragca. I don't give a damn who you think you are," he tells the four most dangerous dragons in this school. You don't tell the royal guards' what to do unless you're the king. The royal guards only protect my family because they are cursed to do so. *Until we are all dead that is.* It doesn't mean they would be punished for killing my uncle as he isn't a royal, so I'm surprised he just told them what to do.

"Hell, no," Dagan chuckles, which dies away when he looks at my uncle.

"Now, get out," my uncle commands, a dark-sounding threat lacing his words, and to my surprise, the guys walk out without a word. I go to follow them, but my uncle stops me.

"Isola, you will stay. Shut the door behind them," he says. I shut the door, but not before I see Dagan pulling Elias away from Thorne. They are both glaring at each other with anger in their eyes, and look close to fighting. *What the hell is that about?*

"You will need constant supervision now, and I am trusting you to get your powers under control. We need you to be strong, not out of control," he says, and gets up, walking to the window. "Every Sunday morning, you will fly to the mountains with Dagan and Korbin and train with them, because they are the best fighters we have. Every Saturday, you will spend all day with me, and I will teach you valuable lessons. Thorne can teach you the history of Dragca after classes on Friday, your least busy day of the week. I trust him, and he is smartest of them all in history anyway," he tells me.

"And Elias?" I ask.

"Is too out of control to be trusted to train or teach you anything. He will protect you, as he is a dragon guard, but I don't trust him alone with you. I wish for you to stay away from

Elias, unless you need him to save you from danger," he says, growling slightly.

"Fine," I say, wondering what exactly Elias has done to make my uncle trust him so little. Also, I'm hating the small part of me that wants to spend time with Elias, just because my uncle told me not to. *Like he is forbidden fruit or something.*

"I hope I don't have to remind you that relationships between the royal family and the dragon guard is a death sentence for you both. The curse–" he starts, and I cut him off.

"I know about the curse, I read it this morning," I tell him.

"Good, then you understand why it is so very important that you stay away from them, and keep your relationship strictly business. Think of them as bodyguards, nothing more," he tells me. I don't say anything as the words run around my mind, this is why my family has never mixed with fire dragons, because of the risk of this curse.

"I still love Jace," I admit.

"The dead do not need your love," he states, almost gently but still strict with every word like I'm coming to expect from him.

"But, he has it, and my vow of revenge," I say, and he bows his head to me.

"Revenge is a much better feeling than love. As you already know, love is a weakness to us. Revenge is a strength, it gives you determination, a reason to fight," he comments.

"Love is not a weakness," I argue, and he laughs, looking back at the window.

"It is the weakness of every dragon and human alike. Every species known to us that can love is weak because of it. Love makes you weak, and you are proof of that. You are weak because of Jacian's death," he says.

"That's not true, I am not weak," I insist, my dragon backing me in my mind.

"You are, and you being weak makes the whole of Dragca weak," he scolds me as I cross my arms and glare at him.

"Focus on revenge, Isola, not other feelings," he tells me firmly before I can reply to him. I walk to the door, looking back at my uncle as I rest a hand on the door handle.

"Who did you lose?" I ask, hearing the pain of his loss behind his angry words. No one is that angry without losing someone close.

"Everyone I've ever loved is dead, every person I consider family. Now, leave," he demands. His voice is so detached that I don't how to reply to him. Instead, I choose to just open the door and walk out. Thorne is leaning against the wall, his hands in his pockets, and his hazel eyes look up at me.

"Interesting first day, Issy," he says, walking over, and stopping right in front of me.

"Only attempted to kill my whole class, got myself extra training, and I bet I made a whole lot of enemies here," I shrug, making him laugh. I feel my lips turn up in a smile before I end up laughing with him.

"Classes have been cancelled for the day and–" he stops when he sees my hands, and he picks them up.

"How did you do this?" he asks, looking at my blood-covered knuckles, and I flinch when he rubs a finger over one of the cuts. I had actually forgotten about them.

"I had to break through the wall of ice I made, well, that my dragon made when she got mad," I respond automatically. I see the realization float across Thorne's face at what my words mean. My ice can hurt me, and my dragon healing doesn't work to fix the cuts. It's a well-kept secret of ice dragons, not many people know it and for good reason.

"I don't know much about ice dragons or anything, but come back to my room, so I can clean that up. I can stitch a few places up to stop the bleeding," he says gently as he lets go of my hands.

"Alright," I say, knowing I can't go to my uncle for help, and I don't want anyone else knowing how vulnerable I am to my own powers. Thorne walks close to my side, our arms brushing as we walk up the stairs, and past my bedroom. We walk past the others until we get to another staircase. This staircase leads all the way up to the top of the tower, and you can see all the way up, and see the hundreds of rooms lining the tower.

"All the guards staying at Dragca Academy live in these rooms," he tells me as we start to climb. We pass two doors on the walk up before he stops and gets a key out of his cloak. He opens his door and waves me in. Thorne's room is like mine in size, but he has a tiny window and a small bed with blue sheets. There is a pile of books on his bedside cabinet, with one still open. I walk over and see it open to a page on the history of ice dragons.

"Sit, I have a first aid box in the bathroom," Thorne instructs as he shuts the door and undoes his cloak, hanging it over the bathroom door. I keep my eyes on the way the tight leather is stretched across his muscular frame, showing off his toned stomach and chest. When I look up, he is watching me as he sifts through a cabinet above the sink, but he quickly glances away. I shake my head, reminding myself that he is just helping me, and it doesn't matter how damn hot he is.

"What happened in the lunch room?" he asks, as he comes and kneels in front of me. I watch as he opens the box, pulling out everything he needs and laying it out on the floor. He gets some alcohol and pours it on a cloth, before he grabs my right hand. He starts cleaning it as I bite down on my lip from the stinging pain.

"If I answer that, can I ask you something?" I bargain. He looks at me, and nods once before focusing on my hands again. He wraps the knuckles, clearly deciding they don't need any stitches before taking my left hand, which is the far worse of the two.

"Dagan and Korbin, they said something about Jace . . . I lost control," I say, not being able to look at Thorne as I speak.

"Understandable, it hasn't been long since you lost him,"

Thorne says gently. When he tilts his head to the side, I see a smudge of what looks like brown paint on his neck.

"Do you paint?" I ask, pointing at it, and he quickly rubs it away.

"No," he says, his voice colder than before.

"Why do you hate Elias?" I ask, watching how he completely tenses up and squeezes my hand a little tighter.

"He killed someone close to me," he says, his tone gruff as he reaches into the box and gets some butterfly stitches out, sorting my left hand before wrapping it up.

"I'm sorry, who was it?" I ask.

"I don't owe you another answer, Isola," he snaps, the iciness of his tone makes me pull my hands away from him. I stand up, walking around him, pausing as I open the door.

"No, you owe me nothing, but I am sorry. I know what it's like to have the people you love murdered when there is nothing you can do to stop it," I tell him. I quickly walk out of the room before I do something stupid, like let him see me cry.

8

ISOLA

"Wake up," a voice shouts, and then there's loud banging on my door. I roll over and groan into my pillow as I rub my tired eyes. I look over at the gap in the curtains, only to see that it's still dark out. Sliding myself out of bed, I move to shout at whoever is stupid enough to wake me up this early. *It's inhuman, that's what it is; no one should be awake before the sun rises.* I walk over to the door, pulling it open and glaring at Korbin who is jogging on the spot outside my room. He has a short vest on, showing off white tattoos that trail up his arms and disappear into the vest.

"Eyes up, doll," Korbin says, laughing when I glare at him and rub my eyes.

"I'm half asleep, and this *doll* is not fucking impressed, what the hell do you want?" I snap, making him laugh louder.

"I like you already, but we have a two-mile run to do. So, *doll*, get some running gear on as we only have two hours before class," he says, making my jaw drop open.

"I don't run, not unless something is chasing me, and even then, I'd rather take my chances with it," I grumble. He steps closer to me, before leaning down to growl into my ear.

"You can get your butt in there and get changed for our run, or I can throw you over my shoulder, take you to the woods, and throw fireballs at your ass to make you run," he warns me.

"Seems like you're focused on my ass a lot in that sentence," I respond, making him grin at me.

"Get changed, flirting with me won't make me be any nicer to you," he says, moving back and starting to do that annoying jogging thing again. *Why is he so happy, and more importantly, awake at this time in the morning?*

"I wasn't–" I snap, and he interrupts me.

"Get changed."

"So bossy," I groan, giving up because I'm pretty sure he would throw fireballs at me and enjoy it. *I'm also pretty sure I wouldn't.* I turn around and walk back into my room, slamming the door shut behind me. I quickly dive through my suitcase to try to find my active-wear. I really need to unpack. Finding what I need, I pull the yoga top, leggings, and small jacket on.

"Hurry up," Korbin shouts, banging on the door once. I resist the urge to throw my trainers at the door, deciding to put them on, and pull my hair up into a ponytail instead. I brush my teeth, then throw some water on my face before walking out of the room.

"About time," Korbin begins before pausing. His eyes trail over me, starting at my feet and making their way up my body slowly, as he rubs his beard with one hand.

"Is this what humans wear? Tight, bright clothes?" he questions, and I look down at my bright-pink leggings and black crop top.

"Some people live in clothes like this, but never actually work out in them. They are designed for working out," I shrug, so used to seeing humans wearing them that I never considered that it would be weird at all.

"Humans are strange," he states before turning and running down the stairs. I start after him, but he goes so fast that he is standing leaning against the wall when I finally reach the bottom. He smiles arrogantly, before taking off and running out of the room. We run straight down the corridor to the entrance hall, where he holds the door open for me.

"So, where are we running?" I ask.

"In the forest. Don't worry, it's protected, and Dagan is out flying in dragon form, keeping an eye out," he says, just as a loud roar shakes the trees.

"Well, he is closer than I thought," Korbin laughs, before running straight towards the trees. I run after him, getting to his side as we get to the path in the woods. He keeps at a steady pace as I take the opportunity to look around. The path is smooth, and there are little hills at the side that drop down into more trees. I look up at the sunrise, seeing the pinks and purples spreading across the sky around the two suns. The large green trees stretch so high that they almost look like they are touching the sky, it's amazing. I have to look down and focus on my breathing when running gets harder, making me realize how out of shape I am. *I seriously don't run.*

"How much longer?" I ask as the trees all start to look the same. I stop, breathing heavily as I put my hands on my knees.

"The path takes an hour and a half to run at this speed, and we have been running for twenty minutes," he says plainly.

"Oh my god," I pant out. "It felt like forever, I'm done," I state, making him chuckle, and I look up.

"We have an hour left. Don't make me get the fireballs started," he threatens, and I just glare at him.

"I'm not going to do this every day. What is the point?" I ask as I get my breath back and lean against a nearby tree. Korbin sighs, holding his hand in the air and making a small fireball.

"Now, doll, I wasn't kidding about throwing fireballs at your ass if you don't start running. I'm not paid to explain anything to you," he says, making the fireball in his hand larger. I move away from the tree, walking straight up to him, and placing my hand into the fire. It warms my hand, but it doesn't hurt me one bit.

"Fire doesn't hurt me, so there would be no point, other than burning my clothes. Do you really want to see my ass that badly?" I ask, watching his eyes widen in shock. I lower my hand when he stops the fire and steps closer. I have to tilt my head up to meet his eyes as we both glare at each other.

"I think you're the one obsessed with your pretty little ass, not me. You keep bringing it up."

"I think you're in denial," I chuckle, and he narrows his eyes at me.

"Well, being *princess* and all, I guess you would be right about everything," he says, the amount of venom and sarcasm in his words makes me want to back away from him. I don't, I just end up staring into his green eyes. They are a dark-green with black around them, and in places, they have little tints of hazel. They are amazing, so deep and different from anyone else's I've seen.

"Why do you hate me?" I ask, seeing his dislike in his eyes.

"Do you have any clue what it is like to be a slave to the throne? Knowing that your only place in the world is to die for the royal family. That the curse will always ruin every part of your life, and knowing you can never really be free?" he asks me.

"Who says I'm free? There is no curse on the throne, but there is a burden that no one, particularly me, wants," I reply.

"But you *can* run, you can escape. Magic won't make you choose to allow the curse to kill you, or come back to a king that would kill you for deserting him," he spits out.

"He wouldn't do that," I shake my head as Korbin takes a step back and laughs.

"Tell my parents and sister that. Oh wait, you can't, because they are dead for wanting to be free," he growls at me. His vehemence makes me stumble back with a slight bit of fear, but then he turns away from me. I take a deep breath before stepping closer, feeling like I need to tell him something, anything that I can to make this better. I didn't know my father was like that, I didn't even know the words of the curse until yesterday. I place my hand on his shoulder, his skin burning hot under my touch.

"I'm sorry, I didn't know about my father, or even the specifics of the curse until recently. I would never do that to anyone."

"Then you should know not to touch me. I have to be nothing to you, not even a friend," he says, glancing over his shoulder and shrugging my hand off.

"I know that," I reply, feeling stupid for trying to comfort him.

"There's still a lot you do not know, doll," he states cryptically as he narrows his eyes at me and walks away. "Run or don't, but being in the best physical shape you can makes your dragon stronger," he says, just before he runs off. I stand and watch for a second before taking off after him, and we don't say a word for the rest of the run.

9

DAGAN

"**W**hat happened in there? Why did you tell her about your past? You know we can't be friends with her, we can't be anything to her," I ask Korbin as we watch Isola run towards the academy, dressed in the tightest bloody clothes I've ever seen. *What the hell is she wearing, and why does she look so fucking hot in it?*

"I don't know, she messes with my head when I'm near her, and I forget everything planned," he says with a groan, rubbing his face as he watches Isola, like I do, until we can't see her as she gets inside the academy.

"She can't mess with your head. Your parents–" I say.

"I know, I'm not an idiot," Korbin interrupts, looking over at me.

"I get it, she is attractive and damn innocent in all this. But, it has to stop, and she has to bear the price in the end. Being her friend–it's not part of our job, and is fucking dangerous," I say, making sure he is looking at me. "Don't get close."

"Who are you trying to kid? I've known you my whole life, and I know when you want something," Korbin says, making my dragon growl low.

"You don't know anything, just like you told her," I growl.

"I know something is up. You looked shocked to see her yesterday. Why?" he asks. I try to ignore how my dragon is thinking about her, how we watched her all the way around the woods, and I couldn't get my dragon to focus on anything but Isola. It's a total mind fuck when your dragon finds a treasure he wants, and you can't explain why we can't have her. It's more confusing when I can't stop thinking about her either.

"I remember meeting her, but I don't want to talk about it," I refuse to even think about it. I won't be thanking her for anything.

"Then keep your eyes off her," he warns.

"It's all my dragon," I growl, watching as Korbin's eyes turn slightly black.

"I get it," is all he says.

"What are we going to do about Thorne?" I ask, needing to discuss him. I don't know why he's here, he wasn't meant to be.

"Watch him, and hope he doesn't drop us all in it," Korbin says as I roll my lip ring between my lips, and look back at the castle.

"We should all take turns watching both him and Isola. We need Elias to actually help us and not fuck around while he is here," I mutter, knowing my brother can't be trusted to do anything that doesn't benefit himself.

"Talk of the devil," I mutter. My brother's dragon is diving out the sky and flying straight towards us. Elias' dragon is all black with red claws and a nasty temper, not far off from my brother's. He lands with a thump in front of us, roaring loudly before shifting, and my brother is left kneeling on the ground. He stands up, reaching inside his leather jacket and pulling out a cigarette. He lights it up before walking over to us.

"I heard my name," he says, blowing smoke at Korbin and smirking when he doesn't look impressed.

"Where have you been? You're meant to be watching Isola this morning," I question him.

"I'm here, aren't I?" he replies, shrugging a shoulder and looking back at the castle.

"She is inside, in the shower by the sounds of it," he says and smirks at me, "I wish I could join her," he taunts. His eyes turn black as his dragon says something that makes him grin around his cigarette.

"No fucking her, no messing around, or you will get kicked out of this place, just like you did when we went to school here," I warn him.

"Sleeping with three of the teachers was worth it," he shrugs.

"We need to be here, and you know why. If he finds out–" I stop talking when my brother's face goes serious.

"I'm going to fucking watch the *princess*," he snaps and turns around, walking towards the castle before I can say anything else to him.

"Do you trust him?" Korbin asks when Elias is out of sight.

"He's my brother, of course I do," I reply.

"And if he chooses the wrong side?" he asks.

"He won't, so it doesn't matter," I state. My brother may act like a complete asshole, but he knows the end goal of being here. We have a job to do, and nothing can mess with that job. It could mean the end of everything, and even my brother isn't stupid enough to mess that up.

"Your judgement is too clouded by the fact he is your brother. You don't see how out of control he is, and always has been," he replies.

"Don't Kor," I warn him, and he places his hand on my shoulder.

"I'm your friend, if I didn't say it, I would be lying to you," he says gently.

"Elias has never loved anyone, never given a shit. I don't care what some prophecy says. He won't fuck this up," I shrug his hand off and walk away. As I get closer, I pick up the sweet, icy scent of Isola.

"*Mine, she will be mine, and you will save her,*" my dragon whispers to me. For the first time in years, I slam a barrier down between us before punching the wall near the door.

"For fuck's sake," I mutter. The third prophecy says one of the brothers will fall. Everyone thinks it is Elias, yet it's my dragon that already thinks of Isola as his. The third prophecy, the one that no one knows except for the king and us. Well, and the fire rebellion. The only one who can never know is Isola. It would destroy her—and us.

10

ISOLA

"How was your run?" Thorne immediately asks when I answer the door. He asks nicely, no sign of the ire from our talk last night. I decide to not mention it and forget he acted weird as I walk out of my room.

"Good but painful, what classes do I have today? Please tell me it's nothing physical," I groan.

"It's Herbololgy, and I'm escorting the princess today," I hear said behind me, and I turn to see Elias leaning against the wall of the stairs just above me.

"I have to stay with Isola at all times, you are not needed," Thorne sneers. He places a hand on my waist and stares up at Elias, who just seems focused on Thorne's hand.

"Guys, we are going to be late. You can argue, fight, or measure each other's dicks to see which is bigger later. I need a guide to class," I say, stepping away from Thorne as he coughs on a laugh, and I see Elias smirk.

"Mine's bigger, I'm sure, but let's go," Elias says, and jumps over the bars of the staircase. I look down to see him land perfectly on the floor below.

"Cocky asshole," Thorne mutters, walking down the corridor, and I quickly follow. When I get to the bottom of the stairs, the guys are just staring at each other. Both of their eyes are turning black, and Thorne even has fire sparks falling from his fingers.

"Guys?" I ask, trying to get their attention. They both ignore me, and I just give up. Clearly those two can't work together.

"Why are you even here, Elias? Don't you have work for the king to do? Innocent families to kill?" Thorne asks snidely. Elias steps closer, pulling up his fist and slamming it into Thorne's face. Thorne crashes into the wall, shaking the tower before standing up.

"Don't you like the truth, or do you not like the princess knowing what you really are?" he asks.

"Don't bring me into this, I barely know either of you," I say, holding my hands up. They continue to ignore me. I might as well just walk away, but I'm scared they might actually try to kill each other, and bring the castle down in the process.

"I don't care what she knows or thinks," Elias says loudly, and then lowers his voice, "but your family wasn't innocent. You need to get the fuck over it because you know what they did." Thorne stares at him, not replying. Elias walks past me in the doorway and down the corridor.

"Come on, my naughty princess, you're going to be late for class," Elias calls. I look back to see Thorne looking at the ground, his arms burning with fire, but he doesn't say a word.

"Go," Thorne says so quietly that if I wasn't a dragon, I wouldn't have heard it. I run to catch up with Elias, stopping at his side as we walk down the corridors, mixing in with the students going to class.

"You must think I'm a monster, eh?" Elias asks me, after a few moments of awkward silence.

"Are you?" I question.

"We are all monsters, I think. It's inside of us," he says.

"I don't think you're a monster, perhaps just damaged and broken. Maybe working for the wrong side, I don't know. I'm not going to judge you, especially not on something I don't fully know the details of," I comment.

"Like you," he chuckles and stops walking. Elias moves close enough that I'm overwhelmed by his scent. It's a smoky musk, like a bonfire on a cold night, and I can't help but want to be closer.

"What?" I end up asking like an idiot, forgetting what we were even talking about.

"Broken in here," he steps closer and places his hand on my heart. Reaching forward with his other hand, he pushes a bit of my hair behind my ear as I suck in a ragged breath. I end up just staring at him, lost in his eyes. Those light-blue eyes are so much like Dagan's, but Elias has a black ring around his pupil. Both are seriously stunning to look at.

"You are so, so dangerous for someone like me, princess," he murmurs, stepping back, and nodding his head at the door like nothing just happened.

"Your class is in there. I'm not listening to that shit about plants again, so I will be out here," he says. I nod, speechless, walking to the door and opening it up, rather than replying to him. I feel his eyes on me, and it makes me look back, and Elias smirks before lightly chuckling.

"What's funny?" I ask. He doesn't reply to me, only pulling out a cigarette and lighting it up with his finger.

"Nothing you want to know, my naughty princess," he grins. Shaking my head, I open the door further and walk in.

"Miss Dragice, we have been waiting," the male voice says as I walk into a room covered in plants. It's a bit of a surprise in here, considering that you can't see the walls or floors from the amount of plants and trees in here. Actually, I don't even think there is a floor when I look down to see grass beneath my boots. I walk around a bush near the door to get to an old man standing in the middle of five students. He has a weird, green top hat on, a matching suit and holds a walking stick, which he taps on the floor.

"Come on, come on, we don't have much time today. I am Mr. Oneen," he urges. I move closer, standing next to a girl who glares at me as she pushes her strawberry-blonde hair over her shoulder before moving away. I've never had a girl as friend, with human girls hating me from the moment they saw me. It seems nothing is different here, except for the reasons why they hate me. I wonder if she, or any of the others, were in the cafeteria yesterday. It would make sense of all the hate-filled glares I'm receiving. I doubt it would make them feel better to know it was by accident that I nearly killed them.

"Welcome to Herbology. As you know, we live in a magical world full of unusual and rare plants. We also have rare creatures that roam the forest, but that is something you will learn about in wildlife class with me later in the week," he says as he smiles at me. "No, this class is about the plants, trees, flowers, and even the grass you walk on. It is about how magic is woven into this world and how the plant life can help us, like we can help them," he tells everyone before walking over to a plant pot and bringing it over.

"Come and see," he waves us closer, and we all gather around as he puts the pot on the ground. In the soil, there is only a tiny plant with light-green leaves.

"Watch this," Mr. Oneen chuckles at our confused faces before he starts to whistle. We watch as the plant shakes, and then starts growing as Mr. Oneen whistles more loudly, occasionally changing pitch. The plant continues to get bigger, and branches stretch out, with little purple shells hanging from them. Mr. Oneen stops when the tree touches the ceiling, surrounding us with its branches that hang low. I watch as he breaks one of the purple shells off the tree and comes back to the middle of the circle. He goes to open it and then seems to realize we are all still standing here. He waves one hand in the air.

"Will you all please get one, and open it for me," he asks. I reach for the nearest shell, pulling it off of the branch, and picking open the tough shell. Inside is a small purple round-shaped object.

"As Isola knows, humans have 'sweets' which are copied off the idea of these trees," he says and pops his purple sweet into his mouth, crunching it around. "These sweets have healing properties, say if your dragon throws too much fire," he pauses to smile at me, "or ice, this will heal your sore throat. "In this class, I will teach you about the magic of the plants around you," he says as he places a hand on the tree. "The magic of the plants, the forests, and even the mountains are what protect our world from the human world. They even look after us by making natural healing elements for dragons," he says as he steps away and places both of his hands on his walking stick.

"Please go around the room, find a plant of your choice, and take it back to your room," he instructs, but none of us move.

"What do we do with the plant, sir?" I ask when no one else seems inclined to speak up, and he laughs.

"Oh, I forgot to mention that. I want you to study the plant, tell me what it does, and how it can be used. You will pass the class if you can figure it out," he waves a hand around the room. "Go."

I walk out of the cluster of branches, away from the other students and down the rows of potted plants of different sizes and colours. I stop when I see an ice-blue plant. It's tiny, with only two leaves in a black pot filled with soil. I pick it up, walking back to the teacher, who looks down at the plant.

"Perfect," he nods his head, gently stroking the plant.

"Perfect for an ice dragon, I guess," I smile at him. He nods, a surprised look on his face, as he looks at me once more and then back to the plant.

"Did you know—your mother chose the exact same plant," he tells me, shocking me.

"No," I say quietly.

"There is something about the BlueTay plant that calls to ice dragons I believe," he smiles. "You may leave now, and take it back to your room," he says and walks away to help another student before I can ask him anything else.

11

ISOLA

"**I**sola?" Thorne's voice shouts after the door is knocked on three times. I run over, pulling it open, and he is standing with three books in his hands, then his head tilts to the side.

"Are you going to let me in?" he asks, almost cheekily.

"Are they for me?" I ask, as he walks past me into my room and drops them onto my bed.

"Well, sort of, I'm going to teach you tonight. Remember?" he asks, and I remember what my uncle said about him teaching me something. *There goes my plan to sleep for the rest of the afternoon.*

"What exactly are you going to teach me about?" I ask, scrunching my face up at the idea of studying all night.

"Politics," he says and smiles at my pulled face.

"Really? That's what you have to teach me?" I ask, groaning.

"Yes, really. You want to rule, yet have no idea of the councils and five selected that rule the five parts of Dragca," he states simply.

"I've never even heard of them," I say honestly, and he shakes his head, opening one of the books and sitting on the rug on the floor. I go and sit next to him, leaning over to see the picture-less book written in another language.

"It's written in Latin, but I will read it to you," he says.

"You can speak Latin?" I ask, watching as his hazel eyes turn to lock with mine.

"And French," he says, leaning a little closer and picking up a piece of my hair, twirling it with one of his fingers.

"Tes yeux sont comme de beaux trésors," he says softly as he lets my hair fall onto my chest.

"What does that mean?" I ask, and he looks away breaking that contact between us.

"Just that your eyes are bright," he says, but I have a feeling he is lying to me, not that I can prove it.

"Okay, so what are the five selected?" I ask, changing the subject onto what we should be doing.

"So, you know each major town, all five of them in Dragca have councils. In each council, there are four members, and they vote for one of them to become the selected. The selected has the final say, more power, and speaks directly to the king with any issues," he explains.

"That makes sense," I nod.

"Here it explains that the council have open meetings every Friday, where anyone with an issue can come and speak," he pauses for a second. "I went to one once," he tells me.

"What did you go for?" I ask.

"I went to get justice for my adoptive parents, against Elias," he tells me, his anger looks like it is almost vibrating through him until I move closer and rest my hand over his. He doesn't move, but he doesn't move his hand away from mine. I know I shouldn't comfort him, he is a dragon guard, yet here I am. *I never said I was smart.*

"You don't have to tell me if you don't want to," I say, and he leans back, putting the book down on the floor with his free hand.

"I might as well tell you before Elias tells you the twisted version," he says, and I stay quiet. I don't think Elias would bother making up any excuses, he seems like the type to own the deaths he has caused. The dragon guards do kill, and I'm sure Thorne has killed to get to where he is now.

"My adoptive parents, my father to be exact, helped his brother to kill someone very important, but he was made to do it," he shakes his head.

"Who?" I ask, wondering who his uncle killed, and why his father would be killed for helping.

"It doesn't matter, what matters is that he shouldn't have been made to help, and Elias was ordered to find him and kill him for it. My mother killed herself because of the loss of her mate two days after his death,"

"I'm so sorry," I say, and he looks over at me.

"So am I. I wanted to save them, but I couldn't. I hated feeling weak."

"I felt that way when I saw my mother dead, when I saw Jace dead. I'm never there to help them, always late," I whisper and he nods.

"How old were you?" I ask.

"It was two years ago that he was killed. I was training and didn't know they had been found. They had been on the run for years," he explains.

"Can you help me with something else?" I ask him after a lot of silence has passed between us.

"Sure," he smiles sadly.

"I have this plant, and I wondered if you could take me to the library, so I could find some books on it?" I ask.

"Yeah, let's go now, I'm not in the mood for studying," he says, jumping up and holding a hand out for me. He pulls me up before walking to the door and opening it for me. We walk down the quiet corridors, only passing a few students the whole time. The library is right at the end of the longest corridor in the castle, and it has big dark-wooden doors.

"This is the library, I can wait outside for you if you want," he offers, and I nod, walking a little away from him before stopping and walking back. I gently wrap my arms around his frozen body, hugging him and walking away before I look back at his reaction.

12

ISOLA

"What are you reading?" Elias asks, jumping onto the sofa next to me in the library and ruining my perfect silence. The library is even better than Thorne said it was, and I will have to remember to thank him later for bringing me here. It's the perfect mix between human technology and the ancient magic of Dragca. They even have chargers in here for Kindles, and modern books that the librarian told me they import from Earth every month. *I swear I'm never leaving this place.*

"Nothing," I quickly try to shut the book, but he easily takes it off me. I cover my face with my hands as he starts reading it out loud.

"His hands slide down my body, as his mouth devours my own. I can't help the moan that escapes my lips when Enzo-" Elias begins reading louder. I jump over to his side of the sofa, slapping my hand over his mouth, and he laughs. I pull my book away, sliding it on the side as Elias keeps laughing.

"You really are a naughty princess, aren't you?" he asks me with a smirk. I roll my eyes at him before getting up and walking away. I hear him follow me as I walk down the aisles full of books, both modern and old mixed together in their respective categories. I get to the charging table, and picking up my Kindle, see that it's fully charged. I unplug it, practically giddy at the thought of logging myself in and finishing my book.

I take one more look at the massive library, the rows of bookshelves, the big windows, and pause to appreciate the old-fashioned, cozy feel to the place. I love it, it reminds me of the library from *Beauty and the Beast*. I keep walking when I hear Elias behind me, hoping to get back to my room before he comments on anything he just read.

"I'm only winding you up; it's cool that you read. Though, I had you down as a classic kind of girl, not the girly porn type," he says as he jumps out from behind a bookshelf and blocks my way out of the library. I find every word out his stupidly attractive mouth downright insulting to females. We should be allowed to read whatever we like, without being told it's porn.

"It's not girly porn," I stop walking and face him, as he laughs at me.

"Yes, it is. Books like that are written to get bored girls all hot and bothered," he says, stepping closer to me. I swallow when his rich, smoky smell hits me, and my dragon basically purrs in my mind.

"Don't even think about it," I tell her, watching as Elias tilts his head to the side.

"Mine," she replies simply. It's not a demand exactly, but it sounds like she has made her mind up on something she is keeping. She never said that about Jace; well, honestly, she only tolerated him, and I never really knew why. But he was still family in her mind, and she misses him as much as I do. Yet this damaged, kind of crazy and dangerous dragon, she wants to keep? *You have got to be kidding me.*

"I've never seen an ice dragon's eyes before," he says into the silence, only the sound of pages turning and the librarian falling asleep at the desk can be heard in the room.

"They're normal for me, but I couldn't remember fire dragon eyes, not until I saw them here," I comment.

"What *do* you remember from when you lived here?" he asks me, leaning back on the bookshelf.

"Why do you want to know?" I ask him in return, and he only smirks.

"I heard that before the queen was killed, there was peace in Dragca. I was too young when she died to remember that time, and I lived out in a poor village. I'm curious what the royals and the rich called peace," he states. I don't know that I really remember much to tell him.

"I remember big parties, long dresses, and beautiful dragons. I remember how my mother would travel to villages and give the people food," I say, thinking of how I remember my mother looking. She always had her long, white-blonde hair up in a bun, with two plaits on the sides and little curls that escaped. She always wore white or blue, never any other colors, and she smelled like sweets. I miss her so much. Honestly, I miss more of the dead than I love any of the living.

"You used to go with your mother," he tells me.

"Once, I went once with my mother, but she hid me. No one knew I went, how did you?" I ask, curious about how he could ever know that.

"Don't you remember? You gave me and Dagan food and your gold rings," he says, making a flashback pop into my mind.

"DON'T GO FAR," my mother warns me, her hands full and unable to grab on to me. She holds two baskets of food, and several guards with her also carry as much food as possible. I slip out two rolls of bread from the carriage and smile at her.

"I promise," I say cheekily, almost tripping on the deep mud on the ground that sticks to my white dress. I walk around the fountain, stopping when I see two boys my age sitting on the edge. One of them is drinking the water, and the other is staring at the ground, his black hair hiding his face.

"Hello," I say as I walk up to them, and they both turn to look at me.

They are brothers, and are kind of cute, even as their dragons take over, making their eyes go black. I watch as they look at the bread in my hands.

"Here," I offer the bread to them, and they both shake their heads.

"Well, I'm just going to leave this here then," I say, placing it on the side of the fountain and stepping back. I look down at the three gold rings on my fingers and back to the skinny boys that won't even look me in the eye. They are starving, and I'm wearing gold that my father gave me that could help them. I slide the rings off, putting them in the middle of the bread. One of the boys watches me the whole time, whereas the one with long, messy black hair doesn't look my way.

"Isola! Where are you?" I hear my mother shout, sounding worried.

"Goodbye," I say to them, but they don't reply as I turn around and run back to the carriage.

"YOU WERE the boy with the messy black hair," I say in shock. I hadn't thought I would ever see those boys again. I was so proud I had helped them, proud that I was like my mother and could do something beneficial for others. We made up stories in that carriage of how when I was queen, I could sneak out and feed the villages, even make some changes, so they weren't so hungry all the time.

"Dagan remembers you, just as I do, but he is too proud to thank you for saving our lives. Our mother had been killed by one of her clients, and the whorehouse had kicked us out that morning," he admits, the strain on his face suggesting it's hard for him to do so. I can see why Dagan would never bring it up, it must be a bad memory. I could only imagine how strong they both had to be to survive a life like that.

"I'm so sorry," I whisper, feeling a lot of respect for him.

"Don't feel sorry for me, princess. Your rings got us a room to rent in a house, where an old dragon guard found us and told us we had dragon guard blood. He trained us, and the rest is history," he says, looking down at the ground, much like he did when he was a child. Over the years, I had thought about those boys. I'd felt a connection to them that I've never really understood. I kind of get why my dragon likes Elias now, she must remember him and think he is someone important to her. *At least that's what I'm going to convince myself, and not that my dragon thinks he is the perfect mate for us.*

"My mother was killed two weeks after that," I say quietly and hold my Kindle closer to me as he looks back up. Our mothers were killed close to each other, our lives forever changed, and in so many different ways.

"What do you have on that?" he asks me, changing the subject. I hand him my Kindle after logging in, watching as he unlocks it. I can't even believe this place has Wi-Fi, but apparently it only works in here for some reason.

"All girly porn, the topless guys on the covers tell me that. This one even has three topless guys on it," he chuckles. "Interesting, what is reverse harem?" he asks me, giving me a look that would make most girls want to grab their Kindles and run.

"I'm not embarrassed about what I read, so stop looking like that. It's one girl with three or more men," I say, and he chuckles.

"Sounds like a lot of fun," he winks but then ruins it with his next words, "though I doubt someone like you could handle more than one guy."

"Just when I was starting to think you weren't a complete asshole," I say, snatching the Kindle back and setting it on the bookshelf behind me.

"I don't get why you read this stuff when real men are *much* better," he says.

"Maybe I read them because no men could ever compare to the men in these kinds of books," I taunt. I know my book boyfriends are all fictional fantasies, but still, it's true.

"Maybe you just have never found the right kind of man, *princess*," he says, stepping closer and making me rest my back against the bookshelves.

"I did," I whisper, and he tilts his head to the side.

"No, you didn't," he tells me.

"You don't know anything," I say, slamming my hands into his chest. He laughs, grabbing both of my hands and pinning them above my head as I struggle against him.

"Let me go, Elias," I spit out, and he leans down, his head close to my ear.

"You may have loved Jacian, you may have *thought* he was everything to you, but he wasn't the man for you," he tells me, like he thinks he knows everything.

"How the fuck would you know anything?" I ask him, my dragon growl escaping my lips.

"Because you're still alive, still fighting for every breath, and your heart speeds up whenever I'm close to you. If he was the kind of love you would die for, the kind of love that burns away everything inside of you, you wouldn't be here now. You would be destroying the world for taking him from you. You wouldn't be able to think of anything other than revenge and death," he says.

"How could you possibly know that?" I reply quietly, hating that he could possibly be right.

"I had a woman I wanted to mate with, and I had to watch her die while I could do nothing to stop it. But I knew when she died, that I never really loved her, at least not like I should have. I still wanted to live after she was gone," he says.

"Then why did you want to mate with her? If you didn't love her?" I ask breathlessly, still pinned to the bookshelf, with his body pressed against me.

"I thought I did. I listened to my tutor when he told me our bloodlines would have made a powerful dragon guard, that we should be together because of our blood," he smiles, an almost sad smile. "Like you and Jacian were kept together, made to fall in love, because you were the last of the ice dragons. Not because you chose each other, or even loved each other."

"You may not have loved your mate, but I loved Jace," I snap.

"You did love him, sure, but you were never *in* love with him.

There is a big difference, *princess,* and if anything, I hope you never fall in love with anyone. Because of who you are, you will lose them," he tells me, then lets me go. He walks off down the aisle as I try not to think about his words, though I know I will never be able to forget.

13

ISOLA

"**Y**ou're quiet today," Korbin says as we run, and I don't immediately respond. Elias pissed me off way too much last night with everything he said, everything he made me think about. I know he was right, and I hate him for it. I did love Jace, but was I *in* love with him? Did I really even know the meaning? Every memory I have of Jace keeps flashing through my mind, and in not one of them can I really remember loving him. He was just there for me, and I kind of hate that Elias was right. We *were* pushed into being together. There wasn't another option. Everything was planned, from our first date at fifteen, to every date after that. We were such close friends, but I don't remember any moment that really made me think, I love this man. *I hate myself for these thoughts, it feels like such a betrayal.*

"I'm just tired, I didn't sleep well," I finally reply lightly, running faster to try and get the images out of my head that have been running on a loop all night. Thinking of my true feelings for Jace inevitably led to thoughts of his murder, and they have spiraled from there. Jace with the dagger in his heart. His dead eyes staring back at me. How similar he looked to my mother's dead body. They were killed in the same way, and I know I am next on the hit list. *Will I die just as they did?*

"Isola, watch out for the hill!" Korbin shouts at me. I'm so lost in my thoughts, I don't see the edge of the hill until I'm rolling down it. I scream as I hit trees, bouncing off them as I reach my hands out to try and grab onto anything, but it's pointless. I finally get to the bottom, rolling across the dirt and rocks, coughing as I pull myself up.

"Isola! Isola, I'm coming down!" I hear Korbin shout. Looking up, I see him jumping from tree to tree as he makes his way down the hill. *How the hell does he do that?* He jumps onto the tree closest to me, and slides down it, avoiding all the branches, and runs over to me.

"You're hurt, but it should heal," he says as he grabs my chin to examine my cheek. I lift my hand, feeling the warm blood drip down my face as he shakes his head.

"What is going on in that head of yours that you weren't paying attention to where you were going?" he asks me, still holding my chin and making me look at his green eyes that are practically swirling with anger.

"Why do you care? This is just a job to you lot," I spit out, jerking my face away from him and walking a few steps away.

"I don't know why I give a damn about a spoilt fucking princess, but for some reason, I do. I don't see many other people lining up to be your friend," he says.

"Friend? You seriously want to be friends with someone you call 'a spoilt fucking princess'?" I ask, and he chuckles.

"That's right, doll, I do, and you look like you need a friend, but don't tell anyone that I'm yours," he warns, and I just laugh. The one person volunteering to be my friend, and he doesn't want me to tell anyone.

"Why should I trust you?" I ask him carefully.

"I never said to trust me–just that you can talk to me. I'm a good listener," he says walking over to me. He takes my hand off my cheek, before quickly pressing it back.

"It's a deep cut, and my dragon senses that your ribs are broken. We'll need to stay here for about half an hour to heal," he tells me. I nod, already knowing that from the pain.

"Let's find a log or something to sit on then," I say as I place my other arm around my waist, and he nods. We walk silently through the woods for a little bit until we find a ring of logs. As we get closer, we notice the small, green plant in a pod in the center of the logs.

"What is that?" I ask, smelling something magical and pure, but not having a clue what it is.

"It can't be," Korbin whispers as he shakes his head, looking in absolute shock at the pod.

"Kor?" I prod. He rubs his beard, staring at the pod before looking at me and then back to the pod.

"You should touch it. If I'm right about what it is, it's here for you, not me," he says, looking at me in wonder.

"Is it dangerous?" I ask, and he shakes his head.

"I don't know exactly, but ancient magic is in the air, and it's not calling me. It's yours, whatever it is," he looks down at me. "Can't you feel the pull, doll?" he asks as I look back at the pod. I do feel something that makes me want to walk over to it.

"Go, I won't let anything hurt you. I'm your dragon guard, and I don't feel danger here," he tells me. I know he can't lie to me about that, the curse won't let him put me in direct danger. It would be extremely difficult for him to get around it. I walk forward slowly, feeling the urge to touch the pod grow stronger with every step. *I wonder if I fell on purpose...I wonder what kind of magic is calling me.* This world was said to be full of magic years ago, both light and dark magic, but war destroyed so much of it over the years. It is said there is nothing pure left anymore, making dark magic more powerful than it's ever been. *But then, why does this pod smell so pure?* I was hidden on Earth to ensure dragons that use dark magic couldn't get to me. There is no magic on Earth, it doesn't work there for most people. I've heard of seers powerful enough to have magic there, but it's rare. I step into the circle of logs, kneeling down in front of the pod. I feel a force pushing from it as I lower my hand towards it.

"Be careful," Korbin warns, just as I touch it with my hand. I get thrown into the air, flying backwards, before smacking into a tree and sliding down. I open my eyes, and feel a burning sensation on my right hand. I lift it and see a green tree tattoo, right in the middle of my palm. It almost shines, a green glow emanating from it. I look over to see Korbin running towards me, but he stops when I stand, looking back at the pod. It's open, a small green fairy-type thing in the middle of it, fast asleep.

"What is that?" I ask as Korbin looks away from it and comes over to me.

"A baby tree spirit," he whispers and lifts my hand, swearing under his breath before dropping it.

"It has marked you as its own, and you have to look after it now. It's a blessing," he explains to me, staring in awe at the tree spirit.

"They are very powerful when they are older, blessed with magic. It's said the dragon they mark is destined for greatness. There hasn't been a dragon blessed by a tree spirit in thousands of years, doll," he says, looking down at me. He steps closer, rubbing a finger over my cheek. "It had to be you, didn't it?" he says so quietly that I'm sure he didn't mean to say it aloud.

"Kor," I whisper, wondering what he is thinking as he stares back at me. His eyes glaze over, fire burning across them for a second, before he shakes his head and steps away from me.

"The tree spirit must have healed you, your cheek is completely mended. Pick her up, we can leave," he says, walking away to stare up the hill.

"Are we friends now, Kor?" I ask him.

"Seeing as we have cute little nicknames for each other, I would say so," he says, a hint of humor lacing his words that makes me chuckle a little.

"Can I call you Kor-Kor? Or Korby?" I ask. When he glares at me, I put my hands in the air. "Too far? Okay, I get it," I say, laughing as I walk over to the tree spirit. I lean down, scanning her long, glittering green hair, her pale green skin, and the tiny leaf she's wearing. She looks like a doll, albeit an odd one. Picking her up with both hands, I tuck her into my jacket and button it up, so she's tightly snuggled in.

"Let's go," Korbin says, pointing to the left of the hill.

"We need to walk this way for about half an hour, and then we can climb a small set of rocks to get to the castle," he tells me. We walk silently for a while, as I keep looking down at the tree spirit.

"There's a game called *The Sims*, and there's these plant *Sims* you can get in the game. She looks just like one, but with longer hair," I say, and Korbin gives me a strange look.

"What does the game do? We get a few games from Earth, but they are of no interest to me," he says.

"You make your own humans and houses. And you're able to control them," I explain.

"So strange, but I imagine that it is good practice for when you are queen and have a real world to control," he comments after clearly thinking about it.

"Not exactly. It takes hours to build a castle on that game, and there are no dragons," I say, and he gives me a confused look.

"I know, right? No dragons, no fun," I say, remembering how Jace used to think it was funny that I wanted dragons in the game.

"There's that look on your face, the same one you had when you fell," he says.

"I was thinking of Jace, you know the ice prince that is dead?" I repeat his words, and he flinches.

"I am sorry I said that to you. I have an excuse, but I doubt you want to hear it," he says.

"Tell me," I reply, kinda wanting to hear it.

"My girlfriend, intended mate, is here at the castle. I didn't tell her I was going to be here for a few weeks to protect you. I wanted to surprise her," he chuckles, a deep and dark chuckle that is a little frightening.

"What happened?" I ask, not understanding why I feel sick at the thought of him having a girlfriend. It's not like I could be interested in him like that. *He is a dragon guard; it's so forbidden it's not funny.* Besides, it's not like I can stop thinking of Jace, so it doesn't matter.

"I walked in on her screwing some dragon. She had the nerve to say it was my fault because I didn't tell her I was here," he growls.

"If you ask me, you are better off without her. She clearly didn't deserve you," I say, and he looks back at me for a second.

"After I found her, I came into the lunchroom, and I didn't think before I spoke. I can't apologize for Dagan, he is just a dick, but I didn't mean to upset you," he says.

"Apology accepted," I say, nearly tripping on a rock but able to catch myself. Korbin looks back, shaking his head.

"Come on, doll, before you break anything else," he teases. I grin, walking after him and deciding that maybe Korbin isn't that bad after all.

14

ISOLA

F ire, fire, and more fire is everywhere I look. I can't see anything
through the flames as they warm my skin. I look up and see the
top of a building, strange lights hanging from the ceiling with
wire hanging between them. This can't be Dragca. I feel myself turn
around, and I see a figure walking through the fire. I run towards them, a
sword in my hand that I hold up in the air.

"Don't," a female voice warns, and I stop, looking over to see a
woman my age with black hair that touches the floor, a green dress, and
black swirl tattoos on her face.

"Who are you?" I ask. I see the flames are frozen in place, and I look
back at the woman.

"A friend, and what happened here, cannot happen," she smiles, and
steps away. "This is your warning, my friend," she says, and then everything suddenly goes black.

I SIT up sharply in bed, holding a hand to my head and feeling
like tiny daggers are being shot through my skull. *What in the
world was that dream? This is the second one since I got here.* I jump
when I hear a smash from my bathroom, followed by the sound
of water being poured. I slide out of bed, walking slowly over to

the bathroom, and open the door, not knowing what to think. The tree spirit has made a bath in the sink, with bubbles everywhere, and she is floating in it.

"Err, hello?" I ask, watching as she sits up in the water, swinging her hair around, and splashing water all over me.

"Bee," she says simply.

"Bee?" I ask.

"Bee," she says again, pointing at her chest this time.

"Is your name Bee?" I ask her. She nods, before swimming over to the plug and pulling it out as I just stare.

"So, Bee, you chose me or something?" I ask, and regret it instantly when it sounds like I'm quoting *Pokémon*.

"Bee," she says standing up as the water drains and putting her hands in the air. A ball of green glitter appears in her tiny hands, and she lets it go. It dries all her clothes as it lands on her, and she floats up into the air, flying past me back into my bedroom. I walk back into my room to see her land on my pillow, pulling my quilt over herself, and promptly going to sleep.

"That's rude, and cute. Hell, I don't know," I mutter, and I see her lips turn up in a little smile.

I groan when I realise it's Saturday, and I have history lessons or whatever with my uncle. I go into the bathroom and get ready, dressing in the leather uniform. I look back once more at a sleeping Bee before walking out. Thorne is leaning against the wall opposite my room, and he silently lifts a chocolate muffin and a coffee cup in the air.

"An apology muffin? I heard humans buy food to say sorry," he says, holding out his offerings. I accept them and laugh.

"Sometimes they do, but I've always preferred flowers or wine," I wink at him.

"Aren't you a little young in human years to drink?" he asks, but it's playful.

"I lived in Britain; the drinking age is eighteen, but they don't reinforce that much. I was drinking with Jace from fifteen," I say, thinking about how out of control we used to get because we knew we had so much responsibility in our future. It was just a good way to let off steam, to relax.

"When I mess up next time, I will remember the wine," he says, knocking my shoulder in a playful way. I eat my muffin, throwing the wrapper in a bin on the way to my uncle's office. It's clear everyone sleeps in on a Saturday, as we only see a few dragon guards as we walk. I drink the coffee slowly, wondering how Thorne knew I liked a lot of sugar in my coffee. *Thank god for dragon high metabolism, or I'd be the size of a house.*

"Good luck, and I will wait here, as usual," Thorne says, running his hand through his brown hair, before lowering it back to his side.

"Thanks," I smile at him before knocking on my uncle's office door and hearing him shout for me to come in. I open the door and walk in, seeing him sitting on his chair behind his desk. In the middle of the room is a map of Dragca. It's huge. I've seen maps of Dragca before, but this really shows the intricate details. It looks like a dragon eye. The main part is the land around the pupil of the eye, which is where we are. The pupil is mainly mountains, with two gaps in them. One is the castle my father lives in, and the other is the academy.

"Have you seen this map before?" my uncle asks.

"Yes, we had one sent with us when we were left on Earth. I have looked at it a few times, but never studied it," I say as he gets up and walks over to me. He picks a long walking stick up off the side of the wall and points the tip on my father's castle.

"The royal castle of Dragca, where you were brought up. It's on top of a mountain, making it impossible to penetrate from the ground. As you know, massive dragonglass spears are kept on the top of the castle, and the guards will shoot at any enemies that get close if the guards wish it. Not to mention the dragon guard who fly around defending the castle," he says, moving the tip of the stick across the map to the academy.

"This is us, and again, we are in a good position. We have

dragons in the mountains, to keep us safe, but what is it that makes us safer than anywhere else in Dragca?" he asks me.

"I don't know, I think I remember something about a barrier," I reply, and he tuts.

"Every queen should know where to find the safest place in the world she rules," he warns me, and I nod, knowing he is right.

"Ten thousand years ago, there was a war between dragons and the dark magic users. When dragons use dark magic, it corrupts their souls, and there is no saving them. The dragons fought the war on the very ground we are standing on, but there was a huge price. We can't use light magic anymore. The abilities we were said to have, were lost that night," he tells me.

"What could we do? Why is it safe here?" I ask him.

"We could heal, we could see magic in the air, we could make portals, and most of all, we could connect to the magic of this world to do incredible things," he says and sighs. "Most magic is lost, as are the spirits we had as familiars and the magic they gave us. Dark magic still exists of course, but not dark familiars, so the dark magic users will never be that powerful," he informs me.

I start to tell him about Bee when my dragons whispers, *"Not to be trusted, must keep Bee safe,"* and I pause, closing my mouth before I say anything, deciding to trust my dragon. My uncle keeps talking anyway, not even noticing my pause.

"The land is safe because of the blood spilt here. It keeps those who want war and destruction away, literally stopping them from entering. Anyone that sides with the fire rebellion, would never be able to get in here," he says, and I nod. He slides the tip of the walking stick across to the land of the eye, and to the area just above.

"Any clue what all this is across here?" he asks.

"The poor villages," I say, remembering from my visit as a child. We flew across the purple ocean to them, and the villages are all the same from my memory. Mud huts, muddy ground, and full of the worst of our kind in some places, like the whore-houses and drug dens. There are also people who are just born into that life and don't deserve to be there, but have little choice. Not all dragons have rich parents, so they don't get an education or any way of escaping the life they have.

"A blight to our proud world, but every world has them," my uncles goes on.

"My mother used to say the most beautiful things in the world can be lost in the dirtiest and most dangerous places, which is why you should never give up hope," I say, remembering her telling me that before she tucked me into bed one night. She really was the sweetest person, so loving and kind.

"She was too kind for a queen, too full of hope, and it was her downfall," he says, and I turn sharply to look at him.

"Being kind is something a queen needs to rule fairly, and hope is something she should inspire in her people," I tell him.

"In a peaceful world, yes. In a world drenched in blood and war, no," he says and moves his walking stick to the left side of the map.

"This is where the fire rebellion live, in the old castles. They are able to see our every move with their army of seers. We cannot get too close to them, or they move around the castle so that it's empty when we do get there," he tells me.

"We have never fought with the seers before. How can we beat an army that can see our moves before we make them?" I ask, wondering about how it's even possible to win.

"That is something your father should answer, not me," he says and moves the stick to the other side of the map.

"What is here?" he asks me.

"Our farms. Our water farms and, well, everything we need to survive, comes from the East," I say.

"Correct. Without this, we would all starve. Or worse, our dragons would leave and go to Earth. Could you imagine thousands of dragons appearing through the portals? It would be a war on Earth," he says, and he isn't wrong. That would be horrible, and the humans would never just accept dragons there. My uncle moves his stick to the bottom of the map, the black lands.

"What is here, Isola?" he asks.

"Nothing, just death and dead lands. No one can go there, ever, or they don't return," I say, knowing about those from the little I listened to Jace. He always wondered what made the lands dead, why they were lost.

"Your father sends traitors to the throne there, and you are right. You would never want to be there, Isola," he says and pulls his stick away. He rests it against the wall, and picks up a notebook and a pen.

"Here," he says, holding them out to me. I put my coffee cup down on the desk next to me and take them off him.

"I want you to write down the five main towns, the villages that surround them, and memorize them all," he tells me.

"There must be over three hundred villages, I couldn't possibly memorize them all," I admit.

"How do you expect to rule, if you don't even know the land," he shakes his head. "This is something you must learn, so get on with it," he says. I sit down on the floor, cross my legs, and start my list with the main cities. I know my uncle is right, and this is something I need to learn.

Mesmoia . . . Iaarita . . . Kenzta . . . .

15

ISOLA

"Bee?" I ask as I leave the door slightly open behind me and look at the empty place on the pillow, balancing my tray of food. I nearly drop the tray when I see the plant, well, now mini-tree, in my room. What was the small plant from my class, is now a blue tree with long leaves. There is a pod hanging from it, and the pod has a door. *An actual door, do I knock?*

"Isola, I was just thinking–" Thorne says, coming into the room and stopping to stare at the plant, just as I am.

"What the hell is that?" he asks, quickly shutting the door behind him. I sigh and put the tray on my bed, knowing that I'm going to have to explain the tree spirit. I look at Thorne, who is watching me with surprise, and I wonder if I can trust him. I guess he has given me no reason not to.

"My tree spirit, Bee, must have made it grow and made herself a house by the looks of it," I say, and Thorne couldn't look more shocked if he tried. "Honestly, I don't know. I'm thinking about knocking on the plant door, but that sounds bloody weird," I say, and then laugh a little. I start shuffling my feet when it's silent between us for a long time, to the point of getting awkward.

"Thorne, are you okay?" I ask him, and he narrows his eyes

at me. I step back as he walks over and grabs my hand, turning it over to see the tree mark.

"Why does it have to be you, *fucking you, of all people*," he growls, staring at the mark like his eyes could burn it away.

"Thorne?" I whisper, feeling like anything I may say could set him off right now. I don't know why he is so angry, but his hand is warming up and getting hot enough to burn anyone but me. When he looks up to meet my eyes, his are black. His dragon is in control.

"Thorne? Snap out of it, whatever this is," I tell him. He just growls at me, making me jump and try to move away, but his grip on my hand makes that impossible.

"You can't tell anyone about this, no one, Isola. I mean it," he says suddenly as he drops my hand. He seems to talk to his dragon before it fades away.

"*Mine,*" my dragon whispers in my mind, in such a silent whisper that I almost miss what she says.

"*You can't have every damn hot guy here, get over it already,*" I whisper back and glance up as Thorne's eyes turn back to normal.

"My dragon thinks this puts you in more danger," he explains, like it makes up for his behaviour. It's all confusing, when he shouldn't care, let alone his dragon.

"Korbin knows about my spirit, but no one else," I tell him, and he walks around me, looking at the pod hanging from the blue tree.

"I've never seen a light one. No one has, not in years," he says as he opens the door a little and stares inside. I move closer, leaning over his shoulder to see Bee sleeping on the base of the pod. She has a green leaf blanket covering her, and she is snoring lightly. *She is super cute.*

"She sleeps a lot," I shrug as Thorne shuts the door.

"My grandmother used to tell me she talked to the tree spir-its, and she used to leave sugary sweets out for them. She said they need sugar, it makes them happy and more active. Maybe she wasn't crazy like everyone thought?" Thorne says. I walk over to the pile of snacks, picking up a chocolate bar and opening it as I walk back. I break off two pieces and gently place them inside the pod, before shutting the door.

"Thanks," I say, feeling a little awkward after how he flipped out, and now is acting like nothing happened.

"No problem," he replies, rubbing the back of his head.

"Would you like to help me eat all this? And maybe hang out?" I ask. Thorne looks at the food and then back to me, clearly undecided.

"I guess I could eat," he shrugs. I climb onto my bed, moving the tray in the middle, as Thorne sits on the other side, putting his feet up. I watch as he pulls out a phone, a charged phone.

"Where did you get a charger? I can't find a plug anywhere except the library, and they only have Kindle chargers," I ask him.

"In here," he says, leaning up and opening a compartment in the headboard with a button that is shaped like a rose. Inside are three chargers, a row of different wires, and a spare iPhone that looks fully-charged.

"Holy shit, I think I love you," I say, sliding off my bed and going to my suitcase. I pull my phone out, and jump back to the bed to charge it.

"I think that's the first time a girl has said she loves me," Thorne comments, picking up a sandwich off the tray and opening it.

"I didn't mean–" I say, and he laughs.

"I'm joking, Issy, chill," he says, and I pick up some crisps and begin eating them.

"Tell me something random about yourself?" I ask Thorne, who finishes his sandwich and leans back on my bed.

"Why?" he asks me.

"I feel like we have only talked about our problems, and not what normal teenagers talk about," I comment. I know something happened with his parents, but we aren't close enough for me to have any right to ask him about it. I can see the shadows, the brokenness in his eyes, though he tries to hide it. I have a feeling Thorne has a lot of secrets hidden behind his hazel eyes.

"What do normal teenagers talk about? I don't think I've ever been one," he says.

"Okay, for starters, how old are you?" I ask.

"Twenty, and you're eighteen tomorrow," he says.

"Don't tell anyone that, I don't want to celebrate it. I never have liked my birthdays, to be honest with you," I say.

"Your secret is safe with me, but you might get a gift anyways," he grins.

"Don't," I throw a crisp at him, and he catches it, throwing it into his mouth while he grins.

"Favourite music?" I ask.

"The River Song, I loved to hear it as a child," he says, referring to the slow song that is played at mating ceremonies.

"I loved it, too, but I can barely remember it," I say. Automatically, I think back to the last mating ceremony held in the castle, the one where my father married my stepmother.

"It must have been hard, to watch your father remarry so quickly," he suggests, assuming when I must have last heard the song.

"I didn't understand back then, honestly. I was confused to see him with another woman, and I hated my father for it. I hated him more when I was taken to Earth and left alone for weeks until Jace was brought there," I say, and Thorne doesn't reply as we hear my phone buzz on. I lean up, pulling it down, but keeping it on charge as I unlock it.

"Jace," I whisper, seeing the photo of us laughing at some party on the screensaver. Jace didn't like photos, but we both had been drinking, and he let me take this one. He looks so happy, charming, and everything I remember Jace being. I suck in a breath when Thorne leans over, wiping a finger across my cheek. I didn't even know I was crying.

"I was there, do you remember speaking to me? You asked me to make sure he had a dragon's burial?" he asks me.

"That was you?" I ask, remembering the young guard whose face I couldn't see, but he had given me that little time with Jace that I needed.

"Yes."

"Thank you," I say quietly.

"Don't thank me, Isola, just remember that you're not alone," he says, nudging my shoulder.

"Neither are you," I say, looking back at the photo of Jace, rubbing my finger over it. Despite how much I miss him, this picture seems to make it a tiny bit easier. It makes him seem more real, and not just a memory.

16

ISOLA

"Not even one smile?" Dagan asks after he and Korbin dragged me out of my room at four am. I rub my tired eyes, feeling particularly murderous this morning. It's my eighteenth birthday, and I'm out of bed at four am. That is not fair, not even one little bit.

"It's four in the fucking morning, no I'm not smiling," I state, crossing my arms, and carry on walking between them.

"Not a morning person then?" Korbin asks me, and I just groan.

"Breakfast?" I ask. *Food will make this morning livable.*

"Your dragon will hunt, there isn't any point of you having breakfast," Dagan says.

"My dragon doesn't hunt, or she never has before, at least," I tell him. He laughs, before he looks at my face and realises how serious I'm being.

"Shit, you're serious?" he asks.

"It's not like she is a vegetarian or something, but she is never interested in hunting. Jace used to hunt and bring it back for her while she watched," I say.

"Makes sense that your dragon is a little stuck–" Dagan goes to say, but a long growl from my dragon slips out, and he quickly rethinks it.

"You meant my dragon is lovely," I tell him. He smirks, not replying, just rolling that lip piercing between his lips instead.

"So, what are we doing in training?" I ask them.

"Flying, we will start off with flying and see if you can control your dragon," Korbin says as we get to a building outside the castle, where they've evidently been leading me. It's open-topped, and looks like an ancient arena with stone walls and stone seats.

"I have a little confession before we try this," I say when we get to the middle of the arena and stop.

"What?" Dagan asks me, and Korbin gives me a curious look.

"I haven't let my dragon out in . . . well, months," I admit, watching as they both give me matching looks of horror.

"You have no control over your dragon because you never let the poor creature out!" Dagan shouts at me, and I cross my arms, glaring back.

"I know, okay? I lived in the human world, where for years, all I worried about was who would win *I'm a Celebrity, Get Me Out of Here* and when I last checked Facebook," I say, completely avoiding the real issue with anything I could think of saying. I don't want to admit why I stopped letting my dragon out, that the loss of control scared the living daylights out of me the last time.

"What is *I'm a celebrity*?" Korbin asks, stroking his beard with his hand like he seems to always do when he is thinking.

"A show where they put famous humans in the jungle and film them. One wins, becoming queen or king of the jungle," I tell him. He looks over at Dagan, and then back to me.

"Do the others die? This sounds like it could be an interesting show," Dagan comments, and Korbin nods his agreement.

"No, they don't die. What is wrong with you two?" I protest.

"Shame, as that would have been funny to watch," Korbin

says, and they both look at my disgusted face before they burst into laughter.

"Lighten up, princess, we have training to do," Dagan says, walking off, and still laughing. *Jackass.*

"I will shift first, and then Dagan, and then you," Korbin says, before walking a good distance away from me. I watch as he spreads his arms wide, a black mist covering his whole body. It gets bigger and bigger until a large black dragon slams its claws into the ground. Korbin's dragon has big green eyes, and a long neck with dark-red stripes down it. It spreads its large wings out, where I can see the red lines that spread down them.

"Amazing, so much red," I comment, and Korbin's dragon huffs a puff of smoke at me.

"I changed my mind, you shift first, princess, so I can watch in case something goes wrong," Dagan says as Korbin flaps his wings and flies up into the sky. I have to cover my eyes with my arm from the dust he blows at us.

"Fine," I say, taking my coat off and throwing it on the ground. I spread my arms out, whispering to my dragon.

"Will you fly with me and not take over?" I ask her, feeling her press against my mind. She doesn't answer me, instead just pushing for the change. I scream as I fall to my knees, fighting her with everything I have.

"Answer me, or I will not let you," I demand. She roars, and it comes out of my mouth with a slight strangled feeling.

"Isola! What is going on?" I hear Dagan ask, and a pair of warm hands lift my face. I blink my eyes open, feeling tears run down my face as my body shakes, fighting my dragon. As I fight part of who I am, because I can't let this happen.

"I can't do this, I can't let her control me," I scream out, and she finally roars once more before backing down a little.

"What happened?" he asks me as the shaking calms down, and I feel my dragon sliding back under my control.

"I don't want to talk about it–" I say breathlessly.

"Isola, I need to know in order to help you," he demands,

pulling my face, so I have to look at him. I focus on his dark hair; how perfect it is and the opposite of his brother's out of control hair. Dagan's serious look makes him even more addictive to stare at, but it's just the distraction I need to escape my head.

"Isola, tell me," he demands once more, and something makes me want to tell him. I never even told Jace, because I was so ashamed. I'm an ice dragon, it's part of me, and yet, I was powerless back then. And I've been scared ever since. *What kind of princess is scared of herself?*

"She killed a human, an old man in the forest, because she started to hunt him. I couldn't stop her, she wouldn't let me have any control back and wouldn't listen to me. The human was covered in blood from a cut on his head, he had fallen or something, and once she got the scent . . ."

"She wouldn't stop, would she?" he asks, not saying the words.

"She didn't eat him, but the shock of seeing a dragon gave him a heart attack. She wouldn't let me shift back. I couldn't call an ambulance or help in any way. I just had to watch him as he died," I say, remembering how it was a student at school's grandparent. I had to watch them cry, when I knew I could have helped. I could have saved his life if I had gotten help there.

"Have you talked to your dragon? Told her that's why you don't trust her anymore? That what she did was wrong," Dagan asks gently. He sits on the floor in front of me as he lets me go. I almost miss his touch when it's gone, and I have to shake myself from that thought.

"How would I know if I tell her it was wrong that she'd believe me? How do I trust that she listens to me? What if I let her take over, and she never lets me back?" I ask all these questions quickly, and then look away from Dagan's almost sympathetic face.

"I was training once when I was younger, and I read something in a study book on the relationship between us and our dragons," he pauses, "want to hear?" he asks, and I nod.

"Some people believe their dragon is like a demon that possesses their body, that they are two separate beings that live inside one person, but we know that isn't true," he comments.

"How?" I ask.

"They are us, and we are them. Dragon or person, animal or human, it doesn't matter. They are a part of us, and we have to protect them as much as they protect us, or we lose everything that makes us good," he says.

"You're quite wise for, like," I pause, "wait, how old are you?" I ask.

"Twenty-two, and you get wise in this world or you die stupid," he grins, jumping up and offering me a hand. I slide my hand into his, letting him help me up.

"I remember you," I say, feeling his hand tighten around mine, and he pulls me close to him, a light growl coming from his chest.

"I don't owe you anything, don't expect a thank you," he warns me, already back to the asshole I've gotten used to.

"I don't want a thank you," I say, pulling away from him, but he doesn't let me go. Instead, he places his hand on my hip, pulling me closer to him.

"Yes, you do. Why else would you bring it up?" he asks me, still in a growly voice, though it's not as threatening.

"I said it because I wanted you to know, not because I expected anything from you, Dagan," I say, breathing as heavily as he is, both of us just staring at each other. Anger flits through me, as much as I think it's controlling him. Korbin's loud roar shakes us apart with a jolt. Dagan lets me go and walks away, running his hands through his hair. He opens his arms wide suddenly, and black smoke fills the space where he was as he shifts into a massive dragon. He is much bigger than Korbin's, with long red wings and black spikes on its back. It turns to look at me with its bright-red eyes, before turning around and flying up in the air. I hold a hand above my eyes as I look up to see Korbin and Dagan circling around in the sky.

"Let me fly with them, I miss my wings and being free," my dragon whispers into my head with such sadness that I almost feel sorry for her.

"What you did, with the human, was wrong. You cannot ban me, as much as I should have never banned you," I admit. It was wrong not to sort this with her, not to let her inside my head. I know I should have done this much sooner.

"The human could have hurt you," she whispers, but I hear the guilt.

"No, he couldn't have, and you didn't trust me to make that decision. Promise me that will never happen again, that we work together, or this is all pointless," I tell her, feeling her sorrow in my mind, but she doesn't reply to me.

"We need to be strong to get revenge, to stay alive, and I'm not strong without you," I whisper.

"You are strong as you are me, but I promise to listen, to work with you. Now fly with mine," she insists, almost begging.

"Not mine, but alright we can fly," I reply.

"Mine," she states forcefully this time, and I shake my head.

"You can't collect hot guys like treasures, it doesn't work like that," I tell her.

"Why not?" she almost sounds like she is laughing in my head, and it makes me smile.

"Let's just shift," I say, needing to get her mind off the guys and onto something else. Her desire to have them, it's overwhelming me. I stand up, widening my arms and letting her take over. White smoke appears in front of me, blocking me from seeing anything as I relax, my body feeling like it's burning before she takes over. It's surreal watching my dragon run forward, stretching her long light-blue wings out, which are covered in ice, and taking off into the sky, as fast as a bullet.

"Free," she says as she goes further up into the sky and into the direction she can smell Dagan's and Korbin's dragons. They are flying around each other, flames coming off their wings as they flap them in the air, and they both turn towards me. My

dragon lets out a long roar, icy breeze shooting out of her mouth, but it's not to harm them. They don't feel like danger to me. Dagan's dragon flies around me in a circle, before shooting off towards the mountains. I follow, feeling Korbin's dragon at my side, the wind pushing against my wings.

"*Together*," my dragon whispers, but I don't know if she means me and her together, or her and the dragons she keeps claiming as hers.

17

ISOLA

"Y ou did well today, perfect even. Next week we will be training with swords, the week after flying, and so on," Dagan tells me as I pull my coat on. I look up at the dark skies, see the clouds and know it's going to rain soon. I raise my arms up and stretch, feeling all my muscles groaning.

"I forgot how tired shifting makes you," I reply.

"I like it," Korbin says, basically looking like he could go for a run or something. *Weirdo.*

"Want to have some fun and meet some of the students? It is your birthday, and you shouldn't be stuck in your room alone," Dagan asks me suddenly.

"How did you know?" I ask him, but Korbin answers.

"It's our job to know everything about you, to keep you safe," Korbin says, but he doesn't look at me as he says it.

"Alright, well, what kind of fun did you have in mind?" I ask them both this time.

"The bad kind," Dagan taunts. If I didn't know any better, I would think he was flirting with me. Maybe he just has that natural flirty nature some people have.

"There's a party out in the woods, they do it every month," Korbin explains.

"Will there be wine?" I ask.

"I know there will be beer," Korbin answers.

"Well, I'm sold then, let's go," I say, watching as they both smile at each other before we start walking towards the woods.

"Will Elias be there?" I finally ask, after we've walked in silence for a bit to get to the tree line.

"Yes, no doubt picking up a girl for the night," Dagan says, and I have to swallow the enraged rumble from my dragon.

"Kill the–"

"Oh my god, no, Dragon," I whisper to her.

"What is your dragon saying? Does she not like Elias?" Korbin asks me, clearly seeing the annoyance on my face and that my eyes have turned silver.

"Something like that," I reply, trying to avoid the question as much as I can. We come up to a clearing with a large bonfire in the middle. Some students are sitting on logs around it, and others are dancing to music from a speaker nearby. A few people stop what they are doing when they see me, just staring and looking none too friendly. They hate me because of my father, and the war, and maybe just because I'm not one of them. Oh, and I'm pretty sure me freezing the entire cafeteria didn't help with the whole people liking me situation. I may be a dragon, but I wasn't brought up here, and they know that. It makes me an outsider, in a place I don't need to be one.

"Maybe I should just go back to the castle, I need to get a new book from the library anyway," I say and start to turn back. Dagan puts an arm around my shoulder, drawing me back. It makes me go tense, whereas my dragon sends me waves of happiness. *Betraying little hussy.*

"Let me get you a drink and then introduce you to some people. You should try to get to know them," Dagan says, and I look over to see Korbin nod.

"He is right. You're pretty nice, sometimes, perhaps try to show them that?" he suggests, before walking over to some guys who pat his back.

"Alright, what's the worst that could happen?" I shrug, letting Dagan lead me over to a cooler box. He opens it up, grabs two beers out, and hands one to me.

"They are a little warm as we have to hide them out here weeks in advance," Dagan says, and I chuckle. I grab his bottle off him and close my hands around both of our beers. I let my dragon out a little, making my hands go cold and cover the bottle in frost. I stop when they are cold, pulling my dragon power back and handing the bottle to Dagan.

"Neat trick," he comments, rolling his lip ring across his lips. I find myself focusing on it until he drinks some of his beer, and three girls walk over to us.

"Dagan! Have you seen Elias?" the blonde one in the middle asks. She has waist-length blonde hair with red streaks throughout it. The other two girls just spend the whole time eye-fucking Dagan, completely ignoring anyone else.

"Nope, how are you, Lisa?" he asks.

"I'm good, baby," she grins, stepping closer, and I move before I even noticed I'm doing it.

"I'm Isola, nice to meet you," I say after I've slid right in front of Dagan, and I hear him chuckle behind me. Lisa looks me up and down before putting on a fake smile.

"Lisa, nice to meet you, princess," she says and looks over my shoulder.

"Come and find me when your done with your *work*," she nods her head towards me with a snide look as she says work. I roll my eyes as she walks off.

"That didn't go well," Dagan says, stepping to my side as I drink my beer.

"You don't say," I reply sarcastically.

"Some might say you were jealous," he comments, watching me very closely for my reaction.

"And those same people would be wrong," I say, finishing my drink and reaching for another one. I pull the bottle cap off, chucking it in the box and walking off from Dagan, who is still chuckling. I stop when I get near the people dancing and down the rest of my drink, before sliding into the crowd. I close my eyes, dancing to the music and trying to forget everything. Trying to ignore how jealous it makes me to think of Dagan with that stupid girl.

"You're dripping snow on the ground, what's making you so mad," Dagan whispers in my ear, as his hands slide around my waist, pulling me against his toned body.

"How much have you had to drink?" I ask, still not opening my eyes but letting him control my hips, keeping our bodies moving in time to the slow music. Every movement is sensual, and he knows what he is doing. *I hate that I like it.*

"Not enough," he whispers to me. We both dance silently for a long time, moving our bodies together like we know each other much better than we actually do.

"This isn't smart," I say, feeling how turned on he is as he's pressed against my back.

"No, it isn't," he agrees and breaks away from me. I turn in time to see him pushing through the dancers, his hands in tight fists at his sides. I mentally curse myself over and over as I maneuvre through the people and look around to see the castle in the distance. I can't see Korbin anywhere, or Elias, but I have a feeling he isn't here at all. My dragon can't smell him, or Korbin near for that matter. I walk away from the party, straight towards the castle as I try not to think about Dagan, Korbin, Elias, or hell, even Thorne. I should be thinking about Jace, my boyfriend who just died, and yet, here I am. My dragon is clearly already over him, but she is an animal, so it's expected in a way. She relies on instincts, not her heart, and I just can't process my own feelings right now. Whatever she is thinking can never be, because they are dragon guards. To let them love me, and allow myself to love them, it would break the curse, but they would lose their dragons.

"*Danger,*" my dragon whispers, just before I hear a branch

broken to my left. I stop in my tracks, sniffing the air. I don't catch a scent, but I trust my dragon.

"Which way?" I ask her.

"Left," she replies, so I do the smart thing, and run to the right. I scream when a dagger flies past my arm, cutting my shoulder, and I nearly hit a tree with the distraction. Another dagger sails past my head, landing in the tree beside my head, and I duck around it. I look around as I keep running, seeing nothing but trees, and I realise that my best shot is to shift or shoot some ice at them.

"I got you," a voice says, just as I slam into a hard chest. I glance up to see Elias looking over my head. He pushes me behind him, and both his hands light up with fire. I jump when Elias darts forward, grabbing a dagger with a hand that's literally on fire. He spins, throwing the dagger back in the direction of my attacker. We hear a grunt, and then the sound of a body hitting the ground.

"Problem solved, are you okay?" Elias asks, the fire disappearing from his hands as he walks over to me. I lift my arm, turning it so I can see the cut isn't healing.

"It must have been dragonglass, or I would have healed by now," I comment, and my eyes widen as Elias pulls off his shirt. The tattoos I have seen on his arms also cover his entire chest. There's a large red dragon across his ribs, and a row of symbols I don't recognize over his heart that continue all the way down his v line into his jeans. *I wonder where they stop.*

"Don't get too excited, we need to stop the bleeding," he laughs at my wide eyes, which I narrow as he steps closer.

"Eh, I've seen better," I shrug, trying to ignore the six pack on display, and the way his chest is so toned. Bloody hell, all I can think of is licking it. *There is something seriously wrong with me.*

"Really? Somehow, I doubt it, my naughty princess," he chuckles, brushing his naked chest against my body as he lifts my arm.

"Try not to scream, this might hurt," he says, as he wraps the shirt around my arm, and then pulls hard. I rest my head on his shoulder as I try not to scream, but a whimper escapes despite my best efforts.

"That will stop the bleeding, but I bet your tree spirit could heal it up for you," he says, and I lift my head off my shoulder to meet his dark eyes.

"How did you know?" I ask.

"I broke into your room tonight because I smelt a dragon in there that shouldn't have been. It seems your little tree spirit had put a barrier up anyway, so I couldn't get in. I followed the scent of the dragon out here, and I'm glad I did," he comments.

"You broke into my room?" I ask.

"Out of everything I just said, that's the bit you're focused on? Technically, I just walked in, as the door was open from the dragon that broke in first," he replies.

"I suppose it's not that bad then," I say dryly. He laughs and steps closer to me, boxing me in against the tree at my back.

"There's just something about you . . . what is it that draws me in?" he asks, making my breath catch. I can't escape or look anywhere other than into his eyes.

"Is it you or your dragon that is interested?" I ask, wondering how much of him is in control, because his eyes are naturally dark, and I can't tell.

"My dragon and I are divided on you, princess," he says, and goes to say something else, when we hear Korbin shout.

"What is going on here?" Elias moves away from me, and I look over to see Korbin standing watching us, blatant anger all over his face.

"Kor . . . I need you to take the princess to her room. She is hurt, and I need to deal with the body of the attacker," Elias says.

"Hurt? What the fuck happened, Eli?" Korbin demands, somehow looking even angrier than before as he walks over to us. He steps right in front of me, lifting my arm.

"Ow, that hurts," I say, pulling my arm away.

"We can't leave her alone, nowhere is safe, apparently," Korbin tells Elias, who looks at me for a long time before answering.

"You need to stay with her tonight, and I will find Dagan and explain. We should sleep in her room for protection now," Korbin comments.

"That's not–" I go to protest, but they both ignore me.

"I don't want a damn roommate!" I shout at them, and they finally pay attention to me.

"Well, you have three now, get over it," Elias says.

"Four, you're forgetting Thorne," I say, not knowing why I feel I have to remind them.

"He can't be trusted," Elias says, but Korbin shakes his head.

"With her, he can, trust *me* on that," Korbin says. They stare at each other for a while before Elias gives in.

"Take her back. I'm taking the body to her uncle," he says and walks off into the forest. I stare after him, until I can't see any trace of him anymore. *What is Elias Fire doing to me?*

18

KORBIN

What the fucking hell is wrong with me? I can't get the image of Elias pressed so close to Isola out of my head. My dragon was ready to fight him, one of my oldest friends, over a girl that isn't mine. *A girl that can never be mine because of the curse.*

"Elias thinks Bee will heal me," Isola says quietly, as we climb up the steps of the castle, heading towards her room.

"Bee?" I ask her, having no idea what she is going on about.

"Bee is the tree spirit's name, or what she told me," Isola shrugs.

"Interesting, so she can speak?" I ask.

"Not exactly, she's only said Bee," she chuckles, her laugh light and sweet. It's annoyingly attractive, but then everything about her is. From her shiny, soft-looking blonde hair to her curvy body that I find my eyes admiring far too often. We get to her door before I have to answer her. I open it, seeing the massive blue tree first.

"Did Bee do that?" I ask, closing the door behind us and walking over. The tree has a green pod hanging from it, and it has an actual little door on it.

"Yep, on her first night. I'm meant to take the plant back to the teacher with knowledge on what it does," Isola says as she sits on her bed and starts undoing Elias shirt, "but I can't take that tree back. I can't even move it, and I still have no idea what it does."

"I can help you find out. You need to test the leaves or any fruit it makes," I say, stepping closer to the tree and stroking a blue leaf. The door to the pod bursts open, and Bee pops her green head out, looking up at me.

"Isola needs you," I tell Bee, who immediately flies out the door and straight over to Isola. She lands in Isola's lap, and I watch as they stare at each other.

"You don't have to help me; I'm sure I can sort it out myself," she tells Bee, who flies around Isola, looking for something before flying back over to the tree. She goes inside her pod, and comes out with a tiny white bag.

"Where did you get a bag?" Isola asks.

"Bee make," Bee answers in a tiny voice.

"Remember that elder tree spirits make dragon clothes, woven with magic. It makes sense that Bee could make small items," I comment.

"Bee," Bee says with a happy nod, and flies over to Isola. I watch as she gets a handful of what looks like glitter, and sprinkles it onto Isola's arm above the cut.

"Damn, that hurts," Isola whimpers, as she closes her eyes. I walk over, kneeling in front of her as Bee keeps sprinkling the magic powder on the cut. I take Isola's hands in mine, letting her squeeze them as tightly as she needs.

"Sleep," Bee comments, just as Isola falls forward onto my lap, and I catch her, lifting her in my arms. She tucks her head into my shoulder, her lips brushing my neck as her breathing gets heavier.

"Bee done," Bee comments, making me look away from Isola and watch as she carries the bag back to her pod, and slams the door closed behind her. *That's one interesting tree spirit.*

I slip onto the bed, rolling Isola down next to me as gently as

I can, remembering to make sure she doesn't sleep on her hurt arm. She immediately cuddles into the pillow as I reach down to take her shoes off. I pull the blanket up, tucking her in, and she whines softly in her sleep. I don't know what I'm thinking as I stroke a finger down her cheek, and tuck a little piece of her hair behind her ear.

"Sleep well, doll," I comment quietly, and look at her arm before moving away, seeing it's nearly completely healed.

"Thanks, Bee," I whisper to the pod as I walk past and go over to the window seat. I look over at Isola, seeing how peaceful she looks as she sleeps. You wouldn't know she was just attacked a few hours earlier. I like that about her, that she doesn't destroy herself because of everything that's happened to her. It must have been soul-crushing to lose Jacian, the boyfriend she grew up with and likely loved. *What would have happened if he lived?* I doubt the fire rebellion would have as much support if there were two heirs to the throne. I get as comfy as I can before closing my eyes and trying to drift off to sleep, when someone knocks on the door. I groan, getting up and walking over, pulling it open to see Dagan on the other side. He pushes into the room, heading straight over to Isola and looking down at her.

"Is she alright?" he asks me, his voice gruff and deep, almost a growl.

"She's fine," I say, shutting the door. I wait for him to notice the tree spirit, but he doesn't look away from Isola for a long time.

"It was my fault; I left her out in the woods, and I damn well shouldn't have. I knew you had gone back to the castle, and I still left her alone," he says.

"They would have gotten to her either way," I comment, knowing whoever it was would have planned some way to get her alone.

"I saw the body, it was a student. Her uncle has sent the guards after his family and kicked his brother out of the school, just in case," he says. I hate that the punishments for attacking the throne are so high. There is a good chance his family didn't know anything about the attack on Isola, but her father won't care. He kills anyone that is an enemy, no matter what.

"Damn," I comment, running my hand over my beard as I look away.

"And when the fuck did she get a tree spirit?" Dagan asks, pointing at the pod and knowing straight away what it is.

"Bee, the tree spirit, marked her when we were on a run. I think Isola might even be able to use light magic, but I haven't told her yet. It's probably not a good idea when she needs to be in perfect harmony with her dragon before even attempting magic," I say, looking back at Isola. She could be the most powerful dragon in years if she is able to use light magic. She could be the most powerful queen Dragca has ever seen.

"Light magic and tree spirits, it all sounds like fairy tales. There hasn't been a tree spirit familiar in thousands of years, or a dragon that can use light magic," Dagan replies.

"They say that when dark magic rises, light magic will rise to fight it," I say as Dagan steps away from the bed.

"I don't know a thing about magic, but I don't like this. It doesn't feel right," he tells me.

"Nothing has felt normal since Isola got here. Something feels wrong, and I know that," I reply, "but we have a job to do, and we can't focus on anything else until it's done," I remind Dagan.

"I will see you in the morning after your run," he calls as he walks out of the room. I go back to my window seat, laying my head back, and getting some much-needed sleep.

19

ISOLA

Two hands grab my face tightly, almost hurting me, as I hear a voice shouting, but I can't understand it.

"Who?" I ask, looking up to see a blurry face staring down at me, mouthing words I can't really understand.

"I know you think you hate me, but not like this, not before I can tell you how much of a fucking idiot I am," the man says, but I can't make out who it is.

"I hate you," I spit out, but for some reason, it feels like I'm lying.

"No, you don't, and you do hate that," he replies, before picking me up, and I look away from him. He walks us through a room I can't see, it's all blurry, but I look over to see the same girl from my last dream is standing in the middle of the room.

"Remember this moment, he is not all evil," she says vaguely. I want to shout at her, demand to know who she is and why she keeps coming into my dreams.

"Who?" I ask, only able to get one word out. I don't even know if I mean her, or the man holding me.

"Yours, always yours," the man replies as my head rolls to the side, and I feel like I'm falling.

I open my eyes to my bedroom. Unhooking my arms from my pillow, I sit up feeling amazing. I honestly feel like I've drank ten energy drinks or something, and that isn't normal for me in the morning. I nearly jump when I see Korbin sleeping on my window seat, looking relaxed and peaceful. I look down at my leather outfit, and see that someone took my boots off last night and tucked me in. I look at my arm, seeing a little white scar and some dried blood, but other than that, it's all healed. *That's incredible.* I slide out of my bed, stretching as I walk over to Korbin, hovering my hand over his shoulder, ultimately deciding not to touch him because that might be a little weird.

"Did you sleep on my window seat all night?" I ask Korbin as he opens his eyes and looks over at me from the weird angle he is resting at against the window. His brown hair is messier than I've ever seen him, actually making him look relaxed, and less serious than I'm used to. He looks cute in the morning, but I'd best not tell him that.

"Pretty much," he yawns, standing up and stretching out.

"Can we skip the run today?" I ask hopefully, and he laughs.

"Nope. I'm going to my room to shower, and I'll bring back breakfast," he says, walking around me to the door.

"Thank you for looking after me; I know you didn't have to," I say, and he laughs.

"I'm your dragon guard, of course I have to," he reminds me. I feel stupid for thinking he stayed because we are friends, not because he felt he had to stay. I wonder if that's how they all feel–Dagan, Elias, and Thorne. I'm just a job to them, work, like Lisa said last night. I turn away and walk to the bathroom, shutting the door behind me. I switch the shower on, stripping all my clothes off and getting in. There's something about a hot shower that lets you calm down, and makes everything seem a little bit better for some reason. I try to remember the girl in my dreams, who has said such weird things, and wonder how she can even get into my dreams in the first place. But none of the ideas I come up with make any sense. I wash my hair before getting out of the shower, plaiting it, and then getting into my active-wear clothes. It's really weird how they are clean and folded every morning. I pull my trainers on before getting a chocolate bar out of my chest of drawers, and breaking the pieces up, placing them gently in the pod where Bee is sleeping. She doesn't even notice me open her door.

"Thanks for last night, even though it hurt, there's no lasting mark or anything," I whisper, and one of her eyes opens slightly.

"Bee help," she yawns, and then pulls her green leaf sheet closer around herself and rolls over. Clearly that's the end of that conversation. I walk out of my room, stopping when I see Thorne and Korbin talking quietly. They instantly stop their conversation when they notice I've come out, and look me over.

"Hey, guys," I smile, feeling more awkward by the second as they continue to stare. Thorne snaps out of it first, walking over and lifting my arm, turning it to see no mark.

"I didn't know until this morning, and Korbin said you are okay. I'm sorry I wasn't there. I failed you, failed as your guard," he says angrily.

"You couldn't have known," I reply.

"Still, I think Elias' plan to have someone with you at all times is for the best," he says.

"I have been called to see your uncle, to tell him everything I can about last night, and what our plans are from here. Thorne has offered to take you to class, and we can skip running for today," Korbin says, passing me a paper bag and a bottle of orange juice.

"She prefers coffee," Thorne comments.

"Duly noted," Korbin laughs, patting his shoulder before walking off.

"We have an hour before class, anything you want to do?" Thorne asks me as I lean against my door, drinking the orange juice. Opening the bag, I peek inside and see a cinnamon roll.

"What do you usually do?" I ask him.

"Training," he shrugs.

"What kind of training?" I prod as I start eating the cinnamon roll, and he sighs.

"Why don't I show you instead of trying to explain? It will just sound dorky if I don't," he says and walks off. I jog to catch up with him, chucking my empty bag and bottle into a bin as we go past.

"Have you been studying?" he asks me.

"Nope, being attacked and all this training has been a little bit of a distraction. I haven't even gotten my books out my locker from my first day," I admit, and he shakes his head.

"You need to study, that's all I'm saying," he comments, and I whack his arm with the back of my hand.

"Don't be so . . . so, erm . . . annoying and teacher-like," I say, making him laugh.

"You don't find me annoying, though," he grins as he opens the front door to the castle. We walk across to the arena in silence, with me not sure how to reply to him without lying. He is right. I don't find him annoying at all, and that's a real issue. I shouldn't find him anything, he's just Thorne. Thorne with his brown hair, his hazel eyes, and impressive body. Thorne who is kind and yet dark in a seductive way that makes you want to figure him out.

"Do you have a favourite weapon?" I ask him.

"I'm about to show you mine."

"If you show me yours, that doesn't mean I will show you mine," I say, joking with him a little, and he laughs.

"When you want to show me yours, Issy, I promise you can see mine," he winks at me before opening the doors to the arena as I stand in utter shock from his flirting. I don't know how serious he is, but, holy crap, my dragon seems to like the idea, judging by the way she is purring in my mind. I walk in, following Thorne straight across the arena and to the other side, where there is a row of targets set up.

"Bow and arrows? I should have guessed, considering you don't carry around swords like Korbin and Dagan, or daggers like Elias," I comment.

"And you don't carry any weapons at all, Issy, not the best idea," he says.

"On Earth, it's not normal to train with swords or daggers. I did self-defense classes with a Bo staff, and some archery classes, but I was never very good at either," I confess to him.

"You should be, with your dragon sight," he gives me a confused look.

"I've never used it," I admit. I know that you can tap into your dragon's eyesight and focus on things, but Jace and I never had anyone to teach us that. We had to learn everything from flying to hiding by ourselves. I know it was because we were safer away from any dragons, but that doesn't mean we didn't struggle to fit into a world we weren't meant to be in. I wonder how Jules is, if she has moved out or just carried on her life.

"Really?" he asks, and I nod, "Let me help you," he says, picking up a silver bow and five arrows in a quiver that he slides on his back. Thorne brings them over to me, and we walk over to an 'x' marked on the floor a good distance away from the target opposite us.

"Stand sideways, and hold this," he instructs me as he offers me the bow. I stand how I remember being told in archery classes, and suck in a breath when Thorne's warm hand adjusts my waist, as he steps behind me.

"This way a little," he says and then offers me an arrow. I nock the arrow and lift the bow, lining the arrow up with my lips and keeping it close to my cheek as I was taught when I was younger.

"Now, don't call your dragon, just focus on her eyes in your mind, only picturing her glowing blue eyes. Focus only on them," Thorne whispers in my ear, his body still so close to mine. I struggle to focus on anything other than the way Thorne is holding me, though I know I need to forget he is here for a moment. I close my eyes and take a deep breath, focusing on my dragon's eyes like Thorne suggested. I imagine the glowing blue I've seen in my reflection when I've looked into a body of water. I open my eyes, suddenly feeling a change spreading across them. Everything is super-focused when I look around, and I move my bow to the left a little. I can see the direction it will fly, like it's mapped out in my mind, and I let it go. It flies straight into the middle of the target as I release my dragon's power.

"That was amazing, thank you!" I exclaim, dropping the bow and turning to throw my arms around Thorne's neck. He holds me close, his hands on my waist as I lean back.

"Seriously, thank you. I didn't know it was like that," I tell him, and he just stares down at me.

"No problem," he says gruffly, and draws back from me, reaching inside his cloak. He pulls out a small blue box, and offers it to me.

"I can't wrap anything, but I saw this and thought of you," he says as I accept the box. I open it up to see a small ring, silver dragonglass by the feel of it. The ring has a frozen blue swirl, with blue leaf-shaped crystals on it. I slide it onto my finger, feeling my dragon's love for it as much as my own.

"Thank you! As you know, all dragons love shiny things," I say.

"You shouldn't have a birthday without a gift. That's all it is," he says, and I look up, both of us locking eyes with each other momentarily. I can't tell what's going on from his eyes as he walks away.

"Thorne, wait!" I shout after him, but he doesn't stop. *What just happened?*

20

ISOLA

"You are extremely late, Miss Dragice," my uncle scolds me as I walk into class. I mentally groan when I realise he is my teacher, and this had to be the class I was late for. Of all the damn classes.

"I got lost," I say, telling him the truth. After Thorne left me in the arena, apparently not giving a crap about my security, I had to figure out which class I had and how to get there. Not an easy feat. Thankfully, I found Korbin in the corridors, and he took over guard duty and taking me to class. *I need to find a damn map of this place.*

"Sit down now," he demands, and I glance around the room at the ten or so students in the class before finding a seat in the middle of two girls and quickly sit down.

"We shall start from the beginning to see if any of you were listening, I want each of you to tell me something about each race," he says, and there are several groans. I don't even need to look around to know everyone in this class now hates me even more than they did before.

"Welcome, Miss Dragice, to the Races class. We study each of the races that lives in Dragca, and we even spend some time studying humans, which I'm sure you will excel in," he says with a small smile at me. "Now, who can tell me about the seers' race? That was what we were discussing before Miss Dragice came in," he asks, and the girl next to me puts her hand up. She has long red hair, and her hazel eyes narrow on me before she answers.

"The seers have been around as long as the dragon race has, as long as humans have been around on Earth. Seers cannot shift, they have human life spans that are not extended like ours, and their magic comes from Dragca itself," she says.

"All correct, Miss Lamar. Seers are powerless on Earth, the very magic they need is lost to them if they travel over. Now, anyone else?" he asks, and a guy near the front puts his hand up.

"Seers have different bloodlines that determine their powers. Some can only see the future and others the past, and then there are seers that can warn their family of events that will happen as well as seeing the future. They only usually see the future of their close family members," he says.

"How do they warn their families?" I interrupt, and the class all looks at me, but it's my uncle that answers.

"Dreams. Seers can connect with their close blood relatives through dreams," he tells me, and I sit back in shock. I don't hear anything else they say as I think back on the dreams I've had since I got here. They aren't fake. The girl close to my age in my vision must be a seer, and she must be a relative of mine. What's worse are the dreams she showed me, this means they have to be real, and not a single one of them looked like anything good.

"Now, come and get a textbook from the front, and I want you to find something new to tell me about seers from it by the end of class," my uncle says, and I get up robotically to get a textbook as my mind goes over and over who the girl is and how she is related to me at all. *Dragons and seers cannot mix, it's never been heard of . . . but how else can she exist?*

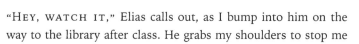

"HEY, WATCH IT," Elias calls out, as I bump into him on the way to the library after class. He grabs my shoulders to stop me from walking away from him.

"Where is Thorne? He is meant to be watching you today," Elias asks.

"I don't know, we–" I start to explain, but I honestly don't know how, "it doesn't matter," I reply, and he lets me go. I walk away, only to have him fall into step next to me.

"Don't you have dragon guard things to be doing?" I ask him, and he shakes his head.

"I trained all morning," he grins, "so, where are we going?"

"The library, I want to find some books on seers and the bloodlines, then to my locker to get my text books, so I can study," I tell him.

"What do you want to know about seers?" he asks, more seriously this time.

"It's nothing," I shake my head, trying to walk faster, but he catches me around the waist. He pushes me against the wall and presses his body into mine, holding my hands above my head.

"Let me go," I seethe, shocked that he could maneuvre me into this position so damn quickly.

"No, because you lied to me, and I don't like it. Now tell me what you're doing, and I might help you, my naughty princess," he says, making me growl at him.

"I'm not your naughty princess, stop calling me that! It makes it sound like I do naughty things to you," I reply. Elias chuckles darkly, pressing his body harder into mine, and I hate that he smells so good, and feels even better against me.

"We could, it wouldn't have to mean anything. As long as I don't fall in love with you, which would never happen, the curse wouldn't be triggered," he suggests, leaning his head down, so our lips are just inches apart. I lift my knee and slam it into his balls. He groans and falls to his knees, letting me go as he drops.

"Dragon or not, that had to hurt as much as your ego will when I tell you I'd rather fuck myself," I fume. I will never be someone's fuck buddy, especially when they don't respect me. If I decided to sleep with anyone, it would be because I want to and because it meant something. I may be old-fashioned like that, but I don't care. Plus, I have a feeling Elias would end up crushing my heart, whether he meant to or not, when he walked away from me, which he already said he would.

"Isola, wait," Elias shouts after me as I hurry away. I'm kind of glad no one is around.

"Fucking wait!" Elias yells after me again. I hear him right behind me seconds before he jumps in front of me and places his hand in the air to stop me.

"I'm a douchebag, and I'm sorry. I fancy you, alright? My dragon does, too, and he is flooding me with desire for you," he says. "I'm not thinking straight right now."

"I get it, my dragon isn't any better," I say, "but fucking isn't a good idea. I've never slept with someone that I wasn't in love with, and I won't start now," I say firmly. I know I'm worth far more than that.

"No one-night stands? Just for the pleasure?" he asks, flirting again.

"I'm eighteen and lived with my boyfriend until he died, so no," I say, and he steps closer.

"Friends, then? Even if we fancy the pants off each other?" he says with a wink.

"Friends, just friends," I say, shaking the hand he offers me.

"Now, about the seer bloodline, explain what you need to your *friend*, because he might have had a seer friend as a kid and know some shit about them," he grins, making me chuckle.

"Of course you did, but I don't think we should talk here," I gesture to the empty corridor.

"My room then," Elias says, not waiting for my answer as he turns around. I know I need to follow him for the answers I need, despite my hesitance. I guess I can't go through life never trusting anyone, though Elias Fire might not be the best dragon to trust. But, I guess a part of me does anyway, because I walk after him.

21

ISOLA

"**Y**our room is much brighter and cleaner than I expected," I mutter, eyeing the light-blue sheets on the big bed, matching curtains, and the white rug. There's a wardrobe, a box by the window seat with a pile of notebooks on top of them. But everything is put away and in order, there are no clothes on the floor or rubbish anywhere.

"What did you expect?" he asks as he shuts the door.

"Black everything, posters of half-naked women, and dirty clothes on the floor," I reply, and he laughs. He takes his swords off his back and places them near the door. One of the swords is black and the other a dark-red. They are kind of beautiful to look at. I watch as he pulls his jacket off, and then his boots, putting them neatly by the door.

"Sorry to disappoint, princess, but I like my shit sorted," he says with a grin. I walk around his room, lifting one of the notebooks up and looking over at him.

"May I?" I ask him.

"Sure," he nods, and I open the book up. Inside are pages and pages of tattoo designs, some in 3-D and others not, but they all are so amazing. There are roses, dragons, and one of several vines swirled around inside a circular drawing.

"Did you design these?" I ask.

"Yep. I designed my own tattoos, as well as Dagan's and Korbin's. Maybe you will let me design yours, and I could take you to my friend for a tattoo," he suggests with a wicked smile.

"The princess covered in tattoos? That would be interesting, and I think my father would kill you."

"So? Do you always play by the rules?" he teases as I put the notebook down.

"Maybe one day," I chuckle.

"I'll design you something," he says in a cocky tone, and I shake my head at him, knowing he won't give up.

"Tell me everything," he says, jumping onto the bed and patting the space next to him. I slide my boots off before sitting next to him and he grins over at me.

"You could lie down," he suggests with a wink.

"I'll sit," I say, ignoring his flirty tone. *Didn't we just say friends only?*

"I've been having dreams since I got to Dragca, of random things I don't understand, but there's always this girl in them. I've realised they are visions of my future, and she says they are warnings for me," I say, watching as his eyes widen. He sits there, seemingly speechless for a little bit.

"Shit," he draws out the word. Elias turns on his side, opening the drawer in his bedside cabinet and pulling out a box of cigarettes.

"Those aren't good for you, they kill humans, you know," I comment.

"Lucky I'm not human then, isn't?" he says and gets a cigarette out, lighting it up and resting back against his bed.

"She must be related to you, a close relative in order to be able to give you warnings," he muses, "but that is unlikely, seers and dragons can't have children," he says.

"How do we know that, though? It's only what we have been told, and I can't see any other way this seer is contacting me," I say, frustrated. I watch him as he thinks, inhaling deeply from his cigarette and blowing it out slowly.

"Nothing is impossible, not ever," he says, eyeing me closely.

"Some things are," I answer.

"I don't believe that," he shakes his head.

"Are we still talking about me having a seer relative?" I ask.

"What else would we be talking about princess?" he grins at me before looking away.

"*Anyway*, I don't think I should tell anyone until I can talk to her some more," I say.

"You shouldn't tell anyone. The fire rebellion already claims to have another heir and this would give them more fire to burn you with," he says.

"How do you know that?" I ask.

"Everyone knows it, everyone is talking about the heir that no one has seen."

"This seer could be an heir and have a claim to the throne . . ." I taper off and lean back on the headboard of the bed.

"What did she look like?" he asks me, putting his cigarette out in an ashtray on the bedside cabinet.

"Long black hair, my age, blue eyes," I tell him, shrugging. "She doesn't look like an ice dragon. She isn't blonde, and from what I remember, her eyes aren't that pale," I say.

"Strange. When I lived in the castle here, there was a seer that was the son of one of the teachers. He was a good guy, and we hung out a lot," he tells me.

"That's how you know about seers?" I ask.

"Yep. He told me a lot of shit, and the most important bit here is," he leans closer to me, dropping his voice, "seers can only contact very close blood relatives with warning: sisters, brothers, mothers and fathers. No one else, because the magic doesn't allow it," he says.

"Impossible, my mother didn't have any other children, and my father would have told me," I shake my head and lean away from him.

"Would he?" Elias challenges me.

"Don't. My father wouldn't lie to me about another heir," I say, shaking my head.

"You don't know him, princess. You haven't seen him in years and have no idea what he is like now," he says.

"I remember–" I start to say, but he stops me.

"Exactly. You remember the father that was mated to your mother and happy. We all know the king who had to give his daughter up after losing his mate, and then savagely hunted fire dragons in order to find out who killed her," he contends. I move to get off the bed, not wanting to hear this, when he grabs me around the waist, slamming me onto the bed and holding me down.

"Get off, I don't want to hear this, Elias," I protest, struggling to get up.

"You need to listen, princess," he insists, as he leans down, and I turn my head away from him.

"I do not," I spit out.

"Do you even know what started the war? How many innocent fire dragons your father killed in the name of your mother? How many dragon guards have died protecting him from the angry families of the fire dragons he's killed?" he asks me.

"Enough!" I shout, feeling my hands freezing the bedsheets under us.

"You don't know a thing, princess, and you do *not* know your father," he tells me, and I look back up at him with tears in my eyes.

"Kings often must make difficult choices, and yes, he might have been wrong. I don't believe he is evil. He is my father," I implore him to understand.

"And all you believe you have left," Elias says softly, searching my eyes for something. I hate that it seems like he can see more in my eyes than I want him to.

"He *is* all that I have left. I don't have anyone else, Eli," I say, and he closes his eyes. When he opens them again, fire burns the colour away, leaving them black.

"I like that, when you call me Eli," he whispers.

"Eli?" I ask when he suddenly jumps off me, climbing off the bed. I sit up and watch his rigid back in the tense silence in the room.

"You should leave before I listen to my dragon and say screw the friends rule we made, princess," he warns me. He never looks at me once as I get off the bed and grab my things. I pause at the door, glancing back at Eli with his head lowered and arms crossed.

"Bye, Eli," I whisper, and his black eyes dart up to gaze at me. I turn and open the door, walking out before I say anything else stupid.

22

ISOLA

"*A*nother warning?" *I ask the shadowy figure in the room full of ice I find myself in. The floor, walls, and the ceiling are all frozen. I look down at my white dress, it's covered in glitter and crystals.*

"Yes," the girl says, as her body comes into focus, and I can see her blue eyes, dark hair, and the long, dark-blue dress she has on.

"Of what? Ice?" I ask, and she laughs sadly, shaking her head.

"Of what happens when fire falls for ice," she waves around the room I don't recognize, "ice always wins."

"Who are you to me?"

"I cannot tell you that, you must discover that on your own," she says, stepping closer, so I can see we are the same height.

"Remember that when fire falls for ice, ice always wins," she states, and everything fades to black before I can ask her what that even means.

I WAKE up to the feeling of something pulling my hair. Turning my head, I see Bee sitting on my pillow, a piece of my hair in her hand, tugging on it.

"Food?" she asks, and I yawn as I reach into the cabinet above my head and grab a chocolate bar.

"Do you eat anything other than chocolate?" I ask her, and she shakes her head, pointing to the tree.

"Leaves food, chocolate food," she says.

"That's good speech," I smile at her as I open the chocolate bar and get out of bed. She flies over to her pod next to me, where I leave some pieces of chocolate for her.

"Bee, do you ever feel like everything is out of your control? Like you're playing a game, but you don't know the rules?" I ask her, resting my hand against the tree.

"No," she says, shaking her head and flying out of the pod. I hold my hand out, and she lands on it, hanging her feet over the side of my palm.

"Fate," she points at the mark on my hand as she speaks.

"What if fate is playing a dangerous game?" I ask her.

"Fate, good," she tells me, but I don't get to respond, as someone knocks on my door.

"Time to hide, Bee," I say, putting her in the pod, and she closes the door. I walk over to my door, opening it up and hiding my body behind it.

"Hey, can I come in?" Dagan asks, and I look down at my cat pajamas and back to Dagan.

"Erm, sure. I thought you would be Korbin for our run," I say, letting him in and shutting the door behind him.

"He is running a little late but will be here soon," he tells me, and then pauses looking at my pajamas.

"Cats?" he laughs.

"Don't, I couldn't find anything to wear last night when I got back," I say, and he shakes his head, reaching inside his jacket.

"I have a letter for you, kitty cat," he says.

"Don't call me that ever again," I groan, taking the yellow letter off him and going to sit on my bed. I open it up, reading a long invitation from one of the area's richest families for their daughter's mating ceremony. The estate is nearby, and prominent families always invite a royal to watch their matings. Normal dragons may mate whenever they like, but it's considered a blessing to have a royal in attendance. I can't see much danger with going, being that it's not far away.

"It's an invite to a mating ceremony, they think it's a blessing if I go, and they have my father's approval," I explain what it basically says.

"Makes sense," Dagan responds, still rolling that damn sexy lip ring between his lips.

"How does that not get removed when you shift?" I ask him, curious. I always thought about having my belly button or something pierced but I assumed dragon healing wouldn't let it stick.

"It's a long story, up to you if you really want to know," he says, leaning against the wall.

"Sure, I'm curious," I reply.

"There's a dragon that lives on Earth, who works in a tattoo parlour. He learnt how to do dragon piercings, tattoos, and all that. Anyway, we had a job to find a young, runaway dragon girl on Earth a few years back, it was one of our first assignments, actually," he chuckles as he rests against the wall and then carries on with his story.

"We tracked this girl, who was twenty, and found her with the tattoo guy, Lucak. They had fallen in love, and her parents wouldn't let them mate, so she ran away," he says.

"Did you take her back?" I ask.

"Nope, I'm not heartless. Besides, the family had told us she was in danger, which she wasn't. She was happy, and Lucak wanted to give us a gift to say thank you for keeping their location a secret. Especially considering we lost a lot of money doing so," he says.

"The lip ring?" I ask.

"Yep, he did this, and Kor's–" he goes to say and then laughs, "I likely shouldn't tell you that."

"What did he have pierced?" I ask, with a cheeky little smile.

"The night before Lucak was to do the piercing, we all had a bet, and the loser had to let us choose the piercing for him," he says.

"Korbin lost?" I fill in.

"Yep, but still not telling you what we chose," he winks at me, but I think I have a good idea what they would have chosen.

"And the tattoos? How does Lucak get them to stick to dragon skin with our healing," I ask.

"As mad as it sounds, dragonglass," he tells me.

"That's crazy and sounds painful," I say, a little shocked.

"It is, but it's not dangerous," he says.

"You have a tattoo like Korbin and Elias?" I ask and he grins, rolling the lip ring around.

"Yep, but kitty cat, I wouldn't ask to see it if I were you. That is, unless you want me to be taking a lot of clothes off," he says, making me blush.

"Anyways," I clear my throat, standing up and handing him the letter.

"It's tonight, and I'm guessing I will need all of my guards," I say as he reads the top of the letter.

"Also, we will need to leave in three hours in order to fly there and give you a few hours to get ready. So, looks like no class for you," he says.

"Some good news then," I grin.

"You and your dragon gonna be okay to fly there?" he asks, and I redirect the question to my dragon.

"*As long as mine are with us,*" she says, and I shake my head.

"She's cool with it," I say, and he nods, walking out of the room.

"See you in a few hours then, I will send Kor to guard your room," he says and walks out.

23

ISOLA

My dragon lands with a loud thump on the ground, shaking the trees nearby, and causing snow from the tops to fall on top of her. She shakes it off before letting me back in her mind, pulling my human body back, and opening my eyes to find myself kneeling on the ground. Dagan and Kor land next to me, shifting back quickly, and I look to the skies to see Elias's dragon flying down. Elias roars, shifting as he lands and making it look effortless. He stands up, shaking the snow off and running a hand through his hair, before pulling a cigarette out of his leather jacket.

"Isola," Thorne says from behind me, coming out of the trees. His cloak is covered in snow. He decided to fly here earlier than all of us to scout the area for any danger.

"Where is the house?" I ask, looking around at the snow-covered trees and the suns setting in the sky. The light catches the snow, making it almost look like it is glowing, and it's beautiful.

"This way, princess," Elias says, and we walk through the woods with him leading the way. I slip on a piece of ice as we round a corner, and Thorne catches me, lifting me back up and smiling.

"Careful," he whispers, and I can see Dagan staring at us both as we keep walking. Thankfully, our surroundings seem to distract him as much as it does me. The trees clear out to a massive house, with a small farm in front of it, and a large metal wall surrounding the property with a big gate. The gate is open as people walk in, their heads covered, but it's clear they are well-off from their cloaks alone. They are all bright colours, with shiny jewels stitched into the partings. The pathway up to the house is lined with pretty white lights and a few trees and plants. The front door is open when we reach it, and the man at the door bows low for me.

"We have a room made up for you, your highness," the man says and turns around. Dagan puts his hand on the middle of my back, steering me into the house when I don't move, still staring in awe. The inside is amazing, with stories of dragons painted across the ceilings and all up the stairs. I can't take my eyes away from the little details, the dragon wings, the villages, and even the snow-covered trees painted on the walls. It must have taken months to paint this, for every little detail. I could spend hours searching it all to see what the story tells.

"It's stunning," I say, not exactly speaking to anyone in particular, as we reach the top of the stairs which lead to a big circular space with doors everywhere.

"Much like the princess," a woman says. I look over to see an older blonde woman walk out of a room. She bows low before stepping closer to me. She has a long gold dress on, with white crystal down the sides. Her hair is up in a complicated bun with lots of plaits and a gold flower on the side.

"This is your room, and I'm here to help you get ready," she points at the door she just left.

"Thank you. Lovely to meet you, you are?" I ask, holding out my hand. She looks at it strangely before accepting my handshake as she speaks.

"My name is Catrina Lowdane. It is my daughter, Elana's, mating ceremony today," she explains to me.

"I can't wait, and congratulations. I haven't seen a mating ceremony in years, and they are always so magical," I comment. Actually, I'm very excited to relax and see some of the magic of Dragca. Mating ceremonies are amazing, and I hate that the last one I saw was my father's and stepmother's. It wasn't a true mating, not that anyone expected it to be. They didn't love each other, and my father was still very much in love with my mother. The mating can take place whether it's true or not, but a true mating is an honour to witness.

"Very true, princess, and we are very honoured to have you here," she says.

"The honour is all mine," I say, bowing my head and looking over at Elias. He is watching me, as are the other guys, but he gives me a little smile.

"Your guards are more than welcome to wait downstairs," she comments.

"The princess must have a guard close to her at all times, I will wait outside the room," Dagan interrupts with a firm voice.

"Of course," Catrina nods and looks back at me. "This way, please, princess."

"It's Isola, if you'd like to call me that," I offer as I follow her back to the room.

"If you wish, Isola," she says, holding the door open for me, and Dagan pulls it closed behind her.

"I have a range of dresses your father sent over, and I'm very good with hair styles, if you would like me to assist," she informs me.

"My father sent dresses?" I ask in reply, wanting to see the first gift he has bought me in a long time. Catrina points to a rack of coloured dresses, most of them are a light- or dark-blue, but there is one long red one. I automatically touch the red dress, pulling it out to admire the simplicity of the dark-red, it's low-cut and has a slit up the side.

"I'm sorry, that one wasn't sent by your father. It was on the rack before I added the others," Catrina says. I hold it up against myself, looking in the mirror and catching Catrina's eyes behind me.

"Red suits you, but I doubt the king would be happy with the ice princess wearing the colour of fire," she advises.

"That's the kind of attitude that I will never adopt, we are all dragons. Fire or ice, it's all the same. I believe it's time for people to see that though I may be an ice dragon, that does not mean I am against fire," I say definitively, and she smiles at me, nodding her head.

"You will make a good queen with that attitude," she replies. I go to the small bathroom, sliding the dress on, as well as the flat shoes Catrina hands me. She sits me down in a chair in front of a mirror as she brushes my hair, curling bits and plaiting the top half, so it almost looks like a crown.

"Thank you, it looks amazing," I say, standing up and looking at myself in the full-length mirror by the dressing table. The red dress sticks to my body, the slit shows off my leg all the way up to my thigh, and the top of the dress is tied around my neck.

"Your father sent this also," Catrina says, stepping behind me and offering me a blue wooden box. I open it up to see a small tiara inside, with three white crystals in the middle.

"Thank you," I say, placing the box on the dressing table and taking the tiara out, sliding it into my hair.

"I will meet you downstairs, your highness. I wish to check on my daughter before the mating," Catrina says.

"Of course, thank you so much for your assistance," I smile at her.

"No need to thank me," she beams and walks out of the room. Dagan steps in after her, and I turn to see him just staring at me. His lips part slightly as his eyes drop down my body slowly, before travelling all the way back up.

"Kitty cat," he breathes out the nickname slowly, making my cheeks light up.

"Dagan," I reply quietly, and he snaps out of it, looking away from me.

"We should go downstairs, the ceremony will start soon," he flips his voice from dark and husky to cold and emotionless so quickly that I end up just smiling tightly.

"Okay," I say simply, feeling almost disappointed. I move to walk past him towards the door when he grabs my arm, stopping me.

"I know I shouldn't say it, and you likely don't want to know. And, fuck . . . I don't even want to say it, but you look absolutely beautiful," he says, leaving me speechless as he opens the door and waits for me. He won't meet my eyes as he holds the door, and I don't even know what I should say to him.

"Wow," I hear Thorne say as I step out of the room and see him near the top of the stairs. He breaks away from the wall, walking over to me.

"Thanks?" I ask, not sure how exactly to reply, and he chuckles.

"Red suits you, but not exactly what I was expecting," he acknowledges.

"That's something you should get used to, guys, I'm not what anyone was expecting," I say with a grin at their shocked and amused faces before walking across the hallway. I head down the stairs, seeing Korbin and Elias at the bottom, talking quietly. Elias is the first one to glance up, doing a double take and muttering something quietly as Korbin looks to where he is staring. Korbin smiles slowly, taking in my dress before meeting my eyes.

"Your highness," his deep voice comments as he bows low before standing up.

"Time to see something special," I say, wanting to get in our seats for the ceremony, and I hear Elias whisper ever so quietly.

"We already have."

24

ISOLA

The outdoor ceremony takes place in the shape of a hexagram, with a raised platform in the middle, and all the people are standing in each of the six points. I stand alone with my guards, in front of them as they stand sentry behind me. I see Catrina in the point next to me, with an older man and two teenage boys behind them. There are twenty or so other people here, divided among the other points, and we are mostly silent as we wait for the happy couple. The wind blows my dress and hair to the side a little, making me shiver. It's freezing, but no one is wearing cloaks. The floor is marked with white powder that is mixed into the grass to make the outline for the shape. The platform has an arch made of three points, raised to meet at the top, and they have white flowers and little white lights wrapped around the pillars. Hanging from the middle of the archway is a small white stone, a mating stone that must be present for all matings.

"I don't know much about the stone, what is its purpose?" I whisper to Korbin, who is standing closest to me. I don't even remember the name of them.

"Dragon stones are said to be found when you need them, and can be discovered anywhere. They are said to appear when a true mating is well-deserved. When love mixes with fate," he whispers quietly, "or that's what I was told." I turn to face him, seeing my own longing reflected back in his gaze. He clears his throat, stepping back a little, and I turn away. I have to stop looking at him, at all of them like this . . . like they are mine.

"They are mine," my dragon whispers adamantly.

"You can't collect them, we have discussed this," I tell her.

"We can," she insists, and I don't reply to her.

I don't have the chance to respond anyway, as three women standing inside one of the points near us begin singing the River Song. The song is deep, beautiful, and full of magic in a way that makes you never want to stop listening to it. I watch silently as the couple we are waiting for walks out of the trees and to the archway. The woman is beautiful, with long red hair and wearing the prettiest dress I've ever seen. It's white, with gaps on her ribs, and flows out at the bottom. There are green leaves stitched up the sides, circling around her in the design and matching the green leaves that are plaited into her long hair. The man has red hair also, a leather suit on, with a green shirt. They look amazing together, but they hardly notice us watching them. They don't take their eyes off each other as they walk up to the platform. They stand in the middle, both of them staring at each other like they are seeing their whole world. It scares me that this could have been Jace and me, doing something I never really wanted. They say mating links your blood to theirs, creating a bond so deep that you never want to be away from the other person. And linking my blood with anyone, scares me. It's not only the bond that is forged in front of us and the exchange of blood, but sex is also a requirement to mating. Thank god, we are more modern now, and don't have to watch that. Jace told me of a story he read about how it was custom for royal dragons to watch the mating, the entire mating, to make sure it was valid. *So gross.* An old man steps out of one of the points, walking up the platform and stands in front of them.

"The ceremony will begin," he says once the music stops, and there's a silence that stretches.

"Please say the ancient words to each other," he says, and the woman starts off first.

"Link to the heart, link to the soul. I pledge my heart to you, for you, for all of the time I have left. My dragon is yours, my love is yours, and everything I am, belongs with you," she says, smiling when her partner leans forward and wipes a tear away from just under her eye. He repeats the same words, and then the old man pulls out a dragonglass dagger from his cloak.

"Please hold out your hands, like practiced," he says, and they both hold out their hands. The man cuts a line across the woman's palm, and then the man's before putting the dagger away.

"Light and dark, good and evil, and everything that makes us dragons, please bless this mating. We bless you," the man says.

The couple link their cut hands as we all whisper, "We bless you."

A light shines out of them, shooting up into the crystal, and it glows brightly as the couple look on in a daze. We are all silent as the light flashes once, and then bursts out in streams in every direction, leaving sparkling little light drops that fall from the sky. We all clap and cheer, and I can't help the smile that lights up my face when I see the happy couple kissing in the archway. *It was a true blessing.*

"The magic of Dragca has blessed the newly bonded. Let us dance and drink to celebrate their future happiness," the old man says, and people cheer more as I turn around to see my guards. They all are watching me, the light dropping around me must make me look strange or something, as they seem a bit dazed.

"Guys? Let's get some food? I'm starving," I say, and it snaps them out of it.

"You're always hungry, doll," Korbin is the first one to speak, and steps away from me.

"Not always, just most of the time," I shrug, walking out of the hexagon and towards the rows of food-laden tables that people are going to.

"I'm going to run a check on the left side of the party, if you can take the right?" Dagan asks Korbin, who nods, but pauses, looking between Elias and Thorne at my side.

"I will watch the princess, don't worry," Elias says, his husky tone sending shivers through me that I try to hide. *Why does his voice have to sound better than melted chocolate?*

"I'm here also," Thorne snaps.

"I can handle them both, go," I interrupt, and they all look at me with little smiles.

"I'm sure you can, doll, but give a shout if you need any help," Korbin says and walks off behind Dagan who shakes his head at him. I head for the food, filling my plate with all the amazing food they have. Thorne and Elias get their own plates, adding twice the amount of food onto theirs as I do mine. *And they say I'm always hungry?* I pick up some little white cakes with snowflakes on the top of them.

"I haven't had these since I was a child, they were my mother's favourite," I say, not really knowing if I'm talking to Thorne or Elias. It makes me almost homesick to look at the cakes. It reminds me of my mum sneaking us into the kitchen, where we would steal some of these before the cook noticed. We would run back to my room to eat them, giggling the entire time. Her laugh could light up an entire room, and then she was just gone.

"I remember these, they are called snowdrops, right?" Thorne asks me, and I nod, sliding one onto his plate.

"You should try one, they are so sweet," I say and look away before he can reply to me. I hurriedly try to swallow the emotions that attempt to crawl up my throat. I grab an orange-looking drink off the side at the end of the buffet, and look around at the seven or so tables surrounding the little dance floor in the middle. The three singers are performing a song I don't recognise, but it's amazing mixed with the sound of the piano that one of the girls is playing perfectly.

"There," Elias nods his head at an empty table in the middle. I follow him over, taking a seat next to him, and Thorne sits on my other side.

"I forgot how amazing the home-cooked food is here," I comment, used to the snacks from the castle. Even though Jules used to cook me amazing food, it was never like this. I bite down on the quiche, and then eat some of the purple fruit pastries as I watch the people dance.

"Do you want to dance?" Thorne asks me, and Elias growls.

"We are paid to watch her, not dance and flirt with her," he snaps, and I turn to glare at him, pushing my chair out and standing up.

"I'd love to, Thorne," I say, walking away from the table and hearing Elias grumbling behind me as Thorne catches up with me. We walk into the throng of dancers, and Thorne stops, looking awkward for a moment. Finally, I wrap my arms around his neck, and he slides his hands on my hips.

"You look nervous," I comment, looking up at him as we sway to the music.

"Not nervous, it's just maybe Elias is right," he states slowly. I feel him lean forward, pressing his lips ever so gently on my forehead. I don't know if they even touched me because they are gone so fast.

"That you're not paid to dance with me? Is everything you do around me because you get paid?" I demand, stopping the dance, and moving to walk away when Thorne pulls me against his body, holding me tightly to him.

"Look at me," he demands as I just let him move my body to the music. When I won't comply, his hand slides under my chin, forcing me to look into his hazel eyes.

"I'm not here because I'm paid. I'm not dancing with you because of money. I don't even know why I'm dancing with you, and that makes me nervous," he admits, his thumb slowly tracing circles across my cheek.

"I make you nervous?" I say breathlessly. *What is it about him that makes me like this?*

"You make me forget why I'm here, forget everything, and I fucking hate it as much as I like it," he says, moving his head closer to mine as I'm left feeling like all the air has left my body.

"I don't know what to say to you, Thorne," I admit.

"Nothing, I can't hear you say anything because this–" he begins to say when he is shoved out of my arms, and I fall backwards. I lift myself up to see Elias on top of Thorne, lifting his hand, and he punches Thorne straight in the face. The music dies off, the girls stop singing, and everyone gets quiet as we watch them fight.

"That was too fucking close to her," I hear Elias say.

"Jealous?" Thorne replies, his tone mocking, and nothing like I expected to hear from him. He punches Elias and jumps up. Thorne charges into Elias, and both of them smack into the stage, where the girls scream, scrambling to get out of the way.

"Stop!" I shout, running towards them as they punch each other, rolling across the stage. When I see Elias getting his daggers out of his jacket, I know this has gone too far. I hold my hands up, calling my dragon ice and shooting it at them, wrapping it around the bottom half of their bodies as they try to charge at each other. They both look in complete shock when they follow the ice covering their legs all the way back to me, and I lower my hands.

"Enough," I say, and they both growl. Elias' hands light up with fire just as Dagan gets to the stage. He jumps up on it and grabs Elias by his jacket. Elias and Thorne quickly burn their way out of their ice holds, both of them looking moments away from attempting to kill each other again.

"Take her back to the castle, Kor, I will deal with them," Dagan demands as Korbin puts an arm around my shoulders and turns me away from the guys.

"What happened?" Korbin asks as we walk towards the house. I don't have an answer for him, so I don't say anything as Catrina runs to catch up with us.

"Thank you for coming, and we won't speak of what happened. May I have a word alone with you before you leave?" she asks after bowing low, her eyes drifting to Korbin who pulls me closer to his side.

"I trust Korbin, whatever you want to speak to me about, can be spoken in front of him," I tell her gently, and she gives him a nervous look before speaking.

"The seers speak of the curses falling, and here you are, so close to your dragon guard. I will make sure no one speaks of the clear signs of how close you are to them, but I do want to warn you, princess," she says, and Korbin stands straighter, almost growling. I doubt that helps to sway her opinion of how close we all are. We are friends, I think anyway, and we certainly aren't anything more. But then I think of how Thorne looked at me as we danced, how difficult it is to take my eyes off Elias, and how much Dagan annoys me in that sexy way of his. And then there is Korbin, who is confusing and yet amazing. When these guards should be nothing to me, they are becoming everything in such a short amount of time. I feel like I've known them forever, not just the one week.

"Nothing is going on–" I argue, and she shakes her head, letting my weak sentence drift off. I doubt she would believe me anyway.

"All curses will fall, and people fall with them. I don't want to see ice dragons fall with the last of the curses. Be careful," she says and then walks past me, whispering, "with both your heart and your life." And I turn to watch her walk away, wondering how right she might be.

25

ISOLA

"Damn, you have gotten quick," Korbin says as we get to the end of our run. We both take a breather, drinking from our bottles of water.

"It's been a month of running, of course, I have," I say, grinning at him. He is the only one speaking to me since the wedding. Elias, Thorne, and Dagan have gone into silent protector mode or something, because they won't talk to me. I've given up trying to figure them out, and decided to focus on my classes. I know I have a new class this morning: wild animals. The teacher cancelled all the classes up till now for some unknown reason.

"Thorne is cancelling his extra training tomorrow," he tells me, and I shake my head.

"And let me guess, we are flying all day Sunday, so Dagan doesn't have to speak to or train me?" I ask, because this is how it's been for weeks.

"Nope, we are training. I've had a word with Dagan, and he isn't coming. So, it'll just be you and me," he says and nods his head at the castle. "Come on."

"Why are they avoiding me?" I finally ask him. I have wanted to ask for weeks, but I just couldn't. I think I know the answer, that whatever happened at the wedding changed things. Made the friendships we were forming so very dangerous.

"Don't you know?" he questions sadly.

"I'm not certain, but I do kinda miss the assholes," I say with a little laugh.

"They can't be your friend, they've tried and failed. It's just how it has to be now, so everyone is safe," he tells me, not meeting my eyes.

"Then we are friends? Because you don't feel that way?" I ask, and he stops walking, tensing up as he looks at me.

"Don't ask me how I feel," he warns me, and then turns around heading towards the castle as I walk silently by him.

"I won't, but that also means you don't get to ask me," I say, trailing my eyes over his tattooed chest as his vest top, sticky with sweat, clings to him. I finally look up to see him staring at me.

"You have class, Isola, and I already know," he says firmly. I snap out of it, running up the stairs, and I look down to see him rubbing his face with his hands before following me up. I get to my room, shutting the door, and looking around to find Bee on my bed, passed out with a load of chocolate wrappers around her.

"Bee?" I sigh, stepping closer and lifting her little body off the bed. She curls into my hand as I take her to her pod and slide her inside, shutting the pod door after tucking her in. In the last month, she has learnt more words and grown more active. She seems to like making a big mess of my room and creating the little handbags she seems to have a problem with collecting. I smile as I look down at the second pod hanging from the tree. It is full to the rim with little leather bags of every colour, some with glitter stuff in them and others without. I grab my leather outfit, cloak, and boots, putting them on my bed. After cleaning up the wrappers, I get into the shower. Twenty minutes later, I leave my bedroom, seeing Dagan leaning against the wall this time. He doesn't look at me as he starts walking down the corridor. I jog to catch up with him, keeping silent as I look over his face. He is still rolling that lip ring between his lips, his blue eyes highlighting his handsome face as they slide over to look at me once, before looking away.

"Here is your class, princess," Dagan says, pointing at the door.

"When is this silent treatment going to end?" I ask, but he doesn't even look at me as he leans against the wall and stares at the floor. I shake my head, turning to go inside the classroom and shutting the door behind me. On each small round table is a little purple egg, and every table is filled except for one near the front. I take the seat, ignoring the stares of everyone else as we wait for the teacher to come. After a month of being ignored, being stared at like you have a dick drawn on your forehead becomes easy to ignore.

"Welcome, class," the old man from plant class says as he hobbles into the room, sitting down on the chair behind the desk.

"I'm sorry this class has been cancelled, but the eggs were not ready until now," he explains to us. I thought he was just ill or something. He hasn't been in plant class either, we were just told to study our plants in our room for the entire lesson each week.

"What are the eggs, sir?" a guy with black hair asks.

"Snakes, jewel snakes to be specific," he says, and several of the girls on other tables move their hands away from their eggs, looking scared. I have no idea what a jewel snake is, but normal snakes aren't that bad. I don't get why people are so scared of them. It's pointless to be scared of something that is likely more scared of you.

"They will hatch any moment, and it's your job to make them like you enough not to bite you, and then let them free in the woods. If you are bitten, you have fifteen minutes to get to the infirmary before you will pass out," he says, yawning as the sound of eggs cracking fills the room.

"If you want to fail the entire year, please run out of the room now," he says, and to my surprise, three people get up and run out, leaving about ten of us in here. I take a deep breath in the near-silent room as I stare at my egg, watching it wiggle a little before a deep crack appears near the top. The egg breaks open slowly as I observe, and then a tiny, green snake with spikes all down its back slithers out of the broken egg. I hold my hand flat on the desk as I hear some students swearing, and others speaking softly to their snakes, but I try not to look away from its tiny little eyes that watch me.

"Hello, little snake, I'm Isola, and erm . . . we need to go outside without you biting me," I say, and the snake hisses at me, sliding across the table. I see a student get bitten by their snake out of the corner of my eye. A quick glance at the teacher tells me he is nearly asleep and not paying attention.

"Great," I mutter, looking back at my snake as someone else screams in the room. The snake gets to my hand, lifting its head as it opens its mouth. Doing the only thing I can think of, I turn my hand around and call my dragon, freezing the snake up to its neck, and it falls on its side. I pick up the frozen snake, keeping well away from the sharp hissing mouth. I stand up and see most of the students holding books out to keep their snakes away from them. I hold out my hand, freezing all the snakes' bodies, and the students slowly drop their books.

"Get them outside, and I will unfreeze them," I say, not waiting for a response from their shocked faces. I walk out of the room, seeing Dagan waiting for me. He just raises an eyebrow at the frozen snake in my hand but doesn't say anything. I walk past him, straight down the stairs to the front door, opening it up and walking outside. I walk to the trees, placing my snake down and slowly unfreeze the ice. It hisses at me before slinking away into the woods.

"Will you do mine, princess?" a guy asks nervously, moving

next to me and putting his snake on the ground as several more students wait behind me.

"It's Isola and sure," I say, unfreezing his snake and waiting for the next student to bring theirs. Everyone's small smile at me makes me think I may have a few less enemies after today.

26

ISOLA

"**W**hat is your plan for the rest of the day, princess?" Dagan asks me after I spent the rest of my lesson unfreezing the snakes, and then explaining what I did to the teacher. He was really impressed with my idea and said everyone has passed for team work.

"Going to the library to read," I say, and he nods.

"I will wait outside then," he says just as cold and impersonal as his very first sentence to me.

"Okay, then," I say, hating how awkward our conversations have become. We walk in silence until we get to the library, and he smiles at me.

"I wish things were different, kitty cat," he whispers.

"So, do I," I say, knowing if he wasn't a dragon guard and I wasn't a princess, this isn't how we would be. I look at him once more, meeting his blue eyes as they drag slowly over to mine. It takes a lot for me to pull away, to force myself to remember who he is, and that he is doing this for the right reasons. Dragon guards and ice dragons can never care for each other, or be anything more than people who know each other. Emotions and curses don't mix, despite how much it hurts to avoid them. I shake my head, knowing I need a good book to dive into and forget the real world for a while. Good books can shake your world, make you forget reality. That's what I need right now.

"Can I help you look for anything, child?" the older librarian asks me as I walk past her, and I pause, turning to look at her.

"Nope, I'm good, thank you," I say.

"Do you know how you can cast a curse? I was just reading a book on them," she explains her random statement, her eyes drifting to the door of the library, and I shake my head.

"Any dragon can call a curse at any time, but you must be desperate, dying, or so close to being destroyed that the curse is all you have left," she tells me.

"That's how Icahn's wife cast the dragon guard curse?"

"Yes, and all curses can be broken, they are made to be," she says, looking at the library door once more.

"Not without a heavy price," I say quietly.

"The heavy price makes it all worth it. You would never risk anything for something cheap and worthless, child," she chuckles, and then coughs a little, smoke coming out of her mouth. She must be really old, as dragons and dragon guards age differently than humans. For us, a hundred years is the same as ten years for humans after we turn twenty-one.

"Can I read this book on curses?"

"Come to me in an hour at the desk, and I will get it for you."

"Thank you, I never got your name?" I ask.

"Windlow Pakdragca, your highness," she bows slightly and walks away. I shake my head at the strange old lady. I know that the information on curses could be useful, but I really don't want to think about curses at the moment. I need to find a good book to get lost in, not a history lesson. I go straight past the romance aisle to the fantasy section, finding a book written about a world full of aliens and then looking for an empty sofa down the aisles. I walk down the middle aisle, stopping when I hear a feminine laugh.

"Elias, come on . . . you remember that night? It was so good, and you're single now. I don't see a reason not to," I hear. Stepping forward, I look down the aisle to see Elias leaning against a wall, and Lisa sliding her hands up his chest. He doesn't move, staring down at her as she kisses her way up his neck to his jaw.

"I can do that thing you like–" I hear her say, and I drop my book, the sentence reminding me of what Jace said to me that morning before he died. Elias and Lisa stop, turning to look at me, and I quickly pick up my book.

"Sorry to interrupt," I say, turning away and walking fast out of the library and towards a confused Dagan. I storm past him, hating how I feel like everything is crushing me, and I start to run towards my room.

"Isola!" Dagan shouts, but I ignore him as I keep running, and then I smack into the chest of someone. I look up, seeing only dark eyes under a cloak as a pain shooting through my stomach has me screaming. I look down, seeing the dagger on fire that he has slammed into my hip, and I gasp, falling to the floor as someone jumps over me. I roll over on my side, seeing Dagan and Elias fighting the guy. Elias grabs the guy's neck, snapping it as Dagan runs over to me.

"Hold on, kitty cat, shit, hold on," he desperately begs me, but darkness prevents me from doing anything other than closing my eyes.

27

ISOLA

"We will meet soon, and this will change everything. Just remember, I will make you remember," the girl's voice whispers to me, but everything feels icy cold, and I can't open my eyes. I don't want to move, I don't want to speak, but I manage one word.

"Remember?" I whisper.

"So you can save us all, Isola. Now rest," she whispers back, and everything slowly fades away into darkness once more.

"Should we tell her what we did?" I hear Dagan question angrily, and a hand tightens around mine. I can't move or open my eyes, as I feel exhausted. Even though I can hear them, everything sounds as if it is getting further away.

"No, she can never know. No one can. This is a secret between us five now, no one will ever know," my uncle commands.

"It's not fair not to tell her," Elias demands, his voice terrifying.

"The world isn't fair, and if she knew what happened, you all know the price she would pay. You saved her life, just deal with it and move on," my uncle says, his voice leaving no room for argument.

"He is right, no one can know," Thorne's voice says, and then everything goes hazy again.

"NAUGHTY PRINCESS, I could do with seeing those crystal-blue eyes of yours pop open and stare at me in that sexy way of yours right about now," the deep husky voice of Elias fills my ears, and I blink my eyes open to see him sitting on a chair next to me. His blue eyes lock with mine, both of us silent as we stare at each other for a long time.

"Eli," I whisper, my voice crackling slightly with hurt as I remember Lisa all over him and then the dagger. I try to roll away, so he doesn't see me cry, and I howl out in pain from my stomach.

"Hey, doll, take it easy. No moving for a little bit while your dragon healing does its job," Korbin says, and I turn to see him smiling at me from his seat on my other side. I take a deep breath, calming myself down a little.

"Who was the man that did this?" I ask, my voice breaking as I rub my tongue over my dry lips.

"Kitty cat, have some water, and let us sit you up a little," Dagan says from near the end of the bed. Korbin gets up, picking a pillow up from the floor and helping me sit forward. He slides it behind me, every movement sending sharp pains through my stomach. I look down at my vest top, lifting it to see the bandaged cut on my stomach. I pull it back down again as Dagan offers me a bottle of water with a straw in it. I take it off him with a small smile, drinking it as he sits on the end of the bed.

"We don't know who he was, but he had a badge with the fire rebellion symbol on his cloak," Dagan explains, and for the first time in a while, I feel frightened. They are everywhere, always out to get me. *How can I ever be safe?*

"He is dead now, you don't have to be frightened," Elias says, picking up on my emotions somehow.

"I'm not frightened of that man, I remember you killing him, Elias," I say, avoiding the point that I'm more frightened of all the other members of the fire rebellion who seem like they will never stop trying to kill me, not until they succeed. I search for my dragon in my mind, feeling her pain as she purrs against me, not strong enough yet to make that connection with me.

"You're awake?" Thorne asks as he walks into the small infirmary room and shuts the open door behind him. Thorne looks as tired as the rest of them do. They all look like they need a long sleep and a shower. I kind of hate that despite the fact it's clear they haven't slept or showered in ages, they still look hot. I bet I don't look hot. I bet I look more like a hot mess that smells.

"Hey," I say, and he smirks, wiping his hands over his face.

"Hey, Issy," he replies gently.

"Are you tired? Do you need anything?" Korbin asks after there's an awkward silence between us all.

"No, but how long have I been asleep? Is anyone looking after Bee?" I ask, and Korbin takes the bottle of water off me and puts in on the cabinet by the bed.

"You've been asleep three days, and no one can get into your room because Bee has put a ward up. I tried to tell her you're not well, but she glared at me like I'm an idiot or something," Dagan explains, huffing.

"There is plenty of food in there, and she knows where it is," I comment, not so worried about her now. She clearly knows how to look after herself.

"I don't think she is strong enough to heal this," Dagan comments, and then explains himself as we all stare. "She struggled to heal your arm, and you passed out from that. I think she needs to be older to wield enough magic to heal something like this."

"Makes sense," I say, yawning.

"I came in for a reason. There was an attack on the left side of the forest. We should check it out with the other guards," Thorne says.

"I will stay with Isola, we need to talk," Elias quickly says.

"No, we don't. You can go," I bite out.

"We do, because assuming things and ignoring others clearly isn't working out well for us," he says, and I just stare at him as I hear the other guys walk out of the room. When the door shuts, Elias moves closer, scooting to sit on the bed next to me. He places his hands on either side of my head.

"What you saw with me and Lisa–" he starts off.

"I don't want to know," I interrupt him, and he chuckles humourlessly.

"You do, don't lie to me. You know I don't like it when you lie to me."

"Eli, I can't want to know. I can't do any of this. I can't because it's impossible for us," I whisper, and he shakes his head.

"Nothing is impossible," he tells me, and I hold my breath as he starts to lean forward. Gently brushing his lips against mine at the start, Elias suddenly deepens the kiss as I let him take control. He slides his hand into my hair as pleasure shoots through me with every brush of his lips against mine until I can't think of anything other than Eli. Eli kisses me like he demands every part of my soul, and won't stop until it is his, and I don't want to fight him. I moan a little when he pulls back, getting off the bed and sitting back in his chair.

"Eli," I whisper.

"You need to rest, but that was real. That is what is between us: chemistry, magic, and fuck knows what else, but I want to find out. What Lisa was trying to do wasn't real, and I wouldn't have let it go further. I'm done letting rules fuck with my mind when it comes to you, the rules of this damn curse."

"You can't, we can't," I say, thinking of the curse. I couldn't let him lose his dragon over me. That would destroy everything between us, it would destroy him.

"Things have changed, and I will explain them one day, naughty princess," he smirks, while I'm just confused.

"What changed?" I ask, trying not to yawn, and he looks up.

"Everything," he says, and I close my eyes, drifting off to sleep with the taste of Eli's lips on mine and his smoky scent filling my senses.

28

ISOLA

"I'm really okay, I can go back to my room now," I tell my uncle, who shakes his head as I lean down and pick up my coat that fell on the floor. I'm still a little weak, and my stomach still hurts, but it has healed over and is not bleeding anymore.

"Fine, stubborn child," he says, but there is a little bit of a smile as he turns to Dagan and Korbin.

"Take her to her room and keep guard. More dragon guards are being sent here by her father tomorrow for increased security. If another attack happens, I'm afraid she will have to be kept under twenty-four-hour watch at the castle," he explains, and they both nod.

"Isola, you must be more careful from now on. The war is coming to a close. I have heard news that your father may have found the rebellion," he says. I'm not sure if that is a good thing, because it would mean a massive fight and fewer guards around both the castle and here.

"That's good, right?" I ask.

"Very good," he says.

"We need you on the throne, and not dead. So, stay close to your dragon guard, agreed?" he asks me.

"Alright," I say, not wanting that, but I get that my life means more than my freedom at the moment. I don't know how I would explain Bee if we had to move rooms. Everyone would find out about her then.

"It's good to see you alive, Isola," my uncle says, placing his hand on my shoulder and squeezing gently before walking out of the room.

"He is an emotional guy, that one," Korbin teases, and I shrug.

"He's lost a lot, I get it," I comment.

"Have you seen Thorne or Elias this morning?" I ask Korbin as he carries my bag of clothes out of the room, Dagan following us out.

"No, I haven't, but they will turn up," he shrugs my worries off, and I'm sure he is right.

"Why don't I go and get you some of your favourite foods?" Dagan asks as we walk past the cafeteria.

"I'd like that," I smile, wondering what the hell changed between us all. They aren't ignoring me anymore; if anything they are always asking me how I am and wanting to do things for me. I don't really know what it is, but they feel like my friends again. I haven't spoken to Elias about the kiss yet, and I'm not sure how to bring it up with him. Or what he said has changed. I look down at my ring, turning it around on my finger and wishing I could talk to Thorne. We haven't had a moment alone, one of the others is always here. I have the feeling he wants to talk to me, I just don't know what it is about.

"So, doll, happy to get back to your classes?" Korbin asks me.

"Kinda, being sick is slightly boring, but I did get plenty of time to read," I say, proud of the five books I've read over the past week. Not so proud of the crazy amount of junk food I ate while reading, but oh well.

"I guess that's–" Korbin starts to say, before he suddenly falls to the floor, dropping my bag and holding his hands to his head. He looks up at me, his eyes burning black and fire spreading across them, as his face is contorted in pain. "Run from me," he spits out, and I shake my head.

"What is going on?" I ask, moving a step back when his hand goes to his sword.

"Isola, run and go to your father. Something is wrong, and I am being ordered to hurt you. I will follow you when I can get back in control," he says and then screams, falling on his side. I do what he says, fear filling me as I turn and run. I head down the stairs of the academy and out the doors, not seeing anyone on the way. I hold my stomach from the pain as I run down the steps and stop.

"We need to go to the castle, so I need you to take over," I whisper to her, and she roars, white mist appearing in front of me as we shift and fly straight into the sky.

"Danger," she warns me, flying faster than she usually does.

"I know, but he is our father," I tell her. She whines, but doesn't stop flying. My fear for my father and my guard mixes with her own fear as she flies through the mountains. The castle slowly comes into sight, and my dragon shoots towards it. The castle is as massive as I remember it being, with five diamond-topped towers, and the main part of the castle in the centre. There are bodies of guards on the floor, their mouths parted in shock as their blood pools from their bodies on the stone. *What has happened here?* I grow more concerned when I don't see any dragons flying around, and when no one stops me as I land right outside the castle. I ask my dragon to let me back in control, despite her apprehension. I hold my side when I stand up in my human form, looking down to see it bleeding a little.

Everything inside me screams as I run through the doors of the castle, seeing the dead dragons lining the floors, and the sight makes me sick to my stomach. I try not to look at the spears in their stomachs, the dragonglass that is rare in this world. *Where did they get this much of it?* The more and more bodies I pass, both dragon and guards, the less hope I have that my father is okay. *No, I can't be too late, I can't lose him, too.* The once grand doors to the throne room are smashed into pieces of stone, in a pile on the floor, and only the hinges to the door hang off the walls. I run straight over, climbing over the rocks and broken stone. The sight in front of me makes me stop, not believing what I'm seeing, but I know it's true.

"Father . . .?" I ask quietly, knowing he won't reply to me. My father is sitting on his throne, a sword through his stomach and an open-mouthed expression on his face. His blood drips down onto the gold floors of the throne room and snow falls from the broken ceiling above onto his face. There's no ice in here, no sign he even tried to fight before he was killed. He must have never seen this coming because he trusted whoever killed him.

"No," is all I can think to say as I fall to my knees, bending my head and looking down at the ground instead of at the body of my father. I couldn't stop this, even when they warned me and risked everything. I hear footsteps in front of me as I watch my tears drip onto the ground, but I don't look up as I know who it is. I know from the way they smell; my dragon whispers their name to me, but I can't even think it.

"Why?" I ask as everything clicks into place. I should have known, I should have never trusted him.

"Because the curse has to end. Because he was no good for Dragca. Our city needs a true heir, me. I'm the heir of fire and ice, the one the prophecy speaks of, and it's finally time I took what is mine," he says, and every word seems to cut straight through my heart. I trusted him.

"The curse hasn't ended, I'm still here," I whisper to the dragon in front of me, but I know he could hear my words as if I'd just spoken them into his ear.

"Not for long, not even for a moment longer, actually. Your dragon guard will only thank me when you are gone. I didn't want to do this to you, not in the end, but you are just too powerful. You are of no use to me anymore, not unless you're gone," he says. I look down at the ground as his words run around my head, and I don't know what to do. I feel lost, powerless, and broken in every way possible. There's a part of the door in front of me that catches my attention, a part with the royal crest. The dragon in a circle, a proud, strong dragon. My father's words come back to me, and I know they are all I need to say.

"There's a reason ice dragons hold the throne and have done so for centuries. There's a reason the royal name of Dragice is feared." I say and stand up slowly, wiping my tears away.

"We don't give up, and we bow to no one. I'm Isola Dragice, and you will pay for what you have done," I tell him as I finally meet his now cruel eyes, before calling my dragon and feeling her take over.

"I wouldn't do that if I were you, princess," a cold female voice says, as a dagger is pressed against my neck from behind, and I stop the shift, knowing I would be dead before I could even get my dragon out.

"THORNE, why don't you get your crown, and then we can deal with the princess," the woman behind me demands in an overly sweet tone. Thorne smirks at me before walking over to my father, and lifting the crown off of his head.

29

ISOLA

"Why?" I ask Thorne, who stands watching me as one of my father's guards handcuffs my arms behind me. The woman with the dagger moves it away from my neck, walking around me to stand next to Thorne. I didn't think I could be more shocked, but I am at seeing my stepmother's self-satisfied smile. Her long white hair is down, and she has a white leather outfit on with a white cloak. Her crown sparkles on her head in the light, very much like Thorne's does. Thorne must have dyed his hair and worn contacts; his once brown hair is now an almost white-blonde colour, and his eyes are no longer hazel, they are blue. A pale-blue like mine. He looks like an ice dragon, he might even be one. He did say he was the fire and ice heir. He doesn't speak a word, only staring at me and not moving. He's like an ice sculpture, but one I want to smash into a million pieces for betraying me. I thought he was my friend, and I trusted him. Hell, I even liked him. My dragon growls low in my mind, her anger towards him is even scarier than mine. Heartbreak and betrayal swim through my mind as I look around Thorne, seeing my father's body once more. *I've lost everything, everyone is gone.*

"I will answer that," my stepmother says, the happiness in her voice is hard to miss.

"I don't even remember your name. You're just the bitch that married my father and clearly betrayed him," I sneer, laughing at her as her eyes narrow. She walks over, slapping me hard across the face, and I fall to the floor.

"Careful now, and it's Tatarina," she says as I look up at her. The door to the left of the throne room opens, and Esmeralda walks in, her red heels clicking on the floor. Her cloak is gone, replaced with a red leather outfit much like her sister's, though hers is dripping with blood. There's blood in her red hair and splattered across her face as she smiles at me. It's a sinister smile, and when she gets close enough, her scent hits me. I didn't smell it before, she must have hidden it, but I know straight away where I recognise it from.

"You bitch, you killed Jace!" I scream at her, trying to get up, but a sword pokes into my back. I turn around to see a dragon guard watching me, his sword placed on my back and threatening to pierce all the way through me. The dragon guard will protect the new royal family, and that's not me anymore. They protect the queen, my stepmother, as she holds the throne. It was never given to me, neither was the curse that comes with the crown. I imagine she plans to give it to Thorne.

"Yes, I remember well. He was not a fighter that one," she laughs, and I growl low.

"I will complete my vow, you evil bitch!" I scream. She just laughs as she walks over to Thorne and my stepmother.

"Everything is done. I will return to the academy to finish the other issues, sister," she says and then bows to Thorne.

"My king, how the crown suits you," she practically purrs.

"You are no king, just an idiot wearing a crown that isn't his," I spit out, and he narrows his eyes on me, still silent like a ghost.

"Let me tell you a story, one that will explain all of this, and then perhaps you will watch your tongue," Tatarina says, walking closer to Thorne and resting her hand on his arm in a loving way as she stares at him.

"This is my son, a son I had with a fire dragon before I was dragged from my home to marry a king I had never even met. My son was hidden with an adoptive family I found, kept safe as I built the fire rebellion up and made the true heir an army," she says, clearly proud, and yet, I can't believe her.

"An ice dragon and fire dragon can't have a child," I say in disbelief.

"Yes, they can," Thorne finally speaks, holding out both his hands. In one hand a ball of flame appears, and in the other a sphere of ice. He smashes them together and grins at me.

"You apparently shouldn't believe everything you hear, princess," he says coldly.

"I would have given you the throne, I never wanted it! You didn't have to kill my father for it!" I shout at them both, and Tatarina laughs, looking behind me. I turn, looking to see Dagan, Elias, and Korbin being dragged into the room. They all look like they put up a hell of a fight, none of them are conscious as they are thrown onto the ground near me.

"Get the seer," Tatarina says, walking over to the guys and stopping near Elias. She moves to touch him, and I roar so loudly it shakes the ground around us, and ice spreads across the floor without me even realising I was doing it.

"You were right, it seems," Tatarina says, moving her hand away and smiling like she just won something.

"We should kill her and them, despite the price," Tatarina continues, flipping a dagger around in her hand as she walks back to Thorne.

"We cannot, not with the tree spirit blessing. I have explained this to you, mother," Thorne replies, clearly frustrated.

"Fine, we will play by the rules and stick to our plan, for now. She won't be a threat, none of them will be soon," she says. No one says a word for a long time, as I stare at my dragon guard with tears running down my face. If they die because of me, I won't be able to forgive myself. Everyone dies because of me, it never seems to stop.

"Was any of it real?" I ask Thorne, wanting to hear him admit it was fake from the start, as I look up at him.

"None of it," he says, his words cold as ice.

"I will kill you, and I promise that will be real," I threaten, and he smiles.

"I look forward to the day you try, and I get a reason to kill you," he replies, looking away as the door to my right opens. A girl, with her face hidden under a cloak walks in, her red dress moving around her as she moves towards Thorne.

"I was called," she says, her voice strangely familiar to me.

"Wipe her memory, and lock their dragons away. We will make her human, with no memory of who she is, and leave her on Earth. As for the guards, I will deal with them," Tatarina says, and I nearly choke on my fear. *Can she erase my memory of everything? Make me human?*

"NO!" I scream. Standing up, I knock the guard out of the way and try to run away when ice freezes my boots to the floor and spreads up my legs, stopping at my knees. Tears fall down my face as the woman in the cloak bows and walks over to me. I keep my eyes locked with Thorne's as the seer puts her hands on either side of my head, and whispers inside my mind.

"Forget everything."

EPILOGUE

Isola

"Time for school. Hurry up, you're going to be late, Isola," Jules says, and I chuckle, putting my Kindle down and standing up off the kitchen stool.

"Okay, okay. I'm going," I say and walk past her, patting her arm before running to the door. I grab my bag and slide my boots on, before leaving the house and walking to the bus stop. I stand there waiting, like I do every day, and it starts to snow, not that we weren't expecting snow at some point. The bus pulls up and I get on, walking down the aisle and stopping as I look at the three guys in the back row. One has black hair, tattoos, and is smoking; another has black hair too, and a lip ring that I watch him twist and play with between his lips. The last guy has a serious look, with dark-brown hair and a big, muscular build just like his friends. The three of them all stare at me as I slide into a seat. I don't look back at the new students, despite the fact they look familiar, which is impossible. I've lived in Barkwood, in Wales, my whole life. It's the smallest town ever. Anyone new or as good-looking as these guys are, I would definitely remember.

"Issy, have you seen the new hotties?" Melody asks as she scoots into the seat next to me. Melody and I have been friends since we were kids. With her black hair and blue eyes, she is a stunner, and a pretty good friend, too.

"Yeah, they are something," I say, and she laughs. We chat about pointless things until the bus stops outside the school, and we all get off the bus. I stop to put my phone in my bag when someone slams into my shoulder.

"Watch where you're going, princess," the guy with the tattoos says and storms past me with his friends into the school.

"Come with me, I want to ask you something," Melody says suddenly and grabs my hand, dragging me through the school. She drags me into the girl's bathroom, checking all the stalls and locking the door.

"This is going to sound weird, and trust me, it is. But it's time you remember. They are here now, and I can't keep pretending to be a student," she says, looking around her and then staring into my eyes again.

"What the hell are you going on about?" I ask her as she walks over to me and places her hands on my head.

"I'm not Melody. I'm a seer, and I took your memory. Not by choice, but it's time you had your memories back and remember who you are. Promise me something?" she says, and I have no idea what has gotten into her crazy ass this morning. Maybe seeing those hot guys have sent her insane or something.

"You're acting crazy," I say, trying to move away, but she tightens her grip.

"Promise me you will bust my ass out of that castle, and get me away from your psycho stepbrother?" she asks. I start to get scared, and I grab at her arms to try and pull her off me.

"Let go!"

"No. Now, remember," she demands, and a white light blasts into my mind.

The End

Wings of Fire link to Amazon...

Four lost dragon guards. Three choices. Two betrayals and one secret . . . .

Dumped on earth with three dragon guards, who have no idea who Isola is, isn't what anyone had planned. With the biggest betrayal still haunting her heart, it's hard for Isola to remember what she has to do, and that she has to return to Dragca. Only making her dragons remember her, isn't as easy as she hoped. The three guards, who she knows it's forbidden to love, are doing everything to make sure they win her heart . . . . So, what could go wrong?
With dreams of her betrayer literally haunting her, and the dangers of earth becoming a problem no one can protect her from, everything seems lost when it's dangerous to be.

The curse must fall, like fire for ice, betrayal and death must be the price . . . .

18+ reverse harem with possible triggers.

PROLOGUE

Every step he makes to get closer to me is dangerous because of what I'm feeling, what I'm thinking. I don't want to lie to him, and yet, I can't let him closer. I can't tell him anything, but he doesn't remember enough to save himself. He pushes me further into the wall, his body pressed against mine. I close my eyes, knowing I can't be trusted to look at him.

"I know if I kiss you right now, you will taste as sweet as a peach and more addictive than anything I've ever tasted in my life," he growls, and I feel a finger tracing down my cheek, towards my neck. His hand slides to the back of my head, gripping my nape and angling my face towards his. Even then, I still don't open my eyes, not even when I feel his warm breath on my lips. I know he is inches away from me, and if he kisses me, I won't have the power to stop him. To fight what feels right.

"Open those eyes and tell me the truth," he urges, yet it feels like a demand. A dark, seductive one that sends shivers through me.

"I can't," I whisper, freezing when I feel his hand tighten on my neck, and his lips ever so gently brush mine.

"Soon then," he promises, and lets me go. He steps back, and I release the breath I'd been holding. I open my eyes, seeing him open the bedroom door and walk out without another word.

What the hell am I doing?

30

ISOLA

F ire must fall for ice, and ice must fall for fire. Evil and good must be equal. Not all evil is truly lost . . . remember, princess . . . not all evil is truly lost . . . .

"Melody?" I shake my head to clear the haze I've been in, looking around at the tiled ceiling, and feeling the cold from the floor I'm lying on. Everything I'd forgotten for the last . . . well, god knows how long, comes rushing back to me like a smack to the head. Thorne betrayed me. My father is dead. My dragon guard don't remember who they are, much less who I am. I shouldn't remember, but I do. I'm back on Earth, apparently in . . . school? And I'm angry, so damn angry. Ice shoots out of my hands, freezing the floor below me, and starts to spread. I close my eyes, begging my dragon to calm down just a little. *We can't do anything now.*

"*You're back? I was trapped,*" she whispers to me, her voice distant in my mind, even now.

"*I'm back, and so are you,*" I confirm and shut her away to get some answers.

"Do you remember? I've never *quite* done that before," Melody says, her head appearing above my face as she stands and leans over me, her long black hair falling over her face. I remember her being my friend in one part of my mind, but then I remember her from my dreams and her voice from when she made me forget everything. She is the seer and a relative of mine. Holy crap, I've been friends with her for what I remember is a long time. Then I remember Elias, Dagan, and Korbin not recognizing me on the bus. She must have taken their memory, too. I don't know if I can trust her.

"You took them from me? And you've been in my dreams! Who the hell are you? You aren't Melody, my childhood friend," I shake my head, getting up off the floor as everything starts to get confusing. It's like two stories are playing in my head, the one where I grew up in this small town with Melody as a friend, and the other where I'm the princess of Dragca, who was seriously betrayed. I have to close my eyes, focusing on the princess story, my real-life story, so I don't get confused. She sighs, waving a hand over herself, and the black swirls of the seer marks appear on her face, and down her arms. Her jeans and crop top are replaced with a long red dress that looks amazing on her.

"My name really is Melody, but people I like call me Odie," she explains, and I just stare at her, gaping like a fish, before I snap myself out of it and walk away. She doesn't follow me, just watching as I go to the sink. I turn on the tap, getting a handful of water and splashing my face. I feel like I've just woken up from a long sleep. I dry my face with a paper towel, chucking it into the bin before turning to look at her. She is all I have left now, no other close family. Except my uncle, but I doubt he is still alive.

"I don't want to know about your name, Melody, who the hell are you to me? A cousin? An auntie? What are you?" I demand, getting frustrated. The happy look finally drops from her face, the seriousness of the moment appearing in her eyes.

"Your sister," she says quietly, a hint of sadness on her face as I step back, shaking my head.

"That's not possible," I say, knowing she can't possibly be my sister. She has to be a distant relative, not this. My parents wouldn't have lied to me like that.

"You're not stupid, Isola. You knew I had to be closely related to you in order to visit your dreams," she says. As she steps close to me, her body shimmers ever so slightly in the light.

"You're not really here, are you?" I ask, and she shakes her head.

"An illusion, one only you can see because we share blood. Others just have memories of me, but I'm not really here for them," she shrugs. "It's complicated magic. It took me months of reading about it in the royal library to learn how to appear solid and not ghost-like."

"Are you my father's daughter? Or my mother's?" I ask, needing to know which of my parents betrayed the other. Melody looks the same age as me, or she must be close, meaning one of my parents was a cheat.

"My mother was the last royal seer, and my father was the king," she says quietly, and I stare at her. She doesn't look a thing like me or my father, no blonde hair or pale-blue eyes, but there's something in the shape of her face. She gives me a look that reminds me of one my father would have when he was sad about something. I step back, looking away from her as pain spreads through me. He is dead, and we never really had any time together. All I have of my parents are lost memories and secrets, it seems. I lost the throne my father worked so hard to keep, I've failed him.

"I can't believe he betrayed my mother like that," I whisper in disbelief, shaking my head, and turning away from Melody. I can't even call him out on it, because he is dead. One of the last things he promised me was that I'm the only heir, that he never had any other children. It was all lies, plus he betrayed my sweet mother. She loved him, I remember that. I remember how they looked at each other, I thought it was love, but I guess no one really knows what goes on behind closed doors. A lot, apparently.

"I'm alone," I whisper, mildly panicking. That thought hurts more than all the other pain in my life, because it's so true. I can't even think about Thorne, not without wanting to walk through a portal, find him, and punch him straight in his good-looking face.

"No, you're not. I'm here, and you are all I have left, too," she says, and I turn to stare at her for a little while, both of us silent. We both share a father, who we recently lost, but she is still a stranger to me. I look at her, really look, and just see the confident friend that part of me thinks I've known for years. But I know that's not who she is, or at least, not *all* of her. The black, tattoo-like designs covering her arms and extending up her neck and cheeks remind me of who she really is. They meet in the middle of her forehead, curling at the ends. I don't remember her mother–only that she died at some point when I was still in Dragca, as a child. Melody is alone, too. I know that, but I still can't completely trust her.

"What is Thorne doing?" I ask her, needing to know if she is still in the castle, and what is going on back at home.

"Your stepbrother is . . . well, actually . . . his mother is making a lot of changes. We need you back, everyone thinks you're dead," she explains, biting her lip a little when snow starts falling from my hands again. It's only because I'm thinking about him, my anger is just too raw to control. I know I need to rein it in, though, when I see Melody's slightly worried face as she steps back from the ice spreading across the floor.

"I'm not going to hurt you," I tell her, and she laughs.

"You couldn't anyway, not without a big fight, and I don't think we are those kinds of siblings. I'm more worried about Thorne," she says, and a flash of jealousy shoots out from my dragon. It overwhelms me, reminding me that she thinks of Thorne as hers. He never was; he's no treasure to hoard or collect, just a viper in a nest.

"I'm going to kill him when I see him next," I seethe, and she just smiles like she knows something I don't. I don't like it.

"Don't ask what you don't want to know, sister," she says, calling me sister like it's a normal thing. Not like it's the very first time she has called me that.

"Where is Bee? She was in the castle last I knew," I say, starting to panic, and I look down at my hand, seeing the tree mark. It looks normal, nothing's wrong with it. *Surely if something happened to her, I would know?*

"I have her. When you come to rescue me, you will get her back. She misses you and is getting powerful. Also, it's getting more difficult to hide her, trickier. I will protect her with my life because of who she is. She is all that is left of the light now." I'm relieved, but still a little worried. I watch as her eyes start to glow blue, and she shakes a little.

"Are you okay?" I ask her.

"I have to go, but you need to get the others to remember, and then sneak into Dragca with their help. Once they remember, they will know what to do," she says abruptly, and I turn to see her move closer, tilting her head to the side.

"Who?" I ask.

"Dagan, Elias, and Korbin. They need to remember who they are, so they can save you. Remember, sister, not everything is as it seems. There is only one way you will get them to remember. I just can't tell you how to do it," she says.

"Why not?" I demand.

"Because it would mess with fate, and fate has messed with you enough, Isola," she explains. Melody then gradually fades away, until I'm standing alone in the bathroom, surrounded by snow and ice. I walk over to the sink, the ice cracking under my boots. I stare at myself, inspecting the changes from the last time I saw myself. My hair is a lot longer, hitting my waist, and my face seems older and is covered in makeup. *Who wears so much of this crap?* I pick my bag up off the floor, putting it on the side. I open it up, seeing textbooks, a pencil case, and my phone inside. I flip my phone on, seeing that it is basically empty of texts or anything, but the date throws me off a little.

"Two thousand and nineteen," I say, dropping my phone back into my bag in shock. It's been two years since Thorne betrayed me; two years since I lost my father because of him. *How am I even still in school? I must be doing my A-levels now, and finishing school soon.* Two years . . . I swear I'm going to make him pay for every single day I've lost and so much more.

31

ISOLA

"**E**verything okay, Miss Dragice? You aren't usually late to my class," a teacher stops me as I walk past a classroom with its door open, so she can see me. There goes the plan of finding the guys and following them, okay, stalking them. *But stalking is okay if it's for their own good, or at least, that's what I'm telling myself.* I stop, turning to face the teacher who is tapping her foot on the floor with an unimpressed look. She is an older woman, with short grey hair tied at the back of her neck, and her skin is covered in wrinkles that pull across her face when she frowns at me. I remember her being a nice teacher, but the memory of the class is fading. I think it's history, no math? *I don't know.*

"Are you coming into class? Or just planning on standing there staring?" she asks me, and I look at the doors of the school once more but look back at the teacher and decide maybe I need to act normal for a while. I doubt Thorne left me here alone, I bet someone here is a dragon in hiding or something, watching me for anything suspicious. Thorne is too smart to leave me on Earth without a guarantee that I wouldn't come back and kick his stupid ass off the throne.

"Sorry I'm late," I say, pulling my bag up on my shoulder and walking into the class. There are thirty or so students in here, and it's weird that I sort of remember them. It's like the memories of being here as a student and growing up in this town are stuck in my mind, but so is the actual truth. This is still the town I grew up in, this is the same school I went to with Jace. I swallow the bitterness I feel that he isn't here. That Esmeralda is still walking around free of punishment when she killed him. My vow to kill her, it just bothers me now because I know I won't be able to keep it for a while. I need to train, get much stronger, and somehow get the people of Dragca behind me, to get back my throne. I slide into my normal seat, two rows back, next to a girl named Hallie. Hallie winks at me, before looking back towards the front of class as the teacher starts talking about William Shakespeare. I suddenly remember this is my literature class, and that was what we were studying. It's all confusing and is slowly giving me a headache. *I guess that is what happens when someone messes with your head.*

"Everyone knows what we have been going over. With your upcoming test next week, I suggest you all start studying. Please come and see me if you have any problems," the teacher says, and everyone starts pulling their textbooks out of their bags. I get mine out, opening it up to the page I remember.

So weird that I remember the page, but not the teacher's name.

"How come you were late?" Hallie asks me, flipping through her own book. I look over at her, and scrutinize my friend. She has black hair, and currently has the tips dyed blue, though she changes the colour depending on her mood. She also covers her brown eyes with blue contacts; she hates wearing glasses and likes blue eyes. I remember meeting her when I was ten in the fake memory, but I also remember seeing her around school when I was here in my real life with Jace. We certainly weren't best friends like we are now, I didn't even know her name then. Yet, she is the only one that isn't fearful of me, like most human females are. I know everything about Hallie now, from her messed-up parents, to the two guys she's sleeping with that don't know about each other. She knows everything about me, too, all of the fake lie of a life anyway. The real me, the princess of Dragca, she knows nothing about. I feel a little guilty that she has been dragged into my mess of a life.

"Complicated," I say, rubbing my temples with my fingers and looking down. *Complicated is an understatement, but okay, that works.*

"Where is Odie?" she asks, meaning she still remembers my seer sister who was in school every day for as long as I can remember. I'd hoped Melody had made her forget, or done something. *Thanks, sister.*

"Erm . . . her family took her on holiday for a bit, and she's going to be gone at least a month," I say, making up the only excuse I can think of right now. It's one that gives me a fair amount of time to stalk the guys and make them remember.

"Lucky cow, the rest of us normal people have to put up with all this rain," she nudges my shoulder with hers, and then looks down at her book.

"Did you see the new students?" I ask her, needing to know where Elias, Dagan, and Korbin are. If anyone knows this school, and everything that is going on, it's Hallie.

"The ones that signed up today? Yeah, Issy, everyone has seen them. Hot damn, they are something else," she grins, pretending to cool herself down with her hand. Clearing her throat, the teacher stares at us, and we both look down pretending to read quietly. After a while, a student walks up to her, distracting her enough for us to continue talking.

"So . . . they aren't in classes today?" I muse.

"Nope, the rumour is they had to fill out paperwork or something, and they start tomorrow," she says, and snaps her head to the side to look at me with wide eyes, "Why? Is the ice queen finally thawing and crushing on someone?" she asks, making me tense up.

"What did you call me?" I ask.

"Ice queen, because you turn down every dude in school," she rolls her eyes at me, and I relax a little bit, "Come on, everyone calls you that. They are idiots, though."

"Maybe," I say, and look down at my own book, wanting to drop the subject. It's no use continuing to talk about them if they aren't even here today. I need to stalk them, like "find their house and then follow them around" kind of stalk. The normal stalking that won't get me arrested.

"I'm sure they will be invited to Michael's party in three weeks, he has an empty house again," she wags her eyebrows. I hate Michael. I hate him now, and I hated him when Jace and I went to school here. He is a jackass, who thinks his good looks mean everyone wants him, and he assumes, for some reason, that I want to sleep with him. It doesn't help that humans here on Earth are naturally attracted to female dragons; it's something to do with the pheromones in our scent. All I remember doing is turning down guys and watching their heartbroken ex-girlfriends glare at me. Hopefully, if I can get Elias, Dagan, or Korbin to be friends with me, then I should be left alone. Male dragons have the complete opposite effect on most humans, they want to avoid them. I doubt the girls here will listen to their instincts when they see the guys; they are all way too hot to evade. I hold back a growl, the thought of anyone touching them makes me want to punch something

"I doubt Michael will want competition there," I say, looking down at my hand where my nails are slowly turning to ice. Sliding my hands under the table, I make sure to keep my eyes down, just in case they turn silver. Dammit, I've got to control my emotions better than this. I did it for years with Jace, I can do it now. Taking a deep breath, I turn the page of my book and pretend to be interested in what it says.

"He would do anything for you, just ask him to invite them to the party. Then, being the good friend I am, I will distract Michael," she suggests. I start to tell her no when I realise I need to get close to the guys again, to make them trust me. It's going to be difficult in this school to do that. No, I need to make friends with them outside of school, and then figure out how to make them remember.

"Sounds like a plan," I say with a grin and start reading my textbook, hoping the day will go quickly.

32

ISOLA

"Jules?" I call when I open my front door. I almost freeze when I see her come out of the kitchen, holding a bowl, and mixing something inside it with a spoon. She looks just like the last time I saw her, her grey hair up in a bun, and she's wearing an older-style dress with a flower and bird pattern. She looks like home, of all the memories I have of her. She wore a similar dress the first time I met her. I remember walking into this house, the dragon guards leaving me at the door, and she made me cookies as I cried. She didn't baby me, but she still comforted me. Since that day, she has always been there for me. I wasn't the best to her in the last couple of years before Jace died and I left for Dragca. I threw parties and got drunk all the time. Overall, I was a total brat, but she didn't quit on me when most would have.

"Hello, darling, I'm making pumpkin pie for dessert, and your favourite casserole for dinner tonight," she says, and I smile tightly at her. I wonder how much magic it took for my sister to erase Jules's memory of me disappearing and to erase her memory of Jace, who she adored. What's more, how much magic did it take to make the whole town forget, to erase everyone's memories?

"Thanks. I have homework to do," I nod my head at the stairs, smiling tightly as my emotions begin to strangle me.

"Okay!" she says with a happy grin, not noticing my mood at all. She walks out of the room, heading back towards the kitchen. I run up the stairs, taking a deep breath when I get to my room. I feel like everything is piling up on top of me as I look around. It's my room, but it's not. There's no familiarities in here anymore, just plain bed sheets, piles of books that don't look read, and tiny holes in the walls where photos of Jace and me used to hang. Pressing my back against the door, I slide down and wrap my arms around my legs. I rest my head on my knees, trying to calm my breathing and stop the tears streaming down my face. It doesn't work; tears continue to fall without my permission as memories begin to overwhelm me, and I remember everything. Every memory of my time in Dragca is different now, my view on everything skewed. Every moment with Thorne is fake; he was lying, tricking me from the start, and I fell for it. He burnt Jace's body, was with me in that final moment that I will never forget, and now it's tainted with Thorne's betrayal. Our every moment spent together is soiled, when he opened up to me about his adoptive family and the reason for his animosity with Elias, when he taught me how to use my dragon sight, and when he was just there for me so many times. I scream into my hands, so angry that he did this to me. *The lying bastard.*

"Isola, can you come down?" I hear Jules shout, making me snap out of it. I can't allow myself to break down; I don't have the luxury of wallowing in my despair. Elias, Dagan, Korbin, Melody, Bee, and the people of Dragca need me. I'm no princess, no leader if I sit here and cry about my problems. No, I need to get up and make a plan of action. I quickly sit up, wiping my eyes and checking I don't look too upset in the mirror. Opening the door, I walk down the corridor to the stairs, following the noise I can hear into the kitchen. I stop, nearly tripping on thin air when I see Dagan, Elias, and Korbin sitting at the table. They don't even look my way, just continue to talk, and I slowly walk up to Jules as she puts a casserole into the oven.

"My brother called, and apparently, his nephews need a place to stay for the next month or so. I don't know everything, but they are enrolled in school. I emailed your father, who replied saying it was fine," she explains, and I tighten my fists, knowing it couldn't have been my father who replied.

"Okay," I reply slowly, and she looks up, a slightly dazed expression on her face. Someone has been messing with her memories. Jules doesn't have any family, I remember her telling me that. It's why she made the perfect nanny for me and Jace growing up.

"They are very good-looking, so it's best you don't go looking. Teenage pregnancies are no fun," she says nonchalantly. I choke on air, coughing a few times as I plainly nod at her. I didn't expect her to say that.

"You don't have to worry about that," I explain to her, and she winks.

"Sure, I don't," she looks at the guys, and I hear her mumble under her breath, "If only I was forty years younger." I laugh a little, and then pull her to me, hugging her side.

"What was that for?" she asks.

"I just missed you."

"You haven't had a chance to miss me, we see each other every day," she says as I pull away. "Now go and say hello to your roommates, silly girl." I nod at her before looking back at the guys. It's weird to see them in jeans and normal polo shirts. Elias still has a leather jacket on, so some things don't change, but it's clear a lot has. I look at Dagan next, noticing his black hair is a little longer than before, but the sides are still shaved, and he still has his lip ring. Korbin and Elias have also grown their hair out, it falls close to their eyes now and just adds to the wild look they both have. I wonder where their dragons are, they must be inside of them somewhere, but just hidden. My sister must be insanely powerful to do what she has, to make everyone forget, and to even appear as an illusion. I wonder if she has a dragon inside of her, as she is half ice dragon after all, and it could boost her power. Maybe her dragon blood makes her seer powers that much stronger. *I guess I have a lot of things to ask her when I see her next.*

"Well, go and say hello to them, they will be your roommates for a while. Besides, staring is rude," she chastises, shoving me towards them. I take a deep breath, telling myself I can act normal and like I don't know them as I walk to their table. They look up, one by one, until they are all staring at me. It's odd for them to stare at me like this, like I'm a total stranger to them. Their eyes assess me, rolling over my body and making me shiver. Their total attention is on me, three powerful, sexy dragons, and they all look at me like they have just found a treasure they want.

"I'm Isola," I say, after clearing my throat a little and sliding my fingers into the back of my jeans. Dagan leans back in his seat, his eyes still travelling over my body while moving his lip ring and grins.

"I-Sol-A," he spells my name out slowly, wickedly, and then chuckles.

"Dagan, right?" I ask him, and he nods, biting his lip a little and giving me a strange look. I look away before I can try to decipher that look, it's not a look of remembrance, that's for sure.

"And you're Korbin?" I ask Korbin, hating that I have to pretend not to know. He isn't even looking at me anymore, and I notice straight away that he no longer has his beard. Damn, I liked that beard on him. Korbin ignores me completely, choosing to mess on his phone instead. *Great.*

"I'm Elias, and no, I don't want you to sneak into my room later," Elias says, winking at me as he gets up and pulls his cigarette packet out of his jacket. His hair is longer, making him have to brush it out of his eyes. It makes him look wilder, more untameable, and honestly, so sexy I'm having trouble not reaching up to touch it.

"Those things kill humans," I say, repeating a warning I once gave him to see if it jogs his memory, but it doesn't seem to have any impact. He just shrugs and puts the cigarette in his mouth.

"Usually the best things in life do kill us, princess," he says, making my heart pound as he walks past me and to the back door.

"Princess?" I ask, wondering if he remembers calling me it.

"You look like a princess, a naughty one at that," he chuckles darkly, walking out as I smile. He might not remember who I am exactly. None of them do, but I have hope because of those two words. There's only one dragon that calls me naughty princess, and I intend to make sure he remembers me.

33

THORNE

"Is it done?" I ask Melody, shutting her door behind me and turning to look at her. She is sitting on a window seat, a crystal ball in her hand and her black hair draping around it until she sits back. The seers' rooms are just as grand as the rest of the castle, and it makes me uncomfortable. I look around at the gold walls, the gold floors, and gold linen hanging everywhere. I didn't grow up like this, I grew up in a muddy hut in the forest. The nicest thing we had was a small, wooden, dragon knight toy I used to play with. Melody is used to this, and yet, I hate it. It's a castle full of lies, secrets, and is dripping with blood.

"Come and see, my King," she says formally, yet the twitch of her lips tells me she is being sarcastic. I walk over, looking down into the crystal ball as it glimmers before Isola appears. She is in a kitchen, talking to Dagan, Korbin, and Elias by the looks of it. Her blonde hair is much longer than it's ever been, soft-looking, and falling in curls down her back. She looks up, almost as if she can sense us looking, and I get to see her pale-blue eyes, doll-like features, and pale skin. It hurts to see her when I know how much she must hate me. I just want to be by her side, able to protect her in the open rather than in secret, behind her back.

She has good reason to hate me, and I doubt she will ever forgive me, or let me even be her friend after all I've done. But I will protect her and ensure she lives through this.

"How long until she can make them remember?" I ask Melody. She waves a hand over the ball, making it go cloudy, and slides off the seat.

"I don't know, I've seen it happen but not the time or date," she admits.

"We don't have long! When my mother goes to the dungeons and sees Dagan, Elias, and Korbin are free . . ." I trail off, looking away from her. I doubt any of us will live when she figures out I've betrayed her, that I chose Isola over her. It's not that I don't love my mother or want the crown, it's just that I know it's what needs to be done. The curses need to end, Isola needs the throne to protect her. *I'm no king if I betray everyone to have the crown.*

"I know. I know she will find her guards, but I've told you before I don't know what happens after that. My visions aren't all seeing," she says, her frustration clear in her voice.

"Fine, I should go in case someone comes looking for me," I say, walking to the door, but her voice stops me.

"You should tell her how you feel, what you did to save her. Maybe more importantly, what you didn't do, Thorne," she tells me gently. I look back, locking eyes with her blue ones as she folds her hands and waits for me to reply. Melody looks nothing like her sister, yet they have the same demanding nature. It must run in the family or something.

"She *should* hate me. I might have fixed some things, but I still betrayed her," I say emotionlessly, not even able to say her name out loud. That betrayed look she gave me before she lost her memory, it haunts me, leaving me unable to sleep. I can't get it out of my head, and I know it's my fault, I brought it on myself. I wish I could have warned her, told her how things had changed for us all, and how I had changed my mind when I saw her father die. But being completely honest with myself, the plan changed the moment I met Isola Dragice.

"When you see her, you won't be able to fool yourself or her. She will figure it out, considering only one person could have saved her dragon guards and kept her alive," she suggests.

"I will always keep her alive, nothing will ever mean more to me than her life," I snap, reining my dragon in as it flares to life, wanting to go to Isola, to protect her.

"*Minnnneee,*" my dragon demands, his claim on Isola is overwhelming because of what I did. When I open my eyes, Melody is staring at me with what looks like sympathy written all over her face.

"Here," Melody says, walking over to a box next to her bed and pulling out a bracelet. It's all black stones, but I don't have a clue what it is or does. She comes over, handing it to me.

"What is it?" I ask.

"Wear it when you sleep, and you will understand. It's a gift, a rare one, so don't lose it. I want it back," she says and then nods her head at the door.

"You should go," she tells me. I don't question her, just open the door and walk out, slipping the bracelet onto my wrist as I go. I walk down the grand corridors of the castle, intending to go to my rooms, when my mother walks out of one of the royal rooms. She smiles at me and walks over, placing her hand on my shoulder. My mother has clearly just woken up, her blonde hair is down, and she has a cloak on over her dress. Nothing like the white leather she usually wears and comes back to the castle with blood spots all over.

"Where have you been so early, son?" she asks, and walks next to me as I keep going. I hate that I have to lie to her, betray her, but I know it's the right thing to do. My mother isn't who she used to be, and it's the king's fault for making her like this. Evil in a way, but I can save her. I will save her and Isola, but not without the price of having them both hate me.

"Just a walk to the kitchens, I was hungry," I say, and her dark-blue eyes look up at me. They used to be clear blue, like most ice dragons, but over the years they have gotten darker.

Now they are so dark, you can barely see the blue, it's almost black. The black would match the black veins crawling up her arms, but I try not to think about it and look away.

"I have to leave the castle with Esmeralda today, we have a job to finish in the north," she explains.

"What job? I should come with you," I ask, curious and desperate to keep an eye on her before she destroys the entire kingdom. I don't know what she is doing, but she comes back covered in black dust, and smelling of fire.

"Nothing for you to worry about, and I told you before, you can't leave the castle. You're the king, and until you are mated, with an heir on the way, it's too dangerous for you," she says, sighing.

"I'm not mating anytime soon. I've told you this," I say, trying to hide my annoyance that she won't tell me what she is doing.

"When the seers are back on our side, or Melody tells us who your future mate is, we will find her," she says, like it's no concern for her. Melody pretends to help her all the time, but I doubt she is helping her much.

"The seers still won't come here?" I ask.

"No, but they will change their minds very soon," she smiles as we get to my room.

"What are you going to do? You can't just kill everyone that doesn't side with you, mother," I warn her, and dark lines crawl down her cheeks for just a second before she shakes her head.

"I won't kill *them*," she says sweetly and walks away. I open the doors to my room, walking across it and straight to the balcony. I have to take deep breaths to calm my dragon down as I look over the mountains as the suns shine above them. I look over at the crown on the side. It's a worthless trinket, considering I have no idea what is going on outside of this castle.

A king with no power is no king at all.

34

ISOLA

"Isola," a voice whispers, the voice both hauntingly familiar and heartbreaking. My mind knows who it is, without me even having to look.

"Hello?" I ask, blinking my eyes open. All I see is smoke all around me. There is a fire in the background, and I quickly turn around, looking for the voice. Part of me doesn't want to find the man who spoke, but a deeper part of me still yearns for him.

"Here," the voice says from behind me, and I spin, seeing a shadow of a man in the smoke.

"I can't see you," I say, and he chuckles.

"You don't want to, you hate me," he says sadly, but then still steps forward into the clearing. Thorne stands still as I get a good look at him. His ice-blue eyes lock with mine, his hair matching the stolen white crown on his head. I can't get used to the blonde hair, as I'm so used to seeing it brown. It has been kept short and suits his face more this way. He has a new outfit, still black leather and similar to his guard uniform, but this one is much nicer. He has a long cloak draped around him, with blue and red dragons stitched down the sides.

"Of course I hate you, you killed my father! The very crown you wear, you stole from his dead body! You betrayed me! Get out of my head, and *fuck off, you bastard!" I shout at him, stepping back when he steps closer. I'm literally shaking with anger, wishing this dream was real, so I could kill him.*

"I can't escape you anymore than you can escape me, but hate me all you want," he whispers, and I barely even hear him as I go over the million different ways I could kill him. I think stabbing him through the heart like he did my father would be the best way. When he only stares at me, not saying anything, I have to reply.

"What the hell does that mean, Thorne?" I snap, and he strides quickly towards me. I back away until I can feel the heat from the fire burning my back. He grabs my face with his hands, pulling me towards me. I hit him, struggling to get away, and even try to call my ice, but it doesn't work.

"Fight me, hate me, but you can't shut me out, Issy, and when you know why, you won't want to," he tells me and leans down, brushing his lips across my forehead. He lets go, allowing me to fall into the smoke.

"I hate you, don't come to me again. I have my dragon guards now," I shout, falling still but not fighting. The smoke takes me away from him, and that's what I want more than anything.

"I sent them to you, protected them for you, but that doesn't mean you shouldn't hate me, Issy," is the last thing I hear him say before everything feels like it is burnt away until only emptiness is left.

I SIT STRAIGHT UP in bed as my alarm blares, covered in sweat and with my heart pounding. Feeling my hand burning, I look at my tree mark and find it glowing red, before it gradually fades back to its normal green colour. When my heart stops pounding in my ears, and I calm down, I realise the dream couldn't be real. *It's just a bad dream, Thorne wasn't really there.* I turn my alarm off, seeing the display saying it's six in the morning, and I lean across the bed, switching my lamp on. Thorne can't contact me, it's impossible for him to do that across worlds, and I doubt he is on Earth. He might be a fire and ice dragon, but the only way to get into someone's dreams is to be a seer and have a blood connection, as far as I know. Thorne and I don't have any connection, so clearly, I'm just losing my mind. My laptop sits open beside me, I must have fallen asleep looking at it last night. Closing it, I look around my room again. I can't help the feeling that someone has taken a part of me, not just everything related to my previous life here. It's not just the photos of me and Jace that are missing, though that's a huge part of it. Anything related to Dragca is gone, all of the books, and it makes me wish I had read them now. Even my phone is different, it's not the one I had before, and that means the last image I have of Jace is just gone.

"Dammit," I swear, wiping the tears away, and knowing I can't be weak like this. I have three of the most stubborn men I've ever met to convince that they are dragons. *God, they are going to think I'm insane.*

"Need to fly soon," my dragon whispers into my mind as I slide out of bed.

"I know, I will find a way to sneak away tonight," I explain, and I feel her comfort at my words before I take over again. I don't need anyone seeing my eyes turning silver right now; that will freak them out. I grab my running clothes, after washing up in the bathroom, and then plait my hair without looking at my reflection for too long. I look just like my father, and I keep imagining him, how disappointed he must be in me. *What would he say if he were alive? How would he save Dragca?* I leave my room, looking at the other five doors down the corridor. I know Jules moved into the room opposite me, leaving the three rooms and the shared bathroom at the end of the corridor for the guys. Her and my rooms have their own bathroom; I guess the guys don't mind sharing theirs. It stings that she is sleeping in Jace's room now, and I know if I went in there, it wouldn't be anything like it used to be. His books wouldn't be littered around, and his guitar wouldn't be leaning against the messy bed. This house feels like it's haunting me more than the messed-up dream of Thorne.

Even his name annoys me, I hate him so much. I shake my head, moving away from my door, and walk down the corridor. Instead of dwelling on the past, or things I can't change, I decide to focus on my plans for the day.

"Good morning!" I say, walking into the kitchen and yawning slightly. Korbin is sitting on a stool, and his head lifts up, locking those green eyes with mine. I knew he would be up early. I miss the smiles he used to give me, and even almost miss our runs and his threats to throw fireballs at my ass if I didn't speed up. He doesn't say anything as he gets up, he just walks over to me and reaches his hand out to get something out of my hair. He pulls back, showing me a little feather.

"It must be the feather duvet I sleep on," I say, and he smirks, brushing the feather down my cheek slowly and almost seductively, making me shiver all over.

"Maybe you should show it to me," his husky voice suggests, sending goosebumps up and down my body. Korbin has never spoken to me like this, and part of me doesn't want him to stop. I trace my eyes over his tight pajama shirt and snug shorts that show off his muscular thighs. *Who knew thighs could be attractive?*

"My duvet?" I ask confused, and he shakes his head, stepping closer to me. We are only a breath apart when he whispers.

"Your bed, doll." My mouth parts in shock, and he steps back, leaving me a little shaky. He picks his phone up off the side and acts like nothing just happened.

"I-I don't think that's–" I start to say, stumbling over my words and acting like a timid little girl that's never spoken to a guy before. *Damn it, get it together, Isola.*

"We could always start off with a date," he suggests, his deep and husky voice making me just want to listen to him talk forever. I don't reply to his flirting. I can't let my hormones control me, not right now, anyway. I need him to be my friend again, we can't risk anything else. It's too dangerous. The fact they don't know about their dragons doesn't mean a thing, they would lose their dragons permanently by falling for me. Or me for them. I don't really know specifics on how the curse works, but I'm not going to test it. Not only would they hate me forever, but I'd hate myself.

"Do you run? I like to run every morning," I say, lying my ass off. I spent most of the night reading about how to jog someone's memory. One of the most successful recommendations is to get them back into their routine. *That means running, oh god, running.*

"I usually run in the evenings, but a pretty little doll like you shouldn't be running on your own," he says, walking past me and towards the stairs. "Get us some water while I get changed."

"Alright," I reply, and he runs up the stairs. I walk to the fridge, pulling out two bottles of water. I head for the door, putting the water down to pull on my trainers. Hearing steps on the staircase, I turn and see Jules coming down. She has jeans and a long tunic shirt on today, and her hair is down. She looks happy, although slightly shocked.

"Wow . . . I didn't expect to see you down here already. Are you feeling okay?" she asks, knowing I don't like mornings. I usually roll out of bed with half an hour to spare, and still spend most of that time reading, before dragging my ass to the bus stop.

"I decided I need to be healthier. I'm going to run every morning with Korbin," I explain, and she chuckles.

"I bet seeing that boy in tight workout clothes and dripping with sweat has nothing to do with your need to be healthy and wake up earlier?" she says, making me choke on thin air, again, as she keeps laughing.

"I used to be young once, I'll have you know. I would have done more than run every morning to get close to a body like that," she teases, winking at me. She walks into the kitchen as I just stare after her in shock. Thankfully, Korbin comes running down the stairs, distracting me from thoughts of what Jules was like when she was younger. With all these comments lately, I'd bet she was a wild one. I try to not appreciate how amazing

Korbin looks in his tight running shorts and loose shirt, but I majorly fail. *Holy crap on a cracker, he looks hot.* I trail my eyes over him shamelessly, and when I finally look into his eyes, he knows I've been checking him out. Thankfully, he doesn't call me on it. *I have no excuse.*

"Ready?" he asks gruffly, and I hand him his water as he gets closer.

"Yep," I respond. I need to use this time alone with him to make him remember, though I'm not sure how.

"Do you know a good route with a path?" he asks when we get outside, the cold morning air making me shiver. It's freezing out. The sun is just rising in the sky, but I know running will warm us up until the sun is fully out. Our house is in the middle of the woods, with a private driveway that leads down to a secluded road. There aren't any other houses for miles, and the only vehicle that comes this way is the school bus. The woods have a track I used to walk with Jace sometimes.

"Yeah, see over there," I point at the post in between the trees to the right, "there's a path all the way around the land and back," I explain.

"We should race. If I win, I get a date with you. If I lose," he pauses, "well, what would you like?"

"Nothing, I'm not taking that bet. We can't date," I say.

"Boyfriend? I should have guessed," he asks, disappointed.

"No boyfriend," I say, and he grins, his green eyes shining with the reflection of the sunrise.

"Then you best think of something you want to win, not that you really need to worry. You won't win anyway . . . I want that date," he tells me and takes off running. I run after him, cursing him with his green eyes and sexy voice for distracting me.

"It's cheating to have a head start!" I shout, and he looks back at me for a second, still keeping up his fast pace.

"I don't play fair, doll," he tells me, and I shake my head as I hustle to catch up to him. We run at a normal pace for most of the run. Then, in the last fifteen minutes of our race, he suddenly speeds up, and it's impossible for me to keep up with his pace. I swear under my breath when he quickly disappears from view, and I sprint as fast as I can to the end of the track. When I get there, Korbin is leaning against a tree, drinking water. I stand there gawking as it drips down his chin onto his chest, I can't help myself. In my distracted state, I trip on something and slam onto the ground. Nothing hurts, well my ego does, but I ignore that as I roll onto my back.

"Shit, here," I hear Korbin say, and he picks me up, letting me straighten myself out. He lifts his hand, picking some leaves out of my hair, and then pushing a strand behind my ear. I don't know what gets into me when he rests his hand on my cheek, but I lean my head into it. I close my eyes for a second and just breathe in his smoky scent. He might not know he is a dragon, but he still smells like one. He still has that comforting scent. When I open my eyes, Korbin is staring at me with such longing and desire, that I can't look away. Something is changing between us. I should stop it, I should run away from it . . . but I don't feel like I can.

"There's something about you, doll, and I want to know what it is," he whispers.

"There's nothing," I answer, wanting to say there's nothing that I can tell him.

"Nothing is definitely not a word I'd use to describe you, you are everything but it," he claims forcefully, sliding his hand from my cheek to my jaw, his thumb lightly skimming across my lips.

"You're a shameless flirt," I say, smiling a little tensely. Pulling away, I wipe the dirt off myself and lean down to pick up my water bottle.

"Not usually, but with you, yes," he replies, watching me carefully as I try to shake off what just happened. *What happened to making him remember? This run accomplished nothing.*

"We should shower before school," I say, walking towards the house, and he swiftly catches up.

"I'm going to guess that wasn't an invite to shower together," he drawls.

"Nope," I giggle.

"I can wait. Our date is Saturday at seven," he says, running ahead of me and into the house before I can even say no. *Damn cocky dragon.*

35

ISOLA

"Want a ride?" Elias's sexy voice drifts over to me, making me jump as I walk out of the house. I turn, seeing him sitting on a massive motorbike, and I have to make my eyes pull away from his leather-covered body. *Holy crap, he looks hot.* I only know it's Elias from his voice, as I can't see his face under his helmet, but I know he can see me ogling him.

"You have a motorbike . . . of course you do," I mutter, pulling my coat tighter around me as I glance up at the dark skies. Dagan and Korbin walk past, going down the drive to the bus stop, looking between Elias and me.

"It's going to rain before the bus gets here in half an hour, you should take the ride," Korbin suggests. Dagan doesn't say a word, only staring at me intensely, like he is trying to figure out a puzzle.

"Make your choice, princess," Elias says. I shake my head, knowing I must be mad, and I walk over to Elias. He offers me a spare helmet, and I slide it on before getting onto the back of the bike. It's a little awkward to get on, being that I've never ridden one before, but I do manage. *Just not very gracefully.*

"You will need to hang on," his voice comes loudly through the helmet, and I realise they must have some kind of walkie-talkie built in them. I'm sure there's a technical word for it, but it just reminds me of the walkie-talkies we used to have as kids. I tentatively wrap my hands around his waist, trying not to feel the flat, hard muscles that are under my grip. He grabs my arms, making me slide forward on the seat until my body is wrapped around his, and he pulls my hands tighter around him. Elias starts the bike, and I close my eyes as it purrs to life underneath me. We begin to move, flying down the driveway by the sound and feel of it. It's scary at the start, but once I relax, it's pretty enjoyable. I'm used to flying or moving fast, it's what dragons do but at much higher heights. I'm still not looking though; my eyes are staying shut.

"Are you going to open your eyes?" Elias asks me after we round a corner.

"Nope," I reply back, and I hear him laugh through the helmet. It's oddly relaxing to hear his laugh, hear him so relaxed and happy.

"It's not that bad, you might like it if you try," he says, and I gently open one eye and then the next. We are driving through town; the shops and people seem like blurs, and it's incredible.

"It's so weird, but in a good way," I say, and he laughs, not replying to me. It's another ten minutes until we are pulling up to the school car park, and he stops his bike right near the front of the school. I get off, ignoring the stares from everyone as I pull my helmet off and hand it to Elias. He puts both of them in the space under the seat, and then unzips his riding gear. As he pulls it off, his shirt rides up, so I get a glance of his tattoos and the v shape that disappears into his jeans. He puts the outfit in the bike, and grabs his leather jacket, putting it on before slipping his keys into his pocket.

"Are you going to show me around then?" Elias asks after I spend way too long gaping at him. *Shit.*

"Yeah, sure, so where are you guys from?" I ask, and we start walking up the steps to the front doors. I need to know where they have been for the last two years and why Thorne said he brought them here. I can't accept that he did, that he helped me in any kind of way.

"A little bit of everywhere, our parents like to travel, but we are stuck here for a while," he explains, and I wonder who Melody made him think his parents are. I doubt they were travelling anywhere, either. Thorne's words keep rolling around in my mind. He claimed he kept them safe, so they must have been near him. Maybe they were kept in the castle or something.

"So, down here are all the classrooms, and at the end of this hall is the lunch room. On the right is the head teacher's office, the reception rooms, and to the left are the toilets," I say, pointing in each direction as I explain them. He nods, looking around as students walk past us, all watching him. He pulls a piece of paper out of his pocket, looking at the table on it.

"I have double English first, what about you?" he asks.

"Same," I say, and nod my head down the corridor, "it's this way."

"Isola!" I hear my name shouted, and turn around to see Michael running over to me. Michael has golden-blond hair and a massive build from all the training he does for football. He towers over me when he steps near me.

"Hey, Michael," I reply briskly, wanting to get to class. I need the time to spend thinking of new ways to get the guys to remember me.

"I heard from Hallie that you're finally coming to one of my parties at the end of the month?" he asks, stepping closer. I look over as Elias wraps an arm around my waist, pulling me to his side.

"We will be coming, I'm Elias," Elias says tensely, holding out a hand for Michael. Michael looks between us, anger flashing over his face, but he instantly schools his expression, shaking Elias's hand.

"You should come and train for the football team, I'm the captain. You have two brothers, right?" he asks.

"He does," Dagan's cold voice comes from behind Michael, just moments before he and Korbin step next to Elias and me.

"Cool. Anyway, can't wait to see you at the party . . . and your friends can come, too," he says, confusing me a little. I flinch when he steps closer, wrapping his arms around me as he pulls me away from Elias and drags me to his chest. I swear I hear someone growl, and I can only hope it was one of the guys and their dragon.

"We are going to be late for class," Dagan says, and you can hear the hostile tone in his voice. Michael lets go, grinning at me before walking away.

"Who is that?" Elias asks.

"Just this guy that goes to school here: Michael," I reply. All the guys watch Michael until he gets to his classroom and disappears from view. I place my hand on Elias's shoulder.

"We really will be late for class," I say, not really caring about being late, but I know I need to distract him from whatever he is thinking. Dagan and Korbin look at me once more before walking off, and Elias steps closer, putting his arm around my waist.

"What are you doing?" I ask, though I don't push him away. This close, I notice he still carries the smoky scent of his fire dragon, and it makes me want to press myself closer to him.

"*Mine,*" my dragon whispers, and Elias's eyes widen in surprise. He grabs my chin to look at me closely as I feel my eyes fade back to their normal blue. He saw them turn silver, he must have.

"Let go," I demand, and he narrows his eyes at me.

"Your eyes, they changed colour," he exclaims.

"You're seeing things, Elias," I reply nervously.

"Don't lie to me, I don't like it," he demands and lets go, stepping back and shaking his head.

"Eli?" I whisper, watching him hold his hands to his head for a few moments. When he finally looks back at me, he seems so lost.

"Class. We need to go to class, and then we *will* have a long chat tonight," he orders. "I don't like lies," he repeats, and I turn around, walking the rest of the way to class.

"I know, but I don't have any choice," I whisper to myself.

36

ISOLA

"Issy, come on, we are going shopping, remember?" Hallie asks as soon as I step out of our final class. I feel Dagan, Elias, and Korbin follow me from the room. Someone has arranged it so we all have the same classes together. Probably the same person who made it possible for them to live with me. Something is going on, and I'm starting to feel like a puppet on a string, yet I don't know who it is that is controlling me. The guys haven't spoken to me much, not even at lunch, though they sat eating their food next to Hallie and me. It's awkward between us all, but I'm clueless as to why it feels that way.

"What?" I ask her, snapping out of my thoughts.

"Shopping? We made plans to go tonight," she says, and I vaguely remember making plans with her in my fake life last week.

"Alright," I concede. When I drop the book I'm holding, I stop to pick it up, and someone slams into me. We both fall to the floor, and I land on something hard. I open my eyes to see Dagan underneath me, his hands on my waist and a serious expression clouding his eyes.

"Are you always this clumsy?" he asks. This moment reminds

me of when we first met, how he jumped on me to save me back then. Not that he is saving me this time, but still.

"No . . . well, yes. I mean, I can be. I try not to be if that helps," I grin, and he shakes his head at me as I get off of him.

"Here," he hands me my book, but doesn't let go. He stands there, still staring at me with confusion written all over his face.

"Thanks, Dagan," I say, as he finally lets go of the book and steps away, rolling his lip ring. He always does that when he's thinking about something.

"No problem, kitty cat, see you at home," he replies and turns around, walking over to where Korbin and Elias are waiting for him by the door.

"'At home'? What have you not been telling me?" Hallie gasps dramatically, pushing her long hair behind her shoulders. I sigh, watching the guys disappear through the doors.

"They all moved in yesterday. Apparently, they need a place to stay for a while, and Jules is completely okay with it," I say, and her eyes widen. I walk to my locker, letting her process the shock, and shove my textbooks inside, before closing it to face her.

"Holy fucking shit!" Hallie exclaims, whacking my arm and making me laugh. I actually like this girl.

"Please, please say you're going to sneak into at least one of their rooms . . . like naked, so they can't resist," she begs, and I laugh.

"I don't think I need to do that, Besides, I have a date with Korbin on Saturday. It's a long story, but I kind of lost a bet," I tell her.

"Then we definitely need to find you something tight and sexy to wear," she wraps an arm around me and leads me to the door. We go in Hallie's car to the shopping centre, parking up and walking in. I look at Hallie, trying to find something from our fake past to ask her about. It's getting harder to remember, the memories becoming more distant.

"Are your mum and dad still arguing?" I finally ask.

"Yeah, and when it's over you, you can't help but feel bad," she admits, and I remember how her father wants her to join the family business after school, and how her mother is completely against it.

"It's not your fault," I reply gently.

"It really is, though. I'm their only child, and dad is head of their business. Mum lets me work with him sometimes, but she still hates what he does. I'm not a fan, but I understand it's needed. It's just complicated at home," she sighs.

"What is the family business? I can't remember," I ask her.

"My dad works for the government and has his own facility, but I can't tell you what they do. It's all top secret and whatnot. I have told you this before," she laughs. I laugh it off with her because the truth is, I don't remember asking her that before. The fake past is slipping from my mind faster than I thought it was.

"I know, I thought I'd just try asking again. But seriously, it's not your fault. You can be anything you want when you finish school," I tell her.

"Not when you have to keep your parents happy, and have responsibility thrown at you from birth," she says and then shakes her head. "Anyway, less depressing talk about things we can't change, and more shopping." I smile at her, and let her lead me towards the clothes shops we usually buy from. We have a lot more in common than I ever knew. Neither of us ever really had a choice about our futures and what we get to do. Freedom was never an option for us.

I WALK UP the stairs quietly, holding three bags at my sides, and make my way into my bedroom. I put the bags on the floor by the door, shutting it, and switching on a light as I go. I turn around and jump at the sight of Elias on my window seat, smoking a cigarette out through the open window.

"What the hell are you doing in here? You have your own room!" I exclaim. Internally, I groan when I realize my plan to sneak out later and go to the woods to let my dragon out won't be happening. I feel her grumble in my mind, her annoyance isn't too bad, though.

"I said we would talk, and I meant it. I don't forget things," he says, and I mentally cringe. He *has* forgotten things, he's forgotten everything. Everything that makes him Elias Fire, the deadly dragon guard I know. I watch him finish his cigarette, flicking it out the window and shutting it before facing me. I keep my back against the wall near the door, unsure whether to approach him or not.

"What do you want me to say?" I ask, knowing I can't tell him about the real reason my eyes changed colour, or why I lied to him. I have a feeling Elias knows when I'm lying, and at the moment, I'm having to lie about everything. How I feel, what is real, what isn't, and my entire life.

"I dream about kissing you, not in a made-up dream, but an actual memory. I remember kissing you. How is that possible? We have never met, but I know you're mine. That dream fucking haunts me even when I'm awake," he tells me as he gets up and stalks over to me, never taking his eyes off mine. Every step he makes to get closer to me is dangerous, because of what I'm feeling, what I'm thinking. I don't want to lie to him, and yet, I can't let him closer. I can't tell him anything, but he doesn't remember enough to save himself. He pushes me further into the wall, his body pressed against mine. I close my eyes, knowing I can't be trusted to look at him.

"I know if I kiss you right now, you will taste as sweet as a peach and more addictive than anything I've ever tasted in my life," he growls, and I feel a finger tracing down my cheek, towards my neck. His hand slides to the back of my head, gripping my nape and angling my face towards his. Even then, I still don't open my eyes, not even when I feel his warm breath on my lips. I know he is inches away from me, and if he kisses me, I won't have the power to stop him. To fight what feels right.

"Open those eyes and tell me the truth," he urges, yet it feels like a demand. A dark, seductive one that sends shivers through me.

"I can't," I whisper, freezing when I feel his hand tighten on my neck, and his lips ever so gently brush mine.

"Soon then," he promises, and lets me go. He steps back, and I release the breath I'd been holding. I open my eyes, seeing him open the bedroom door and walk out without another word.

What the hell am I doing?

37

DAGAN

"I can't stand this anymore," I yell, slamming my hand into the stone wall. Korbin looks up as he does another sit up, and then rolls back into a crouch.

"Keep it down, Elias never gets any rest. Work out, keep yourself occupied, do anything but think. It's what I do," he snaps, nodding a head towards Elias sleeping in the corner. I look into the other dungeons, seeing the other dragons in here. Most have no idea why they were taken, others have said they side with the ice throne and its true leader. Isola isn't here to save them, or to be on the throne, and she needs us.

"It's been two years! Two years of living in this cage, stuck in this dungeon, while we wait for him to bring us food!" I growl, though I quickly lose my bluster. Sighing, I lean back against the wall and think of the only person that makes all this worth it. Isola.

"I miss her, too, and the connection makes separation painful for us all," Korbin says as he sits down next to me. I don't reply, I don't need to confirm how I'm feeling. We all know, because we're all experiencing the same emotions. When we saved her life, we didn't expect to be separated from her.

"I can't even connect to her," I growl again.

"It's because we've been weakened, and she is lost in her own mind. Connecting to her dreams is impossible," Korbin replies.

"Maybe she is better lost, because when she remembers . . . it will break her," I say quietly. She is strong, one of the strongest people I know, but none of us expected Thorne to betray her the way he did. Never expected him to kill her father, to imprison her guards, and take her throne.

"But she will have us," he comments.

"Yet, she won't. We can't escape this," I mutter back, getting angry all over again. Flames burst out of my hands, and I roll them around, forming a dragon. We are silent as I play with the flames, but eventually, I put them out and watch the door to the dungeons. Thorne should be here with food soon. He always shows up like clockwork every five days, around the same time of day. Elias wakes up, but stays quiet as he waits for the door to open with the rest of us. The door soon opens, but instead of coming in with the usual two guards, Thorne arrives with the seer at his side. The one that made Isola forget.

"Get up," Thorne demands as he lifts his hand, showing us keys and unlocking our cage. We all stand to hurry out, but Elias is first through the open cell door. He immediately walks over and drives his fist into Thorne's face.

"What the fuck? I'm getting you out of here, you moron!" Thorne sputters, rubbing his jaw as his nose bleeds.

"That's for Isola. Don't even say you didn't deserve it," Elias says as they stare at each other. Thorne eventually nods, and turns away, walking up the stairs.

"Come on, we don't have long to get you out. Be ready to fly," he says, and we follow him out of the dungeons.

"And be ready to forget, it is the only way because I've seen all your deaths if you just go to her. Including my sister's, and I will not risk that," the seer says, just as darkness blurs everything.

"Anything for Isola, even my memories, even my dragon," are the last words I manage to hear myself say.

I WIPE my face and give myself a shake, trying to clear my mind of the dream I've had every night since we arrived. I force myself to focus on the fact I'm in class, and it's not real. I glance over at Isola, staring at the beauty sitting two rows in front of me. Like she can feel my eyes on her, she turns, and her pale-blue eyes lock with mine. Everything disappears, the classroom, the school, until there is nothing but us gazing at each other. Her blue eyes are like a pool of clear water, they suck you in until you don't want to escape. Her blonde hair is light, so natural, as it frames her face, falling in perfect waves. She is stunning and utterly irresistible, and I've only known her a few days.

"Mr. Fire? Do you know the answer?" someone asks, and reality rushes back as I realise the teacher was talking to me.

"I completely missed the question, miss, what did you say?" I ask.

"Perhaps try listening next time, Mr. Fire. I asked what made Juliet decide to kiss the poison lips of Romeo when she awoke?" she asks me. I look at Isola as I answer.

"Juliet knew she couldn't live without the one person that made life worth living. She wanted to follow Romeo anywhere, and that included death. She made the choice that he was worth more than herself," I answer, and Isola takes a deep breath, before turning around and facing the front.

"Correct, Mr. Fire. Now can someone tell me what happened when the poison didn't work?" she asks, and Isola puts her hand up. "Go on, Miss Dragice."

"In her utter agony at the poison not working, she picked up a dagger and stabbed herself through the heart. She was certain that the only way to be with him was in death, so she guaranteed it the only way she knew how. Many people were sad and jealous of such a tragic love, that death was the only way for them to be together," she answers. The teacher claps, turning to the white board as she keeps talking. I don't hear a word of it as I watch Isola, like I have since I got to this school. There's something different about her, and there's something different about me when I'm around her, too. *I can't stay away, and I have no plan to try either.*

38

ISOLA

I look up at the gym, the building I've avoided ever since I remembered who I was. The place where Jace died, the place that holds a memory I don't want to replay, but I need to. The final bell rings, and I square my shoulders, holding my head up as I walk in. The normal smells of socks and body odor fill my senses as I walk through the small room and into the main part of the gym. I stare at the spot where he died, seeing nothing other than a newly painted floor. Any sign Jace died here is gone, everything about him is gone from this place. Meanwhile, I'm forced to stay here and pretend every-thing is normal. Ignoring my teacher's shouts for me to return, I turn around and leave the building. I can't act normal in that class, in that room. It's too much. I wipe my tears away as I walk out of the school and head towards the bus stop. I just want to go home and feel like shit for the rest of the evening. Everything is just so fucked up, and damn if I have a clue what I'm doing.

"Hey!" Dagan shouts, and I slow down so he can reach my side.

"Skipping class? I didn't think you had it in you, kitty cat," Dagan says as he catches up to me on my way to the bus stop.

"It's been a shit day," I tell him dryly, looking away as I can't deal with trying to get him to remember right now.

"So, I have Jules's car today as she wants me to do a food shop for her. Problem is, I have no idea how to find the supermarket," he says, grabbing my arm gently, so I stop walking. "Would you show me?"

"Why are you shopping for Jules, anyway?"

"Apparently, the three of us eat too much and keep her busy with all the extra washing we've caused. Jules is tired of constantly having to go to the shops, and told us we needed to start helping," he says, rubbing the back of his neck and making his shirt ride up. I quickly pull my eyes away, looking up at him and sighing.

"Fine. I could use some chocolate and ice cream," I reply. I follow him back to the car park, and he opens the door for me, letting me in.

"Take the main road out of town, and then it's three rights to get to the Tesco," I explain to him, as it's pretty hard to find. I don't know why they didn't just buy a building in town to put the store in, but they didn't.

"So, why are you skipping class?" Dagan asks me after he starts driving.

"Why are you?" I counter.

"I don't like gym," he explains simply, no excuse, he is just stating a fact. "You're turn."

"I don't want to talk about it."

"Come on, I want to know," he nudges my shoulder gently. Dagan catches and holds my gaze when he finds me looking at him, "I want to help, let me."

"You can't help, not with this," I mutter.

"Explain, and then we will see," he replies.

"Fine. My boyfriend died in the gym, and I went there today. I don't know, it just freaked me out, and upset me," I tell him, and he nods.

"How did he die?"

"A fire a few years ago," I say, because I can't really tell him the truth. That my step-aunt stabbed him through the heart with a dagger.

"I'm sorry, I really am. They say you never lose someone close to you, not really. Not in here," he points at his chest.

"But you miss them. You miss them so much it hurts, some-times," I say, and he reaches over, lifting my hand and just silently holding it.

"I can't relate to you, I can't tell you how to feel. So, I won't, but I can be here as your friend, or whatever you want me as, Isola," he says, more serious than he is ever usually like with me.

"I sometimes wonder if Jace would hate me for moving on, for even thinking of someone else that way."

"If he loved you, no, he wouldn't. He would want you to be happy, to love, and to live life to the fullest. That's all anyone wants for someone they love, and I'm sure he felt that way about you," he says, just as we spot the Tesco. We take two more turns until we pull into the car park and get out. I hadn't realized until he lets go, but he'd been holding my hand, lightly stroking it with his thumb, the entire time we'd been talking.

"Did she give you a list?" I ask, wanting to change the subject. From the look Dagan throws me over the car bonnet, he realises, but still allows it.

"Yeah, not that I have a clue what half the things on here are," he shrugs, pulling a list out of his pocket.

"Okay, you push the trolley, and I'll put things in, nice and simple," I say, opening the list and seeing mainly herbs, meat, and fresh food. There is also, in big bold letters at the bottom saying, "Buy your own junk food."

"Apparently, you need to buy your own junk food," I show Dagan, who chuckles as he gets a trolley, and we walk into the store. It's really strange how normal this is, shopping in the human world with Dagan, a big scary dragon. I'm sure he never would have done this if he remembered who he is.

"Okay, so let's get the junk food first. It's near the entrance," I muse, and Dagan claps his hands.

"You should hold the trolley then," he grins as he starts throwing god knows how much junk food into the trolley. When it's basically full, we are at the end of the aisle.

"You can't possibly eat all this!" I say, just not believing it.

"I don't want to come back to the store, and Korbin and Elias will eat shit-loads, too," he shrugs, and then steps backwards. Everything seems to slow down, just like in the movies, as Dagan bumps into a stack of dozens of cereal boxes piled on top of each other in a triangle shape, and they go flying everywhere.

"Whoops," Dagan says, straightening up, and we look over to see an angry shop assistant glaring at us.

"Dagan," I hiss, turning the trolley around and getting the hell out of there. Dagan and I basically run down the aisle and into the next one, both of us stopping to stare at each other before bursting out laughing. By the time we stop laughing, we have tears running down our faces.

"Come on, before they find us and we get kicked out," I tease him. He takes the trolley as I get the list back out. This was just what I needed to cheer me up. Dagan is just what I needed.

39

ISOLA

"I 'll go get the last bag, don't worry about it," I say, stopping Dagan from walking out of the kitchen. He chucks his keys at me, and I reach out a hand to catch them. I eye the twenty or so bags lying all over the kitchen and mentally sigh. It's going to take forever to unpack all the junk food he has bought.

"Okay, I will start putting everything away. Can you lock the car when you're finished?" he asks me, rolling that lip ring between his lips, and totally distracting me enough to drop the keys. I reach down, picking them up as I mentally curse myself. *Gotta get it together, Isola.*

"Sure," I smile at him, and walk out. The sun is bright today, making it almost warm, unlike the usual cold, wet weather we have. I walk out to the car and reach into the boot.

"*Danger,*" my dragon's voice warns me, hissing the word in my mind. I open my senses, still trying to act normal. As I'm reaching for the last bag, I hear it, the sound of something flying at me from behind. I turn, and hold both of my hands out, making an ice wall just as two daggers slam into it, one cutting my hand.

"Shit," I hiss in pain as I lower my hand, seeing the deep cut but knowing I have bigger problems. I slowly look around the ice wall, keeping my senses open, but see nothing. I can't smell anyone around either, only the residual scents of the people living with me.

"Dragon? Can you sense them?" I ask her, trusting her senses.

"Gone," she whispers. Looking back at the wall of ice, I spin around and kick the bottom, and it falls to pieces. I reach down and pull one of the daggers out of the ice. It is dragonglass, with a red dragon symbol etched into the wooden handle. The second one is the same.

"Isola?" Dagan shouts from inside, and I quickly throw the dagger into the boot of the car. I pull the second one out, shoving that in too. I will have to remember to get these out before Jules sees them and has a heart attack. I grab the last grocery bag with my good hand, cursing at the blood dripping freely from the other, and shutting the boot. I look at the ice briefly, hoping it will melt before anyone sees it. I run up the stairs, looking behind me once more for any threats, before shutting the front door.

"What the hell happened?" Dagan says, dropping the cereal box in his hands, and rushing over to me when I get into the kitchen. He lifts my cut hand, pulling me into the kitchen, so he can see it under the spotlights, and picking up a towel, placing it on the cut.

"I, err . . . shut my hand in the boot door," I claim, the only thing I can think of, as I put the plastic food bag down on the floor.

"When you said you *try* not to be clumsy, you weren't lying, right?" he asks, a small concerned smile on his lips, making me chuckle.

"Yep," I reply, and he shakes his head at me.

"Hold this on it while I go get the first aid box," he presses my free hand on the towel and steps away.

"It's under the sink in the bathroom downstairs," I tell him. He nods, heading in that direction. I watch him walk away, as I run the image of the dagger through my mind. It wouldn't be Tatarina's or someone she sent, because I have no doubt she would use a dagger with an ice dragon and fire dragon on it to make a point when killing me. I guess it could be her, yet she would make a curse by killing me because of Bee, and she isn't that stupid. Thorne doesn't want me dead, he made that clear by stopping his mother from killing me before. *So, who would do this?* Dagan comes back, and I try to relax, attempting to forget that someone just tried to kill me. *Even though that's impossible.*

"Let's go upstairs. Jules will be home any minute, and I don't want to explain this to her. She will only freak out and want me to go to hospital," I say, hopping off the seat after Dagan nods his agreement.

"If it needs anything more than butterfly stitches, we still might have to go," Dagan says once we get to the top of stairs. When we reach my room, I open the door with my elbow.

"I heal fast, so don't worry," I reply, walking into my room. Dagan switches the light on, and I sit on the bed, moving the towel to look at the cut. It's pretty deep, straight across my tree mark, splitting the tree in half. It has begun to heal a little already, and I doubt it even needs butterfly stitches, just a bandage will do. Dagan sits next to me on the bed, pulling my hand to him, and inspecting it. He gets some antibacterial wipes out of the box and starts slowly wiping the blood away.

"I didn't know you had a tattoo," he says, admiring the tree mark. "Do you have any others?" When he slides a thumb over it, a burst of warmth shoots through me, and he quickly moves his thumb away. Dagan continues to clean my hand, though he keeps giving me strange looks.

"Nope, just this one," I answer, clearing my throat and wondering what the hell that was.

"The green ink is amazing, so unique," he comments, and I flinch as he wipes the cut, the cleaning solution burning the cut.

"Sorry, kitty cat, I should have warned you that would sting,"

Dagan comments, stroking my wrist with his fingers in a soothing way.

"It's okay, thanks for helping me," I reply. I close my eyes and inhale his smoky scent as he wipes the cut again, and I have to bite my lip at the sting. He smells like home, like everything I really didn't know I needed.

"Anything you need, you come to me," he commands as I open my eyes. Looking up, his blue eyes hold such promise as he stares at me. I still remember the Dagan that didn't like me, who would never look at me like this–wouldn't help me, not unless he was forced. It's still him, but he is a lot nicer, that's for sure.

"What are you thinking, kitty cat?" he asks, and I pull my eyes away from his. When I look back, he is reaching into the box for a white bandage and tape.

"I was wondering about what you like to do in your spare time?" I respond, saying the first thing I can think of.

"Other than catching you from falling, and fixing your injuries?" he jokes, making me laugh. "Well, I like to work out. The basement gym here is pretty good." I smile tightly, remembering all the times Jace and I would train and fight in that basement. How our first time was actually in there, on one of the sofas. It wasn't romantic, we were both drunk and had no idea what we were doing, but it still meant something.

"Hold still a sec," Dagan says, letting go of my hand. Putting the bandage underneath, he wraps my hand tightly before ripping some tape and tying it. This reminds me of when I cut my hands in Dragca, and Thorne fixed me up. All that time he was planning to betray me, but as I look up at Dagan, I just feel confused. Sending them to me was helping me somehow; it couldn't have been done for any other reason.

"Tell me about your childhood, your parents?" I ask Dagan, needing a change of subject, as he puts the spare stuff away. I pick up the wrappers, walking over to my bin and dropping them in. I sit on the window seat, pulling up my legs.

"My mum and dad work for the army, so there's a lot of travelling. We went everywhere, moving every month or so. It wasn't much fun moving all the time," he says each word like a robot who was programmed to say this speech. I smile tightly, wondering how far I can push his memory. I remember seeing Elias hold his head, the pain of remembering before it was time overwhelming him, I suspect. I need to push Melody into talking to me, telling me what she knows of my future and how to make them remember.

"What about you, your parents?" he asks.

"My mother and father are dead, but I have a half-sister and uncle. They just don't live around here," I say, feeling weird about talking about my sister so casually when it still feels so raw.

"Jules said she talks to your father, and he pays her?" he asks me, his suspicious eyes narrowing on mine.

"She means my uncle, he claims to be my father sometimes," I lie, and I know he knows it when he tuts.

"You're not a good liar, you should work on that, kitty cat," he says and picks the first aid box up, walking to the door. He stops when he opens it, looking back at me.

"When you came back in that kitchen, you were scared. Is it safe for me to leave you?"

"Of course, it is," I say, trying to wave it off.

"If you need a guard, a friend, or *anything* . . . I'm only two doors away," he says and walks out, the look in his eyes staying with me. He knows I'm hiding something. Even when he doesn't remember who he is, or who I am, he still wants to guard me. For some reason, it makes my heart flutter.

40

ISOLA

I shoot my eyes open, seeing a gun pointing at another version of me. My hair is up in a ponytail, and I have my dragon leather outfit on, which gives me hope that I get back to Dragca at some point. I can't see who is holding the gun, only the slight wobble of the person's hand as they hold it in front of my face. I don't move, just hold my hands up, and speak words I can't hear. I can't even see the room, only a smoky blur instead.

"Hey, sis!" I hear Melody say cheerfully, making me jump. Why do people keep appearing out of nowhere? I turn to see her walk through the smoke, wearing the same red dress as last time I saw her. Her hair is up in a bun this time, and her marks on her face almost glow in the dimly lit room.

"Another warning vision?" I ask.

"Oh this, no . . . well, yes. It doesn't matter, I only use them to be able to talk to you, as the visions won't change," she waves a hand like someone holding my future self at gunpoint isn't important.

"Someone tried to kill me, with daggers," I tell her, and she sighs.

"Thorne thinks he controls his mother, that she isn't stupid enough to kill you. He doesn't know her at all. Watch your back," she warns me.

"I wish people would stop coming into my dreams, it's just annoying now," I give her a pointed look, but she just raises an eyebrow at me.

"And I wish I didn't have to use my power every day to keep you safe, but we all don't get what we want. Now grow up, get over it, and listen," she tells me off, and surprised, I decide to listen. She does have a point.

"What is going on in Dragca? Has anyone seen my uncle?" I ask, needing to know what is going on. He is all I have left who is on my side over there, that I know of anyway. If I can get to him, then I can figure something out. I don't think walking back into Dragca with no plan is a good idea. I remember how Tatarina looked at me; she wants me dead, and I have a feeling Bee and the curse is the only reason I'm not.

"No, we haven't found him, but that's a good thing. He is hiding with the seers, somehow; smart man," she pauses to wink. "Anyway, your step-brother is being ruled by his mother. She is an evil bitch, just in case you were unsure, and his dear auntie is her executioner. The whole of Dragca is split with those who are scared but secretly hope you are still alive, and those who support Thorne but are scared of his mother. Then there are others who don't know who to choose, so they are going to the seers, who will not choose a side anymore," she explains.

"I will come back soon and convince the seers to side with me. With you by my side, it shouldn't be too difficult," I promise.

"Oh, I know, only . . . it's not going to be as easy as you think. Once you come back, I'm not seeing all your future, just bits, like this gunshot . . . it's bothering me. I see you coming for me, and then it's black. I'm missing something," she says, frustration written all over her face.

"Can I stop Thorne from coming into my dreams? Is there any way you can tell me how to make the guys remember?" I ask her, knowing this dream can't last forever, and talking about the future isn't what I need to know.

"No, it's fate, and good for you both," she says, with a sad smile. She looks over her shoulder at something, but I only see smoke. When she looks back, the sad smile is replaced with tight lines.

"Which is?" I ask.

"All of this, it's what has to happen, and there are so many outcomes that could occur. I could tell you the clearest route, but then it would risk that future. First rule of being a seer, you don't tell your closest family their futures, unless you want them dead," she says, seeming happy, and

then she looks behind herself again. Her smile disappears, and worry fills her face instead.

"What are you looking at?" I ask.

"I'm projecting from my room while half-asleep, and Thorne is knocking on the door," she says and turns back. "I don't have much time as he wants me to look for you again, tell him what you are doing, and that means his mother is out for a bit," she explains.

"I hate him, Odie! I can't and don't want to see him in my dreams. Also, I don't want you telling him what I'm doing!" I shout at her.

"Have you ever heard the saying 'there's a fine line between love and hate'?" she asks, but a gunshot makes me jump before I can yell at her about her ridiculous idea. I don't love Thorne, I detest him. I can't stand him for what he has done. I look over to see the future me holding my stomach, the person with the gun actually shot me. Who is it? I try to walk over, but something stops me, like a glass wall I can't see.

"Time to wake up, your dragon guards need you, and time is short," Melody tells me. I go to correct her about the love and hate thing, and the stupid saying which is bugging me when I know there are more important things to find out. Like who shot me.

"I've been shot, who is that?" I bite out.

"Oh, that's nothing, and you know I can't tell you. I know you live . . . if that helps," she chuckles, and then everything blurs away. Being shot isn't nothing, but I don't get to tell her that.

THE SHRIEKING of my alarm makes me wake up. I'm feeling a little hazy as I rub my eyes and grab my phone. The memory of the dream flashes through my mind. I'm going to be shot in the future, which I bet really hurts. Why didn't I defend myself, fight them? It doesn't make any sense. I don't even want to think about that knowing look my sister gave me, like I could love Thorne. That's impossible, so fucking impossible. I turn the alarm off, scrolling blankly through my Facebook messages from Hallie. I guess she went on a date last night with some guy, and apparently, he's really good in bed. *At least someone is getting laid.* I think I'm starting to forget what sex is like. I send her a quick text about how lucky she is, and then start to get out of bed, when someone knocks on my door. I run over, open it up, and keep myself behind the door as my banana-covered pajamas aren't cute. Neither are the Dorito stains all over them.

"I can't run this morning, I have to go and look at a car that's for sale across town. Elias is coming with me, and Jules as well, because she just wants to get out of the house," Korbin says. I nod as I run my eyes over his styled brown hair, green eyes, and the tight shirt and jeans he has on. They cling to his body, showing off how damn impressive it is.

"It's Saturday anyway, I don't run on weekends," I make myself look away as I reply.

"Cool, that works out then. Be ready at seven tonight," he instructs, stepping back.

"Seven?" I ask.

"I'm a little insulted you forgot about our date, doll, but you can make it up to me tonight," he says with a wink. I mentally sigh as he turns around and walks away. We can't date, it's too risky for them, for me. Yet, somehow the thought of going out on a date with Korbin turns me on much more than it frightens me. I shut the door, mentally cursing myself, and try to decide whether or not letting my hormones control me is the best idea. I pull the bandage off my hand and, despite the cut being healed, get a plaster out to replace it. I should have something covering where the cut should be, just in case Dagan sees it. I get changed and grab my Kindle, intent on spending the day reading a romantic wolf-shifter book. Running down the stairs, I freeze when I see Dagan in the kitchen, cooking something that smells amazing. He even has an apron on, no shirt underneath, and I just stare at all the muscles on his back. There are a few scars littered around, but mainly it is all muscles, and damn fine-looking ones at that.

"I didn't have you down as the cooking type," I grin, and he turns to look at me.

"Oh, and what did you have me down as?" he teases.

"A guy that lifts weights all day and likes to fight," I shrug, as really, he does seem like that type, and back in Dragca, there was no need for him to cook at the academy.

"I do fight, so you're right there. In fact, I have a self-defence class today that I'm going to for the first time," he chuckles and then looks over at me as he pours batter into the frying pan.

"Want some pancakes?" he asks.

"I'd love some," I reply, walking over to the table. Dagan serves the pancakes up before sitting opposite me. After pouring some maple syrup on the pancakes, we begin eating in earnest, not really speaking. Every so often, I feel his eyes on me, but whenever I glance up, he is looking away and pretending like he wasn't. I need to do something to get some alone time with him, where we have a chance to talk, and he isn't so awkward with me.

"How's your hand?" he asks, reminding me that I need to get the daggers out of the car before Jules sees them.

"Fine," I respond, and he nods.

"Can I come to self-defence? I used to go to the local one a few years back," I blurt out.

"Really? You did self-defence?" he asks, leaning back in his chair, and looking me up and down. *Why do guys think females can't fight simply because we don't look strong?* Usually, the strongest people in the world are hidden behind a pretty face.

"Yes, I did, and I bet I can kick your ass," I say, totally bluffing. Dagan is like twice the size of me, and most likely could break me like a twig.

"I'd like to see that, but you hurt your hand. It's not a good idea."

"It's all healed, I swear I'm fine," I say, and he narrows his eyes at me.

"Alright then. We have Elias's bike we can ride there, as he took the taxi with Korbin and Jules earlier," he tells me.

"I will clean up, you cooked," I say when we have finished eating, but Dagan picks his plate up and moves to get mine.

"Nah, I don't mind, and you need to get dressed. Class starts in an hour, and we'll need to leave in ten minutes to get there," he explains.

"Okay," I say, getting up and keeping my eyes on him. "A hot man that cooks and cleans, most girls would do anything to find a guy like you." I instantly regret it when I realise I said it out loud.

"You think I'm hot?" Dagan teases, as my cheeks light up.

"That was meant to be a comment in my head, not spoken out loud," I explain, which only makes his grin grow. He rolls the lip ring in-between his lips and puts the plates down, walking over to me. He stops when we are mere inches apart, and I have to arch my neck to look up at him.

"Go and get dressed before I show you just how *hot* I think you are, kitty cat," he warns me, and yet, I don't move as I stare up at him. His blue eyes are brighter now, the black specks from his dragon are gone, and I kind of miss them.

"What are you thinking about?" he asks me, his voice deep and husky as he strokes his fingers down my arm. His touch snaps me out of my thoughts and brings me back to my senses. I step back, clearing my throat.

"About how a girl is going to beat your ass in class," I say with a grin, and turn away before I do something crazy, like jump on him and kiss him until we both forget everything else.

41

ISOLA

"Ouch," I groan as Dagan flips me onto my back, and I wheeze out in pain. He looks down at me, his hands on his hips, and his dark eyebrows raised. I huff mentally, knowing I'm not using all my strength, because to do that would be to call my dragon for help. I have to put a large barrier between us, just so she doesn't take offence at Dagan's smirk every damn time he wins. *Cocky asshole.*

"How long has it been since you trained?" he asks, offering me a hand which I push away and get myself up. There are a few other people training, and they look our way, but they don't stare for long. Most of the humans are scared of Dagan, and have been since we walked in, which works well to get them to leave us alone. The training hall is right in the middle of town, at the back of a warehouse. The place is used for all sorts of sports, I believe; the stench of sweat, dirt, and blood is overwhelming me.

"Months, years, I don't know," I manage to pant out. Dagan rolls his lip ring as he watches me. All I can think about is how I want to kiss him, want to feel that cold silver of the ring against my own lips. I shouldn't be thinking these things.

"You need a lot of work before you would stand a chance of

beating *anyone*," he says, and the teacher chooses that point to walk over.

"Isola had a lot of skill from what I remember; with some personal training she could be a worthy opponent in a fight," Miss Dale says, smiling. Miss Dale is thirty-something with bright-pink hair cut very short, and a muscular, toned body that most people would die for. She also has a serious expression that makes you want to run away from her. She is tiny, like five-foot-three, but she could kick all our asses without even getting breathless. Well, maybe not Dagan, but then he has trained all his life, even if he doesn't remember it.

"I don't see any skill now," Dagan comments drily, like I'm not right in front of him.

"Maybe you should give her some lessons. The skills on your paperwork indicate you don't really need this class anyway, so why not train someone in need, instead?" Miss Dale suggests.

"I'm not in need," I protest.

"You are, and being the good person I am, I will help you," Dagan cockily replies, and I just glare at him as Miss Dale claps.

"Excellent," she says with a sweet smile towards me. "Why don't you get the Bo staff and fight with those? I remember you being amazing with one," she suggests, nodding her head towards the large fighting ring in the middle of the hall. The Bo staffs are lined up next to it. It's a common way to fight here, and I used to be able to beat everyone other than Jace. He was something else as a fighter, but everyone has forgotten him here. This is a place he came to every week, and they can't remember him. I close my eyes, looking away for just a second to calm down from the rush of anger that makes me feel.

"Okay," Dagan says, walking over to the ring, and I follow reluctantly. This is going to hurt both my ego and my butt when he beats me. I grab a Bo staff from the rack, and climb into the ring after Dagan. He stands, swirling the Bo staff around with one hand as he watches me from the other side of the ring.

"This might hurt a little, but I promise to be gentle," he

comments, and runs at me before I'm ready to even reply. I lift my staff, whacking it against his and spinning around straight after, meeting his next hit. Dagan jumps to the left, swinging the staff for my legs, which I manage to avoid with a backflip. I land with my staff up, ready to protect myself, as he attacks again. He pushes all his strength down onto me, and I have to take several steps back, keeping my eyes locked onto his blue ones.

"Is that what you tell all the girls? That you will be gentle?" I tease him, trying to distract him enough to escape the corner I'm backed in.

"Wouldn't you like to know what I tell them," he answers, just as my back hits the ring's barrier.

"Not if that's what you tell them. I don't like *gentle*," I say, biting my lip, and he pauses. That moment of hesitation is all I need to push him back. I sweep my staff under his legs, and he lands hard on the floor, on his back. I place the end of my staff against his neck before he can even blink.

"Kitty cat, I'm impressed," he coughs out.

"You haven't seen anything yet," I laugh, moving the staff and straightening up. "Again." I grin at his shocked smile.

"I think I'm going to like you, kitty cat," he says. He jumps up, slamming his staff into mine with the slight distraction his words cause, and all I can do is laugh.

"WILL I be seeing you here next week?" Miss Dale asks me as I come out of the changing rooms.

"Yes, I think I will be coming every week for a while," I reply, and she smiles, placing her hand on my arm.

"Does that have anything to do with a certain dark-haired hottie?" she asks, and I chuckle.

"Dagan? No, it's not like that with us," I deny.

"No one looks at each other the way you two do without there being something between them," she squeezes my arm once and walks away. Standing still, I roll her words around my mind as I watch her walk out of the hall. I want to deny it all, say she is wrong, and there's nothing between us . . . but I hate lying, especially to myself. I just have to keep my distance from him and the others. I can't risk it all, not just for my feelings. Not when there's a curse that could take everything from me, from them. I watch Dagan walk out of the male changing room, chatting to some guy who pats his shoulder like they are friends. Dagan looks around for me, a small smile playing on his lips when he spots me. He says something to the guy, who looks over at me, and then smirks at Dagan before walking off. Dagan walks over to me, his eyes staying locked on mine like there isn't anyone else in the room. The moment is so intense and breath-taking that it's hard to control my own desires and continue to try to convince myself there's nothing between us.

"Kitty cat, let's go and get some lunch. Where is best to eat around here?" Dagan asks me.

"There's a deli two doors away, they do amazing sandwich-es," I say. "They have these peanut butter bacon sandwiches which are my favourite."

"Peanut butter and bacon in a sandwich? That sounds gross," he shakes his head at me.

"Don't knock it until you try it," I say, making him laugh as he opens the gym doors for me. I walk out, and he immediately follows.

"It looks like it might rain, we should hurry up," he says, and I look up, seeing the dark-grey clouds and feeling the chill in the air. He is right. We rush around the corner, but we're too late as the skies open up, and rain pounds down on us. I see the deli not far from us, its purple door is easy to spot.

"Shit, run, it's not far," I say, grabbing Dagan's hand and running down the street to the deli. I pull the door open and rush inside, trying to catch my breath.

"We are both soaked," Dagan comments. Something in his tone has me looking down at my white shirt and yoga pants. A blush rises up my cheeks when I notice my shirt is see-through, and you can see my pink bra underneath. I look up, seeing Dagan's eyes drift over my body, and then back up to my eyes. There's a moment where we stare at each other, and I'm sure we are thinking and feeling the same things, but neither of us move. We just stare, until he decides to step forward, leaving us only a breath apart. Just as he reaches forward to touch me, a voice interrupts.

"I got you some towels, the weather is awful this time of year," a sweet, older-sounding voice says. I turn to look at the lady speaking to us. She is about fifty, with hair dyed purple and cut short, and a big smile on her lips as she looks between us, holding out some white towels.

"Thank you, it just came down so quick," I say, accepting one of the towels and stepping back from Dagan.

"Why don't you sit over here, the heater is under the table, so it will dry you off," she points to a small table for two by the wall.

"Thanks, can we have two peanut butter bacon sandwiches and some teas, please?" I ask, seeing Dagan glare at me from the corner of my eye.

"Perfect, I will get right on that," she says, writing the order down on a notepad and walking off.

"I'm not eating that," Dagan says as we walk over to the table.

"Come on, you have to try it. Fair enough if you don't like it, but trying new things is fun," I say, and he shakes his head at me as he slides into his seat opposite mine. I glance around seeing the empty deli, and out the window where it is still pounding down with rain. Thank god Dagan parked the bike in the car park opposite the gym, so it won't be wet when we get to it.

"I'm not leaving here until that stops," I say, and Dagan looks at the rain outside briefly before turning back to me.

"It's likely just a shower, and will be over soon," he says. The lady brings our drinks and food over a few minutes later, placing them onto the table. I practically drool at the sight of my favourite sandwich. It's been so long since I've had one of these. I pick it up, taking one big bite, trying not to moan out loud at the amazing taste.

"I know what to buy you if I piss you off," he comments, making me chuckle.

"When, *when* you piss me off. Now man up and try yours," I nod my head at his plate. He narrows his eyes at me as he picks the sandwich up. He sniffs it before taking a bite, and I watch like it's almost in slow motion.

"Soooo?" I ask as he puts the sandwich down.

"It's okay," he says, and I laugh.

"You like it! You just won't admit that I'm right," I say, raising an eyebrow.

"I have no idea what you are talking about," he says with a grin and picks up his sandwich. He takes a big bite, and I try not to laugh. *Stubborn dragon.*

42

ISOLA

"This is a bad idea, such a bad idea, Issy," I say to myself, smoothing down the tight red dress. Pushing my curly hair over my shoulder, I stare at myself in the mirror. I glance at the clock on the wall, seeing it's nearly seven and time for my date with Korbin. I'm kind of hoping the red dress I bought will jog his memory of the mating ceremony. I'm running out of ideas on how to make the guys remember me, and that's not good. The more time I spend away from Dragca, the more I have no idea what's going on. I keep thinking about the seers, wondering how I'm going to convince them that fighting for me and protecting me is a good idea. How I'm going to convince anyone to help me get the throne back. I still jump a little when a knock sounds at my door, even though I'm expecting it. I walk over, picking up my leather jacket hanging on the back of the door before opening it.

"Wow," Korbin mutters as I just stare at him, speechless at how amazing he looks. Korbin's hair is styled a little, making his eyes pop, and he's wearing a blue shirt, black trousers, with a long black coat.

"Oh, snap," I say, and then shake my head as my cheeks

burn. "That was really lame. You look good, is what I meant to say," I blurt out. He laughs, stepping closer.

"You're cute when you're nervous, Issy," he tells me, and I chuckle.

"Cute and weird, you sure you want to take me out?" I ask.

"Certain," he grins seductively.

"So . . . where are we going?" I ask, as he hasn't told me a thing about this date. Korbin clears his throat, holding his hand out for me. I slide my hand into his, feeling the roughness of it from his training, I expect.

"It's a ten-minute drive, and no, I'm not telling you where we are going as it's a surprise," he says, leading me down the corridor, and still holding my hand. We're walking to the door, when someone clears their throat, and I turn around to see Dagan leaning against the wall. His eyes drift down my dress, and feel like they are burning my skin with every part they touch until he looks up.

"Have a good night," he says gruffly, his hands tensely held in fists at his sides. We trained all day, and something seems to have changed between us. Like it has been changing with Elias, like it's changing with Korbin. I don't see them as just friends, and when I'm with them, I forget the curse. I forget who I am and wish we were just normal people who could be together without any danger.

"We will," Korbin answers when I don't speak, opening the front door.

"Bye, Dagan," I say, and he nods tensely before I turn around and walk outside. It's lit up by the solar lights attached to the house and the ones running down the sides of the driveway. Parked up is a black car, which Korbin unlocks with his keys.

"It's a Vauxhall Antara, we got it today. What do you think?" he asks.

"That I'm clueless about cars, but it's nice?" I say, making him laugh as he opens my door for me. I get in, and he shuts the door as I pull my seatbelt on and wait for him to get in and do the same.

"Are you really not going to tell me what you have planned?" I ask him, and he winks at me as he starts the car.

"Don't you trust me, doll?"

"Fine," I pout, rolling my eyes at him, and making him laugh. Korbin turns the radio on, and to my surprise, starts singing along with the lyrics of the Taylor Swift song.

"Look what you've made me do," he sings as I just sit watching him with wide eyes.

"What?" he asks, finally noticing me.

"I didn't have you for a Tay-Tay fan," I grin as he shrugs.

"I like to sing, it's meant to be good for you. You should try it," he suggests teasingly. I like this playful side of him, he is usually so serious and grumpy. Well, not as grumpy as Eli and Dagan, but still.

"I don't sing, and the world can thank me for that one at any time," I say, making him laugh.

"Come on, I won't tell," he winks, and I chuckle, still not singing with him. He just carries on singing like nothing happened, without a care in the world. I gently start humming along after a while, and he reaches over, taking my hand in his for the rest of the drive. I know it's only holding my hand, but it sends little warm feelings straight through to my heart. Feelings that I need to ignore in order to get through tonight. I can't really date him. It's just hard to remember that when Korbin is like this with me, winning me over with every damn look from his deep, sexy green eyes.

"Here we are," he pulls up to the beach port, a place I've never really been in all my years of living here. I give him a questioning look as we get out of the car, and walk down the pier. When the dock with five large yachts tied up comes into view, and one that is lit up with a man waiting at the end, I have a good idea what the date is.

"A yacht date?" I ask, and he nods, looking nervous.

"I love it, I haven't actually been on one before," I say, and he looks relieved as he lifts our joined hands, gently kissing my knuckles. I end up blushing at the sweet movement. *Damn, this night is going to be harder than I thought.*

"I've rented it for the night," he explains as we near the human waiting by the walkway to the yacht. The human has a suit on, dark hair, and a serious expression.

"Mr. Dragoali and Miss Dragice, I presume?" he asks, and Korbin offers him a hand to shake.

"Lovely to meet you, Mr. Gregory," he says.

"Come on board, I will be steering my yacht for the night, but you won't see me, you have it all to yourselves. So lovely to see such a happy young couple," he comments, and we walk up the ramp. Korbin slides an arm around my waist.

"One more thing, the music speakers are playing up. They might turn on and off, but let me know if it becomes a problem, and I will switch them off altogether," he tells us.

"Thank you, Mr. Gregory," I reply.

"Let's look around, I've only seen the photos online," Korbin says as we continue on. I nod, resting my head on his shoulder as we walk around. The yacht has an entire glass level, with three sofas, a bar, and other normal things spread around. It's all shiny, new, and stunning. There are doors that lead outside to the front of the yacht, where you can look over the ocean. Korbin walks down a set of stairs, and I follow, my mouth dropping open at the room below. The entire bottom of the room is glass, so you can see underneath with the bright lights in the four corners of the room. There's a table, with bowls of covered-up food on it, but I barely notice as the yacht moves.

"This is incredible," I say, moving around the room as we begin to see fish swimming below the glass. Korbin lies down on the floor, looking down, and I chuckle before lying next to him. *It's a good idea, really.*

"It's kind of like you're floating through the water," I say, "it's so beautiful," I whisper, and look over to see Korbin staring at me.

"So are you," he says, reaching for my hand, and linking our fingers together. We don't say much more as we watch the fish and the sea for a long time, until the yacht slows down. Every time I point something out, Korbin is never looking, his eyes are always on me instead. I don't know why, but the idea that I'm more fascinating than the beautiful sight in front of me is scary. Not scary because of him, but because what is happening between us isn't just nothing. It's something special, and something like this could break the curse and I don't know if that is something I want to happen while we are on earth.

"We should eat," Korbin suggests, jumping up in one smooth, sexy movement, and holding a hand out for me. I grab his hand, getting up as I clear my throat.

"It's hot in here," I comment, taking off my leather jacket. It doesn't really help, as it's not the temperature, but rather Korbin that's making me hot. Korbin takes his coat off at the same time as I do, watching me for something. It's almost like he knows what I'm thinking, but he doesn't call me out on it like he could do.

"Here," he takes mine from me, and goes to hang them on a hook near the staircase. I lift the lids on some of the plates, seeing a range of sea food, and a chocolate dessert that makes my mouth water from just one glance. I sit down as Korbin gets back to the table.

"I hope you like seafood, I should have asked before we came," he says as he takes his seat on the other side of the table.

"I love seafood. Jace couldn't stand the smell of it, so I didn't have it often," I say, mentally laughing at the scrunched-up face he used to make when it was anywhere near him. *I miss him, but his memory seems to drift further away every day.*

"Who is Jace?" Korbin asks as he picks up his knife and fork to begin eating.

"My ex-boyfriend, he died a few years ago," I say, even
though it feels like it was just yesterday that I found him dead.

"I'm sorry, I truly am," he says, reaching across to hold
my hand.

"I can't eat with one hand, you know?" I tease him, trying to
lighten the mood a little, and needing the subject change. It's
not that I don't want to talk about Jace with him, but just not
this Korbin who can't really understand my anger or need for
revenge. And it would all be a lie, I can't tell him how he died,
and I don't want to lie to him any more than I must. It doesn't
feel right.

"Yes, you can, watch," he grins and throws a chip in the air,
catching it perfectly with his mouth.

"Not all of us are that good. If I tried that, I'd end up poking
my eye out with the chip and we would be in A&E," I say, and he
laughs, letting go of my hand. We eat our food, occasionally
commenting on how amazing it all tastes, though I still try to
keep my eyes away from him as much as possible. This date is
feeling too real, too much. Some slow, romantic music starts
playing just as we finish, making Korbin laugh.

"So, the music is working again, and perfect timing. Would
you like to dance?" he asks.

"I don't know," I mumble and he gets up, holding a hand out
for me. I can't really say no when he looks at me like that,
despite how dangerous this is. I place my hand in his, and get
out of the seat, walking away from the table a little. Korbin pulls
me close to him, with hands on my waist, and I slide my arms
around his neck as I look up.

"I had this dream, that I was watching you dance, in a red
dress, with someone else. All I wanted was to dance with you,
hold you, but I couldn't for some reason. That dream keeps
running through my mind, almost as much as your blue eyes
do," he admits, making my heart pound. He is dreaming about
the night I danced with Thorne at the mating ceremony, meaning

he is starting to remember something. I wonder if any of the others are having dreams.

"Some people say dreams are our deepest wishes, that they could even be true," I reply, and he chuckles, taking my hand and spinning me around, before pulling me back to him.

"I don't know about wishes, but desires, yes. Dreams are definitely our deepest desires," he says, leaving me breathless as I can't look away from him. Korbin leans down, taking my lips with his when I'm not expecting it. But I can't stop the reaction I have the moment our lips meet. The kiss is deep, passionate, and perfect. Groaning when I pull him closer, Korbin lifts me up by my ass, and I lock my legs around him.

"Kor," I moan, when he kisses down my jaw, getting to my neck and sucking, making me want him so much.

"Isola," he whispers, pulling back, his thumbs rubbing circles on my ass where he holds me to him. I slide my hands into his hair, and any hesitation he had is gone as he slams his lips into mine, lowering us to the floor. I should tell him to stop as he pushes my dress up around my waist, but I can't, I don't want to stop. Pulling the top of my dress and bra down, Korbin exposes my breast and flicks his tongue over my nipple. I moan, and in response his hand drags my underwear down my legs slowly, until I can kick them off. He slides his hand up my leg ever so slowly, teasing me as he leaves my breast to kiss me again.

"Doll, stop me," he almost begs.

"I can't, and I'm on protection. I don't want to stop," I breathe out, not lying about protection exactly, but female dragons can't get pregnant unless they are in heat, and that only happens once a year.

"Doll," his deep gravelly voice whispers next to my ear as he slips a finger inside me. I moan just as he moves his hand, each movement getting me so close to the edge.

"Damn . . . you're tight," he groans, moving his finger out of me and making me miss it already. I hear him undo his trousers, the sound of his zipper coming down making me desperate for him as I lie down on the floor, and he follows after me. I don't have to wait long as Korbin moves his body over mine, sliding inside me with one long stroke. I feel a slight coldness of a piercing I can feel on him, shocking me a little, but it's so pleasurable that I don't care after a second. He looks down at me, buried inside me, and pushes a hand into my hair.

"Mine," he growls, and his eyes turn completely black, his dragon taking over. I moan as he starts slamming into me harder and faster.

"Mine," I moan back, my dragon agreeing with me as Korbin picks up speed with my words. I push him over onto his back, seeing his surprised look, and knowing he let me take control. I grab his shoulders as I ride him, his fingers gripping my hips tightly as I drive myself to the brink.

"I'm close, Kor," I moan out, my words barely making any sense. Kor sits up, taking my nipple into his mouth and flicking it with his tongue, and that's all I need. I come hard, and a few thrusts later, he finishes inside me, grabbing my hips hard as he bites down on my shoulder.

"Damn, I didn't expect it to be like this," he pants out, and I kiss his cheek, as he turns to look at me.

"Do you remember?" I ask, hoping that the black I saw in his eyes means he does, but the confused look he gives me proves he doesn't.

"Remember what?" he asks.

"Nothing," I say, kissing him before he can read my expression, letting his kisses erase any disappointment that he doesn't remember, and I let myself get lost in him. We stay like that a while longer, as I try to forget the fear that when he *does* remember, he'll hate me for not stopping this because of the curse. I couldn't stand him hating me, and it makes me sick to think he might. What have I done? *When did my life get so complicated?*

43

ELIAS

Black shadows surround me, pressing against every part of my body as I try not to scream out from the pain. The bitch won't hear me scream, that's for sure. My dragon beats against my mind, but I can't let him out, the fucking seer has locked him away. I imagine Isola as the pain floods every part of me, remembering what she looks like, how sweet her lips taste. How she is mine, and once I get out of here, I will tell her that. Even if she doesn't want me, even if the curse takes everything, I will be at her side. Friend, protector, guard, or lover. It doesn't matter, I just want to see her.

"Enough, stop this!" I hear someone demand, but they won't be able to stop her, no one can.

"I said no more!" the man shouts, a growl reverberating with his words this time. The black shadows move away, dropping me onto the floor. I cough blood out, wiping my mouth as I look around for Dagan and Korbin. I finally find them both passed out on the floor. The bitch started with them before me, and they couldn't handle it for too long, not that I'm far from passing out myself.

"We should kill them, they will only try to escape and help Isola. They aren't loyal to you, my son," I hear Tatarina say in her overly sweet voice. I turn to see Thorne watching me as he stands next to his mother.

"I don't want them dead, I want them available to use against her.

Think about it, mother, if Isola ever remembers, or anyone tries to help her, we need someone to use against her," he explains, and I push myself up.

"You betraying bastard," I spit out, but he ignores me, still watching his mother. She pushes her pale-blonde hair over her shoulder, and I see the black veins crawling all up her arms. If it wasn't for the darkness around her, she would look so sweet and innocent with her big doll-like eyes and features. She is using a lot of dark magic, so she must have a dark spirit, the very opposite to Isola. That makes Isola her biggest threat, yet, she isn't dead. I would know if anyone killed Isola, it would destroy my soul.

"Fine, fine. We will keep them alive . . . for now. Let them starve, no one helps them," she says and walks away. Thorne watches until she shuts the dungeon door behind her, and finally meets my eyes.

"How could you? You know what she is to you, what she could be," I growl.

"Don't, I don't need advice from you," Thorne spits out, anger burning in his eyes as his dragon turns them silver. Thorne shakes his head and reaches into his cloak, pulling out three little bottles. He puts them on the floor just inside the cage.

"Drink these, they will heal you and the others," he says, confusing me.

"Why do you care? You have your throne and everything you wanted," I ask.

"I don't care, but Isola does. For that, I will keep you alive and help you escape when the time is right," he says, and I step back, not understanding why.

"Are you going to let us go, only to use us against her somehow?" I ask. "I can't believe you would just to help her."

"Does it matter why?" he replies, but I know it's a lie, I can see it in his eyes. I don't question him on it, knowing I'm missing something. And I need to figure it out, I need to figure Thorne out.

"FUCKING HELL," I mutter, sitting up in bed as another one of those messed up dreams bothers me again. *Haunt me.* Ever since I came to this town, I can't stop dreaming of dragons, of a beautiful girl with blue eyes so clear they almost look like you can fall into them. I dream of a castle, of being locked away for years, and a guy named Thorne bringing me food–looking after me and the others. For some reason, I hate that bastard, and I want to punch him. Then there are dreams of a girl in a red dress, dancing, and looking so happy, so free. It's always Isola, but it's like she is someone else in these dreams. A princess, and a forbidden one at that. It's a total mind fuck that makes me want her more than anything. I slide out of bed, leaving my room in only my pajama shorts and walking down the corridor, pausing outside Isola's room. I've always been able to smell people, which I know isn't normal, but it's not like I can turn it off. I can smell her, mixed with the scent of Korbin. *So, their date went well, I guess. For fuck's sake.* I run down the stairs, taking the right through the lounge, and heading to the stairs that lead to the basement. I walk straight to the punching bag, lifting my hand and slamming it into it. I pour all my frustration, my hate, and my confusion into every punch, closing my eyes and shutting the world off until my hands burn.

"Eli!" I hear shouted, and I stop. Breathing heavily, I turn to see Korbin standing a few feet away from me. His hair is messy, and he's just wearing his pajama shorts, smelling so much like Isola that I want to hit him.

"You're bleeding," he points out.

"I heal quick, always have. Don't worry about it," I say, and he offers me a towel. I place it on my hands and quickly step away from him.

"How was your date?" I ask tensely, and he picks up on it.

"Good. She is mine now, Elias," he states, the possession in his voice isn't hard to pick up on. He has another thing coming if he thinks I will just walk away.

"For now, I'm not backing off. The naughty princess isn't something I'm willing to give up on," I warn him, and he walks over, until he is standing straight in front of me.

"Back off," he bites out.

"Make me," I say, being deadly serious.

"What the fuck is going on?" Dagan shouts, being the voice of reason like he usually is between us. He comes over, pushing his way in the middle of us, and I try to calm myself down. I don't really want to fight with Korbin or Dagan, yet it's hard to think of anything else right now.

"What the fuck is going on with you two idiots? Explain," he demands.

"I'm not sharing Isola, and fuck-face doesn't get that," Korbin replies in a dry tone.

"I'm guessing your date went well then?" Dagan says, and I hear the growl in his voice, making me smirk.

"You like her, too," I state, but he doesn't answer or look at me. There's a tense moment between all of us, none of us saying a word. We can't, or won't, give up on her. That means there is only one way we can have a happy ending with Isola. I think she means more to us than just some random girl. It's been more than that for me since I first saw her. I don't need them to tell me how they feel, I can see it in how they watch her.

"Yeah, you could say that," Dagan finally replies.

"Right, well, shouldn't this be Isola's decision? If she isn't interested in anyone else, you have nothing to worry about. Though, I will warn you of something, Kor," I say, stepping away from them both.

"What?" Korbin snaps.

"Isola is stubborn and smart, and I doubt you telling her what to do will go over well," I say, and he shakes his head, looking up at the ceiling. He knows I'm right, this has to be her decision.

"She can't date us all," Korbin finally points out what we have all been skirting around.

"Why not?" I'm the only one brave enough to point that out. They just stare, in complete shock, as I walk out of the room.

Sharing or not, I can't stay away from Isola Dragice, and I won't even try.

44

ISOLA

I don't need to open my eyes, I can sense him here as soon as I feel the smoke blowing around my body. I can feel him near me, I can smell his smoky scent as it surrounds me. Like it's trying to slowly choke me to death with its seductive smell. My dragon is practically purring in my mind, wanting to be closer to the man I hate.

"Issy," he says, and I finally look. Thorne is standing close to me, about a footstep away, with his hands held behind his back. His cloak moves in the breeze, swaying around the guard uniform he is wearing. The leather is stretched tightly across his chest, and when I look up, I see his blue eyes gazing at me with a look I don't understand. He isn't smiling, or frowning, just standing like a statue. Like a predator waiting for its prey to run or face him. I hate that he looks good, so attractive to me, and I pull my eyes away from him.

"Thorne, you don't get to call me that. It's Princess Isola to you," I reply coldly.

"I will never call you that, you will always be Issy to me," he says, stepping closer. I keep very still as he reaches a hand out to touch my hair. He tucks a stray piece behind my ear, and my heart pounds against my chest as I stare into his blue eyes. I actually wouldn't even describe them as blue, more silver than anything else. They are like silver pools, mixed with *blue dots and darkness around the corners. The silver blue colour bounces off his blonde hair, which only serves to remind me of who he is.*

"I hate you," is all I can think to say, and then I move away, clearing my throat. *Telling him I hate him has become a defence mechanism, because I can't say anything else. I can't feel anything else.*

"I deserve for you to hate me, I don't expect anything less," he says, his words hollow as I hear the pain in them.

"Why? Why are the guys here with me? It doesn't make any sense the more I think about it," I ask, trying to ignore any pain I can hear in his words. *Ignore that it mirrors my own pain, and forget that I can see his own loneliness reflected in his eyes and words.*

"I sent them to you and kept them alive for you," he tells me, and I want to call him out on lying, but I can't. *I know he is telling me the truth, I see it in his eyes. I've seen him lie to me enough to pick up on it now. Plus, I don't think the guys could have escaped without help, and Melody would have told me if it were her.*

"But why?" I demand, and he looks away.

"Let me tell you something, and I promise if you still want the answer . . . I will tell you," he asks, and I shrug.

"It's not like I can escape you here, so go on," I say, waving a hand at the circle of smoke we are inside. He frowns, but doesn't call me out on it.

"My mother was a happy woman once. She had a good life, and was mated to a fire dragon guard. One day after she found out she was pregnant, my father was killed protecting your mother and father from an attack. My mother kept the pregnancy a secret, knowing I would be in danger if anyone knew who I really was. She left me with my adoptive parents to keep me safe. She was one of the selected, and one of the last ice dragons. It was too dangerous to have me close to her and keep me hidden at the same time. She was happy with her life, seeing me in secret when she could. She was happy with her close childhood friends bringing me up, and it likely would have stayed like that forever . . . but then your mother was killed," he pauses and shakes his head as snow starts falling from his hands.

"We all know what happened after that," I say.

"Yes, your father's side of the story," he says bitterly, and I just nod, *almost wanting to hear the side he has been told. I want to know what makes him so sure about following his mother's orders while they sit on the throne I'm meant to be on. I have a feeling Thorne isn't in control at all, just being used by his mother for what she wants.*

"My mother was commanded to marry an old man, a king twice her age. She was forced to sleep with him, and she had no choice in any of it. I bet your father never told you that, huh?" he growls.

"She got to be queen, and from what I remember, she liked her power, but I didn't know she was forced. For that I'm sorry, but you are punishing me for something I had no control over," I say, struggling to feel sorry for the person who started the fire rebellion and ordered her son to kill my father. Who most likely ordered her sister to kill my intended mate.

"Don't be sorry, you have no idea! No idea what is going on or what works are in play," he turns away from me, running his hands through his hair.

"No, but I know you're a murderer! I know you killed my father!" I spit out, losing all sympathy for him when I picture my father dead on his throne.

"I didn't," he says quietly, but it shocks me to my core, just the same as if he'd shouted the words. I stumble back, all the hate I feel for him, all the times I've pictured killing him for what he has done flashing across my mind. He still betrayed me, but he didn't kill my father . . . how did that not happen?

"What?" I ask.

"I was meant to kill him, but when I looked into his eyes, I saw you. I saw the girl I sat telling stories to about my bad past, and how she made me laugh in the darkness. The brave girl who lost so much but didn't let it corrupt her. I saw the innocence and the beauty of his daughter. The daughter I couldn't get out of my head, and I couldn't do it," he admits, and I step back in shock.

"Who did?" I ask, seeing the truth in his eyes as he looks up at me.

"My mother, and I didn't stop her. You should hate me for that," he tells me. So, Tatarina is the one that should be on the throne, she is the one that killed the last king. It makes no sense for her to put Thorne on the *throne, unless it was because of his blood. Yet, that wouldn't make anyone respect him.*

"Why do you want me to hate you?" I ask him, and he doesn't answer me. He only stares, a hopeless stare which says more than I want to know.

"Why do you listen to her? You know she is evil, right? You can choose to be good, to be different, Thorne," I beg him. His eyes glaze over, the silver almost glowing, and it reminds me so much of Jace that it hurts. But Thorne is different, darker, and more messed-up than anyone I know. It makes me want to fix him, help him, because I have a feeling he isn't all bad. I can feel it inside of me, and it's not something I can ignore anymore. I feel a connection to him, like I do Elias, Korbin, and Dagan. Yet, I have no idea what it means, and it makes no sense. Being connected to any of them means death.

"You're asking me to choose you over my family," he whispers.

"I'm asking you to choose the side for good, to choose someone that could care," I say, my voice catching.

"Could care? Issy don't lie to a liar. You care more than you can even admit to yourself," he chuckles darkly, and everything becomes hazy.

"How are you connected to me?" I ask, feeling myself falling back-wards into the smoke, and I can't see him anymore. I just feel him near me.

"Fate," is the last word I hear him whisper before darkness takes over.

I BLINK MY EYES OPEN, hearing my phone ringing, and am momentarily blinded by the light blasting through a gap in my curtains; it's in my eyes. I pick the phone up, seeing Hallie's name flashing on the bright screen and answer it.

"How was the date?" she asks straight away, sounding like an excited bunny. *How is she so happy this damn early?*

"Erm . . .," I say, blushing when I think back to the date, and everything comes flashing back. I can't believe what happened last night, but I wouldn't change it.

"You totally slept with hottie number two, didn't you?" Hallie asks, laughing.

"Why is Korbin number two?" I ask, curious and not answering her. She knows, I don't need to confirm it.

"Height. Elias is the tallest, then Korbin, and Dagan is the shortest, which isn't saying much, as they are all built like towers you just want to climb," she says, making me laugh.

"You have that right," I say, groaning as I fall back on my bed and look up at the ceiling. Things were a little awkward between Korbin and me when he drove us home last night and walked me to my room. He kissed me, making me want to invite him into my room, but Jules came out and checked on us.

"Any plans for today?" Hallie asks, and I hear the sound of beeping in the background.

"Nope, I don't know what the guys do on Sundays, but I want to eat junk food. Oh, and catch up on *I'm a Celebrity, Get Me Out Of Here* and then read, and read, and read," I say, knowing I need to clear my head of everything I learnt from the dream last night. I need to clear my head in general, and remember who I am, who the guys I'm falling for are. This isn't a fairy tale where the curse is broken in the end and we all have a happy ending . . . No, this is a nightmare, and they will pay the price. Everything is so seriously messed up. I was meant to make the guys remember, not fall for any of them. Yet, I've slept with Korbin, and I damn well know how I feel for him; it sure isn't nothing. I can't keep my thoughts off the others, and the man I thought I hated, now I'm just confused about. *These kinds of thoughts are why I need a reading day to escape.*

"Oh my god, it's the finale tomorrow. You totally need to catch up, so we can discuss who will win! Have a good day, hun," she says, and I hear someone shouting for her in the background.

"Later," I say and put the phone down. I pick up my dressing gown, put it on, and go to the bathroom. I brush my teeth, and run my fingers through my hair, just leaving it down and sliding my slippers on as I leave my room.

"Hey," I say when I run half away down the stairs and see

Elias walking up. I pause when he gets closer, leaning sideways on the bannister.

"What did you do to your hands?" I ask, seeing the blood.

"Nothing," he mutters the word quietly, but the tone makes it clear he isn't telling me. He must have been working out, as he is dripping with sweat, his hair pushed roughly out of his eyes. He only has shorts on, so I can see all the tattoos that cover his chest. I want to reach out and touch him, to trace the red dragon design. I want to ask him what the symbols on his heart mean.

"Do you like tattoos?" he asks me, following my eyes to where I'm looking. I don't breathe as he leans into me, pressing me against the side of the stairs. I don't hold back, moving my hands onto his chest over his heart, and tracing the symbols like my body wants me to.

"What are these?" I ask him, looking up when he stays silent. He is just staring at me, his blue eyes blazing with something.

"Kiss me, and I'll tell you," he promises, a devilish smirk on his lips.

"Eli," I breathe out. I can't believe myself when I inch closer, moving my face just below his. Every part of me wants to kiss him, but I feel like that's cheating on Korbin. That I'm betraying him, somehow, even though we never spoke about being serious. Even though he is likely going to hate me when he remembers who I am.

"Your choice," he whispers, his warm breath blowing across my lips. I close my eyes once more, just breathing in his smoky scent.

"I . . . can't. Korbin and I–" I start to say, but he presses a finger on my lips, stopping me. I open my eyes, seeing he's watching me seriously. He moves his finger, sliding it slowly down my chin and to my neck as he speaks. Every space where our skin connects sends shivers through me. It's like every touch of his skin is branded against my own.

"I don't mind sharing, so you being with Korbin isn't going to prevent me from wanting you," he tells me. He pulls away, walking up the stairs while I try to get some oxygen back into my body. Once Elias is out of view, my dragon perks up, pressing herself into my mind, and making it nearly impossible to move.

"We need to fly, it's been too long," she whines.

"I know, I'm sorry. I've just been distracted," I explain to her. It's not like I don't want to fly, I could use the time to myself.

"Now, I need to fly," she demands this time, even going far enough to push into my mind a little, and ice slides across my palms. I shake my hands, seeing the ice drip onto the floor, and hope no one sees it before it melts.

"Fine." I shut her away, groaning that my day of catching up on TV is gone. Instead, it looks like I'm taking a hike through the woods, and then a flight around the cold mountains.

"Good morning, Isola," Jules says, walking down the stairs. I turn to face her with a smile.

"I'm about to go to the shops, do you want to come? I've never seen boys eat as much as our guests do," she chuckles and walks past me to put her coat on.

"No, thanks, I have a day of books, and drooling over the hot guys in them, planned," I lie, and she laughs, pulling her keys out of her bag.

"Wait, I left a bag in the boot when I went shopping with Dagan, can I just go and get it?" I ask her, holding out my hand for her keys.

"Sure, I could use checking the fridge once more before I leave. You never know, I could have left something off my list," she says, sliding the keys into my hand. I slide my boots on, pulling my dressing gown tighter around myself as I walk out of the house and to the car. I pop the boot open, picking up the daggers and putting them inside a spare plastic bag Jules always leaves inside the car. *Thank god for the ban on free plastic bags in England, that's all I can say.* I walk back into the house to find Jules waiting in the hallway, looking through her bag. I slip my boots off and hand her the keys.

"Okay, hunny, see you later tonight," she says, eyeing my plastic bag for a second, before she walks out the door. I watch through the small glass window until her car pulls away and drives off before getting ready. I pull my dressing gown off, leaving my pajamas on as I will just have to take them off anyway. *No magic clothes here.* I pull my wellies, thick coat, and hat on before stepping outside, still holding the plastic bag. I look up, seeing the dark clouds and smelling the rain in the air. It's actually a good thing; the rain will hide my dragon well when we fly up. I shut the door and start walking towards the woods, keeping an eye out around me to make sure no one is following. Once it's just me and the trees, I look down at my tree mark on my hand. I miss Bee, even though we didn't get that much time together. It just feels like it's been such a long time since I've seen her. It's almost like I can feel our bond growing weaker by the day.

"*Do you miss Bee? Can you sense her?*" I ask my dragon, wondering what the bond to Bee is like for her.

"*Bee is bonded to you like I am, but she is not bonded to me. She is your human side, not your dragon side, Isola,*" she explains to me.

"*I understand, that's why I miss her as much as I do,*" I say.

"*Like you miss me,*" she replies sadly.

"*I will never lose you,*" I reply, feeling a wave of warmth and love come from her. I smile, walking more quickly through the woods. About an hour later, I get to the clearing I used to shift in with Jace.

"*Jace,*" my dragon whispers.

"*I miss him, too, so much more now that I'm here and surrounded with our memories. Do you think he would hate me for moving on?*" I ask her, being that she is the only one that remembers him. Even if she is an animal that relies on instincts for everything, she still loved and bonded with him in the same ways I did. She still felt heartbreak, she felt the same fear of being alone like I did.

"*No, it was never your fate to be with just one,*" she replies, sounding so sure of herself.

"*How do you know anything about fate, dragon?*" I ask her, and she just laughs.

"*Seers and dragons came from the same land. Fate brought us all into existence. It's not what I know, it's what I feel.*" She says, gentle almost. I open the plastic, pulling out one of the daggers. I flip it over, looking closely at the fire dragon on it. I know I won't get any answers from the dagger, but I still commit the crest on the dagger to memory. Someone came after me, and I want to know who. I pick the other dagger up, holding them both at my sides and look over at the tree about fifty feet away from me. I spin around, throwing both the daggers at the same time and they slam into the tree, buried to the hilt.

"*Now shift,*" she tells me. Our conversation makes me wonder what else my dragon knows but decides not to tell me. I pull my coat off, followed by my boots, and finally my pajamas. I walk away from the tree I leave them near, and take a deep breath, smelling for any humans nearby and finding none. I open my arms, calling my dragon, and white mist appears in front of me slowly, swallowing me inside of it. She takes over with a roar that shakes all of the trees near us, and then she stretches her wings out, ice falling off them onto the grass. She looks up at the skies, her sense of freedom improving even my bad mood. She then lifts herself off the ground and shoots into the sky.

45

ISOLA

My dragon lands in the clearing many hours later with a huff, her annoyance at the dark skies and knowledge that she needs to let me back flooding her thoughts. The rain pours down on us, soaking my dragon, and I know it will be worse when I'm in human form.

"*Again . . . soon?*" she asks me as she lets me shift back, my human form kneeling on the cold ground, naked and freezing everything off as my wet, cold hair drips down my body. I look up at the skies, just as the rain stops slowly.

"*Soon,*" I reply and stand up, freezing when I hear a branch snap somewhere near me. I don't move, looking around as I open my senses. I jump to my right when a shadow of a man steps out from behind the trees where my clothes are hidden. He walks into the clearing, pausing as he holds my clothes in his arms. His eyes widen and quickly look away. *Shit, I'm naked and not the kinda naked I'd like to be with Dagan.*

"Dagan," I say his name carefully, very aware it's unlikely he didn't just see me shift back from a dragon. He watches me, his black hair dripping rain water down his face, his blue eyes almost glowing in the darkness. His white shirt is wet, his jeans too, and they stick to his impressive body as he breathes deeply.

It's the only sign he is even alive, the movement of his chest. I hope he didn't see me shift, but when he meets my eyes, the fear is too hard to just avoid. *He knows, and how the hell do I explain that?*

"What . . . the . . . hell?" he asks slowly, his usual calm voice is replaced with a nervous, gruff one. He keeps his eyes locked on my face, and not looking anywhere else. He doesn't look scared, or even that shocked . . . but fearful. *Which is understandable, I mean most people would just go running in the other direction, screaming.*

"Can I have my clothes and then explain?" I ask, and he nods, walking closer and handing me my clothes slowly before stepping away again. It's awkward as I quickly get dressed, sliding my boots and coat on over my pajamas. I squeeze my wet hair, the rain dripping on the ground before shaking it and pushing it out of my face. He just waits the whole time silently. It's unnerving to me.

"You're a dragon?" he asks finally.

"Yes . . ." I say, and he steps back, shaking his head.

"A . . . dragon . . . dragon," he mutters, rubbing his lip ring between his lips and not really making much sense, "dragons aren't real. Just damn fairy tales, but that doesn't explain what I just saw."

"Do you want to sit down or something?" I ask, making him laugh. A sarcastic and mean laugh as he glares at me.

"No, I don't want to sit down, Isola! I want you to explain what you are! How dragons even exist?" he says, frustrated. "How one minute this huge dragon flies out the sky, and the next, white shit appears, and you are there. Naked."

"Technically, what *we* are," I say, just needing to point that out, but regret it when his eyes widen in shock. I try to think back to the paranormal books where the main guy usually has to explain to the female main character how she is one of them. *How did they do it?*

"I'm not a dragon, I would have noticed that," he huffs, waving a hand at his body.

"Erm, well, you are, but a seer has blocked your dragon away in your mind. Made you forget who you are and your past," I say, and for a second I think he might believe me, but then he steps back.

"You're crazy," he tries to walk away, and I hold my hand out, making a wall of ice appear in front of him, and he stops walking just before he would have hit it. He turns, looking at my hand and back at the wall of ice.

"What the fuck?" he exclaims, stepping away from it, shaking his head.

"You need to believe me, I'm tired of trying to do things to make you remember who you are, Dagan," I say.

"Like what?"

"When I asked you about your parents? Your childhood, it was like a robot repeating a story with no details," I say, and he shakes his head.

"You're mad," he says.

"Nope, I'm not. So, Dagan, what was your favourite ice cream as a child? Where did you hide when you played hide and seek? Where did your parents take you when you did something good in school?" I ask, and he gives me a confused look.

"I . . . I."

"You don't know, because it's not real. The real Dagan was brought up in a whorehouse, the bastard child of a fire guard, and his mother was killed. I know this because your brother told me, because I met you as a child," I say, and he glares, a glare that almost makes me want to run away from him. But I don't, I hold my ground. I need him to see I'm telling him the truth. I need him to remember.

"I need to tell Elias and Korbin about this, about you," he says and starts pacing. I stay silent for a while, letting him pace as my wall of ice melts slowly, and the moon starts to come out. It's getting dark quickly, and we should get back home, but Dagan is still pacing.

"They won't believe it, and they are dragons, too. Can you

stop pacing and freaking out for a second?" I ask, placing my hands on my hips.

"What do you suggest I do? Just act like you don't turn into a massive blue ice dragon, and you're not telling me I'm one?" he asks me sarcastically.

"That would be great, yes," I say, nodding, and he gives me a nasty look.

"Look, it's getting dark, and I'm worn out from flying all day. Let's go back home, and you can freak all you want there. Go ahead, and tell anyone you want, no one will believe you," I say walking past him, and pausing before I get to the trees.

"When you want the real truth of who you are, you know where I am," I tell him, thinking I've heard that in a book somewhere, and it's good advice. I walk off into the woods after one more look, seeing the angry look crossing over his face as he stares. After walking for a while, trying to avoid logs and rocks, I hear Dagan stalking behind me. I turn to see him looking at the ground. Clearly, he is thinking but likely doesn't want to talk to me yet. *I guess it's a big shock.* I turn back, walking to the light from the house in the distance, and when we get there, Dagan walks past me through the front door and straight up the stairs. I shut the door, sighing against it for a moment until Korbin walks out of the kitchen with a bowl of popcorn.

"Long day?" he asks, eyeing my dirt-covered clothes and messy hair, and then to Dagan walking up the stairs.

"I went for a hike, Dagan came too," I explain, and his eyes narrow.

"Right, I see how it is," he says, accusing me of something I haven't even done.

"Kor–" I get out, but he cuts me off, pissing me off.

"Don't," he says, walking up the stairs, and I just close my eyes, wondering if this day could get any worse. The house phone starts ringing, and I run over, picking it up.

"Hello?" I ask in a tired voice, I just want to go to sleep and pray this day couldn't get worse.

"Hello, is this the home of Jules Donald?" a man asks, the sound of beeping and people talking filling the background.

"Yes, I don't know if she is in as I've just gotten home, but I can take a message," I say, picking the pen up off the side and going to grab the paper when the man speaks.

"Madam, Miss Donald is in hospital, and I would like you, or her next of kin, to come in. She asked for an Isola Dragice," he says, making my heart pound against my chest. This can't be happening, not Jules.

"That's me, I'll be right there, is she okay?" I ask.

"I can't tell you any more on the phone. Please don't worry and come in," he says, and I say goodbye before putting the phone down. I run up the stairs, knocking on Elias's door and waiting. He opens it up a few moments later, looking like I just woke him up, with his messy hair, and just his pajama shorts on.

"What's up?" he asks.

"Jules is in hospital, and I need a ride there. Dagan and Korbin aren't talking to me, so could you please take me?" I ask, and he nods, reaching for a hoodie off the back of the door and pulling it over his head, hiding the body I can't even focus on because I'm so worried about Jules.

"Yeah, anything for you, princess. Is she okay? What happened?" he asks, and walks past me out the door.

"I don't know," I admit, and he slides his hand into mine, squeezing once before letting go. I wait for him to get his coat and some keys off the side.

"I'm sure Korbin won't mind us borrowing his car," Elias smirks, holding the keys up in the air.

"I'm pretty sure he will," I say, remembering how angry he looked, how he judged the situation wrong and walked away. I walk up to the car, waiting for Elias to unlock it and then getting in. Elias gets in, doing his seatbelt at the same time as me before starting the car.

"So, what happened to Jules to get her in the hospital?" he asks.

"I don't know, they didn't tell me much, just that she asked for me. I'm all they had to call. She basically brought me up, so she is all the family I have in a way," I explain, and he nods, not taking his eyes off the road. Thankfully it's only twenty minutes' drive to the hospital, and there's no traffic around.

"Okay, another question. What happened with Korbin and Dagan?" Elias asks, and I look out the window.

"I don't want to talk about it," I mutter.

"Come on, princess, you can trust me," he says cheekily, and I shake my head, hating how he can make me smile.

"Fine. Korbin thinks something happened between Dagan and me today, when it didn't," I say, still cross about how angry he got without talking to me. I hate being judged for something I haven't done. I can't say I hadn't thought about doing it, but yeah . . . I *hadn't*.

"Okay, have you ever heard the term reverse harem?" he asks me, surprising me a little.

"I read a lot, and my favourite is a series about demons," I say. "But you can't be suggesting . . . and how do you even know about reverse harems?" I blurt out, feeling my cheeks getting red.

"I read, and it's something I'm interested in, with the right people," he says, shocking me silent.

"It wouldn't work, you guys are all too possessive," I say, knowing dragons are naturally possessive about those they consider theirs. They see their mates like treasures, and they don't like to share those. Like my dragon seems to think they are all hers, and I know she would lose her shit on me if I tried to date anyone else. I never got why she put a claim to them in the first place, why she calls them mine. I want to ask her, but I can't with Elias watching me so closely.

"Yeah, I am. I don't know why, but the idea of anyone touching you . . . It's not good, princess," he admits, tightening his hands on the steering wheel. "Then I think about you and Korbin and Dagan . . . I wouldn't hurt them for loving you."

"You wouldn't?" I ask, curious.

"No. But I know you're not ready to be with us all, and to be honest, none of us are even close to figuring out what is between us," he tells me, and honestly, as I meet his blue eyes, I know he is right.

46

ISOLA

"What did the doctor say?" Elias asks, using his shoulder to open the door as he carries two hot teas in his hands. The door shuts behind him as I look at Jules on the bed, plugged into dozens of wires and looking as pale as the bedsheets. I wipe a tear away, numbly repeating what the human doctor told me.

"Jules had a heart attack and fell over, banging her head. They said they have her in a medically induced coma to stop the swelling on her brain before waking her up," I say, struggling with the worry I feel for Jules.

"Here, a cup of tea always helps everything. Or that's what Jules told me two days ago," he says, making me chuckle.

"Yeah, she is British through and through, thinking a cup of tea fixes everything," I mutter, but he hears me.

"I never really liked it," he says, sipping his drink and pulling a face.

"Shhh, don't let her hear you say that," I say, smiling. Elias always knows how to make me smile somehow. I drink my tea, still holding onto her hand with mine. I knew I'd see her die one day, as a human her lifespan is so much shorter than mine. It still hurts, it still crushes me to know she will be gone, and every connection to a massive part of my life is just gone with her. I stand up, putting the cup down and walking out of the room, not really thinking or looking where I'm going.

"Isola, wait!" I hear Elias shout, but I can't listen as I start running and going down corridor after corridor until I find some stairs. I open the door, running up the stairs and getting to the very top, and to the emergency-only door. I pull it open, running out onto the roof and just stopping. The view is amazing up here: hills, trees, and lit-up houses for miles to see. The stars above make a beautiful backdrop, but all I can think about is how much pain happened in this world because I don't belong here. I can feel it, I always felt it. This isn't my world, and I feel trapped here. Haunted by ghosts.

"Isola . . ." I hear Elias say behind me, the sound of the door shutting behind me makes me jump. I turn, seeing him standing a few steps away from me. There's such tension between us, so many unanswered questions running across his eyes, such passion. I want to run to him, let him hold me like I know he would. But I don't, instead I take a step back, protecting myself from doing anything I know I might regret. Not that I would regret being in his arms, but I would regret the curse taking any price for any of my actions. I have already risked Korbin, and I know him hating me now is only a slight fraction of what he will feel when he remembers.

"Tell me, what is it you're hiding? What are you running from?" he asks me, his deep and seductive voice making me close my eyes.

"You will be the one running if I tell you what I am," I say, meaning every word.

"I don't run, I will never run from you," he says, a promise laced into his words. I pull my coat off, chucking it on the floor and kicking my boots off as he gives me a confused look. I laugh, a long laugh as I call my dragon, and shift. He stumbles back when I land on the roof as my dragon stretches out her wings. She turns her head to the side, seeing the ice dripping off each little spike on her wings, before turning back to Elias. I watch him, fully expecting him to run from me, but he doesn't. He stands up and walks slowly to my dragon, each step full of a confidence I would expect the old Elias to have. When he gets closer, he holds a hand out, and my dragon pushes her nose into his hand, a purr vibrating through her.

"*Mine*," she whispers, and I don't disagree with her, because it feels wrong to say she isn't right. My dragon steps back, feeling my need to shift, and I close my eyes, pulling my human form back. I look up, my long hair falling around me as Elias stands utterly still. I pick my coat up, seeing my torn clothes on the floor but once my coat is done up, it's good enough. *Only a little bit cold.*

"You're a dragon? A shifter, or whatever you call yourself?" he asks, and I nod, not wanting to tell him he is one, too, as that didn't work so well with Dagan.

"What else can you do?" he asks, reaching into his pocket and pulling out his cigarettes. He puts one in his mouth, lighting it with a lighter, and then resting against the door.

"Ice and snow," I say, holding my hands into the air and closing my eyes. I focus on the clouds above, freezing them slowly and then open my eyes.

"I don't see anything . . ." he drawls.

"Just wait," I chuckle, just as it starts to snow. Slowly at first, and the wind starts blowing it around us.

"Amazing," he says, his voice full of wonder, and he keeps smoking. We are both silent, both of us close to freezing until he finishes his cigarette and puts it out under his boot. He walks over, stopping right in front of me.

"Any more secrets you want to tell me?" he asks, and he watches me so closely for my reaction that it hurts when the lie slips from my mouth.

"Maybe, but not yet," I answer, and he nods.

"You don't trust me," he says, and for the first time, hurt

appears in his eyes. I can see it and he steps back, walking to the door.

"Eli, it's–"

"You don't trust me, and I'm not going to make you, *princess*," he says and opens the door, slamming it closed behind him. I look up at the star-filled skies, the dark clouds, and the snow falling slowly. I mess everything up, and I don't know how to stop doing it.

47

ISOLA

"So, why are the sexy guys annoyed with you?" Hallie asks me as I open my packet of crisps and lean back in my seat, following her gaze to Dagan, Korbin, and Elias who are sitting at another table. Each one of them has ignored me since the weekend, but all for different reasons. Korbin thinks I'm sleeping with Dagan, and clearly can't deal with me. Dagan knows I'm a dragon and overall looks freaked out by me. And Elias . . . well, I think is just working out what I'm still hiding from him, but at least he isn't freaked out like Dagan is. I'm actually not sure about Elias at the moment, what he is thinking anyway, but I don't tell Hallie any of this.

"I don't know, they are just moody," I say, and then stuff my face with food and hope it makes me feel better. It doesn't, but hey, the chocolate buttons are just amazing.

"How is Jules?" Hallie asks.

"She woke up two days ago and is a little groggy, she will need a lot of medical care, but they think she will make a full recovery," I tell her.

"I'm glad, I know how much you care for her," she tells me, and I nod, not really wanting to speak about Jules. I know I have to return to Dragca, so I can't look after her long-term like I wish

I could. Like she deserves. Instead, I had to use the stupid amount of human money in my account to buy her a place in a nursing home for when she gets out of the hospital. I hate that it's all I can do.

"Hey, sexy Issy," Michael says, sliding into the seat next to me, and in some ways, I'm thankful for the distraction from my own thoughts and stuff I can't change. Hallie just rolls her eyes, stabbing her fork into her pie. I mentally groan as I turn to face him. He slides his giant arm around my shoulder, pulling me into a side hug. I try to pull away, but he doesn't let for me for a while, making me super uncomfortable.

"Michael, you're hurting me," I say, when he doesn't let go, squeezing me too tightly, and he does straight away, grinning as he pushes his blonde hair out of the way of his eyes.

"Sorry, I forget how small you are," he comments, using that as an excuse to look down my top and not raise his eyes for far too long. *Urgh.*

"Michael, don't you have an interview with my father tonight? Shouldn't you be . . . I don't know, training or research-ing, or something other than hitting on Issy?" Hallie asks, cutting in, and I flash her a thankful smile.

"You're working for Hallie's dad?" I ask Michael, moving across my seat and towards Hallie.

"Our parents are good friends, so he offered me a job. It's a brilliant one," he says, and Hallie laughs, but she doesn't say anything as Michael glares at her.

"Shut it," he snaps at her, and she still laughs. It gets seri-ously awkward as I sit between them, having no idea what they are talking about. I wish I knew what her father does, what she is so sure she doesn't want to do.

"So, erm, how was your weekend?" I ask Michael when there's a very uncomfortable silence between us all for way too long.

"Didn't do much, I'm just looking forward to my party. You are still coming, right?" he asks, like an excited child.

"Yep," I say, not really wanting to go, but the puppy dog eyes he is doing right now makes me feel a little guilty. I look away, seeing Dagan, Korbin, and Elias all watching me, wearing matching faces of anger. I want to get up and go to sit with them, explain myself to each of them, but I can't. I've already messed up with Dagan, and risked the curse with Korbin. Even with Elias if I'm honest with myself. I might not have kissed him since Dragca, and he might be hurt because of me right now, but there's something between us. *Some princess I am, making the guards lose their dragons because I can't control my hormones.* The bell rings, snapping me out of it, and I quickly stand up.

"Time for class," I say, walking away, but Michael grabs my arm as he stands, roughly pulling me to him.

"Let go," I say carefully, not liking how strong he is, and how my dragon hisses in my mind. I look up as he grins.

"I only wanted a hug, sexy Issy," he says playfully, and I pull my arm away.

"You should wait for me to offer, not demand. Goodbye, Michael," I tell him, seeing his bright-red face as he glares at me. Hallie links her arm with mine, walking out of the dinner hall at my side. I rub my arm, looking behind me to see Michael still watching me, anger flittering in his eyes. Humans and dragons never date, because the human always gets obsessed. It was one of the things Jace made sure I knew, not only for my protection but for my understanding of why guys like Michael won't leave me alone.

"You should stay away from Michael, he is pretty obsessed with you. I don't want to see what he would do when he realises you're not interested," Hallie tells me, looking back at him when I turn around.

"I plan to stay away, don't worry," I reply.

"So, you're not going to the party?" she asks, relief flittering over her face.

"I will if the guys go, they wouldn't let anything happen to me, and I need to get them to speak to me," I say.

"Why? They might be sexy, but so are you. You don't need to chase them," she says gently.

"I'm not chasing them, it's complicated," I say, and she smiles.

"Good, I'm not having you chase anyone," she says, and I quickly pull her in for a hug. She hugs me back, laughing.

"What's that for?" she asks.

"For being a good friend. Whatever happens, I'm your friend," I tell her, and she gives me a slightly confused look as I pull away.

"What would happen?" she asks, and part of me wishes I could explain all this to her. Explain that I'm a dragon, and I have to go back to Dragca soon. That I won't see her for a long time, and I might die trying to save the world I was born in. Not that I can tell her anything, only enjoy the little time I have with a true friend now.

"Nothing, I'm being silly," I reply, lying.

"Come on, you weirdo, it's Mr. Dread's class, and you know how much of an arsehole he is if we are late," she says, tugging me along to class.

"ISOLA!" I hear my name shouted as I walk out of the school, and I look through the students, seeing Dagan walking through them and towards me like a man on a mission. He looks stressed, his black hair looks like it has had his hands run through it a million times. I look down, seeing the shadows under his eyes and the tight-lipped expression he is giving me. He has a black coat on, tight black jeans, and a grey jumper underneath. It makes him look like a normal guy, a hot god-type guy, but still not someone I'd expect to be a dragon.

"Hey," I say, wondering what he wants when he nods his head to the left of me and walks around me, not stopping once. I follow him, looking over when I hear Elias's bike roaring, and seeing him driving out of the car park. I don't see Korbin's car, so I think he must have left without Dagan. Dagan walks to the bus stop, sitting down on the empty seat as students walk past us. There are three other students around when I sit down next to him, but they have their headphones in, or they aren't paying attention to us. Both of us are silent for a long time, just watching nothing. I just wait for something from him, any sign that I haven't messed everything up when I need his help.

"I have fucked-up dreams," he says quietly.

"Yeah?" I mumble.

"Yeah, kitty cat, dreams that make me believe what you are telling me," he says and reaches over, taking my hand in his and linking our fingers. His hand feels warm, rough and right.

"Do you believe me?" I ask him.

"Yes, I believe you. Or I want to," he admits, sending relief crashing through me.

"I need you all to remember, only you can help me. Or I'm not going to make it long, and people will suffer in our home world if I don't try to fix things,"

"Tell me some things you know about me? About my home land?" he asks.

"Honestly? We only knew each other for a month or so. You are a dragon guard, and I'm a royal. Even though I haven't known you that long, I know a lot. I know you're one of the bravest, most stubborn men I've ever met. You are cocky, protective, and sometimes even charming," I chuckle when he grins.

"Seems you liked me."

"Sometimes," I laugh, but it dies away when the seriousness of everything rushes back. "Dragca needs me, needs us. I'm meant to be on the throne, meant to be ruling and uniting everyone. But right now, it's got Thorne, one of my old guards on it."

"Old guard?" he asks.

"Longer story, you kinda dislike him. Elias hates him, but I see something in him, even though most of me hates him for the things he has done," I say quietly, and Dagan leans over, moving a little bit of my hair over my shoulder, before trailing his fingers down my side.

"You are so much of the light, you know that?" he asks me, staring at me strangely.

"What?" I ask, wondering why he would say such a strange thing.

"In my dreams, a girl I've never seen before, tells me you are the light. All the light left to save us from dying in the dark," he tells me, and I stare wide-eyed at him.

"What does the girl look like?" I ask quickly.

"Honestly, green. Like a green Barbie doll, and the size of one, too," he says, making my heart pound. Bee told him something, I don't know how it's possible, but she did.

"A lot of things are so uncertain for us, maybe it would be best if you got up and walked away. Lived a life as a human, and I go back to my world, face what I'm running from alone," I say, and he shakes his head.

"Every little bit of me tells me I could never let you do that alone, Isola," he bites out, anger clouding his blue eyes.

"Dagan, get Korbin and Elias, and go. I can't do this, I can't let you try and fight with me," I suddenly realise. I can't lose them, and taking them back to Dragca would mean I could. They are safe here, safer than another place, even if they don't remember who they are.

"All I know is that I want to be close to you, and this distance between us is driving me fucking insane. I'm with you, no matter what," he says as the bus turns up, but neither of us moves as we stare at each other. Our faces are inches apart as he leans closer, and a car beeping makes us shoot apart before he can kiss me. We shouldn't anyway, no matter how disappointed I feel.

"You shouldn't want me, we can't be together. There's a curse, a curse that says you will lose your dragon if you fall in love with me," I blurt out loudly to him and then look around quickly, noticing all the people have, thankfully, gotten on the bus, so they didn't hear us.

"Apparently, I've already lost my dragon, so what more could any curse do to me for doing this," he says and moves over, slamming his lips onto mine. I slide my hand into his hair, fully accepting his kiss, loving how his lip ring feels as it slides across my own lips. He groans, pulling me as close as we can get without me climbing in his lap, sliding his hands into my hair.

"Kitty cat, I feel like I've wanted to do that forever," he whispers against my lips and then kisses me again before I can answer. Maybe he has wanted to kiss me for a long time because I know in this moment, I've wanted to kiss him for just as long.

48

ISOLA

"I t's about time, I've been waiting in this place for an hour. Go to sleep on time please," Melody's voice comes through the haze, and I open my eyes to see her standing over me as I lie on the floor.

"I made the mistake of checking on my future girlfriend and her life, only to see her with another guy," she says, as I stare up at her.

"Is she not out of the closet yet then?" I ask.

"Nope, but I've seen us together. It was my first vision, and the only one I've had about myself," she tells me. I always wondered if she sees a lot of her own future, and how creepy that must be.

"You must be excited to meet her then," I say.

"We already met, but it's complicated as she doesn't remember me. Anyways, you should get up as we don't have much time as you didn't go to sleep," she says, offering me a hand. I stand up, looking around at the trees and more trees that surround us. I look up, seeing two moons, so I know it's Dragca.

"What is this a warning of?" I ask her, ignoring her whining about me not going to sleep on time. I didn't know she was waiting for me, it's been over a week since she last came to my dreams.

"Wait for it," she waves a hand behind me, and I turn, seeing myself running through the woods in the distance, three men are chasing after me. I look desperate, broken, covered in blood in a long dress that catches on *everything I run past. I watch myself run, and I step forward, wanting to save myself. A person walks in after the guards and me, following them but not looking in any rush, dark smoke trailing after her cloak on the ground. The smoke slides up the trees next to her, burning them into dust. I've never seen anything like it, and it honestly terrifies me.*

"What happened to me?" I ask quietly.

"I don't know, I only see this one after you come for me. There will be no more warnings for a while, sister," she says sadly, and then I hear myself scream. The scream goes on and on, and then there's a loud bang that makes Melody and me cover our ears. Fire shoots up in the air, blasting out in every direction and heading straight for us. It burns all the trees in its path, and blue lights come out the trees, floating up into the air. I can feel their sorrow; the lights seem to look into my soul. The fire goes around us, like we're immune to it and yet part of me wants to stop it.

"This moment feels massive, yet, I don't understand it," Melody admits, and I look over at her, seeing fear in her eyes for the first time. She has always come across so fearless, so sure of herself, but not right now. And that scares me, more than anything has scared me for a long time.

"Melody . . . Dagan and Elias know what I am but don't remember. My relationship with all of them is advancing more than it should. Thorne is . . . well, I don't know, but he confuses me. He didn't kill our father," I ramble out.

"I know, I see it," she taps her head.

"Tell me what to do, how to make them remember," I ask.

"I can't. What has to happen, will happen, and they will remember because of it," she says, a tear dropping from her right eye.

"Because of what?" I ask.

"Because of the emotion. The hate, fear, and the love. It's the only way, and I'm so sorry I can't stop it," she says, stepping closer, and placing her hand on mine.

"I need you, and Thorne does. Don't forget about us," she asks.

"I wouldn't forget, not unless you make me," I joke, making her smile for a second, but it soon fades.

"The curse will fall, and so will you, but remember, Isola. Remember what you have to fight for," she says, pulling me into a hug, and holding

on tight. I return the hug, feeling strange about hugging my sister I've never known.

"I'm going to show you something you must tell Thorne when you have a moment alone with him. A real moment, not a dream, and you will know when," she begs me so seriously.

"How can you show me?" I ask her.

"By using all my power, it just hurts me a little bit, and I will sleep for a few days. No biggie," she says, shrugging a shoulder, and moving to stand right in front of me.

"No biggie? That sounds big, I don't want you hurt. You're my sister," I say, grabbing her hands.

"And that's exactly why I must show you this, you must make Thorne see the truth because I can only show you, and he won't believe me. My mother showed me this, just before Tatarina killed her, and I know it's the only way to save everyone," she says.

"How can one vision save everyone? And I'm sorry about your mother," I ask.

"Because it shows you who the real villain is, who really killed both of our mothers," she says and puts her hands on my head. A blinding light bursts into my mind. When I can see again, it's like I'm floating above the ground in an empty hut. The hut has stone floors, a fire in the fireplace, and a small table. The door opens and Tatarina walks in, a much younger version of her anyway. She is stunning, a perfect image of an ice dragon with her long white-blonde hair and pale-blue eyes. I'm sure her eyes aren't that pale anymore, I've never seen them like this anyway. Two other people come into the room, a couple about her age, and the man with brown hair shuts the door.

"We have to kill the queen. She is evil; I've told you this, but I can't do it. You can get close enough when you go to the castle tomorrow," she says, shocking me. I didn't expect her to say that. I knew she was evil, but to ask someone to kill my mother?

"We would never get close, but I will try because of everything you have told me about her. She tortures dragons and humans, she kills children, and the king hides it because he loves her. She must die," the man

says, and I shake my head, wanting to scream at him that none of this is true, but no sound comes out my mouth.

"Thank you, my friend," Tatarina says, and the door opens again. A little boy runs in with blonde hair, covered in dirt, and blue eyes. He runs up to Tatarina.

"Mummy!" the boy shouts, and when I look closer, I know it's Thorne.

"Go with your parents, we had a good day together, but you can't stay late," Tatarina says, hugging Thorne, who nods and walks over to the couple who open the door. I keep my eyes on the man's face, and I know this is the man that killed my mother. Thorne's adoptive father killed my mother. He knew and lied to me, he made me feel sorry for him and his parents. Bastard. Thorne and his parents leave, shutting the door behind them. Tatarina grins, looking up at the ceiling near where I am floating as if she can see me. She raises her hands, and a dark spirit flies in from a hole in the ceiling. The dark spirit has dark blue skin that almost looks black, black hair, and smoke drifting off its body. It looks just like Bee, a light spirit, only dark-skinned instead. The dark spirit lands on Tatarina's hand, and she grins at it.

"Our plan is starting. We will have the throne and an heir because of my son, who can rule. I will kill the princess and any other ice dragons that stand in our way. Then we can enact the second part of our plan," she says, and the dark spirit nods. Just before I float away, I hear, "My son will be king, but I will rule. He just doesn't know it yet."

I SLAM AWAKE, my heart pounding against my chest, and it takes me a moment to realise someone has their hands on my shoulders, rubbing their thumbs in a comforting motion. I look up to see Elias looking down at me with worry, his hair is messy, and his t-shirt is all wrinkled. I take deep breaths, breathing in his smoky scent to calm myself down. I'm safe, I'm not there anymore, and the dark spirit is gone. I repeat the same line in my head over and over until I can breathe normally. That vision, or whatever it was, felt so real. It was overwhelming, terrifying, and it makes so much sense. Tatarina planned this all, she planned for my mother to be killed, to become queen, to put Thorne on the throne and control him. *What else has she got planned?*

"You were screaming. I'm sorry, but I had to wake you up," he explains to me, removing his hands and sitting on the edge of my bed. "Bad dreams, princess?" he asks carefully.

"Something like that," I say breathlessly, looking at my phone and seeing it's only three in the morning.

"Sorry I woke you up," I tell him, and he shrugs.

"I went outside for a cigarette, and I was walking past," he explains.

"Outside? I thought you smoked them in your room," I chuckle.

"Nah, not since Jules walked in on me once. She hit me with her shoe and told me she wouldn't have me smoking in her house," he smirks. "I like the old lady, but she can half hit with that shoe," he tells me, making me laugh.

"That's better, you laughing is much better than seeing you frightened," he says gently.

"It just takes a minute to realise some dreams aren't real," I mutter, and he tilts his head to the side a little. We don't say anything, but I push my hair out of my eyes when it falls and look down at my pajamas. Thank god I'm wearing plain blue ones, and not the ones with cupcakes all over that I almost put on.

"Yeah, I get that, princess," he squeezes my hand and stands up, dropping the notebook he was holding.

"What's that?" I ask, remembering his notebook at Dragca Academy. I wonder if he draws the same type things. It would make sense for him to have the same hobbies, enjoy the same things he always had. He is the same dragon I met, just with a few little changes.

"Here," he offers me the notebook. To my surprise, he walks around the bed, pulling off his leather jacket and boots. He slides into bed next to me, tucking himself in like he sleeps in my bed all the time or something. He rolls on his side, raising an eyebrow at me as he rests his head on his arm.

"Comfy?" I ask sarcastically, and he smirks.

"*Very,*" he replies, somehow making one word seem seductive and panty-dropping. *Damn him.* I shake my head, looking back at the notebook to get my eyes off him. I open the first page to see a drawing of me, not what I was expecting at all. It's a beautifully drawn image of me sitting on the school bus, and looking over my shoulder. It's the first time he saw me here on Earth. He makes my eyes look bigger than they are, like I'm a doll or something. My hair is layered down my back in perfect curls, and my face looks perfect, not one imperfection. Which I know isn't true, I know I have a slight dent on the right side of my nose where I broke it falling out of a tree in Dragca when I was seven. I know I have freckles littered across my nose, too, and they spread to my cheeks when it's summer. I'm not perfect, not in any way.

"You make me look pretty, way too pretty," I say, and he chuckles low.

"I don't make you anything other than what you are," he argues. I look back, flipping through the notebook, seeing more and more sketches of myself. All little moments in class, all times when I never saw him even looking at me. I turn over a page and stop, seeing a different drawing. It's a tattoo design, with four red dragons flying around an ice dragon in the center of them. They almost look like they're protecting her. The main dragon looks like mine, and the little ones are all slightly different. There are swirls coming off the ice dragon, connecting them all together, and it's remarkable. I can't look away, I just end up staring at it. I feel Elias slowly look over, to see what I'm so fascinated by.

"I love this," I say, tracing my finger over the design.

"It's yours, I designed it for you. I don't remember when I exactly started drawing it, but it was way before I met you in another notebook and then re-drew it here. Yet somehow I know it's yours," he says, making my heart pound.

"Thank you, Eli," I whisper, tracing the design with my finger.

"I love when you call me that," he says gruffly, his voice almost a whisper like mine. Neither of us say a word, and without communicating, I know neither of us wants to ruin the moment. I can see it when I look over at him, I know him well enough to read it in his eyes. I put the notebook on my side, and then lie down in bed, facing him. I reach up, placing my hand on his cheek, and he closes his eyes at my touch.

"What if I told you that kissing you could trigger a curse? That it could destroy everything you don't even know you have?" I ask him, my words coming out more breathless than I intend them to be.

"A curse?" he asks, frowning at me. As he opens those blue eyes, I find myself instantly lost in them.

"Yes, a curse that was meant to do good for my family, but right now it feels like it's destroying the very family it was meant to protect," I say, meaning every word. *Why does it have to be like this? It's not fair.*

"You're not making much sense, princess," he says, and I shake my head, lowering my head to his chest after he rolls onto his back. I reach over, switching the lamp off, and then placing my hand on his chest.

"Stay the night?" I ask him, not really giving him a choice as I'm already comfy, and don't want to move.

"You don't have to ask, princess," he whispers, kissing my forehead. Only seconds later, darkness makes me fall asleep as I lay listening to his beating heart.

49

ISOLA

"Someone is knocking on your door. It's too fucking early for me to be a gentleman and answer it for you," a voice grumbles. The feeling of a face pushing into my neck has me blinking my eyes open. I pull myself awake to find Elias practically lying on top of me, and he looks up, his messy hair makes him look cute in an early morning way.

"How much would you hate me if I said how cute you are in the morning?" I ask, and he glares at me, rolling over and pulling a pillow over his head. *Someone doesn't like mornings.*

"Get the door," he groans, his voice muffled by his pillow. I laugh, getting out of bed and walking to the door, opening it a little to see Korbin standing outside.

"Hey?" I ask, sounding like a dork.

"Running? I know we haven't been speaking recently, but I–" he says, and then Eli's loud shout interrupts him.

"Keep it down!"

I look back at Korbin as his whole face tightens, and then he turns, walking away. "Korbin, wait!" I shout, running out the door and down the stairs after him. I catch him just before he gets to the front door, grabbing his arm.

"Let me explain," I plead.

"Explain what? Am I nothing to you? Or was it only me that felt something, Isola?" he fires all the questions quickly at me, never giving me a second to reply.

"Kor, it wasn't nothing. It meant *everything* to me. You have no fucking idea how hard this is for me. What I'm doing, it is killing me as I don't want to hurt anyone," I tell him, and he turns, pushing me lightly into the wall and stepping close. He presses me against the wall as he slides his hand to the back of my neck, and he makes me look up at him. His green eyes blaze as he stares at me. It's almost unnerving to see the emotion in his eyes, but I don't look away. I know he needs to see the same passion in mine, he needs to know that I don't feel nothing. I feel everything, and it frightens me.

"I don't know how to cope with how you look at Dagan and Elias," he admits, his thumb stroking the back of my neck.

"I don't know what I'm doing, only that I can't stay away from any of you," I reply truthfully.

"Then for now, this is how it is, because, fuck, Isola, I can't lose you," he says and slams his mouth onto mine. I moan against his lips, returning the kiss the best I can when he is taking total control, leaving me no break between each punishing kiss. He brushes his lips down my jaw, angling my head with his hand on my neck, and then breaking away.

"Now, get your cute butt back to your room, and get your running gear on," he says, an actual smile on his lips for the first time I've seen this week. He lets me free from against the wall, and I jump when he slaps my ass playfully as I pass him.

"Cheeky," I say, but I can't keep the grin off my face.

"Oh, and Isola?" he stops me when I get to the bottom step.

"Yeah?" I turn to ask.

"Make a lot of noise as you get changed, I don't think Eli was awake enough yet," he says, and I laugh as I walk away, intending to do just that.

"HOW WAS YOUR RUN?" Dagan asks when Korbin and I come back into the house, both of us worn out. I look out the window to see it just start to pour down, and I'm damn thankful we got inside before that started.

"Good, but the more important question is whether or not those are waffles?" I ask, smelling them before I even get to his side and see the waffle maker he has out. I look over to the table, seeing cut fruit on a plate and all the sauces lined up. There are even plates and cutlery set out.

"Sit down, I've made you all some," he says, winking at me. The back door opens, and Eli walks in, the cigarette smoke clinging to his clothes letting me know what he was doing outside. He shakes his wet hair, before using his hand to push it out of his face. He takes his jacket off, resting it on a hook by the door.

"Morning," he says as I sit down, and Korbin hands me a bottle of orange juice before sitting next to me.

"Morning, cutie," I reply, seeing Eli narrow his eyes at me as Korbin laughs.

"Cutie?" he asks with a laugh, looking between us.

"Don't ask," I reply, and he chuckles. Eli sits down opposite me, still glaring and gently kicks my leg under the table, and I laugh. I pile some fruit on my plate, popping a strawberry in my mouth as Elias still looks annoyed.

"So . . . any plans after school today?" Korbin asks, cutting an apple up with a knife.

"I'm going to see Jules," I tell them.

"Want a ride?" Elias asks.

"Nope, Hallie is taking me as she wants to see her, too. They got along since Hallie was over here often. She wants to take her some grapes," I explain. Although she was only over here in memories Melody made up, they are real enough for Hallie. I doubt Hallie even remembers Melody now, it seems like no one really does. I haven't had to explain to any teachers where she is, Melody is so powerful she has messed with all their heads. Dagan slides the waffles onto my plate, and I grin up at him.

"Thank you," I say, and he puts another plate full of waffles in the middle of the table.

"Are you not serving mine up? I feel left out," Elias says, with a wounded, jokey expression as he pours maple syrup on my waffles. Dagan whacks him on the back of his head on the way back to his chair.

"When you're as pretty as Isola, then sure," he says, and Elias smirks, but doesn't reply as he starts pulling waffles onto his plate. I smile, looking at them all and enjoying how well we all just fit together like this. Having breakfast together, just relaxing together. It's so normal and perfect. I cut my waffles up, sticking a piece into my mouth, and try not to moan at how amazing it tastes. They must have cinnamon in them or something, because seriously, these waffles are better than any I've ever had.

"I'm kinda jealous of the waffles right now," Dagan comments, and I look up to see all the guys watching me, a mixture of amused and turned-on looks in their eyes.

"Why?" I ask, my voice muffled around my waffles. I'm not stopping eating to talk, this is too good.

"They make you smile more than anyone else," he says, and the guys all laugh.

"I was thinking they make you moan as much–" Elias starts to say, and Dagan leans over, whacking his head again.

"That hurts," Elias glares at his brother.

"Not as much as the stupid shit that comes out of your mouth does," he says, and I decide to intervene before the brothers start fighting and get in the way of me and my waffles.

"Yes, yes they do. My relationship with your cooking is becoming addictive, I may never let you out of my sight now," I joke, though he doesn't reply. We eat up, and when Dagan leans down to take my plate from me, he slants his lips close to my ear.

"Sounds good to me, kitty cat," he whispers and then walks off, leaving me with bright-red cheeks that I try to hide from the others, but they know and surprisingly, they don't say a word.

50

ISOLA

"Don't be silly, you look good," Hallie grins, and Jules laughs, waving a pale hand in the air. I spent the last hour brushing her hair, putting some dry shampoo in it for her, and then plaiting it. I couldn't stand to see her hair so messy, when she usually has it in a tight bun and styled, unless she has just gotten out of bed. Jules happily let me help her, and in some ways, it helped me feel better, too. I've been carrying so much guilt about not being able to look after her when I go back to Dragca, despite all the time she took care of me.

"I look awful. I have seen a mirror, little one," she replies to Hallie. Jules sits up a little in her bed, and pats the side next to her. Hallie goes to sit next to her with a worried expression. I lean back in my seat, letting them have their moment alone together as I look out the window. Outside, rain is pouring down, hitting against the roof of the small side building of the hospital. It makes a soothing sound in the otherwise quiet room. I hate hospitals, it smells of death and loss in here. I can hear all the beeping machines trying to save people, and the cries of the families who lost someone close. It reminds me I haven't had time to truly grieve my father or Jace. I don't have somewhere to go to remember either of them. I try not to get lost in my own thoughts any more than I have to. I can't live in the past, with the people I had to leave behind there, there is only the future now.

"Come here, Isola?" she asks me. I get out of my chair and walk over, sitting on the edge of the bed, and holding her hand as Hallie gets up.

"I'm going to get us some drinks," Hallie says, patting my arm as she walks out of the room.

"You really don't look bad," I tell her, and she chuckles.

"And you have always been a terrible liar," she responds, making me smile because she has no idea that I lie to her all the time. That so much of my life is a lie, that there is little truth left here on Earth and in my life with Jules.

"You will be back home soon, I'm having to put up with Dagan cooking and takeaways. I miss you," I mumble out. Not that Dagan is bad at cooking, because he really, really isn't. But I'm not going to tell her that.

"I'm glad the boys are looking after you. They tell me you are well every time they come to visit me," she says, and I frown at her. *What boys?*

"They come to visit you? Elias, Dagan, and Korbin?" I inquire.

"Every day, one of the boys comes to see me," she explains, making me smile. They didn't have to do that, and I didn't even know they were. I love that Jules hasn't been as alone as I've worried she was. I wonder why they didn't tell me they were going to see her. They must have made a plan between them all or something.

"I haven't been able to email your father about being in here, have you spoken to him?" she asks. I close my eyes, looking away from her blue ones as I answer.

"No, I haven't. But I will," I say, hating that I'm lying again.

"Okay," she answers. "Isola, you can tell me anything. You know that? I see you as the grandchild I never had," she says, and I look back, squeezing her hand tighter.

"I see you the same, but that's why I can't tell you everything. You are safe here and at the nursing home I chose for you
until you are better," I say. She smiles, but there is an unspoken
sadness clouding over her eyes. I want to tell her everything, but
I doubt she would believe she has been raising a dragon her
whole life. Nor that she has four living in her house right now.

"You will visit me?" she asks, her brown eyes watching me
like it means everything to her for me to say yes.

"One day, when everything is settled, I will. I promise," I say,
and I mean it. I will come back when I have the throne, and
there is no war. When I can make her safe and maybe even bring
her back to Dragca, show her my world. She could live out her
days in the castle, with people to help her. I wonder if Bee could
heal her a little, take away some of her pain.

"I know you lie to me all the time, and that you have your
reasons. I know you're protecting me from something I don't
need to know about. I'm just glad that sentence wasn't a lie,
because I do want to see you at least one more time before I pass
away," she says, and I frown.

"What—" I go to say when the door opens, and Hallie walks
in. I pull my eyes away from Jules, intending to ask Hallie to give
us some more time. I don't get the chance as Hallie starts talking
quickly.

"I'm so sorry to cut this visit short. My father called, and I
have to get back home. It's urgent," she says, putting the drinks
on the side.

"Okay," I respond, seeing the worried look on my friend's
face. I stand up, leaning over, and kissing Jules's forehead.

"I will see you soon, and we can discuss what you just said,"
I say, and she laughs.

"A lie, but I will always forgive you. It's what people do when
they love someone," she replies, making me wonder if that's
true. Hallie comes over before I can tell her she means a lot to
me, too.

"I will come back on the weekend, and you can tell me that

chocolate chip cookie recipe. I can't live without those in my life," Hallie says, making Jules laugh.

"I will write it down for when you come next, Hallie," Jules replies. Hallie gives her a hug before we both leave. I look back once more at Jules as I open the door, and she gives me a small nod. There is a look of love in her eyes that I know I won't forget. Yet, it's still hard to shut the door and walk out. I have a feeling I won't see her for a long time, and I hate it. It shouldn't be like this.

"What's so urgent with your dad?" I ask Hallie as we walk down the empty corridors of the hospital and neither of us have said a word.

"I can't really say, but something big has happened. He thinks I need to see it," she rolls her eyes.

"You confuse me," I bump her shoulder, "but I love you anyway."

"You best do, biatch," she grins, making me laugh.

51

ISOLA

"H ey, you're back, how was Jules?" Korbin asks as I close the door behind me, and start pulling my coat off, shaking the rain out of my hair. *Does it ever stop raining around here?*

"She is doing good. She is just wanting to get out of bed and start doing stuff," I say, pulling my boots off after hanging my coat up.

"Good to hear. We are watching a movie, and pizza is on the way. I've ordered your favourite: pepperoni and chicken," he says with a grin. He should know my favourite by now as we have all been taking turns ordering food for each other. I walk over, sliding my arms around his waist, and resting my head on his chest.

"Sounds perfect, and just what I need right now," I admit, and he kisses my forehead. Dagan walks down the stairs, stopping as he gets to us, and I let go of Korbin. It still feels a little awkward to hug or be close to any of them when there's another one of them around. Something to get used to, or not. *Who knows, they might suddenly change their minds and try to kill each other.*

"Welcome back," Dagan whispers, his fingers brushing my hand as he walks past me into the lounge.

"Go and sit down. I'll get you a drink," Korbin says, and walks off to the kitchen before I can reply to him. I walk into the lounge, loving how it's my favourite room in the house. It's the cosiest place in the house. It has three black-leather sofas, a fur rug on the floor in the middle, and they all face the stone fireplace. The television above the fireplace is on, and someone has lit the fire, so it's toasty warm in here.

"Come here," Dagan pats the space next to him on the sofa, and I go over to sit next to him. I rest my head on his shoulder as he flips through the movies on the Sky box.

"That movie looks good, I like end of the world movies," I comment. I have a weird fascination with them.

"*San Andreas?*" he asks, and I nod.

"Okay, we have the movie picked then," he replies, renting it and pausing the movie when it starts up. Dagan holds me close to his side, seeming fascinated with twirling a strand of my blonde hair around his finger.

"Hey, princess," Elias says coming into the room. He puts his drink down near the sofa and sits down, stretching his legs out.

"How was school?" I ask him, just as the doorbell sounds. Elias and Dagan stare at each other, neither one of them moving to answer the door. I go to get up, myself, but Dagan's arm stops me.

"I'll get it then," Dagan says sarcastically, getting up and walking away. Elias grins, grabbing his drink, and moving to sit next to me.

"That's Dagan's seat," I laugh.

"I know, that was the plan. I miss you," he grins, wrapping an arm around my shoulder and pulling me to him. I laugh, snuggling into his side and not arguing, I'm sure Dagan won't be impressed when he gets back, but that's his argument to have.

"Asshole," Dagan grumbles when he walks in with the pizzas and sees Elias in his seat. Korbin walks in next, putting a glass of Coke on the floor for me and sitting down. Dagan passes the pizzas around to us, and I open mine up, inhaling the smell.

"Give it here, fucker," Elias grumbles as Dagan holds his box in the air, slowly opening the box.

"Nope," he says, and Elias gets up lazily, grabbing the pizza, but not stopping Dagan from grabbing a slice, which he shoves in his mouth.

"And they say *I'm* the asshole brother," Elias grumbles, moving back to his seat next to me.

"Damn, I love pizza, it's just amazing," I say, picking up one of my pieces and eating, okay inhaling, it in seconds. I look up to see all the guys looking at me, with matching smirks.

"I like a girl that loves her food," Elias grins as he picks the remote up and presses play. When I finish my pizza, I rest my head on Elias's shoulder and smile. This is a perfect moment, all of us here together, but it feels like I'm missing something. *Or someone.*

~

"Issy," Thorne's voice comes through the haze. I force my eyes open, but I can't see anything other than darkness. It's an unsettling and scary darkness, one I just want to wake up from.

"Thorne? Where are you?" I ask nervously.

"Here," he says, and a hand grabs my arm. I turn, trying to see him, but I still can't, just a black shadow of a hand holding my arm.

"Why can't I see you?" I ask, feeling for his hand. It doesn't feel right, not solid but like air instead. It's so weird, and for some reason it scares me.

"I don't know why, but I think it's because we have been apart for too long," he tells me, his voice wavering at the end.

"Thorne," I mumble, wanting to tell him everything I learnt from Melody, but not like this, not when I can't even see his face.

"Your adoptive father killed my mother," I say, angry with him. Angry would be an understatement. I'm furious.

"Yes, but he was brainwashed into thinking your mother was evil,

brainwashed into believing he was doing the right thing. It's no excuse, though, I don't blame you if you hate me for it," he says sadly.

"He still killed her, and you made me feel sorry for him and you!" I say, trying to move my arm away from him, but he doesn't let go.

"He did, hate me for that as well if you wish, just don't go," he whispers.

"Why do you want me to hate you?"

"Because I messed up, and I don't deserve forgiveness," he says, each word is more distant and faint than the next.

"Who brainwashed your father?" I ask quietly.

"I don't know, I never knew. My mother and I will kill whoever it was," he vows, but I can barely hear him.

"She doesn't know?" I ask, needing to know how much she has lied to him.

"No, she doesn't," he whispers.

"Stay safe, Isola, I don't think I'm strong enough to keep doing this," he says, and for some reason it makes me feel sick; the idea of never talking to him again, never seeing him again.

"You want to let me go, Thorne?" I ask.

"Never. I never want to let you go, but you should run from me," he whispers, and then everything goes black.

I BLINK MY EYES OPEN, hearing the television on in the background, and feeling my body resting on top of something hard and warm. I look down to see Elias underneath me on the sofa, my head on his chest, his heavy breathing tells me he is sleeping. I hear light snoring, and turn on my side to see Dagan sleeping on one of the sofas, and Korbin sleeping on the other. I slide off Elias slowly, careful not to wake him, and avoid the pizza boxes on the floor as I escape the room. I go through the kitchen and to the bathroom, turning the tap on and splashing my face with some water to wake me up. That dream was weird, and why am I suddenly so worried about Thorne? All I can think is that something is wrong, and there is nothing I can do. I'm tired of being here, helpless and not being able to do anything. I'm the princess of Dragca, the last ice royal, and my ancestors didn't back down. They didn't hide when everyone needed them, no, they went to war. They took the throne, demanded peace, and never let anyone beat them. The door opens behind me, snapping me out of my thoughts, and in the mirror, I see Dagan come in the room.

"Shit, sorry. I thought you had gone up to bed," he says. I shake my head, words escaping me as I still can't stop thinking about how much of a disappointment I am. How I'm meant to be making them remember me, instead I'm just falling for them. It's a massive cluster-fuck. I don't know if Dagan sees something written on my face, but he doesn't walk out, only holds the door as he looks at me like he can read my every thought.

"I only just woke up," I admit, and he shuts the door behind him. Dagan walks up to me, wrapping his arms around me from behind, and resting his head above mine. Our eyes meet in the mirror, neither of us looking away, and just finding some comfort and security in each other.

"Things are changing for us all, and it's getting complicated. Sure you don't want to run, kitty cat?" he asks, seductively in that panty-dropping voice that I swear these dragons have mastered. I could run from everything and live a life in hiding. But I would always be running once I started, and I would be heartbroken. I know I would, I couldn't leave them.

"I'm not running from anything anymore, especially not with how I feel. Life is so short, my life has taught me that, and it's pointless to fight what is right," I tell him, keeping my eyes locked with his. I want to make sure he understands every word. I will find a way to break the curse, to set them free and able to keep their dragons. Even if they don't want me in the end, even if I die making sure it happens, I'm going to do it.

"Tell me to stop, and I will," he says, as he tilts my head to face him as he kisses me. The kiss is slow and leisurely as he holds me close to him. I moan as his hands tighten on my hips, sliding towards my stomach slowly. Every kiss teases me to the point of begging him. His right hand flicks open my jeans, as he slides his hand slowly into my jeans, and underneath my lacy underwear.

"You're a tease, Dagan," I moan, as his finger glides up and down my slit.

"I want to spend hours teasing you, learning your every reaction. What you like," he rubs a finger around my clit making me moan out in pleasure as he whispers, "what you love, and what makes you scream my name." He slowly slides one finger inside me, before taking it out and adding another.

"Watch me as I pleasure you, I want you to remember this," he demands, and I look at his eyes in the mirror, as he gets me closer and closer. So much passion, so much devotion is blazing in his eyes. He means every word, and I know after this, I will be his. I know I already was.

"Come for me, Isola, I want to see and feel you come," he whispers in my ear as his thumb finds my clit, and his masterful hands send me over the edge. I moan out, keeping my eyes locked with his–even though it's difficult–and my body pressed against his. He keeps his fingers inside me as I calm down, enough to tilt my head and look at him. I slide my hand to his belt, but he stops me with his other hand.

"No, beautiful," he whispers slowly, removing his fingers and stepping away. I watch breathlessly as he walks to the door.

"Don't you want to?" I ask.

"Not yet, there are plenty of things I want to do to you before I finally get to be inside you, kitty cat," he says with a seductive smirk, and walks out of the room.

52

ISOLA

"How was your exam?" Hallie asks, rubbing her forehead as we walk out of the dinner hall where we have been writing our exams for the last two hours. I didn't even see the point of trying to study for it, so I just drew the royal crest while I waited. I know I'm going to fail every class. The memories of being here for the last two years have nearly all gone, and all I remember are certain things, only the big things that happened. And that wasn't much, or anything to do with school.

"Shit, I know I failed it, but it doesn't really matter," I reply, and she sighs.

"You're lucky your parents aren't on your case like mine. My dad would lose his shit if I failed," she says, and I reach over lifting a bit of her hair.

"Is that why you dyed the tips red?" I ask. I've never really known why she changes the colour.

"Yeah, I thought it would give me some confidence with the exam and dealing with my parents," she laughs sarcastically, "but it didn't."

"I'm sorry," I give her a side hug, trying to ignore the pangs of jealousy I feel. I wish my father was here to get angry that I didn't pass a test. That we could do simple things like that. Yet, even when he was alive, he didn't make much of an effort with normal things, because the crown came first. I remember reading a saying in a book once about becoming a queen or king. They say you give everything up for the crown, for the people you are chosen to rule. Maybe that was just the case with my father, he gave everything up in the end, even me.

"What happened yesterday after the hospital? You never said," I ask as we keep walking towards the front doors of the school.

"Nothing, he was just being overdramatic," she says, smiling tightly at me. I open the door, deciding not to call her out on lying to me. I really need to do some stalking of Hallie to find out what her father does. I literally have no idea from the clues she has given me. Something is going on, though, and I need to know what.

"Hey, princess, can I have a word?" Elias asks, leaning against a pillar, putting a cigarette out under his boot. *Does he ever stop smoking?*

"Have fun," Hallie winks, and walks off as I chuckle.

"What's up?" I ask him after I walk over. He looks down at me, his blue eyes sparkling and drawing me in.

"A date, we are going on a date," he announces.

"That doesn't sound like you're asking me," I raise an eyebrow. I don't like to be commanded to do anything.

"I'm not asking, you had one with Korbin, so I'm feeling left out," he says playfully, stepping closer, smoothing his hands down my arms.

"That's a shame, isn't it?" I tease. "If you ask nicely, I might go on a date with you," I say, making him laugh.

"Isola Dragice, will you go on a date with me?" he asks, somehow making the awkward question sexy. *Dammit.*

"Where did you have in mind?" I ask.

∾

"ICE SKATING? NOT WHAT I EXPECTED," I say as we walk around the corner and stop in front of the ice skating building. It has ice boots glowing green next to a sign that says *"Skate for Ice."* A nice classic sign that I'm sure took someone hours to think up.

"You are an ice dragon, I'm pretty sure you like ice," he whispers next to my ear, his lips lightly grazing them.

"Okay, I'm an ice dragon that's never been ice skating," I admit, making him laugh. He tugs me towards the doors of the building. We walk in, get our boots after Elias pays, and go to sit on a bench to put them on. There aren't many people on the ice, or on the steps around it. It's a small ice ring, with plastic protectors and rails all the way around. The place looks like it could use some new paint, and overall is not in the best condition, but I bet it doesn't get a lot of visitors in this small town.

"Do you know how to skate?" I ask him, doing up the laces and pulling them tight. I stand up slowly, wobbling a little, even when I'm not on the ice. *This is not going to go well.*

"Maybe, I think so. I don't know, my memories are a little hazy," he says, getting confused because he doesn't remember what is real, and what is not. This is Melody's fake memories messing with him.

"Let's just go out, and see if you can," I say, and he stands up, not wobbling at all and reaches for my hand.

"Don't pull me over if you fall, princess," he requests, and I know if I fall, he is coming down with me. This was his idea, not mine.

"I promise I will," I say, grinning. I look away as we get to the ice, and let go of Elias to hold onto the rail. I slip straight away, grabbing the rail for dear life to make sure I don't fall over and hurt my ass.

"Princess, need a hand?" Elias says behind me, and I turn to see him skating around in circles. *Show off.* Of course he would be good at this.

"Nope," I bite out, determined to do this myself. I can make ice, so surely I can skate on it? Right?

"Ahh!" I scream as I fall over after letting go of the bars, smacking my right side on the freezing cold ice.

"I've got you, my stubborn pain in the ass," Elias says, picking me up and putting me on my feet like I weigh nothing. He holds me close to him, neither of us moving.

"I'm not stubborn," I point out, needing to say it.

"Yeah, princess, you are," he says, and then moves back a little, letting me grab his arms with my hands.

"Okay, come forward two steps, and then just glide. And repeat. It's easy, and I won't let go," he tells me, and I narrow my eyes at him.

"I'm not a kid," I say.

"Oh, I know," he says, his tone deeper and gruffer than before.

"Sorry, I just don't like not being able to do something," I tell him, taking two steps forward like he suggested and then letting the boots glide me along.

"Again," Elias says when I slow to a stop. I repeat the action, until I'm doing it without thinking, and we are skating around the ice together.

"Sometimes, you can't do everything alone. You need to accept help, in whatever forms it comes in," he tells me, and I know he is right. It's like going back to Dragca, I will need help. There is no way I will be able to win the throne back on my own. No, I have to start asking for help when I need it. Elias is right, but I'm not going to tell him that. His ego is big enough already.

"Even from the sexy biker man I'm on a date with?" I ask, and he pulls me to his chest, making me almost lose my footing as he holds me close to him.

"Even me," he whispers, and then kisses me.

53

ISOLA

"**A**re you sure you don't want to come with us?" Korbin asks me, as he and Dagan pull their coats on. I lean against the wall, shaking my head.

"Nope, you need to do a food shop. I'm not going with you after last time," I shoot a pointed look at Dagan, who laughs.

"It wasn't that bad," he grumbles, walking out the door.

"It was! Watch out for the big pile of food this time!" I shout after him. Korbin chuckles and follows him out.

"Do you want anything special?" Elias asks as he comes out the kitchen and gets his coat.

"Chocolate, lots of chocolate."

"I should have known that answer," he grins. "What are you going to do today then?"

"I'm going to sit and read this book that came out today I've been waiting forever for!" I say excitedly, and he laughs, kissing my cheek before walking out and shutting the door. I grab my Kindle from my room, and run down the stairs, sitting on the sofa as I open a new book. I love the feeling when you start reading the first line of a new book and you know you are going to be hooked from just that one line. You also know you won't be putting it down for a long time. I settle down on the sofa just as my phone starts ringing.

"You have to be kidding me," I groan. I put the Kindle down and run into the kitchen, finding my mobile on the side. I just miss the call, but there are five messages from Hallie.

> *Hey! I decided to go to the party. Hot guy is going!*
> *Okay, the party is boring.*

I skim through the next couple of messages (who is hooking up with who at the party, and some girl was sick on a guy) to the last message.

> *Help me! I can't drive, and some guys won't leave me alone.*

Shit. I grab my coat, looking down at my leggings and green tunic top that stops at my knees. I don't look too bad, and she needs me; what I'm wearing isn't going to matter. I quickly call a local taxi firm and then wait outside, deciding not to call the guys. I'm stronger than they are right now anyway, and I can freeze anyone that touches Hallie. The taxi turns up ten minutes later as I keep calling Hallie's phone, and it goes straight to voicemail every time. I give the taxi driver Michael's address and sit back, still wondering if I should tell the guys. I quickly text Elias.

> *I'm going to Michael's party to pick Hallie up. Won't be long. X*

I REST MY HEAD BACK, worrying more and more about Hallie. She takes self-defence like I do, and I remember her telling me her father taught her how to stop an attacker in seconds. She will be okay, she likely just needs a lift, and her phone is flat. Michael's house finally comes into view, a massive house in the middle of the woods on the other side of town. It must be five floors, with white panels and massive windows. There's loud music blasting from the house that I can hear from inside the car, even as we head up the driveway. There are students all over the lawn in front of the house, some making out, others smoking, and then I spot one student throwing up. *Gross.* I quickly pay the driver and get out, walking up the footpath and stepping over a passed-out guy in the middle of it.

"Issy!" I hear Michael shout my name from in front of me before I even get in the door. Michael jumps up from his seat in the living room I've walked into, like he was waiting for me or something. I look away, searching the room and seeing half of it is a smoky dance floor with loud music making it hard to hear anything, and sweaty teenagers dancing with each other all over it. The other half is full of sofas pushed together, teenagers all over them, doing things I quickly look away from when I don't see Hallie. *Shit, where is she?*

"I'm so glad you came!" Michael says, grabbing me and holding me tight to his sweaty and alcohol-stinking body.

"Have you seen Hallie?" I shout near his ear, smelling the beer and smoke on his clothes. He stinks so badly, and not in the good way.

"Upstairs, I will show you where she is. She is okay, don't worry, just a little drunk," he shouts back, taking my hand and pulling me through the people to another room with a large staircase. I don't trust when he says she is fine, but I don't have any choice but to let him lead me to where he said she is. He drags me up two floors, as we avoid drunk people on the stairs, and the sounds coming from the rooms.

"In this one, she was pretty drunk," Michael says, pointing at a door in the middle of three. I pull my hand away, walking over and opening it up. I walk in, seeing an empty bed and nothing else in the room. I turn as something sharp slips into my neck, and an arm wraps around my waist. Ice spreads down my hands as I try to fight the person holding me.

"Don't fight, little dragon, you're mine now," Michael whispers, licking my ear as everything goes black.

54

KORBIN

"Those look gross and seriously bad for you, man," I tell Dagan as he picks up his eighth packet of some tube of sweet powder things and chucks them into the trolley. I think I'm the only one that likes healthy food. Not pure sugar.

"I like sweet things," he winks at me, and I just groan, giving up on him. The whole trolley is full of crap, I know why Isola didn't want to come shopping with us now. I bet it took a year to put everything away.

"Come on, two trolleys full is enough," I say, staring as Dagan gets two more random sweet packets, and we walk to the next aisle where Elias is getting the last of the things on the list.

"Got everything?" I ask, seeing him searching his pockets.

"Yeah, I think," he says, "I just left my phone at home." He slips the note into his pocket and spins his trolley towards the other aisle. I'm half way down when I fall to my knees, screaming out from the pain and panic I feel. No, not that I feel, what Isola does. I can feel her, and she is in trouble. I go to open my eyes when a roar escapes my lips, and everything goes black as I hit the floor.

. . .

I BLINK MY EYES OPEN, seeing another version of myself on the floor. I'm much younger, about ten, covered in mud as a man shouts at me. I don't know the man, yet I feel like I do. I can't look at this child version of me anymore, something makes me want to run away from it. I look away, at the ice behind me, so much ice.

"Hello?" I ask, as a green little doll creature floats through the ice.

"She needs you. Save her, fire dragon. Save ice, save the light," the little doll says and suddenly a flash of memories hits me. Everything comes back. Isola. The throne. Dagan and Elias. My dragon.

"Save her," Bee pleads with me as I start falling, and I can't fight it.

"KOR, WAKE THE FUCK UP," Elias's voice comes through the haze, and I feel a hand slapping the side of my face. "For fuck's sake."

I jump up when water is thrown over my face, and I wipe it away, looking around at the shopping aisles, to Elias standing over me with a bottle of water.

"Help me wake Dagan up, we have to find Isola. Something is wrong," Elias says, panic all over his face as he runs to his brother. I pull myself up, feeling for Isola, but not sensing anything. *How is that possible?*

"Get lost," Dagan grumbles as Elias shakes him. Elias starts pouring water over him when he doesn't wake up.

"Isola, wake up for Isola," Elias demands, and Dagan sits up, rubbing his face. My dragon pounds in my mind, its relief at finally being back clear.

"Find princess, find mine," it hisses, trying to push me to shift in the middle of a store.

"Are you guys alright?" a woman asks, running down to us as Dagan gets up. I reach into my jeans and pull out my wallet.

"Can you put all this away for me? I'm so sorry," I say, as her eyes widen at the packed trolleys and then the wad of cash I get out, leaving it on top.

"Wait!" the woman shouts, but we all ignore her as we stumble out of the store and into the parking lot.

"We have to do what we were tasked with, we must protect Isola and get her to Dragca," Elias comments.

"The curse . . ." I let my sentence drift off and start pulling my coat off.

"We will pay the price," Elias says, but there's no hate in his words. We all shift, shooting off into the skies as we hear the screams from humans that see us.

"*Protect mine, and the curse will fall,*" my dragon says. He is prepared to lose himself for her. I know it.

"*I will lose you,*" I reply.

"*But you will have her, and she will be safe,*" my dragon whispers, and I know he is right. There isn't anything I wouldn't do to save her, and I've known that for quite some time.

55

ISOLA

Everything is blurry as I open my eyes. I feel cold, and someone is ripping something. A shadow is lying on top of me, pulling at my clothes, kissing my neck, and pushing their hardness into my stomach. Fear swallows me as I try to fight the darkness, I feel so out of sorts. Everything is cold again in a blink, and when I open my eyes, my surroundings are still so blurry that I can only make out shapes. Yet I can hear them, I feel the body moving off of mine.

"Shit, she is waking up and freezing stuff. You said that stuff knocks dragons out for a whole night!" I hear Michael shout at someone.

"Just be quick, and then I want my go before she really wakes up. My dad will lose his shit when he finds out I stole that stuff from the labs," the other guy says, in a whiny voice. Oh my god, I need to move, I can't let them do this to me. Fear strangles me as I try to do anything, only to fail, only to feel like I don't control my body.

"Shut up," I hear as I feel Michael pulling at my leggings. I try to move, to fight him as he pulls my underwear down, but I can't move. I can't do anything as I hear a belt being undone, every little sound making me utterly terrified. This is worse than dying, I would rather die than let him do this to me. I feel a tear slide down my cheek, the tear being the only thing I can focus on as I try to forget where I am. Panic, fear, and revulsion fill me as Michael spreads my legs and puts a knee on the bed, making the bed dip a little. I scream in my mind for my dragon, but I can't hear her. I can't do anything, and no one is coming to save me. The sound of a door slamming open fills the room, followed by the smell of smoke.

"You will die for this," Thorne's growly voice exclaims, but my mind refuses to believe it. He isn't really here. *He can't be.*

"It's not–" I hear Michael beg, and then he screams and screams. The smell of burning flesh fills the room as more screams follow Michael's. I try so hard to move, to know if what I'm hearing is even real, to see anything other than the blurriness in front of me. The warmth of the fire in the room eventually takes over the sound of Michael's and the other's screams, and then something is wrapped around me.

"I know you hate me, but not like this, not before I can even tell you how much of a fucking idiot I am," Thorne whispers near me, and I feel hands on my face.

"I hate you," I mumble, trying to make the words ring true. I don't even know what I'm saying, I don't even believe it's really him.

"No, you don't, and you hate that," he says gently, and picks me up in his arms. I try to reply, but I can't, only seeing a shadow carrying me out of a fire. When Thorne's face comes into view, I can finally see the burning house just behind his head.

"You saved me, why?" I ask, feeling numb.

"Because in the end, I always will," he tells me, kissing the top of my head. I rest myself against him as I let darkness take me away.

56

ISOLA

"I didn't do a thing to her! I saved her, you fucking idiots!" I hear Thorne shout as I wake up. The memories of Michael and my resulting terror making me jump, and I fall off the sofa I'm on. I slam onto the wood floor, flinching at the coldness and how the room spins. I put a hand on my head, and I look around, somehow expecting him to be there, trying to force himself on me. I feel down my body, knowing I'm not in pain, so he couldn't have . . . . *I can't even say the word.*

"Shit," I hear Elias say, and then he is standing above me, leaning down to help me up. I grab the blanket, scooting away from him, and he holds his hands up.

"Hey, it's me, princess," he coaxes gently, not taking another step closer. I look around the lounge, trying to relax now that I'm home and not in danger.

"I told you what happened, don't push her," Thorne says, coming to stand next to him.

"I remember, princess, we all do," Elias says gently.

"How?" I croak out, and clear my throat a few times. Dagan walks over, seeing me hiding in the corner of the sofa, and frowns. I look at the glass of water in his hand, but I don't really want him close enough to me to take it.

"Here, it's just water," he offers me the glass of water he was holding, reaching out, so he doesn't get too close. I accept it, and he backs away, sitting on the edge of the sofa. They all watch me with fear in their eyes, all of them look as worried as the next one. Elias and Thorne sit on the floor where they were, and it shocks me that they aren't arguing. Or not trying to kill each other.

"I got you some clothes," Korbin says as he walks in the room. He places them on the back of the sofa I'm hiding next to and then backs away, knowing I just don't want anyone near me right now. He sits by Dagan, all of them looking at me as I pull my blanket close around myself.

"How?" I repeat, needing to know what happened to make them remember, and they all look at each other.

"We were shopping, just about to check out another aisle, when it happened. We felt your fear, your pain, and it overwhelmed us into remembering. We shifted outside and flew straight here just as Thorne carried you in and explained," Dagan explains. "I think we all passed out for a moment at the store."

"That's not possible, only mates or blood bound souls can feel each other's emotions in times of need," I point out, and they all look at each other.

"How do you know that?" Elias is the one to ask.

"Jace wanted to share blood with me before we mated, so he would know if I was in any danger. I decided I didn't want to, because I wanted our blood to be swapped at our mating," I explain, and there's an eerie silence between us all. They are hiding something from me, and I'm not sure I even want to know what it is they did.

"Tell me what you did, what you all did," I demand, knowing guilt when I see it in each of their eyes. I keep looking over at Thorne, not really believing that he is here.

"Wait, before you answer that, how are you here? How did you know?" I ask Thorne.

"I didn't know, but Melody must have as she came to me. She demanded I leave right then. She said she would meet us when we come back to Dragca," Thorne tells me, and I look down at the floor, taking a deep breath. I have to thank Melody and Thorne at some point.

"Is Michael . . .?" I stumble over his name, and I'm not sure Thorne even understood what I said until he answers.

"Dead." He says the word firmly, unapologetically, and full of protective tones. I clear my throat before looking at Dagan, and nodding for him to tell me what they all did.

"When you were stabbed, you were also poisoned and dying. Your uncle told us that you needed to have the poisoned blood taken out, and it had to be replaced," he says, his sentence drifting off as my eyes widen.

"You gave me blood to save me?" I ask.

"We all did, you needed a lot, and there was so much poison it was turning your blood black," he says, his haunted eyes communicating how horrible it was for him.

"We are blood bound, all of us?" I exclaim.

"Yes, we made the choice to die for you. We made the choice to give you our life then, because you are our queen. You are the one we fight for, and that hasn't changed in all the weeks we have been here," he says firmly.

"What has happened, the curse . . .?" I ask, and they look between each other.

"The curse doesn't work on Earth, but if we ever go back . . . we will lose them," Korbin says and then drifts off.

"I have to return, you don't," I tell them, and I mean every word. I might be their queen in their eyes, but I won't demand this of them.

"We do have to return home, and we made our choice a long time ago," Dagan says as Elias and Korbin nod. I look back at Thorne, and his next words crush my heart.

"My dragon is gone, it was the moment I made the choice to come here for you," he tells me, pain laced all over his face.

"Thorne . . ." I choke.

"Don't, it's done. Melody and Bee need you to get up, put your clothes on, and return home. They are waiting for you in Dragca," he says, and his firm words make me want to move.

"Don't let a stupid human win. You are Isola Dragice, and you don't give up," Thorne tells me. I close my eyes, calling my dragon.

"Will you fight with me? Are you ready for this?" I ask her.

"I am with you, always," she replies.

"It's time to go home," I whisper a reply and open my eyes, knowing they are silver as I stare at all my dragon guards.

Home to fight and win.

"Who are you calling?" Thorne asks me as we walk through the woods and to the nearest portal.

"My friend, Hallie. I can't just vanish from her life," I say as I ring her house phone, knowing Michael must have stolen Hallie's cell, and he nods. I doubt Hallie was even at the party, and the more I think about it, I was stupid to fall for that trick.

"Maybe you can tell me about her one day?" he asks and every instinct in me wants to say no, while other parts just want to run to him. Let him hold me, and tell me everything's okay. I don't know why I feel so safe with him, whether it's because he saved me, or if it's because we share a blood bond. I don't know, but it's hard to resist the pull. It also makes sense how he was getting in my dreams now, even across worlds. If our connection is so strong already, I don't even want to think about how powerful it could be if we mated. Not that I'm thinking about mating. *Not at all.*

"Maybe," I say quietly as the phone rings and rings, finally going to voicemail. I wait for the beep before I start talking, and I see Elias look over to me as he speaks quietly to Korbin and Dagan to my left.

"Hallie, this isn't going to make much—or really any—sense. But here we go. I have to leave, for a long time, and I have no idea when I can come back. Jules has a nursing home set up, and she knows where the cash is in the house, but can you please check on her?

"Also, I never had a best friend, or anyone that close to me, but you are that to me and that will never change. I love you, Hallie, and stay safe for me." I go to say more when it starts beeping, and I know I have to put the phone down.

I wipe some stray tears away, and even though Thorne doesn't look my way, he says quietly, "I will make sure you see her and Jules again, this isn't the end." I don't reply to him, I can't tell him how much comfort I received from his words. We walk silently to the portal, seeing the shimmer in the trees in the dim morning light.

"You don't have to come; in fact, I won't allow it. I can't let you give your dragons up for me," I stop in front of the portal, turning to my dragon guards. If they walk through this portal, they won't be dragons anymore, just guards. It won't change how I feel for them, but it might change how they feel about me. I still shake a little when they move near me, even though I know they would never hurt me like Michael tried to. I have to close my eyes, and force myself to push what happened into a little box in the back of my head. I can't cope with it right now. *I just can't, more urgent things are going on.* Thorne nods sadly, walking to the portal, whispering where we need to go, and giving us some alone time.

"We all knew what we were doing when we gave you our blood," Dagan says.

"But the last few weeks, I did this. You didn't know who you were, what you were!" I exclaim.

"You did try to tell us, princess," Elias replies.

"It doesn't matter, I did this. I caused this," I say, getting more and more upset.

"Isola . . . just trust us. There are things we need to tell you, things that will make you understand," Dagan says, keeping an eye out for anyone around us. Not that there will be anyone, we are in the middle of the woods.

"Then tell me?" I ask them all. "I can't believe that you would choose this."

"It's my choice, princess. I told you once already . . . I've made my mind up about you, and I never lie," Elias says with a smirk, but I see the fear flash over his eyes. He doesn't want to lose his dragon, and yet he is still going to walk into Dragca for me. I watch as he walks past me and straight into the portal without stopping once. Thorne nods once at me before following him, and there is a long silence between us all.

"I do have to come with you, I'm yours. I don't need to tell you anything else, doll," Korbin smirks. I can see his fear, too, but like Elias, he walks past me and into the portal. My heart pounds against my chest as Dagan steps closer to me, placing his hands on my face.

"Stay here, please don't do this," I beg him, not wanting him to lose that part of himself. I can't bear for the curse to destroy that part of him.

"Isola, stop it," he demands as I try to move away from him.

"No, this is crazy, what you're saying and going to do . . . It can't," I mumble and then trail off when his dragon takes over, the blackness burning over his eyes. I stumble away from him, walking backwards towards the portal.

"Stop!" he shouts and storms over to me, pinning me to a tree, and levelling his eyes with mine, so I can't look away.

"If it's a choice between my dragon, a part of my soul, and you, I. Choose. You." he says, growling out all his words.

"Dagan," I whisper.

"It would crush me more to lose you. *That* would destroy my soul more than anything any curse can do to me. My dragon agrees because, you know what?" he asks. I shake my head.

"He would die for you," he tells me, kissing me gently and stepping back. He walks through the portal as tears stream down my face. The curse meant to protect me is destroying the only things I care about. I step forward, closing my eyes, and walking through the portal as I hear whispered by the sweetest voice:

"The last light returns, and the darkness will be stopped."

58

ISOLA

The portal lets me out on the other side, and the bright light from the suns blinds me for a little bit, until I can open my eyes and see what's in front of me. Elias, Dagan, and Thorne are standing to one side, and Korbin is right in front of me, with a long red sword resting under his chin. A tiny amount of blood is dripping down his neck. I follow the sword to see Esmeralda holding it, a smug smile on her painted red lips that match her red cloak. Guards come from all directions to surround us, raising their swords that shine in the sunlight. I know she has won, I can't do anything other than lower my hands. She would kill Korbin in a second because he means nothing to her, and I won't let her kill anyone else I care about again.

"You are all coming to the castle, and then meeting your *true* fate," she glances at Thorne, "even you, who dares to betray his mother for a stupid girl."

"Not a girl, a queen. I didn't betray my mother, I'm putting right the mistakes we have made. The throne isn't ours, and my mother is going mad from the power!" he shouts at her, and she shakes her head.

"So, so disappointing," she tuts.

"No, that would be you. You should really tell your dear sister where you go next time, Esmeralda, and maybe get some more guards," Melody's voice comes from above us, and I look up just as she jumps down, slamming Esmeralda to the ground. Korbin grabs her sword, as Esmeralda throws Melody off her. From the corner of my eye, I see Elias slam a hand into his guard, grabbing his sword and running it through the guard's stomach. Korbin runs to help them just as all hell breaks loose, and my dragon guard make quick work of killing the guards surrounding us.

"Are you going to fight me fairly, princess?" Esmeralda taunts. "Or die quietly, in shock, just like your pretty ice dragon and dead daddy did."

"You never played fair, and neither will I," I say, stepping forward. I raise my hands out in front of me, making a long Bo-shaped ice staff, with deadly spikes on either end. Esmeralda doesn't wait for more than a second, shooting three arrow-shaped fire sticks at me. I raise my staff, hitting each one as I walk slowly towards her. She shoots more and more, until I can't see her over the fire in front of me, until I'm standing right in front of her. I whack her legs out from under her, holding the spike at the bottom of the staff right above her heart.

"Don't even think about it," I say, leaning down as she looks up at me with fear-filled eyes.

"You . . . will . . . regret . . . this," she whispers each word as I lift the staff and slam it into her heart, without a second thought. Her eyes widen, her lips parting as blood drips down the side of her face.

"That is for Jace, you goddamn bitch," I say, making sure she hears every word before letting go of the staff. I look around, seeing the guys still fighting three guards. I make three ice spikes, spinning around and throwing them at each guard using my dragon's eyesight, pinning them to the trees with the spike in the middle of their stomachs. Thorne and Korbin run to my sides, protecting me even though there is no one left to hurt me now. I run to Melody, shaking her a little, and she groggily wakes up, holding a hand to the back of her head. I help her sit up as Elias and Dagan get to us, surrounding Melody and me.

"You did it, sis," she says, pulling me to her and holding me tight.

"Sister? What did we miss?" I hear the guys talking and remember I never told them. I hear her sharp intake of breath from Melody before she pulls back. I follow her gaze to Esmeralda's body.

"We have to leave, you shouldn't have killed her. I see her alive no matter what you did here," Melody tells me, pulling my arm, and I look away from Esmeralda to see the desperation in her eyes.

"The future is changing, and it's darker than ever. That's why we are here. We must run before she gets here, the light must live," a small voice says, a green head of hair popping out of Melody's cloak.

"Bee," I shout, as she flies to me, landing on my hand. She is bigger and brighter, her skin almost glows now. I feel so relieved to see her, to have her close to me. "I missed you, I thought I'd never get to see you again."

"Stop darkness, light must win. We *must* win," she demands, her voice older and far more serious than she has ever been. I lower my hand as Bee flies to my shoulder, holding onto my hair as I stand up. Melody stands with me, and we look around at all the bodies. So much death.

"I made a vow, and I won't regret it," I tell Melody.

"Death always comes with a price," she says, nodding her head to the left of me. I look around to see Melody's face full of worry, Elias wiping blood off a sword, Dagan staring at the ice. That is until I see Thorne, who is just staring at the body of his aunt. I killed his aunt. Our families . . . we have all killed so much of each other. With so much death, can there be anything left but hate? Or just pain. I still walk over to him, softly placing my hand on his arm, making him flinch, but he doesn't move away.

"I'm sorry, I know she is family," I whisper.

"She wasn't family, not after the choices she made and the deaths she caused. You have no idea the amount of destruction she has caused in Dragca since you have been gone," Thorne snaps out, walking away from me. I go to follow him when I hear a pained grunt.

"Issy," Korbin whispers, and then falls to the ground as I turn to look at him. I drop down next to him as the others run over, and I look to where he is holding a hand against his shirt, and it's bleeding. I lift it up, seeing a deep cut, with purple lines spreading out from it slowly. I panic, pulling my hoodie off and pressing it against the cut.

"I'm going to be fine," Korbin says, but any fool could hear the pain in his voice.

"Don't lie," I say, and he holds my hand, squeezing it tightly.

"Here, out of the way," Dagan says, kneeling next to me.

"I'm going to burn the cut, seal it and stop it bleeding. It's the best we can do until we find somewhere to go," Dagan explains, moving my hoodie off the long cut.

"Do you even have your fire still? Without your dragon?"

"I can't hear my dragon anymore, but yes," Dagan says, holding out a small flame in his hand. "Only I can't do it for long. Nothing like the power I used to have."

"You can't do that," I say and look to Bee. "Can you heal him?"

"Not from poison, not without power," she says sadly, and my dragon growls, whines, and demands I do something in my mind. Anything to save him.

"Look away," Korbin demands of me, and Elias pulls me away, turning my head into his chest as I hear Korbin scream and scream. I don't think I will ever forget the sounds of his screams, I don't want to. It reminds me that I could lose him, it reminds me what I need to fight for. When it stops, I fall to Korbin's side next to Dagan. I examine the cut, it's burnt and no longer bleeding, but the purple lines look darker and longer.

"I'm okay, don't worry, doll," he tries to reassure me, reaching up and wiping some of my tears away.

"He is poisoned, we need to find a town, and a healer quickly," Melody says nervously, looking over my shoulder.

"Can you walk?" I ask Korbin, and he shakes his head with a tired look. Elias and Dagan lift him up, keeping an arm around their shoulders. But I know he won't be walking fast.

"Save mine," my dragon whimpers, before disappearing away in my head.

"What is the nearest town? Where do we go now?" I ask, but I don't really know who I'm asking. I don't know where we are, it's just trees and mountains for a long time.

"To the seers near here, we have to show them you're alive. To show that you want to fight, and hope they will let their healers save him," Melody says.

"We have allies here, things you don't know, Issy. We have a lot to tell you," Dagan comments.

"I could fly ahead and get help," I suggest.

"No flying, they will be looking for an ice dragon in the skies, and the reward on your head is high. Poor people do desperate things, and we will be lucky if they even help you save your guard," Melody says.

"Let's go now. They *will* save him, or I will kill anyone who thinks to let him die," I promise, turning around. Looking once more at the ice staff melting into Esmeralda's body, I wipe a tear away. *Jace finally has his justice, but why do I feel like I just made a huge mistake, a mistake that could cause me to lose everything that is alive, for a promise I made to death?*

EPILOGUE

Tatarina

"There are rumours the king was seen this way with the princess and other guards," one of the royal guard says, a nervous look flitting across his young face as he stares at me. I smile, placing my hand on his shoulder and feel him shaking. I laugh, and walk around him in the direction he pointed at. I can't believe my son would betray me, not for that spoilt princess. He wouldn't do that to me.

"Your highness, we have located your sister," a guard says

running over to me breathlessly, placing an arm out in front of me to stop me from seeing what is behind him. Like I need to be hidden from the darkness that is this night. I lift a hand, a hot breeze of fire whacks into him, and sends him flying out of my way. I stop, staring at the bodies littering the ground and the one right in the middle.

"NO!" I scream, running over to my sister, dropping down to my knees at her side. There's a hole in her chest, blood surrounds her which mixes in with her long red hair. Too much blood, and it's too watered down. Someone used ice here. My beautiful sister is lost. *Who could have done this?*

"Queen," a hushed voice says, making me look up as a dark shadow hovers above us. My dark spirit, Nane, flies out the shadow, floating down to me.

"Nane, she is dead," I say, refusing to cry. I haven't cried for many years, and I won't now. I will get revenge, I will destroy this world for what it has always done . . . taken everything from me.

"The light killed her, the light must pay," she whispers to me, and lands on the stomach of Esmeralda, lifting a blood-covered hand. "Blood and ice."

"Isola? She did this?" I question Nane, who nods, and I close my eyes as a scream leaves my lips. Black shadows spread out from under me, going in every direction and burning away the trees near me as I try to reel in my anger. They burn the guards, and I hear them, their screams are almost pleasurable to hear. Someone has to suffer for this, for my sister.

"I. Will. Kill. Her," I bite out as I open my eyes and lean forward, tucking a lock of Esmeralda's red hair behind her ear. *My sweet little sister.*

"We can bring her back, bring her back stronger than ever. Bring her back linked to your life, and she will never leave you," Nane suggests, looking up at me with a wicked grin.

"Will she be the same?" I ask.

"She will have a dark soul, much like yours," Nane says, and I laugh.

"She had one before death, but now she will want revenge," I say, a large smile playing on my lips as I place both my hands on Esmeralda's head.

"Call darkness," Nane whispers, and sends a blast of darkness straight into me through our bond. Black lines spread down my arms, onto my sister's face. They crawl up her face slowly and painfully for me. When they hit her eyes, I pull back, catching a breath, and stand up. I wait for a long time, knowing it takes a while for a body to come back. Finally, Esmeralda's eyes open slowly. She looks up at me as I stand over her, her eyes blood red, and a sinister grin on her lips as she stands with my help.

"Time to hunt a princess, my sister," she says, her voice darker and almost sweet. Like a sweet berry that you don't know will kill you, until you're dead.

"Then let's hunt," I say, and Nane laughs as she floats into the shadows once more, but I hear her dark whisper in my mind.

"Darkness will win; not only Dragca will fall, but Earth, too . . ."

The End

Wings of Spirit link here (Protected by Dragons book three).

Three secrets. Two fights. And one broken curse.

Isola is finally back in Dragca, but nothing is the same when she is hunted and betrayed by everyone she meets. With one of her dragon guards fighting for his life, time is running out.

When the seers come to her aid, lies and blood are their price. With two battles on her hands, one for their freedom and one for her dragon guards, Isola has a lot to fight for . . . and a lot to lose.

The dragon guard curse must be broken, for fire has finally fallen for ice . . . but is death the final price?

18+ Reverse harem romance.

PROLOGUE

No! I scream in my dragon's head as we fall through the trees and land on the ground, his claws finally coming free of my wings, so I can move. I shoot ice onto his wings as he tries to fly and keep shooting it until his entire dragon is frozen to the ground. His dragon's eyes almost dead as I stare at him encased in the ice. I look up, not seeing Thorne or any other dragons flying around.

"It has been a long time, Isola, don't you think?" Tatarina's cold, detached-sounding voice says from behind me, and my dragon turns to roar at her. I feel down my wings, knowing the damage to them is too much, and I won't be able to fly out of here for a bit. There is only one thing we can do, even if it makes me vulnerable.

Let me take over? I ask my dragon, who doesn't hesitate as we shift back. I stand up straight, keeping my head high as I face Tatarina. She stands still like a ghost; her dark, nearly black hair blowing in the wind is the only movement. Her eyes are completely black, and they match the dark glow her skin now has. I look over as a woman moves out from the shadows of the trees, making me take a step back.

"Bu-but, I killed you!" I gasp as Esmeralda stands by her

sister's side, smiling widely with her blood-red lips. Her eyes are now as red as her hair, and her pale skin is littered with black veins.

"Death was not my ending," Esmeralda replies, her voice croaking and broken in places. Her head twitches as she speaks, and Tatarina places her hand on her sister's arm.

"I will remember to chop your head off next time," I sneer. "Just to be sure."

"There will not be a next time, for this is *your* ending, Isola," Tatarina says, holding her hands out at her sides. "You are all alone, and I am queen. Is this what you always thought would happen?"

59

ISOLA

"Isola, we need to take a break," Melody gently urges, as I step over another fallen branch and pause, looking back. Melody is resting against a tree, looking breathless and tired, but watching me. I feel like crap, too, but I know we can't just rest now. Resting could mean death, and I don't want to risk it. Bee strokes my cheek from where she sits on my shoulder, making me turn my head to stare into her green eyes. I can almost feel her sadness like it's my own.

"Your sister is right, we need to stop. We have been walking for about ten hours, I believe," Dagan says quietly, walking to my side. I automatically step away from him, shaking my head as I look at Korbin. His arms are around Thorne's and Elias's shoulders, and he is struggling to stand up as they all wait for me to say something. I know he needs to rest, but we need to get out of this damn forest and find somewhere safe.

"We can't, look at him," I wave a hand at Korbin. The purple lines of the poison are crawling up his pale face, and he can barely hold his head up. He is sweaty, pale, and looks on the verge of death. The poison is killing him.

"Isola, we are stopping. Korbin needs to rest, too," Dagan says, nodding his head at Thorne and Elias who carefully set

Korbin down next to a tree. He is barely conscious, and not strong enough to even hold his head up. "We are all worried. I get that, but we need to rest. We won't stop long. I promise."

I turn to Dagan, nodding in acceptance before walking over to Korbin and sitting next to him. I place my hand on his forehead, feeling how burning hot he is, and his green eyes pop open, a little smirk appearing on his lips.

"You make a sexy nurse, doll," he tells me, and I chuckle, shaking my head. "I like hearing you laugh," he coughs on his words, and I see blood on his hand even as he tries to hide it from me as he lowers his hand to his side.

"I like hearing you awake and talking. Do you want some water?" I ask him, clearing my throat as I try to speak through the fear I'm feeling. He nods, and I pull the small water bottle out of the bag that Melody brought with her. We have pretty much emptied it already. There wasn't much in there to start with, but it's better than nothing. We don't have a lot of water left now, but we have to find a village soon, and we can re-stock. I open the plastic bottle, holding it to his lips and helping him drink. Before I put the bottle back, I take a long drink for myself. I rest the bag on the ground near Korbin. I look up as Bee flies off my shoulder, landing on Korbin's lap and smiling up at him. She is growing; she even looks bigger than when I first saw her again.

"Dying," Bee says, pointing a tiny hand at his stomach, and Korbin laughs, even though it makes him cough.

"Thanks for telling me that, Bee. I think I know, though, and don't need a reminder," he says playfully, and Bee shrugs, looking over at me with worry in her eyes.

"Food?" she asks, holding out a hand.

"We don't have any food left, I'm sorry. There is water . . ." I say, and she sighs dramatically, flying up past us and sitting on a branch hanging over Korbin. She lies down, her long green hair blowing in the wind, and I think she is going to sleep, but who knows. She hasn't talked to anyone much on the walk here.

Well, none of us have really spoken, and I think it's about time that changed. It's been years since I was last in Dragca, and I'm worried what I'm going to find when we get out of this forest. I look back at Korbin, seeing his eyes are closed and light sounds of snoring are coming from his chest. I end up just watching his chest move for a while. The movement reminds me that he is alive, and we still have time to save him. A branch cracks behind me, and I turn to see Elias standing there. His hair is messy, and his dark-blue eyes don't have that glow to them anymore. He looks crushed, just like all my dragon guards have since we got here. Since they lost their dragons because of me. I struggle to swallow the guilt I feel as I look at Elias.

"We are all going to sleep for a bit, and I'm on first watch. Get some rest," he says.

"I can't sleep," I say, frustrated, and stand up. I don't want to sleep, because all I can think about is what happened when I last let myself be vulnerable. How I couldn't stop him and needed someone to save me. I can't sleep because I'm scared I'll wake up and Korbin will be gone. He needs me. Sleep is the last thing on my mind, but I can't make the words leave my lips that I want to tell Elias. I look over to see Dagan making a fire, and the simple, normal act makes me relax a little. Reminds me that I'm safe, for now anyway. I look away to see Melody is resting against another tree, her hood covering her face, and Thorne is standing not far from us, watching the forest.

"You should try," Elias says gently, moving to touch my arm, but stopping as I flinch.

"I'm sorry, it's not you," I blurt out my excuse. I can't believe I just quoted every terrible clichéd movie quote as someone gets dumped. Not that I'm dumping Elias. I literally can't as we share blood. We share a bond, and I don't want to dump him anyway. I just feel scared to let him touch me, to let him hold me and tell me this is all okay when it's so far from okay. I can still feel Michael's hands on me, still feel how weak I felt and how powerless.

"It's him, I know. When you're ready, I will always be waiting," he tells me, and I nod. I want to reach out and hold his hand, but I just can't. I almost hate myself for it when I see the longing in his eyes.

"It's impossible to make you walk away, isn't it?" I slightly tease him.

"You know it," he smirks.

I walk over to Thorne, stopping at his side. He doesn't move, doesn't speak for a long time as I follow his gaze through the forest. It's silent and almost peaceful.

"What has changed in Dragca while I've been gone? I need to know what your mother has done," I ask quietly, and Thorne finally looks over at me, his pale-blue eyes still so hauntingly open to me. I can see what he feels, almost guess exactly what he is thinking, just by looking into them. He doesn't hide anything from me, but it's still not enough for me to trust him again. Saving me wasn't enough for me to trust him with my heart again, but I know I can't let him walk away from me yet, either. His pale-blond hair moves around his face in the wind, and his cloak floats just behind him as we watch each other. *I wonder what he thinks as he looks at me?* Does he see a scared princess, or someone else? Someone that is worth all of this. He still wears the royal cloak, the ice and fire dragons embroidered into it. It's just a reminder of what happened to get us to this point. I hate that I can't trust him, and I hate that it hurts my heart every time I think of our past.

"A lot," he answers. Two words are not enough to explain everything I need to know. I'm tired of this; I won't settle for these non-answers anymore. How am I meant to save Dragca, convince the seers I'm their queen, and somehow get my dragon guard their dragons back when they treat me like a clueless girl?

"Simple answers are not enough right now. Tell me everything, Thorne. I will never trust you, never accomplish all I'm meant to, if you don't tell me what I need to know. I'm not the same girl you met at Dragca Academy, the girl who didn't know what she wanted or who she was . . . I am Isola Dragice, and I want to know what has happened to *my* world," I demand, getting frustrated with him as he still silently watches me. I feel Dagan's approach, just before he steps to my side and places his arm around my waist. I don't know why I can let Dagan touch me, hold me. Maybe it's just because he doesn't ask permission to hold or support me. He just does, and once I'm near him, I don't want to pull away.

"Why don't we all sit by the fire and discuss this? There are things we haven't had a chance to tell the princess, also," Dagan asks Thorne as he rolls his lip ring in typical Dagan fashion. Thorne doesn't seem to notice as he seems more focused on my proximity to Dagan than listening to him.

"Like what?" I ask Dagan, wondering what he could possibly be talking about.

"Your father gave us a mission before he died, before we even met you. A mission based on a prophecy that no one other than the old king knew about," Dagan says, keeping his light-blue eyes locked on mine. I try to hold my dragon's growl in as I move out of Dagan's arms and feel ice on my fingertips as I get angry.

Too many secrets, my dragon whispers in my mind, and I couldn't agree with her more.

"Tell me everything, and no one leaves out any secrets this time," I demand, shooting a fierce look at both Dagan and Thorne before stepping away and walking over to the fire.

60

ISOLA

"Start from the beginning," I say, standing with my arms crossed as Dagan, Elias, and Thorne walk to the fire, crowding in close to me. It's strange to see them all together like this; my dragon guards who I've been falling for and the dragon guard that has been haunting my dreams. I can't stop myself from stealing glances at Thorne every so often because the dreams didn't do him justice. I forgot what it was like to be near him, to have that inexplicable connection I feel. A connection that makes me forget about his betrayal, which I never want to do. Melody looks up from the tree she is resting against, listening in as her blue eyes lock on mine. My sister has yet to say much, though she's always watching me every time I look at her. I have a feeling she is hiding things from us, but calling her out on it won't work. I imagine she is as stubborn as I can be. I hear a cough, and I look over to find Korbin sleeping, chest heaving. He sounds like he's in pain, and it's worrying me. This isn't Earth, I can't just take him to a doctor and demand they fix him. We need a healer that doesn't work for the new queen. It's like looking for a needle in a haystack, but with that haystack on fire. I can't even bring myself to acknowledge that I might lose Korbin, not with how I feel for him. I love him, the pain I feel every time I look at him confirming it.

"Maybe you should start," Elias suggests, giving Dagan a pointed look before his dark eyes drift back to me. Elias's black hair is messy, and he looks tired, yet still so incredibly hot. It's easy to get lost in my thoughts when I look at Elias, and the smirk on his lips lets me know he knows what I'm thinking.

"No, Korbin should be the one telling this to Isola as he started it all, but here we go," Dagan says, clearing his throat and not looking my way as he starts to speak. "Korbin's parents were both close to the king, and your father asked them to find three dragon guards he could trust implicitly. Of course, they chose their son, and Korbin asked us, trusting only us to keep a secret," he says, pausing to look at Korbin, and Elias takes over.

"We were brought to the king, and the first words he said were, 'The ones that come when called, will fall for ice. When fire falls for ice, darkness will have its price.'" I muse over his words, completely confused. *Why would my father say that?*

"I heard about the lost prophecy from my mother, but she never told me what it said. I think she feared it, hated it maybe," Thorne admits, and we all look at him for a second. If his mother fears this prophecy, we need to know everything about it. Thorne keeps his eyes locked on mine for only a minute, and I see so much guilt. It reminds me that I still need to tell him what Melody showed me, what his mother has done. I just need to find time alone with him. He shouldn't have an audience when he learns the truth.

"What is it? What else did it say, and who made it?" I rapidly ask questions as the cold wind blows against all of us, and Dagan holds his hands over the fire, warming them up as he answers.

"He didn't share the full prophecy with us. Only that single sentence and one other thing, before demanding that we meet him at Dragca Academy in two weeks when you were to return to Dragca. He told us to stay quiet and follow you," he tells me. I stay silent for a while, just staring at the fire. My father was keeping more secrets from me, and it doesn't even surprise me anymore. I don't know how he expected me to take the throne when it was built on so many lies. I look over at Melody, who doesn't seem shocked. She is a prime example of those lies.

"Tell me?" I look towards Dagan and ask carefully.

"He told us that ice cannot rule anymore, that ice and fire must find balance. That light and dark must find their way to survive, together. He said that we would be crucial in the war that was coming. A war that will destroy Dragca, destroy Earth, and anything light or dark in our worlds unless we stand in its way. Unless we change what everyone has always known," Dagan says, and there's a tense silence between us all as I look into the fire, trying to collect my thoughts before I reply to them. My father knew something, something bad, and he sent my guards to me. He knew they would fall for me, like I would fall for them, but why didn't he say anything to me? I look over at Melody, who just pulls her hood back up, hiding her face in darkness and not saying a word. I bet my sister knows more than she is admitting right now.

"So, let me get this straight. We have four dragon guards who don't have their dragons, one of which is injured and dying. One seer who doesn't talk to us, and one accident prone princess that is supposed to be dead. . . *and* we have to save two worlds?" I blurt out. *Nope, sorry, we are all going to die.*

"You forgot Bee," Thorne points out, and looks at me seriously. "You are not just some accident-prone princess who is powerless. You can control light magic, the most powerful magic known to Dragca. You are an ice dragon, and you can fight. Don't count yourself out just yet," he says. At least he admits I have some faults like tripping over my own feet sometimes, rather than ignoring them.

"I don't know how to *use* light magic, and Bee isn't old enough to tell me," I say as an excuse, but even my voice falters with my weak retort. Honestly, I haven't thought about light magic. I have no idea what it can do. I don't know what dark magic can do either, and the fear of both is making me not want to find out.

"Have you tried asking her? She isn't a baby anymore," Thorne points out.

"You still haven't told me what has happened in Dragca since I've been gone," I counter, because I don't want to admit I haven't asked Bee about it, and I'm not sure how to. Light and dark magic are unpredictable, and that's the last thing we need right now.

"Remember that my mother isn't evil, she really isn't, so don't you all look at me like you feel sorry for me. I don't agree with what my mother has done, and I'll admit the power has gone to her head, but there is still good in her. I only need to get close enough to talk some reason into her. She will stop this and place Isola on the throne. I'm sure of it," Thorne insists, and I briefly glance at Dagan who shakes his head in exasperation. This isn't the time to disagree with him, and Thorne keeps talking before I can even think of replying, anyway. "My mother has destroyed the councils. Esmeralda killed the selected that ruled them and placed one ruler she trusts in each of the main towns. My mother has started a culling for new dragon guards, making them join her without giving them any choice. I don't know too much about how she is forcing them to join, but the dragon guard is growing far larger than it's ever been," he admits to us, and I close my hands into fists in anger.

"She is forcing them to join the guard? Making them curse themselves?" I gasp in shock. My father never did that. Anyone can join the dragon guard, but it was always a choice, and they knew the price. Forcing them . . . it sends shivers of disgust down my spine. No queen should force her people to do that. Ruling with fear is not ruling at all. It's a path to destruction.

"The people don't have a choice. She threatens their families if they don't join . . . or kills them outright. I met a few in the dungeons that she had imprisoned for refusing to join her,"

Dagan tells me, reminding me they spent the last two years trapped in the dungeons. They must know some things that could help us. It reminds me that I still haven't thanked Thorne for keeping them alive, for setting them free, and helping Bee and Melody. There is a lot I haven't thanked him for, but I just don't trust myself not to blurt out a load of other things I'm thinking when we are alone.

"What else?" I ask tentatively, almost not wanting to hear the answer. The guilty look in Thorne's eyes lets me know there is more to this story.

"She has raised taxes, cut down on food provisions, and gained total control over Dragca with fear," Elias answers instead, and Thorne glares at him.

"You make it sound worse than it is. She only did that to feed the army, and she offered anyone who wants to join a place there, with their families protected," Thorne snaps back.

"Every dragon would rather die than join the dragon guard and curse their whole family. Your mother gave them no choice," Elias spits out.

"Enough!" I shout at them, and they both stop instantly, turning to me. "We cannot fight amongst ourselves like this, not when Korbin needs us to find him help, and we have true enemies everywhere."

"The princess is right, but my mother is not completely evil," Thorne contends, and walks away from us all. I want to follow him, tell him everything I know about his mother and that he is wrong about her, but I don't.

"It is not yet time, sister," Melody's voice drifts over to me, but I still watch Thorne as I reply.

"I know."

61

ISOLA

"I finally know where we are," Dagan says, and I stop, looking back at him as he helps Thorne hold up Korbin. Thorne has a royal cloak on now, covering up his eyes and hair, much like I do. We both stand out way too much otherwise. The only difference, I have my ice power, and he doesn't. It would be a death sentence if anyone spotted Thorne. Elias and Melody are behind them, watching their backs as I stay in front. As Melody and I are the only ones with any powers currently, it's smart to have us at the front and the back. I follow Dagan's gaze to our left, where there is a row of trees and a path in the middle of them. The trees have dragons engraved down the trunk, painted in red.

"Where are we?" I ask, curious. I don't see any towns, but the path looks well worn.

"Where we first met you, kitty cat," Dagan says playfully, but I can see the pain in his eyes when he looks at me. His old home, where he lost his mum, which, no doubt, holds some awful memories for them. I glance around Dagan to Elias, who looks tense, staring at the ground. Of all the places we could have ventured to, it had to be their old home.

"Which town is it?" Melody asks.

"Mesmoia," Elias answers gruffly.

"Perfect! Mesmoia is only two days away from where the seers are hiding, and where I saw us meeting them," Melody answers happily. She opens her bag up, and Bee flies off my shoulder straight into it, knowing she has to hide for now.

"But we still need to get through the town without anyone recognising us and get help for Korbin," I tell Melody firmly. She looks at Korbin, and then nods.

"We don't really have the time, but he won't make it to the seers like this. I guess we have no choice," Melody states, looking away from us all as she puts her bag back on.

"I know someone in Mesmoia that might hide us. If he is still alive, anyway," Dagan tells me.

"Can he be trusted?" I ask.

"No idea. He was a friend of our mentor growing up. I don't want to trust him, but we don't really have much of a choice," Dagan says, looking down at Korbin, who they are just dragging along the floor at this point. He isn't conscious, and his breathing is shallow.

"Let's just go. Like you said, we don't have a choice because I refuse to let him die. We risk this for Korbin, he's worth it," I say, making my mind up and knowing they feel the same when none of them disagree with me. This could be Korbin's only chance, and there is no way I'm not taking it. Elias catches up to my side as we get to the row of trees, and we start walking down the path. I pull the hood of my coat up, hiding my blonde hair and knowing I need to keep my eyes on the ground when we enter the village.

"How are you?" Elias prods quietly, his hand brushing mine with every step. He doesn't push to hold my hand, but the little contact feels like he needs it.

"Fine," I answer quickly.

"Tut, tut, naughty princess. You know I don't like lies," Elias calls me out on my crap, and I sigh, looking back at Korbin and then to Elias.

"I'm worried, scared, and I can't think of anything other than saving Korbin right now. My problems can wait," I explain, and he gives me a dark look, full of understanding. I love that with Elias, he just gets what I mean. He knows what I'm feeling like he can feel it himself. And that one kiss with him, just stays on repeat at the back of my mind. I find myself staring at his lips, and then I don't know what happens. I just freeze, pulled into a memory of being defenseless on that bed in Michael's house, and ice starts dripping from my hands.

Safe. Mine keep us safe, my dragon comforts me, and I try to shake the panic off.

"When you're ready to talk about it, let me in. I was brought up in a whorehouse, and it wasn't a pleasant childhood. I might be easier to talk to, than just holding it all in that pretty mind of yours," he says, not looking my way as he speaks. It's hard for him, too, I can feel that. I think my blood bond with them is making my emotions more connected with theirs, and I need to find out more about blood bonds. I know it means we can find each other, no matter where, and we can feel great emotion or physical pain. It's not the same as a mating bond, that bond is far more.

"Why didn't your mum move you out of the whorehouse? Let you live anywhere else?"

"She couldn't afford to after our dad left her. She wasn't always a whore, we know that. It was only the last three years of her life she was in there with us. We were safe, most of the time anyway, but we saw things no kid ever should," he admits, and I only pause for a brief moment before I grab his hand, linking our fingers.

"Your dad left?"

"Yeah, my mum said he left her for another dragon and that was the end of it. He must have been a dragon guard, because we are, but we don't know much else. If I ever see him, I'm going to kill him," he tells me firmly, and I feel his hand warm up in mine. Even though he doesn't have his dragon, his hand can still burn hot. I call my ice to my hand, just to cool it down, and it melts instantly.

"Life seems to like making us stronger before it allows us to be happy," I say, and he squeezes my hand.

"I'm happy with you, even in these little moments I manage to steal. I know you're hurting, and that's on me. Once again, I didn't protect you, and I can't begin to tell you how much I regret it," he says, almost gently, but there is so much anger in his voice that he just can't hide from me. I wish I felt angry, and not just scared of a human. Of what could have happened.

"He was a human, and I still wasn't strong enough to stop him. If Thorne . . ." I stop, feeling hot tears streaming down my face as I talk about what happened for the first time, and I can't even look at Elias.

"It's no secret I dislike Thorne. I think he has his own motives for everything he does and loves no one but himself and his mother. But when I saw him walking through the door with you in his arms, he was so angry, so furious that anyone had tried to hurt you. He was destroyed with his anger and pain for you. I will always owe him for saving you, and I believe he would do anything to keep you alive," Elias tells me, making my eyes drift over to Thorne for a moment. He is watching me, but I can only see his blue eyes as he is hidden in his cloak.

"I still don't trust him. Betrayal changes everything, particularly anything we once had," I say.

"You still don't get what I'm trying to tell you, princess," Elias says, almost teasingly.

"Explain then," I respond, smiling a little.

"Thorne has betrayed everyone that is close to him. His mother. His aunt. You. Everyone . . . but it was *you* he came back for. It was you from the very start, and that's why you should let him, and us, protect you. What happened on Earth, it was all of our fault. I remember feeling like Michael was a threat, and if I had known who I was, I would have killed him before he ever had a chance to lay a finger on you," Elias growls out.

"He didn't . . . you know. Thorne killed him just before he could . . ." I let my voice trail off because I can't say the word. I have to remember I'm in Dragca, not Earth, and that I'm safe from Michael. I don't need to worry or panic. Everything is going to be okay.

"I'm glad to know that, but don't let him win. He is just a bug, a bug your dragon guard stomped on, so you can rise above him. In ten years, a thousand, no one will remember him, but Dragca will always remember you. No matter what happens, they will know you fight for Dragca, for them," Elias firmly tells me, and I nod, agreeing with him as his words fill me with pride. I'm not the only one that will be remembered if I get my way. Elias, Dagan, Korbin, and Thorne should be, too. I ignore the little whisper that drifts in my head, the thought that they will be remembered as my mates.

Minnnee . . . my dragon demands, and her urge to shift and fly brushes against my mind.

It isn't safe. Soon, trust me.

Soon, I want revenge, she growls, before settling down. I focus back on Elias, who is watching my eyes closely.

"I love seeing your sexy eyes shift. They are stunning," he tells me.

"I miss seeing yours, it's like I can feel the emptiness of your dragon," I tell him honestly.

"The last thing I heard my dragon tell me, was to protect you. That you are his," he says softly. "He is happy with the choice I made. He never argued once as I stepped into the portal and said goodbye."

"I don't remember much about Mesmoia as a child, what is the town like?" I ask, needing to change the subject. Elias nods his head in front of me, just as we walk over a small hill.

"Why don't you see for yourself?"

62

ISOLA

I stand still, staring at the massive town of Mesmoia and taking in the beauty of it. I don't remember it being beautiful like this, but then, I was so young when I was last here. It is a town full of blue-slate buildings, a massive clock tower in the center, and a wall surrounding the town that is made of dark blue stone, with five large defence towers in the corners with bright blue fires on the tops of them. Seeing the fires, reminds me of my mum taking me here all those years ago. She loved the fire and how its blue light can be seen from our castle. I look back, seeing there is only one way in and one way out, through the large gates I can barely see from here. I look up as three fire dragons shoot across the sky, flying towards the entrance and shifting back.

"You can't fly in or out of the town. In each tower, there is a seer orb, and it has magic that protects Mesmoia," Melody explains as she stops at my side. "Much like my own orb, it needs a seer to re-fill it with magic every few months. I doubt Mesmoia will have its protection for much longer now that the seers aren't on the side of the throne."

"Amazing, and that might be good for us if we need a quick escape at some point," I say, still staring at the town. There is a surprising amount of trees and large bushes full of flowers all around it, making the town seem more alive than I expected.

"Isola, make sure you keep your hood up, and don't look directly at anyone. You, too, Thorne. You're both too easily recognisable," Melody tells me firmly, just as Korbin coughs, and blood drips down his cheek as I run to him. I wipe the blood off his chin with my sleeve, and tilt his head up, seeing how completely out of it he looks. He doesn't even seem to notice me in front of him, and the purple lines are now covering his face, his neck, and I bet, everywhere else. *How long until the poison kills him?*

"We don't have time, Korbin doesn't have time. Let's hope your friend can help us, or I'm freezing the whole goddamn town until someone does," I say, keeping my voice calm despite the fury flowing through me as I let Korbin rest his head down again. I turn around, walking straight down the path towards Mesmoia. Melody catches up to my side, and Dagan stays on my other as Elias swaps places with him to hold Korbin up. We walk as fast as we can down the hill and come to a group of people that are walking towards the entrance. There are five of them, all in ragged clothes, and they are pulling a cart behind them that has two children on it who don't look in any better of a state. They both have dark-red hair, and one of them sits up to stare at me, pushing her messy hair over her shoulder. I look away, but I know we are too close to let her see me. The kid might have seen my eyes, or even a little bit of my hair. Or I might be para-noid. . . who knows?

"Come here, kitty cat," Dagan holds an arm out for me, and I quickly realise he wants to hold me close to keep me hidden. I step closer, letting him slide an arm around my waist, and I bend my head close to his chest, breathing in his smoky scent. I keep looking to the side as we walk behind the people and their cart, the children still watching us.

"Guards," Dagan whispers close to me, his lips gently brushing the tip of my ear, and I inch my hand to his sword on instinct. I know I can pull it out and attack anyone to get us a distraction to escape. I briefly look up after I feel us starting to walk on stone to see five dragon guards at the gate. They watch us all for a second before another guard walks over to them, and they get distracted talking to each other. I look away just in case I catch any of their gazes, and, thankfully, none of them stop us as we walk straight into the town and join the crowds of people. I lift my head, still keeping close to Dagan's side as I look around. Dozens of people surround us, a mixture of red, black, and brown-haired dragons. Some dragon guards are in their dragon leather, and nearly everyone else has cloaks on, covering themselves up. I spot people huddled together on the ground near a building, begging for food or money, but people walk past them like they aren't even there. The cracked blue-stone path we walk down leads to the clock tower right in the middle of town. The tower is surrounded by little stalls selling foods, powders, clothing, and many other things. There is so much colour, so much life . . . it's amazing and nothing like any human town I've ever seen.

"This way," Dagan pulls at my waist, leading me and the others past all the stalls. We get to an alleyway behind the tower that looks dark, and Dagan walks us down it. We get to the other end which opens up into a quieter part of Mesmoia, and there is a water fountain. I pause, remembering this place as I stare at the stone dragon, the water shooting out of its mouth and spraying into the fountain. The water isn't blue like Earth, it's more of a purple colour. I know humans can't drink the water here; it would kill them and has done so many times. Dragca isn't made for humans, I guess.

"I met you and Elias right here, didn't I?" I ask Dagan, and he nods, making me walk past it and over to a row of small, blue-stone houses like he can't stand for me to stare at where we met for too long. "What's the rush?"

"We need to get inside, but yes," Dagan says, but he doesn't seem to want to linger here for long. Not that I can blame him.

Dagan walks us to the house on the very end, with a white door and a dragon-shaped silver knocker, which he knocks a few times. We all wait for what seems like a long time, but is likely only seconds, before the door is pulled open, and an old man stands in front of us. The man has long grey hair plaited in one long plait, and brown trousers, with a brown cloak covering his white shirt underneath. The cloak has a silver dragon crest, my father's crest. My family's crest. It almost hurts to see it, a reminder of how that crest doesn't symbolise the throne anymore. He looks between us all slowly, before scrutinizing me, pausing at Thorne, and his eyes landing on Dagan with a long suffering sigh.

"You bring trouble to my door, boy," the old man states tightly, tipping his head at me.

"Darth, I wouldn't come unless I had nowhere else. Korbin is dying, we need help," Dagan tells him, and he looks over at Korbin, pausing.

"Is that Janiya and Phelan's kid?" Darth asks, seeming curious as he squints his eyes. "They have been looking for him. There's a big reward for his safe return."

"Yes, and you can have the reward, if you help us," Elias says firmly, and Darth steps back, holding the door open.

"You best get him in here then, boy, and the princess, too. We don't allow royalty to stand outside in the cold in this house. My wife would be turning in her grave if I allowed that," Darth mutters, ushering us into his house. I walk in after Dagan, and Melody follows.

"Take him to a bed upstairs," Darth says. We wait as Thorne and Elias carry Korbin into the house and take him straight up the stairs. Darth closes the door behind them, mumbling something under his breath that I don't quite manage to catch. The house is all one massive room downstairs as I look around. The back of the room is the kitchen, with a large fireplace, and then there is the lounge, with two ratty brown sofas and a worn-down rug. There are hole-filled curtains on the windows, which

Dagan goes around and closes, so the only light is from the fireplace.

"Now, kid, you'd best start telling me the story of what happened while I find my medicine box," Darth grouses, heading for the kitchen.

"You're a healer?" I ask as he opens a cupboard and starts pulling random pieces of paper, old unrecognizable junk, and some saucepans out. I watch as he chucks them on the floor one by one, making a huge mess. I briefly look at Dagan and Melody, who are watching Darth like I am, wondering why he has so much junk as Darth finally answers me.

"Back in the old days, yes. I worked for your father as a royal healer, until I got too old," he deeply chuckles.

"That's how you knew who I am?" I ponder.

"No, I saw your eyes. They are the mirror image of your mother's, that's how I knew. That's how anyone would recognise you. You should hide those eyes, princess Isola. Then again, it's much like how I knew one of your guards is the son of the current queen. He has her eyes also, well, before the darkness spread into them," he tells us, never pausing as he moves to another cupboard and starts chucking things out of that one, too.

"You knew my mother when she was younger?" Thorne asks, walking down the stairs having clearly overheard our conversation.

"I knew both of your mothers as children, when they were friends, before jealousy got involved and darkness entered Tatarina's heart. We all watched as your father chose your mother over Tatarina, which was the start of her heart being destroyed with darkness," he pauses to look back at us, noticing our shock. "Such a shame, she was so young for darkness to take its hold, but then she was weak."

"Lies! My mother didn't know the queen, they weren't friends!" Thorne exclaims, and I place my hand on his shoulder on instinct; a need to comfort him, and his eyes flash to my hand before he looks up.

"It makes sense. They were the last ice princesses, and there was only my father they could marry. They would have made them all grow up together, like my father did with me and Jace. That's where he must have gotten the idea from in the first place," I say gently, and Thorne nods, anger in his eyes as he stares down at me.

"She lied to me then. My mother said she never met the queen, not once," he growls.

"You mother lied about a lot of things, you silly boy," Darth chuckles, and Thorne pulls away from me, storming out the door as Darth still laughs. "So much anger, if he doesn't control it, he will end up as bitter as his mother."

"No, he won't," I snap.

"Ah, I see. He belongs to you . . . well, you should tell him the truth. Lies do not make a relationship, they only destroy it," Darth tells me. "Ah, here it is." I watch as he pulls a big box out of the back of the cupboard, holding it up just as Elias runs down the stairs.

"Something's wrong, Korbin needs help! Now!" Elias shouts out, and we all run up the stairs with Darth following. My heart pounds, feeling like it could be destroyed at any second if I lose Korbin.

63

ISOLA

"**M**ove," Darth pushes Elias out of the way in the hallway, opening the first door to the right and entering the dimly lit room. I follow Elias in, seeing Darth holding Korbin down on the bed by his shoulders as his whole body shakes. Korbin's eyes are rolled back, blood drips from the corner of his mouth, and when I hear him cry my name in pain, I nearly fall to my knees with panic.

"Oh god," I whisper, not feeling attached to my own body as I mentally pray Korbin will make it through this. I can't lose him. I just can't. I don't notice the ice spreading under my feet until Elias nearly slips on it as he rushes into the room. Darth opens the big box he placed on the floor, pulling out a small blue bottle that has white liquid inside. He gets a needle, extracting the liquid. I feel two hands on my shoulders, one is Dagan and the other is Melody, I instinctively know from the way my dragon relaxes a tad at their touch. Darth rubs his face, looking over at us and back at Korbin after a moment.

"Show me where he was poisoned, girl. Elias, hold him down," he orders.

"Can we do anything?" Dagan asks.

"You and the seer girl, go and get hot water from the middle of town. There is gold on the fireplace in the pot, you can pay me back later," Darth tells us, and I rush forward at the same time Elias does. I hear the others rush down the stairs in the background, but I can't focus on them as I watch Elias get closer to Korbin. I know they aren't as close as Dagan is to Kor, but I can see the worry flash across Elias's eyes when he briefly glances at me. Elias holds his shoulders firmly, as I lift Korbin's shirt up and try not to feel sick at the awful smell coming from the now black cut on his stomach. The lines are crawling from the cut, all over his chest and spreading in every direction. Some are massive purple lines and others are tiny little ones.

"Oh mighty. We have work to do," Darth almost chuckles, like a crazy person, before slamming the needle straight into the cut without pausing once. Korbin calls out my name several times, and I grasp his hand, not knowing what else I can do. Korbin gradually stops shaking, settling down but still out of it as Darth pulls the needle out and places it on the side.

"He needs blood and a bond made, or he dies," Darth says simply, looking straight towards me.

"We have shared blood before and have a bond, he can have mine," I reply, knowing that I don't care about sharing blood with Korbin. Even if we weren't bonded already, I would still happily give him my blood.

"It will make you weak, and with the amount of blood he will need, it will create a permanent bond," Darth warns me, and my eyes flash to Elias, who simply nods. I know he will support me no matter what I choose. I look down at Korbin and squeeze his hand tighter.

"I know you're not awake to make this decision, but I will save you," I tell him and look up to Darth who is watching us with a sad smile.

"We are permanent, anyway. I will *not* lose him," I say, keeping my eyes locked on Darth's, and he nods, a small smile on his lips.

"Let's get you all set up in the other room then. I will take as much blood as I can without hurting you, every two hours. Our dragons speed up blood loss, and that should be okay for Korbin. This isn't a fix for the poison, but it will give me time to examine and figure out what he needs to heal him," Darth explains to me and Elias.

"Take what you need," I reply.

"Your dragon needs to be okay with this, is she?" Darth enquires, "I don't want an angry dragon bursting out in my room and freezing me."

"*Save minnnee,*" my dragon hisses in response, and I watch Darth almost smile as he sees my eyes change.

"She will do anything to save him. We have always been in agreement about my guards," I reply, and I feel Elias gently stroke my arm with his fingers.

"Right then, let's get started," Darth says, picking up a bundle of things from a box and walking out of the room. I move closer to Korbin, leaning down and kissing his sweaty, boiling hot forehead and hearing him mumble my name.

"I'm here. I'm always here for you, Kor," I tell him gently, seeing him slowly relax and his breathing even out before I straighten up. I don't want to leave him, but I know I have to. Elias waits for me by the door, holding it open with his back. I slip past him, and he stops me, grabbing my hip with his one hand and using the other to place a finger under my chin, making me look up into his swirling blue eyes. I raise my hand, moving a stray piece of black hair out of his eyes and trailing my finger down his face as he carefully watches me.

"He will survive this, for you. Don't look so scared, I hate seeing it in your eyes," Elias admits in a whisper.

"I've never felt like this, not for anyone until I met you three. I thought losing Jace devastated me, but I know if I lose any of you, I would be completely ruined," I say gently, placing my hand on Elias's chest. He closes his eyes, leaning forward to rest his forehead against mine. The little contact soothes me, reminds me that I have them and that they are not going anywhere.

"Neither have I ever felt like I do for you, and it scares the fuck out of me, princess. You know, I thought I was brave and fearless, but I'm *nothing* compared to you. You make me so proud with how brave you are. You are my inspiration to keep fighting, to push through, even though I've fought my whole life for nothing but survival," he whispers, as I watch him so closely, taking in every part of his complexion, his handsome features as he makes my heart flutter in my chest.

"Eli," I sigh, my emotions leaking out into that one word, and he moves a tiny inch closer as he opens his eyes.

"Excuse me. Now, I don't need to see you two kissing when I have things I need to be doing, like saving your friend's life," Darth's slightly amused voice comes over to us, and Elias backs away, letting me pass through the door. Darth is standing in the open doorway of the room opposite, and nods his head towards me, inviting me in.

"I'm going to keep an eye out downstairs," Elias tells me as I look back at him, seeing desire and longing swirling in his eyes but knowing there isn't anything we can do about it right now. Something always seems to come between us, every time we start to get close. It's like fate is finding it fun to keep us apart, with only brushes of stolen kisses to keep us going. Elias turns, walking down the stairs as I go into the small bedroom where Darth is waiting for me. There isn't much in here, but it's cosy. There is a double bed, with torn blue sheets covering it and matching blue curtains on the window. In the window is a vase of flowers, but they are all dead and look like they have been there for years.

"Sit on the bed, girl," Darth says distractedly as he looks through his box that he has placed on the floor. I watch him searching through the box, taking things out and putting others back, so focused on the job at hand, and all I can think about is how he knew my mother once. There aren't that many people alive who knew her and a deep part of me wants to know as much as I can about her. I guess I could ask about my father at the same time, but I don't. Every time I think about him, I just remember Melody. How my father betrayed my mother, had a child with another woman, and couldn't even man up enough to tell me about her.

"What was my mother like? If you don't mind me asking. It's only, I don't remember much, and there is no one alive to tell me more things about her," I ask.

"Tatarina is alive and knew your mother more than anyone, well, before she married your father at least. After the marriage, they never spoke because of your father," he says, with a slight chuckle as he carries a handful of things over to the bed, placing them next to me and sitting next to them. "Take your cloak off and pull your right arm sleeve up." I do what he asks and place the cloak on the pillow. Darth taps the inside of my arm a few times before sliding a needle inside and taping it down. The needle has a long tube connected to it, that goes into a jar.

"Are all these clean?" I ask, seeing that the jar isn't a great colour and doubt the needle is.

"Clean as we can get when we are poor and not in the castle. Your dragon blood will keep you alive, do not worry. You aren't human after all," he says, watching my blood pour into the jar. I decide to leave it for now. It doesn't much matter, like he said, and I have to stop thinking like a human. I remember his comment about Tatarina and decide to answer it.

"Tatarina would sooner kill me than tell me anything about my mother. Not that I could trust a word she speaks, anyway," I say, still not fully processing the fact that mine and Thorne's mothers were so close.

"There isn't much to tell, not much you do not already know. Vivian was kind and gentle . . . and honestly, not built to be a queen. She couldn't make the hard decisions, and a simple life would have been better for her, but she was oh, so beautiful. No man could resist her, much like her daughter seems to have caught the hearts of many also," he says, not looking at me as he stares out of the window, lost in his thoughts and likely his memories. I instantly feel jealous that I can't see his memories of my mother.

"Do you think someone kind and gentle shouldn't have the throne?" I ask.

"No, someone who is brave, selfless, strict, and kind should have the throne. They would be best to make the decisions they will face. Yet, we cannot get all those things in one person," he muses.

"I have to take the throne back from Tatarina," I whisper into the now silent room.

"Yes, but it will not be easy. Tatarina was one of the selected before she became queen, and her son later killed the king." I go to correct him, that Tatarina killed my father, but decide not to as I don't want to interrupt him. "She has always been in power and knows Dragca better than anyone else. Well, perhaps not as well as her son, but he is not strong enough to rule and kill his mother." I don't directly reply, but when he looks over at me, I know he feels my agreement to his statement in my eyes. Thorne is smart, but he cares too much for his mother to do what is right in the end. He is blinded when it comes to her, and I'm anxious about telling him what I know of his mother, worried he won't believe me.

"Why is she like this?" I have to ask, because I want to understand what happened to make her so cruel. She sent someone to kill my mother, a childhood friend, and then she mated to the husband left behind. Only someone truly evil could do something like that. Only someone with no soul.

"Some say a dark spirit came to her on the day of the royal mating between your father and mother. Her jealousy, hate, and anger called out to the dark spirit, and since then her heart has been darkened. I truly believe it. I saw Tatarina a few years back, and even her appearance is darker than it's ever been. Her blonde hair is a mustard colour, and her light-blue eyes are now a dark-blue."

"So, the dark spirit, the darkness has changed her?" I ask.

"Yes, and I believe when you start using your light powers, you will change, too," he says, and I wonder if he is right. I guess I will know soon, when I finally get the time to start using the light. I may be scared of its unpredictability, but I'm not stupid enough not to recognize that I can't beat Tatarina without it.

"Can any part of her be saved?" I ask, thinking only of Thorne. She is still his mother, and I know what it's like to lose one. Thorne has already lost his birth father, his adoptive parents, and his aunt. Even if most of them deserved their deaths, he doesn't deserve to lose another relative if it can be avoided.

"He is better off without her alive. The world is. Child, I know little of light and dark spirits, but where there is one, there must be another," he smiles, looking down at the jar that is half full.

"The darkness must be destroyed," I whisper, and he flashes me a sad smile.

"You cannot destroy something that has existed before Dragca, before life, before even time, itself. Darkness and light are equally needed and equally cursed by one another," he tells me, but still seems sad to do so. I don't reply as I look out the window he was looking out of, seeing the two suns high in the sky and how bright they look. Sun comes before the night, and light comes with darkness. *God, my life is starting to sound like a movie, and I won't be surprised if something else goes wrong at this point.*

64

ISOLA

"How is Korbin doing?" I ask groggily, lifting my head from the pillow as Melody steps into the room with a small tray full of food. I rub my arm as Bee flies out of her bag, coming over to me and landing on my hip. She sits down as Melody puts the food on the dresser. I'm not really hungry because the blood loss is making me feel sick, but I will try to eat later.

"Dagan is with him, and he still hasn't woken. The healer is doing his best," she answers, but not really answering the question I asked. I want to know if he is doing better, if he looks better, or anything other than the fact he hasn't woken up yet. It's been a day since we got here, and I've done countless blood exchanges. I lie back on the pillow, feeling Bee stroking my arm as I look at my sister. She doesn't have her cloak on now, and her black hair is down, covering her serious expression as she opens her bag. The look on her face somewhat reminds me of my father. Well, *our* father. Something I don't know how to get used to.

"Did Thorne come back?" I ask.

"He is back, and not speaking to anyone. He just spent the last half an hour cleaning the kitchen," she tells me.

"I didn't know he cleaned," I say aimlessly.

"Tired?" Bee asks me, distracting me from my thoughts as she slides off me and chooses to lie on the bed right next to me instead.

"Yeah, a little. Are you okay?" I ask her, and she nods, curling up in a little ball.

"We need light . . . soon . . . darkness is rising," she mumbles, yawning loudly before falling to sleep. *Nothing like some cryptic, scary words from a spirit to make you feel better.* I pull the blanket up, covering her body before looking over at Melody who holds her orb. I'd seen them at a distance when I was a kid, but I never really understood them or what connection they have to seers. Most seers have their orbs on a sceptre, which I remember seeing many seers walking around with them like a walking stick. Suddenly, I remember Melody's mother as a flashback flitters into my mind.

"PRINCESS, you should not be out here alone," a warm, kind voice says from just behind me, and I spin around, looking up at the royal seer. She has long black hair, brown eyes, and black swirls on her face that look like someone drew on her.

"I had to put the bird outside, it flew into my room," I explain, holding the little bird up to show her, and she smiles.

"That is very kind of you, but you should still have guards with you. You are the princess, and so very important to Dragca. Let's put the bird down and find your personal guards," she says, holding out a hand. I put the bird down on the floor, watching as it hops a little before flying away. I accept the seer's hand, smiling up at her as we walk back through the gardens.

"Your name isn't seer, is it?" I ask, curious.

"No, why do you think that?" she replies.

"Everyone calls you 'seer', or 'royal seer'. It's confusing," I say, gigging a little, and it makes her laugh.

"My name is Savannah."

. . .

THE MEMORY LEAVES my mind as I look back over to Melody, who is staring into her orb. Her eyes glow a warm bright blue, and she carefully places her hand on the orb as sadness washes over her face. She looks so much like her mother. They have the same features, and the same mysterious air seems to surround her, just like it did her mother. Everything good about her seems to have come from her mother, and luckily, she only seems to have my father's eyes. I'm starting to believe my father was never the good guy in any situation. Maybe everyone isn't good or bad though, and my father had good parts in him.

"Bee tried to help Darth heal Korbin, but it didn't work. Bee said the poison is from the dark, and that it is immune to light," Melody tells me, and I frown. How are we going to stop it from killing Korbin, then?

"What did Darth say when he saw her?" I ask, stroking Bee's green hair. It's so soft, fine, and full of glitter.

"He wasn't that shocked. He said he once saw Tatarina's dark spirit, and a light one isn't all that different," she says, and goes back to focusing on the orb. I guess that makes sense. I wonder what makes dark and light spirits look different? I'm curious to find out, but at the same time, I don't want to have to fight the dark.

"What do orbs do?" I ask, snapping her out of the connection she has going with the orb, and she looks up, not bothering to hide the sad look.

"Boosts our natural powers, allows us to see people, but we have to have a connection to who we want to see. It's how I could watch you when you were on earth," Melody explains and stands up, walking over to me. She climbs onto the bed on my other side, and I pull myself up, careful not to wake Bee. I sit with my back against the headboard, with Melody snuggled in right next to me.

"Who were you looking at just now?" I ask gently.

"Hallie," she whispers, confusing me.

"I thought you needed a connection? I didn't know you and Hallie were connected by anything other than fake memories," I say. Melody places her hand on the side of the orb, her eyes glow as smoke fills the inside of the orb, swirling around and around before an image comes into view. The image starts off blurry, then fills out. Hallie is sitting at a desk in what looks like an office. There isn't much in the room, just a grey desk, filing cabinets, and I can see a door behind her. Hallie isn't moving, just staring at the wall, tapping her fingers on the desk. Her hair is dyed purple at the tips, not the blue it was when I last saw her, and she has glasses on, no contacts, which instantly worries me. Hallie hates to wear her glasses.

"Her father has had her locked in this room for the last two weeks. No bed. Little food, and plenty of interrogation from both him and the people that work with him," Melody says, her voice cracking ever so slightly.

"What?" I ask in alarm, looking back down at Hallie. She looks normal like she usually does, though maybe a little paler and tired. The door opens, and a man I don't know walks in, just as smoke fills the orb, and the image disappears.

"Wait, who was that?" I ask Melody. "Actually, that doesn't matter, we need to rescue her from her father!" Melody gently places her hand on my shoulder, stopping me from trying to get up even when how weak I feel stops me anyway.

"If I could do anything to help her, I would have already. There is nothing you can do, and he won't kill her. That's all that matters," she says, but her excuse seems weak. She wants to help, but I don't get why she is so emotional about this.

"Who is Hallie to you?" I ask quietly.

"I told you that I saw my future girlfriend once?" she asks, and it clicks into place as I remember Melody mentioned that she never sees herself in visions, except for one of her and her future girlfriend.

"Hallie is your future girlfriend?" I ask.

"Yep. Sucks that she isn't into girls right now, or at least, she hasn't admitted it to herself. With everything that will happen, I don't know if we will ever have a future like I saw," she says, and wipes one shaky hand across her cheek. It must be horrible to watch someone you know is destined for you with other people and now being hurt.

"You will," I grab her hand on the orb, and it burns where my fingers graze the orb, making me sharply pull my hand away. I look down at my hand and see little burn marks. Fire doesn't burn me . . . but the orb can?

"Crap, sorry. I didn't expect you to touch it. Orbs burn any dragon. They can't be touched by your kind," she explains, moving the orb away a little like she is worried I would be crazy enough to try and touch it again.

"I've never been burnt before," I whisper, kind of amazed.

"I forget you don't know much about Dragca . . . most dragons know not to touch orbs," she chuckles which makes me smile.

"Where did you get your orb from?" I ask.

"It was my mother's. Orbs are passed down within families, well, usually. If the family has no heirs for the orb, it is returned to where all orbs come from," she says.

"Where?" I ask.

"No one knows. I've heard they just disappear," she replies, shrugging her shoulders and making her black hair fall over them.

"That's sad," I comment.

"I thought I wouldn't be able to touch the orb, being half dragon, but, apparently, my dragon side didn't stop my inheritance," she states. I bet she was nervous to try and touch it the first time.

"Do you hear your dragon in your mind?" I ask her, curious. I can't smell dragon on her, not like you would expect. I can only smell her seer side, so her dragon side must be well hidden.

"No. I've never had that, or any powers from my ice dragon

side, except one," she smiles, looking at my hand. "I can't be burnt either."

"That's a good power to receive," I say.

"Can I give you some advice? As your loving sister, as well as someone that wants you back on the throne," she asks, and I nod.

"I wouldn't flaunt your relationships with your dragon guards. If you want the seers to side with you, and if you want the dragons to, you can't be seen to be in love with dragon guards who have no dragons. You can't be seen to publicly choose them over the throne. They are a weakness to you now, one that can and will be used against you by your enemies. Don't let everyone see what they mean to you, don't wear your emotions on your face quite so much," she advises me.

"I don't want to hide how I feel, it's not going to change anything, and I *would* choose them over the throne. If they can't accept my dragon guards as my–" I go to say 'mates' when I realise they have never asked me to mate with them.

"Mates. They will be your mates, I don't need a vision to know that's what you want from those smoking hot dragons, sis," she teases, and I laugh.

"It's all still so new to us, and everything is going wrong. It's not the right time to be planning long-term stuff when none of us knows what our future will hold," I say.

"What do you *want* for your future?"

"I guess I don't really think that far ahead anymore. Everything has become a fight for each day, and it never leaves me time to dream of an ending to this. I guess I only want the dragon guards' curse to be broken, for Kor to live, and for me to kill Tatarina. Those are my main concerns for now," I tell her.

"The seers might know how to break the curse, or at least they might have an idea."

"Really? I could get back their dragons?"

"Maybe, but you need the seers to side with you first. You need them to believe you are the rightful queen, and one who will always put Dragca first before *anything* else," she firmly tells me. I know she has a point, yet I don't want the seers' decision to side with me based on lies. I don't want the throne if deceit and half-truths are the only way to overthrow Tatarina and secure the crown.

"How do you feel about Thorne now?" Melody enquires, trying to sound innocent, but the tiny smirk on her lips gives her away.

"He betrayed me, and then he saved me. I guess I don't know. Thorne has always had the uncanny ability to confuse me, even from the very first time we met. It's strange, because even when he is pushing me away, betraying me, and downright being an idiot, I still want to be near him. I know I could never hurt him, and what's worse is that I understand *why* he did everything he did. I don't forgive him yet, but I do understand most of it," I admit, and she takes my hand, leaving the orb in her lap.

"Love doesn't care about circumstances. It just turns up, wrecks your life, and somehow has the ability to make you the happiest you can ever be," she says.

"My sister is pretty smart, huh?" I gently bump her shoulder, and she laughs.

"About time you noticed," she says with a grin and rests her head on my shoulder.

"When we don't have all this stuff going on, and our lives are kind of sorted . . . I want to get to know you, find out more about your life. We missed out on a childhood together, but we can make up for that," I comment.

"Deal," she whispers.

"Pinky promise?" I ask, holding out my pinky finger and wiggling it, and she frowns at me like I've lost my mind. Whoops, I forgot seers wouldn't know about human things.

"What is that?" she asks slowly.

"Something humans do on Earth that means you promise never to break the promise. I know it's silly, but there were these siblings I grew up at human school with. They always pinky promised things, and I used to be jealous I never had a sister or brother to do that with," I explain to her. Jace wouldn't do it with me, because he didn't like things that humans came up with and said the idea was stupid. Melody links her pinky finger with mine.

"I pinky promise," she says, and all I can do is grin.

65

ISOLA

"Y ou should be resting, girl. It's the middle of the night," Darth chides as I step into Korbin's room, and I softly close the door behind me. Darth is sitting on a chair next to Korbin's bed, but I barely even register his presence. Korbin is sitting up on the bed, his green eyes watching me as his lips tilt up with a little smile.

"She was never good at doing what she was told," Korbin teases, his voice croaky as I run over to him and wrap my arms around his chest.

"You're awake," I say, pulling back, and he smiles widely, looking as happy as I feel at seeing him awake. Korbin still has purple lines crawling up his face, close to his eyes, and he looks extremely pale, but he is awake, and that's an improvement. Any improvement seems like a blessing right now.

"I'm tired, but trying to stay awake for a bit," he says groggily, and I kiss him lightly before sitting back. I hold onto his hand as I look over at Darth.

"Is he going to be okay now?" I ask, and Darth shakes his head.

"A temporary fix. I don't have the magic, or the right medicine to heal him, and I have no advice on where you can find it,"

Darth admits and looks at Korbin. "Your parents . . . they might be able to help, or at least pay for the right kind of help."

"They will be with the seers, and we are going that way anyway," Korbin says.

"Then I will come with you to keep you alive. We will leave in the morning," Darth states, standing up slowly.

"Why are you so willing to help me?" Korbin asks.

"Your parents, I knew them very well. We had a falling out many, many years ago. Let's just say I owe them, and keeping their only son alive is a good start at repayment," Darth explains and then leaves the room as we silently watch him go. I look back up at Korbin, just running my eyes over him to check he is okay. Just needing to see that he is, at least for now.

"Lie with me? I just want to hold you for a bit," Korbin asks, and I do, resting my head on his chest.

"Dagan and Elias told me about what my father said to you. They said my father trusted your parents," I whisper, yet my voice still feels like it carries around the room.

"I wanted to tell you sooner. Every morning, running with you, and keeping a secret from you, it wasn't easy because I fell for you the moment we met. I knew your father was right, that the prophecy was right, as soon as I met you, and I wanted you safe from that moment on," he slowly tells me.

"I felt something from the very start, too. I did with you all, but I tried to play it off because I was grieving over Jace," I voice something I haven't even wanted to admit to myself. It feels like I betrayed Jace by just feeling it, much less saying it out loud.

"I'm sorry Jace died, I have a feeling I would have liked him. You know, after we fought over you and agreed we could both love you at the same time," he jokes, and I sigh.

"Jace would have kicked all your asses," I mutter, but I'm not actually sure who would have won.

"I don't doubt he would have tried. I wouldn't want to share you, not if I met you first and had you to myself for so long," he muses.

"Are you okay with everything? The fact that I want to be with Elias and Dagan, too?" I ask quietly after a comfortable silence between us.

"At first, no. I couldn't swallow the thought of sharing you and having you love someone else. I was scared you would love them more than me," he tells me, his hand holding mine tightly.

"That won't happen," I say, looking up at him, and he stares up at the ceiling.

"Then I realised something. You loved them anyway, had the whole time we were together, and you still loved me the same. Loving more than one person doesn't make you love less, it just makes you love more," he says, his words making me smile like a crazy person because they are so sweet. And so true.

"Such a romantic. If you weren't ill, then I'd be swooning and doing sexy things to you," I say, making him laugh.

"I'll hold you to that offer when I'm better, doll," he whispers. "Thank you for saving me, giving me all that blood when you knew it would make our bond stronger. We never did have a second to talk about that."

"You did it for me once, how could I not do the same for you?" I reply.

"One day, when we have a moment to ourselves . . . would you mate with me?" he asks suddenly, casually like he didn't just ask something very important and life changing. I sharply sit up, leaning over him. My hair falls like a curtain around us as I stare down at him.

"Really? You want me? Forever?" I ask, completely in shock. *He must still be ill.*

"You have me forever, even if we don't mate. I don't care what I am to you, mate, lover, friend, or even ex-lover. I just want to be with you," he says, and I go to answer him when the door bursts open behind us. I jerk up to see Elias running in.

"The guards are searching the houses. They know we are here, we have to go!" Elias shouts, panicked, and runs over to help me get Korbin up as I slide off him. Korbin holds an arm around my shoulder, and the other on Elias as we hurry out of the room and down the stairs.

"Isola needs to fly everyone out, it's the only way," I hear Darth demand as we get to the bottom of the stairs.

"She can't fly us all, and the barrier . . ." Thorne shakes his head as he watches out the window, not looking back at us once as he speaks.

"I *can* fly all of you, at least far enough to make it out of the town. I'll land in the forest, and we can run and hide," I say, sending the thought to my dragon. I know she is bigger than most dragons and strong. Let's hope strong enough as I'm not leaving anyone behind to deal with the guards.

"*Yes, but not far. Tired,*" she replies, sending worry crashing into my head.

"I can drop the barrier for a second, I just need my orb to touch it. It will knock me out though, as it's a lot of magic," Melody explains. "It will also let the seer who made the barrier know where we are. They might look for us, which would be a good thing."

"We will protect you after you destroy the barrier," Dagan tells her, and I nod at her in confirmation.

"They are two doors away," Thorne says, shutting the curtain quickly and stepping away.

"We go into the garden, and Isola you need to shift quickly. Everyone ready?" Darth commands us all, picking up a bag and walking to the fireplace. He picks up a small picture frame, kissing it once before sliding it into his bag.

"Sorry about this, man, but we need a quick escape," Elias says, picking Korbin up by the waist and flinging him over his shoulder. "What the hell do you eat, you weigh a ton," Elias groans.

"Asshole," Korbin groggily replies as we walk to the back door. I go to step out when a hand stops me, and I look up to see it's Thorne.

"Let me go first, we don't know if anyone is out there," he commands, like I should listen to his every word.

"That's why I should go first," I mutter, glaring at his back as he gently pushes past me and out of the door. I don't wait as I follow him out, seeing a stone garden filled with stone ornaments of dragons, wings, and various other beautiful things. They all look handmade, and clearly someone put a lot of effort into making this garden as beautiful as it is.

"I'm going to break everything by shifting out here," I say to no one in particular.

"I'd rather you break my wife's statues than the guards break us. Get on with the shift, girl!" Darth barks out, and I nod sadly at him. I walk straight into the middle of the garden and close my eyes, letting my dragon take over. When I open my eyes, everything is sharper, and I look over to see everyone standing at the door. My dragon lowers herself down, crushing the statues as she does, and even my dragon seems to realise. Elias climbs up my wing first, followed by Dagan, Melody, Darth, and Thorne last.

"Over here!" I hear someone shout. My sensitive ears pick up the sound from what could be a good distance away, but regardless, they know we are here, and we can't fight them like this.

"Fly straight up, close enough for Melody to touch the barrier, but don't let yourself touch it. I don't want you hurt," I say to my dragon, and she bats her wings out, flying up in the air and knocking a stone wall over on her way up.

"Shoot her! Don't let her fly away!" I hear a guard scream, and then dozens of arrows fly at us, hitting our right wing and making my dragon roar. She turns around, mid-flight.

"Freeze," I hear her hiss, and I don't disagree as she shoots a blast of ice at the guards, freezing them all on the spot while they try to reload their arrows. Two guards manage to escape, and I see them shifting moments before they fly up into the air, breathing out fire.

"Get to the barrier! We can't fight them with the others on our backs!"

I try to reason with her, and thankfully, she does as I ask, speeding away even when her wing hurts from the arrows that fall away in the wind. She gets close to the barrier, gliding in the air as streams of fire hit our tail from the dragons following us. My dragon turns her head back in time to see Melody place her orb against the barrier, holding it firmly in place as the orb flashes brightly. A white light blasts out, blinding us all for a moment, and then the barrier falls away in little blue sparks.

"Fly away! Now!" I plead with my dragon, and she flies off, straight into the woods. I hear her cry reverberate in my ears as the forest gets a little blurry, and the surrounding sounds seem to buzz against our ears. I know her wing is hurt, and she can't last long, but those dragons must still be following us. The last thing I'm aware of before darkness claims me is my dragon plummeting, crashing into the forest, and the screams of our passengers as she falls.

66

DAGAN

I brush the dirt and hair out of my face, jumping up off the ground as everything swirls for a moment, and I try to focus on what happened. Isola was flying one second, and then crashing the next. Something had to be wrong for her to fall like that. Thank god, we weren't too high when she turned on her side and dropped us in the trees. I quickly scan my surroundings, knowing I need to find her and seeing no one else near me.

"Isola!" I shout, and no one replies. Shit. A guard steps out from behind a tree, holding a sword, and smirking when he sees me. I quickly pull out my own sword, holding it at my side as I examine the guard. He is young and fairly small. I doubt he is trained well from the way he rushed out here rather than planning out his attack.

"Bring it on," I say, wanting to get this out of the way. He rushes at me, lifting his sword behind his neck and slamming it down on mine, and I elbow his face when he lets his guard down for a second. I kick his stomach as he drops his sword in shock and falls on the floor. I pick up his sword, walking over and holding it against his neck.

"Don't shift, don't move. Now, you can run away and deal

with the queen hunting you, or you die by my hand now," I warn.

"I-I had no choice. The queen made my father join the dragon guard. She said she would kill my mother if he didn't. I have four brothers, and we all got cursed with him," he replies.

"I am truly sorry for that, but make your choice," I honestly tell him.

"I will run," he says dejectedly, his voice an echo as I watch his whole body glow red for a second, and then I see the pain in his eyes. His dragon knows the queen knows he has betrayed her. She will send guards to hunt him now. The curse always makes sure the ruler knows when they have been betrayed. Which means I need him to run and get as far away from Isola and me as possible.

"Run and don't stop running," I say, moving my sword away, and he runs into the forest, never looking back once.

"Watch out!" I hear Melody shout, and I look up just in time to see her jump down. I quickly move out the way as I put my sword back in its sheath and throw the other in a nearby bush.

"You okay?" I ask her, and she shakily nods. Bee flies down to us, following Melody.

"Isola?" Bee asks, searching for her in the trees and frowning.

"Bee, can you fly up and see if you can find anyone? If you notice any other dragons, don't let them see you," Melody asks her, and she nods, flying up the tree.

"Isola was hurt, we need to find her," I state.

"Agreed. We need to find the others and get out of here. The guards will be searching for us," Melody tells me what I already know. Thankfully, at least one of them isn't searching for us, and there were only two that shifted and followed us. That only leaves one guard, and I'm hopeful he won't find us. We wait silently until Bee flies down, sitting on Melody's shoulder.

"That way," Bee points to our left, where we can see nothing but more trees, and we have no choice but to trust her.

"Keep your eyes open," I tell Melody, who nods, sliding a

dagger out her pocket as I pull my sword out. We carefully step through the trees, our feet crunching on branches with every step, and I'm way too aware of how loud we are being. Any guards would be able to hear us with their sensitive hearing from their dragons. We trudge through the forest until we come to a clearing of smashed trees that leads to a little cliff, and I know Isola must have crashed here and skidded all the way down. I run out of the clearing, only seeing more trees at the bottom of the cliff.

"Damn, we will have to climb down," I say, rubbing my jaw.

"Dagan!" I hear my name shouted, and I turn, freezing at the sight of a man I don't know holding Isola in his arms. She is unconscious, her head hangs from one of his arms, but she doesn't look dead, though blood drips down her right arm. It doesn't look good, not with the three arrow marks I can see from here. The man keeps his eyes on me, and I see that he is massive, with dark-red hair and red tattoos littered down his arms. I breathe a sigh of relief that she is alive, and step forward, only pausing when Melody stops me.

"Give her to us," I demand.

"No," the man says simply, a large grin spreading across his face as he looks down at Isola. *The fucker.*

"Enough. We didn't come here to discuss anything, and we cannot stay long," a woman says, stepping out of the shadows of the trees. About twenty other people follow out after her, all covered in weapons, and they aren't dragon guards. I keep my eyes on the woman that spoke. The way she stands slightly in front of them all tells me all I need to know; she is the leader here. The woman has long black hair, tanned skin, and most of her face is hidden in her cloak. She lowers her cloak, showing me her black eyes and the black marks on her face.

Seer.

"Let the princess go," I command, and she laughs.

"You have no authority here, Dagan Fire. Do not push me," the woman says, and I let out a loud growl, my eyes never leaving Isola in that idiot's hands. I'm going to kill him for touching her.

"We were looking for you," Melody says, stepping in front of me with Bee on her shoulder. The woman's eyes go straight to Bee, as do every other seer's and dragon's here. I've gotten used to seeing her, but for most, it is still a shock.

"It's true. The light has returned," the woman says, breathing out her words slowly like she can't believe them.

"Do you support the dark?" Melody asks, and there is complete silence except for a few gasps of shock.

"No." The one word answer comes from the woman, and she steps closer.

"We request safe travel, for all of us, and for you to give Isola a chance. My mother was your last leader, and Isola is my sister. Will you refuse me?" Melody asks, holding her head high as she glares at the woman. If Melody's mother was the last leader, surely Melody should be the one leading them now?

"You side with the lost princess?" the woman asks, almost laughing.

"The princess is the one that *should* be queen, as she is who the light has chosen. Not everything is clear, but unless you plan to kill the last light today . . . you will help us," Melody states.

"My name is Essna, the current leader of the seers, and I accept your request. We will take you all back, as prisoners, and wait for the princess to wake up. She may yet be the queen we need," Essna says, and Melody bows, stepping back to my side as I rush past her.

"Let me hold the princess, and we need to find the others before we leave," I say, seeing the smirk on the asshole's lips as he holds her close to his chest. I'm going to knock that smile off his lips the first chance I get.

"No. She needs a healer, and yours is currently unconscious from the fall. We have taken the other dragon guards. The one is very ill, and the other put up a good fight. You will behave, or I

will put you in the prison until you control your emotions,"
Essna says.

"I'm sorry for this, but I know your stubborn ass will fight
them," Melody says from my l left as she quickly places her hand
on my head, sending blinding white light flashing through
my mind.

67

ISOLA

I sola. Isola. Make the deal, make the trade. Light must win, and darkness cannot fade. Make the deal, make the trade, but remember that balance must be gained . . . .

I groan as I wake up, hearing the echo of a female voice singing the song like a whisper in my ear, but when I open my eyes, the unfamiliar room is empty, and I'm just left feeling cold. I flinch when I try to use my arm to sit up, and I look down to see the white bandage covering my entire arm, stopping at my wrist and at the top of my shoulder. It's spotted with my blood, but it's not too painful. I frown as I realise I have no clothes on, terror filling me until I feel like I can't breathe. I pull the brown sheets tighter around me, moving back on the bed and closing my eyes, trying to calm down.

I'm not on Earth. Michael is dead. I need to relax. I repeat the same words, time and time again until I can think a little more clearly. It comes back to me that I shifted and lost my clothes, but it doesn't stop the panic from rising again that anyone could have found me naked in the forest. *Dagan. Elias. Korbin. Thorne. Home.* Repeating those words in my head instead of thinking of anything else helps me breathe, helps me calm down. When I can finally open my eyes, I see I've frozen most of the sheet and the straw walls of the hut I'm in. *Hut?* I look around, seeing it's a basic circle hut made out of straw that is tied at the top. A small firepit in the middle of the hut, the bed I'm on, and a dresser next to a fabric door are the only furnishings.

"What happened?" I ask my dragon, but say it out loud, figuring she'll be listening.

We fell. I do not know more. We must find mine, she hisses, and I feel her frustration and worry ramping up and blending with my own. She thinks she hurt them, and she knows my arm is not going to heal for a while, so I can't shift. I'm torn from examining my dragon's emotions when the fabric door is pushed aside, and a woman walks in. The woman is wearing a brown cloak tied in the middle with a belt. Her brown hair is up in a bun, and she doesn't look my way as she closes the fabric door behind her.

"Who are you?" I ask firmly, sliding off the bed and standing tall, even as I hold my blanket up with one hand. The woman bows her head, and her scent hits me. *Human.* "Am I on Earth?" The woman doesn't answer my question, walking over to the dresser and opening the drawers. She pulls out a bundle of leather clothes and a cloak before coming over to me.

"My name is Jenny. I am human, but you are not on Earth. I fell into Dragca twenty years ago after running away from my family. I serve the seers, and in return, the seers keep me alive. I was sent to help you get dressed, as our leader wishes to meet you," she says and finally looks up at me, her harsh eyes meeting mine.

"Where are my dragon guards? My sister?" I demand.

"I cannot give you the answers you want, but I can only suggest that letting me help you get dressed and meeting our leader might get you the answers you need, princess," she answers, but her voice is still hard and cold. There is nothing warm about her, and I wonder if that's why she was sent to me, because she can't be swayed.

"Fine," I mutter, moving aside, so she can place the clothes on the bed.

"I will be over here if you need help. Your arm should not be moved much. The healer said you would need help getting dressed," she says.

"I don't need help, but thank you," I reply, because one way or the other, I'm getting myself dressed on my own. Jenny sharply looks away and walks over to the dresser, facing the wall. I drop the blanket, picking up the leather tank top and sliding it over one arm, before carefully putting my injured arm though the hole. I bite my lip as I pull the tight tank top down over my head and down my body. It stops just under my boobs, holding them up like a sports bra instead of a shirt because it's so tight. They must have been made for someone a lot smaller. I sit down on the bed, pulling the tight leather trousers on, that resemble three quarter lengths by the time I get them up and then click the cloak around my neck.

"Let me sort that hair of yours out. No princess should see anyone with that rat's nest of hair. I washed your hair when you were sleeping, and washed you down, if you wondered why you are clean. You smelt bad, and I found more dirt in your hair than actual hair," Jenny says in disgust, but it makes me laugh in relief that it was her that looked after me and no one else. I look up to see her holding a chair out with a hairbrush in her hand. I smile, walking over, and sitting down.

"Thank you," I say, and flinch as she roughly brushes my hair. I guess it was messy. It takes twenty minutes for her to brush it all, and she plaits the top of my hair, so it falls into a long plait down my back in the middle of the waves of blonde curly hair.

"Now, that's much better," Jenny claps, and I stand up, my long hair falling to my waist, and smooth down my cloak. "There is a mirror over there." I follow Jenny's pointed finger to where there is a full-length mirror hanging on the wall. I stare at myself for a second, noting how much older and worried I look. I don't look confident. I look scared, and my blue eyes seem to show my every emotion. Melody is right. I need to hide my emotions better if I want to make it through this. I steel my gaze, lift my head up, and straighten my back. I am Isola Dragice. This is my world, and I will not be a frightened little girl anymore.

68

ISOLA

I'm blinded by the sunlight for only a moment as I step outside the hut and smell the scents of multiple dragons and seers, all of them unfamiliar. There are five huts on each side of a white stone path that has lanterns on wood sticks following along each side. Jenny walks down the path, and I follow just behind her, glancing around, taking stock of my surroundings to get an idea of where I am. There isn't much to see, other than woods and the sun shining high in the sky. We could be in any forest, and unfortunately, Dragca is full of them. I don't have any more time to look as I notice Jenny is nearly out of my sight, and I jog to catch up with her. The path winds around more huts until I can see a massive crowd of people gathered around something.

The people turn one by one to stare at me, some lowering their heads in respect, but many just stare blankly. I spot some seers, some dragons, and even catch the scents of a few humans in the crowd. As we get to the people, they part to make a small path through them, but I feel the eyes of so many of them on me, judging me. I keep my eyes forward and my head high as we walk into the clearing. I see a woman sitting on a wooden chair, one that almost resembles a throne. She has long black hair, seer marks on her forehead that are similar to Melody's, and a very serious expression. Next to her, are two sets of seers in cloaks, each holding long sceptres with orbs on top in front of them. I skim the crowd, searching for any of my dragon guards or my sister, but not seeing them.

"They are here and on their way, princess," the seer woman says, like she knows my thoughts.

"Good. Are they well?" I ask, continuing forward and leaving Jenny in the crowd. I stop right in front of the woman, and she stands up, towering over me as she is much taller. I still keep eye contact and hold my ground.

"Is that really the only question you wish to ask, lost princess?" she chuckles and starts walking around me with measured steps, examining me slowly. "Don't you want to ask if you are a prisoner about to meet her death . . . or if we side with you?"

"I will not ask either of those because I already know the answer. Yes, I am your prisoner, and you do not know whether you want to side with me or not. If you didn't want to truly consider which queen you want on the throne, I would be dead already," I reply, and she nods, going back to her seat and sitting down. We watch each other closely, neither one of us saying a word as the warm wind blows my hair around my face.

"Isola!" I hear Dagan shout, and I turn, seeing him, Elias, and Thorne being dragged through the crowd in handcuffs. They all look a bit worse for wear, especially Elias, who is covered in dirt and has a cut on his cheek. I go to step towards them when Melody walks out of the crowd, shaking her head as she stops next to Elias. She isn't handcuffed, and she has clean clothes on. A light-blue cloak, leather clothes, and she has clearly showered. So, they apparently trust her.

"The princess that is always lost wants us to fight for her!" the woman shouts out, catching my attention, and there is laughter in the crowd as my cheeks light up.

"Essna, you must hear her out," Melody shouts back,

pushing past a seer that tries to stop her and comes to stand at my side.

"I have listened to you all day, and I understand what you need . . . but I know from one look where her loyalty lies. What the princess *truly* wants," Essna says, her blue eyes watching me like she has won some great prize.

"What do you think that is?" I ask Essna, and her eyes purposefully travel to my guards and stay there.

"Them, you are in love with your dragon guards. The only dragons in this world who you are forbidden to love, and yet, you fell. Why would we want a rebel who doesn't follow or respect rules to be our queen? Who would trust a princess who let a curse take her loves' dragons?" she asks, her voice echoing around the crowd, and everyone hears. I glance at my guards, who don't seem upset by her words like I am. If I could have stopped the curse, I would have. I never wanted the curse to take their dragons. I wouldn't wish that on anyone.

"I want to break the curse. The curse should never have been placed upon the guards," I say firmly.

"Yet, you are here to ask for help to take the throne back. Which is it you want more, Isola Dragice? Your dragon guards free and the curse broken . . . or the throne," she asks, and I know she is testing me.

"Both," I answer.

"You cannot have everything in life. So, I will make you an offer. I will fight for you, and my army will side with you . . . only if you choose us over your guards. Make it clear to me that the throne means *everything* to you, and when you get it back, you will dedicate your entire life to fixing the mistakes of your father and his wife," she says, but the calculating smirk on her face tells me all I need to know. This isn't a real offer because she knows my answer, and she wants to drag it out for our audience.

"I will always fight for my dragon guards. I will always choose them. They are mine, and I am theirs," I state, walking up to the seer and not backing down. I'm their queen, not simply some stranger asking for help.

"The queen can only belong to the throne and the people it rules. A queen lost to her guards is no queen we want to follow or support," the seer responds, raising her hand, and I see several seers in cloaks walk over, surrounding us. Melody gives me a worried look, but my focus is on the little flash of silver I see at her hip as she steps closer to me.

"I am not asking. I am demanding," I say, and I reach across, sliding the dagger out from Melody's belt and holding it to my neck as shocked gasps fill the air.

"No, Isola, don't!" I hear Thorne shout. Growls emanate from my dragon guards as they fight their way over to me, but I don't look away from Essna. This is about me and her, nothing and no one else matters right now.

"I will use my last words to cast a curse, a curse on you that will make sure no one ever forgets the name Isola Dragice. I *am* the rightful queen, and I demand you give me fair trial to win your favour . . . or you should hope the magic is kind to you upon my death," I say, trying not to swallow with how nervous I am. Essna stares at me and finally lifts her hands into the air, stopping her people from coming near me. I wait for her people to move away, and I feel my dragon guards right behind me as I lower the dagger, holding it at my side.

"Impressive. There may be more to you yet, Isola Dragice," Essna says quietly, and stands up, raising her voice. "The princess is offered two trials for two prizes. The first will be the answer to breaking the dragon guard curse. The second will be to win our help in the war that she will bring to Dragca."

"What are the trials?" Melody asks Essna, who smiles like Melody is asking exactly what she wanted.

"On the blue moon in one week, she must enter the cave of memory. If she can make it to the other side, she will learn how to break the curse. The second trial will be on the yellow moon, three days after the blue moon, and you will not be told in advance what it entails," Essna tells me, and I glance at Melody, who shakes her head.

"This is unfair! No dragon has survived in the cave! Seers can barely make it through without losing their minds!" Melody exclaims, not exactly making me feel better about this cave. I watch as her eyes glaze over, and she stands very still. I think she is having a vision when suddenly her eyes pop open, and she stares right at me.

"She is no normal dragon, and she may take her light spirit with her. I'm sure she knows enough light magic that she will not miss the loss of her ice powers that the cave will take," Essna waves a hand as she speaks, and I finally look away from Melody.

"Make your choice," Essna says to me.

"I have one request first," I ask.

"Go on," Essna retorts, looking annoyed.

"My guards, my sister, and Darth are all to be treated as guests. Not as prisoners, and you must heal Korbin," I state, holding my hands on my hips, the dagger still in my hand.

"Korbin has been healed already. His parents have taken him," Essna says flippantly, and I try not to show the emotion on my face, though my relief is immense. "As for your other wishes, they are allowed as long as you take the trials. We are seers, and we look after those who we side with."

"Then I agree to your offer. I will take the trials," I say, knowing that I've likely just signed my death warrant. The cave of memory sounds like the last place I want to be or will be able to survive alone, without my powers.

"Can she take someone into the cave with her?" Thorne asks, stepping to my side, close enough that his arm brushes against mine.

"If anyone is going with Isola, it will be me or my brother. Not you," Elias snaps, pulling Thorne's shoulder, so he has to step back from my side as he shakes Elias off.

"Don't fight, now is not the time," I turn my head to whisper harshly at them as they glare at each other, clearly seconds away from fighting once again.

"No, the trial is for Isola only. She must do this alone," Essna snaps.

"I see him benefitting from travelling the cave. The past needs to be revealed; you should allow it," Melody says, and Essna narrows her eyes at her.

"You are not your mother. You are not even a full seer, so do not think you have the right to tell me what I should and should not do!" Essna practically growls, standing up.

"I meant no disrespect," Melody starts, but her expression says otherwise. "I only speak what the visions have shown me. He is meant to travel the cave with Isola. Thorne even feels the pull to his past, and that is why he is asking to go. We never *used* to ignore the visions that we are sent to guide us. I didn't realise things had changed so much since my mother was in charge." Essna's face narrows on Melody as people whisper in the crowds, and Melody simply smiles like she just won a prize at a circus.

"Nothing has changed. We still respect the magic of Dragca and trust in the visions she blesses us with," Essna snaps out, and slowly sighs as she glances at the people. "The fake king shall go with the princess. That is all for today." Essna quickly holds one hand in the air, and all the people copy her move.

"One more thing . . . is my uncle here?" I ask her, and she breathes out an aggrieved sigh again.

"No. He was, but he went to Earth to look for you. We haven't seen him in a while, but I'm sure he will return here when he realises you are no longer on Earth." She lowers her hand with her sharp words, and quickly walks away. The crowd all walk back to wherever they came from until there is just us, all standing together quietly. Jenny walks over, handing a key to me which I accept before she scurries off without a word. I quickly realise the key is for the handcuffs on my guards, and I turn to Thorne first.

"That was stupid. I could die in that cave, and now you might, too," I mutter angrily, undoing his cuffs which fall to the floor. Thorne catches my hand before I can turn away, making me look up at him. I hate how attractive he is, even with his blond hair all messy and littered with dirt and leaves. His stupidly perfect face stares down at me like I'm his everything, and all I can feel is anger. *And hate. I hate him, remember that Isola.*

"I've told you before, hate me all you want, but I am *not* leaving your side. You will not die in that cave. We will get through it together, or I will at least make sure to find a way you will survive," he tells me, locking his eyes with mine and making me stare into those pale-blue eyes that remind me who he really is.

"Let's hope so, or Dragca will have no dragon heirs to the throne left to stop your mother," I pull away, and he lets me go, averting his eyes because he knows I am right. If we both die in that cave, there is no one left. I sigh as I rub my forehead, knowing things just got a million times more complicated. I walk over to Dagan and Elias who are talking quietly. Their conversation stops when I get to them, like that isn't suspicious at all. I raise my eyebrows at them, just as I notice something.

"I guess we all have a lot to talk about, but first, where is Bee?"

69

ISOLA

"Bee is with Korbin. She didn't want to leave him alone. Darth went with them, and he said he would watch over her," Dagan tells me as I unlock his handcuffs after undoing Elias's. Dagan rubs his wrists, looking at me through his fringe, which has fallen into his face, and frowning. He gently places his hand on my cheek, rolling his lip ring around as I relax into his hand for a second. "It's going to be okay." Melody clears her throat, snapping me and Dagan out of the little moment we had.

"Do you know where Korbin is?" I ask. I want to see him, even if his parents are looking after him. I need to see that they have a cure, and if there is anything else I can do to help.

"Yep. In fact, his parents want to meet you," Elias grins. "Ready to meet the parents, naughty princess?"

"I didn't think of it like that, but erm, yes," I say, suddenly feeling nervous. What if they don't like me? What if they don't think I'm good enough for their son?

"They will love you," Melody says, clearly guessing what I'm thinking and smiling at me. "I'm going to sort out accommodations for us all and have a snoop around. I want to find out what the second trial will be. I don't like that she didn't tell us. Seers have many ways to kill dragons, and I'm not letting my sister go into an unfair trial." I smile at her words, loving how protective we have become over each other in such a short time.

"We shouldn't have split up. I don't trust everyone here not to try and kill us," I say before she can walk away from us.

"I will go with her," Thorne offers, stepping to Melody's side.

"Thanks," I tell him, only glancing his way briefly.

"Come on then, blondie," Melody says, not looking entirely happy about Thorne following after her, but I know she sees the reason in it. We can't trust this place, not yet.

"Princess Isola. Princess Isola's dragon guards," Jenny says from behind me, and I turn to see her standing behind me, bowing her head, and two other women stand next to her. I instantly scent that they are human, and when they lower their hoods, I believe they must be Jenny's children. The teenagers look like her, anyway. They have the same hair, similar features, and they give me a nervous glance.

"We wish for you to come with us and choose your weapons for the trials. I am also to take your guards to select new clothing to wear while they are here," she says, and Dagan places his hand on my shoulder as he steps to my side.

"I will choose the weapons for the princess and the clothes for myself, my brother, and Thorne," Dagan says, and I watch the two teenagers giggle as they stare at Dagan.

Kill, nice meal these humans, my dragon growls, pushing for me to shift.

No! Dagan looks like a god, you can't blame them for finding him hot, I try to reason with her, and she huffs.

"Everything okay?" Dagan asks me, snapping me out of my head. I turn to him, leaning up and kissing him thoroughly, loving how his lip ring pushes against my lips.

"Everything is fine, my dragon was just getting a little jealous," I admit to him, forgetting that there is anyone else here as Dagan slides his hand to the back of my head and takes my lips passionately. His lips press against mine, marking me, and making me completely unaware of anything other than his kiss until he breaks away.

"There is nothing to be jealous of," he whispers against my lips, the chill from his lip ring a direct opposite of his warm lips. It feels amazing, and I wish we were alone.

"I wouldn't say that," Elias drawls from my other side as Dagan and I break away and see Jenny narrowing her eyes at me with her hands on her hips.

"Young people, always frolicking. Come on with me if you think you can manage to pry yourself away from the princess, Mr. Fire," Jenny scolds, and I try not to laugh at her annoyed face as she turns, walking away with her daughters trailing behind her. Dagan winks at me before following her, and I turn to Elias, who holds out a hand. I slide my hand into his, and he pulls me close to his side as we walk across the clearing towards a path in the trees. I look over at two women watching us near a table as they fold clothes. I still see the look of desire they flash Elias. The growl slips from my lips before I can stop it, and they jump, giving me a fearful look before scampering away.

"That's not the way to make friends, princess," Elias laughs.

"My dragon is a little possessive," I reply, not apologising for it. They could clearly see us close together and should have figured out he is off limits.

"Mine, too," he kisses the side of my head. "But yours has nothing to worry about." I don't answer him, knowing nothing is really certain between any of us, and that's why my dragon worries. She won't stop being jealous and irrational until mating with them. Dragons are naturally territorial of what they think of as theirs. Unfortunately for me, my dragon thinks sexy guys are like jewels. And she wants to hoard them all, keeping them for herself.

"How is your arm?" he asks, and I automatically glance at it. It's really weird how you have to look when someone asks about something.

"It's okay, I don't think it will be long before I can take it off,"

I answer. It is feeling a lot better. I will be glad to take the bandage off later.

"You were amazing today, you know that?" he says, watching as two seers pass us, not even looking our way.

"I don't think amazing is the right word to describe it. I haven't gotten any of them on my side or believing in me," I respond quietly. "How did my father and my family before him just get people to follow them?" I ask the question I keep wondering. I know one of my ancestors won a war and that made him king, but how did my family never get kicked off the throne until now? I know we are stronger than fire dragons, but there are only so many of us, and every generation there are less. I always wondered what would have happened if I had a child with Jace and who that child would have mated with. With no ice heirs, it would have had to be a fire dragon, and then everyone would find out that fire and ice dragons can have children together like Thorne. Fire was always heading towards the throne, one way or another. My father wasn't a stupid man, he would have thought this all through, so what was his plan?

"By being a leader, a ruler. By being a light they could follow when it felt like darkness was all that was left," he tells me. I don't reply as we follow the path, walking past more huts until we are quite far out in the woods.

"How do you *become* a leader?" I ask, because it's clear I do not have a clue.

"By being inspirational," he shrugs. "I always used to hear tales of the king and queen, and how even though they had their issues, they were inspirational to see."

"Then this is hopeless. I'm not an inspiration to anyone. I'm a princess of a world I wasn't even brought up in, a princess that let her father be killed and then forgot who she was. A princess that didn't even *want* the throne in the first place," I say, starting to panic as everything collapses in on me. What the hell am I doing trying to get the throne back? Why aren't I running away like a smart person would? Elias pulls me to him, tucking my head under his chin as I try to calm down. When it becomes hard to breathe, I start to panic more, not knowing what is happening to me.

"You're having a panic attack. Breathe nice and slow and listen to me talk. Just listen and think of nothing else," Elias says calmly, trying to soothe me, but it doesn't work. I just feel like I can't breathe, and everything I don't want to remember or think about is rushing through my mind.

"I-I can't do this," I breathe out, my words catching and likely not making any sense.

"Isola Dragice, you know what I thought when I first met you?" he asks as I try to take deep breaths and just relax in his smoky scent.

"No," I shakily exhale.

"I thought, 'wow, she is pretty gorgeous'. Then a few hours later I thought, 'wow, she is going to die super quick because she is so clueless'," he says, and it makes me laugh a little.

"If you're trying to make me feel better, you suck at it," I eventually say, loving the soothing circles he rubs into my back with his thumb.

"It took one week for me to know I was absolutely wrong about you. So wrong. I saw how strong you are, how kind, and how utterly special. Isola Dragice walked straight into a world she could barely remember, clueless and heartbroken . . . and held her head high even when everything was stacked against her," he pauses, lifting my chin, so we are looking at each other. "If that isn't inspirational, I don't know what else is. Everything you have been through, everything you have lost, and you are still standing here. That alone is amazing. You still fight for what is right when we both know it would be easier to run away."

"Why do you believe in me so much?" I question quietly.

"Because I love you," he whispers, and my eyes widen in shock as I just gape, momentarily at a loss for words. "Because I've loved you, an inspirational girl I met once as a boy, since you gave me that second chance at life. I spent years dreaming about her, even when I discovered she was the princess, and I knew she would never look at me twice. I love you because you never gave up on me, not once, even when I didn't know who you were. I love you, Isola Dragice, and I will always be yours."

"I love you, too," I whisper, and lean up, pressing my lips against his, only able to do it once before he loses all control and slams his lips firmly on mine and picks me up in his arms. Elias walks us through the trees, away from anyone or any path, as we fervently kiss each other. I pull his shirt off when he stops, and he slowly slides me down his body, gently biting my bottom lip before letting go and stepping back.

"I want to see you, all of you," he tells me, and I nervously unclip my cloak, letting it fall to the ground. I pull my top off, careful not to hurt my arm, and watch as Elias's eyes widen and fill with heat. I wriggle out of my trousers as I scan my eyes over Elias's chest, the dragon tattoo, the words on his heart, and finally down to the trail of dark hair that disappears into his jeans. I look up as my trousers fall to the floor, and I step out of them, standing completely bare in front of him. When I meet his eyes and see the desire, any embarrassment disappears as I see how much he wants me. How nothing he sees is anything other than what he wants, what he needs.

"I'm yours, Elias. Isn't it about time you show me what it's like to belong to Elias Fire?" I whisper, and my words make him snap, taking one big step forward and picking me up. Elias lies me down on my clothes, holding my uninjured hand above my head as he keeps eye contact with me and presses his body against mine. Even with his jeans on, the friction makes me gasp as he knocks my legs apart. Elias slowly kisses down my jaw, pausing to graze his teeth against a sensitive part on my neck before moving lower. I moan as his lips find my nipple, sucking it into his mouth and biting down gently. The mixture of both pleasure and pain drives me crazy until he breaks away and spends time with my other breast.

"Isola, you are so fucking beautiful," Elias comments

between kisses as he makes his way down my body until he finds where he was looking for.

"Eli," I moan as his talented tongue finds my core and starts twirling in slow, perfect circles that get me so close, but aren't quite enough to push me over the edge. The asshole is teasing me.

"Enough, I want you now," I say, and he lifts his head, seductively licking his lips as he looks down at me.

"Are you sure you can handle me?" he asks with an amused grin as I slip my hands to his jeans, undoing the button and sliding my hand inside. Elias's grin disappears when I wrap my hand around him, stroking him firmly and making him groan as he closes his eyes.

"Are you sure you can handle me?" I mimic him, and his eyes leisurely open as his hand grabs mine, pulling me away only to maneuver his body on top of mine.

"No, I know you are going to drive me insane when I'm inside of you. You already do just when we kiss," he tells me and kisses me, stopping anymore talking. I kick his jeans down his legs, writhing against him as his hands explore my breasts and his lips devour my own. I gasp as Elias thrusts into me, every inch of him feeling amazing as he slowly fills me up.

"Eli, I love you, don't stop," I mumble out around kisses, arching my back as Elias kisses my neck and groans loudly as he slams into me again and again.

"I won't. God, you're everything," he says, leaning up and kissing me roughly as he picks up his pace. I moan as an orgasm unexpectedly slams into me, and Elias bites my neck, speeding up his thrusts until I feel him finish. We both lie together, our foreheads resting against each other, and our heavy breathing is the only sound.

"It's impossible how much I love you," he whispers, and I smile as I whisper back.

"Nothing is impossible."

70

ISOLA

"Okay, are there any more leaves in my hair?" I ask Elias after shaking my hair out once again. I don't want to meet Korbin's parents with flushed cheeks and messy hair that is full of dirt and leaves. They will know straight away from our scent alone, but I'm not hiding my relationship from anyone. I couldn't even if I tried. The whole camp must be talking about how I basically claimed my dragon guards when Essna asked me to choose them or the throne. Starting off on a lie isn't the best way to do anything. Elias chuckles, pulling his shirt on and walking over to me. He reaches a hand into my hair and pulls out a leaf.

"Just the one, and now you're perfect," he grins, making me laugh. Elias helps me clip my cloak on, and I'm just about to start walking back to the path when he speaks.

"I was worried what happened with the Earth boy would affect us. You would tell me if I scared you, right?" I turn at his unsure voice and walk straight up to him, placing my hands on his chest.

"You could never scare me. I didn't think about–" I have to clear my throat before I can say his name, "Michael. What he almost did, well, it's not going to ruin my life. Do I get scared sometimes? Yes. But never when I'm with any of you. I know I'm safe, that you'd never hurt me, so I don't need to be scared." I stop rambling when he kisses me, and I can feel the smile on his lips before I even see it.

"You're *always* safe with us. I'm glad you know that," he replies, linking our hands together, and we walk through the forest. We are silent for most of the walk once we get back on the path and pass a few huts with people milling around. Most of them stare, and a few children run past us as they sing songs with big smiles on their faces.

"The people look so happy here," I say quietly.

"Yes. I know the fire rebellion was once a group of dragons, seers, and humans that believed in the old ways of Dragca to guide them. They trusted light and dark magic, fire and ice, and all that Dragca naturally gave to them. Your father did not hold those same beliefs. He did not think dark magic should be respected, or even practised. I don't believe he trusted magic of any kind, purely because I heard of many missions where guards were sent to find and stop practisers," he says. I rest my head on his shoulder as I look at the children and their mother watching them from the door with a big smile on her lips. How could my father destroy people for loving Dragca and magic?

"Why would he hunt light magic users? It makes no sense, as far as I know you cannot use it for anything, and the only magic we've known for years is dark and destructive," I say, thinking back to the stories Jace told me about. He said his parents told him that dark magic had taken over a farm boy, and he had killed an entire village by accident. His parents told him that story when he was twelve, and three weeks later they disappeared. We never did find out where they went, but Jace always said he felt like they were alive somewhere, though I'm pretty sure they are dead.

"Lies. I know others were connected to the light magic, but not on a scale like you are and like Tatarina is to dark. They didn't get spirits and the protection from that. They could just use it for tiny things, like healing plants and making light," he says tensely. "Nothing that could hurt someone, not like what you are capable of."

"Did you see Tatarina a lot in the dungeons? Did you see her use dark magic to hurt someone?" I ask, because we haven't had time to talk about where he was and what happened during those years I didn't know he existed. It couldn't have been easy, even with Thorne protecting them for me.

"Yes. She liked to use her dark magic on us and the other prisoners, who she regularly killed by accident. I believe it made her stronger, and her dark spirit, Nane, enjoyed watching," he answers. I know he is hiding the worst of it from me, and I squeeze his hand tightly, letting him know he can talk to me whenever he wants to. *When did we all become so broken?*

"I don't think we can kill Nane, not without killing Bee. I've heard several times now that there must be dark and light alive at the same time. I worry that destroying one, will destroy the other," I whisper, but he hears me. I won't let Bee die, not for anything. I'm too attached to the little green Barbie doll that eats like a horse and, I'm pretty sure, likes food more than me.

"I don't know enough of light and dark magic to advise you. I just know that Nane must be controlled if she is kept alive. Also, she won't survive without a new host, not if you kill Tatarina," he tells me, and I suspected as much.

"Let's hope Nane's next choice is better than her first, or we will just end up killing one host after another, and that isn't something I want to do," I admit, and we both walk in silence to the end of the path where a large hut sits. The hut is two put together, but I imagine they make one house. There is smoke coming out of the hole in the middle of the main part of the hut, and I can hear quiet talking inside.

"Time to meet the parents," Elias teases me with a big grin on his lips, and I roll my eyes at him as we walk to the door. I lift my hand, knocking twice. The door is opened a few seconds later by Darth, who smiles when he sees us. He has a few cuts on his face that are stitched up, his grey hair looks brushed, and he has new clothes on, with a long cloak clipped at his neck. They have been looking after him, but I still feel a little bad about dropping him in the forest and cutting his face. Hopefully, they won't scar.

"It's about time you got here, girl," he says, and holds the door open as I walk in, and he shuts the door behind us.

"I'm glad you're okay after the fall," I reply with a smile.

"I was lucky to land in a rather large pond with Korbin and Elias. We swam out, carrying Korbin of course, and then the seers found us," he says and points at his face as he chuckles, "though I managed to hit a few sharp rocks under the water somehow. I've always been a little unlucky."

"You were lucky my son was found right then. I doubt he would have survived much longer in the state he was in," a woman says, stepping through a fabric curtain in the room and standing still, assessing me and Elias. The woman is stunning, with long black hair in braids, light-brown skin and green eyes that are the image of Korbin's eyes. Even without her saying anything, I would have known she was his mother, or at least a close relative.

"That was not my fault, Janiya," Darth says, shaking his head.

"You should have called me straight away, father! He is my only son, and if he had died, there would be nothing left!" Janiya shouts, fire lighting up her arms as her eyes turn black, and she looks away sharply as she calms herself down. I stare at Darth with my mouth gaping open.

"You're Kor's grandfather?" Elias is the one that speaks before I can.

"Yes, not that we ever met. I was a terrible father, always working. Janiya joined the dragon guard when she turned eighteen to escape," he explains.

"That's not the only reason I joined, father; not everything is about you," Janiya huffs, and Darth smiles indulgently at her.

"You are just as stubborn as your mother," he says, and

shakes his head. "I will leave you to meet the woman your son is in love with." Darth says, walking around us and out of the door as I lock eyes with Janiya.

"Princess Isola Dragice, I presume?" Janiya says, crossing her arms and making the bangles on them clang against each other. It's only then that I notice she has a dragon guard uniform on, a purple cloak and three metal, circular necklaces around her neck that match the bangles on her arms.

"Yes, it is nice to meet you," I say as I step forward and hold a hand out for her to shake. Janiya stares at my hand before sliding hers into it, gripping me tightly.

"Thank you for keeping my son alive for as long as you and your guards did," she says tightly, like it pains her to thank me. She stares at my eyes for a long time, seeming like she has just seen a ghost or something as she whispers under her breath. "You look just like your father."

"It's nothing, I would never have let him die, and thank you. I've always heard I have my father's eyes, but I look like my mother," I say, pulling my hand away and glancing through a small gap in the curtain, seeing Korbin on a bed.

"No, your mother had a kind face and your father was more . . . determined. You will find you are much more of your father than your mother, Isola Dragice," she says, shaking her head.

"I don't think it matters who I am most like in looks, I know I am different to them both. More importantly though, I came to see Korbin. I need to know if he is okay," I say, stepping closer to the fabric and the gap where I can see Korbin sleeping.

"Unfortunately, I don't wish for you to see my son anymore. You will cause his death, and I won't allow that," Janiya says, stepping in front of the gap and glaring at me as she crosses her arms again.

"You can't stop me," I state firmly, crossing my own arms and holding my ground.

"I *will* stop you if that's what it takes, but instead, hopefully, you can be reasoned with. You are the princess, a princess that over half of this world is looking to kill or dedicate to a throne for the rest of your life. If my son is at your side, he will die protecting you, or worse, be used against you. Have you even thought about the risk of having my son at your side? If you care about him at all, you will walk away," she asserts, making me question my own decision until I remember that I can't make Korbin stay away from me. Even if I walked away, he would still protect me, and he could die at any point because life isn't certain. Death is, but how we live our lives should be our choice. I won't make that choice for Korbin. He knows the risk of being with me.

"Janiya, love, enough of this. We have talked about our son's decisions, and you know what he wants," a man says firmly, after stepping out of the curtain and standing next to her. The man looks like an older version of Korbin as they share a lot of facial features, but he has light-brown hair, tanned golden skin, and kind-looking brown eyes.

"Phelan, this is insane. He can't mate with her! That would make a dragon guard a king, and no one will ever accept that! So, what is the point of letting them be together? She will get our son killed! Royals get everyone killed, and besides, her father killed my mother!" she growls out, pushing Phelan away and slamming her shoulder into mine as she passes me and walks out of the hut.

"I didn't know what my father did," I whisper into the silence of the room. No wonder she hates me. My father killed her mother, and in her eyes, I'm now trying to get her son killed.

"We cannot be held accountable for the actions of our parents. I am sorry for my mate's reaction. She just fears for Korbin's life, and things have been touch and go for the last two days. I don't think she has slept since he came back," he explains.

"I understand that. If I could walk away from him, I would have done so by now. I can't, and ultimately, it is up to Korbin who he chooses to love and fight for," I say gently.

"My son has told me all about you, and I know there isn't a chance in Dragca that he is leaving your side," he chuckles. "You can thank his mother for his stubbornness. They are very much alike and are usually butting heads over something."

"Why did my father kill Korbin's grandmother?" I ask.

"I do not know everything, only that Janiya's mother knew something, something she shouldn't have known. The dragon guards were sent in the night, and they murdered Janiya's mother while Janiya was training in the dragon guard. She found out the next morning and left the guard with me, running to the only place where the king couldn't track us. The fire rebellion," he tells us, and I glance at Elias, who looks as confused as I am.

"I don't understand. How did my father ever trust you two again? I mean, you are dragon guards."

"He didn't know who we were, we changed our names, and your father had long forgotten Janiya over the years of hunting her. When you run from the curse, it does eventually give up on chasing you. The magic isn't endless, and the king had many runaways to deal with. When Korbin was old enough, we knew he had to return because of the curse. We followed him back, became the best dragon guards your father had, and Korbin got the training he needed," he clarifies.

"Still, I am sorry for what my father did," I say and look away, "I seem to be apologizing for a lot of his actions recently. I didn't have a clue who he really was and what he did as king."

"Just be different than he was, that's all any of us want. Tatarina is very much like her departed husband, and no one wants her on the throne. Make good choices," he says, and pats my shoulder before walking to the door.

"Where is Bee?" I ask, making him pause and look back. "In the kitchen, which is at the back of the hut through that curtain. I found her a bunch of human chocolate and sweets, and she has ignored us since. Now, I better go find my mate," he grins, one much like his son's, before walking out. I walk to the right, peeking through the open curtain and seeing Korbin fast asleep on his side. One leg sticks out of the blanket, and his light snores fill the room.

"Let's check on Bee before we wake him. He looks comfy," I whisper to Elias who peers over my head at Korbin.

"Sure," Elias replies, and I step back, walking across the little living room in the hut. There are sofas in here, a fireplace, and brightly coloured, worn rugs on the floor. There is a makeshift wall at the back of the hut, made out of a purple, nearly see through fabric. I move it aside and walk in, laughing at the sight that greets me. Bee is on a table, lying in a glass bowl full of bubbly water, sunbathing from the beam of light coming in from the window. There are dozens of wrappers from sweets and chocolate all around the bowl, and Bee is currently trying to eat a chocolate bar that is bigger than her head, as it melts in the water.

"Bee?" I ask, hearing Elias chuckle behind me. Bee drops the bar into the water, flashing me a chocolate-covered grin.

"You back," she says, and I sigh.

"I missed you too, Bee. I need to train on how to use light tomorrow. You can rest, or do whatever it is you are doing now, but tomorrow, things have to change. I need to be able to use the light to survive now," I say, and she yawns, looking unimpressed.

"Good," she says, pushing her green hair out of her face and picking up her chocolate bar, clearly done with our conversation.

"Are you sure you are ready to use light magic?" Elias asks as we walk out of the small kitchen.

"No, but then again, I don't think I have a choice. This is who I am meant to be, and Dragca needs magic once again."

71

ISOLA

"Hey, sleepy head," I call softly, stroking the side of Korbin's face. His green eyes open slowly as he jolts up, relaxing back into the pillow when he sees it's me. Korbin looks amazing, so much better than he was. The purple lines are gone, his skin has colour, and he looks, well, more alive.

"What is a sleepy head? It sounds kind of dirty," Elias asks from where he is leaning against the wall.

"It's an expression. It just means you have sleepy, cute, messy hair. Don't worry, you look cuter in the morning. I think Korbin has the sexy look instead," I wink at him, and he growls.

"I'm *not* cute. I'd rather be sexy. Sexy tops cute," Elias grumbles as Korbin and I laugh. Korbin sits himself up on the bed, only flinching in pain slightly before relaxing back against the wooden headboard. He coughs a few times, and I place my hand in his, trying not to show how worried I still am about him.

"I'm fine, honest. I just could do with a glass of water," he says, and I go to get up, but he holds my hand tightly. "I can wait, though, I'd rather you stay with me."

"I'll get it, man," Elias says in understanding before I can reply, walking out of the room.

"How did they heal you?" I ask, curious. Korbin pulls his shirt up, showing me the purple leaves stuck over the cut.

"There is a plant called Tunits, and their leaves absorb anything. They are rare in Dragca, and the leaves are expensive to buy. Of course, my parents sent for the leaves the moment the seers brought me here. Darth helped heal me with your blood until the leaves could be found," Korbin explains.

"You know Darth is your grandfather?" I ask, and he chuckles.

"Yeah, I was shocked at first. The old dragon is good at keeping secrets, and I can't scent him because . . ." he stops, pain flickering in his eyes at the mention of losing his dragon, and I squeeze his hand. "Anyway, my mum slapped the silly out of him when he first walked in here."

"Your mum is erm . . . scary," I say, and he laughs loudly, holding his stomach as laughing must hurt him.

"You braved my parents to come and see me? I'm impressed you made it in here," Korbin comments.

"Actually, it was just your mum I had to brave. Your dad seemed to be okay with me," I tell him, shrugging, and he laughs, even though it seems to hurt him a little.

"They will love you, just like I do. It will just take time. Especially if you ever answer that question I asked you before Eli came in," he says with a nervous grin on his lips. There are a million reasons why I should say no. Responsibility of the throne. The timing. The fact I haven't spoken to Elias or Dagan about all this. Yet, there is one reason I know all that stuff doesn't matter. I want Korbin as my mate. I nearly watched him die, and I know my life would be empty without him.

"You know my answer, it was always yes," I whisper timidly, and he grins, tugging me down with his one hand, so he can kiss me. I break away just as Elias comes into the room, but I can't look away from Korbin and the massive smile on his face. I lean forward and kiss Kor again, grazing my lips against his, and he laughs, gently holding me back.

"I love you, too," he says with a chuckle. "But remember I'm not well enough to really show you how much."

"Don't stop on my account," Elias says playfully, coming over and handing Korbin the drink. Korbin drinks most of it before handing it to me, and I hop off the bed, so I can reach the dresser to put the glass of water on top.

"Isola just agreed to mate with me," Kor suddenly blurts out, and I turn, giving him a wide-eyed look that suggests he stop talking, but he doesn't seem to get it. He shrugs his shoulders and explains. "Almost dying made me realise I love her more than anything, and I don't want to wait years to make a decision when I know what I want. We could be killed any day, and Isola is it for me. Thank god, she said yes."

"What? Don't you think that is something we all should discuss?" Elias exclaims, and I turn in time to see him run his hands through his hair.

"I'm not taking her from you. I would never stop her from also mating with you or Dagan. I just need Isola to know how I feel about her. I know how serious mating is, and we have made our choice. I want you to accept it. It was you that suggested the idea of sharing and all of us being together in the first place," Kor says. *When was this conversation?*

"But being mated . . . that's something else. I never thought that far ahead," Elias mutters, flashing me a guilty look when he finally looks my way and likely sees all my emotions on my face. *He . . . he doesn't want me?*

"Are you saying you never see yourself mating to me?" I ask quietly, and Elias shakes his head, walking over to me and trying to reach for my hands, but I jerk back away from him.

"It's not that, it's just mating is forever. It's a blessing and a big step. We are young and–" I cut him off as I don't want to hear it. He was just telling me how much he loved me, and we were having sex, but *now* he isn't sure? He certainly wasn't unsure when he was inside of me. Why are men such assholes sometimes?

"You know what, Eli? Just get out, or I'm going to leave," I shout, my words coming out a growl as my dragon's anger fills me, making everything seem doubly as painful. I step back, hearing a cracking noise, and I look down to see the floor around me is frozen, the ice spreading towards Eli and Kor's bed.

"Isola . . ." Eli starts, but I can't look up at him as I try to stop the ice. It doesn't work, instead the room starts snowing. As snow falls on my cheeks, I look up to see Eli just standing there, looking bewildered as snow covers him.

"Leave, just please leave. You're right, I didn't think any of this through. Me, you, Kor, and Dagan. How can we possibly all get blessed and be mated when it's clear you never even *thought* about being that serious with me?" I ask, my heart pounding in my ears in fear of anything Elias might say.

"Isola, it's not that I don't love you–" he starts to say, and I shake my head, the snow falling inside the room increasing.

"You just don't want to mate with me, I get it. Now get out," I say quietly.

"Isola–"

"Just get out!" I shout, covering my face with my hands, and my voice trailing off into a whisper. "Please go. I can't deal with this right now."

"Leave, Elias. Don't make me try and get off this bed to kick you out. You've said enough for today, don't you think?" Kor says firmly as I stare at the wall and try not to cry. I hear Elias walk out of the room and the sound of the door slamming only moments later.

"Come here, doll," Korbin gently coaxes, and I run over, burying my head into his neck as he drapes an arm around my waist.

"Elias is scared, you know that, right? He's scared of losing you, and I bet he thinks mating with you will kill him more if he lost you. I know he loves you, and whatever is stopping him from mating with you, it is in his head. It's fear, not lack of love," he tells me soothingly, but nothing seems to help with how my heart feels like it is shattering.

"I get being scared, I'm scared every day, but I don't get not wanting or planning a future with the people I love," I whisper, my words not making much sense as I wipe my tears on Kor's shirt.

"I know, doll. Give Elias time to calm down. His shock over you agreeing to mate with me, everything that is going on, and losing his dragon is messing with his head. Give him time," he says.

"He shouldn't have to think whether he wants me or not. I never had to think like that about any of you. I just knew, deep down inside, I knew," I reply.

"Me, too, doll," Korbin says, kissing the top of my head. "Stay with me for a while? I could do with holding you close."

"I'm not going anywhere," I mumble, wiping the tears off my face and relaxing in Korbin's arms. *If Elias doesn't want me, fine, but I'm not going to allow it to destroy me and distract me from the trials. I can't, because if I'm destroyed, what becomes of Dragca?*

72

ISOLA

"These are the huts they have given us to live in while we are here. I think someone should stay on guard, and no one should be alone anyway. I don't trust Essna. There is something else going on here," Melody says, waving a hand at the two huts in front of us, but keeping her serious eyes on me until I sharply nod. I don't trust Essna either. I look back at the huts, seeing that one is massive and looks like it could fit dozens of people inside. The one next to it is rather small. Bee flies off my shoulder, flying into the hut through a gap in the fabric before I can stop her. She wasn't pleased that we had to leave Kor at his parents' and with Darth until he is better. I can't say I'm happy about it, but I know he isn't well enough to be moved yet, and his parents will care for him. I also know I need to start training as soon as possible with Bee, and I'm going to be distracted until the trials.

"I will check it is safe first," Dagan says, walking past me and through the fabric door. I roll my eyes over his black trousers and shirt, and the two swords on his hips attached to his belt in holders. He also has a new dark-blue cloak which he holds rather than wears. It isn't cold, and I might take my cloak off soon as it feels like the middle of summer here. I aimlessly look around the trees surrounding the huts, noticing that they have put us far away from anyone else. I don't know if that's to protect us or them. More likely them.

"Where is Thorne?" I ask, remembering that he was supposed to be with Melody for protection.

"With Elias getting food for us all. We bumped into him on the way back here," she explains.

"That's good," I say tightly, even hearing his name makes my dragon growl, and my heart pound in my chest.

"What's up? You've looked like someone killed your puppy since you left Korbin's," Melody says, nudging me with her shoulder.

"I don't have a puppy," I reply dryly, really not wanting to talk about anything.

"It's a metaphor, now come on, out with it," she demands, and I'm thankful for the distraction when Dagan comes out of the hut.

"It's clear, come on in. It's actually pretty nice," he calls to us, holding the fabric door open. I quickly walk in, happy to get away from Melody and her questioning gaze. The hut is nice, with three red sofas and a matching red and yellow woven rug in the middle of them. There is a fireplace, which is already lit and makes the room really warm. I see five doors, and I'm guessing they lead to the bedrooms, bathroom, and kitchen areas.

"I'm taking the hut next door. It's made for one, anyway, and I want to watch my orb for a while," she says, placing her hand on my arm for a second.

"You could stay here," I say.

"No, it's yours, and there are some things a sister never wants to hear through these thin straw walls," Melody pulls a disgusted face and walks back out of the door as I smile. She has a point, or at least I hope she does. I walk into the room, sitting on the couch and laying my head back, staring at the ceiling.

"What happened? Did Kor upset you? His parents say something?" Dagan asks, moving to the back of the sofa and looking down at me, rolling that lip ring around. I stare up at him, noticing how long his hair has gotten in the last couple of weeks. Dagan usually keeps it short, and it needs a cut, but the dark-brown, wavy hair makes him look dangerously sexy.

"Nothing happened," I mutter, standing up and walking to the fireplace, looking at the little wooden dragon statue in the middle of the mantle. I pick it up, smoothing my hands over the wood and thinking of the detail that must have gone into making it.

"What the hell happened, kitty cat? Talk to me," Dagan asks, and the fabric door opens, with Elias and Thorne walking in as I stiffen up. My eyes immediately lock with Elias, seeing the guilt and maybe even fear in his eyes as he stops and stares at me. I don't seem to be able to focus on anyone else, or anything going on in the room other than Elias.

"Leave me alone with Isola. I'm the one that pissed her off because I'm an idiot, and we need to talk," Elias says, looking awkward as I glare at him.

"Sure," Thorne agrees, putting the bags on the floor next to the ones Elias put down. "But if you hurt her, you're dead," Thorne says calmly, but with just enough protective tones that it sends shivers through me. Elias doesn't look his way, keeping his eyes on me the whole time.

"Fix whatever stupid shit you said. We need to be united at the moment, not apart," Dagan whispers adamantly to Elias as he passes him, but Elias still keeps his eyes locked on mine. In the corner of my eye, I see Dagan pat Thorne's shoulder, before practically pushing him out of the door.

"You don't need to apologise. I've had time to think about it. If you think I'm not worth mating with, if you don't want me for more than just fun, then I will break the dragon guards' curse, and you can leave," I say as I turn away, annoyed when my voice catches when I try so hard to be emotionless. Elias walks over, taking my face into his hands and holding on tightly. He forces me to look into his eyes that show his every emotion, and all I can see is fear. He is scared.

"I love you. I fucking *love* you, and everything I said about mating, it had nothing to do with how I feel about you," he growls.

"Then I don't get it, am I not enough? Do you never want to mate with anyone?" I ask, and his thumb wipes a tear away that falls down my right cheek.

"I am scared, not of mating and you, but of being a disappointment to you. Mating with you would make me a king, would make me a leader, and I'm definitely not that. I can't be what you need, and I don't want you to mate with me, then regret it down the line," he admits, his voice quiet like he doesn't want to tell me this.

"I would never regret that. I would never regret *you*," I breathe out.

"Yes, you would. People will never accept that you have more than one mate, let alone all of them being dragon guards, Isola. Mating with you, it could ruin everything, and I don't want to risk that. We can be together as much as we want, without me being a king," he says gently, almost like he's trying to soothe me, but I don't agree with a single word he says.

"The people need a queen who isn't cruel, isn't dead inside, and isn't lost. If I don't have all of you as my mates, if I have to give you up for the throne, I might as well leave Tatarina on it. They would not have a better leader if I were destroyed. Dragca is changing, and it will change with me. I want you as my mate, and I don't care what anyone else, other than you, thinks. If you care about the opinions of strangers more than me, then there is nothing worth fighting for between us," I pull away from him, walking over to one of the doors as he lets me go.

"Make your choice. I won't make anyone love me, mate with me, or be with me if they are scared of what that means. You have always known who I am and the price that comes with being with me. If we have no future, please tell me now and don't break my heart any more than you already have," I watch as he tensely watches me speak, never moving, and I know I have to get away from him before he sees me break down. I turn and open the nearest door, which leads to a small bedroom. Quickly closing the door behind me, I slide down the door, finally letting the tears fall.

73

ISOLA

"Isola? Elias?" I hear shouted, making me sit up from where I've been slumped on the floor in the tiny bedroom for god knows how long. My dragon whines as I stand up, stretching my arms and wiping my dry lips. It's funny how time seems to stop when your heart is breaking. I feel like I've already lost Eli in a way, and what's worse, I'm more broken than when I lost Jace. How could I love Eli more than Jace, when I knew Jace nearly my entire life? The only conclusion I come to is that I'm a crappy person, and Eli is likely better off without me. Then in the next thought, I'm furious at Eli and think I need to woman up. *Or princess up? I actually have no clue.*

"I'm in here," I shout back, not even remembering who called until Dagan opens the door and, at seeing my face, closes it behind him in one smooth motion. He steps into the room and pulls me into his arms. I tense up for second, but when his smoky scent hits me, it relaxes me as well as my dragon.

"I'm okay," I whisper, feeling how tense he is as my head rests against his chest.

"Elias is in a room with the door locked, and I'm betting he is regretting whatever the hell he said. I don't want you to tell me what happened, but I do want you for the night. Let me take you out somewhere," he asks. "A date, because we haven't actually had a real one."

"We went to the café in the rain and had sandwiches, that's totally a date," I tease him, and he chuckles.

"Eating those horrendous sandwiches is not a date. Plus, this is Dragca, not Earth. I want to take you on a date in our world," he says.

"Where? We can't leave . . ." I trail off as he pulls back from me a little, so he can see my face as I look up at him.

"Trust me?" he asks, kissing my forehead.

"You know I do," I chuckle, and he steps back with a big grin, linking our hands and walking us out of the room. Thorne is sitting on the sofa, sharpening a sword while Bee sleeps on the sofa next to him. She even has Thorne's dark-blue cloak covering her. Thorne looks up, but I can't focus on anything other than the fact he doesn't have a shirt on. Holy crap, he has nice abs. There are eight of them, covered in sweat, and his man nipples even look attractive. *Oh god, now I can't stop thinking about licking man nipples. I don't even know if that is what you call them, or how they can be attractive, but his are.* Thorne flashes me a smile and flips his sword over in his large hands as his wavy blonde hair falls into his face.

"Isola?" Dagan's amused voice calls, snapping me out of my drooling, and I physically have to close my mouth. Why are all these dragon guards built like damn gods? It's so unfair and distracting. I can't even manage to collect my thoughts until I look away.

"Have a good night," is all Thorne says, looking back down at his sword and going back to what he was doing. I look back at the doors in the room for a distraction. Knowing Elias is behind one of them just makes me sad, and it's worse that he didn't come to me, but in a way I'm glad he didn't go far. Maybe he doesn't want me anymore? I try to redirect my thoughts, forget everything going on, and focus on where Dagan is taking me. We walk out of the hut together and see that the lanterns are all lit, lighting up the dark forest, so you can only see them. I look up, seeing the outline of the two moons and the dozens of stars lighting up the sky.

"What kind of dates do you go on in Dragca usually?" I ask Dagan, who tugs me closer, wrapping an arm around my waist as we walk.

"I think it depends on the girl. If I could take you anywhere, it would be to the biggest library in Dragca. There are thousands of books in there, both modern and old. It's amazing, and I would take you to a nice meal, then of course back to my place for dessert," he tells me, and I chuckle.

"I like the sound of your date," I grin mischievously, and he laughs. "But I will admit I'm slightly jealous of the previous girls that went on dates with you."

"I never really got to date while growing up, to be honest with you," he tells me.

"Why?" I ask, glancing up at him as he watches the forest as we walk.

"Well, I had to train, and then Elias was always getting into shit. I was the one getting him out of trouble all the time or taking the blame, so I would get stuck with extra training on our days off," he says.

"That must have been crap," I say.

"Maybe. Maybe not. I'm a pretty amazing fighter now because of it, and Elias isn't dead like he would have been if I hadn't helped him. Either way, it all worked out for the best because I'm here with you," he says, tilting his head down and to the side slightly as he watches my reaction.

"So, you wouldn't change anything?" I ask.

"No. There is only one thing about my past I wish I could know," he says with a sigh.

"About your father?" I guess.

"Yes. We didn't know who he was, and we never knew if he

had family. Sisters. Brothers . . . just nothing. Our mum was so heartbroken she wouldn't say a thing, and we were too young to remember," he explains.

"Sometimes, you have to accept you can't know everything you want to," I whisper. "If I could know why my father did the things he did. If I could know why he sent you guys to me, why he never told me about Melody, or told me about anything important . . . well, it would change my life," I say.

"He loved you, you know that, right?"

"I don't. He left me on Earth, lied to me all my life. How could he have loved me? I don't even know if he ever loved my mother because he cheated on her. How could he have?" I ramble out.

"I can only tell you one thing. When we first met, when you and your father were attacked, I knew he loved you. His reactions to everything happening in those moments, were to protect you. I ran and told you to duck, only because your father was running towards you, and I knew he wouldn't make it. He was going to run straight into that dagger, no matter if it killed him, in order to save you. Whatever mistakes your father made, I believe he loved you very much," he tells me, and I smile to myself as we take a right, away from the sounds of the people and the campfire in the distance.

"I didn't know he did that. Maybe you're right," I concede quietly as I start to hear the sound of the sea and waves.

"I'm always right, kitty cat. Haven't you learnt that by now?" Dagan teases.

"You're always lacking modesty, but I don't know about anything else," I laugh, and he tickles my side, making me jump away from him as we start to see some lights.

"Where are we?" I ask as Dagan holds a branch out of the way, and I step through, straight onto a beach. We are on the rocks that lead to the water, which have several glowing white stones littered around.

"What is this place? What are those stones?" I ask Dagan as I walk over, stopping in the sand, just before the waves can reach my boots.

"Glow Stone Beach. A nice simple name, and in about ten minutes, something amazing happens. So, let's get in," Dagan explains, and I turn around just in time to see him pull his shirt off slowly and drop it on the rocks where he has already taken his cloak off. The moonlight shines on his chest, where his chiselled chest leads to a defined set of abs and distinct v shape dips into his jeans.

"Kitty cat, do you not want to swim?" Dagan asks, his voice full of amusement, and my eyes flash up to his, seeing the playfulness there. I clear my throat.

"Yep, I want to swim. But you are getting in first," I say, crossing my arms, and he laughs loudly. He kicks his boots off, pulling his socks off next, and then drops his jeans until he is completely naked, totally shameless as he stands in front of me. I don't let my eyes drop from his, which only seems to amuse him more as he walks past me, straight into the water. *Holy crap, he is going to kill me with his hotness. If that's even possible.*

"Hurry up, kitty cat," Dagan says, snapping me out of my thoughts. I quickly strip down, leaving my clothes piled next to Dagan's before running into the warm water. I swim out to the nearest glowing rock, grabbing it as I place my hands against it, feeling how warm the stone is.

"Boo," Dagan says next to my ear, his hands slipping around my waist. I relax my head back on his shoulder as we float in the waves quietly for a while.

"Turn around, it should be any second," Dagan whispers and helps me turn in the water. I rest my arms around his shoulders, looking up as he tucks a bit of my hair behind my ear.

"What's this surprise then?" I ask, feeling curious now, but I'm also a little overwhelmed by how close we are and the way he looks at me.

"This," he says, turning us sideways so I can see the millions of little blue lights in the water that are being pushed towards us by the waves. It looks like a wave of blue, sparkling diamonds, but much brighter.

"What are those? It's beautiful," I gasp in shock. This is what makes Dragca amazing.

"No one really knows. The people call them Sealights, and they come to this shore every night around this time. I've always wanted to see them," he says as the little lights surround us in the water. They don't touch us, just float around us. I wave a hand out in the water, watching how they move around my hand as I wave it in the sea.

"This is amazing, unforgettable," I mumble, still waving my hand in the sea.

"Just like you. This place reminds me of you. That's why I was so happy when I found out where we are, and I realized I could bring you here with me. This place is special, unique and so alive. It just shows, in a world where light magic is meant to be rare and practically impossible, there is this," he whispers to me. I lean closer, sliding my hand into his hair as I kiss him, and his hands tighten on my hips, pulling my body hard against his.

"I didn't bring you here for that, we can just stay and enjoy the water," he says. I almost worry he doesn't want this, but I can feel how much he wants me from where our bodies are pressed together. I drag my hand out of his hair, down his chest, and find his hard length, wrapping my hand around him.

"I want to enjoy you," I say, and he groans as I speed up with my hand.

"Isola," he rasps, pulling my hand away and gripping me tightly to him. I wrap my legs around his waist as he kisses me. Moaning when his hand grabs one of my breasts and flicks the nipple, I rock myself against his length. I slowly inch myself down on him, and he easily slips in with how turned on I am. Dagan growls as he kisses me roughly, his hands holding my hips as I move up and down, getting closer and closer to the edge.

"Mate with me?" he asks against my lips suddenly, and I stop with him still inside me. Dagan doesn't let me completely stop as he moves my hips.

"You haven't even told me you love me yet," I gasp, and he chuckles as my back hits a stone, and Dagan presses me against it, somehow pushing deeper inside me and making me moan. He glides his hand slowly up my legs as he kisses me and breaks away.

"I love you, and you know it. I know it, though I'm a damn idiot for not telling you sooner. I want you to be mine, but the choice is yours. I just thought you might want to know what I am thinking about nearly all. the. damn. time," he says, punctuating his words with kisses as he pounds harder into me.

"Yes," I moan out, and his right hand moves between us, rubbing circles on my clit as he carries on thrusting. His other hand drifts to my throat, angling my head so I have to look at him.

"Yes to what, Isola? Say the words," he taunts, not letting me go, and no part of me wants him to either.

"I will mate with you," I manage to whisper.

"Good, kitty cat. Now come for me. I want to feel you come around my cock," he growls out, and I cry out as the orgasm that was just out of reach suddenly slams through me at his words. He picks up speed, and only a few thrusts later, I feel him finish inside me as he kisses me deeply.

"Damn. I wanted to spend months getting to know you, learning everything you like, but no part of me regrets this," he mutters against my lips, and it makes me giggle.

"Good?" I ask, and he pulls back to frown at me.

"That was more than good. In fact, I think we should get out of the water, onto the sand, and see if we can do a longer repeat," he teases, sucking my bottom lip into his mouth before letting go so I can answer as he pulls out of me.

"One thing first, though," I say, pushing off the rock and wrapping my arms around his shoulders. "I love you. I needed to tell you that."

"And I needed to hear it. I won't ever forget this moment. It's the beginning of us, our future, and I'm never letting you go," he vows lovingly, and then kisses me once more.

74

ISOLA

"That's just gross. You can't drink the milk you just had a bath in, Bee," I say, watching in disgust as she shrugs at me and carries on drinking through the straw she has put in her bowl of milk. I look over the table where Thorne is quietly eating his toast, watching Bee with the same revulsion I am. He meets my eyes, and we both laugh, shaking our heads.

"Hey, sis, where are Dagan and Elias?" Melody asks, picking up the glass jug of milk and a bowl off the side before sitting at the table. Melody frowns at Bee for a second as she gets the box of chocolate cereal off the table and starts pouring some into her bowl.

"I don't know for certain about Elias, but Dagan told me he was going to see Kor. I bet he took Eli with him," I answer, ignoring the sharp bite of pain that shoots through my heart at the thought of Eli walking out of here and not even attempting to talk to me.

"Makes sense," Melody says, pouring her milk.

"A more important question, how do they have so much human food here?" I ask, pointing at the boxes of food they gave us.

"There is a portal here that opens into the back of a supermarket in Scotland. They send a team into the portal every night there to steal a little food. The humans think there is a stock problem, and our people are fed. It's a win, win. It's part of why they chose this place, that and its close connection to the memory cave," she shrugs.

"That's kind of amazing, and what is the memory cave? You haven't told us anything about it, and I think we need to know," I say, and Thorne puts his toast down, turning so, like me, his focus is solely on Melody.

"It is where all seers go when they come of age. The cave is, in the simplest way to describe, alive with the memories of Dragca. When I went in, it showed me my mother as a child and then her being killed. It also showed me my birth and my death," she explains.

"It shows you your future?" Thorne asks.

"Yes and no. For some people, what it shows comes true, and for others it does not. Like my death, for example. I was shown that I would die protecting you in the castle when Tatarina killed the king, but that didn't happen. I wouldn't worry, the cave mostly shows you the past and helps you find where you need to go," she waves a hand.

"So, it's like your powers? They might not come true, but there is good chance they could?" I question.

"Yes, and another thing . . ." she drawls out with a slightly worried expression.

"Out with it," I say.

"The cave walls are made of the same glass as my orb. You cannot touch it, and it blocks all dragon powers," she explains.

"All we have to do is get through the cave," I say, taking a deep breath.

"You don't understand," Melody shakes her head at me as she speaks.

"Then help me," I coax her gently.

"The cave is dangerous. It will show you things that will make you want to follow it, and then you will be lost forever. It will try to break you. Hundreds of dragons have tried to survive the cave and failed. Only one has ever survived going through it," she says.

"Who?" I ask.

"Your ancestor. The very first ice king," she says quietly and reaches for my hand on the table, covering it with her own. "If he could do this alone, then you can do this with Thorne by your side."

"It's been done before, so we can also do it," Thorne declares firmly, and when I look over at him, I don't see any fear. Just pure determination. I have to do this for them. I have to give them their dragons back, or I will never be able to live with myself. I sharply nod at Thorne, letting go of Melody's hand and standing up.

"Bee, are you ready to go train?" I ask her, and she sighs, flying up and landing on my shoulder.

"Sure. Must walk north," she says, her voice full of attitude. I raise one eyebrow at her, and she just crosses her arms.

"I am coming with you. You shouldn't be alone," Thorne says, standing up and stretching before taking his plate to the sink. I spot the quiver of arrows on his back, a sword underneath it and the bow resting on the table. It makes me think back to the time he helped me use my dragon eyes to shoot an arrow, how I hugged him like he was my best friend, and how I felt something more than friendship in that moment. It's hard not to think of our past with a tinted vision now I know he was deceiving me, plotting to betray me the whole time. I turn around, walking out the door and into the living room. I pick up my cloak off the sofa, pulling it over me and tucking it underneath Bee on my shoulder before clipping it. I wait by the front door until Thorne comes out with a bag on his back as well as his weapons.

"I can carry the bag, all of that has to be heavy," I say as we walk out, and he shuts the door behind him before answering.

"No, I've got it," he replies with a smile and looks at Bee.

"Where to then?" he asks her, and I look up as she points to my right, where there isn't a path but just endless forest.

"To there," she says, looking at us like we should know the way.

"That's not a lot of information to go on Bee. We don't have time to be messing around. Why can't we train here where we know it is safe?" I ask.

"Trust?" she asks, shrugging and not blinking as her green eyes watch me closely. It's like she is testing me in a way; I can see it in her expression and feel it deep down inside of me. I nod, looking back at Thorne who doesn't say a word, simply following me as we walk into the woods.

75

ISOLA

"**B**ee, are we near yet? It's been ages," I ask her, not wanting to walk much further. We have been climbing over rocks and up hills, for the last god knows how long since we ventured into the forest. I look up, seeing the sun is right in the middle of the sky, so it must be midday already. I finish the energy bar I was eating, tucking the wrapper in my pocket as I wait for Bee to say something. "Bee, come on."

"Nearly," she responds finally, smiling at me as she sits on my shoulder. Her green hair is so long it covers her body now, and her green eyes look so innocent when she smiles at me. Like she hasn't just made me walk for miles with no explanation. *It's like all that pointless running all over again.*

"Bee, I'm worried we won't be able to get back to camp before dark if we keep walking before we even get to training," I say, and she huffs, flying off my shoulder and floating in the air in front of me, with her back facing us.

"You've pissed her off now," Thorne jokes quietly, and I laugh a little as I step up to Bee's side to see what she is seeing. There are four rocks on the mountain side, each one at least three times my size, and they are covered in dark purple vines that look like weeds. They stretch over the rock, killing the grass that is now yellow, and the flowers are all wilted.

"What is that?" I ask in shock, looking over at Thorne who seems just as confused as I am.

"Dark. Too much dark in Dragca, not enough light. No balance," Bee says, like her random statement should explain everything. Thorne walks closer, lifting his sword off his back.

"Don't get too close, be careful," I warn him, and he glances back at me with a grin.

"Didn't know you cared, Issy," Thorne says, and I roll my eyes at him before he turns back. Thorne slowly lifts his sword, touching one of the veins with its tip and a black flash of light sends him flying across the rocks.

"Thorne!" I scream, running over to him as he lands and rolls on the ground a few times. I fall to my knees next to him and turn him over onto his back. He coughs a few times before opening his eyes, and I breathe out a sigh of relief.

"Fuck, that hurt," he coughs, sitting up with my help.

"You okay?" I ask.

"Yeah," he says, managing to smile at me, but he still doesn't look great. "I might have cracked a rib, but my limited dragon healing will sort it out soon. I just need to rest for a bit to heal," he explains. I help him pull his bow and bag off his back before he leans back on the rock. I still don't move for a while, worrying that he might be more hurt than he is admitting to me.

"Go and learn, just don't touch it," he insists, studying my expression.

"Are you sure you are okay?" I ask, needing to hear him say it.

"I'm good, now go, Issy. We need you to learn whatever the hell Bee has brought you here for in order to survive that cave," he says, reaching for my hand. I don't move as he carefully pulls my hand to his mouth, kissing the back once before letting go as my heart pounds in my chest at every little movement. I'm sure when he stares into my eyes for a second, he can read my every emotion and hear my heart pounding, but luckily for me, he doesn't call me out on it.

"I should go," I say nervously, stepping back and practically running over to Bee, who is sitting on a normal rock near the weird ones. *Dark covered ones? Rocks I don't want to touch? Who knows what their name should be.*

"Bee, I think it's time you explain," I tell her, and she sits up, crossing her legs and pointing at the rocks.

"Light can destroy dark. You must find it and use," she says, moving her hand to her heart, pointing at it with her little green finger. "Feel the light, call it." I try not to laugh at the fact she sounds like someone out of Star Wars.

"That doesn't sound so easy," I say, and she laughs, floating up in the air and holding her hand out for me.

"Together now, but you can do this alone," she says, and I reach a hand out, letting her wrap her own hand around my little finger.

"What now?" I ask.

"Connect. Feel," she instructs and closes her eyes. I watch as her whole body starts to glow white before the white glow travels to her hand and touches me. I close my eyes in awe, a gasp leaving my lips. It feels like someone just threw cold water over every part of my body, and then it disappears, leaving only a weightless feeling.

"See, connect," I hear Bee say, feeling like she is all around me as I open my eyes. I smile as I see we are floating above the ground, and when I move my other hand, I notice all my skin is glowing white. I glance over at Thorne, who is sitting up watching with wide eyes, and I smile at him in reassurance. I can see something in his chest, like a yellow light.

"What is the yellow in Thorne's chest?" I ask.

"His soul. Babies are born with a white, pure soul. The soul can be tainted, and you can see the taint in time. Yellow is close to white, because Thorne is not tainted by the dark too much," Bee explains, her voice like a sweet echo, and I'm surprised how well she has learnt to speak. I look away from Bee and towards the rocks, seeing them glow with almost a black light that covers it.

"Destroy," Bee urges, letting me go, but the power never leaves me as I feel my feet graze across the floor before I land. I don't look away from the rocks as I walk over, knowing that I am meant to help them. *Help the land. Help destroy the darkness.* All these thoughts run through my head as I place my hand against the rock and a sharp pain shoots up my arm, like an electric shock. The shock buzzes through me as my hand warms up, and a bright light flows out of my hand until I can't see anything other than light.

"Isola! Enough! Stop!" I hear Thorne shout, but I ignore anything other than the need to stop the darkness, and only when I feel nothing but light, does everything fade away.

76

ELIAS

"Any change?" Dagan asks, stepping into the small bedroom and closing the door behind him. I look back over at Isola as she lies in the bed, her eyes closed, and her skin still lightly glowing white. Her blonde hair surrounds her on the pillow, and her pink lips are the only other colour to her pale face. I think back to seeing Thorne running across the woods, holding her in his arms as she glowed like a flashlight, and Bee following not far behind them. I don't think I've ever been as scared as I was in that moment. It reminded me of the time Isola was stabbed and how helpless I felt. *And I didn't even love her back then.*

"Same as the last *six days*," I growl out, standing up from the chair and walking to the window. I stare at the morning suns, just as they peek out of the tree line and slowly rise into the sky. Bird fly past, the trees sway in the breeze, and everything seems so peaceful, all while I feel nothing but panic inside of me.

"Bee said she will be fine. Try not to worry, brother," Dagan reassures me, and I glance over at him. His face is tired and tense as he strokes Isola's cheek with the back of his hand, steady rolling his lip ring around in his lips. I'm not the only one worrying and not sure if Bee is right. Bee is young, and she's not even a dragon. *What if she doesn't have a clue what she is doing?*

"The last thing I said to Isola is that I didn't want to mate with her," I lament, keeping my voice quiet as I look back at Isola, running my eyes over her beautiful face. "She doesn't even know how much I regret being a coward, or how I love her enough to be anything she wants or needs."

"Why did you tell her no?" Dagan asks as he steps back from Isola, his voice free of judgement, and it shocks me a little. I fully expected he would beat the shit out of me for hurting her because I'm an idiot.

"I'm–no, we–are children of a woman who worked at a whorehouse, and we did a lot of bad shit to just survive. I've killed so many that I don't even remember them all, and I can't make myself regret the life I've lived. What kind of mate would I make for a queen?" I say, turning away and facing the window as I clench my fists. *Who in their right mind would want me as a mate with my past?*

"A fierce mate, a mate any queen would be damn proud to have," Isola's sweet voice says, and I turn abruptly to her as she sits up, staring at me with tears on her cheeks. Her blue eyes look like they can see straight through me, like they always have done. There has been no one like her in my entire life, no one who can know me with one look like she does.

"Isola," I whisper, feeling like my feet are glued to the floor as we just stare at each other. I hear the sound of Dagan walking out of the room and closing the door behind him, but neither of us move an inch.

"No one is perfect, especially not me or my family, who have been the kings and queens, princesses and princes for thousands of years. I don't care what anyone else thinks, and I hope you don't either, because in my eyes, Elias, you are everything. Please don't think I judge you, please don't think I ever will," she whispers, and my feet finally move as I walk to the bed and fall to my knees next to her. She leans over, placing her soft hands on my cheeks, and slowly kissing me. I groan at her taste, at the feel of her, until I have to pull away.

"I don't want to fuck this all up. I've never been scared of anything as much as the thought of losing you scares me. I've always believed I was strong, brave and not a coward, until the second I hurt you the other day. I never wanted to do that, and I was a fucking idiot," I admit, and she shakes her head.

"I get it, the fear anyway. I remember when you told me once not to fall in love, because if I did, I would lose them in the end. You were right. I'm dangerous to love, and that won't change anytime soon. I get it if you want to walk out this room and never look back," she chuckles humourlessly. "Most would."

"I'm not most, naughty princess. I'm here fighting for you . . . if you will still have me?" I ask resolutely, knowing I made my mind up the second I saw the pain in her eyes from my stupid words the other day. I love her, and even if loving her is dangerous, every moment is worth it.

"I love you, but please don't hurt me again. If we keep hurting each other, there won't be anything left of us that is worth fighting for," she says, taking a deep breath.

"Never again," I say and slam my lips onto hers in a harsh, brief kiss before I break away and keep her beautiful blue eyes locked on mine. "Mate with me, Isola Dragice? I can't offer you anything other than myself and my heart, but I will be yours forever. I will always love and protect you," I say, and she smiles widely, her eyes drifting to silver as she speaks to her dragon. I watch silently until her eyes turn back to blue.

"Yes, even my dragon agrees . . . but says she will ice your feet to the floor for a week if you hurt us again," she says, and I laugh, pulling her to me. I hear the door open behind us, and Korbin walks in with Bee on his shoulder.

"Light is awake," Bee says, and Isola pulls away from me, confusion rolling over her face as she looks at me and asks one question.

"What happened?"

ISOLA

"**M**ade light," Bee answers my question, flying into the room and sitting on my lap. I look away from Elias to Korbin leaning against the door frame. Kor has a leather dragon guard uniform on like the others, and I wonder who made them it for only a second as I see how well Kor looks. His tanned skin looks healthy, and his green eyes are blazing with mischief and love as he watches me.

"You're here and looking good," I say and he grins, walking over.

"Thanks, doll. You don't look too bad yourself," he jokes and places a tender kiss on my forehead.

"So, guys, how did I get from the woods to here? Everything is a little blank," I admit, looking between Kor and Eli, as they both sit on the edge of the bed. Eli puts his hand on my leg, comforting me.

Fly soon. Need mates with us, my dragon hisses in my mind.

Do you know what happened? I ask her, and all I get in return is a yawn as she ignores me, and I focus back on Eli and Kor.

"I can answer that, if I can come in?" Thorne asks from the doorway.

"Come in," I say with a smile, waving him in. Eli and Kor

tense but don't openly say anything as he walks in. Thorne sits on a chair in the room, clearing his throat before talking.

"You glowed like a flashlight, and then you touched the rocks. You lit up like nothing else; I couldn't see you, I couldn't see anything but light. I tried shouting, telling you to stop," he explains, and I have a vague memory of Thorne shouting.

"I heard you, but I just couldn't stop," I say, "or I didn't want to. The power was addictive."

"What happened next?" Kor asks, sliding his hand into mine on the bed.

"The light just suddenly cut off and Isola was lying on a rock, still glowing but passed out. Bee was watching her and clapping her little hands," Thorne tells us. "Bee seemed really proud of you and told me I didn't have to worry about you not waking up." I stare at Bee who just shrugs, her cheeks a bright-red colour.

"I'm sorry, that must have scared you," I say, looking at Thorne, but he only stares out of the window.

"I knew you weren't dead, our blood bond told me as much as I ran to you. Isola," he pauses, looking back, "the dark-purple things that covered the rocks were gone, and the rocks were covered in bright flowers and vibrant grass. You had brought the entire place back to life."

"Light can heal, right, Bee?" I ask her, and she nods, landing on my open hand.

"You are strong," she says and looks at the door.

"Food is ready," I hear Melody shout, and Bee doesn't hesitate as she flies off my hand and out of the door. *I swear Bee loves food more than anything else. I can't say I blame her.*

"How long was I sleeping?" I ask everyone.

"Six days, doll," Korbin answers, and it suddenly dawns on me.

"The trial, it's tonight, isn't it?" I ask, and Eli nods.

"You don't have to do it, you know that right? We can live

without our dragons as long as you are alive," he says, squeezing my leg.

"I need to do this. If I don't, I wouldn't be able to live with myself," I say, making sure to catch each of their eyes.

"You could die," Kor whispers hoarsely, reaching over and pushing a strand of hair behind my ear.

"The dragon guard needs to be free of this curse. Not only so you can get your dragons back, but so Tatarina doesn't have an army who can't think or act for themselves. Once the curse is broken, the dragons could leave, and the fight for the throne would not be as great," I explain. "Plus, it will earn the seers' respect and, hopefully, their help."

"We are meant to meet Essna in half an hour to start the trial," Thorne states, standing up. "Isola needs to shower and get ready."

"Are you saying I smell?" I ask, and he smirks, shrugging his shoulders once.

"Maybe," he says.

"Cheeky bastard," I mutter as he walks out, and all the guys laugh. It takes me by surprise a little at how relaxed they are around Thorne now; how I am, too.

"Thorne has a point, and I want to get your weapons ready before you go," Eli says, kissing my cheek before walking out of the room as Kor stands up.

"These are your new clothes," Kor says, picking up the pile of clothes next to him on the end of the bed and passing them to me. I smooth my hands over the supple, light-blue leather, never having seen anything like this leather before. There are even snowflakes etched into the design and a long dark-blue cloak rests under it.

"Where did this come from?" I ask Kor, still rubbing my fingers over the material.

"Bee. She made it for you while you slept," he says and points at his own clothes. "She made these, too. We all have new clothes."

"Wow," I say, speechless and amazed how she has become strong enough to make this.

"I will get some food ready for you, and the shower is through there," Kor says, going to step off the bed, but I catch his hand, stopping him.

"I love you," I whisper, and he turns our hands over, kissing the back of mine sweetly.

"I love you more," he says and lets my hand go, walking out of the room and shutting the door behind him. I slide off the bed, walking straight to the other door in the room, and catch a glimpse of myself in the full-length mirror in the bedroom just before I open the bathroom door. My whole body is slightly glowing white, my eyes look brighter, and I feel so much stronger than I was. *Let's hope I'm strong enough to survive this trial, because nothing else matters now.*

78

ISOLA

"**I**sola Dragice, looking every bit like the princess you are," Essna says as I walk into the clearing where she sits on her makeshift throne. Her calculating eyes watch my every step, only briefly glancing at my guards at my side, until I'm right in front of her. She has a long cloak on, her black hair is up in a tight bun, and her sharp eyes are decorated with black makeup which matches the black seer marks on her face. The marks make me think of Melody, knowing my sister has my back if Essna tries to attack me.

"Where is your sister and the light spirit?" Essna asks first, folding her hands together.

"Safe," I answer simply, and her teeth grind together, the only sign of her annoyance as she keeps her face blank. I know she wants my sister dead and to have Bee near her in case I die in that cave, but that isn't happening. Now that we know light magic isn't going to help me in the cave unless I need to heal plants, we all agreed that sending Melody and Bee to hide was the best plan. If anything happens to me, Bee will bond with Melody and that is the best option we have. *Not that I plan on dying any time soon.*

"Let's go then, we do not have time for talking. The blue

moon will be upon us soon, and we must be at the entrance in time," Essna says, rising up and walking around her throne, with her seer guards following just behind her. Ten more guards surround us as we start to follow her through the crowds of people and when I look back, the crowd is walking behind us at a little distance, all whispering amongst themselves.

Safe? my dragon hisses in my mind, but I don't have a response for her. I don't think we will ever be truly safe for a long time. Essna slows down a little, falling back to walk at my side after Dagan steps away when I nod at him to say it's okay. I still feel Eli and Kor step closer, and glance over to see Thorne has his hand on his sword, watching Essna closely.

"Tell me, princess, what are your plans for Dragca if you reclaim the throne?" Essna asks, never looking my way once as she speaks.

"I want peace, something Dragca hasn't known since my mother was alive," I say determinedly, and she laughs.

"There was never peace for the poor, for the hunted, or those who didn't want the dragon guard curse and paid the ultimate price. There was peace for the rich, but that is it, and I know that well," she chuckles, and there is a silence between us as I think about her words. *Was there ever peace when half the dragons were slaves to a curse?*

"How did you know there was never peace? It is true I only had my view from the rich side, but they seemed happy," I ask, curious.

"I was only ten when my family was killed in a fire that destroyed my village. The fire was caused by an accident, but no ice dragon came to put it out when they could have easily done so," she sighs. "I was the only survivor, and for years I travelled around Dragca, looking for food and, well, a home."

"I am sorry that happened to you," I say, though I'm still confused about why she's telling me about her past.

"Most are, but being sorry does nothing for my past or for your future. When I turned eighteen, I found this place, secretly run by Melody's mother. I was her second in command before she died," Essna explains. "I respected and loved her dearly, even with her mistake of loving your father."

"Does Melody know this?" I ask quietly. Melody seems to hate Essna, maybe she wouldn't if she knew how close her mum was to her and how her mother trusted her enough to place her as her second in command.

"Melody does not want to ask the questions she is scared of the answer to. I may be strict with her, but only because when I am gone, Melody is the rightful leader. She is too young, too strong-willed to lead the seers at the moment, but I see so much of her mother in her," Essna says, and for a moment, I think I may understand her a little better. Sometimes you can't act how you wish to in order to get the right outcome.

"When I am queen, I will change what my father always should have done. I know my words feel like an empty promise, but I can only offer you words for now. Dragca needs to unite and fight for itself, rather than being at war like it always has done," I say, looking up at the sky and enjoying the warm sunlight that streams onto my skin. It reminds me of the light and for a second, I call the light and feel it spread over me like a wash of cold water. I glance at my hand, seeing I'm glowing a little brighter than usual, but you can't tell in the bright sunlight. Essna keeps her eyes forward as I stare at her, seeing the yellow light of her soul and knowing she isn't tainted. I glance back at Kor, Elias, and Dagan, seeing they all have normal souls too, even if Elias's is the darkest yellow out of them all. The power slowly leaves me as I turn back to Essna, and she finally replies to me.

"I see you bringing change, but I also see you bringing about our destruction because of who you love," Essna says, placing her hand on my shoulder briefly, before walking ahead. "I only hope it is peace you love more."

79

ISOLA

"This must be it," Dagan says, and I follow his gaze to the small cavern at the bottom of a mountain we are approaching. The mountain is well-hidden in the forest, and I doubt you could see it unless you flew over it. The cavern has a massive door, with what looks like dozens of etched dragons flying around in a circle on it. The dragons are painted red, blue, black and white, which sends goose bumps all over my skin as I look at them. My eyes travel all over it, to the middle where in the center of the dragon circle is a circular hole that looks like something fits in it. There are dozens of lit candles on the ground near the mountain, many looking old and some newer. Essna walks back to me, stopping at my side with Thorne moving to her other side. We wait for the other people following us to catch up and gather around us. Some of them carry new candles over to the other candles, lighting them and bowing their heads as they whisper.

"Seers have a tradition, every time we lose someone, every time a new seer is born, every time there is a blessed mating, we leave a candle outside here. Our tradition says the memory cave is where the first seer was born and gifted her sight. Therefore, we have always respected this place," Essna explains from my side as we come to a stop.

"Come Isola, Thorne, it is time," Essna says as the crowd parts around us, and she walks over to stand by the door. Dagan skims his hand over my face, making me turn to him, and he kisses me lightly. His blue eyes look darker than usual, with worry, I expect. I place my hand on his cheek, and he leans into it, closing his eyes for a second.

"Good luck, and come back to me, kitty cat," he whispers, stepping back as my hand falls away. Kor and Eli both kiss me goodbye next, neither one of them needing to say a word that hasn't already been said. I know they are worried, so am I, but this has to be done.

"Stay safe," I tell them all, knowing there is nothing else I need to say. They know how I feel and that I will fight to survive this for them. *And for myself.* In nearly every romance book I've read, the main girl always wants to live for her guy, when she should want to live for herself, too. She is just as important. *I miss reading, why are there no books here, or any time for reading?*

"We will wait for you here. None of us are leaving until you return," Elias states, making me smile as I walk over to Essna. I glance back to see Elias's hand on Thorne's shoulder, whispering something to him before letting him go, so he can catch up with me. I slide my hands over the two daggers on my hips, feeling the soft material of the new leather dragon outfit, and keep my head up high as I stop near Essna. Essna pulls a flat, glass, circle-shaped object from inside of her cloak, and turns around, walking to the door. We follow her over, standing a few feet behind her as she places the object into the gap in the circle. Nothing happens for a long time, and I glance at Thorne, who shrugs in confusion. I'm about to say something when Essna steps aside, placing her hands high in the air. She looks up at the sky behind us, and I follow her gaze. The moons slowly appear out of the tree line, rising in the late evening sky as the blue light shines through the trees. Both of the moons are a bright blue colour, shining so brightly that it could be mistaken for daylight. When the moons are high enough, the light shines on the door, and we hear a clicking noise. Each one of the etched dragons lights up blue, and then the door opens itself gradually.

"Go, and good luck, princess," Essna says, and Thorne walks in first, not hesitating at all. I slowly follow him in, looking back only once as Essna closes the door and her words follow us through, echoing in the cave. "Beware of the past, because it is just that."

"HERE," Thorne says as he clicks a flashlight on and hands one to me, before clicking his own one on. Thank god he thought ahead and has a bag full of useful things.

"Thanks," I say, flashing the light around the room. It looks just like a normal cave with brown dirt, rock walls, and what I'm sure is a rat that runs past our feet. *Gross.*

"We should be careful not to touch any crystal in here," Thorne says and starts walking down the silent cave. "The burns aren't bad, but I don't fancy risking it."

"Thanks for coming with me. You didn't have to do this," I say, and Thorne chuckles as we walk quietly.

"I *did* have to do this, and not only just for you. Since I met you, I've repeatedly dreamt of walking through a cave. The same dream all the time, and something urged me to come with you. Call it what you will, but I believe fate wanted me here," he says, pushing his messy blond hair out of his eyes. He hasn't cut it in a long time, and it's long enough that the ends are starting to curl.

"Do you believe in fate? That some things are meant to be?" I ask.

"Yes. Though, I believed in it more the day I met you," he says, glancing back at me once as my heart pounds in my chest, and I look away. I don't look back as we continue walking in silence, my own thoughts not straying far from Thorne and what he means to me. The more time I spend with him, the harder it is to deny there is something between us, but it still hurts when I think of how he betrayed me. It's an an odd mixture of pain and possible love, and I know it could destroy me if I'm not careful.

"Stop," Thorne says suddenly as I walk into his outstretched arm, which he uses to hold me back as he shines a light on the massive room right in front of us. The floor, walls, everything is smooth crystal, looking almost like a mirror.

"Mother?" Thorne says suddenly, dropping his arm and running into the room. I dash into the room after him, grabbing Thorne's hand, and a shock vibrates through my arm. I turn to where Thorne is looking and see two girls running through a woods in the glass. The image is so clear that it's like we are in a cinema or something.

"Mum?" I whisper.

80

ISOLA

The two girls run through the forest as we watch, holding hands and laughing loudly, glancing back every so often with big smiles on their faces. They must only be ten or so, but the one on the right is clearly my mother as a child. I've seen paintings of her in the castle, her long blonde hair and blue eyes are so much like mine that I would recognise her anywhere. The girl next to her I don't know, but she is an ice dragon, too, with short blonde hair and blue eyes, too, but hers are darker and her features sharper. The girls both have blue dresses on that sway in the wind and knock against the flowers on the ground.

"Let's stop, Tata. He won't be able to find us, we ran too quickly," my mother giggles, dramatically throwing her arms in the air.

"Okay," Tata shrugs, lying down on the grass, and my mother lies next to her.

"Is that your mother?" I ask Thorne, sliding my hand into his without noticing I'm even doing it. I turn to him, his expression full of sadness as he watches our mothers. Everything must be clicking into place for him, everything that his mother has lied about. I look back at Tatarina, wondering how this little, innocent girl became the monster we all know now.

"Yes," he whispers back, just before my mum and Tatarina start talking.

"Everyone is saying that one of us will have to marry Ofen and become queen," Tatarina says, staring at the sky. She speaks of my father, and it hurts me to even think of him right now.

"I don't want to be queen, or marry a stinky boy, even if he *is* a prince," mum replies, and it makes me laugh as well as Tatarina.

"Nope, me neither. Boys suck, and I love you anyway," she says so innocently that I want to believe she is lying, when it's likely she isn't.

"I love you, too. You're better than anyone else," my mum says, and then they fade away. There is just a crystal mirror left behind, reflecting the image of me and Thorne. We stare at each other's reflection for a while, neither one of us breaking the growing tension with words. My heart breaks for him. I know what it is like to have the image of your parents smashed to pieces by finding out what they were really like.

"Our parents were friends . . . what Darth said was true. It's all true," Thorne says in shock, shaking his head and stepping away from me as he unlinks our hands. "My mother lied."

"Melody showed me a vision of your mother, a vision that showed me Tatarina had convinced your adoptive parents to kill the queen. It was all her. You might as well know all the entire truth. Somehow, they went from best friends to Tatarina wanting my mum dead and making sure she got her wish," I say, knowing he needs to know this. He needs to know who his mother really is. Thorne doesn't look at me as I go to him, placing my hand on his tense shoulder.

"No!" Thorne shouts, rubbing his hands through his hair. He jerks away from me, refusing to look my way.

"I think she did all of this because she wanted to be queen. She wanted to rule. Your mother killed mine and then married my father," I whisper. "We have all tried to tell you any parts of her that were good are gone, but I think you can finally see it now."

"Why?" Thorne shouts, walking to the crystal wall and kicking it. "Show me why!" I gasp as he slams his hands against the wall, and it burns his skin, but he doesn't stop.

"Thorne, stop!" I shout, running over and grabbing his arm to stop him, just as the crystal wall blurs again, and an image eventually comes into view. We step back together, watching as two people appear, and it becomes apparent they are Tatarina and my father, only much younger. They look like teenagers.

"It's not you, Tatarina. I'm sorry, but I love her," my father exclaims, pushing away Tatarina's arms as she tries to cling to him. She is a mess, tear-stained cheeks, messy hair, and desperate eyes that watch my father. He looks worried, but no other emotion is on his pale face. My father smooths his hair down, straightening his cloak as he watches Tatarina fall to pieces.

"We slept together just last week! You told me you loved me and wanted *me* as your queen," Tatarina pleads, and tears stream down my face as I witness her heartbreak. My father pushes her away, and she falls to the floor. My father's face is cold as he walks to the door, pausing with his hand on the handle.

"It was a mistake, and I am sorry I hurt you, but I love her," he says, and Tatarina bursts into tears as my father walks out the door. We both silently watch Tatarina break down, pulling her beautiful blonde hair out in chunks and screaming on the floor. She does eventually get up, walk past us and out of the door. The image in the wall follows her down the corridor of the royal castle, through a little door that leads to the gardens. Tatarina stops as we all see my father down on one knee, offering my mother a ring. Proposing to my mother just after he destroyed Tatarina.

"Yes! Of course I will! I love you!" my mother's sweet voice sings, and she laughs as my father picks her up and swings her around in joy. The last thing we see is Tatarina's heartbroken, tear-filled face as she walks away, and the wall turns back to the crystal mirror. Thorne falls to his knees, his head bowed. I kneel next to him, putting my hands on his shoulders and resting my head against his. I pull his hands up, going to call my ice to sooth them when I notice I can't do that. I can't feel my dragon or her emotions in here, it's like she is locked inside my head by the magic in this place.

"My whole life, even before I was born, she has lied and destroyed everything good around her, out of nothing but pure jealousy," Thorne whispers, the anguish in his voice painful to hear.

"Life is cruel at times, and it has different effects on us all. When I saw that, I only felt anger towards my father, sorrow for your mother, and sadness for my mum," I admit. No one other than my father won in that situation. Both of our mothers were hurt, because I doubt my mother knew her soon to be husband had slept with her best friend.

"All I felt was anger at my mother," Thorne says, lifting his head and locking his eyes on mine.

"Your mother killed mine, or at least made the order, and I hate her for that. I always will, but I understand her better now. She was lost from that moment we just saw, but I'm sure there is some part of her that still loves you. You are her son," I say gently.

"She doesn't love me. I was just a way for her to get the rebellion on her side," he whispers.

"You don't know that," I reply, and he laughs.

"I do. It's always meant to be like this for me. The people I love, they don't feel the same way. I might as well finally start accepting it," he says, pulling away from me and standing up. He clicks his flashlight on as I stand, and I place my hand on his shoulder.

"You don't know what she, or anyone else, feels for you," I

say, and he looks down at me for a second, something shining in his eyes that I can't understand.

"Then tell me," he pleads, dropping the flashlight and grabbing my face with his hands. I don't–no can't–say anything for a while as I just relax at his touch.

"I can't say it yet. I'm not ready to admit it, but I will say that you are wrong. You are so wrong about how I feel for you," I whisper. "And you might be wrong about your mother. It's hard not to care for you, even when someone doesn't want to, or isn't ready."

"Then I will say it, and I can only hope that you do feel the same and are willing to forgive me one day. I get that I still have a lot of making up to do, and you can hate me forever if you want, but I do love you. I loved you from the first moment I saw you, and it killed me to betray you for my mother. I was torn between two women, and not knowing which side to choose. I really did believe my mother was still good, and she was doing the right thing. I wish I realised how lost my mother was, but I didn't, and I can't change the past no matter how much I wish I could," he says, and I lean up, brushing my lips against his ever so gently before pulling away before it can become a real kiss, and I'm honestly surprised that he lets me.

"You're right. I can't just forgive and forget, but I can't let you go either. This is so complicated between us, but I'm not denying there is something more here than just our past. There was something from the moment we met, and together we can build again," I assure him, and he pulls me to him, holding me close.

"Thank you. I promise I will never let you down again. Never," he says into my hair, kissing the top of my head.

"You best not," I chuckle, wishing I could hear my dragon's thoughts on the matter, but she is still locked away from the magic in here. I don't even want to know Eli's, Kor's, and Dagan's thoughts on this when we get out of here. They are likely going to flip a lid, but I won't lie to them.

"We should get going. We need to get out of here," I say, pulling away but keeping my hand linked with his. He carefully picks up the flashlight from the floor without touching the crystal. Thorne flashes the light around the cave, and we both see the cave we came through is gone, and there is just a wall in its place now. There is another tunnel on the other side, and I guess that's the only way we can go.

"Are your hands okay?" I ask, feeling a little bit of the burns on his knuckles with my hand as we walk towards the tunnel and step off the crystal.

"Yeah, they don't hurt much," he shrugs, but I bet they do. *Men and their egos.*

"What is that?" I ask, seeing a light at the end of the tunnel just ahead of us.

"Maybe it's the exit?" Thorne asks.

"I don't think so . . . That would make it too easy . . ." my voice trails off as we walk into the light, and I take in the sight in front of me. The clearing is a meadow with white, glowing grass and five black trees in the middle of the grass. There are white flowers which smell amazing as we walk closer to the trees, and everything suddenly starts to feel a little hazy.

"Thorne . . ." I manage to whisper as his hand lets go of mine, and he falls to the floor. My legs can't seem to hold themselves up as I drop right next to him, seeing his lips form my name just before everything goes black.

81

ISOLA

"Hello?" I call, opening my eyes and staring at the empty ballroom in front of me. This room is from the castle. How did I get here? Where is Thorne? The ballroom is covered in flowers, a table full of presents is in one corner, and there's also a table full of food. I turn and look at the thrones at the front of the room. One large one, and one a little bit smaller. There are three pairs of thrones in different rooms of the castle, if I remember correctly, and I used to love watching my mother and father sitting on them, their crowns shining. They always looked so proud and happy. When nothing happens for a while, I start to panic, turning in circles. Where is Thorne?

"Thorne?" I shout, though my voice doesn't seem to make a sound around the room. The double doors suddenly open behind me, and I turn, seeing my mother walk in, her stomach large with pregnancy, and my father right behind her. My mum looks furious as she stops in the middle of the room. My mother has a long, stunning blue dress on, that matches my father's blue shirt. All blue, all representing the ice dragons that are nearly extinct now.

"All this time . . . all this time you never told me you slept with Tatarina? Then you cheat on me with the royal seer who is now pregnant! How many others?" my mum demands, screaming at him, and ice starts spreading across the gold floor as she shouts.

"Mum," I croak out, trying to go to her, but I can't move an inch, it's like I'm glued to the spot.

"No one else. Those were mistakes, grave mistakes," my father pleads, reaching for my mum, but she steps back.

"Liar! I know about the maid you just slept with, during our child's blessing ceremony of all things! While everyone is here to celebrate the fact that our child is nearly here, and you are too busy fucking the maid! A maid who was my friend!" mum spits out and walks over to him, slapping him hard around the face. He lets her, not moving as blood drips down his chin.

"I am sorry," he says.

"Tatarina was my best friend, and I never understood why she hated me so much like she does now. You took her from me because you are a spoiled brat who thinks he can have anyone and anything he wants!" mum growls and walks around him, towards the door. "I tell you now, you will never have me again. Publicly I will be a queen for you, but that is it."

"And our child? You can't tell her, she would hate me," he pleads.

"I will tell her everything about her father and what he has done when she is old enough to understand. Now never come near me again unless it's business about the crown," she says coldly and walks out of the room, leaving my father standing, watching her go. He falls to his knees, his head in his hands, and as I watch, I just hate him.

The vision suddenly blurs, and the room spins rapidly. I have to close my eyes as I fall to my knees as everything shakes. When the shaking stops, I open my eyes and look down at the long red dress I'm wearing. The dress is massive, something a queen would wear. I stand up slowly, staring out at the ballroom, which is completely on fire now. Pieces of the ceiling fall around me as I stand still in the middle of it. So much fire.

"I always knew you would bring fire and darkness. This is your future," a cold voice says behind me, and I turn, seeing Tatarina watching me with a huge smile.

"No," I whisper.

"To Dragca, may it burn eternal," she laughs, and everything, thankfully, fades away.

. . .

"ISOLA? ISOLA, WAKE UP!" Thorne's voice calls to me, but everything seems groggy as I force my eyes open and look at the cave ceiling. "Here," Thorne says, helping me up slowly and offering me some water from his bag. I drink some quickly, looking back over at the trees and meadow in the next room as I try to collect my thoughts.

"The blossom in the trees must be some kind of herb. Made to make you pass out and see visions. I saw some weird stuff, but Melody gave me an herb before we left. She said to take it when we entered the cave," he says, and I chuckle, wiping my eyes to wake myself up. "I guess it woke me up."

"Sounds like Melody. Mysterious and random," I say, my mind flashing back to the vision I saw. My father and mother hated each other, they always did. The vision of the future, of everything burning, and Tatarina winning.

"What's wrong?" Thorne asks, clearly seeing something in my expression.

"The vision showed that my father was always cheating on my mother, that she knew and hated him for it my entire life. Then it changed, showing me a version of the future that we cannot allow to happen," I whisper.

"The vision showed me that my mother never loved my father, and she just used him to further her plan," he says, smoothing his hands down my arms and leaving goose bumps. "I think we qualify for the most fucked-up parents award, don't you?"

"Yep," I laugh.

"Our parents are not us, and we can be better than them. That's all the vision was trying to show us, that we are better than they were. That somehow, we learnt right from wrong, even if it wasn't taught to us by both our parents," he says, helping me stand up as the room still sways a little.

"My mum taught me right from wrong, and I now know she is the bravest and most selfless woman I ever met. She put me and the crown before her own happiness," I say.

"You won't ever have to do that," he insists.

"Who knows what the future will bring? Now we need to find a way out," I say, straightening up and holding onto Thorne's hand. He puts the water away, and we start walking down the path we are on. It leads through a few more rooms made of crystal until we get to a much bigger room, full of treasure.

"It looks like a pirate hid all his treasure here," I gasp, staring at the piles of gold, jewels, and various other things littered around.

"Yeah, more like ten pirates and an army of jewel thieves maybe," Thorne mutters.

"I don't think we should touch anything. On Earth, they have tales of dragons hoarding jewels and gold, that they love shiny things and will do anything to protect them. Maybe there is some truth to it?" I suggest as we walk through the piles of gold.

"Humans are smarter than they look, children of Dragca, and the rumour is very much true," an old lady's voice drifts over to us. We look over to our left, seeing an old woman sitting on a gold throne, holding an old but deadly-looking staff. She has a black, ragged cloak on that covers her body, and her long grey hair falls around her shoulders.

"We didn't come here to steal. We just want to pass through here," I say, locking my eyes with her blue ones. I don't know why, but some part of me is cautious of the woman.

"I know. Yet you want something, you just do not know what," she says, speaking in riddles.

"Can you offer me something I want?" I ask.

"For a price, yes," she says, a big smile appearing on her dry, cracked lips.

"What is the price?" I ask hesitantly. Her haunting laugh fills the room as her next words frighten me.

"A price you will never give willingly."

82

ISOLA

"Explain? What wouldn't I give?" I ask, holding my hands on my hips. The old lady laughs again, lifting her staff and pointing it at Thorne.

"Love, the throne, and most of all, your people. You care too much to be a queen," the lady says. "A trait you have from your mother. Though, I do like people who care more for others than themselves."

"What is your name?" I ask, wondering how she knew anything about my mother, but learning her name might be the best start.

"Secrets are best kept that way, don't you think?" she says, moving her eyes between me and Thorne.

"You've lost me with all these riddles. We want to get out of this cave, not stand around talking. Let's go, Isola," Thorne says in a frustrated tone, and the old lady shoots a white light at him from the staff, making him fall to the ground with a thud.

"Thorne!" I scream, kneeling next to him and feeling his neck, thankfully finding a pulse.

"Don't you go worrying, he will be fine. I needed him out of the way, so we ladies could speak about the important things," she says, chuckling as I glare at her. "Men only get in the way, especially a sexy one like him."

"Talk about what?" I ask, standing up and staying in front of Thorne, though I cringe at her words. She suddenly loses all traces of amusement from her face.

"There must be balance, and very soon the balance will tip all the way in the favour of darkness. Now dark does not mean evil, nor does light mean good," she says, and I'm sure I have heard that somewhere before, but I can't remember where.

"Balance?" I question.

"All the worlds must have balance. We all have a choice, but none matter as much as your choice does," she says, her random sentences not making a bit of sense to me. It's like she jumps from one thought to another without explaining the last.

"Choice about what?" I ask.

"If you wish to become the balance or not," she says. "Though, you were born to be. Every time a balance is born here, they are either destroyed by the power, or they reject it. I do look forward to your choice," she says, smiling at me like she is proud of me or something.

"Lady, this isn't making much sense to me. What is the balance? What choice? What price?" I ask, shooting questions off rapidly, and she sighs deeply.

"Children," she huffs. "They have no patience at all these days."

"That doesn't exactly answer my question," I mutter as the lady carefully stands up and beckons me over. I glance once more at Thorne, who looks fast asleep and safe, before walking over to her because I know we need answers. She then walks through the piles of gold, and I follow until she stops so suddenly that I slam into her back. I collect myself before walking to her side and stare at the row of rocks in front of us. Ten rocks, all different colours and each one is floating.

"Balance is important in all worlds. Earth. Dragca, Frayan,

and many others that are interlinked," she says. I know of Earth and Dragca, of course, but not Frayan.

"Frayan?" I ask.

"There are portals on Earth to it, it's where fairies are from. Did you really think you were the only supernatural being alive? I believe there is even a war on Earth as we speak, destroying one of its main cities. The one with the pointy tower," she clicks her fingers in the air as I try to process her information. "Never mind the name of the place, Earth is not important right now."

"Who the hell are you? How do you know all this?" I demand, staring at her.

"Earth people call me a goddess, others call me a fate, and I have many, many other names you will never have heard of. I travel between worlds to do my job, to keep my power," she explains.

"Fate? You are fate?" I ask.

"One of many, at your service." She grins, a toothless one at that. "That is the human saying, yes?"

"Erm, yep," I reply, completely weirded out.

"Where were we? Oh yes, balance," she snaps her fingers, and the stones shake a little.

"Are the stones the balance?" I ask.

"No. You are. The people on Dragca, the dragons, the humans, and every being here. If darkness takes over, light will have to defend it," she says. "Dragca cannot fall, because Earth and Frayan would not be far behind. Millions, billions will die."

"You mean Bee and I have to defend it?" I ask in a hoarse whisper from the pressure her words create, and she smiles.

"Ah, the light spirit. Funny little things, aren't they? What is your dark spirit called again?" she asks, and I give her a confused look.

"I don't have a dark spirit, only a light one," I explain.

"Oh, I forgot. Silly me," she smacks her head with the staff. "I also forgot that this is for you." She hands me the staff, and I have no choice but to accept it, as she lets it fall into my open hands. I lift it up, examining the two deadly spikes on either end, and the twirls engraved all the way down it. The lady pushes a red gem right in the middle of the staff, and I step back in shock as the staff goes all bendy and snake-like as it gets smaller. It suddenly swirls around my arm, stopping with the red gem on my wrist.

"What the hell?"

"I've been to Hell, and it is not a nice place. Nasty demons there, child," the lady chuckles as I stare at my arm as I move it around.

"How does it work?" I ask, holding my arm out, and she looks at me like I'm an idiot.

"It's a royal weapon, a magic staff that can channel your ice and light powers. Only your blood line can use and wear it. The staff will change with you when you shift, and if you need to use it, you only have to push the red gemstone," she says in exasperation, like I should know all this.

"Thank you," I say honestly, knowing the staff could be very useful and very well might save my life one day.

"It belongs to your blood line, your very first ancestor made it. I would know, I was there," she laughs. "He was a funny man. I did like him very much."

"How old are you?" I ask as she continues to laugh, and she shakes her head, tapping the side of her nose to let me know I don't have a chance of getting that answer. I'm willing to bet she is pretty old.

"Now, we must discuss a price for the gift," she hums, rubbing her hands together.

"What gift?" I ask, guessing she doesn't mean the staff.

"I can tell you how to break the dragon guard curse. It is rather easy, actually, I'm surprised no one thought of it before, but you will need my help," she chuckles.

"You know how to break it?" I ask.

"Yes. Why else would Essna send you in here? She isn't a bad girl that one," the lady winks, and then the playfulness leaves her eyes.

"What is the price?" I whisper, dreading her response. From the look she is giving me, I know I won't like it.

"The price for the answer you seek is dear. In many years, when your firstborn turns eighteen, she is to be sent to me. No one will see her for three years, and my price will be taken," she says, almost singing the words, and I feel the power connected to them.

"What will you do with her?" I ask, my voice a mere rasp.

"I cannot tell you more, only that it is her fate. You must also never tell her of the promise you make me today. She cannot know in advance," she says and places her hand on my arm. "Do not worry, I see many children in the future you seek."

"You're asking me to hand over my child to you, my first-born, the heir of Dragca, if I win the throne?" I whisper.

"Yes. It is not an easy price to pay, but without my knowl-edge, you will never have a child to give me anyway," she says simply. "I cannot offer the help of a fate without a price. I do not wish to cause you more pain, Isola Dragice. I know your life has not been kind to you so far."

"Can you promise me her safety? That she will not be harmed?" I ask, needing at least that much to be answered.

"I promise that she will be under my protection. That is all I can say," she says, and steps over to the rocks. As I watch, she grabs the glowing blue one, crushing it in her hand and when she opens her hand, a long silver chain holds a tiny blue rock.

"You must wear this every day, until the time comes for you to fulfill your promise. Give it to your daughter when you bring her here in several years," she says.

"There isn't really a choice, is there? The curse must fall at the final promise. That's what the prophecy says. This is my fate, and my child will be the price and promise," I whisper and walk forward, tears streaming down my cheeks. I wrap my hand around the chain, lifting it and placing it over my head, so it falls around my neck.

"I promise," I breathe out roughly, and the stone glows briefly before settling back down. I look back up at the lady, who is smiling widely.

"Brilliant," she claps. "Let's wake your man, well, one of them, up. We will be needing him to break the curse."

83

ISOLA

"Thorne," I shake his shoulder a few times before he abruptly sits up, his hand automatically going to his sword. His eyes focus on me, and he seems to relax a little as he sees that I'm okay.

"What happened?" he asks, and I rest my hand on his that covers the sword and shake my head.

"It's okay, the lady just needed to talk to me alone," I tell him, and he looks over my head, where the old lady–well, goddess–is sitting on the gold throne again. She just smiles widely, and in a pretty creepy way, too.

"Don't do that again," he warns her, and she chuckles as I help Thorne stand up.

"I promise," she winks at me, and I roll my eyes at her playful attitude.

"What is this?" Thorne asks, first holding my arm out to look at the staff and then looking at my necklace.

"A long story, and something that can wait," I say, pleading with him to trust me. He does, nodding his head once, and he links our hands.

"How do we break the curse?" I turn and ask the lady.

"Simple. You must mate with the half ice and half fire prince.

The curse was made so no dragon guard and ice dragon could ever be together. So that dragon guards could never get the throne, and no half-blood would rule. If you two are mated, the curse will break. The curse was made from a place of love, from a mate desperate to save her king. The curse was never there to stop this. Fire and ice must rule, and the curse must break," she says, muttering the end as I stare up at Thorne.

"It can't be that simple!" Thorne refutes, shaking his head.

"Love is not simple, boy, you know this," the lady says, tutting at him.

"So, any half-blood could have stopped the curse by marrying a royal?" I ask.

"Yes. There is a reason the mixing of ice and fire dragons was kept secret. Your father knew how to break the curse, but that would have risked his army. So, he sent dragon guards to kill any half-bloods, just in case, to prevent you from ever falling in love with one. Seems he didn't find them all," she says as she winks at me again.

"Wait, we never agreed to mate," I whisper, looking up at Thorne.

"I won't push you for this. I know you don't love me fully yet, and it's too soon," Thorne tells me.

"You only need to say the words, share the blood, and I can bless you both. The rest of the mating can wait. Many have been mated without love or feelings. You do not need them," she informs, and pulls out a white stone. "I happen to have your mating stone right here."

"Isn't that meant to appear to me? To us?" I ask.

"Who do you think drops them for people to find? Sounds like a job for a fate, no?" she winks at me once more. *What is with all the winking?*

"Can Isola and I have a second alone?" Thorne asks, and she nods, leaning back in her chair. We walk around a pile of gold, and Thorne starts pacing the moment we are hidden.

"Stop a minute," I say, grabbing his arm.

"I can't make you do this; you don't want this. You don't want *me*. I don't want you to mate with me out of obligation. I want you to choose this and want it, want me," he sighs, pushing my hand away, "and I can see it in your eyes that you don't."

"I do want this, Thorne. Maybe not exactly mating yet, but I'm already bound to you in a way. I hate that I want this when I should still hate you. I hate that I can't tell Dagan, Kor, or Eli before we do this. I hate that we don't have more time to get to know each other, but I don't hate *you*. If anything, it's the opposite," I say, placing my hand back on his arm, and this time, he doesn't push me away.

"Isola, you don't have to say that," he says, and I grab his other arm, making him look down at me.

"I would never mate with someone I wasn't sure I want in my life. This curse needs to be broken. Let me give you back your dragon, and we can spend the rest of our lives working on us. Even if we end up as just friends, I want you in my life, and we will always mean something to each other," I say, and he smiles.

"You sure?" he asks, tucking a piece of my hair behind my ear.

"Positive," I grin, and he kisses my forehead. I lean in, closing my eyes, and breathe in his smoky, almost frost-like scent.

"I haven't got all day, you know!" the lady shouts, and I chuckle, linking my hand with Thorne's as we walk back over to her. She stands from the chair as we get closer, making the white mating stone float into the air above our heads when we stop.

"How are you doing that?" Thorne asks, and she laughs as she pulls a dagger out of her cloak, not answering his question.

"Thorne, why don't you start off with the ancient words? Do you know them?" the lady asks.

"I do," he says, taking my other hand in his and holding them between us as he speaks. "Link to the heart, link to the soul. I pledge my heart to you, for you, for all the time I have left. My dragon is yours, my love is yours, and everything I am, belongs with you." I repeat his words, watching as the white mating stone starts to glow, growing brighter with every sentence we speak. Our mating is blessed.

"Please hold out your hands," she requests, and we both do. She cuts Thorne's first and then mine as I hold in the pain-filled cry that threatens to escape my lips from the sting.

"Light and dark, good and evil, and everything that makes these ones dragons, please bless this mating. We bless you," the lady says, and I lock eyes with Thorne as we link hands. A blast of white light shoots out of the mating stone, sending us both flying apart. I roll as I land on top of a pile of gold, the white light making it impossible to see anything. As the light dims, my eyes widen at the sight of Thorne's dragon standing on a pile of gold. I've never seen his dragon before, and it's amazing. The wings and body are red, but covered with blue spikes that match his blue eyes.

"Isola, my dragon is back," Thorne's deep, shocked voice floats into my mind, as well as a touch of his elation I can sense. *We are mated. Holy crap. The dragon guard curse is broken.*

"I can hear you in my head," I chuckle, and I hear his laugh as his dragon snorts out ice and fire at the same time.

"None of that, I do not want my home on fire or frozen, thank you very much," the lady shouts, stamping out the fire with her foot and shaking her stick at Thorne. I slide down the pile of gold, tripping a bit, but managing to land somewhat gracefully.

"Thank you," I tell the lady as I walk over to Thorne and place my hand on the side of his head.

"Do not thank me just yet. Anyhow, you must leave," she says and points a stick up in the air to the ceiling. "That is your way out. Good luck, Queen Isola Dragice. I do look forward to the day we meet again."

"Goodbye," I say, watching as she walks through the gold, looking back at me once more.

"When you meet a woman called Queen Winter, make sure you tell her that her aunt says hello," she states cryptically, totally confusing me. Her body seems to slowly fade before she disappears altogether. I guess I will be meeting another queen. *Let's hope she is friendly.*

"*Well . . . that wasn't weird at all,*" Thorne mutters in my head, and I nod, still looking at the space where she once was.

"I can't call my dragon in here. I have no idea how you are, now that I'm thinking about it, but I will climb up, and you can fly us out of here," I say out loud, turning and pulling myself up onto his back after he leans down.

"*If you wanted to ride me, you only had to ask,*" he chuckles in my mind.

"Get your head out of the gutter. Besides, you need to prepare yourself. It's likely Eli and the others are going to try and kill you for mating with me once we get out of here," I laugh, hearing his own grumble in my head. I slide myself between two of the spikes on his neck and wrap my arms around the one in front of me.

"*They can try, now hold on,*" he warns, and spreads his wings out, knocking over everything as he bats his wings and pushes down with his legs, shooting up to the top of the cave. I hold my head down as Thorne slams into the ceiling of the cave, breaking out into the night sky. He flies up into the sky, levelling himself out as I look at the stars.

"*Can you see that? Something is wrong,*" Thorne's worried voice drifts over to me in my mind, and I lift my head, seeing the forest on fire in lots of places, seconds before I hear the screams.

Danger. I sense Tatarina, my dragon hisses.

"Dragons incoming," I shout, spotting five of them flying straight towards us, suddenly appearing out of the trees. They don't look right; their dragons are flying way too shakily, and they look almost grey. *What the hell are those?* I move myself from between the spikes and walk down Thorne's body as he tries to fly us away.

I'm going to shift in the air. We haven't done this before, but we need to now. You ready? I ask my dragon, and she roars in my mind.

Be right back, mate, I say to Thorne, who doesn't seem to realise what I'm about to do. I run and jump right off his tail, falling and opening my arms as my dragon takes over.

84

DAGAN

"What the hell is wrong with them?" I shout, driving my sword into the heart of another dragon guard. I look down at him, examining his black eyes and the black veins all over his pale skin. They are almost like zombies, and they fight like them, too. The dragon guards should be more trained than this.

"Tatarina has done something to them!" Elias shouts back as he kills two of the guards in one broad swipe of his sword. I look around, seeing only a few more of the dragon guard coming for us. I'm running straight through the woods when I see a little girl screaming as she runs away from three dragon guards who are trying to kill her. She can only be eight, and they are attacking her. I catch up to the little girl and push her behind me. She's shaking and absolutely terrified.

"Stand by that tree and close your eyes," I tell her. She does as I ask with a single nod and tears streaming down her dirt-covered cheeks. I turn to face the guards, anger burning through me.

"Come on then, don't you think you should play with someone your own size, you bastards?" I shout as they run at me with their black eyes. I kick the first one, slicing my sword across his neck and swinging to meet the next guard. He slams his sword against mine as the third guard runs for the girl. From the corner of my eye, I can see where she stands, still holding onto the tree with her eyes closed.

"No!" I yell, pushing against the sword with my other hand, cutting it, and slamming the guard back. I quickly pull out a dagger from my belt and slam it into his chest, and I keep moving, running at the girl, trying to reach her before she gets hurt. Kor appears from behind the tree, throwing his sword into the guard's chest just before he can get to her, and the guard falls to the ground.

"Good timing, man," I breathe out, going back to yank my dagger out of the other guard and sliding it back into my belt. Kor kneels next to the girl, who won't open her eyes and shakes her head of red hair. I walk over, placing my hand on Kor's shoulder. He looks between us and stands up.

"I will keep an eye out," he says, standing behind me as I kneel in front of the girl.

"Hey, what is your name?" I ask gently.

"Isie," she mumbles, sobbing on her words.

"Isie, I need you to open your eyes and answer something for me," I tell her.

"Okay," she says shakily and finally looks at me. "You saved me. You are like a brave prince." I smile at her words and pull my cloak off my back, wrapping it around her shoulders.

"What happened in the seer village? We don't know anything as we were here waiting for princess Isola to come out the cave," I explain to her, spotting Elias walking over to us. She grips my cloak tightly before she answers.

"The guards came while we were all sleeping, and the woman with black stuff all over her was telling them to kill us all. The guard killed my mummy, and my father told me to run," she says, bursting into tears again. I pick her up, holding her close as I turn around, hearing the sound of footsteps.

"Someone is coming," Elias says, stepping in front of me and the child, guarding us with Korbin. We watch the treeline anxiously as we hear people running, and a woman comes into view. She runs, holding a baby, and five other small children are with her. They all look covered in dirt and blood. *Maybe whoever did this let them go?*

"Auntie!" Isie shouts, wriggling in my arms to get down, and I let her. She runs to her aunt, who holds her close as we come over.

"What happened?" Elias demands. The woman is clearly panicked and scared, her cloak is covered in blood, and her brown hair is littered with leaves. The children all hide behind her, looking terrified.

"The queen has done something dark to all of those guards. I was in charge of the nursery for the night. We barely escaped. They don't know who we are, who they are, and have no control over who they kill," she blurts out and looks behind her before staring at us. "We have to leave. The children are not safe. You could come with us and protect us."

"We have to wait for the princess, but keep running. We won't let anyone follow you," I say firmly, and she nods.

"Good luck. If we make it, we will pray for the princess. The true heir of Dragca," she says, bowing her head, "and her mates." I nod back before she runs carefully through the forest with the children trailing close on her heels. Isie waves once before following them, clutching my cloak.

"I don't like this. Melody and Bee are in the village," Kor says, rubbing his face. "My parents are, Darth . . . we have to go back." I catch his shoulder as he starts to walk that way.

"No. Isola needs us," I remind him.

"She will never forgive us if we let Melody and Bee get killed," Elias points out, and I shake my head at them both.

"We can't–" I stop as a light bursts in the sky, a bright light like nothing else I've ever seen, and a warm feeling slams into my body, causing me to fall to my knees.

Fly, my dragon hisses in my mind, the shift taking over before I can even think or comprehend what just happened.

You're back, I say, feeling so relieved and whole. My dragon stretches out its body after the shift, and I know somehow Isola has broken the dragon guard curse. I roar, looking over at Korbin's and Elias's dragons. They seem to be in shock, just standing there, shaking their heads.

Minnnee, my dragon hisses, turning its head to the sky just as a dragon breaks out of the mountains and into the sky. I instantly recognise the blonde head of hair as Isola riding on Thorne's back through the skies.

Danger, I shout to my dragon, seeing five other dragons flying towards them. My dragon stretches its wings out just as Isola stands up and jumps straight off Thorne's back.

85

ISOLA

Fight, my dragon hisses in my mind as her wings spread out in the air, and she starts to fly. We turn around mid-air, feeling Thorne's dragon at my side as we face the others as they get closer. They shoot fire in the shape of spheres at us, and my dragon drops under them, shooting straight towards them.

Kill them! I demand of her, and she shoots her own spheres of ice at them in a flurry of ice and fire that Thorne shoots with me. I drop down as the dragons get too close, and Thorne does the same, but he goes above them. My dragon looks up just in time to see two of them get hit with Thorne's attack of ice, and they drop into the trees. One of the dragons slams into me while I'm not looking, digging his claws into my wings as we fall together, and I cry out in pain. I look up, seeing three more dragons flying towards Thorne as he fights two off on his own.

No! I scream in my dragon's head as we fall through the trees and land on the ground, his claws finally coming free of my wings, so I can move. I shoot ice onto his wings as he tries to fly and keep shooting it until his entire dragon is frozen to the ground. His dragon's eyes almost dead as I stare at him encased in the ice. I look up, not seeing Thorne or any other dragons flying around.

"It has been a long time, Isola, don't you think?" Tatarina's cold, dead-sounding voice says from behind me, and my dragon turns to roar at her. I feel down my wings, knowing the damage to them is too much, and I won't be able to fly out of here for a bit. There is only one thing we can do, even if it makes me vulnerable.

Let me takeover, I ask my dragon, who doesn't hesitate as we shift back. I stand up straight, keeping my head high as I face Tatarina. She stands still like a ghost; her dark, nearly brown hair blowing in the wind is the only movement. Her eyes are completely black, and they match the dark glow her skin now has. I look over as a woman steps out from the shadows of the trees, making me take a step back.

"Bu-but, I killed you!" I gasp as Esmeralda stands by her sister's side, smiling widely with her blood-red lips. Her eyes are now as red as her hair, and her pale skin is littered with black veins.

"Death was not my ending," Esmeralda replies, her voice croaking and broken in places. Her head twitches as she speaks, and Tatarina places her hand on her sister's arm.

"I will remember to chop your head off next time," I sneer. "Just to be sure."

"There will not be a next time, for this is *your* ending, Isola," Tatarina says, holding her hands out at her sides. "You are alone, and I am queen. Is this what you always thought would happen?"

"I kinda hoped I would have killed you by now, but I still have time," I say, feeling for the staff on my arm and knowing I can fight her.

"You could join me," she says simply, and I just laugh.

"The throne is mine! I am the heir, and I will claim it back when I have killed you! You killed my mother, my father, and had your sister kill Jace! There is so much death on your hands, and you do not deserve to live!" I spit out at her, and for only a brief second does she flinch at my words.

"Mother, don't do this," Thorne says from behind me, and I turn, seeing him walking to my side with Kor and Dagan next to him. Thorne and his mother stare at each other, and a flood of pain enters my body from Thorne's emotions, not that I would have expected any less.

"Where is Elias?" I hiss at Dagan as he gets to my side.

"During the fight with those other dragons, we got separated. I'm sure he will find us soon," Dagan whispers back, and I try to swallow the worry and guilt that floods me. I know he isn't dead, with our blood bond I would feel it. *So, he must be okay.*

"Do you really choose her? I'm your mother, and I can give you the throne! All I ask is that you kill her!" Tatarina gets more and more frustrated with every word, and I swear there is actually some kind of emotion coming from her.

"This isn't a choice," Thorne replies, glancing at me. "It never was. You have lost your mind, do you really want to lose your son, too? Is the throne worth it?"

"It's me or her," Tatarina growls, never taking her eyes off Thorne.

"Is that what you asked my father? I mean, when he chose my mother over you," I ask, and she growls, black ice dripping from her hands as she steps closer, focusing her attention on me instead of Thorne.

"No!" she spits out.

"It was, wasn't it? All of this because my father was an asshole and didn't choose you. You don't have to do this, you don't have to lose your son and make him choose," I say, and she laughs.

"I can smell your mating, he has already chosen," Tatarina says.

"Mating?" Dagan hisses, and I can't look away from Tatarina and Esmeralda as they step forward together to answer him.

"It's time you ran, little girl. Change is coming, and there is no room for the light on Dragca anymore," Tatarina says, and a dark spirit flies out of the trees, landing on her outstretched hand. The dark spirit looks so much like Bee, but with dark-blue skin and black hair. She is still beautiful, even if she is dark. Her dark eyes meet mine, and there's a shock that flitters through me as we stare at each other. I almost step forward, but Kor grabs my arm to stop me.

"There is always a place for light and the true queen," Melody says, just as I feel Bee land on my shoulder. I glance over to see her stop next to Dagan, nodding at me, even as she is covered in blood, missing her cloak and holding her orb under her arm.

"Good, you are all in one place. It will make this so much easier," Tatarina says, and I see her smile widely.

"There is a portal to our left, we run," Bee whispers in my ear as I look back at Tatarina. *We need a distraction.*

"Are you really so bitter over one man turning you down that you will destroy the whole world?" I ask her, and she growls loud.

"Once I've destroyed *your* love, let me know if you feel like destroying the world in revenge," she counters and clicks her fingers. Two guards walk out, carrying an unconscious Elias who hangs between them, his hair covered in blood. I scream, going to run forward, but both Thorne and Dagan hold my arms, stopping me. I swallow the panic in my throat and force my eyes away from Elias as Tatarina smirks at me.

"No," Dagan growls out, fire feeling like it is burning my arm where he holds me, but it doesn't actually burn me. I honestly don't really notice as I stare at Tatarina's every movement. Tatarina walks over to Elias, and I clench my fists, trying to hold myself back. She lifts his head by grabbing a fistful of his hair, showing me his bruise-covered face before letting his head drop back down.

"This one is pretty, such a shame he has such bad taste in women," she says, twirling a piece of his hair around her finger.

"Let him go," I demand, my hands shaking as ice drips onto the floor, mixing with the blood on my arms from the cuts. My dragon roars in my mind, and I have to push her away to stop the shift.

"Why?" she asks, laughing deeply, still touching my Elias. I'm going to kill her for this. *Slowly.*

"You can have me if you let him and my friends go," I say, starting to panic as I spot the thirty or maybe more guards surrounding us, hiding in the trees.

"No," Kor growls, pulling me back by my arm.

"Best listen, you cannot beat me," she laughs. "But you can watch as I destroy all the light. Nane?" she asks, looking at Nane who flies towards her hand once again.

"What are you doing?" I ask, just as Nane touches her hand, and she kneels down, digging her hand into the dirt. Her whole body glows black, and thick smoke flows from her body, spreading quickly.

"This place, it's the source of all of Dragca's magic. What do you think happens when I flood it with darkness?" Tatarina asks, and my eyes widen as I realise what she is going to do.

"Stop!" Bee shouts and falls off my shoulder as Tatarina slowly destroys all the light, and I can't stop her. I catch Bee, and Melody takes her off me.

"Protect me, sister, and the light will soon be gone," Tatarina says, a black orb of smoke surrounding her body as dozens of guards appear out the shadows, walking towards us. Esmeralda pulls out two swords and runs towards us suddenly. I growl, stepping closer and ready to fight when Dagan grabs me. He throws me over his shoulder and takes off running the other way. I look back, pushing against Dagan as I see the guards drag Elias away into the shadows. My heart shatters and panic floods me.

"Let me go, what are you doing?" I demand, fighting him, but he is too strong. My dragon fights me, too, trying to make me shift, and my arms still burn from the cuts, knowing I couldn't fly even if I let her. *I can't save him.*

"Saving you. It is what Elias would want and what has to happen. Tatarina is destroying the light, and you are all that is left," Dagan says harshly, and I turn in time to see Thorne slam his hands on the floor, making a large ice wall stretch up between us. The circular wall completely covers us, only leaving a small gap behind us to escape as we see Esmeralda slam her sword against the ice on the other side. Dagan holds me tightly as he darts through the gap, and I fight him, desperate to get back.

"Stop! Let me go! We can't leave him with her! She will kill him!" I cry as we run through the forest, following Melody.

"Doll, we don't have a choice! Do you think we want to leave him with her? No," Kor says from my left, and I growl at him. I catch Thorne's eyes for only a second, feeling his sorrow through our bond, but he still runs.

"I will hate you all if he dies, let me go!" I plead, my words turning into sobs.

"We are nearly at the portal," Melody shouts over her shoulder. Thorne and Kor shoot balls of ice and fire at guards that get near us. Dagan finally drops me and lets me go as we come to a stop, and Melody whispers to the portal we are at. I push him away as he tries to hold my hand, and he grabs my shoulders firmly, making me look at him.

"You would have frozen me if you truly believed you could save him. You can't, and you know it," Dagan says, wiping my tears away as he takes my hand. "She won't kill him, not when she can use him against you. If I thought there was any way to save my brother, I would be back there. We need to make a rescue plan, and we can do that on Earth. Okay?" he says, and I finally give up, even as it makes me sick to do so. One day on

Earth to make a plan, that's it. She can't do too much to him in a day.

"Okay," I agree shakily, still hating that I can't run back now. I follow Melody through the portal back to Earth, knowing we will be back soon to get my dragon.

86

ISOLA

"A supermarket, great," Kor mutters as he comes through the portal last, and we stare around the empty place. Melody grabs a bottle of water off a shelf, opening it and drinking some before passing it to Kor.

"We should run, they could follow us," Kor says, accepting the drink. I just turn and stare at the portal, wishing Elias would run through it, escaping somehow.

"Is Bee okay?" I ask, glancing at her in Melody's arms. She looks less bright, less like Bee, and something isn't right.

"Earth isn't good for light spirits, and I don't know what Tatarina did back there," Melody says, looking both confused and worried at the same time. I have an idea, but not a good one.

"We will go back after we make a plan and clean up. Oh, and we need to get weapons," Dagan says, and I nod, walking through the aisle we have come out at.

"Is-o-la," Thorne strangles out my name, and I turn, seeing him holding his neck where a dart is sticking out of it. He falls to the floor as Dagan shouts out in a pain-filled grunt and drops to his knees. I grab him as he falls, pulling out the dart that is stuck in his neck and looking at it. *What the crap is that?*

"Run!" Kor demands, and I turn, only to stop as a figure

walks down the aisle. I hear Kor and Melody fall behind me as Hallie steps into the light, holding a gun at me. She looks so different from the last time I saw her that I almost don't recognise her. Hallie's hair is up in a ponytail, the tips dyed a green colour that doesn't match her brown eyes that are narrowed on me. I look over her clothes, or outfit rather, that is black army gear or something. She is covered in guns, daggers, and there is even a sword on her back. *What happened to my friend?*

"Shoot her!" a man demands behind Hallie, and she holds a hand up as she focuses on me, and everything goes deadly silent. I can't help the brief smile I give her as I missed my friend, but I know something is wrong. They have done something to my dragons and sister.

"Isola," Hallie says coldly, and I hold my own hands up in surrender as she raises the gun higher.

"I don't understand. What are you doing? Hallie?" I ask her, and she shakes her head, holding the gun firm.

"My father told me what you are, but I didn't believe him! I didn't believe that monsters were real, and my best friend was one!" she shouts, locking her eyes with mine.

"I'm not a monster," I explain gently, seeing the five guys stepping behind her, wearing masks and holding their own guns up.

"My father hunts monsters like you, keeps us safe. You are a dragon, much like the monsters that took over Paris and destroyed it while you were gone! Thousands of people are dead or missing because of your people!" she spits out. "My mother was in Paris. My mother is gone, and it's all your fault!"

"I don't know anything about Paris!" I shout at her, getting frustrated. "I only want to save my own world. That is it."

"Same, and this is why I have to capture you and take you to my father. To the hunters' organisation," she says, her voice cracking as her hand shakes.

"You don't have to do this. You could let us go. I have to go back to Dragca for Elias, and I'm no threat to you. I'm your best friend, Hallie!" I plead, and I spot tears streaming down her face as she pulls the trigger, shooting a dart into my stomach. I hold my hands over it as I fall to my knees. She kneels down, too, looking straight into my eyes, and I can see nothing but hate reflecting back in them.

"You burnt down Michael's house and killed five teenagers. You are a monster and *not* my best friend. I clearly don't know you at all," she says, walking away. Everything gets blurry as I try to speak. I can only hear her footsteps on the floor as the world goes dark and one word leaves my lips.

"Eli."

EPILOGUE

Elias

"Elias Fire . . . you are so, so lucky," Tatarina taunts, grabbing my shoulder with her cold hand and digging her nails in as she smiles widely. I smirk before spitting in her face. She slams me back into a wall of the dungeon, my chains slamming against it as I stand up again.

"Kill me and get it over with, you bitch!" I shout. I close my eyes and picture only Isola. I feel content in the knowledge the others would have her safe on Earth by now.

"Death is not my plan for you. No. Isola will come for you, and when she does, I want her to know the pain of having the man she loves choose darkness over her," Tatarina says, chuckling to herself.

"I will never choose anything or anyone over Isola," I growl, opening my eyes again. Tatarina just smiles widely at my response.

"Darling, when I'm done, you won't even remember who she is," Tatarina laughs, holding her hand in the air, and a black cloud of smoke spreads from her hand.

"Isola," I shout as the smoke smothers me, and everything blurs away.

Pre-order Wings of Fate here...

Two worlds and only one light left to save them both...

With one of her dragon guards left in Dragca, and Isola trapped on Earth, everything is spinning out of control.

Isola fights to overcome her memories of Earth as she discovers more hidden secrets than she could have ever imagined.

Curses have been broken, but so have minds and hearts as the war for Dragca continues...
18+ Reverse Harem

PROLOGUE

HALLIE

"Hallie, dear, I didn't expect to see you today," Jules surprised voice greets me as I walk into the room. I close the door behind me before looking at Jules, who sits in a chair by her bed, a closed book in her lap. Jules smiles at me like nothing is wrong as she places the book on the side, but little does she know that everything is so wrong. The woman I love and her sister are in terrible danger…and I put them there. I carefully pull the small, green, doll-like creature out of my zipped up jacket. Isola, Melody and the other dragons came through the portal with it, and the last thing Melody told me in a dream was to protect this creature with my life. I risked everything to hide the creature in my jacket when none of the other hunters were looking. The creature has silky long hair, and very much looks like *Tinkerbell* but more green.

"Oh my…what is that?" Jules gasps.

"Melody told me her name is Bee, but I don't know what she is," I try to explain. "Melody said Bee needs plants to survive here, or she will die." Jules slowly gets up off the chair with an awed expression aimed at Bee and walks over to me. She picks Bee out of my hands and looks around the room.

"I have a bonsai tree. It will have to do until I can get some more plants tomorrow morning," Jules says. She carries Bee to the small tree in the corner of the room and places her so she is resting in the branches. Bee shines a bright green and smiles as she wraps her tiny hands around the branch near her face.

"She seems happy," I say with a little sigh. I can't mess this up. My Melody wouldn't have told me to keep her safe if it wasn't very important.

"But you are not, my Hallie," Jules kindly mentions. "Where is Isola and this Melody you speak of?"

"My father has them, and I can't do anything," I say, lifting my hands to my face and rubbing my eyes. "I need a plan and maybe some help."

"For those who listen...help can be found," Jules cryptically tells me, walking over to her bedside cabinet and picking her phone up. "Dragons are not the only creatures that are magical in this world. I think it is time we told the supernaturals in this world about your father's work...and how to destroy it."

87

ISOLA

I lie on the cold floor, staring up at the rocky ceiling above me, listening to the sound of deadly silence. The room smells of damp and a lot of bleach, which makes my nose twitch. I stretch my fingers out, feeling nothing but cold, rough stone under my hands. I try to move my body on instinct, but nothing other than my fingers move. Panic starts to set in just before I hear his voice which instantly calms me.

"Isola, you're okay. It's just the drugs wearing off. I'm here."

I know it was Dagan's voice, but I'd like to see him and reassure myself, yet moving isn't an option right now. As I lie in the dim light, staring at the ceiling and hearing Dagan's deep breathing not far from me, I remember coming through the portal. I remember those people shooting us with darts, and Hallie being with them, looking so different from when we last saw each other. Hallie shot me. I wasn't even fighting her, trying to run, or defending myself, and she didn't hesitate for more than a moment before she pulled the trigger.

I try not to panic when I realize we have been gone from Dragca a lot longer than I thought, and that Eli needs me to get him back. *Elias needs me, and all I can do is lie on the ground, wishing to move.* I know some part of me is thinking this is all still some big mistake, and Hallie will save us somehow. Then I remember everything she said about Michael. Paris doesn't sound good either as she clearly thinks dragons killed her mother. If I can get her alone, I can explain what happened with Michael; at least I might have a chance of getting her to understand. A million questions run through my head as I'm forced to lie still and remember everything. *This is all so confusing, why would she let her father do this? What exactly does he want us here for?*

After a while, I manage to pull my head with all my strength to the left, seeing thick bars right next to me as the feeling starts to come back to my body. I focus on the other side of the bars where Dagan is. He is lying on the floor, looking dazed as his blue eyes meet mine, filled with worry and as much pain as I am in. Dagan's hair is messy, and he looks very pale but not much different from when we came through the portal. I notice he still has his dragon guard clothes on, and so do I, by the feel of it. I reach my arm up, feeling for the necklace on my neck and am relieved to know it's still there. I promised never to take it off, and breaking a promise to a fate might not be the best idea. I'm hoping it hasn't been too much time while we slept, and I hope I can move soon to find answers. *Before getting the hell out of here.*

"Are you okay?" I question Dagan, my voice sounding dry and cracked even to my ears. "Have you seen the others? Where are we?" The questions rapidly spew from my mouth; I know I'm mumbling them, and I doubt Dagan can understand me.

"I'm okay, princess," Dagan whispers back, his voice sounding as bad as mine, but at least he understood that bit. I feel relieved, even if he doesn't look as okay as I'd want him to be and free from here. I watch as he pulls himself into a sitting position, before slowly making his way to the bars, sweat pouring down his forehead from the struggle. He doesn't say a word, just being there for me as I keep testing my body to see if I can move. I slowly start wriggling my legs after a long time. Even though I'm not strong enough to move like Dagan yet, my strength is coming back which is a relief. I reach for my dragon in my mind, feeling her presence, but she feels dazed and sleepy, before I focus back on Dagan.

"Was that your human friend with the people who knocked us out?" Dagan asks me, clearly remembering Hallie. "I didn't know humans were so trigger happy."

"Yes, it was. Hallie believes I killed Michael and four other teenagers. She thinks I've got something to do with her mother dying in Paris," I mumble. "I don't know if she is my friend anymore or if we can trust her. The look in her eyes when she shot me...it was empty of emotion."

"I'm sorry, Isola. Losing a friend is never easy, but we can't focus on her right now. What happened in Paris?" he asks me, and when I stare into his eyes, he reminds me of Elias for a second which makes this whole situation harder than I know how to deal with.

"I don't know what's going on any more than you do. We need to get out of whatever this is, because Eli needs us," I whisper, my voice cracking when I speak his name. *My Eli.* My dragon guard is in danger, and I know I could never survive losing him.

"My brother is alone with that psychopath who hates us all. God knows what she is going to do to him, but we have to save him before she destroys him. The last time we were there wasn't pretty, but at least he had us with him. Elias has a dark side, and being around a dark spirit won't be good for him," Dagan growls, getting angrier with every word before he slams his fist onto the ground. "Fuck's sake, I can't lose him."

"Hey!" I shout getting his attention, and his now red eyes lock on mine. "We can't lose it right now. We need to figure something out and keep calm."

"I know that, princess. I don't like being weak and defence-less. We can't make our dragons come out with these around our necks," he points at the metal collar strapped around his neck. It's only then that I realize that I have one on as well, the cold metal is tightly pressed around my neck. It no doubt stops us from shifting, and I reach a hand, feeling the thick metal and the small box attached to the left side. I'm sure the collar is for more than just stopping us shifting.

"I'm going to look in the cell next to mine. Maybe Korbin, Thorne or Melody are in it," Dagan states and pulls himself up with the bars as I watch silently. I call out for Thorne in my mind, feeling that he is okay, but his lack of response suggests he is sleeping still. Dagan comes back after a little while, sitting close to the bars and looking down at me, catching his breath back.

"Thorne is in the next cage, but he is still asleep. As I'm sure you already know, he is fine," Dagan tells me, looking tense. I don't need to ask what is wrong because I can see it in his eyes. He is upset about Thorne and me mating, and I don't blame him one bit. I want to comfort him, explain things, but I know it is not the right time.

"Can you make any fire?" I ask, because I am too weak to make ice right now, but if Dagan could burn the bars, we could get out.

"No. I tried it when I woke up, and the collar electric-shocked me until I passed out. Either whoever knocked us out is clearly watching us, or these collars somehow have some kind of sensor in them. Whatever it is, don't try to call your ice," he warns me in a frustrated voice. *Well, there goes that plan.* I know he isn't frustrated with me, just the situation, and he is right to be. It sucks. I take his advice for now, but the moment I can get this collar off, I am going to let my dragon free to do whatever she wants. It's not like I can call my powers or my dragon at this moment anyway, but it is nice to look to the future.

"Isola, I need you to get up and try to move. The drugs wear off quicker when you move, I think. I know it hurts, but come to me." I keep a brave face on as I focus on sitting up, every little movement sending pain throughout my body and making me want to just take a nap. Though I do notice it gets slightly easier and less painful after the first few movements. I manage to sit myself up slowly, every movement is still a little painful, and it takes me a long time to do anything. I move my arms a little when I'm sitting up, seeing the spear is still wrapped around my arm. The necklace and spear bracelet must be magically attached to me, because there is no doubt the people that took us here would have tried to take them off. I need to pretend it's a piece of jewelry, as it would be a good way to defend myself when the time is right.

I feel around my two pockets, not finding anything useful. Dagan is silently watching me, and I know I need to get to him at least. I crawl myself over to the bars where Dagan is resting, even though every part of my body aches and protests against the movement. It reminds me of whatever Michael injected me with, but worse. *Much, much worse.* Even thinking back to what happened with Michael, and how familiar this drugged out feeling is, freaks me out. Michael must have had something to do with whatever Hallie's father has gotten Hallie involved in here. I try not to feel terrified at the thought, but my hands shake, and my mouth goes dry. When I get to the bars, sliding down to the floor, Dagan reaches through and holds my clammy hand in his tightly.

"I will get us out of this, Isola," he whispers to me, pressing his head on the bars, watching me like he can understand my every thought without me saying a word.

"How can we get out of something when we don't know what's going on?" I ask, resting my head on the cold bars next to Dagan's, needing the brief closeness for the comfort he gives me. I stare at the door to the cell for a long time, which is the first in the corridor of cages, by the looks of it. After a long time, my legs finally feel like I'm strong enough to move. I stand up and walk around the room, shaking the bars to test them, but knowing it is pointless.

"They wouldn't have put us in here if we could just get out. Come and sit with me," Dagan softly suggests, and I sigh, knowing he is right, before going to sit back down next to him. I go to ask Dagan how Elias got caught by Tatarina, but the door to the corridor opens, flashing a bright light in. A moment later, someone turns on the lights in the room, which blasts against my eyes so I can't see for a second. When I can see again, I briefly look across Dagan's cage, seeing Thorne on the floor in another cell, still sleeping. The cages next to his are too far for me to see in, but I see shadows of people on the floor which gives me hope that they are Korbin and Melody. I look back to the door in time to see a man walk into the room, stopping right in front of my cage.

"It is lovely to finally meet you, princess Isola Dragice, sole heir to the world of Dragca," the man smoothly says, confusing me a little with how he knows my title and name. "My daughter and your father told me so much about you that it's a pleasure for us to finally meet," the human man states. The human has familiar features, with short brown hair that matches his brown eyes. His expensive suit has a yellow dragon symbol embroidered into the breast pocket. I recognise him as Hallie's father after a moment's pause, though his cold eyes lack any human emotion like his daughter has. I freeze when I process his sentence, and the part where he claimed my father told him about me. *That is impossible.*

"My father told you what?" I demand, and he grins widely at me.

"Why don't we go for walk, and I can explain everything to you as I give you a tour of your new home, Isola," he suggests, though I don't think for second he is asking me to walk with him as much as he is making a demand. The human holds all the power here, and from his tone and the look in his eyes, he knows it as well as I do.

"My Isola isn't going anywhere," Dagan sharply snaps. I shoot my eyes to him as he roars out in pain, his hands going to the collar, holding it as it electrocutes him as he falls to the floor. Dagan growls and screams as he tries to stay awake. The awful smell of the collar burning his neck floats over to me, making the whole situation terrifyingly real. My heart pounds in my chest, feeling like it's breaking into pieces as I watch the dragon I love being tortured.

"STOP!" I scream, pleading with anyone to stop this. Nothing changes, and thankfully a few moments later, I watch in horror as Dagan passes out on the ground, his hands falling away from the collar. I have to watch his chest rise and fall in the silent room before I can even take a breath.

"That is just a taste of what I will do to him—and the others —if you don't behave. Now, let's have a talk like civilised people," the man states coldly, like he didn't just cause my dragon immense pain before he passed out from it. I pull myself up with the bars, keeping my expression neutral as I face the man, but I promise myself that he will be the first one I kill when I get the chance. *No one touches my dragons without paying for it.*

88

ISOLA

The man clicks his fingers in the air, and two men in black army-type uniforms come through the open door into the corridor. They are dressed similarly to how Hallie was when she shot me, all black army clothes, but these men look more serious with their shaved heads and scary expressions. I remind myself they are only humans, and even with this collar on, I could fight them. *Or try*. One of them unlocks the door to my cage and stands waiting, waving a hand, signaling me to walk out. I walk to the door, and the other man holds his hand in the air with a pair of handcuffs, stopping me from leaving.

"For safety. I am not stupid enough to allow you out here without your hands in those. Especially since we cannot get that thing off your arm, and I do not know what it is," the man in charge says, flashing his eyes towards Dagan in the other cell. I know he is warning me that I have to do this or the others will pay for it. I grit my teeth, hating that I have no choice but to do as I am told. I put my arms out in front of me, and the man holding the cuffs quickly snaps them onto my wrists. I slowly walk out between them, towards the man in charge. I stop right in front of him, having to look up as he is a little taller than I am, and he grins widely like this is all a game. *I highly doubt he will think this is funny when I kill him.*

"My name is Mr. Graves. Though your father used to call me Graves, so you may, as well. I do wish for us to get along," he says, referring again to the fact he apparently knew my father. I almost don't want to reply, knowing that there is a very good chance my asshole of a father did something evil with this human. I already know he was not a good king, mate or person. If he had something to do with this human, I might as well call him evil and be done with it. I know it's immature to want to cling to some hope that my father made one good decision in his life. That he did one pure, selfless thing that means I can remember him without hating him. The more I learn of the past, the more I know that will never happen.

"I don't believe you. What was the king of the Dragons doing talking to a *human* like you," I growl, and the man's face tightens in anger. "Humans were nothing but slaves to a king like my father."

"I have already warned you once to behave, and I will tell you now that I do not lie or give second chances. I want us to have an agreement, purely because I respected your father and had a good agreement with him," he says, calming himself down as he speaks. I resist the urge to roll my eyes at his lie. This man used my father as much as my father likely used him. The only question is: *what did my father want with humans?*

"What kind of agreement are you talking about?" I ask, instinctually going to cross my arms but the handcuffs don't let me. I lock my fingers together instead, feeling lucky the middle part to the handcuffs is a chain, so it's possible.

"Come with me, and I will show you," he simply replies, nodding his head towards the door before walking towards it. Again, I know he is demanding I follow him and not asking. The sound of the guards behind me unclipping their guns tells me as much. I walk just behind him, looking behind me once to see the two human guards staying close, with the guns once clipped to their belts now in their hands. Apparently, they don't trust the collars all that much, and it gives me hope that I might be able to break them somehow.

The door opens out to a massive white room that is circular, and there is a banquet table in the middle, with empty metal trays where I assume food is served. There are doors littered around the room and tables with chairs pushed up to them in the middle. Graves walks straight across the room and opens the door directly opposite the door we came out of. This room is similar to the one that we woke up in. There are cages lining the sides of the corridor, and it is all made of stone except for the thick metal bars.

Graves stops next to the first cell, and I stare in at the little metal bed, a small desk and chair. A young boy dressed in white clothes sits on the chair with his back to us. He turns and faces us, and I step back in shock because he is the very image of Jace. The boy can't be more than seven, but my god, he looks like Jace when I first met him as a child myself. They have the same white hair, blue eyes and even similar facial features. For a second, I make myself believe that he is a human that just looks familiar, but when I scent him, I know that he is an ice dragon even if he smells a little odd. *I'm not the last ice dragon.* The fact sends shock through me. The boy doesn't say a word, he just goes back to whatever he was drawing, like he is used to people staring at him and that it is no surprise to see another dragon. I wonder how many of my people are in this place. Graves doesn't say a word as I stare at the boy, feeling shocked to my core.

"Who is that?" I finally demand, but instead of my voice coming out strong, it is like a hushed whisper.

"Now you see my proof, let us go back and sit in the main hall as we have a talk. This conversation is not meant for little ears," Graves states, and I run my eyes down the row of cages, seeing little flashes of other people, possibly children in the other cells.

"Fine," I mutter, but Graves is already walking around me

and back to the door we came out of. I follow him back into the massive room and he sits at one of the tables. I walk around the table and sit opposite him, folding my hands as I wait for him to speak.

"That child, like many here, is a dragon we bred," he starts off, placing his hands together. He speaks about the boy in such an impersonal way, and it annoys me, but he doesn't seem to notice as he keeps talking. "Though not many of his kind did survive. This boy, and the others which we mixed with different gene lines, did. Creating a pure ice dragon is a lot harder than we thought, but add in some different strands of DNA, and we have things that live."

"Bred? Things? What the hell? They are people, not animals! They are just innocent children who didn't want you to mess with them!" I shout, a long growl slipping from my lips, and he smiles.

"Do not lose your temper with me, little dragon princess. Remember you are not in Dragca, you are not a princess here, and you are in my world now," he responds, flashing his eyes at his guards behind me before looking at me. The warning is clear enough.

"Are you claiming Earth belongs to you?" I muse. "I wasn't aware they named you king of Earth."

"Not king, but simply, yes, I claim to protect Earth. We are the only thing that stands between the Earth falling to ruin by creatures like you destroying it," he explains, making us sound like emotionless monsters. "The Hunter's Organisation is the last defence for mankind now."

"We are not here to attack you," I bite out, ignoring his statement on how he is some kind of protector of Earth. He is just a human with a big ego.

"Maybe you're not. Maybe you are. It is my job to protect my people, my world; and your kind is a threat to that either way," he states firmly. His mind made up.

"So, putting children you *bred* in cages is your way of dealing with dragons?" I ask. "Don't you worry those dragons you capture are going to bite you in the ass one day for treating us like shit?"

"We give them—you—a home. We are being reasonable, rather than killing the creatures like every human wants," he replies smoothly.

"Children. They are children, not creatures," I spit out. "We are not creatures, we are people, but if you treat us like monsters and bring those children up thinking that's all they are, you won't be able to control them when they decide they want to be free."

"Children that will grow into monsters will never be free. They are creatures that humans cannot stop on their own, therefore they must be controlled," he says and lets out a long sigh. "Though this is wasting time. I am not here to convince you that my job is the right thing to do."

"What are you here to convince me of then?" I ask.

"The Hunter's Organisation has been around for almost one hundred years, and we were set up by your grandfather as a way to keep dragon prisoners he didn't want to kill," he points at the yellow dragon crest on his coat. "This shows our past and is our symbol. Your family designed it."

"Excuse me? I don't believe you!" I growl, shaking my head before looking away.

"Then your father took the throne, and we made a new deal. He wanted us to make more ice dragons and mix them with different supernatural gene lines. He wanted to see if we could make an ice dragon more powerful than ever before," he pauses, fixing his coat. "So, your father sent us any ice dragons that he could make go missing, and the company got to work. We also made a deal that he could hide his daughter and another male ice dragon on Earth, and that we would watch over you. I loved my chats with your father as he checked in on you. Your father was a very smart man."

"We can agree to disagree on that one," I mutter to myself,

trying to hold in my burning anger. My father was clearly a fucking disaster.

"All this was working out well for our company. Unfortunately, not many of the created dragons survived in the early years, but in the last twenty years since I took over, we have made amazing advances," he says proudly, even though it just makes me feel sick.

"That child…is Jace's brother?" I ask, almost not wanting him to tell me the answer, but I'm not stupid. He showed me that boy to rattle and upset me.

"Yes. Jacian's mother was taken by us, and unfortunately died giving birth to the child in there. Jacian's father died in early testing," he says. "Such a shame."

"You're disgusting," I spit out.

"It is work, nothing more or less," he states. "Now we have a problem. I have spies in Dragca who claim you have lost the throne and you are meant to be dead. With your father dead, there is no one else to deal with Dragca, and we have decided, after the instance in Paris, to keep all supernaturals here until they pass away."

"You're keeping us here?" I ask.

"Simply, yes," he says with a smile. "Though do not worry, we do not treat you badly. We plan to continue our testing for advances in medicines, which I'm sure you will not mind helping with to keep everyone you love safe."

"You're a terrible person and human. I will never help you or stay here!" I spit out and slam my hands on the table. "I am getting out of here, and I will kill you before I leave!"

"All you dragons are so uncivilised. I had hoped you would be different, being a princess brought up on Earth, but it seems not," he sighs dramatically.

"You are treating us like monsters, so that is what you will get in return. Let us go, and I will walk out of here without killing you," I suggest. "That is the only way you are getting out of this."

"Isola, dear princess…you don't have any power here. I could kill you with the snap of my fingers, but my daughter has convinced me it would be smart to keep you alive. The other dragons will listen to you, follow you, and you will listen to me. See, we all can win here. Don't push me, this is your only warning," he threatens and then changes his tone into a sickly sweet one, "Enjoy your time with your dragon guards and sister. We will talk next week when you have had time to settle in."

"I will make sure you regret this. I am not some simple dragon that you can control," I tell him as he stands up and looks down at me with a big, happy smile on his lips.

"But that is exactly what you are, Isola Dragice," he responds and walks away, laughing. I grit my teeth as I watch Graves walk out of the room through one of the doors, knowing there isn't anything I can do to fight him just yet. *But there is always time.*

89

ISOLA

The guards lead me back to the cage, taking off my handcuffs before pushing me into it with a harsh slam on my back. They laugh as I bounce across the floor, smacking my shoulder on the cold floor. I quickly turn over, glaring at them as they lock the door, and my dragon finally comes back from her sleep in my head. As I pull myself up off the floor, she pushes into my head for control on pure protective instinct until I can't do anything but focus on her.

We can't shift, I tell her, and she stops for a second, only sending waves of worry, panic and anger through me. It's not emotions that aren't already in my head anyways.

Mate. Sister. Mine all in trouble. We must fight. She pleads with me, and every part of me wants to go with her plan, if it weren't for these damn collars around my neck. I ignore my dragon for a moment to walk to the bars and sit on the floor, reaching my hand through them to try and reach Dagan who is still passed out.

When it is time, we will fight. That time is not now. Rest. My dragon thankfully listens to my advice and settles down with a huff, and I look over the cages to see Thorne slowly starting to move. It takes a while before he is sitting up, looking dazed, and there is blood covering the one half of his face. A growl slips out of my lips before I can acknowledge it, and he turns to me, relief spreading across his handsome features.

"Isola, fuck, are you okay? Kor and Melody are in the cages next to mine, but they are passed out, by the looks of it," he tells me, not needing to use our ability to talk into each other's minds as he is close enough I can hear him. I'm filled with relief to not only see him awake, but to know Kor and Melody are okay and close. The only thing that panics me now is where the hell Bee is. I have to tell myself they wouldn't kill her. That she must be somewhere safe, or I would know. *Right?* We are bonded, and I don't feel like she is in danger. I know he can feel that I am not hurt, but I think he means if I'm okay emotionally.

"I don't really know right now. This place, everything about it, is nothing like I expected," I tell him, and he crawls as close as he can to the bars, as I try to think over everything that I have just learnt. I know I don't want to believe what Graves said about my father, but it is hard to ignore the proof that he showed me. *I have to admit, my father was a monster.* That boy looks so much like Jace that there is no way he is not related to him, and it doesn't make any sense how there are ice dragons here if my father didn't help these humans. I thought I was the last ice dragon, but it is very clear that I'm not. Some part of me is relieved, but other parts of me worry. I am starting to think that something bad happened in Paris, and if it has to do with us, then humans are always going to hate us. I need to talk to Hallie. She is the only one who could make any sense of all this. I also need to talk to Melody. Considering that she and Hallie are meant to be together in the future, she might be able to knock some sense into my friend.

"What is going through your mind, Issy?" Thorne asks me, snapping me out of my own thoughts and back to the reality of the situation. I know we have to take one day at a time.

"The man that runs this place states that my father made a deal with him and my grandfather did before him also. He must have meant my grandfather who died shortly into his rein," I reply, my voice sounding like it echoes when I wish I could keep it quiet.

"What kind of deal?" Thorne asks.

"My father and grandfather gave the humans dragons. They gave humans dragons like they weren't people, like they were theirs to sell rather than protect. I saw an ice dragon boy that was the image of Jace. Jace's parents went missing, and now I know they were brought here because my father must have betrayed them. Jace's brother is here, and god knows who else," I angrily reply.

"Isola...fucking hell. This is complete crazy," Thorne gapes in shock.

"I know, right?" I reply, staring over at him as he looks at me with a desperate need to get to me, to hold me close. "We need to get out of here, but I don't see any way of that happening unless Hallie decides to help us."

"Isola!" Dagan grumbles, shaking his head and picking himself up off the ground quickly. When he looks over at me, there is relief on his face, and he comes closer, reaching through the bars to hold my hands for a brief moment before straightening up and turning to look at Thorne like he can sense he is watching.

"Good to see you awake, Dagan," Thorne says.

"Do either of you want to explain how you ended up mated?" Dagan asks us but turns to stare at me. "And what I mean is: Thorne piss off for a second and leave us alone so Isola can explain."

"Isola?" Thorne asks me, his tone telling me he just wants to know what I want to happen. I stare at Dagan for a moment, seeing the hurt in his eyes and how lost he seems. I need to explain everything and make sure Dagan and the others understand this wasn't me picking Thorne over them. I have no doubt Dagan's dragon is losing his mind right now.

"Give us some time. See if you can wake the others up," I ask, and I'm happy to see he doesn't look mad, just accepting.

"Others?" Dagan asks.

"Kor and Melody are in the cages near me. I can't reach them, but I can see them. I will give you two space," Thorne says, nodding once at me before walking off into the shadows of his own cell. Dagan moves closer to tightly hold onto my hand as we look at each for a second. This isn't the place for romance. This isn't the time for love and feelings when we need to fight to survive, but every part of me knows we need this moment.

"To break the dragon guard curse, I had to mate with a half fire and ice dragon guard. The curse was made out of love and honour, but it caused nothing but pain until right at the end when Thorne and I mated. That was happiness, and I know it upsets you, and you have every right to be mad at me for loving him—"

"You love him?" Dagan interrupts. I meet his blue eyes, knowing I need to be confident as I admit the truth.

"Yes. I tried to fight it, but it's always been there with Thorne. Even when he betrayed me, part of me still loved him. There is just something between us. The same feeling I have for you, for Kor and for Elias. I love each of you more than I knew it was possible to love anyone," I say. "I know the world we live in expects me to choose one of you, but I can't do that. I will let any of you walk away if you want...but this is where I stand on all of us."

"I will admit I'm fucking mad and jealous...but I think I can get used to this, and I will never make you choose. Thorne is in love with you, always has been, and he has proven it over and over. He made a mistake, a big fucking one, but he has earnt your love and trust back with his actions. Thorne has earnt my trust back. That is enough for me," he says, lifting our hands through the bars and kissing my fingers. "But I want us to mate as soon as we get out of here. No more wasting time. I need to know you're mine...if you'll have me."

"My answer has always been yes. I love you," I whisper, and we kiss awkwardly through the bars, and I giggle as I pull away, holding him close. I nearly jump out of my skin when there is a loud buzzing noise just before the doors automatically open. I stand up, watching as the main door to the big room opens on its own too, just before a sweet female voice talks over a hidden loudspeaker.

"The cage doors are open from seven a.m. until five p.m. Please remember, we do not tolerate fighting or the breaking of anything inside the building. If anyone is not in a cage by five p.m., their collars will activate. Have a good day."

90

ISOLA

I slowly walk out of my cage as Dagan does the same, I see out the corner of my eye. We both pause in the empty corridor, expecting to fight for a moment, but nothing attacks us. I'm not sure which one of us moves first, but the next second, I'm in Dagan's arms, breathing in his smoky scent as we both hold each other as tightly as we can. Dagan holds me close and only lets go when I feel Thorne moving near us. Thorne pulls me into his arms, kissing the top of my head as I breathe in his scent for comfort much like Dagan. Having them both close to me gives me a second to breathe and get my emotions under control.

"What is going on?" Dagan questions, but it's more rhetorical as he knows we don't have any answers.

"I will get Melody, you two get Kor awake," I suggest, and Thorne lets me slide out of his arms as Dagan nods at me. I quickly make my way down the cages, briefly stopping outside Kor's cell, seeing him knocked out on the floor and wanting to go to him. I feel better when Thorne and Dagan lift him up and his eyes open, locking on mine for a second before I make myself walk to the next cage where Melody is awake, trying to stand up. I run to my sister, sliding an arm around her waist as she leans heavily on me. Melody looks okay, but some of her clothes are torn, and she is covered in dirt. I imagine it was from the fight in Dragca more than anything here. I don't see her orb or her cloak anywhere around us.

"The drugs will wear off soon. Once you wake up and start moving, it gets easier," I explain to her, and she rests her head on my shoulder as I walk her out of the cage and into Kor's, sitting her next to him with Thorne's help.

"Come here, doll," Kor grumbles in a gravelly voice, and I don't hesitate as I go to sit next to him, wrapping my arms around his waist, and he wraps his arm around my back, pulling me closer to his side.

"Eli will be okay, and we will get out of whatever trouble we are in now," Kor whispers to me, trying to comfort me, but it isn't working.

"Eli is with her, and the longer we are here, the more he and Dragca suffer. I don't even know where Bee is, and I'm freaking out," I admit. We don't have time to be stuck here with these goddamn humans when I need to get back to Dragca.

"Bee is safe," Melody randomly whispers, and I sit forward, meeting her eyes as she looks at me. "This is how it has to be."

"Is Bee here?" I ask her, focusing on that part and not the "meant to be" thing. *Seers and their riddles just confuse me.*

"I can't tell you anymore, only that Bee is safe. Maybe you should speak to a girl with green-tipped hair," she cryptically states and closes her eyes, resting back against the bars.

"Melody, what do you know? And no bloody riddles, please!" I demand, shaking her arm.

"You know I can't tell you anything, and I'm tired. Go and look around, and do something stupid," she mutters in annoyance, not opening her eyes once, and I know she is done with the conversation when there is silence after her words until Kor speaks.

"Go and look around with Dagan. Thorne can watch us until

the drugs wear off, right?" Kor suggests. "I feel like me and Thorne need a chat anyways."

"Are you sure?" I ask quietly, not really wanting to leave any of them.

"Go. We woke up as they were driving us into this place, so they knocked us out again. It will be a while before we are back to normal," Kor says, explaining why they are still dazed from the drugs.

"Alright. I think it's best we look around anyway," I say, being brave and lightly kissing Kor, before pulling myself to my feet. Dagan wraps an arm around my waist as we walk past Thorne out of the cage, and Thorne's fingers brush against my own.

Call if there is any trouble. I'm always here. I smile at his overprotectiveness and the way he can make me feel safer now just by speaking to me in my mind.

I promise. Behave with Kor, I reply as we get closer to the door at the end of the corridor, and I start to feel a little nervous. I keep my expression as neutral as possible, knowing I can't afford to show weakness in this place. They already know my dragons and sister mean everything to me, and I will do anything for them... they don't need more ammunition.

Anything for you, Issy, Thorne replies, but I don't think a single word back as we step through the door and into the massive room which is full of people. There must be at least fifty people in the room, and every single one of them slowly notices us and pauses in whatever they were doing. The room slowly goes silent as I stare around at the people. There is a mixture of children of all ages, men and women...and each one of them is a dragon. I'm surprised at how many of them look like ice dragons, and all their scents are so overwhelming that I can't focus on what smells strange about them. Not human or dragon... it's weird.

"Why are they staring?" I ask Dagan.

"Maybe they don't get new people in here often," he replies.

"Dragons turn up here every day, Dagan Fire...but not a royal that is meant to save us all," my uncle Louis says, walking to the front of all the people. He slowly bows his head, and every other dragon in the room does the same. I'm happy to see him for a moment, but I am unsure of how to deal with him. My uncle was always cold with me, and I don't know if it is a good thing having him here. I notice how his eyes go to Dagan's arm around my waist.

"Uncle, what are you doing here?" I ask, noticing him slightly flinch as I call him "uncle" instead of his name. I walk over to him, trying to ignore how everyone in the room rises when my uncle lifts his hands as he stands. They listen to him, which is interesting.

"I came to Earth to find you, to tell you something very important, but then I got caught by the hunters," he explains. "I had hoped they would never get you, but here we are."

"Is that what they call themselves?" I ask. "Hunters?"

"A lot changed in this last year, you might want to sit as I tell you all of it and about this place," he suggests. "Then you can explain what the hell has been going on in Dragca, and why you are here with your dragon guard's arm wrapped around your waist, and why you're not on the throne where you belong."

91

ISOLA

I carefully watch my uncle as we find an unoccupied table, which has empty food plates in the middle, piled up. My stomach rumbles, reminding me that I can't remember when I last had something to eat. I know finding out what is going on is more important than my hunger, so I ignore it, but Dagan doesn't.

"I will find us some food and take some to the others. Louis Pendragon, the legendary fighter, won't let anyone hurt you. I'm sure of it. I will be close either way," Dagan tells me, keeping his voice low enough for only us to hear him, but my uncle can clearly hear as he nods once at Dagan. He trusts my uncle, like I think I do, but not the other dragons in this room. I stare back at my uncle, seeing how he has a long beard now and his hair has grown to his shoulders. My uncle still has that cold, detached feeling to him as before, but I know something has changed. The uncle I remember as a child was a killing machine my father loved, and the uncle I met again at Dragca Academy was detached from life as he lost so much of it. He couldn't even see me as his family back then. He could only see me as a reflection of my mother when she was younger. He only saw his sister, not his niece. This version of my uncle is strange to me...he is treating me like a queen, which I am not, and like family, which he has never done before.

"Alright. Thank you and be careful," I tell Dagan, who squeezes my hip with his hand before walking off and leaving us alone.

"I am going to explain something to you…something hidden from Dragca and its people. Only your father and mother knew, and your mother told me," he starts off, crossing his arms and resting back in his seat as I don't respond. "Dragon shifters and seers are not the only type of magical beings in the worlds."

"Fates are as well. I met one," I respond, trying not to seem too shocked.

"Well, I've never heard of fates before, but considering Earth has more magic than any of us thought possible, hearing another creature exists isn't surprising," he says, muttering it under his breath, and I'm not sure if he is even talking to me.

"What magical beings were you talking about then?" I ask.

"Wolf shifters. Witches. Vampires and angels. I've even heard of fairies, demons and pixies being real," he responds.

"That's just human fairy tales," I laugh, but I stop laughing when I see how serious my uncle is being.

"Like dragons are?" he retorts. "Don't be so naive, Isola." His scolding tone makes my dragon growl, and my lips itch with the need to say something snarky back, but I know that would be proving his point further. I take a deep breath instead, reminding myself about the collar and knowing I need to relax.

"Have you seen these supernaturals?" I ask him.

"Yes. There are five buildings here, and each one contains different supernaturals. This is clearly the dragons' buildings. On Fridays, they let us go outside into a gated field, and you can meet these people yourself," he tells me.

"What day is it?" I ask.

"Wednesday. There is a clock up there for the time," he points at the giant clock on the wall that I don't know how I missed. "Being observant clearly isn't something you have learnt these past few years."

"What happened to Paris?" I ask, ignoring his insult.

"There was a war between demons and the supernaturals. Paris and most the people inside it were destroyed...or worse. The supernaturals won, and humans declared war on them, and now they are in hiding—or caught and put in here," he replies like that is nothing. Paris is a massive city, the capital of France and a place Hallie's mum used to love to go on holiday to. I remember Hallie telling me she was spending the winter in Paris...and if that happened while she was there, no wonder Hallie hates me.

"Hallie's mum was in Paris," I whisper to myself, knowing that must have destroyed her, and I can see why she shot at me first before asking questions. I did constantly lie to her about who I was before disappearing, and she had to find out the truth from her father instead of me. I have no doubt Graves twisted everything.

"Millions of people were in Paris," he responds. "Millions died. That doesn't matter to us now."

"What does?" I ask.

"The dragon curse is broken. We all felt it. What else is going on in Dragca, and why are you here?" he asks me. "Our home is important, not Earth."

"I broke the curse just before we got here. That's not the point though. Tatarina is on the throne, and she has Elias Fire. I need to get him back and kill her. She has a dark spirit, and she was doing something to the magic of Dragca as we fled," I explain to him, and he doesn't look one bit surprised.

"You are mated to a half?" he asks. "I wanted to tell you how to break the curse, but I never got a chance."

"Thorne..." I say, drifting off as his eyes turn red, and he glares at me, huffing out smoke.

"You made her son your mate?!" he angrily questions. "Her son?!"

"Thorne is *not* like her, and yes, I did. It broke the curse, and I love him. Get over it as I'm not explaining myself to you," I say.

"I see. Stubborn like your mother," he responds rather calmly considering his eyes are still red. The mention of my mother does nothing but make me so angry. My uncle must have been around, known what my father was like. He lived in the castle for years, and yet he never helped my mother, as far as I know.

"Did you know that Tatarina was in love with my father? That all of this was for revenge and bred out of jealousy?" I demand. "Did you know how my father cheated on my mother throughout their entire relationship? Did you know how much of a fucking bastard he was because he did all that and allowed a place like this to exist?" I spit out in anger, knowing I'm mad at my father and taking it out on the only person alive that knew him well.

"I begged your mother not to marry him, and she knew from her wedding day exactly what he was, but she also knew that you were on the way. A seer told her if she didn't marry him, if she didn't attempt to love him, you would not exist. A queen that could save everything. My sister was too good, too kind to let the dream of you die. Dragca needed you, and she knew that. After you were born, my sister knew you needed the protection only he could give his daughter. My sister stayed with him because she loved you...even before you were born," he solemnly replies, "and she died for you."

"She stayed with that monster, that heartless bastard, to protect me," I whisper back, gulping the ball of emotion stuck in my throat away and praying that I don't cry right now. I don't move from the shock, knowing that moving would give me the chance to break down. My uncle covers my hand, almost making me jump from the contact.

"I am not good with emotional things since I lost so much, but you still have family. We will get out of this and put you on the throne. Well, if there is anything left of Dragca when we get there," he says. "You have a fate to finish and a war to win, Isola."

"My people are in danger both on Dragca and here. The war she has made will destroy everything good in Dragca," I whisper, looking around the room for a brief moment. I lock eyes on Jace's brother, a boy I don't even know the name of, as he eats his food with two little girls at his side. They both have white hair and look like ice dragons as well, but thankfully they don't look like Jace or his brother one bit. I don't know why it would be harder to cope with knowing that Jace's mother had more children in here, but it would. "Everyone has lost a lot for the throne, for Dragca, but we still do not have peace. It has been war, secrets and a shit storm of wrong for too many years. We will get out of here, and we will build an army with what we can and go back home."

"Yes, my queen. Luckily, there is quite an army here, if we can all get out, that is," he suggests, nodding his head around the room. "They will follow you home. We all want a home and a queen to fight for."

"A queen to believe in, to fight for, is something I can promise they will have when I take back my throne," I state firmly, and he smiles, patting my hand before moving it away and resting back again.

"With more than one king at your side, it seems," he suggests, finally bringing up the elephant in the room. I expect him to say it in disgust, but there is nothing in his voice that suggests he doesn't like the idea of the queen having more than one king.

"Yes, there will be more than one king. Is that a problem?" I ask, following my uncle's gaze to where Kor, Thorne and Dagan are walking over to us. They look powerful, determined, protective and every bit the men I want at my side. We have come a long way from where we met in Dragca Academy to here, yet the way each of them look at me hasn't changed one bit. They always saw me as their queen. *Theirs to protect.* Just like Elias did too. Once I have Elias back, we will be complete.

"Not one bit, your highness. It seems the silly, innocent princess that stumbled in Dragca Academy is long gone," my uncle muses, and I keep my eyes on my dragon guards, wishing that Elias was with us with every bit of my soul.

"I'm still that princess, but they have taught me how to be a queen."

92

ISOLA

"**H**ere you go," Dagan says as he slides a tray of food on the table in front of me and sits down at my side. Kor sits next to him, and Thorne sits on my other side, pressed close to me. I can sense their protectiveness as much as their need to be close to me. I'm not complaining one bit, I want to be just as close to them. I look down at the bowl of creamy soup, the fried chicken and apple on my plate. It's an odd break-fast, but looking at the trays Kor, Dagan and Thorne have for themselves, there wasn't a good choice of food. Actually, it looks like they got me the best stuff. It's super cute.

"Where is Melody?" I ask.

"We gave her food, but she didn't want to come see you like Kor and Thorne wanted to," Dagan answers.

"Melody is acting like we are taking a holiday rather than being captured. It is odd," Thorne mutters. "She knows something."

"Seers are usually wise," my uncle states as I eat my food rather than replying. "One as powerful as a half royal ice dragon and half royal seer should be observed." I briefly wonder how my uncle even knows of Melody, but then again, he did spend time with the seers' army before coming here. There is no doubt Essna told him everything she knew. I hope Essna is still alive and her people are okay. I know it's going to be a long shot if she is.

"Still, it would be useful if she told us what she knows," Kor muses.

"The curse of any seer is knowledge, and anything they can tell you, they will. If Melody won't tell you something, it means you are safer not knowing," my uncle replies. We all sat in silence after my uncle's strange statements on Melody, the whole situation feeling awkward as my uncle stares at Kor, Dagan and Thorne the entire time before he randomly speaks. "Food is served at that table every morning and at three p.m. I usually take food back to my cell for snacks, as the doors lock automatically at five. It gets tiresome," my uncle points at the long table in the middle of the room where Dagan got the food from.

"Thanks for the tip," Dagan replies.

"The shower rooms are through that door; the library and rec area are in that room, and the rest are cages except for that one." I follow my uncle as he points at the doors around the room and commit them to memory. My dragons take in my uncle's words, and all I think is "library" until I force myself to remember where we are. Though a book always makes any situation better. Even when you're kidnapped.

"Thanks," I reply when the guys don't say a word and it gets beyond awkward. Uncle Louis seems to be giving them the "dad stare" I've seen other parents do to their kid's new boyfriend or girlfriend in movies.

"The showers are good places to talk...alone," my uncle suggests, meaning they don't have cameras in there. I nod at him once, looking at Dagan who briefly glances at me with a look that suggests a shower talk later with no one around. When I see the heat in Dagan's eyes, my cheeks go bright red with the thoughts of shower time with him.

"Do the hunters come around often?" I turn and ask my uncle. I need to talk to Hallie, and I hope she will come around here at some point, but I need to know when to look. I only need her to talk to me.

"Why?" he asks. "The hunters won't be easy to make friends with. I only know of one who even talks to one of the dragons here."

"I need to talk to one of them who is already my friend. A girl with green-tipped dyed hair," I explain, and he looks at me curiously but answers anyway

"The hunters are around from four p.m. to five p.m. to make sure we get back into our cages. They don't like killing us for no reason," he explains.

"Thanks for the information," I reply with a tense smile.

"Though the hunters won't speak to you while the cameras watch. It's pointless," my uncle states. "Unless you can somehow get them where the cameras don't watch."

"Maybe. It will be difficult, but I have to try," I shrug.

"Can I have a moment alone with your dragon guards, Isola?" my uncle asks, and I pause, looking at them all who give me little nervous smiles.

"I don't think it is safe for Isola to be wandering around alone," Kor replies first.

"No one here will hurt Isola. The hunters won't try to kill her because they clearly want her to control us all. Isola is the safest one here. You should be more concerned with them hurting *you* to control *her*," he remarks, basically speaking my greatest fear of this place. I remember Graves's cold eyes and how the human felt like he would do anything to control this place.

"As long as they don't touch my Isola, it doesn't matter," Thorne replies, and a low growl escapes Dagan's lips when Thorne says "my Isola". I place my hand on Dagan's knee, and it seems to calm him a little.

"Young love. I forgot how much I despise it," my uncle

scowls at Thorne's answer and looks back at me, waiting for my choice. Dagan nods at me, making it clear he is back in control and okay with me leaving.

"I have someone I want to speak to anyway," I say, standing up as the guys give me a worried expression. From the look on my uncle's face, I wouldn't want to be them either. I hold in my smirk as I walk away from them, hoping my uncle doesn't scare them too much.

Making my way over to Jace's brother, I know I need to speak to him for Jace's memory, let alone anyone else's. I won't leave here without any of them, but this kid is different. Jace was my first love, my best friend and family to me. I thought I'd lost every part of him when he died, and I never thought I would be lucky enough to have some part of him in this world. *This is Jace's brother, and I will protect him.* The boy looks up at me as I get to his table. He is alone now, his friends are playing and running around behind him.

"You again," the boy drawls nervously, looking up at me with eyes just like Jace's. My heart hurts as I stare down at him and pause, speechless, for a moment.

"May I sit here?" I ask.

"Sure," he says cautiously, and I try to ignore how it's not fair a child his age is so cautious and has so much fear in his young eyes.

"I won't hurt you. You don't need to look at me like that," I tell him, wanting to comfort him and shut the boy away from the world he is in.

"They said that too, and they hurt me," he replies, and I try not to show the heartbreaking emotion I feel at his words and instead remind myself that the people here will pay for what they have done.

"I am not them. We are not heartless humans like them, we are dragons," I growl and regret it when he seems more scared. "I'm sorry. I didn't mean to scare you. I'm Isola." I hold out my hand, and he stares at it for a while. I'm about to put my hand down when he reaches for my hand and shakes it.

"The people here called me number forty-two, but a friend of my mother told me she called me Jonas when I was in her tummy. You can choose," he shrugs. I pause for a second before I answer, wondering why they would call him forty-two, but it dawns on me that Graves said the others didn't survive. I bet he was number forty-two of the experiments. Forty-two dead dragon children before him. When I get my dragon free, Graves is going to pay for all of this. All the hunters are

"You are not a number, and your name is Jonas LaDrac. Remember it. I knew your brother very well, and he told me stories about your parents. You are the only one of their line left. Wear that name proudly," I tell him firmly before letting his hand go. It hurts to even say Jace's last name after such a long time, but it's important he knows it. Jonas stares at me like I'm crazy for a few moments before he speaks.

"My father is still alive, but they don't keep him in here because he is a witch," he tells me, shrugging his shoulders. "So, I can only see him on Fridays, but he doesn't like to talk to me."

"You're a half witch?" I whisper, believing my uncle more now than before because the child seems too confused by my expression to be lying to me. I sit back in my chair, rubbing my face as Jonas nods his head. I look around me at the other children here and wonder if they are mixes of these other supernaturals and our kind. If they are, how dangerous could they be, and how will they ever know what world they belong in? I know that it's impossible to know all these answers right now, and I guess it's a problem for the future. If we have one, that is.

"I had a brother?" Jonas asks me, and I take a shaky breath as I try to speak about Jace.

"Yes. His name was Jace. I was going to be mated to him. We grew up together, and we were dating before he was killed," I explain to him.

"Will you tell me about him? About my mother?" he asks, and I nod.

"I'd love to. It's hard being the only one keeping his memory alive," I whisper, more to myself than Jonas before starting to explain everything I can to Jace's little brother, knowing it somehow helps to keep Jace's memory alive.

93

THORNE

I lean back in my seat, taking my eyes off Isola's uncle—Louis—to watch Isola walk over to a table where a young, familiar-looking boy is sat down. He looks at Isola with slight fear, and yet some part of him clearly trusts her, as he doesn't walk away when she sits down. Though Isola isn't easy to say no to. She has that quality every leader needs—respect. It doesn't take me long to remember why he looks familiar to me. The boy looks like Jacian, Isola's first love and the guy whose body I burnt because she asked me to when we first met.

With the amount of ice dragons here, even if all of them look like teenagers or children, something weird is going on. There are at least four fire dragons here, by the looks of it, and mostly men. If we can get them on our side, maybe we could have a chance of getting Elias back and stopping my mother. I think back to the last time I saw my mum, how she looked nothing like the mother I grew up visiting. That dark spirit has changed her too much, taken her soul and corrupted it further than what Isola's father did once.

"Do you love her? Love her enough to die for her even if she wouldn't want it?" her uncle suddenly asks us all, drawing my attention back to him. Isola's uncle looks nothing like Isola at all, and his time on Earth hasn't changed that. His dark red hair has grown much longer—and greyer—than when I saw him last. His burning red eyes lock onto me, and I know from the anger in them, he hasn't forgotten how I betrayed Isola and his trust all that time ago.

"Yes," Dagan, Korbin and I state confidently at the same time. Dagan takes a moment to glare at me before sighing loudly.

"We have all proven how much Isola means to us. She is Thorne's mate, and soon to be mine," Dagan tells him.

"Mine as well," Korbin smoothly adds in. Part of me and my dragon want to tell them to fuck off, and my dragon briefly takes over in my mind, feeling possessive. I glance over at Isola again, staring at her long blonde hair which is somehow in perfect waves, the pale soft skin that glimmers in the bright lights of the room, and her slender body that I wish I could hold in my arms. I know I am not strong enough to protect her alone and love her as much as she needs. I know that she needs Korbin and Dagan in her life to be safe, to be complete and happy. She needs Elias too. There is something about how each of them seems to bring out a different side to her that is always content. Dagan makes her strong, Korbin makes her empathic, and Elias makes her a fighter. I don't know what I make her, but she seems to want me in her life as much as I need her in mine.

"Your mother is on a war path, and I know she will destroy Dragca, and then she will come here," Louis states, and I nod once at him, leaning back in my seat. "Either way, there will soon be nowhere to hide Isola that she won't find."

"I am aware of my mother's plans," I reply.

"If you love Isola, you will make a plan. When we escape here, which we will, you need to go to Dragca alone and face your mother," Louis states.

"Why do you think I could stop her?" I ask, remembering the way my mother looked at me the last time I saw her.

"She loves you, and she will not kill you straight away. Dagan and Korbin, with my help, will make a distraction, and you must go back alone," he explains. "You're her son, and there is a reason you are still alive."

"Tatarina will kill him," Dagan practically growls, and I give him a surprised look at his protectiveness. He shrugs at me with a small smirk. "You mean a lot to Isola. If we helped you walk into your death, she would hate us. You might be an asshole, but you're family now." I suppose his logic makes sense, in a messed up way, and Korbin nods his agreement.

"Getting the closest people to Isola killed is not a good idea. Isola has lost enough, and any more…there won't be a queen left for the throne. Just a broken woman," Korbin retorts while I stay quiet.

"You all just told me you love her enough to die for her. Even if she wouldn't want it," Louis states. "Sometimes we have to make the hardest choices for the people we love."

"There are hard choices, and there is sending her mate to his death bed," Dagan replies, but Louis ignores him to look over at me.

"Isola needs you to kill your mother and give her the throne in the ashes. I know my niece's plan is to escape here and go to save Elias. Tatarina wants *exactly* that, and it will get Isola killed," he says. "At this point, it is your life or hers."

"I will do it," I say, ignoring Dagan and Korbin's instant disagreement as I look at Isola as I speak. "Elias being taken was my mother's only way of getting Isola to come back and fight her. I stand a chance…Isola does not, and I love her too much to risk it. If I die, don't let Isola ever come back to Dragca, and keep her safe here."

"I can't do this to her," Kor disagrees.

"Then you don't love her as much as I thought you did, boy," Louis snaps. "Did you think being in love with a royal was going to be easy? I do not want my only family to die for nothing! Tatarina has destroyed everything that means *anything* to me, and she will not stop until Isola is dead. I will not let her be killed for simply being my sister and the king's daughter. I won't let her be killed because of jealousy."

"I didn't know you care so deeply for Isola," Dagan replies, leaning back in his seat, taking in Louis.

"I've always cared for Isola. I loved my sister and watched as her whole world lighted up because of Isola, her sweet little girl," he replies. "I watched in secret as that child turned into a lost princess of a world she didn't understand or want to be part of. Then the woman that walked into here today was every bit the queen her mother was. If Isola falls, so does Dragca. So, make your choice. Love...or her life," Louis tells us before getting up and walking away as we all sit silently processing his words.

"Your mind is already made up, isn't it?" Korbin asks me, leaning forward, and I glance towards him.

"She is my mate and my everything. If there is even a slight chance I can save her, isn't that worth risking it all?" I ask, my mind made up. I owe Isola, and I know Louis is right. If I don't stop my mother, no one can.

"We will help you leave, even if it costs us everything. Isola must live, because I know none of us can live without her," Korbin replies, and Dagan still sits silently, clearly thinking it over.

"I don't know. When the time comes, I will make my choice. If I can see another way to save Isola, my brother and you, I will take it," he states.

"We should explore and talk to the dragons here. We need alliances," Korbin interjects when none of us say a word. "And one of us is staying in the cage with Isola tonight. The collars say we need to be in a cage, not which one."

"Good plan...but it might get one of us killed if the collars shock us for not being in the right cage," I reply.

"It's a possibility...that's why I'm thinking you should take the first night," Korbin says with a deep laugh as he gets up, and Dagan chuckles too. *Maybe being killed might come sooner than I thought.*

94

ISOLA

"Isola," Dagan says from just behind me as I laugh with Jonas. It's taken a few funny stories of Jace to make him lighten up a little. I want to get him out of this place so much and let him have a real childhood. Jonas doesn't even talk or act like a child, and it's so sad he has to feel that he can't be free. I hate that he was born in here, and when I get this damn collar off, I'm freezing the entire place and having my dragon guard burn the rest. They say we are the monsters they need to keep in here, but really, they are the monsters who cannot see themselves as what they truly are. *Evil.*

I look up to see Dagan smiling down at me, before introducing himself to Jonas. At least my uncle didn't scare or hurt him. I remind myself to ask what they talked about later when we are alone. I look around the room quickly, spotting Thorne and Korbin together, talking with a group of five fire dragon men who seem entranced by whatever they are saying.

"I'm Dagan Fire. Anyone who makes my Isola laugh is my friend," he says, and Jonas shyly smiles at him before reaching to shake his hand.

"Jonas LaDrac," Jonas says, making me smile widely at the use of his name. "It is nice to meet you."

"A LaDrac, huh? I heard your family were known as some of the fiercest ice dragon warriors Dragca has ever seen," Dagan tells him, and it is true. The LaDrac fought alongside the Dragices in the ancient wars of Dragca. Our families were always close to each other, always fighting at each other's sides.

"Really?" he asks in wonder, looking eager to learn more about his family history.

"Yes, really. I have to borrow Isola for a little while, but I will come to find you another day to tell you what I know," Dagan promises, making Jonas's whole face light up.

"I'd like that," he replies and turns to me. "Are you going to talk to me again? Please?" he asks. I slide out of my seat, walking around the table and crouching down right in front of him, lowering my voice so only he and Dagan can hear me.

"I will be here every day to see you, and one of these days, I am going to free us all. I need you to be brave and be ready," I tell him. "You need to be a strong boy for just a little longer like your brother and mother."

"I can do that," he replies with a nod of his head. "I promise."

"Good," I grin at Jonas before pulling him into a hug I know he doesn't expect. He doesn't push me away like I somewhat expected him to, but instead he wraps his arms around my neck. I eventually pull away, standing up and stepping into Dagan's arms. He squeezes me gently before letting me go to lead me around the table.

"I thought we should look around. Korbin and Thorne are introducing themselves to the dragons here, so we have time to explore," Dagan says, kissing the side of my head in a comforting way.

"Good plan. What did my uncle say?" I ask. I'm surprised to see Dagan seeming so calm after a talk with my uncle. I thought my uncle would drill into them all about how they will be kings once I take the throne and the important responsibilities they will bear. I know Thorne will be a good king because he has so much knowledge of Dragca. Dagan and Korbin might not know as much, but they have good hearts, experience of both the good and bad in people, and that gives them good judgement.

"Nothing more than you'd expect an overprotective uncle to say," he replies, amused at my slightly confused grin back.

"I never knew he cared," I reply, keeping my eyes on the seductive way Dagan rolls his lip ring between his lips and how tempting it is.

"None of us did, but for what it is worth, you have an uncle that cares deeply for you," he tells me, leading me through the tables but holding me close. I meet the eyes of a few of the dragons as we walk past their tables, and each one of them bows their head in respect. I don't expect them to bow, but it is good to know I have their support, even in a place like this. It makes me sure that I might have some chance of an army when we get out of here.

Going back to Dragca alone isn't the best idea, but nothing will stop me from going back to Elias. Everyday I'm here, is another day Elias is with her, and I know we can't stay here long in this collar because Elias will suffer for it. My dark dragon has always been lost in darkness, and he never wanted to be saved. I know he needs me to save him now. I don't answer Dagan, I just lean my head on his shoulder as we get to the door my uncle said was the library and rec rooms, and Dagan opens it. I walk into the big room, which has three bookcases, sofas and some cabinets lying around.

"Why don't we look through the books, so you have some-thing to read tonight?" Dagan asks, and I smile up at him.

"We could pretend this is a date, and you, being all romantic, chose a library," I say, and we both laugh.

"So, Isola, my soon-to-be mate, would you come on this date with me?" he asks, and I giggle out a "yes". Dagan keeps his arm tightly around my waist as we walk to the bookcase. There are two other dragons in the room, two women with dark red hair, and their faces are locked into the books they are reading. They don't even look our way. I move away from Dagan when we get to the bookcase and start looking through the books as he folds his arms and rests against the bookcase end, watching me. A lot of the books are history, geography and non-fiction, but when I get to the end near Dagan, I find the romance section. I pick up a book about a girl who gets sold at an auction to vampires. This sounds awesome. Dagan takes my hand and leads me to a sofa, sitting down first, and I sit next to him, resting on his shoulder as he wraps his arms around me. I start reading, engrossed in the story after page one.

"I love the way your eyes light up when you read. The way you seem to automatically relax with a book in your hands," he whispers, putting his head next to my ear and kissing the tip.

"I like pretending I'm in another world sometimes. That I don't have tons of pressure on my shoulders."

"As long as you come back to me when the book is done, I'm happy," Dagan whispers just for my ears, and I relax into his arms, letting him hold me tight as I drift off into the world this writer created.

95

ISOLA

"Hello?" I shout into the room of dark smoke. The smoke swirls around my feet, and when I hold out my hand, it twirls around my hand in an almost beautiful way. I turn around slowly, looking for anything in the room other than smoke, and wondering how exactly I got here. I was just with Dagan, reading a book…right? I pause when I see something in the corner of the room, then I walk towards it, the smoke moving out of the way for me with every step. I stop right in front of a man I would recognise anywhere, his dark hair covering his face as he looks at the ground. His hands are wrapped around his knees, and he doesn't move as I kneel down.

"Eli?" I whisper, reaching to touch his hand. Just as I'm about to touch him, his hand shoots out, roughly grabbing my wrist. Elias slowly lifts his head, and instead of his dark blue eyes I expect to see, there is nothing but darkness in his gaze as he stares at me.

"Guys, it's nearly four p.m., and the hunters are coming out to make sure everyone is back in their cages. We should all get back," Korbin suggests in a quiet voice, but it still makes me jump because of the strange nightmare as I wake up on Dagan's lap on the sofa, my book in my hands. *Was that Elias or just a dream?* Dagan kisses my forehead, making me push the strange dream away and wake up more. I stretch as I get up, wondering when I fell asleep in the first place. My heart hurts as I remember how much I miss Elias and how worried I am. That Elias in my dreams couldn't have been my Eli, not with the way he looked at me. I must have been more tired than I thought. The drugs have probably worn me out and somehow made me have very realistic and scary dreams.

"Everyone back to your rooms. The boss wants an early night today," a male voice shouts from behind us, and I look back to see two hunters come into the room, holding guns directed at the door to further their point. The hunters look around our age, but they don't give us eye contact, instead looking around us like trained soldiers. Dagan and Kor stay close by my side as we walk to the door and go out where there are hunters in black uniforms walking dragons back to their cages. I briefly catch Jonas's eyes, and he smiles at me before disappearing into the door where his room is.

"We will get him out," Korbin whispers to me, and I smile at him, reaching over to grab his hand, and he links his fingers in mine, squeezing once. I search through all the hunters, looking for Hallie and not seeing her, which is damn annoying. It's likely Graves will keep her away from me anyway, being that she is his daughter and he has been telling her a bunch of lies. I have to tell her the truth. We get to the door to the corridor of cages we have been given, and I look back once more, hoping to see her and feeling more annoyed that I don't. Korbin tugs my hand, pulling me into the corridor after Dagan. We both look back as a hunter reaches in and shuts the door behind us, and we hear it being locked not long after.

"Thorne is staying in your cage tonight," Korbin tells me, stepping in front of me and pushing some of my hair behind my ear. "You shouldn't be alone, doll."

"Is it safe to do that?" I ask, reaching a hand up and stroking his long fringe out of his eyes. Korbin needs a haircut, but it is kind of sexy like this. He grins at me, leaning down and briefly kissing my lips in a teasing way before stepping back. Dagan comes closer and answers my question when Korbin hasn't said anything.

"We think it is safe," Dagan shrugs, not really filling me with optimism as he leans down, kissing me on the lips gently before walking into his cage. Kor runs his finger across my bottom lip before letting me go and walking back to his own cell. I look over at Thorne, who watches me with a small tilt of his lips as he leans against the cage door.

"Are you sure you want to risk staying in the same cage with me?"

"I asked around, and it is perfectly safe to share cages. Everyone does it in here," Thorne answers. "Besides, it is worth the risk." I laugh and look down the row of cages to where Melody's is still open, and the others are closed. Kor and Dagan are both eating snacks on the mattresses that are now in their cages, while I can't see my sister from here. I sigh, knowing I should speak to her before going in the cage. *We have time.*

"I'll be right back," I tell Thorne, who is still leaning against the door to the cage, and he nods once.

"Don't be long," he lightly warns, referring to the warning we had about being in the cages by five p.m.

"I won't be. Just a quick chat," I reply, and quickly jog down the cages to my sister's. Melody is sat on the edge of the mattress someone has thrown into here. By the looks of it, all the cages have a mattress, thin white sheets and one pillow in each. Melody looks up, sensing me staring at her, and she sadly smiles.

"You want to know if I can see his future? Eli's?" she asks, knowing what I'm going to ask before I say it. "You want to know if your dream is real?"

"Yes. Is he going to be okay?" I ask, getting straight to the point it seems. "I also wanted to check that you are alright," I tell her. She looks up at me, and I focus on the black swirls on her face that match her dark hair. I try not to stare at her blue eyes for too long. They aren't exactly like my fathers, but they are very similar.

"I won't tell you those answers, but I will explain this. Elias knew his future...he knew he had to be caught by Tatarina to make sure you live. That Dragca has a future," she tells me, her voice lacking any emotion until it cracks at the end when she sees the betrayal and heartache on my face. I don't move, don't think for a few moments as shock rips through me. *Elias let himself be captured by her? Why would he do that?*

"What?" I whisper, stepping into the cage a little further, as the need to know more overpowers my anger at my sister for keeping this from me.

"I saw something. Something both bad and good," she starts off, not looking at me as she speaks. "If Elias came to Earth with you and the others, we would never return. Isola, we would all grow old here on Earth. We would be happy. But then you would have a child, and that is where the happiness ends."

"I don't understand, why would a child end our happiness?" I ask. I understand that future in a way. As much as I love Dragca and want to save my throne, if I had a chance for a long and happy life on Earth without losing anyone, I don't know if I could walk away from that. Even if it did make me a coward instead of a queen.

"The deal with the fate you made said you had to bring that child back to Dragca when she was older. To the memory cave. When you stepped back into Dragca, nothing but death waited for you, your dragons, me...and your child. No one would live..." she all but whispers, the vision clearly still horrifying her.

"So, he let himself be caught to make sure I would go back? To make sure any child we could have had a future?" I figure out and ask her. I need to hear her say it.

"Yes," she replies.

"The self-sacrificing asshole! That was *not* his choice!" I shout at her, feeling frustrated. "He could die in her hands, and how would anyone be happy because of that?"

"It was his choice! Now we all have a chance of winning this war," she replies. "That was Elias's choice, that is why I told him."

"Tatarina will kill him because you couldn't keep your mouth shut!" I shout. "I love him, and she will destroy him!" I look away from her to the cages next to us where Dagan and Kor are stood, listening in with faces of stone that I can't understand right now. They look a little shocked though, and it's enough to let me know they didn't know about this.

"Eli knew there was a chance she would kill him...or do worse. You are lucky to have someone love you that much, Isola. Now, go back to your cage and wait," Melody says, clearly done with the conversation. *When did she get so heartless?*

"Wait for what Melody?" I spit out. "More secrets and lies? Is there anything else you want to admit to, sister?"

"Isola—"

"You are so much more of our father than I thought! He loved secrets, lies and being a heartless bastard!" I spit out, growling low. I don't know if it's more my dragon's anger or mine, but I struggle to keep in control.

"I love you, Isola, but I also love Dragca. I want a good future for us all, so I am not like our father despite what you think. I know this isn't easy, and I *know* what Eli means to you. I wouldn't have told him anything if there were another way," she says, clearly hurt by my words, but I won't take them back. My sister reminds me of him right now.

"You best be right about this so called chance at a future. If Elias dies for nothing because of what you told him, I will never forgive you," I state, my voice cold before I walk out of the cage, not able to look back at her. I catch Dagan's and Kor's eyes from their cages and shake my head at them as they look close to saying something. *I don't want to talk about it.* I walk to my cage, and Thorne understands from one look, which makes me love him even more. Thorne simply holds the door open for me, wordlessly. I walk to the mattress, pulling the rough feeling sheet around me and lie down, curling up into a ball and closing my eyes. Even if I don't sleep, I don't want to see anything. I feel Thorne slide onto the mattress behind me and wrap an arm around my waist. We are both silent for a long time, just hearing his deep breathing and feeling his warm breath moving the hair on the top of my head. The simple comfort calms me down after a while, but it still feels too raw to talk.

How many more people do I need to lose before this is all over? I whisper to Thorne in my mind, never opening my eyes because I don't want to let the tears fall.

I wish I knew what to tell you. I won't lie to you and say no one else will be lost, but I know you're strong enough to fight until the end. You're Isola Dragice, my beautiful strong mate who is fated to be the best queen Dragca has ever had, he replies, kissing the back of my head. *Fate be damned.* I won't lose anyone else to this goddamn war for Dragca.

96

ISOLA

I push my head further into Thorne's shoulder, and he squeezes my hip where his hand is resting.

"How long have you been awake?" I ask him, and he smiles, rolling me over on the bed and leaning over me. "Not long. I just didn't want to wake you. Are you feeling any better?"

"Sort of, but I'm still angry at her," I whisper, leaning a hand up to trace my finger down his cheek, feeling the rough hairs that are growing out. Thorne's blue eyes stare down at me with more longing than I've ever seen him look at me before, and I quite like it.

"You know, you haven't kissed me. Like really kissed me," I whisper, moving my finger from his cheek to his soft lips. Thorne smirks as he kisses the tip of my finger.

"Like this?" he asks, reaching a hand behind my neck as I lower my hand to his shoulder, and he pulls me into a scorching kiss. I moan as the kisses become deeper, and his tongue battles with my own. I gasp as he pulls away, leaning up and kissing my forehead as he catches his breath.

"You taste like forbidden fruit, and if we don't stop, there won't be anything keeping me from devouring you," he tells me, his words followed by a light growl that sends pleasurable shivers down me. I almost grumble out loud as Thorne climbs out of the bed and stretches. "You might want to wake Dagan up. The doors will open soon, I bet."

"Yeah—I mean, yes. Good idea," I stumble over my words which only seems to amuse him. I climb out of the bed and stretch out my sore muscles from the hard mattress before walking over to the other side of the cage.

"Morning," I say, reaching through the bars to gently touch Dagan's shoulder to wake him up. He rolls over on the mattress, smiling up at me before stretching his muscular arms above his head.

"I wish I could just grab you and pull you into bed with me," he teases, and I laugh as he sits up. The doors automatically open the way they did yesterday, and Thorne comes over to me.

"I think we should take turns showering," Thorne suggests, and I sniff my shirt, knowing I smell, so Thorne has a point. *At least he said it nicely.* I look to the door as Kor and Melody walk past, and Kor comes into the cage while Melody stands just outside, looking awkward, with her arms crossed.

"I want to go and talk to someone," she explains. "I need to talk to someone here today because we are running out of time."

"Kor, could you go with her? I don't want any of us to be alone in this place," I say, and Melody's face lights up.

"You don't hate me?"

"Elias is still alive, so no, I don't hate you. I was shocked last night, and I'm still upset, but as long as Eli lives...we can get past this. You are not like our father. I am sorry for saying that," I reply, looking away from the hurt and understanding on my sister's face and to Kor, who smiles, looking more awkward than the room is suddenly feeling.

"Of course, I will watch your sister," he answers and walks to me, wrapping his arms around my waist and pressing me against him. "Though you're sleeping in my bed—well, mattress —tonight. Have some relaxing time with Dagan and Thorne, doll."

"Thank you, and I would love that," I reply, leaning up and teasingly brushing my lips against his. "Can't wait for tonight."

"You're going to be the end of me, doll," he replies with a smirk before letting me go and walking out of the cage with Melody not far behind him, smiling back at me, but I can't make myself smile back quite yet.

"Come on, we might as well go to the showers early, unless you want to get food first?" Dagan asks, and I think back to the bad, almost stale, food that was served yesterday morning and decide my stomach can wait.

"No. A shower sounds much better right now," I admit, walking to the door. Thorne links his fingers with mine, and Dagan walks ahead of us in a protective manner as we leave. The other dragons in the room briefly pause to bow their heads when they see us, before going back to their food, their eyes still watching us closely. I see Jonas across the room, sitting with Melody, my uncle and Kor. He lifts his hand and waves at me, which I return with my own little wave. I will remember to ask Melody later about why she needed to talk to a child. Melody didn't even know Jace.

We follow Dagan across the room to the doors with a shower sign on them. There are three doors, giving me hope that we might get a shower room alone. Dagan opens the door on the far right, and we go into the pretty, empty cave room. I was expecting white tiled rooms with shower curtains blocking the sections off like you see in the movies, but this is nothing like that. If anything, it looks like a rich person's bathroom from those TV shows where they buy expensive houses. Jules always watched those shows, and I ended up just as addicted to watching humans buy homes. I shake my head from the memories and look around.

The walls are all smooth rocks. Drilled into the walls are four shower heads with faucet handles underneath them. There is a wall in the middle of the room made of more rock, with more shower heads in them. There are drains on the floors where the water clearly goes into, piles of white towels, and a basket for them by the door. The lights are dim in here, little spotlights in the ceiling. I reach for my collar on instinct and know from the lack of cameras in here that the collars must have sensors in them to make sure we don't use magic. I bet I could freeze the collar off otherwise, or one of the guys could burn it into nothing. I look back as Thorne shuts the door.

"We can't shower in here, what if someone comes in?" I ask them both as Dagan smirks at me while he starts to pull his shirt off. I have to close my gaping mouth as I trace my eyes over his six pack and the V-dip into his trousers that he starts taking off too.

"Thorne is going to stand in front of the door and make sure no one comes in. Aren't you?" Dagan asks, his alpha demand sending shivers through me as he finishes taking off his clothes. Dragons have no problem with nudity...and at this moment, with the view, *I like it.* I look up at Thorne who doesn't hesitate as he bows his head in agreement and takes up his stance in front of the door, crossing his arms.

"You can undress now, Isola," Dagan suggests, and I widen my eyes at him as he stands completely naked, proud, with an amused grin on his lips. I don't know whether to chuckle or be nervous with this version of Dagan, but I do smile. Dagan turns around, slowly walking to the shower heads, and my eyes drift down his muscular back to his tight ass.

"I won't look if you don't want me to, Issy," Thorne quietly says behind me, and I look back at him, clearly seeing the desire for me in his eyes. Thorne is my mate...and I don't want to hide from him. Not now. *Not ever.* This moment between us all is important, and I know that. It's building trust...which is something Thorne desperately needs to gain with Dagan, Korbin and Elias. I never thought I'd find myself comfortable enough to even think about being naked with two guys...but right now I can't think of anything I want more.

"No. Watch," I find myself whispering, knowing I want

Thorne to see all of me. He is my mate, even if we haven't taken that final step yet to being complete. He smiles at me as I shakily pull my shirt off and unclasp my bra, watching how his eyes burn with desire, and his dragon briefly makes them flash silver. I turn around as I take my boots off, and then slowly push my leggings and panties down and step out of them. I look back at Thorne as I walk across the cold stone floor to Dagan and to the showers that are now on; desire floods through me at just the look on his face. *Pure longing.* When I look back to Dagan, there is a similar expression on his face as he stands under the steamy water. It drips over his wet hair, down his lickable chest that I just want to run my hands all over.

"Come here, princess," Dagan suggests, rolling his lip ring between his lips in a seductive way that makes my own lips part. My legs are moving towards him at his suggestion before my mind has even caught up. My dragon is practically purring in happiness in my mind. I nearly get to Dagan when I trip on a stone, managing to stop myself falling but crying out a little in pain. Thorne and Dagan run to me as I turn around and lean down. I pick up the smooth white stone that is out of place in this room, and really shouldn't be here.

"My mating stone," I say in awe, wondering how the hell it got here. When I meet Thorne's eyes, I'm pretty sure we are thinking the same thing. *Fate playing games, I presume.*

"What is it doing here? I didn't know they could literally appear anywhere," Thorne asks as I show it to Dagan, who steps up right behind me. I flash Thorne a worried look, wondering if anyone could just walk in now. "I've blocked the door for now, using the lock…which I'm surprised we didn't see at first."

"Thanks, and no clue," I shrug. "The fate had it the last time we used it, so she must have put it here for us." I suddenly become quite aware I'm completely naked, and so is Dagan, when Dagan presses his naked—and hard in some places—body against my back. I shiver from the contact and try to remember to focus when I realize Dagan is talking to me.

"Mate with me. Thorne can say the words, and we can cut our hands with the edge of the stone like they used to do before they realized daggers were easier. This is a gift from fate, and I don't want to wait for some magical, perfect-planned moment when none of us knows if we are even promised tomorrow. Mate with me, be mine," Dagan says, turning my head to make me look at him. I press my lips to his for his answer, and he grins against them before I pull back. I look up at his blue eyes as I whisper.

"Yes."

97

ISOLA

"I didn't expect to be mating with anyone naked in a shower room, with my other mate doing the blessing," I say nervously as Dagan steps in front of me and takes my hands in his. When I was a little girl, I always planned a big mating ceremony...wearing a big dress and all of Dragca watching. I also imagined it would be with Jace, and I would be queen, and that my father would be the one saying the words as he gave his daughter away. Now...I couldn't think of anything worse. I don't want the dress or the blessing from a father who I can't even stand the thought of. This feels private and perfect in the oddest way. I only wish Korbin and Elias were here with us, but I have this feeling it should just be us for now. Korbin and Elias will be my mates at some point, there is no way that isn't happening...but right now Dagan is right. Fate left this here for us...and the crazy old lady might be suggesting we take this time for ourselves. Who knows what will happen tomorrow or the day after. *The future isn't promised to us.*

"Our ancestors always used to be naked at matings. It was tradition until the last hundred years or so," Thorne reminds me, grinning at us as Dagan and I laugh.

"At least we are being traditional in one sense," I reply as he holds the stone out, and his expression goes much more serious as the room fills with a nervous tension. Thorne winks at me before nodding to Dagan, who starts off the ancient words of the ceremony.

"Link to the heart, link to the soul. I pledge my heart to you, for you, for all the time I have left. My dragon is yours, my love is yours, and everything I am, belongs with you," he says, and the mating stone glows brightly as I repeat the words, my voice catching in my throat with joy. Another blessed mating. This was always our fate.

Dagan was always meant to be mine, my dragon whispers in contentment, and I couldn't agree with her more.

"Hold out your hands," Thorne asks, and we both do, holding them next to each other. Thorne cuts my palm first with the sharp end of the stone, in the opposite direction of the scar on my hand from Thorne's and my mating. I flinch from the pain but keep my eyes on Dagan, being strong. Dagan doesn't even flinch as Thorne cuts his hand.

"Light and dark, good and evil, and everything that makes us dragons, please bless this mating. We bless you," Thorne speaks the ancient words, and at the end, Dagan and I hold our hands together. A blast of white light blasts out from our hands, blinding me until I have to look away, but I don't let go of Dagan.

My mate, Dagan whispers into my mind as the light from the stone fades away. Hearing his gravelly sounding voice in my mind is perfect.

"I will leave you—" Thorne starts to say, but Dagan reaches over, placing a hand on Thorne's shoulder and cutting off his sentence.

"No. Watch me take my mate, learn your place in your new family, and then if Isola wishes, you could join in," Dagan demands, his voice is almost a growl, and it sends shivers of desire through me. My heart beats loudly in my chest, my lips feel dry, but I couldn't be more excited or happy right now. I always wondered if Dagan, Kor and Elias could truly accept Thorne into their group like they did me. There always has to be a ranking with dragons, like a pack of wolves. Dagan has always been the alpha, and Korbin comes across as his beta, in a way. Elias was always the defender of the pack, the one who was uncontrollable but loyal. I l slowly became part of their pack, a link between them all. I don't know my place exactly, but I know wherever they are is where I belong. Thorne didn't have a place until this moment, and I am interested to see how he reacts to Dagan making sure he knows who is in charge.

"Isola is the one in charge here. It is her choice," Thorne contests, surprising me.

"True," Dagan replies, looking pleased at Thorne's answer. "We are nothing without Isola...and she will always be the one we follow. I'm glad you know it." Thorne pats Dagan's hand on his shoulder, and I feel like it was a test for Thorne in some macho man way. I pull my eyes away from Dagan to Thorne and beam up at him.

"Stay and watch, please, Thorne. Don't leave," I ask him, and he steps back a few times, leaning against the wall in the middle of the showers and nods once. I feel like he needs to be here, he needs to be okay with sharing every part of me for this work. Dagan pulls me into his arms before I can even blink or look back to him, his lips finding mine only a moment later. I moan into his mouth as he picks me up, his rough hands gripping my ass tightly as he walks back under the hot shower water and presses me against the cold stone.

"My mate," he growls against my neck as he slowly kisses his way down to my chest. I'm not sure who is in charge, Dagan or his dragon, but I don't care one bit. Dagan's tongue circles around my nipple just as his right hand slides between my legs, pressing down on my clit and rubbing. I moan loudly as Dagan gets me right to the edge and stops, leaving me breathless as he lines us up and looks into my eyes as he slides deep inside of me. I gasp as he fills me completely, utterly and perfectly.

Dagan's eyes burn red as he slams his lips onto mine, as he starts thrusting until I can't think of anything but him.

"I love you so much, Isola," he whispers into my ear, before gently biting down on my neck as he thrusts into me harder. I meet Thorne's silver glowing eyes over Dagan's shoulder, the sight of him watching us turning me on even more. I moan loudly as I come around Dagan, and a few thrusts later, Dagan finishes, groaning my name like a prayer. A warm feeling spreads all over my body, flittering around me until I have to open my eyes as it disappears. I can feel and sense Dagan like he is part of me.

"Mating is more amazing than I thought," Dagan whispers, pulling out of me and gently easing me to the floor. The hot water pours down us as I stare up at him in happiness. Dagan kisses me before pushing my wet hair behind my ear and whispering as I lock eyes with Thorne who remains still as he watches us.

"Go and claim your other mate. I will be right outside the door just in case the hunters are getting suspicious." I stay still as Dagan walks away from us, towel drying himself before pulling his clothes on. I wait to say or do something until Dagan opens the door and walks out. The sound of the door shutting seems to shake me into stepping forward. I walk over to Thorne, stopping right in front of him.

"If I move, my dragon will take his mate," Thorne warns as I place my hand on his cheek. "I don't have much control left, Issy."

"Then don't move," I whisper, feeling more confident than ever about who and what I want. Life is short, life is precious, and I'm tired of not taking the leap I want. I slowly slide my hands down Thorne's chest, down his flat stomach to his trousers. I undo the button, before pushing them down and taking his long, hard length into my hand. Thorne groans as I stroke him before falling to my knees and not pausing or teasing as I take all of him into my mouth, stopping just before I choke.

"Fuckkk," Thorne groans as I bob my head up and down, sucking and rolling my tongue around his length. Thorne suddenly pulls me away from him, laying me down on the ground with one smooth movement and lying on top of me. I kiss him harshly as he thrusts inside me, holding himself deep as he breaks the kiss.

"You and me. Nothing comes between us now," I tell him. His silver eyes burn as he slowly moves, drawing each movement out until I feel like I might lose my mind with him deep inside of me.

"I'm yours. You are mine. I love you more than anything in any world, Issy." He makes each statement between slow thrusts, making me moan out of control before he deeply kisses me. Thorne reaches between my legs with his thumb, only needing to rub me a few times before I release once again, and he shouts out my name as he finishes with me. The same warm feeling spreads over me, completing our mating, and Thorne holds me close the entire time, making me feel more content and complete than I have ever felt before.

98

ISOLA

I run my fingers through my damp hair after pulling my clothes on, trying to get the knots out and failing as it is a mess. We found some soap, but no shampoo, so trying to clean my hair with that wasn't good. I give up and put my damp towel in the washing basket.

"Here, I found a comb," Thorne says from behind me, and I look over my shoulder to see him walking to me with a blue comb in his hand. He pauses right next to me, placing his hand on my arm to stop me turning around to face him. "Can I brush your hair?"

"Sure," I whisper back. Even with the shower still pouring in the background, my voice sounds loud. We couldn't figure out how to turn the showers off and concluded that it might be an automatic shut off. Thorne gently combs my hair; the repeating motion is soothing, and I resist the urge to lean back into him as I know it would stop him combing.

"I love having someone do my hair," I admit, and he chuckles, turning me around with his hands after he finishes my hair. I look up at him, placing both my hands on his cheeks and leaning up to kiss him. The door opens to the shower room, and Dagan comes in, spotting us and walking over.

"Hallie is out there with some other hunters. I don't think you should say anything to her, but I'd rather be by your side as you do, so let's go," he says, but I'm already walking to the door and hearing them both sigh behind me. I step out into the large main room and spot Hallie straight away. She is sliding a tray of food on the banquet table in the middle with a blond-haired male hunter at her side. Though she can't sense me looking at her, she looks up and narrows her eyes on me as I storm over to her without a second thought. Hallie still looks like an army brat, but her green-tipped hair stands out like a sore thumb. Two other hunters are stood just to her right, both older men with gelled, short, brown hair and bulky bodies under their uniforms. They glare at me, and I stare for a second at one of them, wondering why he looks familiar to me.

"What do you want, Isola?" Hallie asks with a sigh when I get to her side, and she turns to look at me. The hunter next to her slides his gun out slowly, but it still catches my attention before I lock eyes with my best friend, though no part of her looks at me the way she used to. She looks at me like I am a stranger and nothing to her. I glance around the room, seeing all the dragons watching me, and Korbin is being held back by two hunters stood right in front of him. His eyes meet mine, and he shakes his head, clearly warning me to behave, but that isn't going to happen until Hallie listens to me.

"You're my best friend, Hallie. Won't you even pause to listen to my side of the story?" I ask her and notice how the entire room is silent. The two hunter men come over to stand right at Dagan's side next to me, and Thorne stands silently a little distance away. The tension is thick in the air as there is nothing but silence.

"You and your kind are murderers!" she spits out at me, seeming so angry, and her words are so hurtful. I know she lost her mother, and I know they were close.

"Should we take them back to their cages?" the blond hunter at Hallie's side asks. Hallie shakes her head at him; clearly, she doesn't want this conversation to end. I might have some chance of getting through to her.

"Is Jules okay?" I ask Hallie, needing to hear the answer first.

"Of course she is. Jules is human, and none of this is her fault," Hallie replies, crossing her arms.

"Good...thank you," I say, before clearing my throat as I start to explain. "I am so sorry about your mum. I don't know everything about Paris or what happened to her, but I am so sorry. What happened with Michael wasn't like you said. I didn't kill him or the others, but I wish I could have. He drugged me, and then he tried to rape me. I won't say sorry for my dragon guard ending his life, he deserved it." Her eyes widen in shock, looking briefly away from me to the two hunters nearby. When she looks back, there is fear on her face.

"What did you just say about my son?" one of the male hunters demands, walking over to me, but Dagan slides between us before he can get close. Fear shakes through me as the man's eyes meet mine, and they are the image of Michael's.

"You heard," I bravely reply. "Your son tried to rape me after drugging me with something he clearly stole from here. I will never apologise for your son's death...he deserved it."

"You're a liar! My son would never do that! You killed him because you're a monster and that is what your kind do!" the guard shouts, trying to push Dagan to the side to get to me. Dagan lifts Michael's father by his jacket and throws him across the room, his body slamming into the wall, and there is a sickening crack as his head hits the wall before his body drops to the floor. I scream as Dagan and Thorne fall to the ground, each holding their collar as it electrocutes them. It's only seconds before my own collar starts shocking me, sending incredible pain throughout my body, causing my legs to collapse underneath me. I slam onto the floor, my eyes still open to see Hallie's pale face as she stares down at me.

"I'm sorry," she mouths, before the pain sends everything into darkness.

99

ISOLA

"I warned you not to test me. Yet here we are, and only the second day of you being here, and you cause chaos. I am *very* disappointed," Graves's voice drifts into my ear as I slowly come awake, feeling my face pressed against the cold floor. Every part of my body still hurts, and my neck feels worse than any of it. I can smell a slight burning and taste my own blood in my mouth as I blink my eyes open to see shiny black shoes behind bars. I roll on my back, looking up to see Graves standing outside the cage, his arms crossed with an expression suggesting he wants me dead.

"I only told the truth," I gasp out, clearing my throat a few times to try and make my voice come back. I must have screamed to make my throat feel so raw, but I don't remember anything past Hallie mouthing that she was sorry. Why would she be sorry? A little part of me hopes I might have gotten through to her, and she might help us escape. Though I need to remember it won't be that easy. There is no doubt Dagan killed Michael's father, and Graves will make us pay for that.

"Well, maybe you will learn to shut your mouth in the future. Don't expect your dragons back anytime soon," he threatens, grinning down at me as I start to panic at his words. Graves walks away as I pull myself up with a grunt and look into Dagan's empty cage. I stare through the cages and only see Melody in the room with us. She stands in her cage and shakes her head.

"I'm sorry," she says loudly, reminding me of what Hallie said for only a second, and I wonder if that means something. I search my mating bond, sensing Dagan and Thorne are alive, but I can't hear them. I can't feel them like I usually can either. My dragon roars to life, freaking out just as much as I am at Dagan and Thorne's lack of response.

Get the collar off, my dragon demands.

If I could, I would, I growl back, and she huffs, letting me have control because there is no choice here. I pull myself up to stand shakily and look over at Melody in her cage through the bars.

"Where is Korbin?" I ask, pretty much hoping her answer isn't what I am expecting her to say.

"They took him too," she answers like I expect her to. I grab the bars, trying to shake them before resting my head against them in frustration. I was stupid to risk talking to Hallie, and now my dragons will pay for it.

"At least they didn't take you," I finally reply to Melody.

"No, they don't need me to control you," she replies emotionlessly. "It's nearly time. You can save them."

"Time for what?" I look up, meeting her eyes as I ask her.

"Fate," she quietly replies and steps back, disappearing into the shadows of her cage.

"Come back! You can't just say that!" I shout at her, but there is silence for a reply. *Damn seers.*

I pace around my cage for what feels like ages, knowing every moment, my dragons are in danger. I don't know how long it has been, but suddenly the walls and ground shake, knocking me to the floor, and my head slams against the ground. The lights flicker before the room goes pitch black, and I hold my hands over my head as the ground shakes more. When I open my eyes, the lights are flashing and flickering, and there is a loud alarm blasting somewhere nearby.

"Melody? Are you okay?" I shout, worrying when I don't hear her for a while as I pull myself up off the floor.

"I'm good. Just a little shaken," she shouts back as I hold onto the bars, just in case. I look around, seeing that my door has come off the hinges a little in the shake. I go over to it and pull at the gap, making it a little bigger and bigger before I can climb out. I fall out the door just as the ground shakes again, and I hold my hands over my head as pieces of the ceiling fall. When the shaking subsides, I sit up, pushing my dusty hair out of my face, blinking as I look up to see a woman my age standing in the corridor entrance. She has long brown hair, glowing blue eyes and a leather outfit on that reminds me of some kind of assassin or something.

"Who are you?" I ask the woman, who tilts her head to the side and smiles.

"Winter—well, I'm kinda the queen—but it doesn't matter right now as you don't have to call me anything but Winter. Sorry, totally mumbling. We need to get going," she pauses as we both hear a long growl that oddly sounds like a wolf. A very scary and unhappy wolf. A few screams follow after the growl which worry me a little while I still have this collar on.

"What was that?" I slowly ask her, feeling like the woman looks familiar somehow, and I'm not sure why. Why does her name sound familiar? The ground shakes again, and we both duck as more ceiling falls near us, the sharp rocks hitting my arm. Winter just gets up, shaking the dust off and answering my question like nothing happened.

"Jaxson, my mate, is dealing with the guards. Let's just say they should be scared, he is pissed off since one of them *tried* to shoot me. Anyways, Dabriel and Wyatt are sorting out the other buildings since we got a tip about this place," she says with a grin. "Let's go, we have people to save, right?" she asks as she walks over to me and holds out a hand. I slide my hand into hers as she helps me stand up, and we both look behind us as Melody walks over, brushing off dust from her clothes.

"Time to go. Nice to meet you, Queen Winter. My sister's soon-to-be close friend," Melody says, walking around us like we aren't even here and never stopping as she speaks. Winter frowns at her and looks back to me.

"How did she know my name?" Winter asks.

"My sister, Melody, is a seer. I'm Isola, by the way," I say, figuring I might as well introduce myself before we walk to where Melody waits for us by the door. Winter slides two daggers out of her belt, looking between Melody and me like we are strange. If anything, Winter seems strange to me...or just very brave. *I'm not sure which yet.*

"Here, you need a weapon," she offers one of the daggers to Melody, who waves a hand. "Give it to Isola. I don't need it." Winter shrugs and hands it to me, and I accept it. *If a seer says you might need a weapon, you find a weapon.*

"Is everyone in this building seers? My mates and army have got our people out, but you guys were the most protected, so it took longer. They really didn't want to let us in here," Winter explains as we walk into the war zone of the main room where most of the screaming is coming from. There are wolves everywhere of different colors and sizes, there are people shooting fire, and angels flying around the room, fighting with the hunters who are having no luck shooting them. A massive black wolf picks up a hunter in its mouth like it is nothing and throws the hunter across the room with his other paw. *Damn.* I jump back when a man appears right in front of us. The man looks like a Greek god with his long blond hair and his black cloak clipped at his neck. The man doesn't even seem to notice us as he looks at Winter, assessing her in a loving way. I know that look because it is how Dagan, Kor, Elias and Thorne look at me when they are worried about me. Right before becoming all overprotective.

"Atti, did you work out how to get the collars off?" Winter

asks the man, apparently called Atti, who grins at her in a cheeky way.

"Of course I did! What do you take me for, love? It only took me a few attempts to get it right," he replies, laughing.

"Yes, I'm sure the ones you tested it on where not thankful for your attempts," she replies, arching an eyebrow as he pulls her into his arms, and I look away as he kisses her. I spot my uncle as he snaps the neck of one of the hunters and picks up a little girl with white hair, before running out the room with her.

"It was only two of them, and these guys are stronger than they look," he replies, laughing, and Winter shakes her head at him. They are in the middle of a war zone and making jokes. Whatever these people are, they are weird.

"Isola, do you want your collar off?" Winter asks me, pulling away from Atti and gently touching my arm to get my attention.

"Is it safe?" I ask Atti instead of answering her, and he nods.

"Perfectly," he replies, and I nod, knowing I don't really have a choice if I want this thing off me. Atti steps closer and holds his hand on the collar on my neck. It burns for a moment before it makes a loud beeping noise and unclicks. Atti pulls it off for me, and I rub my neck, loving the feeling of being free. Atti steps away from me as snow starts falling from my hands, and my eyes must be turning silver.

We find them and get revenge. I don't have to reply to my dragon, knowing that we are on the same page. I close my eyes and try to sense my mates, knowing Kor is most likely with them. It takes me a few moments to realize that something is still blocking me from actually finding them, but I know they are near.

"Thank you," I tell Atti and Winter. They look between each other and back to me like I'm a puzzle to figure out, but I ignore them and look to Melody. "Where are they? I know you can find them when I can't."

"This way," Melody nods her head to a door, like she was waiting for me to ask. I grit my teeth and run after her, only

looking back when I hear footsteps to see Winter and Atti
following after us.

"We are coming with you, for back up. I don't know why, but
I think you might need us," Winter replies, but I don't have time
to reply to her as I turn and run after Melody who is heading for
a door. She stops, suddenly spinning around, and kicks the door
open in one fluid movement that looks badass, before running in
with me right behind her. The room is a long corridor, full of
wooden white painted doors. Melody doesn't pause, heading
straight for the third door down and kicking it open. There are
screams as I follow Melody in, and I watch as she punches one of
the hunters in the face, and they fall to the floor with a smack.
One of the other hunters tries to run past us, but I grab the back
of his coat, calling my ice and freezing the hunter from top to
bottom.

"Okay...that was freakin' cool, Isola," Winter says in awe, but
my eyes widen as I look around the room. Dagan, Kor and
Thorne are all in one cage, strapped to the wall by metal grips.
There is various tubing taking blood from their arms and likely
pumping some sedative into them to keep them half asleep. Each
of them looks up when we walk in, their faces each covered in
bruises and cuts. They look like someone has beat the shit out
of them.

"Get them out. I have to find her," Melody tells me, but I
barely hear her or see the hunters running down the corridor
behind us as I head for the cage. I grab the bars of the door,
freezing the parts near the lock until they snap. I step back to
copy my sister's move, spinning and kicking the cage door which
falls to the floor with a bang.

"I could have just found the key," I hear Atti almost sarcastically say behind us as I get to Korbin first. "But that works too."
I pull the tubing out of his arm, holding my hand over the
bleeding for a moment until it naturally heals. I pull the metal
straps off his arms and then his legs, and he pulls me into an
embrace the moment he is free. I breathe in his fire scent as I

wrap my arms tightly around his neck and try not to break down just yet. We are so close to being free, and I can only let anger rule me right now.

"You okay, doll?" he asks me, and I nod. Kor follows my gaze over towards Atti and Winter who are pulling off Dagan's and Thorne's straps. "Who are your new friends?" he asks me quietly.

"Winter, who is apparently a queen, but I don't know what of, and her friend, Atti. They saved me, so they are my friends now. I owe them," I explain to Kor, and just like that, I can see any hostility towards them gone. They saved me, and dragons always respect those who they owe a debt.

"My mate, Atticus, actually. I am the queen of the supernaturals, but just call me Winter," Winter chimes in as I get to Dagan who she has just undone. I wrap my arms around Dagan, silently seeking his comfort, and he squeezes me tightly in response. I meet Thorne's eyes over Dagan's shoulder as Atti undoes his collar.

Time to get out of here, Thorne speaks in my mind, and to my surprise, Dagan is the one that replies as he can apparently now hear us. I love how we are all bonded now.

Not before we kill the hunters that put us here.

ISOLA

"So, blondie can make ice from her hands, what else can you guys do? What do you call yourselves?" Atti asks as he gets Kor's collar off as we wait, and we are finally all free then. "I would suspect a version of witches, but you don't seem like a witch like me."

"Isola..." Hallie whispers, stepping through the door before I can answer Atti. Melody steps in behind her, and they are holding hands which surprises me into silence. Dagan doesn't seem too surprised as he protectively wraps an arm around my waist. I always knew Melody and Hallie were meant to be together, but after everything Hallie has done, this is hard to swallow. I look between them, ignoring the gentle shake of the ground behind us and the distant screams, growls and scent of fire in the air.

"Seriously, Melody? We can't trust her," Dagan growls. "She was the one that put us in here in the first place! Her father runs this place and tortured us!"

"We can trust her! I love my sister, and I would never put her in danger if I had any choice!" Melody exclaims, wiping a tear away and looking over at Hallie. "Hallie, please explain everything while the witch king takes off my collar." Melody leans over, kissing Hallie's cheek before letting her go to walk to Atti.

"How did she know what and who I am?" Atti asks Winter as I stare at Hallie like she is the only one in the room.

"Apparently, she is a seer and knows stuff," Winter replies as Hallie nervously puts her hands together and steps forward towards me. Dagan lightly growls, pulling me back, but I put my hand on his chest and shake my head at him.

"First, you should know Melody has been visiting me for months in a faded, almost ghost like form. She told me everything. I am so sorry for what Michael almost did. If I could bring that bastard back to life, I would, just to murder him more painfully next time. I fell in love with Melody, and I knew one day we would get to be together...just not like this. It was just an instant thing, a feeling of finally belonging and being happy with her. Melody is my world...and you have always been my best friend," she whispers. "I hate my father, but after my mum died in Paris, he went insane. I didn't have a choice but to pretend to be on his side. I couldn't do anything but pretend."

"I don't remember you pretending anything when you shot me," I reply, not knowing if I can trust Hallie or not.

"Yes, even then. I shot you to save you, funny enough," she tells me, completely confusing me.

"I don't feel like you saved me at all," I retort. "All you did was get us stuck in here and my dragons tortured. You did nothing that saved me at all. Winter saved me."

"I didn't know you were going to come through that portal when you did. I wasn't expecting it when you all came in and everyone saw you. There were hunters everywhere around that portal, and I knew we could never have fought them all off. I had to pretend I hated you, even when it broke my heart to see the betrayal in your eyes as I pulled the trigger," she whispers. "You have to believe I didn't want to shoot you. You're my best friend."

"You shot your best friend? That's not cool," Winter says,

clearly only hearing the end part of the conversation as she steps to my other side. Melody—now free of her collar—goes to Hallie and they link hands. I glance at the bag on Melody's shoulder, where her orb just sticks out, knowing she must have stopped off for that too. When Hallie and Melody look at each other for only a moment, I see the love and adoration on both their faces. I don't doubt for a second they love each other, but it's hard to swallow that Hallie did all this because she was trying to protect me.

"Hallie has protected you for a long time. She even hid Bee from them all, and took her somewhere safe," Melody tells me, changing everything. If she really kept Bee safe all this time...I might actually believe everything. Why would she do that otherwise? I glance at Dagan, then Thorne and Kor who seem just as shocked as I feel.

"You saved Bee?" I whisper, looking back at Hallie, feeling tears prickling my eyes.

"Of course I did. My father couldn't have seen Bee because who knows what he would have done to her. I took Bee to Jules at the nursing home. Jules and all the old people there love her," Hallie explains. That sounds like my Bee. *I miss the little spirit.*

"She is okay?" I ask, remembering how weak she seemed when we came through the portal.

"Bee and Jules, both of them are okay, just weak for different reasons. I know it will take time for you to forgive me...but I am so sorry. I just did what I could to keep you safe, and Jules helped me call the supernaturals, because she clearly has her own secrets, to tell them about my father's work," Hallie says, looking down at the ground. I step away from everyone and go to Hallie, wrapping my arms around her as I wonder how Jules knows anything about supernaturals. She cries silently as we hug, and I pull away as I know we have other things to do. Hallie is right, it will take time for me to trust her again, but we are on the right track now.

"Sorry to interrupt, but my witches have got everyone out.

We should go now so they can destroy the buildings," Atti says to us all. "I can make us move outside if everyone holds hands." I look at Winter, who nods her encouragement and holds a hand out to me as she holds Atti's hand. I slide my hand into hers, and Dagan, Kor and Thorne place their hands on my back while Hallie and Melody hold my arm. A cold wash of magic, much like going through a portal, drifts over my skin, and I close my eyes. As I open them, we are stood in a forest, with five buildings in the distance, which I bet is where we were being kept. I let go of Winter's hand as I see Graves getting into a car with some other hunters in the distance, a low growl slipping from my lips as my dragon locks onto her target. My hands drip with ice as anger burns throughout me.

"You want to see what we are?" I turn and ask Winter with a grin. She nods, looking a little confused. I run forward, letting my dragon take over after a few steps, everything turning white as I shift. I roar as I spread my wings out, knocking down trees and hearing gasps behind me.

"You're a freakin' dragon!" I hear Winter shout in amazement.

"We rescued dragons...that is cool. Where is Jaxson...the wolf isn't the biggest creature on Earth anymore. He will fucking love that," I hear Atticus say, followed by his loud laugh. My dragon focuses on the car as it speeds away down a path, ignoring anything else.

Graves will not escape. Let's hunt, I tell my dragon and she takes off into the sky, heading straight for the car like there is nothing else in the world.

Human will die for touching my mates, my dragon growls as she swoops down, catching the car in her claws and flying up with it like her prey. My dragon looks down at the car as she hovers in the air, seeing Graves's panicked face in the window as he tries to escape, and the driver jumps out of the car, falling to his death. My dragon looks over to see Dagan's and Korbin's dragons next to us, and they fly for the buildings. They shoot fire, setting the buildings alight and roaring proudly. My dragon doesn't even need my instruction; she flies us over the biggest building, hovering with the car just above it.

Bye, asshole, I mutter, seeing Graves's terror-filled eyes as my dragon lets the car go, and it falls into the fire. Some part of me feels bad for killing Hallie's father in front of her, but when my dragon finds her, standing next to Melody, she nods with a firm gaze. *He didn't deserve to live or have a daughter like Hallie.* My dragon roars loudly, the sound echoing around the forest, and we hear cheers from the people on the ground. I shoot a stream of ice all around me before my dragon lands us back in the forest on top of the ice and snow. I shift back and stretch as I stand up tall. Winter and Atticus run over as Dagan's and Korbin's dragons land behind me and then shift back. All the dragons and other supernaturals in the forest run out too, with my uncle not far behind them, his hand holding the little girl's and Jonas's hands. I nod at him, thankful that he got the children out safely, by the looks of it. I stare at all the ice dragon children in the crowd, knowing that when Dragca is safe, they will return to their home, and I won't be the only ice dragon left. As I look around, taking in everyone's smiling faces, I notice one missing.

"Where is Thorne?" I ask, not seeing him anywhere. I search for him in my mind, frowning when I can't sense him near, and he keeps getting further away. *Thorne?*

I did this because I love you. I will get you the throne, he tells me. My mouth parts in shock when I realize he has gone back to Dragca alone. He is going back to see his mother.

No! Come back. We do this together. Your mother will kill you! I plead with him, but I know he won't reply to me, because all I can feel from him is how certain he is. Everyone finally makes their way to me as I stare angrily at the ground, tears pricking my eyes that I can't let fall.

Why would he do this? Why couldn't he wait? my dragon whines in my head, making me not only deal with my emotions but hers as well. I won't lose my mate because he is an idiot that thinks he can do this alone. I am the one that is meant to stop Tatarina. If Thorne kills her, he will never forgive himself. No matter what Tatarina is…she is still his mother.

"Isola…he had to do this," my uncle says, coming to my side, and I glare at him as I lift my head.

"Did you tell him to do it? Tatarina won't pause before she kills him, and I thought Thorne knew that," I say, growling low.

"He is her son. He has a better chance than you do," my uncle says, shrugging like it is a done deal and not important that Thorne might be killed. I ignore him to look back at Dagan's guilty face, and to Korbin who seems just as guilty as he stares at the ground. I don't even need to ask if they planned this, if they let him go while I was distracted. I know they would be behind a plan to save me fighting Tatarina…but nothing is going to stop that. Part of me understands the need to try and save the ones I love, but it doesn't mean Thorne is right to fight her alone.

"We are going to Dragca now!" I growl out, and I look up when a snow flake falls on my nose. The dark clouds in the sky start letting it snow, and I stare at the white flakes falling from the sky, watching the way the wind moves them. They stick to the trees, making everything seem so alive. It somewhat seems perfect that it is snowing as we leave Earth, and I know I won't be returning for a long time. Not until I am queen. Dragca is my home and where I want to spend the last of my days. Where I want to build a future, not only for myself and my mates, but for the people of Dragca.

"I'm sorry, Isola. Thorne is the only one that can get close to her," I hear Dagan say to me as I continue staring up at the sky.

"No, he isn't. Tatarina wants me the most because I am all that is left of her best friend and the man she was in love with. I am her enemy and the only thing left she feels she needs to destroy. That is why she hasn't killed Elias, it is why she will hold Thorne hostage…to get me to come to her. Tatarina has *my* throne and she is destroying *my* home. I am going after her, with or without you all," I tell them all and finally look away from the snowing sky to see not only Dagan, Korbin and my uncle watching me but dozens of other dragons. And other people.

"We are with you. Always," Korbin agrees and Dagan nods.

"I'm sorry for letting Thorne go...you are right. We are with you, our queen," Dagan tells me, bowing his head a little before meeting my eyes. I'm still mad at him for letting Thorne go, but I know he is only doing this to try and save me. *I can tell him off later for being a know-it-all douchebag.*

Jonas comes running over to me with snow-covered blond hair, pointing at his collar-free neck. Someone has given Jonas a big adult's jacket, so he won't get too cold.

"The witches are taking the collars off. I'm free," he says, grinning up at me like it is Christmas. His happy, innocent face almost makes me forget everything and smile. Almost. I pull him into a hug, and he doesn't resist, staying at my side when I let him go. "I've never been without this on unless they were testing me. You said we would be free, and you were right. Thank you."

"Freedom isn't something a child should have to be given. Children should always be free, Jonas," I whisper to him. "You will always be free, from this point on. No more collars." Jonas gives me a shaky nod, before resting his head on my arm as I look away from him to Dagan who smiles down at Jonas before glancing at me.

"We need the dragons that can fight free from the collars before we go back to Dragca, and also somehow get them weapons. I will go with your uncle to figure out who will come with us," Dagan says, and I nod once to him. *I love you,* he whispers in my mind, making my lips tilt up for a second before I remember that both Thorne and Elias need me. *Urgently.*

"What is Dragca?" Winter asks, walking over from the trees and stopping right in front of me. She has a big cloak on now, the hood pulled up to protect her from the heavy falling snow. Though with a name like Winter, I doubt she minds the snow.

"The land of Dragons. We come to Earth from a portal, and

our worlds are linked. I am the last ice dragon princess, but I will soon be queen when I take my throne back from the murderer sitting upon it," I explain, and her eyes widen, taking it all in. I step back as a huge black wolf walks to Winter's side, and she places her hand on his head. The wolf growls, baring its huge teeth, and Winter tuts.

"Jax behave," she says and looks to me. "Wolf shifters can be a little territorial, but it seems your own dragons are just the same." I follow her eye when she looks to my left, seeing Dagan and Korbin talking to Atti, but their eyes are constantly looking back to check if I am okay.

"We have a lot in common it seems, Queen Winter," I reply.

"My friends don't call me Queen. It's just Winter," she replies, winking at me, and I chuckle. "Do you need any help in your homeland? As queen of the supernaturals, I want an alliance between us. I want to help, but we have just been at war ourselves. I'm sure you heard about it, and we lost a lot of our people, but we can still send a small army with you and weapons."

"We need to go in quiet and unseen, so we can not use your army this time, but thank you. Some weapons for the dragons here would be much appreciated. I will always owe you for getting us out of there and even offering to help us after your own war," I say, and Winter nods, both of us standing quietly in the falling snow.

"That was nothing. If anything, we should be sorry we couldn't stop the hunters and save you sooner. Are you sure there is nothing I can do for you other than the weapons? We have time; Atti and the witches will take at least half an hour to get all those awful collars off," Winter offers, and I look over at Melody and Hallie, who are holding hands and quietly talking.

"There is one thing."

101

ISOLA

"Jules…" I whisper, letting go of my sister's arm when we appear in her room, as I can't help the smile on my lips from seeing her. I don't know how to exactly define my relationship with Jules, but she is as close to a second mother as I have. She is family, and I missed her. Jules is sat in a chair by her bed, her very grey hair in a tight bun like usual on her head and a massive smile on her lips. Jules's fashion sense hasn't changed, and I somewhat love seeing the flower-covered dress she has on and the yellow knitted cardigan. I run to her as she opens her arms for me, her watery eyes looking so happy to see me.

"I knew we would see each other again, child," Jules gently says to me as I pull back and pause in shock. I look to the left at the massive tree in her room, and a familiar pod hanging from it. The tree looks like a bonsai tree…but much bigger and brighter than normal. There are dozens of plant pots around the tree, filled with bright flowers that crawl half way up the tree's trunk. Everything in the room is so bright and colorful; when I look back at Winter, Atti, Hallie and Melody, they look as surprised as I am. That is not what you expect to see in a regular nursing home. "Your little friend is quite the gardener." I laugh at Jules's unasked response.

"Seems so," I mutter out as I still laugh, and Jules smiles up at me.

"You have changed in the time we spent apart. You seem older. Stronger. It is what I have always wanted to see you as," Jules says, taking my hand in hers and squeezing it tightly. "I always knew this strong woman was inside of you, but you just had to grow into her." Jules's statement brings tears to my eyes, and I gently release her hand to wipe my cheeks. I go to reply when the pod flap opens, and Bee flies out. We both stare at each other, as I take in the rush of our bond coming back into place. I open my arms, needing to have her close, and she flies straight into them. I stroke her hair gently, happy to have her back near me. Pulling her off me a little, I take a closer look at her, seeing she isn't as bright as she usually is, but she looks okay. We need to be back on Dragca. We need to go home so she can connect with the magic there.

"Miss you," Bee mumbles, flying out of my hands and sitting on my shoulder. "Lady gave me food. Good food." Jules laughs, smiling at Bee and me.

"I missed you too, Bee. We keep getting separated, but never again," I whisper to her.

"That looks like a green less-troll-like female version of Milo," Atti tells Winter, who nods staring at Bee. I turn, remembering that they are still here and I haven't introduced them.

"Sorry, Jules. This is Winter and Atti, they are friends. You know Hallie, and this is my sister, Melody," I introduce them all. They each say hello in an overly kind way, except for Hallie who just smirks at me, and my lips tilt up a little in response.

"I'm glad to know you have friends on your side," Jules remarks. "Family and friends. That is all anyone ever needs."

"Jules is a very wise woman it seems," Winter comments.

"I like this one," Jules replies, winking at Winter who laughs. "Come and let me see you, Melody. I see your sister a little in you." Hallie tugs a nervous looking Melody over with her to Jules.

"I need a favor," I quietly say to Winter, while I watch Jules fuss over Melody who is blushing.

"Anything," Winter answers. "Well, anything I can offer you."

"Hallie, Melody and Jules need to stay on Earth with you for a while. Dragca isn't safe for them," I tell Winter. "I wish for you to protect them until I can send someone back with good news. I am returning to Dragca because it is where I belong, and I will die or rule there. There is nothing in-between. As a queen, I'm sure you understand the hard decisions you have to make to do what is right for everyone...but I can't lose them. They are my family."

"You have my word that your family will be protected. After we are done at the hunters' base, we will come back and move them into our home. The castle is the safest place on Earth," Winter replies, and I place my hand on her arm.

"Thank you," I tell her, before walking closer to Jules.

"Dragca is where you are from, right?" Jules asks me. She has always been smarter than anyone knows, or Hallie has been telling her a lot recently. I nod. "You must leave and save your world. Right?"

"Yes, I have to leave. Dragca needs me. The men I love need me, but I am leaving Melody and Hallie with you and Winter. They need time to recover and relax. Where we are going...well, it isn't safe, and it is a dragon war," I explain, and Jules's eyes widen. I guess she didn't know exactly what I was, but the cat— well, dragon—is out of the bag now.

"Can I have a quiet word, sis?" Melody asks me, and I nod at her before turning back to Jules.

"One day, I will come back and get you. I want to show you Dragca and explain everything," I tell her, and she reaches for my hand. I slide my hand into hers, and she squeezes tight.

"One day, child. I do look forward to it," she says with a big smile. I squeeze her frail hand once more before letting go and walking over to the door, pulling it open. Melody follows Bee and me out into the silent corridor of the nursing home, and she shuts the door, so we are alone.

"I wish I could come with you to Dragca, but I cannot," she says solemnly. "I am not meant to be at your side in this fight. I just had to get you here and hope for the best. For all the futures I see...I do not know what will happen next."

"I figured as much when you didn't disagree when I asked Jules to have you here," I say. "I wish I could have you at my side too...but what is left of Dragca needs to be won by dragons, and I cannot lose you in a dragon war."

"The seers have not all been lost in the war, and I truly believe they will help you. I need to tell you something before you go back, something very important," she says, and I cross my arms as Melody's eyes leave my face and go to Bee on my shoulder, who is holding onto my hair, from what I can feel.

"Light and dark spirits are twins. Both are meant to be together, bonded with one dragon who becomes the balance. Nane—the dark spirit—can only be stopped if she bonds with you like Bee did. No one else could understand and control her. Too much light or dark in one world would destroy it. One dragon is meant to be the balance from the start," she says, shocking me into silence. "I saw a vision just before Tatarina attacked us in Dragca and we had to leave. The vision was of the past, of the last time a light and dark spirit were born. They did both bond with the dragon they chose, but the dragon couldn't handle the power and died from the bond."

"How the hell do I even get close to Nane then? What if I die bonding with her?" I ask in disbelief. I can't fight this whole battle for Dragca just to die at the end, trying to become some kind of balance between light and dark. I glance at Bee, and she smiles sadly at me. Bee already knows this, and I wonder how she feels about Nane. If they are family like Melody says, Bee must care.

"I don't know. Nane has to choose to bond with you because

she must understand you. Bee bonded to you because she saw your innocence, your compassion and love. Nane bonded with Tatarina because she saw her hate, anger, jealousy and mistook it for darkness. You have that darkness inside of you, that anger, and Nane would easily bond with you if she let you in. To be honest though, she has taken in so much darkness without Bee to balance her out that I don't know if you could survive bonding with her now. Bee's light might not survive it either," she says sadly.

"What happens if I don't bond with her?" I lightly ask, needing to hear the answer out loud, even if I have a sneaking suspicion of the answer.

"Dragca needs both light and dark at the same time. There cannot be one without the other. If Nane dies—"

"So do I," Bee interrupts to explain, and I look to her, seeing the sadness on her little face. "My sister will destroy our bond. I chose you...she chose bad."

"I won't let that happen to you because Nane made a bad choice," I tell Bee, and she shakes her head a little, before looking away.

"Then you need to get close to Nane once Tatarina is gone," Melody states. "You must bond with her before anyone else does to save Bee. Nane can't take any more darkness from anyone else...she will destroy every living thing as well as herself if she does."

"Okay. I will sort it," I say, reaching to hold her hand. "You will look after Hallie, alright? I may be mad at her still and you as well, but I love you both."

"More like she will look after me," she chuckles with a grin that soon disappears as the seriousness of the situation hits us once more. "Elias and Thorne need you. You must go," she says, and I nod before walking to the door, and pausing with my hand on the handle.

"Am I going to lose Eli or Thorne?" I whisper, my voice

cracking because I don't even know how to ask the question or if I want to hear the answer.

"There are many futures I see...I just don't know what will be left," she quietly replies, and places her hand on my back. "I only see in every future that they love you more than life, and that makes you one of the lucky people in life. Sometimes just having one person love you that much is worth everything."

"Be safe, sister," I whisper, and open the door. *It's time to save my dragons before they destroy themselves.*

102

ISOLA

"That's everyone free from those collars," Atti exclaims proudly, coming over to us as he burns one in his hand. I stare, fascinated with how these witches can control fire just like dragons. We are more alike than we think. Except that I come with scales and wings...and they have more fur and disappearing acts. I clip the daggers to my new belt, thanks to Winter, and look back at my uncle who is quietly talking to Korbin and Dagan. They all have new weapons, as do all the dragons here who want to fight. Winter really came through with that promise, and we might have a slight chance of surprising Tatarina long enough for me to kill her and take the throne back. I can't even think of Elias and Thorne right now. They would be a distraction when I need to focus on the right now.

"Do I have to stay with them? I want to come to Dragca with you," Jonas says, snapping me out of my thoughts. I glance at him, seeing how nervous he seems as he stares at the group of children the witches are taking back to Winter's home. They are all bundled together in the snow-covered forest, with thick coats on. Behind the children are groups of supernaturals and a few dragons that can't fight bundled in groups with a witch in charge of each group. They are taking all of them to Winter's castle where they will find homes for the ones that want to stay and temporary places for the dragons who wish to return to Dragca in the future. Either way, I know Winter and her kings will keep them safe.

"When the war in Dragca is over, and I am on the throne, I will send people back to Earth to find you. Anyone that wants to come to Dragca will have a home there," I explain to Jonas, placing my hand on his shoulder in comfort. "Jace was my family, and I couldn't save him. I wish I could have, and finding you feels like I have a chance to honor his memory. I will always be here to protect you, and you will have a home with me in the future. Jace was my family...so are you." Jonas stares up at me with teary eyes, and I only look away as someone steps in front of me. Winter smiles at us, before tucking some of her long hair behind her ear.

"It's true that you will always be protected from now on, not only by Isola. Plus, my home is pretty cool, and I have a stepson around your age you might get along with," Winter says, smiling at Jonas who seems to relax a little as he wipes his eyes.

"You will see me again?" Jonas asks me, staring up at me with those eyes so much like Jace's that it hurts. It only reminds me that Jace's murderer is still alive, and I'm likely going to be fighting her soon.

"I promise you I will see you again, Jonas," I tell him, knowing he needs to hear me say it, and I hope to god I can keep my promise and not die before I have the chance to fulfill it. Jonas nods, holding his head high before walking off to the group of children.

"Is he your child?" Winter asks me, watching Jonas like I do.

"Nope, but he is the brother of someone I lost," I explain to her, and she nods in understanding. I look at her for a second and suddenly remember why her name was bothering me.

"I met your aunt. She said hello," I say, and Winter laughs, before realizing I'm being serious.

"My relatives are all dead. You must be mistaken," she replies sadly. "I don't have an aunt alive anymore."

"I'm not, though the old lady could have been lying to me. I met a fate, an old lady in looks, but she was much stronger than she would admit. The fate told me we would meet and to say hello to her niece," I explain to her. "She seemed to know we would meet."

"My mother was a half fate, and my grandmother was a fate. Maybe she had another sister I didn't know about," Winter whispers to herself, looking happy. "If there is another fate out there, then I hope I get to meet her at some point."

"Perhaps you can come to Dragca to visit when I take the throne back," I smile, and offer her my hand to shake. Winter knocks my hand away and pulls me into a tight hug, which I happily return. There is something about this woman that makes me trust her. I don't know what it is, but she feels like my friend already.

"Good luck winning your throne back. The war is never easy, or without great loss, but trust me, peace is worth the fight. You get happiness within peace, I know this," she whispers to me, and lets go. Winter walks away toward Atti, who holds a hand out to her, his other hand touching the head of the wolf shifter who is called Jaxson apparently, and his giant wolf wasn't happy shifting back with dragons everywhere. *I don't blame him.* They all disappear with the children until there are only dragons left in the forest, and the falling snow can almost be heard drifting in the silence.

I turn around, looking down at my arm at the spear, and I press the red jewel. The bracelet uncurls, snapping out into the deadly spear I remember. The spear feels like it was always meant to be in my hand, and I was always meant to fight with it. I place the end on the ground and look over at everyone staring at me. Dagan has Bee sat on his head, Korbin is sliding a sword into his belt, but he looks at me with a determined look. My uncle is ready for war, that is the only way to describe him as the tip of his sword rests in the snow, and he holds both hands on top of it. I have a feeling none of the dragons here have ever had something worth fighting for. Dagan and Korbin never wanted to fight for my father, they were forced by the curse. My uncle was much the same and lost everything, despite doing as he was told by my mother and father. All these dragons have been kept here like animals and caged...with nothing left to show now that they are free. I don't know what inspires me to speak, but I know I have to.

"We return to Dragca today to save whatever is left of our home. I know most of you do not know me, and likely only remember my father or my grandfather...but I am not them. I am not weak, selfish or cruel. I will not keep secrets that will destroy my world, and I will not hide from who I am meant to be. If you support me as your queen, I will fight till my last breath for my people! I will rule with kindness, and I will win us this war! I know how to do what is right and how I want Dragca to be for our children. I want peace, true peace like we have never known it. Follow me to Dragca, let me lead you to a future we will be proud to leave behind!" I shout. Dagan kneels first, then Korbin and my uncle following. Then every single one of the dragons kneels down, lowering their heads with their hands on their swords. Snow falls on them as my skin shivers with goosebumps.

"We fight for our queen! We fight for Dragca!" my uncle shouts, raising his sword in the air as he stands up before walking over to me. "It's time for you to lead us. Where should we enter Dragca?" I wait until Dagan and Korbin get to my side, with the other dragons right behind them.

"The castle. No messing around or hiding. We head straight in," I say firmly, and my uncle nods in agreement.

"It's going to be one hell of a fight," he warns me, and I glance at Dagan and Korbin. Their determination and belief in me I can see in their eyes just reminds me what I have to fight for. I love them...and Thorne and Elias. *Peace is worth the fight.* I remind myself of Winter's words, knowing that is all I need to believe in.

"Thorne and Elias need me. I will always fight for them and Dragca. I won't hide here and die on a world that is not my home. Dragca needs someone to fight for it, and it will be me," I say, firmly. Bee flies off Dagan's head and to my shoulder.

"Then after you, Queen Isola of Dragca. The last ice queen and her kings," my uncle states, using a title that I suppose is right. No matter what happens now, there will be no more ice queens on the throne. Any child of mine will be half fire dragon at least, and Tatarina can't have any more children...so we are the last of the royal ice dragons. We will fight, and one of us will win. I turn, walking into the forest to a portal my uncle said is close. *Time to go home.*

103

THORNE

My dragon lands on the balcony entrance to the castle, feeling a little surprised that no dragon tried to stop me flying up here from the forest and landing. I shift back, knowing if my mother was going to attack me, she would have by now, and I need to talk to her. I try to keep any thoughts of Isola out of my mind as my body comes back and I stand up straight, but I can't stop thinking of her. If my mother kills me, Isola would be devasted. Isola is the only person in the world that cares for me, loves me, and if I didn't have to do this, I wouldn't. Just imagining her sleeping on my chest, and how I was lucky to spend the night watching her...Isola is everything good in my—no, everyone's—world.

The cold air blows against me as I watch the three dragons in their human forms standing like statues outside the entrance door. The wind moves their hair and cloaks around, but other than that, they could be statues. They have black lines crawling all over their faces, matching their new black and white uniforms with a white, dragon-shaped, metal clip holding their cloaks to them. Seems mother wanted a new royal crest. The ice blue royal symbol of the Dragice line is gone. They don't seem to even notice I am here as they stare ahead, only the movement of their cloaks making them even seem alive.

I walk down the stone pathway to the giant doors, every one of my footsteps echoing on the stone. I stare at the burning pots of fire by the doors, and there are more in the corridor ahead, that light everything up. The fire casts daunting shadows over everything, making even the normal dragon statues on the walls seem dark. I walk through the open stone archway, into the silent corridor full of more dragon guards who stand by the walls, with pots of fire between them.

This time, they are much closer, so I can see their dead looking black eyes as they stand still as statues. The black eyes match the black lines crawling over their faces, and the strange uniforms. I glance at how each of them has a hand on the drag-onglass swords clipped to their sides. *What the hell has happened to them?* I wonder if they were dragon guards once, before they became these dead looking people...but the curse is broken, so they should have left. I doubt a single one of the old dragon guard would have wanted to fight for my mother.

I keep walking down the corridor, trying not to feel creeped out by how silent and still these dragons are, before arriving at the entrance to the throne room. The doors are open for me once again, and I walk straight in with my head held high, seeing my mother sat on the throne at the top of the room. She doesn't even move when she sees me, not even a twitch. My mother looks darker than ever before, almost unrecognizable with her now black hair, black veins crawling all over her skin that I can see, and her thin frail-looking body. She has a white leather outfit on, and that dark spirit sits on the seatback of the throne, watching me with clear interest. I meet my mother's dark blue eyes for a second before she looks away again, and I still have some hope there is something left of my mother inside of her.

I stop right in the middle of the room, crossing my arms as I look at her. All the way here, I came up with a million things to say. A million things to ask her, yet when I actually see her, I don't know how to speak. I should hate her for everything, and part of me will always hate her, but she is my mother after all. Isola taught me that the greatest gift is to truly forgive someone, with hope they can change their ways.

"Mother," I say coldly, my voice slightly echoing around the room, and she twitches a little at the sound of my voice before her eyes finally seem to focus on me. I try not to look at the throne she sits on, remembering how she killed Isola's father on it.

"Son. Where is your sweet Isola?" my mother asks, and I tighten my hands into fists, hating that she had to bring Isola up already. From the way my mother said her name, she is still so bitter about Isola's father and so determined to destroy Isola for simply being born and loving me.

"Isola is clearly not here. You will never get to touch her," I warn, and she laughs. A cold, cruel laugh.

"The ice princess must die. How can you not understand this, son?" she enquires. "We kill her together and you can inherit the throne from me. Dragca will be happy...everything will be right for the first time in hundreds of years! Dragices have only brought Dragca pain and destruction."

"Isola has never done anything but fight for Dragca. She isn't her father or even her mother," I exclaim in frustration.

"Don't speak of those betrayers!" my mother snaps, showing real emotion for the first time since I got here. Seems speaking of the people she killed out of jealousy gets her attention.

"I can't understand why you gave birth to me when you clearly only ever loved Isola's father. I saw everything...I know everything you have done and what he did to you," I say, and she briefly seems shaken for a second.

"I didn't love him. He loved her," she growls, ice spreading from her hands down the throne.

"Yes, he did love Isola's mother...but Isola's mother was your best friend, and she loved you. Then you killed her," I say, and she shakes her head.

"I asked her not to marry him, but she told me she had no choice. That Dragca needed a real, true queen," she angrily says. "My best friend and the love of my life betrayed me and had a child they thought deserved to be queen. I will prove she is no queen."

"I wish things were different for you back then...but did you ever love my father? Why did you have me if you only cared about revenge on Isola's parents?" I ask her these questions, knowing I need to hear her answer. I suspect it was because she needed me to get the throne...but part of me wants to know the truth rather than a guess. My mother stands up off her throne, closing her hands together in front of her and looking away from me at the glass mirrors on the one side of the wall. I doubt she even recognizes herself anymore. The sweet little girl I saw in the memory cave is long gone.

"I loved your father...make no mistake of that. But he betrayed me when he died and left me alone. Having you...well, I hoped you would be the first man never to betray me, and yet you did," she almost whispers, not wanting to admit it. "Your father loved the dark side of me and helped me remember there was more to life than death and revenge. Yet he is gone because life doesn't give you what you want."

"I loved you though. I am your son, and I should have been enough! Yet you hid me with adoptive parents, made my adoptive father kill your best friend, and then married her grieving husband. Life didn't give you what you want because you never fought for the things you were given! Like a son that loved you so much, and yet you abused that love!" I shout at her, losing my temper in frustration at her innocent, the-world-wronged-me act. My mother finally looks at me, her eyes filled with tears. "I did everything you asked me to, and you only lied to me. You used me. The sad thing is, I wouldn't have betrayed you if you could have only forgotten your need for vengeance."

"All men betray you in the end. You lie," she says, yet her voice cracks, and I bet she doesn't even believe her own words. I watch as she keeps shaking her head in disbelief, stepping back and then rubbing her face with her hands.

"You are my mother, and I wouldn't have. You only had to believe and love me. In the end, you chose revenge and darkness over your child and still expected that child to fight on your side," I say gently, walking over to her until I'm close enough to touch her. I still pause, not knowing how far I can push my mother now. I know she is lost to the darkness, but I am unsure how lost. My mother doesn't stop me as I place my hand on her shoulder, and she looks up at me with tear-streaked cheeks. There is so much emotion in her eyes that I can't look away, I can't even move. Somehow, I see love in her eyes too. I don't know how long it has been since I've seen her look at me like I am her child and not some massive disappointment. I know it is way too late for my mother and me to have a normal relationship because I could never trust her around Isola, but I want to give her some kind of chance to live a life.

"I love you as well, my sweet son. The day you were born, I cried because I was so happy. I held you in my arms, singing sweet songs of fire and ice to you, knowing that one day you would be something special. That is why it hurts so much to let you die," she whispers, lifting a hand and placing it on my cheek. "If Isola weren't around, you would have been king."

"I will be king when Isola has the throne...but I will support her fully. I know she is meant to be Queen of Dragca, and I wish you could see that," I whisper to her.

"I will never support a child of his...He was evil, and Isola looks so much like her father," she replies.

"That isn't her fault, mother. You could change all of this. All you would have to do is give the throne to Isola and walk away," I tell her, hoping that I can talk some sense into her, but from the look on her face, I know it is too late.

"It is a little late for a happy ending for me now, son," she says and moves her hand, stepping away from me. "I only have the throne, and I will protect it until I die. I know you can't kill your mother, and I cannot kill my son...but there are other ways to deal with the problem here."

I watch her as she goes back to her throne and clicks her fingers in the air, her face back to one of zero emotion. The door behind the throne room opens, and Esmeralda walks out, looking, well, disgusting. Her once beautiful features have faded into dead grey skin, and her red eyes and hair are the only bits of color that make her even seem alive, yet they look close to death as well. She wears painted-on red lipstick and a red leather outfit that is dotted with old and new blood. I don't look at my aunt for long as Elias walks out of the door after her, wearing an all-black leather outfit. His hair is cut short, and his once blue eyes are completely black. I hold my ground as Elias looks towards my mother, bowing his head.

"Elias..." I whisper in shock at his appearance, and his whole body goes rigid at my voice. This is going to break Isola to see Elias like this.

"Kill the traitor and anyone that tries to stop you, Elias Fire," my mother's cold voice demands, and I finally know how she plans to deal with the problem of me. I ignore the sharp pain in my chest that my own mother is sending him to try and kill me as Elias walks towards me, and I have to focus. Elias doesn't even look like himself, his cold and aggressive demeanor is much like my mother's, and his body is thin, the muscles he once possessed faded away. The black eyes are just strange on his pale face, as is the all leather black dragon uniform I've never seen him wear before.

"Elias! What the fuck are you doing?" I shout at him as he keeps walking closer, and I step back a little.

"Killing the enemy for my queen," he replies unemotionally, robotically almost.

"I fight for Isola. She is your queen! I am not your enemy!" I shout, stepping back again as he spreads his arms out, and I know he is going to shift. I could fight him, but my ice dragon side would kill him easily, and Isola would never forgive me.

This is why my mother sent him to do this. She knows I won't really fight Elias, and that means he has a chance of killing me. This is a game and a big fucking trap for Isola. I consider sending a message to her, but we are so far apart that she would never hear me.

"I don't know who this Isola is, but you are a threat to the throne," Elias growls, his eyes glowing red as black smoke covers him. "I am here to deal with any threat." The way he speaks is so sure, and I know straight away that my mother has made him forget Isola somehow. *How the fuck am I going to get Elias to remember?*

"Shit," I mutter, turning and running down the corridor, as I know I don't have a choice in this fight. I call my own dragon, knowing I have to hold Elias off and try not to hurt him until Isola gets here. If anyone can make Elias remember, *it is her.*

104

ISOLA

T he portal comes out in the forest just under the castle, and I stand still, waiting for my army to step through behind me. The trees move in the breeze, and I step closer to one, seeing that the bark is covered in black vines that stretch up the tree. The only light comes from the castle, and I can see all the trees look the same. Dragca feels different. I don't dare touch the trees, not unless I plan to use light magic to get rid of the black vines covering them.

I look up as I hear a dragon roar and the sound of fire crackling in the air, but I can't see what is above us through the tight bunched trees. I'm guessing dragons are fighting, which means we need to be careful or they could see us. I glance at Bee, who seems brighter from just stepping out into Dragca, but her eyes stay on the trees, looking worried. She glances at me, and I sigh, knowing there is nothing we can do about this right now. Using light magic would make too much noise, and everyone would hear us.

"Maybe you should hide, Bee; it will be a war zone in there, and I cannot lose you," I whisper to her. "There is darkness everywhere...and you are not strong yet from your time on Earth."

"No, we together. Dark must be fought," she says firmly, and I sigh in agreement. I don't want her away from me, and I guess I can't shield her from everything. Dagan and Korbin came through first to scout the area before returning to give us the all clear, but they indicated that there was no safe place nearby. So I don't even know where I could hide Bee that would be safe anyway. Dagan and Korbin come out of the portal, both of them walking to my side, staring at the tree like me.

"Seems Tatarina has been busy," Korbin states.

"Hopefully too busy to have time to hurt Elias. I kill her, and then we find him," I repeat the plan we discussed again. "Thorne is still alive, I can feel that. Hopefully she has just locked him up somewhere."

"His mother won't kill him, I'm sure of that. I've grown to like the bastard, so I wouldn't have let him walk to his death," Dagan states.

"Tatarina is bat shit crazy, Dagan. I hope your trust in her not wanting him dead plays out, because I don't believe it. She killed her childhood best friend, and then married her husband. Then killed him, despite apparently being in love with him...those aren't the actions of a sane person," I mutter. "She has to die for everything she has done."

"We love you and follow you, no matter what you choose, Isola," Korbin says, leaning over and kissing the side of my head.

"We are all here," my uncle interrupts, and I turn around to see him standing right behind me, his arms crossed. "If anything —and I mean anything—goes wrong, we meet at Dragca Academy. It's a safe haven against her." I nod once, understanding how Dragca Academy would be the safest place to run from evil to. Part of me misses the academy anyway. Hopefully nothing will go wrong.

"I am going to stay in human form, but everyone else should shift," I say, raising my voice so the dragons behind my uncle can hear. I frown at the sound of more roars, wondering why they feel familiar. When I realize why, I run out of the tree line, hearing Korbin and Dagan shouting for me to stop, but I can't stop. Those roars...they feel like a lost memory. When I get out the tree line, I stare up at the two dragons I love, fighting each other. Elias's and Thorne's dragons are throwing mouthfuls of fire at each other, before flying and slamming into each other in the air. Everything below them is on fire, and now that we are out of the tree line, I can smell and see it. The fight is nasty, but there is no ice anywhere, Thorne isn't truly fighting Elias. He could have killed him by now.

"Why are they fighting?" Korbin asks, his voice full of horror and worry, as my mouth feels dry and I stare in confusion. Elias and Thorne don't pause in their fight, clawing and burning each other every few moments. It is so painful to watch two men I love trying to kill each other and feel completely powerless. I try to reach Thorne's mind to tell him I'm here, but he is too distracted to hear me, and I don't want to become a distraction that lets Elias win.

"We have to stop them before they kill each other!" I cry out, pacing as I watch the fight. If I shift and go to stop them, I won't be able to finish this war and kill Tatarina. Though the more I watch them, the less I care about anything other than stopping them from killing each other.

"Isola, you must kill Tatarina and take the throne. Nothing else can matter at this moment," my uncle says, placing his hand on my back, but I shrug him away, stepping forward with my eyes still locked on the dragons fighting in the sky. I look back at the castle briefly and wonder why Tatarina hasn't sent people out to fight them both. Neither of them can be on her side, surely.

"I will stop them. Kor, you protect Isola," Dagan states and nods at me. *I love you.* I can't help but smile at his words whispered in my mind before he steps away from us all and shifts. The worry sets in as Kor wraps an arm around my waist, and we watch Dagan's dragon take off into the sky. The moment Dagan gets close, Elias goes to attack him like he doesn't even recognize his own brother. Dagan avoids the blast of fire, and Thorne charges into Elias's side.

Isola, Dagan...Elias doesn't remember who you are. He doesn't remember anything, Thorne warns both Dagan and me as we can all hear each other now. Elias doesn't remember me. Tatarina has taken him from me.

Then we knock his ass out and make him remember. Team work time, Thorne, Dagan tells him, sounding strong even though I can feel his emotions and how fearful he is of losing his brother. There must be a way to save Elias's memory, and if I kill Tatarina, we could spend years getting my Elias back.

Got it, Thorne replies just as I watch Elias's dragon slam into him, but Dagan pulls him off Thorne with his claws. I never thought I'd have to watch three people I love more than anything fight with each other. I never knew how much it could hurt deep in my heart to see.

I love you both, be careful. It's all I can think to say, knowing it's only words, but that is better than nothing. When I finally look away and meet Kor's eyes, he doesn't need to say anything for me to know how he feels. The panic, the worry and protectiveness are written all over his face.

"Everyone, shift into dragon form and carry your weapons. We protect the princess at all costs. For Dragca!" my uncle shouts in a war cry, and nods once at me before stepping back and shifting himself. The dragons all move to their own space before shifting, until the whole forest is full of dragons, and I know we have a small chance of winning this. Or of them holding off anyone that supports Tatarina until I can kill her. The dragons pick up their weapons in their claws as I wait for Kor to shift for me. He steps back, his dragon wordlessly taking over in a puff of black smoke until his massive dragon stretches out. I climb up his back as he lowers himself down, and I slide myself between the spikes on his back. I keep my spear tightly in my hand, and Bee moves to sit in front of me, holding the spikes with her little arms.

"To the castle!" I shout, and Kor waits for my uncle and more of the dragons to fly out of the tree line first because I doubt he would want us in the target line first. I lower my head, holding an arm around the spikes and keeping Bee between the spike and me, as Kor flies up with a massive gust of wind nearly knocking me off him. The cold breeze blasts against my skin as I lift my head through the pressure, seeing Dagan and Elias fighting, and Thorne's dragon spiraling away from them after taking a hit. I feel Thorne's and Dagan's pain from the fight, and the fear of losing them threatens to swallow me just as Elias's dragon seems to lock eyes on me. Instead of the blazing red eyes I'm used to seeing, Elias's dragon's eyes are black and cold, vacant of anything. He doesn't recognize me...and the pain from that hurts my chest. There is a moment where it feels like my whole heart breaks as Elias's dragon shoots a blast of fire straight at us, and Kor swoops down low, making the fire miss us before carrying on his flight to the castle.

He didn't mean that, Dagan tells me in my head, feeling my pain, and I realize I need to swallow my emotions because it will affect their fight. I don't want to tell Dagan that I'm sure Elias did mean to try and kill me, and that I'm sure he doesn't even know who I am anymore. When I can look back, Dagan, Thorne and Elias are still fighting, this time crashing into the trees below that are on fire from their fight. I take some relief that they have Elias on the ground now and he can't escape. If Dagan and Thorne can knock him out, then we can talk to him, make him remember who we are. They have all forgotten me once before, and I won't let them forget me again.

I have to force my gaze and mind away from them as Kor lands on the entrance to the castle, and I slide off his back. I'm slightly confused why the towers of the castle and the giant catapults on them aren't being used to defend the castle. We shouldn't have been able to just land here. I look away from the heat as Korbin's dragon shoots a blast of fire at four dragons in white and black uniforms that run towards us with their swords raised high. Two dragons run to our back, but my uncle's dragon swoops low, picking them up in his giant mouth like a snack and dropping them off the edge of the castle before flying back up. I ignore their screams as I hear a loud horn, and then dozens of dragons fly over the top of the castle, heading straight for my army. Out of the corner of my eye, I see Korbin's dragon shift back into his human form and then quickly pick up the sword his dragon carried here.

"Stay low," Korbin demands, pushing me down to hide behind a bit of the castle wall as we see the dozens of dragons aiming straight for my army, and the fight begins. One of them is killed straight away and falls with a thud on the stone floor right in front of us. It's only when we straighten up and step a little closer to the dead dragon that I see how strange it looks. The dragon has black lines all over its red and brown scales, and when I look up, I see that the fire they are shooting is redder than is natural. *What the hell?*

"Looks like we enter this hell hole together, doll," Korbin says to me, and I nod, lifting my spear as I straighten my spine. This is the end game...the end of Dragca being at war. I only have to kill her and take the throne.

"Let's go," I say, knowing we can't put this off any longer, and the dragons above us are fighting to give us this short amount of time. We have a slim chance of killing Tatarina because she wants me here, and the fact she isn't out here fighting means she is waiting for me to come to her. Kor and I run into the main building, which is empty, to our shock, and we get to the end of the corridor, walking into the throne room.

I scream as Kor is blasted across the room with a ball of fire as soon as we enter, and he slams into the wall, falling to the floor, knocked out. I watch his chest moving for a moment, needing to know he is alive before I can calm myself. I angrily turn to look at Esmeralda as she lowers her hand, a smirk on her dead-looking, red-painted lips as she leans against the throne.

Esmeralda looks awful. Clearly, being undead doesn't work for her.

"Where is your sister?" I ask, knowing Esmeralda is not the one I want to deal with tonight. I will fight her if I have to, but killing her won't get me the throne.

"My sister is busy waking up her army…so we have time to catch up. Why don't we start by me killing your little dragon lover like I did Jacian? He seems just as weak. Though you seem to collect the weak ones, like my nephew, for example," she remarks, her red eyes going to where Kor is lying on the floor, and I growl low, making her laugh. I don't collect weak anything, and if the bitch keeps talking, then I will let my dragon show her how strong we all are.

Kill her. Save mine, my dragon growls, and my powers make it slowly snow in the room from my unspoken agreement with her.

"What army? The dragon guard curse is broken; no army serves your sister anymore. I'm surprised there are even a dozen dragons fighting for her outside," I say, and she stops laughing, turning her head to the side in an almost twitchy movement.

"You will soon see how wrong you are," she says, just before sliding a sword out of the holder on her back. "Death is all that belongs to you in Dragca. Like every one of your family and your mates."

"Bee, go to Kor and protect him," I whisper to her without taking my eyes off Esmeralda, knowing she will do as I say and feeling her let go of my hair. Esmeralda runs at me, her sword held high at her side, and there is no doubt she will fight until one of us is dead. I keep still until the last moment and block her sword with my spear, managing to push her away. She swings straight back, this time blasting fire down the sword until it tingles against my skin, but it won't—can't—burn me. I call my ice as I slam my spear against her sword, and to my surprise, ice blasts out of the end of the spear. I scream as Esmeralda pulls a dagger out I didn't see in her belt and slams it into my thigh. I push her away again as dizziness fills me, and whack the spear into her arm, knocking the sword out of it as I try to ignore the pain from my leg which threatens to overwhelm me. Taking advantage of her surprise, I call for my powers as I shove the spear through Esmeralda's heart, and ice slowly crawls all over her skin as her mouth parts in shock. When the ice crawls all over her face making her look like an ice sculpture for a moment, I pull my spear out. It seems like slow motion as her body falls, shattering into millions of shards of ice on the ground, the red and white ice mixing together almost beautifully.

"NO!" I hear Tatarina wail from behind me, her voice echoing around the room in her despair. I turn, holding my spear high as I turn to face her, and bite my lip as the pain in my leg is terrible. I can feel hot blood pouring down my leg, and every tiny movement shifts the dagger a little. If I didn't have the spear to lean on, I wouldn't be able to stand like this. Tatarina falls to her knees, staring at the pile of ice shards as tears silently fall from her face onto the floor. I don't pause as I limp over to her, looking around for Nane and not seeing the dark spirit anywhere, which worries me because I need to see her when I do this. Sweat gathers on my forehead, every step hurting me more than imaginable. It doesn't matter about Nane, I can kill Tatarina and then find her later. All that matters is killing Tatarina and taking that white crown off her head. Though it isn't my father's or mother's crown...she made her own which hasn't been done in hundreds of years. The crowns my parents had were inherited.

I stop right next to Tatarina and move my spear right under her neck as I make myself stand tall. Tatarina finally looks away from the leftovers of her sister and gives me a look that suggests I better run from her or feel sorry for her somehow. I don't know exactly how to read her emotions.

"This is for my mother. She never deserved to die because of your jealousy. Rot in hell, you total bitch," I say, going to push the spear through her neck when she grabs the spear. She laughs even as I apply pressure, so it cuts her neck, and I know if I call my ice, she would be dead. Or if I just push a little more, it will go straight through her neck, and either way I win this.

"If you kill me, you kill Elias," she says, still laughing loudly as my hand shakes with the spear. I shake my head, knowing she must be lying.

"You're lying," I spit out. "Lying won't save you now. I want what belongs to me."

"No, I am not. I killed Elias the first night he was here and brought him back with my dark magic like I did my sister. If you kill me, you kill him," I step back in shock as I gasp out. My hand shakes with the spear, and my mouth feels like there is a giant ball of sadness that I just can't swallow. "He even whispered your name as he died. It was almost sweet how much he hoped you would save him."

"You're lying!" I scream, not wanting to believe it as she stands up, and deep down inside of me, I know she isn't lying to me. She killed Elias. My Elias, and then turned him into a monster.

Isola, are you okay? I hear Thorne's worried voice ask me, and I gasp from the shock and pain. My Eli was killed by this crazy bitch.

"I want you to suffer like I did. You stole my son from me, so I stole the man you love from you. Your dear parents must be suffering so much as they watch you walk away from the throne to save a dragon guard," she remarks, laughing loudly like this is all just a joke. I shake my head, feeling the tears streaming down my cheeks as I fight what she is telling me even now. My body shakes from the shock, from the realization that the price of this war would be Elias, and I won't take it. Elias can't be dead...he just can't be.

"I will save him somehow. You aren't the only one with magic," I growl, hoping that somehow Bee and I could save him.

"Elias wasn't the only one I brought back...maybe you should run, princess, because we both know you won't kill me. You can't do it, and you are never going to be a true queen," she says, smirking as she walks back to the throne she killed my father on and sits down. I shake with anger as I watch her, knowing she is right and there is nothing I can do about it. I won't sacrifice Elias...I just can't.

There are thousands of them...we must leave, and you have less than a few minutes. Get the hell out of there or kill Tatarina, Dagan growls through the bond, sounding panicked.

I can't kill her. Elias will die, I whisper back through the bond, not even bothering to hide my emotions from them. The despair and heartbreak are too much to hide.

What? Run, Isola! Thorne growls into my mind. *We have Elias, but we can't save him without you.*

"Dragca or love? A smart queen would kill me now, but you won't do that. I will let you leave this once, but the next time we meet, I will kill you, princess. It will be fun," she says with a long laugh, and I don't even respond to her. I am no princess...I will never be a queen. I will always choose to love even if it breaks me to do so. I let my dragon take over, shifting quickly with a pain filled roar at the dagger in our leg. My dragon picks up Kor with Bee, holding him tight with her good leg before flying through a wall of the throne room and out into the sky, hearing Tatarina's laugh right behind us as we head straight into a war zone.

There are hundreds, maybe even thousands of dragons in human form on the ground around the castle, and the sky is full of them as they kill what is left of my army. I manage to stay low and go left, avoiding the fight until I'm well into the forest and free. We keep flying, ignoring everything and knowing that there is only once place I want to go to. *There is only one place safe in Dragca for a dragon like me now.*

105

ISOLA

Iland right outside the academy castle, carefully putting Kor and Bee down on the ground before shifting back and collapsing. My dragon doesn't even speak to me, and I can feel her uncertainty of the situation coming from her. Part of her wants to avenge everyone Tatarina has taken from us, but the other part won't let Elias die without a fight. Elias is hers. He is mine...and I can't lose him. Elias was killed though...and what is left of him, I don't know if I can save. I cry silently as I think of how alone he must have been.

I don't feel the pain in my leg or anything until a warm hand on my shoulder shakes me from my misery. Kor sits me up carefully, pulling me into a tight embrace as I breathe in his smoky scent and try to calm myself down. I love how Korbin doesn't need to ask what happened or what is wrong, at first. He just knows I need him close, and that is all that is important. I watch past Korbin's chest as Bee flies into the trees, no doubt trying to find something light, but from the looks of it, the whole of Dragca is in darkness with a queen who found the perfect way to make sure I never kill her.

"What happened, doll? Where are we?" Kor asks after a while of complete, comforting silence. It's too dark to see where we are, and the castle doesn't have any lights on outside. I don't know why I chose to come here when I should have run further, because I don't know how to face my uncle, but it is the only place where Elias, Thorne, Dagan, Kor and I were happy. Since then, something has always been wrong, and now I don't even know if I can fix it.

"We're at Dragca Academy...I was a coward and ran from Tatarina as she sat on the throne. I let her live..." I whisper to him, and he tenses but doesn't say anything for a moment. Rain falls from the sky as I press myself against Korbin's chest, hearing his beating heart, and not knowing if Elias's heart even beats anymore.

We are coming to the academy. Many of us survived. We killed enough to escape, Dagan's worried, tired voice comes into my head, but I can't even make myself reply to him.

"You aren't a coward. I know that for a fact, Isola," Kor finally tells me, kissing the top of my head. "Whatever made you run...I know you wouldn't have had any choice about."

"Tatarina killed Elias," I whisper, bursting into tears again at even saying it out loud. Kor soothes me, holding me tight as he whispers words of comfort until I stop crying and gain some kind of control.

"Elias was alive and fighting Thorne...he isn't dead, doll," Kor says, not understanding anything about what I just said, and I don't blame him. It is crazy.

"Tatarina brought him back to life like she did Esmeralda. She said if I kill her, I kill Elias, and I couldn't do it. I couldn't do it. I couldn't do it," I keep repeating the same sentence throughout my cries, feeling like a massive coward for putting Elias's life before the whole of Dragca.

"Look at me," Kor demands with a growl, lifting my head with both his hands and wiping my tears away with his thumbs as he forces me to look into his eyes.

"Elias is still alive, and we will find a way to save him. You are no coward for choosing love over duty to a throne. We don't want a heartless queen on the throne anyway, and if you did that, there would be nothing left of Isola Dragice. Somehow, we will figure out how to save both Dragca and Elias, I promise you that," he tells me, I nod, agreeing somewhat, even as guilt chokes me still. "Now let me look at that leg."

"Okay," I shakily reply before he kisses me on my tear-covered lips and lets my face go. I flinch when Kor moves me gently off his lap, and he follows my gaze to my thigh where Esmeralda's dagger is still in, and there is blood everywhere.

"I need to pull it out. You ready for this? I don't need to tell you this is going to really hurt, doll," Kor asks me, looking at me for an answer for when I am ready. I nod, resting my head on his shoulder as he places his hand on the dagger, the slight movement killing me. I scream loudly as he pulls the dagger out, chucking it away as everything goes blurry and placing his hand on the wound for pressure which is extremely painful.

"Me help," Bee says from my left, surprising us as I didn't hear her, and she flies out from the trees. Bee floats over my leg, and Kor moves his hand away, letting Bee sprinkle familiar looking powder into the cut. It stings, making me feel dizzy, but I manage to stay awake even as darkness gets into the corners of my eyes.

"Thank you, Bee," I crackle out, not even recognizing my own voice.

"No sad," she says, moving to sit on my shoulder, and her tiny hand wipes at the tears on my cheek as I look at her.

"Sometimes you have to be sad," I tell her, and she doesn't say anything as she hides in my hair and rests against my neck.

"We will fix this all, Isola. Come on, you are stronger than her. Tatarina can't win," Korbin tells me.

"She already has," I choke out, lifting my teary eyes to his worried eyes as I hear the distant sound of wings and feel my mates getting closer to me. "Help me stand up?" I ask Korbin, and he kisses my forehead before jumping up and then helping me stand. I wobble a little, and Kor keeps his arm wrapped around my waist to make sure I don't fall over. I look at my arm, amazed for a moment how the spear transformed with my shift into dragon form and is spiraled around my arm. I soon look away as dozens of dragons land around us, but I focus on the one carrying a dragon in his claws, like there isn't anyone else around. Dagan's dragon drops Elias's knocked out dragon on the ground before landing in front of it and shifting back. Dagan is covered in cuts, bruises and blood, and I worry for a second until I hear his comforting, gentle voice inside my head.

I am okay. Are you? I feel nothing but pain from you. I don't respond to Dagan, only because I don't know what to tell him. *I am not okay.*

"What happened? Why isn't Tatarina and her army dead?" my uncle growls, stepping in front of me with his hands on his hips. Blood drips down his forehead, and he is covered in dirt, claw marks and more blood than I thought was possible to see on someone's clothes.

"I couldn't kill her," I whisper, not wanting to admit it, but I know I have to. I expect to see disappointment, confusion and hate in his expression, but there is nothing but burning anger.

"Why the fuck not? I thought you had long lost the stupid young princess routine and become a queen!" he growls loudly, shaking his head.

"Don't speak to my mate like that," Thorne snaps, moving to my side. "You forget who she is. If Isola didn't kill my mother, there is a reason." They all look to me for an answer, my uncle clearly getting more frustrated with every second I don't reply as I glance at Elias's dragon.

"If I kill her, Elias dies too..." I whisper, and my uncle growls, shaking his head in utter disbelief. I knew he wouldn't understand this, and he is too angry to be reasoned with now. I made my choice, and I have to accept the consequences.

"Stupid child! One dragon is not worth the whole of Dragca!" he growls out, his hands setting on fire in his anger. "Millions of people will suffer because you put a boy before them!"

"Elias is worth Dragca to me! Elias is worth every world to me, and if I can find a way to save him, I will!" I scream at him in reply, my voice echoing around the trees. There is silence as my uncle shakes his head in disgust before walking away from me like he can't bear to be around me. My gaze drifts back to Elias's dragon who shifts back into his human form, still knocked out and looking so different from the Elias I know. I stare at the man I am in love with, barely recognizing his thin, pale and short-haired body. Elias is still him, he just looks ill and close to death. *I know better.* I go to step closer, just as his eyes pop open, and those once beautiful dark blue eyes are now black. I don't know if it's the pain from my leg or the shock of seeing my Eli like this, but my body falls to the floor as my world fades into a deep, anything-but-peaceful sleep.

106

ISOLA

I grumble as I wake up, my eyes and lips feeling dry like I have slept for ages, and some deep part of me just wants to go back to sleep and pretend the world isn't so cruel. So harsh. I know I could stay here, pretending to sleep and be more of a coward than I already am, or get up and fight. Though every part of me doesn't want to, I keep my eyes open. I stare up at the white painted ceiling, wondering where exactly I am, before I sit myself up slowly as my whole body feels exhausted. The room I'm in is plain with white walls and two other beds. I feel my thigh, only feeling a simple scar where the dagger went through and a small amount of pain. I slide myself off the side of the bed, looking down at the oversized men's shirt and long boxer shorts I have on. My hair is plaited when I feel it, and there is no blood or dirt on me, so someone must have cleaned me. I glance around the room, looking for my leather dragon clothes and not seeing them anywhere.

I suddenly remember passing out and the reason why—Elias's cold stare—and I try not to cry. I need to fix him, not cry about it. Not yet. He isn't lost...yet. I walk to the door, only limping a little bit which is impressive, and crack the door open.

I go to step out when I hear talking and pause instead, wanting to listen.

"That boy is lost," my uncle's demanding voice states in annoyance. "Seeing him in that cage proves to me he is better off dead."

"Elias is my brother, be careful what you say next, Louis," Dagan growls out. "If anyone can save him, it is Isola. Dark magic ruined him, light magic surely can fix it."

"You can't let Isola see him like this. There isn't anything left of the dragon she loves, and Isola needs to focus on the war that will be coming. Tatarina let her go for now, but only so she will suffer about Elias before she kills her. Letting Isola near that boy will destroy her," my uncle demands, annoying me because I know he is right. Tatarina wouldn't have let us go with Elias if she thought there was any way I could save him. No, Elias is here to hurt me, but I won't let him. Tatarina doesn't know everything...and I will save him.

"Elias loves Isola, and some part of him is still alive in there. No matter what that bitch did to him," Dagan replies.

"It still stands that Tatarina and Elias are linked by dark magic. Killing her kills him, and we both know Isola won't let anyone hurt Elias. We also know Tatarina has done this on purpose. Elias is the perfect protection against the only dragon that truly threatens her," my uncle states. "I will speak to Isola. Go and see the seers, make sure the academy is protected. This is where we make our stand and the final fight, with the seer army at our side. If Isola won't kill Tatarina, then I will. One way or another, Elias will die, and as her mate, you must prepare her for that," my uncle says, and Dagan doesn't reply as I hear the sound of footsteps walking away.

"You can come out now, princess," Dagan affectionately says, and I step out of the door to see him stood waiting for me with his arms crossed. Dagan looks much better now, cleaned up with a black shirt and jeans on, and a sword on his back clipped by a hold around his chest. Dagan and I only stare at each other for a moment before he is walking to me and pulling me tightly into his arms, his fear for his brother and me slamming into my own emotions. Though it's not like I don't feel the same way.

"Take me to him, Dagan," I whisper into his chest, and he holds me tighter for a moment like he doesn't want to let me go and face reality.

"Elias isn't the same...don't listen to anything he says because he doesn't mean it," Dagan warns me, and I feel him pull away from me a little. "Wait here." I nod, watching as he goes back into the room I came out from and brings out a cloak. He covers me with the cloak and clips it at the front.

"There, covered up. There are a lot of people in the castle," he explains and drops some flat shoes onto the floor for me. I slide my feet into them and flash him a thankful smile. "We could go and get you some food first—"

"I need to see him now, Dagan," I reply, interrupting his idea of distracting me, because I couldn't even think about eating or doing anything until I have seen him. "I have to figure out how to save him. Is Bee around? I want to ask her if light magic can help."

"No one has seen her in days. She went into the forest and didn't come back," Dagan tells me, and I go still in surprise. Bee wouldn't just go off when I was hurt after she healed me. I don't understand that one at all.

"What? She wouldn't leave me, us," I whisper in shock, trying not to feel upset that she would do that.

"I'm sure she will come back. Bee wouldn't have left you without a good reason," Dagan states, and I know he is right, though it is hard to think of Bee being out there alone and so far from me again. *I thought we agreed not to leave each other. Maybe she is disappointed in me for choosing Elias?*

"Let's go," I whisper, not wanting to focus on Bee right now when I need to see Elias. *Even if I know he is going to break my heart.*

107

ISOLA

We walk silently down the empty corridors of Dragca Academy until we get to the stairs, which have gaps in from broken stone and burned black walls. The once grand academy is in ruins now, but surprisingly full of people when we walk down the stairs. They have set up lights, tables with food on them, and there are even children running around laughing. I don't know who they are, but they all pause whatever they were doing when they see me, bowing their heads. Even seeing them bow makes me feel sick with guilt. I chose Elias over all of them, over the whole of Dragca. I shouldn't be bowed to.

A familiar face walks through the people. Essna. She now has a massive scar down her one cheek, and little cuts next to it which have healed but are still red. Her hair is cut very short and shaved on the one side, and she is dressed for war. The black marks are so striking on her pale skin, though that seems like the only thing the same about her.

"I heard you gave up the throne for one of your lovers," Essna states, and I nod, waiting for her to tell me how stupid I am or how disappointing, but instead she smiles. "It seems like something a true queen would have done. Any queen that is willing to kill those she loves for the throne isn't a queen anyone should support." Her statement is somewhat humbling, considering my uncle and likely everyone else thinks I made a mistake.

"Are you here to support me?" I ask her, watching her reaction closely. I'd certainly be shocked if she was.

"Yes. While you were on Earth, I gathered an army for you. Dragca Academy is protected by seer wards, and we can hold off Tatarina for a little while."

"Why would you do that?"

"I had a vision which I believe the last of the magic in Dragca sent me. If there is going to be a future here for any of us...you are our last hope, Isola Dragice," she tells me.

"What did you see?"

"Didn't your sister explain how you should never tell someone what you see? Where is Melody?" she asks me. *Seers and their rules.*

"On Earth," I reply, and she crosses her arms.

"Good. The seers need a leader when this is over, and I doubt I will be alive to be one...or I'm retiring if I am," she laughs, almost making me smile before she turns more serious.

"If the war is won, I'm sure you can retire in peace," I respond.

"Perhaps I might. Do try to save your lover...but know one thing, Isola," she says, and lowers her voice so only Dagan and I can hear her. "When Tatarina finally comes here, I will kill her to save everyone, and if I don't, there will be a line right behind me to finish the job. It is best you kill her though, and then no one will doubt your rule. Or your children's in time to come." My eyes tear at her truthful words, knowing that she is right. I may have walked away from killing Tatarina, but if anyone else gets the chance, they won't pause like I did. If someone else kills her, they have a claim to the throne even if it is decided to be given to me. Then my children could pay the price if one of the killer's children decided to go for the throne.

"Thank you for your advice," I respond, clearing my throat,

and she bows her head with a look of understanding before Dagan leads me away.

"We have time to save him," Dagan whispers to me, and I can't reply as we walk through the people to a door on the other side. Whatever time we have, won't be long. Tatarina will give me time to suffer, not time to save him. I need a miracle.

Dagan opens the door and waves me in, closing the door behind us. There are steps going down, with a light from a fire at the bottom, lighting the steps so I can see where I am walking. I try to connect with my dragon as I walk down, but she seems tired or simply doesn't want to speak to me right now. I don't even blame her, though I sense her pain mixed in with mine. I keep walking down the steps, my heart beating loudly in my chest with every step. I almost don't want to look as I get to the bottom of the steps and see Thorne and Korbin sitting on chairs outside a row of cages. They smile nervously at me, their eyes flashing between me and the cage. I step further into the room, my every step feeling forced as I want nothing more than to run out this room and pretend everything is okay. I have already run from Tatarina...I won't run from Elias. I smile back at them, before looking into the cage where Elias sits on the ground, a collar around his neck that I recognize.

"Your uncle kept one of the collars just in case we needed it one day...and Elias keeps attacking everyone, so we used it on him to control him for now," Thorne explains, but I can't reply as Elias finally lifts his head to look at me. His black eyes are empty of anything but darkness, and I feel nothing but pain as I watch him. The collar was a smart idea, even if I hate the idea of him wearing one.

"Eli?" I question, and he growls in response, standing up slowly. Elias's clothes just hang off him now, and his skin is so deadly pale that it reminds me he really did die. I am so out of my comfort zone here with how I am meant to save him. I need Bee...or a lot of research on light and dark magic.

"Who are you?" Elias asks, his tone horrible and sinister.

"Isola...you know me, Eli," I whisper to him, stepping that little bit closer to the cage, but I know I can't get too close with how Elias is looking at me. He wants me dead. He doesn't know me, let alone love me.

"Princess Isola. An enemy of my queen," he muses with a growing smirk. "Queen Tatarina will be happy when I kill you."

"No. Isola, the woman you are in love with," Dagan snaps from just behind me. "Like I have told you many times, Tatarina is not your queen. She is a monster."

"I don't love anyone, and I serve the true queen," Elias spits out and suddenly runs to the cage door, holding the bars so tightly his knuckles are white. "I will escape and kill you. I will wrap my hands around your neck and break it, pretty princess!" The words are said so cruelly and so loudly that it makes me flinch. Dagan comes to my side, placing his hand on my lower back. I know he expects me to break down...but I won't. I made my choice to save Elias, and I will.

I step closer to the cage, and keep my eyes locked on his as I speak.

"I will save you, Elias Fire, because nothing is impossible."

EPILOGUE

MELODY

Isola stands in the middle of the throne room, covered in blood, with a dagger in her hand as she watches Elias hold a sword to Tatarina's neck. Bee and Nane float near her, both of them fighting with light and dark blasts of magic that are hard to look at.

"Don't kill her! You can't," Isola sobs out, stepping closer with every word, and Elias looks over at her with so much love in his eyes.

"I'd do anything to save you. Anything. Including this," he says, lifting his sword to make the final blow as Isola runs towards them both, screaming in horror. Tatarina shoots a bolt of ice right into Isola's chest before ducking out of the way of Elias's sword and running away. Elias roars as I watch my sister die, and the vision turns into blackness.

I gasp as the vision leaves me, and I sit up off the floor where I collapsed in the empty room, rubbing my face. *Isola is going to die.* No! I stand up and quickly go to the wardrobe in our room, pulling out my orb and grabbing some daggers which I place into the small rucksack. I can grab some more things downstairs before going.

"Melody? Are you okay?" Hallie asks right behind me as she walks through the open doorway, and I tense, knowing she won't like what I have to tell her. I could stay here and be a coward, letting my only family die, or take a massive risk and go to Dragca to save Isola.

"I'm going back to Dragca. I had a vision," I explain to her.

"No...you told me if you went to Dragca again, you would die," she gasps, her panicked voice is hard to hear.

"I know that," I reply.

"I love you, you can't do this," Hallie cries out, walking to me to place her hand on my shoulder. I rest my head on her hand, taking the little comfort she can give me.

"Isola will die if I don't warn her, Hallie. I love you too, but I won't stay here while she dies when I could warn her," I say, turning to face the devastated face of my girlfriend. To my surprise, she wipes her tears away and walks to me, picking up the dagger from my collection in my bag, before pulling the zipper up.

"Then let's go. We will tell Queen Winter, and she will help. Both you and Isola think you have to do everything alone, and that isn't happening anymore," she says, being the strong human I know she is.

"Hallie, this is a world of dragons," I warn her so she knows what she is waking into. "Not all dragons are like Isola, and they don't respect humans. This is a war we will be walking into, and one I don't think I will walk out of alive."

"And like it or not, I'm a hunter. Let's go, because we do this together," she replies, being the strong woman I fell in love with. *Dragca will fall with Isola...so I must save her, even if it means she loses me.*

Pre-order the final book in the Protected by Dragons series here.

WINGS OF DRAGCA

Death or the throne? Queen or survivor?

Isola and her dragon guards are shaken after the events that
forced them into hiding in Dragca Academy.
With the queen of the supernaturals on Earth offering Isola and
what is left of her people a permanent home...will Isola leave
Dragca to save the dragons she loves?
Or will the last dragon ice queen rise and kill her enemy, even if
it means losing her heart?

Death has always been a curse on Dragca, and someone has to pay the price of fate...
18+ RH.

PROLOGUE

ISOLA

"I didn't expect to see you on your mating day, princess," Elias taunts as I get to the bottom step and see him resting on the side wall of the cage, crossing his arms. I run my eyes over his pale skin and dark eyes that match his black hair. This is now or never. I don't have time or a choice anymore. Eli must remember, even if what I'm going to do might kill us both.

"I had to do this. I'm tired of playing this cat and mouse game with you, Eli. You are mine, and you will remember me," I state, keeping my voice firm as I walk straight up to the cage. His eyes widen as I unlock the door, pulling it open and stepping inside. I leave the door open and chuck the key on the ground before standing right in front of Eli who watches me like the cat I know he is. Though he just doesn't know I am his equal in every way, and I will never run from him again.

"That was a bad move, naughty princess," he finally says and pushes up off the bars to walk closer to me. I stay very still as he places both his hands on my cheeks and moves his face inches away from mine.

"Nothing I do to save you is a bad move, Eli," I reply, gulping as his hands slide down my face and to my neck. I'm not shocked when he spins us around, pushing me against the bars as he tightens his hands on my neck. It's a half-assed attempt to kill me, because deep down, I know he doesn't want to. He knows it too, but he is so lost in the darkness, he can't tell me that. He keeps tightening his hands until I feel like I can't breathe anymore, but instead of panic, there is just acceptance that if he can kill me, he never truly loved me. I'd die to test what I am sure of.

His hands tighten further, and I grab his arms as my dragon roars in my mind, begging me to fight for my life, but I won't. Just as black spots enter my vision, tears fall down his cheeks, and I know I have to say something, do something before I pass out and can't. I call my light in the way I have practised, and it blasts out of me in swirls that twirl themselves around Eli. I see the light out of the corners of my eyes, but I can't look away from him as he lifts me off the ground, putting more pressure on my neck.

"E-Eli...k-kill me if that is what you n-need to re-remember."

"**A**re you ever going to leave?" Elias asks, his face hidden in the shadows of the room, so I can't really see him as he speaks. His tone is unmistakeable though, so full of hate and disgust for me. It's been four days since I walked into this dungeon, not recognising the man I am in love with. Four days of him trying his best to get me to leave him alone… and none of it has worked, no matter how much it hurts.

The first day, he didn't stop screaming at me, throwing himself against the bars to try and attack me. Dagan, Thorne and Korbin tried to make me leave, but I knew I couldn't. *Not yet.* It's easier to face Elias down here than to go upstairs and pretend this isn't happening. I made myself a vow to save Elias, to make him remember us. I won't give up on that. The second and third day, he didn't speak a word as he sat against the wall at the back of the cage, hidden in darkness. I felt like silence was my punishment on those days. I almost missed his screams because it was a sign he was at least paying attention to me. The dripping of water, the distant sounds of people moving around upstairs, and Elias's cold gaze on me were all that existed then. Again, my dragons brought me food and tried to make me leave, but I stayed. I will never give up on any of my mates, and even though Elias is not mated to me yet, he is mine.

I almost jump when Elias speaks to me for the first time today. His voice is so familiar, so comforting, even though the coldness in it is something Elias has never shown me until these last few days. Elias always used to be able to make me relax by simply being there. I hope the fact I'm staying here does the same for him, the real him deep down. We soon figured out that Tatarina didn't only turn Eli against me; she spent her time convincing him that Dagan, Thorne and Korbin are the enemies too. That anyone who sides with the Dragice name is an enemy to the throne, to Tatarina who he believes is his queen. Nothing they have said to him has made a difference in his opinion. Although he doesn't react when they speak to him, he loses it when I do. I know I am the key to his memory...I just don't know exactly how to jog it.

"Never. Not until you remember who I am," I eventually reply, crossing my arms in the cold room. Eli leans forward, an evil smirk on his lips.

"You are just a lost, forgotten princess who even her daddy didn't want around. You are no queen, you are barely even a dragon, Isola," he growls in anger, pulling at the collar on his neck.

"More hateful words, Eli?" I ask, crossing my arms. "When are you going to learn I love you so much that I won't ever give up, no matter what you say?"

"When I kill you. That is when you will finally realise how much I hate you." His words are cruel, making my heart ache as he stands up and walks to the front of the cage. The darkness in his eyes seems to reflect off how pale his skin is. There are black lines crawling down his cheeks from his eyes now, and he looks so thin. The bruises haven't healed on his face and arms from the fight it took to get him here.

"Do you remember Tatarina killing you?" I ask him, the words feeling painful to even ask him, but I need to ask the difficult questions, or we will get nowhere. She killed my Eli, and I want to hear every detail because I need to know how much pain she deserves when I kill her. He grips the cage bars tightly, locking his eyes on mine as I stand up off the floor. My hands itch to rush to the cage, to hold him because my heart and body doesn't understand how Eli is different, but my mind knows I can't do that and survive it.

"My queen would never do that to me," he replies, though his voice slightly wavers. "She told me all about you when I woke up from the magic you used to control me." I almost laugh at the crap Tatarina made up. Eli was never under any magic. He just loved me like I love him, even when curses and the entire world told us it was forbidden.

"Tatarina would think love is magic...and it is, in a way, but it doesn't control you. I never controlled you, Eli. You are Elias Fire; no one could control you. And you chose me," I say, rubbing my heart when I feel a sharp pain. In this moment, I can relate to every woman in all the romance books I've read when a guy is breaking her heart. It's never been easy for us. Even so, it feels like Eli is destroying me, but I know I can't give up on him. My Eli is hidden somewhere inside the shell in front of me, I just need to find him. No matter what the price.

"Lies!" he spits out. "You are nothing but a princess that wants a throne that isn't hers. Tatarina helped me, healed me, and I owe her my loyalty. When I get the chance, I will kill you to pay her back."

"I don't believe you," I say, walking up to the cage and keeping a good distance away so he can't reach me.

"Why don't you test it? Come in this cage with me, naughty princess," he taunts. My eyes widen at the nickname, the one he used to call me. I don't care that he is using it to call me to my death by his hand, I only care that he remembers it. He glares at me, scratching at his arms as I stand silent, watching him.

"That isn't happening. Ever," Thorne's cold voice echoes around the dungeon as I turn to see him stood at the bottom of the steps. I was so lost in my shock over Eli's nickname that I didn't hear him come in. My dragon didn't bother to warn me because she has been quiet since we got down here. Eli being like this hurts her too. She thinks of Eli as hers. "Isola, your people need to see you. You need food and decent clothing." I run my eyes over Thorne; his blond hair is brushed neatly to the side, and he looks healthy and handsome. His new dragon uniform fits him like a glove, and his long dark blue cloak clipped around his neck with a Dragice crest pin makes him seem almost royal. His clear blue eyes meet mine just before he speaks privately into my mind so Elias cannot hear.

There is nothing we can do for him right now. Dagan is searching the library for answers, and your uncle is planning the war with Essna. It's important you come and join the meetings. There is news. Come with me and let me help you.

"I can't leave him, and I trust Essna to run meetings without me. I know nothing of war anyway," I say out loud. I know Thorne is right about me leaving the room, not so much about me attending meetings, though I'm scared if I walk away from Elias, he might try to escape or something.

"Elias isn't going anywhere, I will make sure of that," Korbin says like he can hear my thoughts and walks around Thorne who briefly nods at him. Korbin looks different in the little time I've been down in this dungeon. His hair is shaved at the sides, the top part spiked up, and he has a dragon guard uniform on that is black with my family crest in the middle of it. Korbin comes up to me, placing his hands on my shoulders over my cloak. "Go and freshen up. Elias will remember, but until then, there is war going on outside of here, and you are the queen. They can't see you broken."

I sigh, knowing he is right. There is no point to any of this if we don't win the war, and I can't win anything if I am lost down here. I need to breathe and be with my other dragons. I can lean on them for only a moment before lifting my head again.

"Okay," I whisper, leaning up and gently kissing him, hearing

Elias's long growl from right behind me. I turn to see smoke coming off his hands, and the collar is burning his neck as he tries to use his powers. I know jealousy when I see it. My Eli is in there somewhere, fighting to get back to me.

"Tatarina was right about you sharing your bed with more than one dragon. Why would I have ever been in love with someone like you?" Elias growls, harshly shaking the bars of the cage before giving up to walk back into the shadows of the cage. I know this isn't my Elias, but his words still burn a hole in my heart that I don't know how to recover from. Korbin kisses my forehead, whispering words of love before I walk to Thorne's side, letting him hold me close as we walk out of here.

"**M**y old room...it looks almost untouched since I left here," I say as Thorne opens the door, and I walk in first. Someone has made the bed up, lit three fire lanterns around the room, and placed a plate of mixed food on the end of the bed which has fresh white sheets on it. Bee's tree is gone, making me a little sad because I miss her, and two of the windows are boxed up with cardboard. There's one window not covered, and I look out to see three dragons flying past, patrolling the academy. The sight of them makes me feel a little safer. I'm sure my uncle and Essna have the place under strict control and monitoring while we wait for Tatarina's attack. The room smells slightly of chicken from the sandwiches and slightly of lavender from a plant someone has put on the bedside table. Surprisingly, my dragon grumbles in my mind, her eyes locked on the food I know she likes the smell of.

"I spent yesterday fixing it up as best I could. I had to take Bee's tree outside as it had rotted, but everything else was saveable," he tells me as he shuts the door. I turn and wrap my arms around his shoulders, pressing my body into his for the comfort I know Thorne can give me. He knows what it is like to be broken, to love someone who hates them. We were like that once, and we got past it because I knew the depth of my hatred matched the depth of my love for him.

"Thank you. I needed a bit of home, a bit of something to make this all seem better, and this is perfect," I explain to him.

I would do anything for you, Issy. Thorne gently whispers in my mind, and my dragon lets out a light purring noise in my head. She has been quiet the last few days, and the tiny amount of emotion I have gotten from her has been nothing but pain over Eli and indecision over what is best for Dragca. Everything I am feeling too.

"Now, eat while I run you a nice bath. Can you do that for me?" Thorne asks, sliding his hand onto my cheek as I smile at him.

"Yeah, I am pretty hungry, now that you mention it...wait, do I smell that bad too?" I ask, and he laughs.

"No," he says, but I know him well enough to see through that little white lie. I guess I must smell as I've been in a dungeon for four days, only leaving for moments to use a bathroom and go back. I'm still wearing the same shirt and cloak I had on four days ago. I've been just existing the last four days, not aware of anything but what Eli was doing.

"You're lying," I reply, laughing when he winks at me before walking off to the bathroom. I walk over and sit on the bed, practically inhaling all the food as quickly as I can. I am starving because I refused to eat if Elias wouldn't. The thought makes me pause with a sandwich in my hand and put it back down. I could lose him, and nothing has changed while I was down there with him at all. He is still stubborn and unrelenting in believing a word I tell him. I used to love that stubbornness about him, whereas now it is nothing but a pain in the ass.

"The bath is ready," Thorne says, coming out of the bathroom a few moments later. I put the rest of the food down and slowly drink some of the water before getting up.

"Thank you," I say, stroking his arm as I walk past him to the bathroom, leaving the door slightly open. I turn before stepping in, looking over to see Thorne picking up the tray off the bed. "You won't go anywhere, will you?"

"Never, Issy. I am just going to put this on the dresser and wait here for you," he tells me, and I feel his worry from our bond. I sense Dagan's worry as well which, mixed with my own, is difficult. I doubt any of us will be feeling much more than that emotion until this war is over.

"Thanks," I mutter, not liking how vulnerable I am at the moment, but I'm glad it's Thorne that sees it rather than someone I don't trust. I don't know when I started needing to have my mates around me, but everything with Elias and the war is making me want to hold them close.

Save our mates... my dragon hisses in my mind before retreating once again, leaving me stood in the middle of the room with a tear streaming down my cheek. I close the bathroom door before Thorne can see the tear, and I look over at the deep bath which has sprinkles of rose petals in the water. Smelling a sweet scent in the air from the steam rising off the bath, I wipe the tear away and sigh. After taking off my cloak, I fold it and leave it beside the sink. I pull the shirt and knickers I'm wearing off, piling them next to the cloak before getting into the bath. The dirt and blood on my skin are difficult to scrub off, but I manage before finally washing my hair.

After I'm clean, I get out the bath and dry off before brushing my hair which falls to the middle of my chest now. It's so long now, and I think I like it this way. I keep one towel wrapped around me as I leave the bathroom, leaning on the door as I look at my mate on the bed. He is lying down, reading a book, and doesn't notice me for a moment. When he does, his eyes widen, and he puts the book down.

"Th-There are clothes in the dresser for you," he says, clearing his throat, but a wave of pure lust and desire comes through our bond, making my knees weak from the sensation. I shake my head so I don't actually fall over before very slowly dropping the towel on the floor, with my eyes locked on his. Thorne can't keep the lust out of his eyes, even as he opens his lips to protest while I slowly walk over to him, placing one finger against my lips. Thorne keeps still as I crawl on the bed and flip my leg over his hips, feeling how hard he is beneath me. His hands slide from the top of my shoulders down my back, sending shivers through me before he holds my hips. "You should be resting, Issy."

"I know what I should and shouldn't be doing, mate. I need to be close to you, to forget everything but you and me for a while. Can you help me with that, Thorne?" I ask, and he grins, moving his hands around my hips to my front. His one hand slides up my flat stomach to my breast, where he slowly rolls my nipple between his fingers as his eyes run all over my body. I moan, my back arching as I throw my head back, my hips bucking against him. Thorne's other hand finds my core, rubbing my clit in slow circles as he inches a finger inside of me. I cry out in pleasure, digging my nails into his chest as I come around his hand only a few moments later. Thorne flips us over on the bed, kneeling between my legs as he pulls his shirt off. I watch in fascination as he undoes his trousers, pushing them down to reveal his hard, long length. I don't have to wait a moment longer as he climbs on top of me, thrusting deep inside as I wrap my legs around his waist.

"Oh god," I whimper, just before he captures my lips, thrusting his tongue into my mouth and making me forget anything but the incredible feel of Thorne inside of me.

I love you, Thorne whispers into my mind as he thrusts in and out of me, his lips locked onto my own in a fevered passion.

I love you more, I whisper back, letting out a low scream as I feel Thorne come inside me, setting off my second orgasm. My head falls back into my pillow a few moments later, the world feeling like it's spinning in the best way possible. Thorne gently kisses me once more before rolling onto his back at my side. He wraps an arm around my shoulders, pulling me to lie on his chest as I link our legs together.

"I never thought I'd be as lucky as to have this with you,"

Thorne admits to me as I look up at him. He stares down at me with such love and understanding in his gaze.

"Neither did I. I'm happy we found each other, no matter anything else that happened. I wouldn't change a single thing, because I'd never have fallen in love with you otherwise," I tell him, and he pulls a blanket over us, kissing my forehead. We lie together for a while, lost in the gift of being together before we have to face the sacrifice required of us outside those doors.

"You look amazing," Thorne comments as I finish braiding my hair in the mirror and tying the end with a hairband. It falls over my left shoulder, hanging on top of my light blue cloak that Thorne found for me. I've chosen to wear a dragon leather top and leggings, which are black with the Dragice crest embroidered above my right breast. Apparently, all these clothes were just left on the ruined staircase when they came inside of the academy. I don't know where Bee is, but this is a sign she is still on my side at least. Unless there is a hoard of light spirits we don't know about that are on our side, though I doubt it. This is a sign that she hasn't left me like I secretly fear she has. I can sense her in my heart, but I know she isn't near. I don't understand why she would have just left though. I shake my head, knowing I need to focus on anything else besides the thought of my spirit leaving me alone in the middle of a war that could easily take my life.

I stare at myself in the mirror as I lift my head, and for a brief second, I remind myself of a painting of my mother when she was younger—minus a crown. We have the same high cheek bones, bright blue eyes, and pale hair. Before, I always thought I never had the regal presence she did, but something has changed. Even without a crown, I think I am looking more like a queen every day. It's just because so much has happened that has forced me to grow up and face the consequences.

"What are you thinking about?" Thorne asks, smoothing a hand down my back as he steps to my side. I glance in the mirror at his eyes, the small tilt to his lips, and the content feeling drifting through our bond.

"About my mother," I honestly say, regretting it when Thorne's face drops into one of sadness. I feel the same emotion, only deeper, more painful than any look coming from him through our bond. "What happened when you faced her?" I ask. I know he must have spent time alone with his mother, and nothing changed her mind anyway. I hate how much that must have hurt him and that I couldn't be there back then.

"My mother directed Elias to kill me, and that says it all. I thought I could be enough for her. That my mother would choose me over the darkness, but she couldn't, she wouldn't. There was a tiny moment when I thought..." he drifts off, lowering his gaze from mine in what I suspect is slight embarrassment that his mother didn't choose him. She should have.

"Thorne, she made the wrong choice. I don't understand how she could choose a throne over you. I wouldn't. I would give up the entire world of Dragca if you asked it of me," I tell him, and he lifts his eyes to meet mine once again in the mirror.

"I know, I would do the same for you. I have done the same," he gently reminds me, keeping his eyes locked with mine. "But I will never ask you to choose me. I only want your love, my mate."

"You never need to ask for that. It's yours. Even when I pretended I hated you, I loved you," I whisper just as he leans down to kiss me. The moment his lips touch mine, someone knocks on the door a few times. I sigh as he pulls away with a big smile before he walks over to the door, pulling it open. Thorne steps aside as Dagan walks in, flashing me a tired smile as he comes right up to me. Dagan looks exhausted; large dark bags are under his eyes, and his hair looks like he has run his hand through it a million times in frustration. I don't bother asking him if he found any news on how to save Eli in the library as he picks me up in his arms, holding me tightly to him as he briefly kisses me. I know the answer.

"Are you okay?" Dagan asks as he puts me down, and Thorne shuts the door. Dagan keeps his hands on my waist, our bodies close together. "I'm glad you have some colour in your cheeks and look so refreshed." His words make me feel guilty, like leaving Eli for only a little peace is betraying his brother.

"I haven't given up on Eli, you know that, right?" I start off but stop talking as Dagan kisses me again.

"I know you haven't, don't look and feel like that. Sense my emotions through our mating bond; you will see that I'm happy Thorne got you out of there for a bit. You do need to go and see your uncle though, before you go back to Eli," Dagan tells me, and I give him a shaky nod as I sense he is telling me the truth from his emotions. I place my hand on his cheek before gently kissing him.

"I will if you promise to get into bed and sleep for a bit?" I lightly ask, and he goes to argue, no doubt, as I carry on speaking before he has the chance. "And I will bring you food back. I'm not going to accept no as an answer."

"I can find guards I trust to watch Eli for tonight. We all need some time away from him to collect our thoughts. Kor should come up here with you if he doesn't have guard duty. It would be good for him to rest as he hasn't much recently," Thorne suggests, and Dagan nods in agreement with the plan.

"I'm not tired, but alright," Dagan replies, but I know he is lying from how tired he looks. "I could do with a bath before I sleep anyway."

"Yep, you definitely could," I say, and he grins at my teasing, tickling me as I escape his arms to run to Thorne who is laughing at us.

"Get out of here. Good luck with your uncle, and don't let the old fool boss you about. Remember who you are, Isola," Dagan firmly tells me.

"I know who I am now. You've all helped me realise it. I'm soon to be the queen, and I will speak to my uncle. I will not let him try to control me. Don't worry, and get some rest," I say determinedly, and he bows his head with a big grin. I chuckle and walk around Thorne to pull the door open and walk out. Thorne links our hands as we walk down the corridor, passing a few people carrying boxes and weapons who nearly trip when they see me, and they eventually bow.

"Where is everyone sleeping?" I ask once we've walked past them, their hushed whispers drifting to me. They are excited to see me.

You are the queen, my dragon huffs, like she can't understand why I would be confused why anyone is so excited to see me.

Yes, I know you believe that, I reply as she settles down.

"Thorne?" I question him again, noticing how he is watching my eyes, understanding that my dragon is speaking to me. I know there aren't that many rooms, and there must be quite a few people here now, much more than the academy is used to having, though I only have what little information Dagan briefly told me through our bond over the last few days. That Essna has half her seer army here, and the other half are people that cannot fight. There are new dragons coming in every day, survivors of Tatarina. Then adding those that we brought with us from Earth, there are quite a few people in this academy now. I don't think it's enough to actually win this war, not with Tatarina's undead army, but no one needs to actually say that out loud right now. If I can find a way to save Elias, then I can kill Tatarina. Hopefully that means all her army dies with her. I need to kill her so we can all have a future that is worth it. I squeeze Thorne's hand tighter as he answers my question.

"Most are using the old student and guard rooms, but the rest have opened up the old basement which is full of spare beds. There are long tunnels all under the forest which they are sleeping in and storing weapons in. The dining room stores food, and once a day, a team travels to Earth through the academy portal for more food and anything we need," he explains to me as we get to the top of the stairs, and I'm glad to know everything is getting organised, even slowly.

The stairs have been put back together with bits of wood and metal, and there is no dust anymore. I hadn't looked around until now since I had hidden my head in Thorne's chest on the way out of the dungeon earlier as I hadn't wanted to see anyone. Dragons and seers are walking in and out of the main doors, which are now attached and left open. Most are dressed in weapons and cloaks, and there is so much light blue in the clothing. The colour of ice, even though a lot of the people here are fire dragons and seers, all hurt by the ice dragons who were meant to look after them. My father never looked after anyone but himself and his own interests.

There are tables set up, with people sharpening weapons on them and what looks like a lot of dragonglass. At another table, they are making arrows with what looks like dragonglass tips that are handmade. Everyone looks hard at work, getting ready for the war. It makes me feel a little guilty that I have been stuck in the dungeon all of this time. A few people notice me as I get to the bottom of the stairs, and they bow low. When they bow, it's like the whole room suddenly notices that I am here, and they stop one by one to bow as well. I watch it all in slow motion, and it's humbling to see. I gave up my chance for the throne for love and brought this war upon their shoulders, yet they still are bowing to me. Led by Thorne, I walk through the now silent crowd, around the staircase, and towards my uncle's old office.

It doesn't surprise me that it is the office he is using now, even if he isn't in charge of Dragca Academy anymore. I can't help but feel so angry at my uncle for his attitude towards me, how manipulating he came across. I lift my head high while

Thorne knocks on the door, and we hear my uncle shout for us to come in.

"Can you wait out here? I need to talk to him alone. It's about time my uncle and I have a long talk," I explain to him.

"Of course," Thorne says with a little, proud smile before he leans down and kisses my lips. I open the doors and walk into the office, shutting the doors behind me before facing my uncle.

"Hello, uncle. We need to talk."

"I thought I would see you, *eventually*. Have you come to the right conclusion yet?" he asks, placing the book he was reading down and closing it. Every word is manipulative, making me feel guilty for my time wasted with Eli. I don't feel guilty though as I look at my uncle. I only see an angry, frustrated, old dragon who has lost all his family. Who has fought war after war, killing hundreds for the ice throne, the throne I walked away from and caused another war for him to fight in. I'm the last of his family, the last of the throne he fought so hard for, and he can't control me. I understand him, but I do not agree with his demands. I walk across the room to the window, looking out over the field and seeing the dragons and seers training. They are fighting each other, practising while Essna and another man walk around barking orders. Essna holds her head high, spinning a spear and her staff in her hands as she jumps, knocking a man straight across the field like he is a ball. It's almost amusing—the look all the men around her give her. They seem downright terrified. I move my eyes back to my uncle, knowing it's time we have a chat that may make him hate me. I don't want to lose any more of my family, but I will not be forced into what he wants when I do not agree.

"What conclusion would *you* like that to be, uncle?" I reply, knowing his answer before he even speaks it as I eye his long red hair, tied back, and contrasting blue leather guard uniform.

"That one dragon guard boy is not worth the whole of Dragca falling into war and destruction! If that boy could remember who he was, he would tell you to kill him," he growls.

"If you had a choice between my mother and Dragca, who would you choose?" I ask him, glancing over to see his tense expression as he looks over at a painting on the wall. I follow his gaze, seeing it is a painting of two children. The one is my mother, and it wouldn't be surprising to find out the other is my uncle. I walk over, standing in front of it to read the small written message: *The Pendragons*. This painting wasn't here the last time I came into this office, I would have noticed it.

"I would have chosen Dragca," he announces, though I don't believe him.

"You would have been wrong *if* you did, uncle. Dragca might have fallen for another reason anyway. Especially without my mother on the throne," I reply. "The important thing is you would have never been able to forgive yourself because you loved her. It would have haunted you, making you turn into a heartless monster that then could easily become a threat to the world you saved."

"It doesn't matter, your mother is gone, and Dragca is not long after her at this rate. I know I am right about the boy. He is lost, Isola. You have three other lovers, can you not let one go?" he angrily suggests, smoke rising from his hands where he is burning the desk.

"No!" I shout, slamming my hands on his desk, spreading ice across all of it and glaring at him as snow falls from the ceiling around us. "I am tired of you telling me what to do, uncle. I am not some silly child with no clue what she is doing. I am not your daughter. I am *not* yours to command. If all you plan to do is second guess my decisions and ignore my advice, then you might as well leave!" He looks shocked for a second as I keep eye contact, my dragon pushing to come out and fight my uncle to save Eli. There is a long, tense, angry moment before he smiles and leans back in his chair, crossing his arms. I frown, a little confused by his extreme change in emotions.

"Now, my queen, that is what I wanted to see. That is the fire that burned in the heart of your mother. That is the fire that should rule. I will not question you further, but only give my advice and guide you in what you think is right," he says, and my lips part in shock as I watch him, expecting him to change his mind and take it back. I expected anything other than what he actually said. The snow stops falling, but the bitter cold still fills the snow covered room from it.

"Are you suggesting you've been testing me this whole time?" I ask him, sliding into the chair near me.

"There is a good chance we all will die to save Dragca. I want to make sure if there is even a slight chance you sit on this throne after this all, you will be a queen who is *never* questioned. That you will rule for a long time and have children who are respected and loved from their birth by all of Dragca. They will be loved because they are a part of the ice queen who saved Dragca, and her strength made Dragca thrive," he explains to me.

"I want that also," I reply, sitting back in my seat. "Thank you for finally coming to my side without question." He bows his head, before crossing his arms.

"Now, what do you need of me?" he asks.

"I want to find a way to save Elias, so I can kill Tatarina. Do you have any clue how to do that?" I ask.

"I've been reading day and night to find an answer, but I don't have one yet. If you can jog his memory of how he was brought back to life, we may have a clue," he suggests.

"You've been researching?" I ask in utter shock. I look around at all the books on the desk, the ones piled on the floor, resting against the desk. All this time, he has been trying to help me when I judged him for it.

"I have nothing against the boy or your need to save him. I

once had a wife and a child; when I lost them, I lost myself. I understand love. I understand the need to do *anything* to save them. I wish only happiness for you, Isola. If you love Elias Fire, then we will figure out how to save him," he tells me, deep sadness and regret in his eyes as he looks at me. I know it hurt him to even talk to me about this. He has lost so much.

"You had a wife? A-a child?" I stutter out, completely shocked. I never knew that, and it makes some sense as to why my uncle can be colder than my ice at times.

"They died, it's in the past, and I do not wish to relive those emotions. Even with family, Isola. I will say that your mother helped me through that time in my life, and now I will save her child because I couldn't save my own," his words are cold, yet so full of deep, dark emotions that it leaves the room in a deadly state.

"What was your child's name?" I ask, feeling the need to understand him more and a strange feeling I must know.

"Emery," he says, his voice catching on her name.

"I'm so sorry for your loss. For your wife's death. I will remember my cousin's name until the day I die. I hope one day you will tell me more about them," I reply, knowing my words don't hold all that much comfort, but still I say them. He nods before rubbing his face and standing up. He walks around the desk and over to the middle of the room as I watch him, leaving footprints in the snow. He picks up the edge of the red rug and pulls it back, sending snow flying and folding the rug in half to reveal a little door. He pulls the latch to open the door and reaches inside, pulling out an old box by the handle on the top of it.

"This is how I escaped, back when everything went wrong and your father died," he tells me, shutting the door and pulling the rug back. "It leads to the forest, and it's safe, should you ever need to quickly escape."

"Good to know," I reply, watching him come over and sit on

the chair next to me. He turns the chair to face me before putting the box on the floor between us.

"This was given to me by your mother. She gave me strict instructions to only give you it when you are the queen you are meant to be. I know that is who you are now, so it is time. I've never seen what is inside, but I knew my sister well enough to understand it was important," he says before standing up, no doubt to leave, as I'm getting to understand my uncle now. I reach over and grab his arm before he steps away, and he adds, "I am going to give you some time alone to open this."

"Don't. Stay, you are my family, and I need a family member here right now to open this," I ask him, staring into his hesitant eyes. "Please, uncle." He doesn't say yes when I plead with him, but he does slide back into his seat and wait for me. I look down at the old wooden box which has nothing but a crest I don't recognise engraved on the top of it. As I run my fingers over it, Louis explains.

"It's the Pendragon crest. When I die, so will it. Your mother always wanted your father to mix the Dragice and Pendragon crest together to make a new one for you. It just never happened," he tells me.

"It should have. It will one day. The two dragons could have the Dragice rose surrounding them and the swords behind. It will be a royal crest to be remembered," I whisper, though my voice sounds like a shout in the tense, silent room.

"It would be an honour to see a crest like that," he replies and straightens his back. "Now stop stalling and open the chest."

I nod, knowing he has read me like a book, because I'm scared of whatever might be inside this chest from my mother. I'm scared how it might break my heart to open it. I take a deep breath before undoing the clasp and pulling the box open. Straight away, I see the crown, not believing my eyes as I look at how beautiful it is. It's not my mother's crown from the paintings or the one Tatarina stole, so I don't know whose it is. I lift it out of the box, looking at the detailed white and blue stones that are held between swirls of silver and gold. It's very striking for a crown, and I have trouble looking away from it to my uncle, wondering if he knows what it is.

"I can't quite believe my eyes," he mutters, reaching over to gently touch the crown. I look down in the box, seeing a letter at the bottom of the box.

"Here, you can hold it. There is a letter," I say, and my uncle happily takes the crown, holding it in the light as he looks at it in greater detail, though his eyes stray to the letter, and I know he wants to read what his sister has said. I pick the letter up, running my finger over my name that is written on the outside. I open up the letter and take a deep breath before reading it out loud:

To my sweet baby Isola,

When you read this, you will no longer be a baby but a woman—no, much more than that, the queen of Dragca. I write this as you lie in the cot near my bed, happily sleeping after a feed, and it breaks my heart to know you will be in danger. A danger that is impossible for me to even imagine, but I will do everything in my power to protect you.

My Isola, you are the balance that has been waited for. A dragon is prophesied to hold both light and dark magic. You must bond with both the spirits, or the price will be Dragca's fall. I know there is much pain for you to overcome to reach this ending and that I cannot save you from that pain. I know that my life is short, and I will not see you grow up. I wish I could be there on your mating day, but in my mind, I envision how beautiful you will look. How happy. I wish I could be there to see the woman you will become, because I know how amazing you will be. I am so proud of you, no matter the choices you make.

I can leave you a gift, one given to me, but I never wore it as I knew who it should be worn by. It is the crown of the first ice queen. She was the daughter of Icahn Dragice, and she hid this crown when she died, along with her father's legendary spear. This crown is for you to wear as you face the final battle. I know the spear will be gifted to you by the same fate who gave me the crown.

I CAN ONLY WISH *you a life of love and happiness. A life I never had until the day you were born, my sweet girl.*

Hold your head high. Be kind. Be loved and love back in equal measure. Please don't cry for me.

I will love you always, and we'll no doubt see each other in the stars one day.

YOUR MOTHER,
Queen of Dragca.

I TURN THE NOTE OVER, breaking down into tears as I see the crest drawn in the corner of the letter. The perfect mix of Pendragon and Dragice. Just like what I said before, and I know it is my crest she wanted me to wear. I feel like this letter brought a bit of my mother back only to take her away so quickly and so finally as she knew she wouldn't live much longer. This letter is so final. To my surprise, my uncle comes to me and embraces me, holding me tightly to his chest as I cry. It's a long time before I can pull away and take a deep breath as I wipe my face. The crown rests on the desk, and I stare at it for a moment in silence.

"Can you have someone make my new crest? I want to change my royal name as well. To reflect who *I* am. I am not my father's daughter. I am my mother's. Her real name was Vivian Pendragon. My name is Isola Pendragon. Like it should have always been," I tell my uncle. He nods, a tear streaming down his cheek as he accepts the note from me, rubbing his thumb across the crest drawing. I won't hold the Dragice name on the throne any longer. My father was nothing but a cruel king no one should be proud of. I stand up, reaching over to pick the crown up before walking to the window. I watch myself in the reflection as I place my new crown on my head, declaring myself the queen I am going to fight to be. I look like the queen I was born to be. Isola Pendragon.

I pull the doors open to see Thorne laughing at something Korbin said, and they both turn to look at me with wide eyes. The crown seems to have shocked my mates into some kind of silence.

"Hey, are you guys alright?" I ask.

"Wow, you look like a true queen," Thorne whispers, reaching out and lovingly touching my arm.

"Thorne, could I have a word?" my uncle says from behind me, and I turn to let him see Thorne. Thorne looks towards Korbin who nods in some agreement.

"I will be with Isola, and three guards are watching Elias while Dagan sleeps, go on," he says, and Thorne walks past me, gently squeezing my hand as he passes, then shuts the door behind me as I step closer to Korbin. Even though Korbin and I aren't mated yet, at this rate, I'd be surprised if he still loves me enough to make the leap. We really haven't had much time together in ages, and I have mated to Dagan and Thorne in that time. I haven't even asked if he was okay with that. We seem to just be pulled apart right now, and it scares me more than I want to admit. I know he loves me though, I can see it. I love him too, and I hope that is enough.

"It's been a while since we've been alone," I blurt out, and he steps closer to me, placing his hands on my upper arms as I stare up at his dark green eyes.

"I know, doll. I've missed you more than you could possibly know," he tells me before leaning down, kissing me sweetly. I sigh, wrapping my arms around his neck as he grabs my waist and deepens the kiss. It feels like coming home after a long trip when I'm in Korbin's arms. He is my home.

"Son, can we have a word?" Korbin's mother says, and we pause, gently pulling away in shock a little. Korbin keeps his arm around my waist as we both turn to see his mother and father standing a short distance away. They have on long brown cloaks emblazoned with my father's crest, but they look okay after everything that happened before. Well, his mum doesn't look impressed, whereas his father has a big smile on his face. Korbin leads me up to his parents, stopping a little distance away.

"Princess Isola, how lovely to see you again," Kor's father says, offering me a hand to shake. I shake his hand as I reply.

"I am queen now," I inform them both, and his eyes widen only a tad, "though it's good to see you both, Janiya and Phelan. I was worried after everything that happened with the seers and Tatarina."

"That dragon bitch cannot kill us that easily," Kor's mother replies, shocking me with her hate-filled words, and she very slowly runs her eyes up and down me. "I know you gave up the chance to kill her for Elias Fire."

"Yes, I did," I reply, holding my head high because I will not apologise to anyone for the choice I made.

"Until I heard what you did, I did not want you with my son. I did not think his life would be more important to you than the throne. Now I know you chose love over anything else. Can we start over, as I truly believe you are what is best for my son and the whole of Dragca," she asks and offers me a hand to shake. I keep my eyes locked with hers as I shake her hand and nod my head once.

"I'd love that," I reply, and Korbin lets out a long sigh.

"Finally," he says, making us all laugh.

"Why don't we all go for a cup of tea? I've heard humans from Britain love tea," Kor's dad suggests. That is a good idea.

"They do, and luckily I was brought up there, so I know how amazing tea can be. A hot cup of tea fixes literally everything," I reply as we start walking, following Kor's parents.

"Then that's what we shall do. I even hid some chocolate biscuits," Kor's dad says, and I chuckle. We follow them past the stairs and to the left, which leads into the dining room. There are tables everywhere, far more than there used to be in this room, and every one is covered in boxed food, weapons, blankets and everything you could need. I watch as every person we pass stops, staring at me in awe before bowing until I've walked past them. It's an effect I will have to get used to. I need to start believing I will be queen to all if I am going to make the rest of the world believe it.

We walk right to the back of the dining room where there is a row of kettles, clean cups, and containers with what looks like tea, coffee and even hot chocolate in them. We have to wait in a queue for the kettle before making our own drinks, and Kor's dad gets a new packet of chocolate biscuits out of a hidden box under the table. Kor's mum just rolls her eyes before we go outside the dining room to a room just behind it, which is again filled with tables but these are empty. We all sit down, and Kor's dad opens up the packet, putting it on the table in front of us. I dip a biscuit in my tea before eating it and sipping the tea slowly.

"I believe we should plan my son's and your mating ceremony this week," Kor's mum randomly states, and I choke on my tea. Literally. *Way to be cool, Isola.* Kor pats my back as I calm down and look at his mum with wide eyes. "I'm sorry. I didn't mean to take you by surprise, but I am sure you have thought about mating by now."

"Yes, we have discussed it, but a lot has happened since—"

"Have you changed your mind?" Kor interrupts, his voice full of pain as I turn, staring at him with wide eyes.

"No! I honestly thought you might have changed your mind," I admit, and I can visually see his relief as he puts his tea down and cups my face.

"I will never change my mind about you, doll. I'm completely in love with you, no matter what life throws at us, that won't change. I am yours, don't ever question that," he tells me, kissing me hard to emphasise his point before letting me go.

"Okay then," I say, quickly wiping a tear away and turning to Kor's parents, who look happy as they both smile at us. "I think a mating ceremony would be a good idea too."

"I'm happy you think so. The people need some happiness, something to remind them what they're fighting for. A royal mating ceremony would be the perfect way to uplift everyone's spirits."

"I agree," I say, leaning my head on Kor's shoulder as he links our hands under the table. Kor starts talking to his parents about something as I stare down into the dark water of my tea, the darkness only reminding me of Elias and how he won't be at the ceremony. I don't even know if we will ever get a chance to mate with each other, but I know I will fight forever to find a way.

"**D**o you want to come in?" I ask Korbin as we get to my door after a long day of walking around the academy and seeing all the work that has been going on. I was amazed at how much has changed since I've been in the dungeon with Eli. They have kitted the entire academy out for the war everyone knows is coming. I just hope we survive it. I know Tatarina won't give us long. Until then, I'm going to spend my time with my dragons, getting Eli to remember, and with my people. My people were happy when they spoke to me, happy to fight for me despite the darkness we are surrounded in. My heart bangs as I think of Bee, knowing she is out there and still not back with me. I don't like it. "Are you going to sleep in here?"

"I'm on night guard until five in the morning, but I will join you then. Dagan has the night off, go rest with him. He misses you, and though he might not say it out loud, he can't cope with how Elias is right now," Kor informs me, and I nod, knowing that Dagan is taking Eli's condition as well as I am. *Which is not well at all.*

"I don't think any of us are coping well with how Elias is, but we have to just get through it," I reply, and he smiles, stepping closer so my back hits the door, and he pushes his body into mine. I kiss him first, making him chuckle low in his throat before he kisses me back. His hands slowly slide up my body, before gliding into my hair before he pulls back.

"I can't wait for our mating night!" he exclaims against my lips.

"Are you going to make me wait until then?" I ask in frustration, biting down on my lip as his dragon eyes burn red for a moment and then go back to normal.

"I'm going to tease you every chance I get until I can finally have you as my mate, doll," he tells me, sending shivers across my skin as he traces my lips with his own before stepping back and bowing his head slightly. "I will see you later, my queen." I chuckle at his unneeded formality before he turns and walks down the corridor.

Must save our mate... My dragon suddenly rouses to the surface as I place my hand on the door. I know she doesn't want me to go and see Dagan. She wants me to spend more time with Eli...and I can't tonight. I need a night away from him and the pain it causes me to be near him right now.

To save our mate, I need to be okay. Eli is hurting me right now. He is hurting Dagan. Dagan and I can fix each other. I am not giving up on Eli. I promise, I tell her, and she huffs in a mild agreement before sinking to the back of my mind once again. I breathe out the breath I was holding and slowly open the door, letting myself in. I shut it behind me and walk in to see Dagan sleeping on the bed, his arm cuddling my pillow as he sleeps. I smile before quietly taking my crown off, placing it on my desk, and stripping out of my clothes so I'm only wearing a vest and panties. I climb into bed next to Dagan, removing the pillow and letting him pull me against his chest. I breathe in his musky, smoky scent that instantly has me relaxing. I don't know how long I happily lie in his arms, listening to his heartbeat and breathing in his scent like he is my own drug. I never want to move in these moments. I would happily lie here forever.

"Waking up with you is always amazing," Dagan's gravelly voice says, his breath moving my hair as I turn my head to look up at him.

"Even when I have morning breath? Like, that can't be nice," I say, smiling.

"Are you suggesting I need to brush my teeth?" he asks with a grumble, and I laugh.

"No, you smell like fire no matter what time of the day. You taste like fire too," I admit to him.

"Do I?" he chuckles, rolling us over so I'm lying on his chest, looking down at him. "You taste like magic. You taste like peaches but far sweeter and more seductive," he says, leaning down and kissing me like he is desperate to remind himself how I taste. I moan into his mouth, tasting nothing but the fire I spoke of and Dagan. He is addictive, making me want more with every stroke of his lips against mine. The passionate way Dagan rolls my hips against the hard length I can feel tells me he finds me just as addictive. I pull Dagan's shirt off, breaking the kiss for only a moment as he pulls it off. I go to tug my shirt off, and he catches my hand, placing it above my head. I gasp as he uses his shirt to tie my hands together.

"Keep them there for me, Issy. Oh, and trust me," he says, his words turning me on as I nod. I've never seen this side of Dagan, but damn, am I happy to play along. I gasp as Dagan rubs his hands over my breasts, covered only by my top, making me gasp. He chuckles at my reaction and winks before lifting his hands off my chest. He lights his hands up, and my eyes widen as he spreads pure fire all over my skin, burning away my top and panties as they go, making me gasp from the heat. The moment my panties are gone, Dagan is sliding a finger inside me as he twirls a tongue around my nipples. I moan, fighting the urge to move my hands as he drives me crazy. The mix of the danger of the fire and the sexy way Dagan is controlling my body edges me near an orgasm with every second that passes. Just as I get close, Dagan removes his hand and kneels between my legs. I watch him slowly unbutton his trousers, using every second to tease me as he pushes them down, freeing his hard length. He strokes himself a few times as he watches me, teasing me further.

"You are such a tease, Dagan Fire. Are you going to leave your queen waiting?" I ask. His eyes burn with fire for a moment before he grabs my hips, dragging me down the bed. I gasp as he suddenly flips me over, before pulling my hips up and sliding inside me in one fluid motion. I'm so sensitive that I can only grab the sheets, riding out the intense orgasm that instantly slams into me. Dagan thrusts in and out of me, riding my orgasm. I gasp as he suddenly pulls out of me, rolls me over, and holds my hips as he guides himself back into me once again. He leans down and kisses me harshly, both of us breathless and chasing another orgasm.

I love you, my mate, he whispers into my mind, before leaning up and grabbing his shirt tied around my wrists. He burns it away, replacing his shirt with his hands as he thrusts in and out of me.

I love you more, my mate. My Dagan, I reply and cry out as he finishes inside me, setting off another orgasm for me. I collapse to the bed as he lets go of my hands and holds me close to his side as we both get our breath back. When we've calmed down, Dagan pulls the blanket over us, and we face each other. I place my hand on his chest for a moment before he covers my hand with his and links our fingers.

"How was your day?" he asks me.

"Pillow talk, huh?" I tease, and he chuckles low as I answer, feeling my eyes drooping a little as I actually answer his question. "I spoke with my uncle, and the conversation ended with us hugging. Oh, and I changed my name to Isola Pendragon."

"Well, that sounds like you've had an interesting day. I think the name suits you," he says, and I love that he just accepts my choice without questioning me. He just knows it's something I needed to do, and he has accepted it. I know Dagan is always on my side. I smile as I drift off to sleep, not able to fight it any longer but knowing he will keep me safe no matter what.

"**M**orning, Eli," I say, walking into the dungeon, each little noise from my footsteps on the stone seems to echo around the dungeon. There are three lit fire lanterns in the room that were not in here yesterday, and they reveal most of Eli's cage now, so he cannot hide, I suspect. Eli sits silent, unmoving, and looking so close to death that it is hard to look at him. I have to mentally remind myself that my Eli is somewhere in him, just lost for now. It's my duty to find him. I get to the bottom of the stairs and nod at the two guards in here after they bow.

"Welcome back, my queen. We have given him food, but he has not eaten it," the one guard with a deep voice explains.

"Thank you. You can leave us now," I reply, moving my eyes from the shocked expressions on their faces to my Eli.

"A-are you sure?" the other guard splutters out. "He is dangerous."

"Not to me," I confidently reply, stepping aside and waving a hand at the door at the top of the stairs. They quickly bow and walk out of the room, shutting the door at the top. I walk over to my usual spot by the wall and open my book, diving head first into the pages I love so much. It's not long before Elias gets up off the floor and comes to the front of the cage. He speaks just as the main the character in my book gets her first kiss. *Dammit.*

"What are you reading?" he asks, his voice a whisper that no doubt reflects how weak he is.

"It's a romance. There are two people who are soulmates, despite the entire world wanting them apart," I explain, knowing I picked this book up from the library because some part of me understands the love. It's very much like Eli and me. Torn apart by the entire world, but still fighting for each other because our souls know we belong together. Even if Eli can't remember that at the moment.

"Do they end up with each other?" he eventually asks, his eyes locked with mine.

"Yes. Sometimes love can be enough to survive anything," I reply, not being able to hide the emotion in my voice. I don't want to seem weak around him, but I also will not hide myself from Eli.

"I'm not who you think I am. I am not yours," he replies, though his voice cracks.

"What does your dragon say?" I ask, curious. Eli once told me his dragon has always thought of me as his, from the very first moment we saw each other across the corridor of this very academy. It feels like such a long time ago now, though.

"Nothing," he replies, and I frown at him.

"My dragon calls you mine because that is who you are to me," I tell him, and my heart seems like it's beating out my chest as he stares back at me for a moment. His eyes are so black now, so touched with a darkness that I can't see if he is speaking to his dragon or just looking at me. I can't sense much about him either, despite how much that hurts. I used to be able to understand Eli like I understood myself. The more time I spend down here, the more I doubt I can save him and get him back. The thought of that at all makes me want to break down.

"I am not yours!" he growls, making me jump as he shakes his head and falls to his knees, screaming out with pain. I drop my book and run over to him, desperately wanting to stop whatever is causing him pain. I try to reach through the cage to touch him, to see what is wrong, but he crawls away from me, shaking his head. "Leave. Please." His words are softly spoken, a despair-filled plea.

"If you promise to eat, I will go," I finally force myself to say, looking at all the trays of food in his cage. If I have to leave, I will make sure he is at least eating.

"Fine," he replies, to my shock as I didn't expect him to just agree with me. I stand up and walk out, doing what I promised I would do even if it hurts my heart with every step. The two guards are waiting outside, and they bow as I come out the doors.

"Can you watch him again? If he doesn't eat any meal, tell me. Alright?" I ask them.

"Of course, my queen," one of the guards says before they both bow once more. They quickly go back down into the dungeon, pulling the door shut behind them. I stare at the door for a moment, lost in my thoughts of how Elias talked to me just then. There was more of my Eli, but not enough to make me feel any better. I lean closer and rest my head against the cold stone, letting it take me away for a little bit as I focus on only it. I don't know if cold and confused is any less painful than angry and mean with Eli. Either way, every visit with him is hard swallow —and forget. If he doesn't remember before Tatarina comes... well, I want a few moments with him before that fight which I might lose. I want to tell Eli I love him, tell him there isn't anything I wouldn't do for him, and have him be my Eli for a little bit.

"Queen Isola," Essna's voice snaps me out of my thoughts, and I turn to face her. She is dressed for war, with mostly leather clothes, dozens of weapons littered on her, and her staff with her glowing orb held in her one hand. The scar on her face always makes me want to question what exactly happened, but I don't. It doesn't take away from her natural beauty anyway. I wonder if she ever puts the weapons down, as she always looks like this when I see her. I'm glad she is here, as we haven't had much chance to speak to one another recently. Her eyes drift from me to the door and back, before she nods her head to the side, suggesting I walk with her. I don't say a word, only lowering my arms and walking next to her as we leave the entrance to the dungeon, heading through my people to the outside. "How are you? Your dragon guards?" Essna's question takes me by surprise. I never had her down as one for small talk.

"There hasn't been much change. I feel like I will need to do something drastic to get him to remember me," I tell her, trying to keep my voice stronger than how I am feeling. "Dagan, Thorne and Korbin are just keeping themselves busy and trying to help me because they don't know what to do either."

"I believe waiting for your light spirit to return is your best course of action. She would not have left you if there weren't a reason," Essna says as we get to the main doors and walk out into the cold, crisp courtyard. The wind blows against my skin, the bitter cold to it feeling like a slap in the face almost. I pull my cloak around my shoulders as we walk down the steps.

Dragca Academy looks nothing like it used to, and yet I'm so thankful we are safe here for now. The trees look close to falling down, their bark rotting away and their leaves nothing but black shells of the lush green leaves they once were. Winter in Dragca does bring the death of trees, the loss of their leaves, and the fading of their colour, but there is always the promise of rebirth in the spring. Right now, there is no promise. Everything here feels lost in a darkness that will take more than just the trees around us; it will take the very heart of Dragca and destroy it.

"I would have liked if she told me this reason she had to leave first. I feel I am beyond clueless to what spirits are and their actions. I can only trust Bee has something in mind and it is worth me spending every hour worrying about her," I reply. Things are bad enough with Eli and the pressure of being queen to people I am going to lead into war soon; I can't lose Bee on top of that.

"Without a doubt she does have a good reason. You must trust her. I know Bee seems like your child, your responsibility, but light and dark spirits have been around for a very long time. They are full of wisdom we could never understand, and we must trust that Bee has a plan for us all," Essna says as we get to the grass and step onto it, hearing the dead grass crunch under our boots. "I want to test something. Would you give me some of your time?"

"Yes, but I want you to answer a question for me first," I reply, knowing well enough that I might as well try to ask something in return.

"Is it about the future or your dragon guards?" she asks me, her eyes curious. "As I could not tell you anything I have seen of them. It would be pointless anyway; the future is changing every time I look. The world—and its magic—is not in order."

"No, it is not about them. It is about someone else in the present," I ask her.

"Then ask away," she replies, nodding her head.

"How is my sister?" I ask her, and Essna pauses, closing her eyes as she touches the orb on top of her staff. I wait silently for a while, looking down at my own staff swirled around my arm. The red gem seems to glow here in Dragca. Essna finally looks at me, a tiny smile on her lips.

"Melody is alive and well. I cannot tell you more, though I am happy you asked me to look," she says, and I smile as she takes a deep sigh of relief. "Good news is coming swiftly." I don't take in her statement as I focus on the fact Melody is okay, and that means Hallie must be as well. As long as they stay on Earth, they will survive this all.

"I didn't know seers could find just anyone so quickly," I reply after a long silence between us.

"Melody doesn't know it, but her mother was my cousin. Melody is family to me, so are you in a very distant way. I do not need a lot of power to watch those who are related by blood," she explains to me.

"I didn't know that. I'm sorry I ever distrusted you," I reply. If I had known how connected she and Melody were, then maybe things would have been different for us all.

"You were right to distrust me, as much as I was right to distrust you when we met. The throne, the secrets of Dragca, and everything Dragca has become make anyone distrust a stranger. Only a stupid person would blindly trust anyone here," she replies to me, looking into her glowing orb for a moment before meeting my eyes.

"What was it you wanted in return?" I ask her because I want to go to the library, find a book, and get lost in it for a little bit. I miss reading, I miss being me and grounding myself in the way that reading can do. Though I might avoid anything too dark with how I'm feeling. Essna smiles, bowing her head before sitting down on the grass. I stare at her strangely as she pats the ground for me to sit next to her. I do, stretching my fingers into the dead, yellow grass and looking up at the black trees in the distance. It feels wrong to touch the ground, and a deep part of me feels the sickness in my land. *One caused by Tatarina.*

"You are bonded to a light spirit, and a dark spirit did this. I wonder if you can heal the ground a little? If you practised every day, just as far as you can push it without Bee here, you could learn how to heal all of this. You could learn to use light magic on your dragon guard," she suggests, and I sharply look at her. I've never thought of using light magic on Eli. Maybe it could save him, and if it destroys the bond he has with Tatarina, maybe it could actually kill her. It would be a massive risk, one I don't want to do because I have to find a safer way to save him. But it can be a last resort...one I will only use if I believe Eli needs it.

"That might kill him," I finally reply to her, the cold breeze pushing my hair around my shoulders and making me shiver.

"Light magic is pure. It only heals, not destroys. It might be the only way you can truly save him," she replies to me. "I would very much like to see you try to use it now on the ground, Isola. I will be here to stop you if anything goes wrong."

"I will attempt it," I reply, shrugging. "I can't see it doing any real harm."

"Good. Now when I use my power, I don't imagine it. I don't even picture what it can do, I just trust my heart to do what it needs. I trust my body, my soul to use my power hidden in the depths of it," Essna explains to me.

"It sounds like how I connect to my dragon. She and I are one. I can trust her instincts, well, most of the time," I reply, not mentioning how she is a little more kill happy than I am, and I have to calm that down a tad. Light magic isn't like my dragon though, it's different. More powerful than I can imagine. Essna nods.

"Now try connecting to the part of you that can access light magic. I am sure you can do this, Isola," she tells me. I give her a small nod before closing my eyes and feeling only the dead grass under me, the emptiness of it. There is no light here, nothing to pull on, so I must find it within myself. I shut out all the sounds I can hear. I shut out the smell of dead, rotting plants and the distant scent of fire. I block out the comfort of my dragon in the back of my mind, as I know she cannot help me do this. I search for that part of me which is light, pure power. I know when I've found it because it feels like the sun is shining on every part of my body, making me feel so warm and comforted. I sense Bee a great distance away, and I know she senses me as well, as I connect more to the power that binds us. The more I mentally reach for the light, the hotter I feel, the more my whole body seems to be on fire, though I suspect it is not. I gasp when the power suddenly goes, and I'm left shaking as I open my eyes. The sight in front of me is nothing like I expected to see. There is green, healthy grass, as tall as my knees, covering the ground, and flowers growing everywhere around me. Dragca Academy looks more alive than I've ever seen it, and everyone has stopped to stare in awe as I look around. I can't see a dead tree, plant or even a little bit of brown grass for miles.

"Astounding," Essna gasps, standing up with me. I shake a little on my legs, and she reaches out, holding me up for a moment as I see everything surrounding the castle is now green. From the vines covered in white flowers climbing up the castle to the green, red and yellow trees, the grass, the flowers—it's all beautiful. Every dragon I can see suddenly falls to their knees, bowing their heads one by one. I can only stare around me, lost in this moment.

"I'm stronger than I thought," I quietly admit, and she bows her head with a large smile, her eyes drifting around at the beauty I struggle to take my eyes off of too.

"If you can save all this, then with practice, you must be able to save Elias Fire." Her words give me hope, something I didn't know I could have for Eli.

"**A**re you ready yet?" Essna asks, knocking on the door as I look at myself in the mirror and take a deep breath because I damn well need it. I don't remember the last time I was so nervous. At least one thing is certain, I must be wearing the prettiest dress in the whole of Dragca. It's spectacular. My wedding dress is a deep blood red in colour, strapless and tight at the top before falling into a princess gown at the bottom. The top part is lacy, covered in red jewels that sparkle in the light, each one no doubt hand stitched on for this day. My hair curls down my shoulders in lovely waves, each one seeming perfect and soft to touch. Two dragon women came to help me with my dress and hair and makeup. They somehow have made me look dramatically more like a bride on her mating ceremony day, even if I am just a bundle of nerves.

I'm not nervous about mating with Kor. No, my soul knows that is the right thing for us because I love him. I'm nervous about mating in front of every dragon and seer here. I want to do my mother proud, but I so wish she were here to tell me what to do. How to act strong when you are truly scared. Dagan and Thorne are with Korbin, helping him get ready, and it strikes me that I don't have anyone around to help me. Melody and Hallie should be here, they should be my bridesmaids. My mother should be here, she should be doing my hair and whispering words of encouragement. I rub my heart, knowing I can't cry right now, but this dress is like having my mother with me in a way. I remember her letter, how she was proud of me even as a baby. I know deep down that she is proud of me in some way.

"One second," I manage to shout back before picking up the crown and placing it on my head. Now I look like a queen who is ready to mate with one of the loves of her life. Even if one of the other ones is in a dungeon and won't see me without causing me to break down. Every night for the past week, I've gone to see him, and he won't speak to me anymore, but he is eating at least. He looks better each time I see him, but still not my Eli.

I know I need to put thoughts of Elias away for now and enjoy this day with Korbin. A real mating ceremony. Not that I don't love how I mated to Dagan and Thorne, but I've always imagined a day like this. I pick up my dress to turn before dropping it and walking to my bedroom door, pulling it open. Essna is fixing my uncle's tie in his suit, tightening it up and putting it back into place. There is a moment when neither of them seems to notice I'm here, both of them staring at each other before the door creaks and they turn towards me. *That is interesting.*

"Right, you are all done. I will tell them to start in two minutes, Queen Isola," Essna says, dropping her hands from my uncle and bowing her head before very quickly walking away. My uncle watches her go, same as I do before he looks towards me. He bows his head before walking over.

"You look so similar to your mother on her wedding day, it almost hurts to see you, if I am being honest. May I ask why you chose a red dress, ice queen?" he asks, stopping in front of me and offering his arm. I hook my arm in his just as I hear light music coming from the direction of the stairs. The music makes this all the more real.

"The same reason it was rumoured my mother wore a red wedding dress despite everyone telling her she should have worn blue or white," I say, listening to the sweet hum of the music that is romantic and deep in its meaning. "I wear this dress to show that ice and fire dragons are one. It means nothing that I am ice, because I will always care for fire. This dress shows my respect for all dragons."

"She would be so proud of you on this day. Somewhere, your mother is watching, honoured by you," my uncle carefully says, and I have to swallow the emotions that nearly make me cry as we get to the top of the stairs. The music plays in the distance, the people are standing all around the stairs which have a white train down the middle, leading outside. There are white petals scattered everywhere and lights on the edge of the staircase that give it a magical effect. It is beautiful in here, and I can't help but continue looking around at everything.

As we start walking down the staircase, snow starts falling from the ceiling, adding to the magic. I frown, wondering where the snow is coming from until I see Thorne standing next to Dagan by the door. They both look amazing, wearing black suits with red ties. The suits look almost custom fitted, even though I know they had to go to Earth and buy a load of suits and dresses for the day because they didn't have time to have clothes made. The wedding preparations have given everyone a new sense of life, something to be happy about for even a few hours. I'm so glad we are doing this, not only for Kor and me, but for our people. I smile at the beauty, the magic of the perfect moment as I walk to my mates, and my uncle lets go of my arm when we are stood in front of them.

"Your current mates will deliver you to your new mate. It is what is right," my uncle says, kissing the side of my head. "I am ever so proud of the woman and queen you have become. Congratulations, Isola." His words make my voice catch as I nod at him, speechless before he steps back. At some point, Louis has become more of a father figure to me than my real father ever was. I link hands with Thorne and Dagan before we start to walk forward.

You are so beautiful, Dagan whispers into my mind.

Says you who looks so damn good in that suit, I reply, and I hear his little chuckle just as I see Korbin at the end of the white path of petals outside. He is stood under a red- and blue-flowered arch placed in the middle of a star shape that is painted into the grass, his eyes widening before burning red as he sees me. My dragon purrs in my mind at the sight of him too. He is impressively attractive, dressed in a black suit and red tie, with a blue flower clipped into his breast pocket. We are silent as we walk past all the people watching us at the sides. I nod at Korbin's parents stood to one side, who both look so proud and emotional. His mother is crying, and I almost want to comfort her, but I know it is not the right time. I turn back to Kor, locking eyes with him as we get closer, and my mates let go of my hands. They stay right behind me as I take the final step, and Kor lifts one of my hands, kissing the back.

"You look beyond stunning, doll," he tells me, making my cheeks burn as red as my dress, I suspect. I go to say something back when a throat clears, and I turn to see a man I don't know stood behind the arch. He has my mating stone in his hand and is wearing a long white cloak with the hood up, only showing me his dark red eyes and long black beard. I look at him for a moment, trying to figure out where I know him from when I suddenly realise he is a priest. There are few of them left in our world, or any of the worlds, and they only come out to bless a mating ceremony. It was rumoured a priest held my parents' ceremony, though it was not blessed.

"We gather here today for the royal mating ceremony of Isola Pendragon and Korbin

Dragoali," the man says, his voice echoing around as snow falls around us. "As we all know, mating is a blessing and something that cannot be taken for granted." There is silence as both Kor and I bow our heads in acknowledgement, knowing everyone here is doing the same thing. "Now speak the words."

Kor turns to me, taking both my hands in his and holding them between us.

"Link to the heart, link to the soul. I pledge my heart to you, for you, for all the time I have left. My dragon is yours, my love is yours, and everything I am, belongs with you," he says, and I can't help the massive smile on my lips as I repeat the words, trying not to let my voice waver with how happy I am. When we can pull our eyes away, we see our mating stone is glowing brightly. Another blessed mating. We both offer the priest our hands as he pulls a dagger out. I hold in a cry as he cuts my hand and then cuts Kor's next.

"Light and dark, good and evil, and everything that makes us dragons, please bless this mating. We bless you," the priest says, and all the guests, all my people, join in echoing, "We bless you," as we place our cut hands together. The moment we touch, a massive blast of white light shines in every direction, sending off sparks of white dust that fall all around us as I grin at Kor.

I love you, my new mate, Kor whispers into my mind as his emotions flood me. Happiness, love and protectiveness are all I can feel for a long time.

I love you more, mate, I about manage to reply as tears fall down my cheeks just as the priest talks.

"Congratulations, you are one, and blessed by the fates. We bless you," the priest says as he starts fading away into white dust. Korbin pulls me into his arms, kissing me as everyone cheers.

"**Y**ou look so happy," Korbin whispers in my ear as we sway to the music in the courtyard. Dagan and Thorne have had a dance with me and made me laugh. Even my uncle has asked for a dance, though it was more formal, and from the way he looked at me, I know he was seeing my mother instead of me. That's okay though; it feels like part of her is here with me on this day. We have all had some delicious food, laughed, and Thorne even made a funny speech. This is a day I know I will never forget. Dagan and Thorne have gone back to watch Elias for the night to give Korbin and me some time alone. The music relaxes me, letting me sink into it as I hold my mate close.

"I'd be happier when you've taken me up to bed and completed our mating," I seductively whisper into his ear, making sure to brush my lips against him as I pull my head back to face him. His burning red eyes make it clear his dragon likes that idea. Kor gradually comes back, and he slowly kisses me, teasing me with every moment as the song ends. When he lets me go, he takes my hand and leads me out of the dancers and towards the building without saying a word. However, from the way I can sense his emotions, I know what is on his mind as it is on mine. I chuckle when he wraps an arm around my waist and pulls me close to him. I can sense the burning desire from our bond, and there is nothing more I want than to get upstairs with Kor and finish our mating.

We wave and say hello to people as we pass them, both of us just desperate at this point to get away from the number of people here. We hurry up the stairs together, laughing with each other. We run to our room, and I push the door open. Kor closes it behind him and pulls me to him, kissing me like a starving man. I let out a little moan, holding onto him tightly as he pulls at my dress, and his lips press into my neck, nipping and biting gently. My dress rips at the back, and he pulls it off me as I undo his buttons on his shirt. My dress falls off me, leaving me just in red underwear as Kor steps back. He slowly pulls his tie off and then pushes his shirt off, revealing his toned chest, the dip in his lower chest and the six-pack. His hands go to his trousers, but I step closer, covering his hands with mine and stopping him.

"Let me, mate," I whisper before falling to my knees. I undo his trousers slowly, letting my fingers drift across his stomach, and enjoy the deep breath I hear him make every time I do it. I free his length before taking him inside my throat. He groans, holding onto my head and guiding my movements. It isn't long before he is picking me up off the floor and taking me to the bed. He throws me on it, and I bounce, laughing as he crawls over me. He kisses me harshly, pressing his body into mine, before he starts kissing his way down my body. Every kiss makes my skin tingle, makes me let out little gasps which turn into moans as his lips find my nipples. He takes his time sucking and twirling his tongue around each one, driving me crazy before he kisses down my stomach. The moment his tongue finds my core, I scream out the orgasm that slams into me along with the overwhelming desire coming from Kor through our bond. I gasp as Kor climbs up my body, locking eyes with me.

I love you more than I ever thought it was possible to love anyone, Isola. You are my mate, and we will be with each other forever, he speaks the breathtakingly sweet words into my mind as he slides deep inside me, making me moan out his name like a prayer.

I never knew either, but make me your mate. I love you, always, I reply. My words send Kor into a frenzy as he grabs my ass with one hand and holds the back of my neck with his other as he thrusts in and out of me. I can't help the noises that escape my lips with every thrust that pushes me closer to the edge. I cry out as another orgasm slams into me, and Kor kisses me deeply as he finishes too. He rocks into me a few more times, kissing me softly before rolling over. We hold hands, staring up at the ceiling of my room as we both calm down before we clean up.

I sit on the window seat, looking over the courtyard. I should be happier than ever in this moment. I have three mates that I've been in love with since I met them. I have people who care about me, who are willing to fight a war I have made worse...yet my thoughts drift to Elias in the dungeons. I need to get him back, and nothing is going to be right until I make a drastic move. I have to make him remember, no matter what.

I wait until Kor has drifted into a deep sleep before climbing out of the bed and pulling on some clothes. I clip my cloak on before walking to the door, pausing to look over at Kor, and making sure my emotions are as neutral as I can get them before leaving the room. If any of my mates sense how scared I am to do this, they will know something is wrong and come to me. I can't even feel guilt; instead, I try to make myself remember how resolved I need to be. I very slowly open the door and close it before walking down the empty corridors, each one of my steps echoing.

The party is long over, and the academy is happily sleeping after the celebrations, which is why I need to do this right now. I realised as I lay with Kor that nothing could be perfect until I sort out Eli. He has to remember me. I need him back in my life.

I freeze in the corridor when I hear footsteps and quickly step back into the shadows of a corner, holding my breath as two dragons stumble past me, laughing and stinking of beer. I wait until they are gone before walking to the top of the stairs, looking around to see it's empty before I run down the stairs and around the corner. I walk straight up to the two unfamiliar guards stood outside the dungeon doors. They bow when they see me, and I place a finger against my lips when one of them goes to speak.

"Are Dagan or Thorne down there?" I quietly ask.

"Dagan is, but Thorne left to help Essna with a border issue," one of them states, and that is perfect for me.

"Okay, I need you both to go to Dagan and tell him there is a big issue at the border. That you will watch Elias for him until his return," I say, and they look at me with confusion, no doubt going to argue, but I beat them to it. "That is an order from your queen. You will not tell Dagan anything about me being here either."

"Yes, our queen," they finally say and bow their heads before opening the doors. I run to hide under the stairs, keeping my emotions as tucked away as I can as Dagan walks out the dungeons, talking with the guards before storming off towards the main doors of the academy. I wait for a few moments before walking out of my hiding space and to the doors.

"Thank you," I say, walking between them and looking back as they go to follow me into the dungeon. "No, stop."

"Queen, we only wish to protect you," they say, looking between each other with equal amounts of worry. I hate to boss them around when they are only doing the right thing, but it is important they don't stop what I am about to do. Though it might be easier to get the keys off them while I'm being bossy anyways.

"I am your queen, and I will give the orders around here. Now give me the keys to the cell and then wait outside. Whatever you hear, you do not come in here," I say, holding my hand out. They look between each other before one of the guards pulls out the key from his pocket and hands it to me. I take the key and raise my eyebrow, waiting for them to turn around, and I shut the doors before walking down the steps.

"I didn't expect to see you on your mating day, princess," Elias taunts as I get to the bottom step and see him resting on the side wall of the cage, crossing his arms. I run my eyes over his pale skin and dark eyes that match his black hair. This is now or never. I don't have time or a choice anymore. Eli must remember, even if what I'm going to do might kill us both.

"I had to do this. I'm tired of playing this cat and mouse game with you, Eli. You are mine, and you will remember me," I state, keeping my voice firm as I walk straight up to the cage. His eyes widen as I unlock the door, pulling it open and stepping inside. I leave the door open and chuck the key on the ground before standing right in front of Eli who watches me like the cat I know he is. Though he just doesn't know I am his equal in every way, and I will never run from him again.

"That was a bad move, naughty princess," he finally says and pushes up off the bars to walk closer to me. I stay very still as he places both his hands on my cheeks and moves his face inches away from mine.

"Nothing I do to save you is a bad move, Eli," I reply, gulping as his hands slide down my face and to my neck. I'm not shocked when he spins us around, pushing me against the bars as he tightens his hands on my neck. It's a half-assed attempt to kill me, because deep down, I know he doesn't want to. He knows it too, but he is so lost in the darkness, he can't tell me that. He keeps tightening his hands until I feel like I can't breathe anymore, but instead of panic, there is just acceptance that if he can kill me, he never truly loved me. I'd die to test what I am sure of.

His hands tighten further, and I grab his arms as my dragon roars in my mind, begging me to fight for my life, but I won't. Just as black spots enter my vision, tears fall down his cheeks, and I know I have to say something, do something before I pass out and can't. I call my light in the way I have practised, and it blasts out of me in swirls that twirl themselves around Eli. I see the light out of the corners of my eyes, but I can't look away from him as he lifts me off the ground, putting more pressure on my neck.

"E-Eli...k-kill me if that is what you n-need to re-remember."

His hands loosen on my neck slightly at my coughed out words, just as the light blasts to fill the entire room. For the first time in weeks, he looks at me like he remembers us as the light fades, and a hope fills my heart.

"Isola?" he whispers my name, dropping his hands and falling to his knees with a scream as he holds his head. I fall to the floor, gasping for air as the door blasts open, and I feel Dagan running in with Thorne and Korbin not far behind. I crawl to Eli, taking his face in my hands as he lies passed out on the ground, whimpering in pain. *Did I hurt him?*

"Isola, what were you thinking?" Dagan asks, falling to his knees and picking me up as I keep coughing.

"I saved him," is all I can manage to whisper before I pass out.

118

I step out of Isola's room as the healer follows me, and I go to my brother's side. After examining them, the healer says they will both recover, though she cannot tell if Eli is back to himself. I only have what Isola said to go on before she passed out. Thorne and Kor are staying with Isola as she recovers from almost being strangled to death by Elias. I don't know what went through her pretty little mind when she decided to risk her life to save my brother, but I know it comes from pure love. I just hope it actually worked and wasn't for nothing.

I shut the door to Elias's room as the healer leaves and pull a chair over to the side of his bed, looking down at my brother who I don't recognize anymore. I would do anything to save him, anything but lose Isola which we came too close to doing tonight. My brother is deep down inside of this shell some-where, and he is in love with her, that is the only reason she is actually alive, I suspect.

The door opens once again, and I turn with a frown to see who has come in here. Bee flies into the room, looking deter-mined as she lands on Eli's chest with a massive bag of glittering dust in her arms. She drops the dust all over Elias, and it spreads over all his skin as I step back.

"Bee, what was that?" I ask her in shock. Eli starts looking better almost instantly, colour coming back into his cheeks, and his hair looking softer.

"Fix him. Want back," she says and starts glowing brightly as I'm just relieved to see her back with us. Bee should be protected, not out in the world alone like she was. When Isola wakes up, at least she'll be happy Bee is back, even if Eli isn't himself.

"Have you fixed him then?" I ask her, needing to try to understand what is going on.

"For now," she says, nodding her head, and her eyes drift towards the door to Isola's room.

"Isola misses you. You should see her," I gently suggest. I know Isola has been worrying about Bee as much as she has been scared for Eli. I can only hope that at least seeing Bee will make her feel better when she wakes up.

"Must find more. I be back soon," she says, her voice sad and full of longing for Isola, no doubt. She flies out the room before I can even reply, leaving me more worried for her. It's clear she is trying to save Eli for Isola, even if it likely isn't safe for her. I will explain this all to Isola later. I look back as Eli groans, rolling onto his side before blinking his eyes open. We left the collar on him just in case he tries to attack us, though from the way he looks at me, I suspect Isola might have been right.

"Brother?" Eli asks, and I come closer, putting my hand on his shoulder. He doesn't push me away, so that is a good sign.

"You remember me? Do you remember Isola?" I ask him, watching his expression closely.

"You should kill me for what I said to Isola. For nearly killing her," he whispers, his voice filled with so much embarrassment and pain that I only want to fix it all for him, though I can't this time.

"Brother, if you were anyone else, under any other circumstances, you would be dead already. I know you didn't mean it and you love her," I tell him. "Isola knows the same."

"I do love her. I've really fucked up," he mutters, the guilt clear in his voice. "I will fix it, however I can. I never did deserve her, this just proves it."

"None of this is your own making, so stop with the guilt shit and get angry. Tatarina killed you, turned you into this monster to hurt Isola because she knew how much you mean to Isola. Now we will get revenge and live a damn happy life all together afterwards. Got it?" I wait for him to nod, a single tear falling down his cheek. I haven't seen my brother cry since our mother died. The simple fact this is all so fucked up for him kills me. "Good. Now, do you want to sit up?" He nods in agreement, his expression showing he's clearly still in some pain. I help him sit in the bed, pushing himself up on the pillows before I get him some water from the sink in the room. He sips on it for a bit as I glance at him again.

"You look better already," I muse, seeing that he isn't as pale as he once was, and his eyes have a little blue in them that was not there before, "though I'm going to get you some food in a bit. That should help."

"Any chance of a cigarette while you're at it?" he cheekily asks.

"Now I know you are back," I reply, laughing with him.

"You've always been looking after me, haven't you?" he says, and I guess he is right in a way. One of the last things I remember my mother telling us was to look after my brother, and it stuck around, even when he was being a dickhead until he met Isola.

"You're my brother. It's what we do," I reply, chuckling as his expression goes dark as he gets lost in his own thoughts.

"I still hear Tatarina in my head, whispering thoughts and demands to me. Whatever Isola did, it didn't completely work," he carefully tells me.

"Bee is helping too. We will fight this. We will fight her," I tell him, hating how vulnerable he looks for a moment as he meets my eyes.

"Kill her. Promise me no matter what, you will kill her," he asks.

"She is bonded to you," I whisper back, shaking my head. "I would be killing you if I did that."

"I know the price, but Isola needs to be queen. She needs Tatarina dead, and I will pay that price for her. Promise me, brother," he asks, and I know there is a good chance I will regret the next words. They upset me more than I thought words could possibly damage me as I speak them.

"I promise I will kill her if I get a chance. For Isola—and for you."

119

ISOLA

"Come to me, I will let you go if you do, Isola. This war is between me and you, no one else," a dark, mysterious voice whispers to me as I open my eyes to see the fire I am stood in the middle of. There is nothing but fire all around as I twist, trying to find the familiar voice.

"How can I come to you if I don't know who you are or how to find you?" I ask, searching for the voice.

"You may have saved that boy of yours, but one touch from me, and he will be mine again. Come to me, and I will leave him alone. He still will die if you kill me," I freeze in my spot, knowing exactly who is talking to me from the threat alone. Good, I want her to know my thoughts.

"Eli is mine, and you will never have him. Oh Tatarina, I will come for you, but you won't want me there, because it will be the day I kill you. I will make sure Dragca forgets your name, and you will be nothing but a bad memory. I will come for you, but you should run for what you have done," I reply, kneeling down and reaching inside my heart for my light. Bright white light blasts out of my chest, putting out the fire as I hear Tatarina screaming. I smile just as I fall back into the safe darkness of my dreams.

. . .

I GASP as I wake up, sitting straight up as the light of the room burns against my eyes as I remember Tatarina being in my dreams. She knows Eli is mine now, and that means there is no reason why she won't be heading our way with her army. I must tell Essna and my uncle, though knowing them, they already have come to that conclusion. I reach for my throat, feeling how tender it is just before a glass of water appears in front of me. I accept it and down the drink before looking up to see who gave it to me, nearly coughing the water out. *Eli.* My Eli is sat on my bed, his eyes riddled with guilt as he takes the empty glass off me, our fingers brushing each other's before he places it on the side. He looks better, healthier than he ever has, and all I can do is stare. It really worked, and he is here, smelling of smoke but missing the smirk I'm used to seeing on his lips. His collar is gone, so clearly my mates trust him with me. I'm so happy, I feel like I can't even breathe.

"I'm so, so fucking sorry for every shitty word that came out my mouth recently. I will never be able to tell you how sorry I am for hurting you," he admits, looking away from me and down to his hands, no doubt reliving that moment in the dungeon.

"I knew it wasn't you," I say, my voice coming out croaky as I reach out and take his hand in mine, brushing my fingers across the rough skin. "I knew you were hidden deep down inside somewhere."

"Tatarina killed me...I remember it," he tells me, his voice is quiet though, and my dragon roars to life in my mind, letting out a whine as snow starts to fall from the ceiling. Eli doesn't take his eyes off me as it falls around us, he only stares at me like he expects me to hate him.

"I wish I could have stopped her from doing that to you, but she will pay," I vow. "I will find a way to make sure you have a long life...with me."

"I'm still linked to her. I hear her in my head, but Bee keeps doing this light thing that makes me better and her voice goes.

Though she can't keep doing it," he admits. "If things go bad, lock me up again."

"That is never happening, and she isn't the only one that can use light to heal you. Wait, Bee is back?" I ask, reaching up a hand and placing it on his cheek.

"Was she ever gone?" he asks, and I remember that he doesn't know anything that happened when we went to Earth and came back here. I know I need to catch him up soon.

"Yes, she was. She disappeared when we came back from Earth. Where is she?" I ask him.

"She's been outside with Dagan, Korbin and Thorne since she came back again with some more dust last night. You've been out two days from whatever you did to make me remember."

"I used light, but it was different. I didn't want to give up until you looked at me like this," I say, sighing as I move a little closer to Eli on the bed.

"I'm just glad we get some moments before the war. I missed you, my naughty princess," he gently says, picking up a little bit of my hair and twirling it around his fingers.

"I missed you—the real you—so much Eli," I say, and he lets me climb onto his lap, wrapping my arms and legs tightly around him. The moment his arms hold me tightly, I let out a sigh of relief. I have just wanted him to hold me since all this happened.

"So...you don't hate me?" he quietly asks. "I can handle *anything* but you hating me." I slide my hands onto his cheeks, seeing how vulnerable he looks.

"I could never hate you. *Never*. I love you an impossible amount, and I'm nothing but happy you are back with me. We will figure forever out and win the war, but for now I just want to be near you," I tell him, breathing in his smoky scent as I look back to see his eyes. There is a bit of the dark blue I love in there, but mainly his eyes are still so dark, the blackness getting in. I can get used to it as long as I have Eli. Nothing else matters.

"I will spend whatever time I have making sure nothing ever

happens like that again," he promises, and then he finally kisses me. The first moment our lips touch, I only feel how cold he is and yet how perfect he feels. I slide my hands into his hair as I deepen the kiss, and he pulls me closer to him. I rock against him, just wanting to be as close as possible to my Eli, and he lets out a little groan.

"God, I love you," I whisper between kisses, not being able to stop smiling with how damn happy I am. He goes to say something when there is a loud shout somewhere nearby and then a blaring alarm reaches our ears as I pull away from Eli. Seconds later, the door blasts open with Dagan running in through it.

"You need to see this, Isola," Dagan states as I climb off the bed and follow him out of the room, down the corridor which is full of running people who don't even notice us, and he stops, pulling a door open to a balcony. I walk out with Dagan and Eli at my sides as we look over at the trees. They are moving slightly, and the sound of a lot of people heading our way fills my ears.

"Is it Tatarina's army?" I ask Dagan, knowing it is very likely that it is.

"I don't know. You should stay here while we investigate," Dagan warns, and I smirk at him before climbing on the balcony wall and jumping off as I shift into my dragon, and I hear Eli and him swear in annoyance. I fly across the grounds, seeing people ducking below me before I land right on the edge of the forest. I breathe out a wall of ice, leaving only a little gap right in front of me to see who is coming through.

No, danger... my dragon hisses before letting me shift back. I stand still, crossing my arms as I hear my army and mates running towards me just as a familiar face steps out of the tree line first.

"Queen Isola, I heard you need our help."

"Queen Winter...what are you doing here?" I question her as she looks at the walls of ice and walks through the gap. Four men stay close to her side, all of them no doubt her mates from the scent of them. I see a black haired woman stood in the front of the army, dressed in all leather with a giant sword on her back and a brown haired man stood close to her side. Though Winter is dressed similarly in a black leather outfit and her long brown hair is up in a bun, she doesn't seem as intimidating as the other girl is. I pull my eyes from her to the four men that walk over with Winter. One is an angel with big white wings that match his hair. I nod my head at Atticus, but I do not know the other two. One smells like a dog though, so I'm thinking he is the wolf that stayed close to Winter's side but wouldn't shift back.

As I lift a hand, my ice melts very slowly, revealing a big army that stands behind them just in the tree line. All their scents mix together, so I can't really get a read on what they are. Just that they look like an army. I search for my sister, but I don't get to see her before Winter steps in front of me and starts speaking as she crosses her arms. I feel Kor step to my side, his arm brushing mine as Dagan gets to my other side. I sense Thorne close, but he isn't here yet. I'm sure Eli is on his way as well. My heart feels complete, even for a moment, as I watch the Earth queen for answers. I have my men at my side, all of them, and that means I can handle anything.

"Did you really think I wasn't going to come to the world of dragons when you needed my help?" Winter asks, a small smile on her lips. I feel that instant connection with her again, and I don't know what it is, but it makes me want to trust her. I do trust her, even if I don't know much of Winter at all. I move my eyes to her four mates, who are all staring in awe at the dragons flying around the castle. The army behind her all look just as shocked.

"This fight won't be easy. We could all die," Korbin warns from my side.

"I know, dragon, but we won't let Dragca fall. Just like I assume you won't let Earth fall either if we ever need you. We are all linked by fate, and I know I am meant to be here. I know I am fated to fight by Queen Isola's side."

"This is a dragon war, I don't want you hurt in it," I admit to her.

"I can handle myself, much like we all can. I would not come if I wasn't sure you would need us. After Melody explained..." she drifts off, confirming my fear that Melody is here when she should not be. It isn't safe for her, she told me so herself.

"Where is she?" I ask.

"Coming soon. The army is rather large, and she had to come through last with her girlfriend," she claims. I look around the army, wondering if they will even stand a chance in a dragon fight. Wolves, angels, vampires and witches don't belong in a dragon fight. I guess I have to trust they are stronger than they look.

"It is your choice, my queen," Dagan says as I look up at him for a bit of advice.

"We need help. They know the price they could pay," I reply to him, placing my hand on his arm and looking back to Winter.

"If you want to help us win this war, we will happily accept. I will also personally owe you a great debt. If Earth ever needs help, we will answer the call," I tell her, and she smiles, offering me her hand to shake. I slide my hand into hers, and we shake on it before she pulls me into a tight hug.

"I'm your friend first, and I will never let a friend die if I didn't try to help her. Now show me this dragon world you are from as our mates sort the army out," she tells me, and I chuckle as I pull away.

"I'd love that," I reply and look towards Kor and Dagan.

Can you help sort out the army into rooms and anything they need? I ask through our bond.

"Of course," they both reply, before going over and introducing themselves to Winter's mates as Winter and I walk away. Most of my people bow, looking a little confused at the new army, but they all walk over as we pass them. It's about time Dragca's people find out we aren't alone nor the only supernaturals in the worlds.

"This is Dragca Academy, though it isn't in use at the moment. We used to use it as a school for most dragons as they came into their powers," I explain to Winter as she looks up at what is left of Dragca Academy. It's broken in places, but the main part of the castle is intact.

"You know, that is what I want in our home. It is also a castle, very similar to this one, with a protection ward. I want it to be a place all of our kind can send their children to learn to control their gifts. Maybe when this war is over and we have peace, we could work together to set up a Supernatural Academy. One that mixes all of our people. What do you think?" she asks, and as I look at her, I can see our future. All our people travelling freely between Dragca and Earth. Our children growing up together, being friends as they eventually take our thrones.

"It sounds like a future worth fighting for, Winter," I eventually reply, and I can see she is thinking the same thing I am before we both look back at the castle as we get closer.

"It does, doesn't it?" she says.

"How is Jonas?" I ask her, wanting to know about the boy I think of every so often. I feel like I owe the memory of Jace a debt, and I will look after his brother no matter what.

"Happily running around the castle. He and the other dragons have been helping us rebuild some damaged houses," she tells me, and I smile in relief. "My best friend Alex has adopted one of the dragon boy babies we found. She asked me to ask you if it was alright if she looked after him permanently with her mate, Drake."

"Of course. Though when he is older, he might need some dragon training here," I suggest. "I'm glad to know one of the babies has found a family."

"Yes, me too. If anyone can handle a dragon son, it's Alex. She knows he will need to return to his home one day, but she and Drake felt an instant bond with him," Winter explains to me. "He is the cutest baby though. All that white hair that is like snow, and deep ruby red eyes."

"Then he has found a home. I was brought up on Earth and lived happily there," I explain to her so she knows dragons can live on Earth with no problem.

"I didn't know what I was for many years. I grew up with a human mother, went to human schools until I found my stepson hurt in a car park, and my story began," she tells me, which I didn't expect to hear.

"Maybe more than fate links us, perhaps our upbringing is something that links us also. Just think, we are both queens who grew up in normal schools just like any human," I say, with a chuckle as she smiles in agreement. We get to the stairs, and Essna comes down the steps with my uncle at her side. They both bow before lifting their heads.

"I believe we might finally have a chance now that your friend is here. We welcome the Earth queen to Dragca Academy and wish your first time here were under better circumstances," Essna formally says.

"This is Essna, leader of the seers, and my uncle, Louis," I introduce them to Winter. They all shake hands and exchange small nods.

"My mate, Dabriel, is very interested in learning more about seers. He believes they are very connected with their similar gifts somehow. Though he believes we are all children of fates and tied to each other in some ways we will never understand," Winter says.

"I believe a chat with your mate would be very interesting for me as well. We are children of the ancient fates. It is said they breathed life into Dragca, creating both dragons and seers, though no one sees the fates anymore to find out the truth," Essna says, and I share a little look with Winter, both of us have a tiny smile on our lips.

"Essna, we should go and introduce our people," Louis says, gently touching her arm before dropping his hand like she burnt him or something. Her cheeks are a little red as she nods, and they both bow to us before walking away.

"Is it me, or is there some sexual tension there?" Winter whispers as we carry on walking up the steps.

"It's not just you, but my uncle is complicated and lost. I'm sure if anyone could find him, it would be a seer like Essna," I quietly say as we step through the doors, and I see Bee flying through the air towards me with a big smile.

"Oh no, Bee. Where the hell have you been?" I demand, and she pauses with a guilty look.

"I had to fix," she says, and as much I suspect she was finding the dust to fix Elias, I still could have lost her.

"Fix what? Why couldn't you tell me you were going to leave? Let me help you? You have no idea how worried I have been about you! Don't you ever run off in a war again without talking to me, Bee," I say, telling her off, and she nods, flying a little closer and resting her head on my shoulder as I rub her back, holding her close.

"I'm sorry. I had to fix," she mumbles, and I sigh, wiping away a tear as Winter looks at us both, tugging on her rucksack on her back.

"I'm sorry I shouted. I love you, Bee. I can't lose you. Ever," I whisper to her. I was only mad because the idea of anything happening to Bee makes me want to tear the world apart.

"We are one. No lose, but must save Nane. She sister," she whispers into my ear, and I look at her eyes.

"I know, I just don't know how to save her. Yet."

121

ISOLA

"**W**hat the bloody hell is that?" Eli asks, and I turn to look down the corridor just as a blue blur of a creature slams straight into my chest, knocking me to the ground. I cough, lifting the blue creature that looks like a mini troll with strange clothing on into the air.

"MILO!" Winter shouts down the corridor as the small creature—who I assume is called Milo—grins at me before flying out of my hands into the air and making a quick exit in the opposite direction of Winter's room where I just left her. Eli and I were going to find Melody and Hallie to see why they are actually here. Bee went to make a tree in my room to sleep in tonight. I know I need to send Melody home as soon as possible, so I left Bee to it. Melody said coming back to Dragca before the war was over could kill her, and I won't lose my sister for anything in the entire world. Winter, seeming flustered, comes running out the room, looking around before getting to Eli and me.

"Did you see a little blue demon anywhere around?" she asks, and I point down the corridor.

"Wait, did you say demon?" I ask with wide eyes. *Demons are real?*

"Yes, a silly little demon who snuck into my bag when I told him not to come here. I swear, he is worse than Freddy and Josh about following goddamn rules," Winter mutters, not that I have clue who they are, before she storms off down the corridor. I don't want to be Milo when she finds him. Eli pulls me close to his side as I whisper to him.

"Demons, angels and god knows what else we have in the Dragca Academy. I literally could never have predicted this for my future," I say, and he laughs.

"Even if they ride in here with flying unicorns, I don't care. Whatever help we can get to win the war is important," he gently tells me, making me chuckle before he kisses me.

"Hello, sis. I'm glad to see you fixed your last mate as war is coming swiftly," Melody's sweet voice comes to us as I break away from Eli and turn to see her and Hallie walking over. They both have long blue cloaks on and are covered in daggers and swords. Melody's orb is resting on a staff I've never seen before, it looks like it is made of literal gold. I run over to Melody, hugging her tightly as she holds me back before letting her go so I can hug Hallie.

"I'm glad to see you both," I say honestly, before stepping back and pulling my eyes to Melody, "though you said you couldn't come here because it would kill you."

"Futures change, and I need to be here," she tells me, though I sense she is lying to me a little as she doesn't keep eye contact.

"Promise me that I won't lose you and you're not lying to me because you know I will send you back, Melody?" I ask, taking her hands in mine, and she squeezes my hands tightly.

"I will do whatever it takes to save you and Dragca. Trust me, this is the only way," she replies, avoiding my question like seers do best. I will just have to keep Melody close to me. Or get help from my guys and lock her up somewhere safe when the war comes. Either option sounds safe...kinda.

"I won't lose you," I tell her, even if it feels like I lost her the moment she stepped into Dragca for me, and we both know it.

"I'll try not to die. Now, aren't congrats in order? You have a new mate," Melody says, quickly changing the subject, as I glance at Hallie who I can tell is upset, but she is silent.

"Yes, I do," I reply as Eli says hello to them both.

"I will go and help the others and leave you with your sister and Hallie for a bit," Eli suggests, his hand resting on the middle of my back.

"Are you sure you are going to be alright?" I ask Eli, stepping away from my sister before he turns away.

"I'm okay. I will come and see you later. Enjoy your time with your sister and friend," he says, and I kiss him lightly before he leaves. I feel like we haven't gotten much time together since he has become himself, and there is still so much I want to talk to him about, but I know it isn't the time.

"Come on, let's find you guys a room and some drinks," I say as Hallie and Melody step to either side of me, and I enjoy the time I have with them.

"Milo does what?" I ask between breathless laughs, not really being able to stop myself laughing with the others as I sit with Melody, Hallie and Winter in the library in front of a roaring fire. This woman, Leigha, is here too, though she doesn't speak much and never takes off the scary swords she carries around like purses. She is Winter's guard in a way and believes it's her personal job to make sure Winter is safe. So she is standing by the door and refuses to sit with us in case there is any danger. Which doesn't make any sense as Essna boosted Dabriel's gifts with a power exchange, and he saw that Tatarina will fly with her army here in two nights' time. These are our last two nights together before war comes, and I plan to spend it with my guys and my sister.

The guys are checking out the weapon rooms before going to get us food, so Winter has been telling us stories about her little demon friend. He is a good demon, a breed which usually just likes to cause chaos on Earth when they escape Hell. Milo is currently hanging out with Bee since they like each other as they share marshmallows they are toasting on sticks in the fireplace before eating them.

"Yeah, it was a sight I don't think I could forget," Winter says with a little shudder.

"Hopefully he doesn't teach Bee any tricks," I chuckle, leaning back in my seat and looking at my sister who is cuddling Hallie. They look so perfect together. So happy, lost in themselves.

"I'm sure he will, and I'm sorry in advance," Winter chuckles, before sipping on her hot chocolate. I glance behind my seat when I hear a creak of a floorboard and see the old librarian standing near a window. I remember speaking to her not long after coming to Dragca Academy, and if I remember right, she spoke about curses and seemed to know a lot about them. Maybe she might know about light and dark magic.

"I will be right back," I tell them, hearing them muttering okay as I get up and walk over to the librarian.

"Hey, do you remember me?" I ask her, as I can't remember her name off the top of my head. The librarian turns towards me and bows her head.

"Princess Isola, now Queen. My name is Windlow Pakdragca as I can see you have forgotten," she tells me, and I lean against the window, looking out at what she was staring at. Angels fly around the perimeter, dragons above them going in the opposite direction. Not long after, wolves in a small pack walk past. One man stands still at the edge of the forest, and there is one in every direction as their sense would alert us to any change.

"It is strange to see all these different supernaturals all working together to stop a world being destroyed, isn't it?" I ask her, looking back as she watches me closely.

"It is not so strange but humbling to see we are not alone. You are a true queen, much like your mother, though she made the ultimate sacrifice for her people," she says, and I run my eyes over her in confusion.

"What do you mean?" I ask her.

"She married a monster, willingly, because she knew you had to be born. You had to exist in such a dark world," she says, her voice tinged with sadness. "That was her cost, but then she was rewarded with you and knowing you will save the world she loved so dearly. Not just save but improve. The people will thrive with you as their queen."

"Did you know my mother? How could you possibly know this?" I ask her, but she pulls her eyes from me and towards the window.

"I comforted your mother at times. I was the royal librarian, and books were always a good escape in her eyes," she explains to me.

"The more I hear of my mother, the more I realise how alike we are. I only wish I had more time with her, found a way to save her," I admit.

"Don't we all wish we had more time with those we love?" she asks and crosses her arms. "Now, what did you want to speak to me about, my queen?"

"I wanted to know if you had any knowledge on light and dark magic? On their spirits possibly?" I ask, and she nods.

"I know you need to make sure Nane is bonded to you before Tatarina dies. If she dies first, Elias Fire will die with her before you can bond with Nane," she informs me, and my lips part, the only movement I feel like I can make.

"Wow, you know more than I expected," I say with wide eyes.

"I know Elias Fire is bound to Nane, the dark magic she possesses brought him back to life. Tatarina may have used the magic, but it does not belong to her. Much like your light magic doesn't belong to you either, it is borrowed from Bee, and you can use it. If you bond with Nane, then you will be able to save the boy," she says, and then starts coughing out smoke as old dragons sometimes do. I push away from the window to go help her, but she waves a hand. "Return to your family and friends, this time is for you and them."

"Thank you for your help. You will go and rest now, though, right?" I ask her, and she nods, still coughing smoke.

"My time is near, but not yet. You can repay me for my

knowledge one day by taking me to the royal libraries. I do miss the books that live there very much," she tells me.

"I promise," I say, before bowing my head in a respectful way before walking back to my friends and family. Just as I get closer, Melody sees me and sighs in a nervous way before standing up. She offers her hands to Hallie, who smiles at her before letting Melody help her stand up.

"Right, well, everyone is here that I wanted, and I'm more nervous than I thought was possible to ask now," Melody says as she lets go of Hallie's hands, and starts searching her cloak pockets. Hallie gives me a look as I rest against Winter's chair, and I shrug my shoulders. I have no clue what Melody is doing. My eyes widen as Melody drops to one knee, holding out a ring with a large blue gemstone in the middle that reflects the firelight. The ring is stunning, and I hold my hand over my mouth as I realise what is happening.

"Hallie, I have dreamed of you—literally—for years until I got lucky enough to meet you, and you turned out to be a million times better than any dream. I know for certain that you are my future, and I love you so much. So, will you mate with me? Marry me?" she asks, and I feel like we all hold our breath until Hallie nods and jumps into Melody's arms, kissing her as they fall to the floor. Winter and I clap and hug them both when they get up off the floor and get the ring on Hallie's hand.

"So, will you be my maid of honour and secretly attend our mating tonight? I only want a small ceremony with close family and friends," Hallie asks me, and I nod, hugging her tightly before pulling away.

"And mine too," Melody adds in, and I chuckle as I nod my head.

"Right, I'm going to find my dragons and get a ceremony sorted. Want to help, Winter?" I ask her, and she quickly gets up off her seat to follow me out of the room, neither of us can stop smiling the whole time.

123

I clip the final slide into Melody's hair before stepping back and looking at the lovely hair design I've managed to help do. The top half is up in a braid, leaving the rest falling down her shoulders. I've clipped in little white flower slides we found, and overall, she looks so pretty.

"All done," I say, and she stands up, the white dress we managed to find on short notice fitting her perfectly. It's one that is tight all the way down her body, showing off her figure, and strapless at the top.

"Thank you, sis," she says, and then suddenly hugs me tightly, and I hear her little sobs only a moment later as I hold her close.

"I know you think you are going to die, and that's why you want to mate tonight. So that if you die, Hallie will have a good memory," I whisper, understanding my sister more than I even want to. It's something I would do and want to do. I don't know if Eli wants that with me yet, but I can only hope he does.

"How do you know that?" she quietly asks.

"I know you, sis. That is the same thing. I see the fear in your eyes every time we discuss the war. Every time someone speaks Tatarina's name," I reply, my voice a whisper.

"The future can change...that is what I'm hoping for, at least," she explains to me.

"You will not die. I won't let it happen," I tell her firmly.

"If I do, you promise you will look after Hallie?" she asks, and I nod, though I can see she knows I would anyways.

"No more talk of death tonight. We worry about it tomorrow night when we know it will be coming to our doors," I tell her, and she smiles, wiping her cheeks.

"Okay. I know you are right," she agrees. This is a night for celebration, not a night to be scared of what will come either way.

"Come on then, let's go and get your bride," I say, holding my arm out. Melody slides her arm into mine before we walk to the door, and I pull it open before we go out. We walk down the corridor in silence before Melody stops suddenly, jolting me as I stop with her. "Cold feet?" I joke, and she shakes her head.

"I know telling you your future is risky and could make it worse, but I have to warn you. I feel like it is the right thing to do," she says, and I go to stop her saying anything when she starts speaking. "When Elias goes to kill Tatarina, you must duck as she shoots a bolt of ice at you, otherwise you will die." Her words seem to wrap around my throat until I nod, and we carry on walking to her wedding like nothing happened. I know it was a big risk for her to tell me this, but I know I don't have a choice now but to listen to what she just told me. Though Eli can't kill Tatarina until I get to Nane, that is too important.

We walk into the library where we have set up an altar and Windlow has agreed to perform the ceremony. There are rose petals sprinkled across the floor, and my mates with Eli are stood at the one side, and on the other are Winter and her mates. We are all dressed up for the wedding. Luckily, Winter fit into a beautiful blue dress we found, and I am wearing the red dress I once wore to a mating ceremony when I first came to Dragca. I stop at the end, kissing my sister's cheek before letting her go, then I stand next to Eli, who wraps an arm around my waist. All my mates and Eli look amazing tonight, all dressed up in suits that complement them.

I watch my sister and Hallie repeat the sacred words while Windlow holds their mating stone which Hallie found earlier today outside her room. The stone glows a bright white as they cut their hands, and we all cheer as they kiss, completing their mating. I wipe a few tears away as I hug my sister and then Hallie before letting them go off as Eli holds me close.

"You look beautiful, kitty cat," Dagan says, using the nickname I haven't heard him call me in a long time as he takes my hands into his and kisses them. "You really do look amazing," he tells me.

"I'm afraid I need to steal your mates to carry on preparations for the war," Winter's mate, Wyatt, states as he steps over to us. Winter has left with her angel mate and the wolf, leaving us with Wyatt and Atticus.

"That's okay," I say, looking at Thorne, Dagan and Korbin who take turns kissing me before leaving with Wyatt and Atticus. Eli holds me close as they go before we walk quietly through the library.

"Do you remember when I first found you reading in here?" Eli asks, walking me down an aisle and to the sofa seat where he found me. We both sit down, and I cuddle up to his chest, playing with his buttons as I listen to his breathing.

"Yes. I remember you calling my book girly porn," I tease him, and he laughs.

"Well, it was," he replies. "Anyhow, I wanted to kiss you that night, but I knew I couldn't. It was the first time my dragon insisted you were his. He went on and on all night about you, and the moment he left my mind alone, I was still thinking about you."

"What you said to me that night about falling in love? You were right," I gently tell him, lifting my head to meet his gaze.

"I know, but you are much stronger than I ever thought you were. You will not lose anyone, Isola," he tells me, and I crawl up him as he leans back, his dark eyes watching my every movement.

"Kiss me, Eli," I say, and he smirks, sliding his hands up my back ever so slowly.

"No, you kiss me, naughty princess," he replies, and I grin before leaning down and kissing him. The moment our lips meet, we crush them together, and he pulls my hips down, rolling me against his hard length under me. I moan, knowing I don't want to wait as I rip Eli's shirt open, and then we are ripping each other's clothes off in the next moment. He never takes his eyes off me as he rips my dress off and kisses down my body as it falls to the floor. Eli lays me down on the sofa before easily sliding inside me, making my back arch from the pleasure and a moan escape my lips. He chuckles, placing his hand over my mouth and whispering in my ear as he thrusts in and out of me.

"Shh, now. You don't want anyone to hear us and interrupt," he whispers, and I bite down on his hand as he picks up speed. Each thrust sends me closer to the edge until I can do nothing but cry out as an orgasm slams into me, and Eli groans my name as he finishes a moment later. He holds me close as we stare at each other, and I place my hand on his cheek.

"I want to mate to you," I whisper.

"I know, princess, but I can't. Not until this war is over and I know you won't lose me. I can't do that to you, no matter how much I want to be selfish," he whispers, making my heart hurt, but I know deep down he is doing the right thing.

"Okay, but promise we will mate when the war is over?"

"Yes, because I love you and want nothing more," he says and kisses me as a tear escapes my eye, making me more determined than ever to win this war and save my Eli.

Black smoke spins around my legs as I open my eyes, the smoke drifting off in every direction in swirls that look like strange vortexes all around me. I know instantly that this is Tatarina getting in my dreams, using whatever connection she can to mess with me. I'm not overly surprised she would play this trick right before the war. It seems like something she would do.

"Are you going to come out rather than hiding like a little child?" I ask, looking around and waiting to see her, though something seems off about the dream in general. It doesn't feel as strong as the last one. Only a few moments later, a shadow of dark smoke, looking like Tatarina without any features, appears. "Are you not strong enough to really enter my dreams?" I ask her the question, but I know the answer anyway.

"Come to me. We can end this all without so many dragon deaths tomorrow," she purrs, and I have no idea why she is bothering to try and taunt me. Or scare me. Even if I came to her, she would send her army to kill mine. No, this is all a trick.

"No, not yet. Go and hide in the castle, all alone, until the war. I am done having you in my dreams," I shout, and the shadow runs at me, its arms in the air. I go to call my light when suddenly a blast of white light fills my vision, making me shut my eyes. When I open my eyes, I'm in a room filled with gold and jewels. I recognise this place as the cave where I mated with Thorne, where the strange woman who claimed to be a fate and Winter's aunt lived.

"Are you not going to say hello? Or can you not hear me? It has been a while since I pulled a dream, and I might not have gotten it quite right," the old woman muses from behind me, and I spin around, seeing her sitting on a chair, playing with some glittering gold string. She is knitting. How...well, weird.

"Hi, I can see and hear you. I'm just a little confused on the how you are in my dreams and why..." I reply to her, and she looks up at me, still knitting the gold string, though she doesn't have to look down at it as she does. I stare at the string for a moment, feeling a strange pull towards it. Whatever it is, it isn't just string.

"Oh, never mind that. We fate have strange gifts. How are you?" she asks me.

"I have a feeling you didn't bring me here to ask how I am," I reply, "though if you must know, I am worried about war. Worried about a lot of things."

"Oh, I forget how impatient you all are. Right, right. I did not bring you here to ask how you are. Your emotions are clear to everyone," she tuts and sits back.

"Why then?" I ask, sliding my hand to the necklace I like to make myself forget I wear. It is clipped around my neck, the stone a constant reminder of the price my firstborn will pay.

"I wanted to put your mind at ease. I sense you are very troubled about bringing your daughter to me," she says. It's strange to talk about a child that doesn't even exist yet—and may never. Though this fate seems certain she will come into my life at some point, which fills me with a false sense of hope that we might win this war.

"Wouldn't anyone be worried? I don't know you or what you want," I reply, watching the old lady carefully. I can't see any similarities with Winter besides the blue eyes, though they might have shared the same hair colour once, who knows? This woman is too wrinkled, her long hair grey, but she still has this beauty about her that Winter carries. There is just something about them.

"I asked for your daughter to come to learn her powers under my guidance. It is important, as she is to become a new fate. She will be the second child ever to inherit such a power since the old times, the other is yet to return to her lands to claim her powers. Your daughter's power is a gift from the magic of Dragca itself and must be looked after," she explains to me. "Much like a child from Frayan has been given a gift, and a child of the Earth queen will have one too. Power is given to those who can command it and bring about peace."

"That's all you want her for? To train her with this power?" I ask her, and she nods. I avoid the bit about other children getting powers. I will remember to tell Winter about that later though.

"Yes. Then she will return home, unite the lands with that boy..." she stops with a laugh that I don't get. "Oh, wait. I should not say that. It is what humans call a spoiler alert when someone speaks too soon and ruins the book or movie. Never mind, you will see one day." I shake my head at her, wishing she told me whatever she seems to know.

"Thank you for telling me this, it does help," I admit to her. "And thank you for ending my dream with Tatarina."

"The lost queen will not visit your dreams anymore, she does not have the power to do so. You must wake now. Until we see each other again, Queen Isola..." I gasp as the floor below me disappears, and I fall into darkness before I can even say goodbye.

I sit up as I wake, feeling strangely awake and alert like I've drunk a million energy drinks or something as I calm my breathing down, remembering the two dreams. I rub the necklace on my neck, knowing that I have nothing to fear for my child's future. She will be powerful. Though first off, we need to win this war before even thinking about children. I look down at my skin, seeing it glowing a little before it fades, and I rest back against my pillows, feeling restless. There is no doubt the fate sent me back with a little power boost of some sort.

I glance over at Eli, who is sleeping with Bee next to him on his pillow. They look cute together, and I don't want to wake either of them when I see the time on my clock. It's four in the morning, and I know I should still be sleeping. War is coming tonight, and there won't be any more dreams until it is over. The fate was right about that. I have an idea what I can do with my spare energy though.

I quietly slide out of the bed and pull on my clothes before brushing my hair in the bathroom and freshening up. I silently leave my room and walk down the corridors, respectfully nodding at the random person walking around, who I bump into here and there. The corridors feel cold, like there is a chill in the air that mixes in with the tension every person here is feeling. I hope they are spending these last hours with those who they love, saying goodbye just in case. Something I know I need to do.

I find the room I'm looking for and try to open the door, seeing that it is locked no matter what way I turn it. I jiggle the handle a few times before stepping back and looking around. I'm sure no one will care if I break the door handle to get in, and there is no one around anyways. I close my hand around the handle, calling my ice and freezing it until it cracks. I step back and kick the door, and it flies open, revealing the room that looks nothing like I remember it. The once beautiful flower- and plant-filled classroom is all dead now; nothing at all looks alive in it. I guess no one could look after it after the teachers were killed. I suspected as much, but it's still sad to see the room that was so alive now so dead.

I walk in the room and up to the tree, the only thing that doesn't look as bad as everything else in the room. I place my hand on the bark, which is cold to touch, before I close my eyes, blocking out the rotting smell that fills my nose. It reminds me how little life there is left in here, and I want to fix that. I call my light, sensing Bee sleeping upstairs as I do, and seconds later, I feel the light leaving me in waves. The light warms my hand up until it feels like it is burning, and I let go of the bark, opening my eyes to see the now healthy tree I'm standing under. Every branch is filled with bright green leaves that have purple veins on them. The tree feels happy, if that it is even possible.

I look down at my shoes, seeing the soft looking grass under them and sighing. This is why I love light magic. I reach up and pick a pod off the tree, opening it up to find the sweet I know is inside from my old lessons here. It feels like honouring the memory of my teacher and of Dragca Academy by fixing this room. I crunch the sweet in my mouth, enjoying the blast of sweetness as I walk out of the branches. I stop in the middle of the room which is now full of bright, dazzling flowers that make my heart a little happier than it already was. Nature can be the most beautiful thing in the world sometimes, and I fixed this all.

I walk around, touching and smelling some of the flowers before leaving the room and deciding it might be a good idea to have a run outside to burn off more energy. I know it's dark out, but the darkness isn't that bad when there are guards all around the area. I walk to the main doors, pausing when I see Kor and his mother hugging outside the doors. His mother has a letter in her hand as she cries, and I feel Kor's pain through our bond now that I'm closer. I want to know what has happened, but I also don't want to interrupt their moment.

"Isola," Kor says, letting his mum go as he clearly senses me. I know I can't walk away and leave them to it now, so I go over, taking his hand in mine as I look at Janiya who wipes her eyes.

"Darth is dead. We suspected as much, but this letter came back today from some survivors. We sent out two dragons to look for anyone that needed help, and they found a big group of all women and children who claim Darth saved them," Janiya explains, and I reach out, taking her hand.

"I will never forget Darth and how he saved Kor's life. He saved us all, and that is something I can never repay. I am so sorry your father has passed on," I say, feeling overwhelming sadness that such a brilliant man is now gone. Kor kisses the side of my head, wrapping an arm around me as his father comes over and takes his mother away.

"I'm sorry he is gone, Kor," I say, pressing my head into the side of his arm.

"Me too. I suspect he won't be the only one we say goodbye to before all of this is over." His words stay with me as we hold each other, each of us hoping he is wrong.

125

I slowly watch as the two suns rise over the tree line as I sit on the roof of the academy, soaking in the peace of the moment. The suns cast yellow, orange and pink streaks across the sky like a vivid painting. The beauty, so lovely for a day that will bring so much death. It just reminds me that the suns will always rise, no matter how bad the night was. It's something you can always count on. The sunrises are the most peaceful and beautiful thing in every world. I should be training or learning something, but I know unless I calm myself down, I won't be able to focus on what is needed to win this war.

"Hey, kitty cat. You sure pick an easy place to hide," Dagan mutters from behind me, and I turn to see him climbing up the roof with Eli, Thorne and Kor next to him. They all have dragon leather on, making them look even more handsome, and their cloaks fly around in the wind as they climb up.

Must make sure mine survive the war, my dragon protectively purrs into my mind, and I agree with her in every sense as I stare at my dragons.

I will do everything I can to make sure they live. We will do everything we can, I explain to her.

We are strong, she tells me.

Together, yes, we are, I tell my dragon as my guys get to me, feeling a strange sense of proudness from her. They all come and sit down next to me, Eli and Thorne sitting on my sides, whereas Dagan sits by Thorne and Kor sits next to Eli. I rest my head on Thorne's shoulder as he takes my hand in his, linking our fingers. We all happily watch the suns rise together, knowing this very well could be the last moment we all get alone together.

"Whatever happens today, I need you to know I love all of you with every little bit of my heart," I say, my voice catching in my throat as it feels like a ball of sadness is stuck there. I've never even admitted there might be a slight chance we won't make it out of this, and now I need to face that fact. An army of dead dragon guards is coming for us, and it will not be easy to escape this with all of us alive.

"We know, doll," Kor replies, and I look over at him. "Like I'm sure you know how much we adore you."

"I suspect you like me a little bit," I tease, making them all chuckle. "What do you imagine for us when this is all over?" I ask, wanting to know what they think. I've always imagined we will do up the castle and make it more homey for us before moving in. When this is over, I plan to send whatever is left of my dragon guard to the villages to help them rebuild their lives rather than protect me. Dragon guard is no more, so only those who want to be guards can be. There are no more curses on Dragca, and I want to be a queen my people choose to follow. The most important things are making sure my people are safe, have homes, and have food in their stomachs. I will spend the first month travelling around Dragca myself with my guys and healing the land with Bee. I want to see Dragca and really understand my world like I've never gotten a chance to do before.

"I don't know about the others, but I imagine ruling at your side as your equal, helping you set up a council for each village and place rules that benefit our people as well as keep them safe. I also want to wake up with you every morning and get you breakfast," Thorne says, and I agree with the first part completely, whereas the second bit makes me laugh.

"Before your run with me and a fly with our dragons to stretch their wings," Kor adds in, and I scrunch my face at him. I thought we dropped that running every morning thing.

"Then we could train together before we have dinner, and I want to help train a new army of dragon guards. Dragons who are not forced to fight but want to have the honour of protecting the royal family. We could make a future that every dragon in Dragca wants to be part of," Dagan carries on, and Eli finishes the idea.

"I believe in setting your sister up as the royal seer and making a law that recognises seers as people equal to dragons. They shouldn't be living in the woods when this is all over. I also think there should be classes in Dragca Academy, teaching young dragons and seers about light and dark magic. It shouldn't be hunted like it always has been." I nod at Elias's ideas and try not to cry at how he has clearly thought all this out for our future. "Before we sit around a fire every night, with you reading a new book and us watching those Earth movies we like."

"Will there be hot chocolate added into this plan?" I tease, wanting to know the important stuff.

"Of course, doll," Kor replies with a little chuckle.

"Do you think we will win tonight?" I quietly ask them, wanting to know what they think.

"I know that no matter what happens, we will always be with each other," Eli says, his words seem to drift in the wind, all of us not wanting to say a word. It's a long time before Dagan stands up, stretching his arms out.

"We should fly for a bit, all of us together. It will let our dragons have that time together," Dagan suggests, and I smile as I let him help me up. I walk to the edge of the roof and look over my shoulder at my dragons as they walk to me.

"Let's fly!" I shout over the wind before jumping off the roof, letting my dragon take over to fly with her mates.

126

ISOLA

Turn *right,* Thorne directs in my mind, and I swing around with my spear, hitting the moving wooden target straight in the middle of its chest. I pull my spear out and quickly swing back and hit the one I sense a little to my left, right in the middle again. The targets all move around me until Thorne switches them off, and they stay still. This turned out to be the perfect distraction when I needed it more than I knew. I've been running around the academy, trying to help however I can and finding that almost everything has been take care of or attended to. Dagan and Thorne suggested we continue our training. Dagan and Thorne suggested some training might help.

"You've gotten better," Dagan states, smiling at me as I get my breath back in the cold room that smells like sweat and blood. Dagan only has on a thin white shirt with leather trousers, and it makes him look like a sexy pirate. I glance at Thorne as he comes over, putting his bow down along with his arrows after pulling them out of his own targets. Thorne has a cloak on that hides his leather clothes. There is no one but Thorne, Dagan and me in here as not many people are using the guards' training rooms today since they are getting ready at the border for tonight. Even the thought that war is coming in only a few hours scares me more than I like.

"Here," Thorne offers me a bottle of water just as the doors open, and Winter walks in with her angel mate at her side. They are both dressed in leather, kitted out with deadly looking weapons, and seem serious, which worries me. We all walk over, as I smile at Winter.

"Have you come to train with me?" I ask her, curious about why she would clearly search for me. The last I checked, Winter was helping stock the basement where we are hiding all the people who cannot fight. She was also wrestling that little demon of hers down there as Milo wants to fight. I don't know how a tiny demon is going to fight a dragon, but I imagine it would be a sight to see.

"No, I wanted to talk to you about something important that I don't know how to ask," she says, looking nervous.

"Oh?" I ask, crossing my arms and wondering what she could want to speak to me about.

"Why don't you all leave Dragca and come back to Earth? We will destroy the portals, and no one could ever get through again. Tatarina will eventually die, and then maybe one day, someone could go back," she suggests—an idea I've thought more than once about. I love that she has asked, that she is trying to protect me. It just can't happen. There are a million reasons why not, like the fact Bee would struggle to live on Earth, but Dragca is my home. And there is one pressing issue I would never risk. It is a future I will fight for and never run away from.

"It would be best for your people. We can easily find some-where safe for you to live," Dabriel kindly says, folding his arms as he and Winter wait for my reply.

"I can't," I reply, shaking my head.

"Why? This is dangerous here, and we might not win," Winter asks. "Coming to Earth might be running, but it would be safe for us all. I want what is best, but I fought for Earth and my people, so I will understand if you want to stay and fight."

"It's not just about my people, it's so much more than that. If I have a child in the future, I promised to bring her here. To your aunt, a fate. This necklace is my promise, so my child would pay the price of me running away. I won't run, though I do thank you for your offer. I know you are just trying to find a way to make sure I live through this," I explain to her, reaching out and taking her hand in mine before squeezing it tightly. She sighs with a sad look.

"It was worth a shot," she says, glancing at Dabriel. "We will leave you now to get our people ready. We can win this, because I am not losing my new friend."

"I hope so, because I want us to be friends for a long time," I say, and she hugs me tightly before walking off, Dabriel's arm wrapped around her shoulders. Dagan and Thorne watch her go for a while before either of them says anything.

"Come on, I want to show you something," Dagan says, reaching for my hand and linking our fingers. Thorne nods his head as I look back at him and let Dagan lead us out of the training room and down through two doors that look like they lead to a basement. Dagan switches a light on, illuminating a tunnel, as Thorne shuts the doors behind us.

"This is a good idea for a mini break," Thorne tells Dagan.

"I'm the smart one, you see," Dagan cheekily replies, and I laugh as I rest my head on his shoulder as he walks us down the corridor. The corridor opens up into a large room which has steam rising from the floor, making the room foggy. There are wooden benches all around for seating and even some towels folded by the entrance on a cabinet.

"It's the steam rooms, or sauna, as humans call it. After intense training, it is a good place to come and chill out," Dagan says, stepping back from me, and he starts pulling his clothes off. I glance back to see Thorne pushing his trousers down, and I admire the sight of my mates for a moment before I follow their lead. I used to get nervous undressing in front of anyone, but with them, my mates, it just seems natural. I'm surprised they are so okay with being naked near each other though. I finish pulling my clothes off before going to sit down on the wooden seat, and I feel Thorne and Dagan sit on either side of me.

"Do you want children when you're older then?" Dagan suddenly asks, no doubt thinking about it from what I said to Winter.

"Yes. I want a child I can give a good life to. What about you two?" I ask both Dagan and Thorne, looking between them.

"I never thought about a future, a life with children or any of that, until I met you, Isola. You know I didn't have a good upbringing with my mother. I have no idea who my father is...I soon realised that the one thing I missed the most was being loved by my mother when she was gone. She didn't have money, neither could she really look after us, but she kept us fed and happy. I miss her laugh when I think of her. She had the sweetest laugh. I want my child to be loved, unconditionally. I predict we all can have that future, together," Dagan says, making my heart feel happy as I look at him for a moment. I never knew how he felt about children, but there is one thing for sure, any child of mine will have one mother and four dads to keep an eye on them. Love will be one thing that will never be missing.

Thorne adds, "I feel the same. I want a future with you and dozens of children running around, driving us crazy," and we laugh as he links his fingers with mine, pulling them up and kissing the back.

"Dozens?" I chuckle. "I was thinking more like one or two."

"Yeah, one or two is enough. We will never get time alone with Issy if we have more," Dagan says, laughing with Thorne as I rest my head on his shoulder. We all sit with each other for a long time, just content in being with each other and relaxing. I love this moment with them, my mates, but everything outside of here is going wrong, nothing is promised to us, and it makes me just want to be close as possible to those I love before tonight. I move my hand to Dagan's thigh and slowly slide my hand up, finding his length hard and waiting for me.

"Kitty cat, you really do have a naughty streak," he groans as I reach my other hand for Thorne, wrapping my hand around him at the same time. I stroke them both, enjoying the way they buck their hips, and Thorne's hand goes to the back of my head, turning me to kiss him. Dagan moves my hand off him to kneel behind me, turning me on my side. His hand goes straight to my core, easily slipping one finger inside of me. I moan into Thorne's mouth as he gently grabs one of my breasts and starts rubbing my nipple. Dagan kisses my back as his finger thrusts in and out of me, my moans swallowed up by Thorne's mouth.

I move my lips away from Thorne's lips and kiss down his body until I find his length and take it deep in my mouth. Dagan mutters something I can't hear as he pulls his finger out and spreads my legs as he kneels behind me before sliding deep inside me. I cry out in pleasure around Thorne's length as he thrusts in and out of my mouth, his hand still teasing my nipple as his other hand is in my hair. The room is full of only the sounds of my moans and their grunts as we all chase our finish. Dagan reaches around and rolls his thumb in a circle around my clit, as he thrusts in and out of me. Only seconds later, I come, feeling Dagan coming deep inside me a few thrusts later, and Thorne pulls me off him, sliding me onto his hips and thrusting deep. I lock eyes with his silver ones as his dragon roars while I roll my hips, and he groans, finishing with a loud roar that shakes the room. I collapse onto his chest, breathless and completely satiated as I glance at Dagan who is catching his breath with a grin on his lips.

"This is the perfect way to prepare for war," he says, and I laugh, holding Thorne closer as I know this could be the last moments we all have together.

ISOLA

T he wind whips my braid and cloak to the side as I
stand at the edge of the forest with my dragons at my
side, watching the tree line for any movement. My
heart pounds in my chest as I smell the fire and scent of death in
the wind. Whatever is coming our way is not going to be easy to
beat. I only have to find Nane and Tatarina though—and pray my
army with Winter's can beat whoever Tatarina is sending our
way. Winter stands close with her mates, all of us just in the
boundary of Dragca Academy as we wait for the army that is
heading our way. I want to be here for when Tatarina gets to me
as I have no clue how she plans to break the ancient spell that
prevents anyone meaning ill harm to the academy from being on
the land. Bee places her hand on my cheek, and I give her a
worried glance.

"You should be back in the castle where it is safe," I whisper
to her, and she shakes her head, moving her green hair around. I
glance at my mates, catching each of their eyes and feeling their
worry in our bond. They are worried about me, and as I turn my
head to Eli, I know he is feeling the same. I want to tell them it
is all going to be alright, but that would be a lie, and I know it.

"No. End is here, and I am with you. You are balance," she

whispers to me just as I sense something coming our way, and I have to give up my argument with Bee. I press my stone on my staff, and it slides out in my hand as everyone gets their weapons out at the same time. I watch the trees as a single dragon guard walks out, his feet dragging across the ground with every step. His skin is grey, though his eyes are black with black lines crawling down his face that almost seem to move. He stops a few inches away from us. In a seriously creepy way, he tilts his head to the side; his movements seem like a puppet, and we all know who is pulling the strings.

"I h-have a message from the true qu-queen," he grumbles out, his words about understandable to me. "The army will fight here, but she waits for Isola in the castle. Come to her, and the war can be stopped. The war ends in the castle, not in the academy." After his actually well spoken words, he holds a shaky arm up in the air, and dozens of dragon guards run at us as he stands still. I look up as countless dragons with dry black skin slam into the barrier at the same time the soldiers do. It burns them, but the more they push, the more the invisible barrier gets closer to us.

"It can't hold them, we need to get ready," Dagan states, lowering his swords and stepping back, his eyes drifting across the soldiers blasting the barrier, causing little cracks. The dragons above start blasting fire against it, and I know that the moment it breaks, it's going to be hell. There are so many of them here, surrounding us almost. I glance back at our army, seeing how so many of their faces look scared.

"Shift with me, and we will fight in the sky for our queen! For Dragca!" Dagan shouts, and there are loud war cries as people shout for Dragca before shifting, their dragons letting out loud roars as they fly up in the sky. Winter and her mates start barking orders to their men, many of them shifting into wolves, and angels start flying into the sky underneath where the dragons fly around. Dagan comes to me and harshly kisses me, making my lips prickle, before stepping back, and I don't want to let him go. I know he needs to go though. Our people need him more than I do right now. Dagan isn't my dragon guard anymore, he is now guarding all of our people like my other mates. Like Eli.

"You don't go to her, you hear me? She wants you dead," Dagan firmly warns me, but I don't reply before he steps back and starts running. He shifts quickly, turning into his huge dragon and taking to the sky as I look back at Thorne, Kor and Eli at my sides. Melody and Hallie step closer, as do Winter and the giant wolf at her side. Her other mates are with their army, getting them ready.

"Any moment now," I warn, holding my staff up and locking eyes with Thorne.

"We do this, and then we get my mother. It has to be done," Thorne says, and I see the pain in his eyes he tries to hide from me. I feel it through our bond. He knows she has to die today, but she is still his mother. I don't want him there when I do this. It would hurt him even more to see her die.

"I know," I reply, moving my eyes back to the line of soldiers just as there is a bright white light and a whoosh of air hits me directly in the stomach as the barrier breaks, sending me flying backwards into my army behind me. I try to roll as I land, managing to only stop myself after a few spins. I cough and pull myself up to my feet, seeing that we have all been thrown in different directions. I pick Bee up off the floor, seeing a lump on her head where she was hurt from the blast. Thankfully, I can feel her heartbeat under my hand.

I hear footsteps behind me and turn, holding a hand out and blasting shards of ice at the three dead dragon guards that were running for me. They fall to the floor, smashing into black and red dust. I frantically look around as I stand up, not seeing anyone I recognise, but I can sense my mates are alive and some- where near. I look up as Dagan and my army of dragons fight Tatarina's dead army. The fight is all claws, blood, fire and pain as they rip each other apart, moving so quickly that I can't see who is winning.

"Give her to me," Winter suggests, getting to my side just as two of the dead dragon guard get to us. I hand Bee over and quickly hold my hands out, freezing the two guards dead on the spot and kicking them over as they smash into dust before looking back. Winter has a little bag on her back which she tucks Bee into before nodding at me.

"Time to fight," she says, unclipping a dagger, and I turn to look around for my dragons, not seeing them anywhere. I do see a bunch of at least twenty dragon guards attacking my people, and I decide to help them. I lift my spear up and pull back, waiting for the perfect moment as I run and fling it into two of the guards. They scream, burning up where the spear touches them as I slam three shards of ice into more guards.

I watch in amazement as I run, seeing Winter shooting beams of blue energy into more guards, and they turn into dust. She also somehow throws daggers at them as she runs with me. *Damn, she is cool.* When I get to the burnt guards, I pick up my spear and slam it into a dragon guard bent over a woman who is screaming. He explodes into red dust, covering all of me as I cough and kneel down to see the woman, who is in a bad way. I wipe my eyes to see her better, her long red hair mixes in with the blood pouring out from a hole in her neck. She coughs out blood as I hold her hand, knowing she won't have long now before death takes her.

"My queen," she splutters, grabbing my hand tightly.

"I'm here. I'm sorry," I whisper, trying to stay strong for her in her last moments even though I wish I could have saved her, but her body is covered in stab wounds, and I feel powerless in this moment.

"Finish the war," she pleads before her head rolls to the side, and I realise I don't even know the name of the dragon who just died for me. I close her eyes with my fingers, leaving trails of red dust over them before I stand up. I look around at the war around me, seeing nothing but pain, blood and death in every direction. There is so much darkness, so much destruction, and Tatarina caused it all. *She must pay.*

I spot Hallie and Melody across the field just as Winter kills two more dragon guards near me then comes to my side. She looks down at the woman's body sadly before pulling her eyes to me, waiting for a plan.

"This way," I say, knowing I need to get to my sister first and then my mates. We run across the field, and I shoot shards of ice at anyone that gets close. We head for my sister and Hallie who are fighting off at least eight dragon guards on their own, jumping over dead bodies and piles of dust on the ground that I know will be stuck in my memory for a long time. One of the dragon guards gets too close and hits Melody on the head, knocking her to the ground before he lifts his sword for the final blow.

"NO!" I scream, running as fast as I can, knowing I am too far away to stop this. Hallie quickly jumps in front of Melody as the sword comes down, and I scream.

Winter and I blast blue energy and ice at the remaining dead guards as we get to my sister and Hallie on the floor. Melody is holding Hallie in her arms, crying as she rocks her and strokes her face. There is so much blood on all of them. I fall next to her, touching Melody's shoulder as I look down at the massive sword cut all across Hallie's chest. She is crying out in pain but alive at least. A sob escapes my lips as my shaky hand touches her cheek.

"Can you call Dabriel? Can he heal her?" I turn to ask Winter, and she nods, wiping a tear away as she mentally calls her mate. The giant wolf gets to her side, along with Atticus and a bunch of my dragons who circle us, protecting us against the dead guards for a moment.

"I love you. You can't die, this can't happen. It was meant to be me," Melody pleads through her tears as I take Hallie's cold hand into mine and squeeze it tight as she cries. Hallie opens her eyes, staring at Melody and no doubt talking to her in her mind. I look around, hearing more screams, seeing fire blast across the sky as another dragon falls out of the clouds. There is so much pain, and if I don't stop Tatarina, it won't stop.

"I have to go. I have to finish this," I tell them both, and Melody shakes her head, grabbing my wrist as I try to stand.

"No, I have to come with you or—" she starts off as I take her hand off me.

"You've warned me. Stay with your mate, I have to do this," I shakily say. I stand up and step back before looking up at the dozens of dragons fighting in the sky above me. It's going to be difficult to fly out of here, but if anybody can do it, my dragon and I can.

"Winter, please give me Bee," I walk over and ask her. She nods, pulling me to the side a little as more of my army protect us, fighting for us. I know Melody and Hallie will be safe.

"Dabriel is far away. He is trying to get here, but it might not be quick enough to save her," she warns me, offering me the bag off her shoulder. I grab the strap tightly as I take one more look at my best friend and sister, wishing that I could help them in some way. I can't save Hallie and go after Tatarina though.

"Protect them for me as I have to go to stop this war," I manage to say. Winter agrees as I grab my spear and walk back a little before shifting into my dragon form. I knock a few dead dragon guards out of the way as I fly into the air, holding Bee in the bag in my claws. My dragon flies low towards the trees, just as I hear my mates argue with me in my mind, wanting me to come back.

Isola, don't you dare go alone. Wait for us, they plead as I spot two familiar looking dragons flying over to me, closely following me. It's Eli and my uncle, I think. I know Eli won't go back now, and I can't make him, but I didn't want him there when I faced Tatarina. *Dammit.*

I need Nane, but I love each one of you. Always, I reply and block them out before they can say another word as they need to focus on the fight as well. Eli and my uncle get to my side, flying close as the dragon guards simply let us go. She wants me to come to her. I roar as I speed up to the castle, flying as quickly as I can past the dead trees surrounding it.

There is danger. We should leave, my dragon hisses to me, and I sense her fear.

If we leave, there will be nothing but danger and death that will never stop following us. We can do this together, I tell her, and she lets out a loud, confident roar that helps me feel a little better as we get to the castle. It looks worse than the last time we were here, more dead plants climb the walls, and yet there is nobody around this time as we all land after I carefully put Bee down in the bag. I shift back and quickly pull my spear out as Eli and my uncle shift back as well. Bee climbs out the bag, seeming a little paler green than I'm used to seeing her looking, but she is okay.

"Nane is near," Bee tells me, her wide eyes glancing towards the door.

"I know. We are going to save her," I say, patting my shoulder, and she lands on it as my uncle and Eli come to me.

"You shouldn't be here. Tatarina could get control of you again," I hiss at Eli, who just looks at me with a stubborn face.

"She can't control me anymore. I won't leave you alone, so forget it. Now what is the plan?" Eli asks, dismissing my worry. I grit my teeth in frustration, knowing I won't be able to convince him to just leave me here. *It won't matter if I can get Nane.*

"I need to get Nane alone, just for a bit. Can you distract Tatarina?" I ask them, and my uncle nods, rubbing his beard.

"We can, but you won't have long. They will be together, and she is expecting you," he warns me, picking up a sword off the ground he must have carried here. Eli has one too.

"I know it isn't going to be easy, but she can't die until I've bonded with Nane," I warn them. "Understood?" They both nod in agreement, but I have a feeling they won't listen if they get a chance to kill her. I walk forward, keeping my spear ready at my side as we go through the main doors to the castle which have been left open. The inside is a ruin of cracked stone, dead plants and blood on the floor. The wallpaper is ripped, the old paintings lie in ruins on the floor. The beauty of my old home is gone, left in a mess of what remains. I walk across the cold stone to the throne room, knowing this is where it will all end. It's what this war is all about after all.

Tatarina sits on the throne, her eyes drifting to me in an almost unnatural way as she suddenly smiles when I stop in the middle of the room. Tatarina looks worse than ever before, more touched by a darkness she could never control. Her once blonde hair is black, looking dry and horrible as it hangs stiffly around her shoulders. Her eyes are black like the lines crawling down her pale cheeks. She is emaciated, her blue dress barely held up on her body. Nane sits on her hand, though she only looks at Bee and not anyone else.

"Oh Tatarina, what has dark magic done to you?" I question, tilting my head to really look at her and how much she is a sorry state of herself.

"Nothing that doesn't make me better than I already am," she purrs, her voice deep and cracking like a witch.

"This is not better. *You are wrong.* And Nane was never meant to be yours, she was meant to be mine," I say, and Nane lifts her head at the sound of her name.

"NO! You will not steal my power and my throne after you have already stolen my son!" Tatarina spits out, standing up as Nane flies near her, her eyes focused on Bee once again. I don't dare look at Bee as I want to make sure Tatarina stays in my sight.

"Have you even seen what you look like these days?" my uncle asks, stepping closer. "Isola didn't steal Thorne from you; you gave him up to get your dream. Is it all worth it? Are you truly happy as you sit alone in here?"

"You look like death, which you will be familiar with soon enough," she says, though from her tone alone, I can tell she is getting more annoyed as I step to the side, heading for Nane as my uncle raises his sword, walking up to her.

"It is not me that is going to die. I will live with family and find myself a new life. You will die alone, with no one to mourn you. Not even your son," my uncle replies, filling my heart with hope as I take another step towards Nane who starts flying towards me. Well, not me, Bee.

"Oh Elias, how I have missed my slave. One touch and you will be back in the darkness that you belong in," Tatarina purrs.

"No fucking way in hell. I'd rather die," Eli replies just as Nane shoots a blast of dark magic straight at us, sending me flying across the room, but luckily, I catch Bee before I slam against the wall. Looking up, I see Eli go flying in the air from a wave of magic, and Tatarina grabs my uncle by his neck, lifting him off the ground. I scream as she stabs a dagger through my uncle's chest, and he lets out a scream that will forever haunt me, then she throws him across the room like a toy. Tatarina locks her eyes with mine before she begins to talk as she slowly walks over.

"Now the pawns are out of the way, isn't it time for the queens to play?"

129

I jump in the air, pulling out another arrow before I shoot it into the chest of a dead guard who was running at me, then turn around and look for the others as the dead guard explodes into dust. There are dragons dying, screams, and so much pain around me, making it difficult to focus on anyone through it all. I spot Korbin on his own, fighting a big bunch of dead guards and run as fast as I can to him. I pass Essna with a few seers, who are making quick work of killing off the dead guards with their powers, though I know they won't be able to do that forever. Every part of me wants to shift into my dragon and fly to the castle to help Isola, but I know Dagan is doing that. Eli and her uncle are with her, and that has to be enough to give her a chance to win this once and for all. Even if it means killing my mother. A deep part of me knows I am mourning the idea of a mother rather than the person my mother actually is. I said goodbye to her a long time ago, and it's about time I accepted that. I will remember my adoptive parents, because they were really who brought me up in the end.

I let out a long whistle when I get close enough, drawing a good load of the dead guards my way as I pull out some daggers. I get two of them in their chests before going to grab my bow when arms wrap around me from behind, pulling me to the ground as I fight them off. I slide a dagger out from my thigh as the dead guard bites down on my shoulder. *Fucking hell, that hurt.* I slam my dagger into his stomach, making him let me go just as two dead guards run at me with long swords headed my way. I hold up a wall of flames with my hands, burning them to pieces that fall all over me before I stand up, coughing on the ash.

My eyes widen as I hear a noise, looking up to see a dragon falling out of the sky and directly for me. I run and jump over a body, just getting out the way as it lands with a thump. I look around as Kor finishes off the dead guards around him and runs over to me. We stand back to back as we fight more of the dead guards coming at us, and I frown as I see an angel falling from the sky. Isn't that Winter's mate?

"Kor, that way!" I shout, pointing an arm at the angel just as he lands on the ground, sending dust and ash flying everywhere. We fight our way over to the angel, standing over him until Kor gives me a nod to check the angel as he fights the remaining dead guards. I lean down, seeing the burns on his arms that don't look good, but I suspect the cut on his head is why he fell. I nearly jump as Atticus appears out of nowhere right next to us and falls to Dabriel's side. Atticus is covered in blood, his clothes ripped, and he doesn't look in a good state. I guess fighting dragons wasn't so easy. I look around us, seeing that there aren't many of our army left standing here, and there is a massive load of dead guards running our way. The academy steps lay right behind us, and if they pass us, then the people hiding in there will have no one to protect them. That isn't happening. The witch and angel both need to get out of here.

"Wake up, you moody sod!" he shakes Dabriel's shoulder, and Dabriel groans, coughing out dust as we both help him sit up. Kor lights up a ring of fire around us, temporarily defending us for a moment as we take a breather.

"Winter needs me," Dabriel suddenly says, still coughing as he looks at his burnt arms. Atticus lifts him up to stand up before making water appear in his hands and washing Dabriel's arms even though he screams out in pain from it. "Thank you, brother," Dabriel says, and I see that bond between them like I have with Dagan, Kor and even Elias now. We might not be brothers by blood, but that doesn't matter one bit. We are family, all in love with one fantastic woman who we will defend with our lives.

"Grab my arm, dragons, you should come with us. It's dangerous here," Atticus suggests as Kor and I lock eyes before turning away from the witch to face the hundred or more dead guards running at us. We don't have to talk through the bond to understand each other and what we know we have to do.

"Go! We have this. We will hold the academy doors," I tell Atticus, who bows his head before disappearing. The circle of fire disappears around us just as the army get close, and I lift my sword.

"For Isola," I say to Kor, who bows his head, lifting his own sword.

"For our Isola."

130

I crawl to my feet with a groan, feeling my ribs broken from the blast, and it's like all the oxygen has left my lungs with it. I cough a few times as I pick up my spear, seeing an angry Bee fly out of my hands and straight towards Nane, blasting her with a ball of light. Nane fights back, both of them hurting each other, and I know I need to stop it. Light and dark blast against each other, neither of them winning but both of them struggling as the power darkens the room, making all the fires go out.

"You are no queen, Tatarina," I turn to her, knowing I only have to hurt her enough to hold her down, and then I can get Nane and save Eli before killing Tatarina. The plan will still work. I swallow the pain as I lock eyes with Tatarina, not seeing any part of Thorne in her anymore. I thought it might hurt to kill his mother, but at this point, it is all I want, and I hope he will forgive me eventually. *She has to die.*

"And you think you are one? The silly little princess lost on Earth with no parents. Well, you had a daddy, but he was too busy with me to bother with you. Does it hurt that he chose me? That he never wanted you all those years ago?" she laughs, holding her hands out and sliding out two daggers that must have been hidden on her wrists.

"My father was a monster, and you two belonged together. I had a good life on Earth. One I would never change for anything," I reply to her, and her face contorts in frustration. We circle each other, hearing Nane and Bee fighting behind us. My uncle is dying by the throne, and I can't see where Eli is. She flings herself at me, and I duck, slinging my spear across her leg as I go, and she cries out in pain. I spin around just as she throws one of her daggers at me, scratching my cheek, and I gasp. She limps to the left, spinning her dagger around before making a sword of pure ice in her other hand.

"Nice trick," I say, and she laughs as I copy her, making myself a second spear. We run at each other at the same time, her sword blasting into my spear as she tries to stab me with the dagger, but I use my other spear to knock it out of her hands before I push her back. She falls over, and I walk to her as she picks herself up. My eyes widen in horror as Eli appears behind Tatarina, holding a sword to her neck.

"Don't kill her! You can't," I cry out, stepping closer with every word to see if I can stop him. If he kills her, he will die because I won't be able to bond to Nane in time to save him. Elias looks over at me with so much love in his eyes, and it breaks my heart because I know what he is going to do. Melody's warning enters my mind, the one where she told me to duck as I try to figure out a way to save Eli.

"I'd do anything to save you. *Anything*. Including this," he says, lifting his sword to make the final blow as I run towards them both, screaming in pure terror of losing Eli. Tatarina shoots a bolt of ice right towards me, and I fall to the ground, the ice bolt cutting the top of my shoulder. If I hadn't ducked, that would have gone through my heart and killed me. I look up as Eli slams the sword down over Tatarina's neck, cutting her head off, and her blood splatters all over him as her head rolls across

the floor. I cry out, not for Tatarina, but for Eli as he drops the
sword and screams in pain.

"I'm not going to let the darkness take you. Ever," I whisper,
pulling myself off the floor and standing up. "You once told me
our love was impossible, but it is not. I will save you."

"Let me go!" Elias shouts, shaking his head as he cries out in
pain, black lines crawling all over his face. I see Bee and Nane
floating around each other just behind me, trying to kill each
other, and yet they are equal. They are sisters, and they can't do
it. I know what has to happen. *No matter the cost.*

"Nane, you were never meant for Tatarina…You were mine
from the start. You appeared for me when I was only a baby in
my mother's womb. Tatarina found you instead," I say, knowing
with every part of my soul that I am right.

"Run!" Elias pleads, and tears stream down my face as I take
another step forward, right into the middle of Nane and Bee.
They both fly at me, and I hold both my arms out, keeping my
eyes locked with Elias as he realises what I'm about to do.

"No, they will kill you!" he shouts, just as Nane and Bee
touch my hands, and pain ripples through every part of my body.
The dark and light attack me at the same time, making me feel
like I'm being ripped apart. The pain is indescribable, and for a
moment, I can only cry out in agony.

"Stop," I cry out, and the pain slows, only for what feels like
a second, and I can open my eyes. My body is floating, there is a
half white and black orb of smoke surrounding me, and I can't
see the room anymore.

"Light or dark, there must be a choice," Nane demands, and I
turn to her, seeing only a scared spirit who doesn't know who
she is. Or who she belongs to.

"I think you will find I'm good at sharing. I will share with
you both and love you both equally. You are mine, both light and
dark. I am your balance, and I'm so sorry you didn't have me at
your side until now. We were meant to be all together, to bring

peace to Dragca. To save it," I say, and tears stream down her face as she walks up my arm before sitting on my shoulder.

"Save, no more fighting," she says quietly, her little voice filled with pain. "Darkness no more if that is what you want."

"The world needs dark, or you would never see light," Bee comments as she sits on my other shoulder. I smile proudly at her, knowing she is right. I don't want to get rid of the darkness; I just want to cause a balance.

"Let's save Dragca and my Eli. We need balance, and we must drain the darkness that is killing Dragca," I say, watching Nane's reaction because it is important she agrees. She nods, and I float down to the floor. I place my hands on the cracked ground and look up, seeing Elias's body lying on the floor near me, knowing he will never survive if I don't do this. I must drain the darkness out of him as well, pull it back to me, and keep him bonded to me forever.

"For Dragca," I whisper and close my eyes, slamming my power into the ground and pulling all the darkness I can find until everything disappears, and I feel myself falling with no chance of saving myself.

131

ISOLA

Two months later

"Link to the heart, link to the soul. I pledge my heart to you, for you, for all the time I have left. My dragon is yours, my love is yours, and everything I am, belongs with you," I say to Eli, not able to keep the huge grin off my face as our mating stone glows brightly in the priest's hands. We both let the priest cut our hands before placing them together, and the stone glows so brightly I can only see Eli in the room as the priest speaks. *My Eli*. I still relive the moment when I bonded with Nane and Bee; I managed to push enough light and dark into what was left of my Eli and save him. We are bonded in a strange way now, one that means we can sense each other, and I can keep him alive as long as I live. Eli has grown out his black hair, so it is similar to how we met, and his suit fits him lovely, showing off his muscles from the training he has been doing with Dagan and the new dragon guard army.

"Light and dark, good and evil, and everything that makes us dragons, please bless this mating. We bless you," the priest says, and the light blasts brightly as Eli pulls me into his arms and spins me around, making me laugh before he kisses me.

"We bless you," the hundreds of people in the throne room cheer as Eli puts me down and then turns to the priest. He picks up one of the four king crowns on the side as I walk past my other mates to stand in front of my father's throne. There are four new thrones, two on each side of me now, one for each of the kings of Dragca. I glance over at my uncle on the front row of my guests, holding hands with Essna. I was lucky Bee managed to save him after Tatarina's attack, and I was more surprised to find out he and Essna were in love. They mated a month ago while the castle was still being repaired, and now they run Dragca Academy which is being rebuilt, made better for our new generations.

I move my eyes from them to Melody and Hallie, who are talking quietly to Jonas who they adopted when Jonas' biological father didn't want him. I brought Jonas back here with Jules, who sits next to Hallie's side and proudly smiles at me. A few other dragons' children came back from Winter's castle with new families found here, but others decided to stay. It's a good way to keep Jonas in the family as I want to make sure he has a good life. Melody and Hallie can give him that, and they make a cute little family. Dagan, Korbin and Thorne all kneel next to Eli, all of their heads bowed in respect.

"Do you accept the throne? To be kings of Dragca and always defend your queen?" the priest asks my mates, the words feeling so important as this is a massive change for Dragca. We have set up a new council, healed the villages, and with Winter's witches' help, it was easy to rebuild the destroyed homes. The last two months have gone so quickly, and this day has been anxiously anticipated. This is the first day of peace in Dragca, one that I hope will stretch on for generations.

They all have ruby red cloaks on that match my red dress, and their crowns have a mix of red and blue stones. It suits them, and they do very much look like kings of Dragca in this moment. I never would have expected this for our future, but I know it is perfect.

"For my entire life, I will, and I accept," they all say in unison. I watch as the priest places a crown on each of their heads before moving back.

"Then rise, kings of Dragca," the priest says. As my kings rise up, the priest disappears into white dust. My kings come and stand in front of their thrones at my side, and we all sit down at the same time. Every dragon, seer and supernatural in the throne room cheers as I send a message to my mates.

I love you all.

EPILOGUE
ISOLA

I run a comb through my daughter's hair as she sits on a stool smiling at me in the reflection of the mirror in front of us. My daughter is a mini-me, her long blonde hair is the same colour as mine, and she has my blue eyes. Though I don't know who her father is exactly, it has never mattered. She calls them all dad. The day she was born, the whole of Dragca cheered and celebrated the royal birth. The pregnancy was long and difficult, and Jules was with me the whole time. Jules loves Dragca and my daughter, and I hope we still have many years with her yet.

Melody and Hallie adopted a baby girl only a year ago, a seer whose mother passed away. Jonas loves his new sister, and they live happily in the castle with us now. Every day, Jonas looks more like his brother, only his eyes are a little different. It makes me happy because I know Jace isn't all gone from the worlds. He is here with us.

"I can't believe you are five today, Emery. My baby is getting all grown up," I say, braiding her hair as she giggles at me. I slide her silver tiara on her head before sliding some clips in to hold it into place.

"Mummy, I'm a little girl now. Not a baby anymore," she tells me, and I can't help but laugh at her sassy answer. I swear my child is more sarcastic than anyone in the whole of Dragca.

"Oh, I'm sorry, miss little girl. I didn't realise. How foolish of me," I reply, enjoying her laugh. I finish her hair, and she slides off the seat. "Do little girls still hold their mummy's hand as we go to their birthday parties?"

"Of course, mummy," she says, taking my hand as I smile down at her. It seems like only yesterday that she was born, and yet I have to accept she is growing up now. The price all parents deal with, I imagine. We walk out of her very pink bedroom, which is next door to our own rooms, and down the corridor. I hear the children laughing before we even get to the ballroom, and two guards open the doors for us, bowing their heads. Emery lets go of my hand and runs into the room to Dagan, who catches her and swings her around as she giggles. He hugs her tightly before he puts her down and gives her a little present box from his jacket as I walk over. I see Jonas eating the food, Melody and Hallie are laughing with my uncle and Essna by the piano which Jules is playing a sweet song on. All the other children run over to see what the present is. I look back as Thorne places his hand on my back, kissing my cheek as we watch Emery rip the gift open and pull out a yellow collar.

"A collar? I don't understand," she says, seeming as confused as I am. I only know Dagan and Thorne left to go to Earth yesterday to get the present, and it is a big surprise. From the mischievous look Winter gave me when she got here yesterday, I know she had something to do with whatever this gift is.

"Well, you know how you really wanted a puppy from Earth? The ones like the stories mummy has told you?" Dagan asks, and he stands up, waving a hand at Elias and Korbin as they walk over with a black, fluffy puppy in their arms. The puppy is huge, with pointy ears and glowing purple eyes, which looks like no Earth puppy I've ever seen before. It has been a year or so since I went anywhere on Earth except Winter's castle, but still, not that much has changed. Emery squeals and runs over, repeating thank you a million times as they give her the puppy to hold, and it licks her face with a purple tongue.

"A puppy in a dragon castle?" I question Thorne with a long sigh, and he laughs.

"It's not just a normal puppy. It's a little different, so don't worry," he replies. "Adelaide promised it will grow wings soon."

"Wait, wings? It's from Frayan? The crazy fairy place? And what do you mean 'different'? Not dangerous 'different', I hope," I rapid question him and look back over at Emery who is clearly in love with her new friend. I suppose she could freeze the flying puppy if it is dangerous.

"Nope, not dangerous," Thorne says with a big smirk at my over protective nature and kisses me before letting go. "I'm going to check out the food. Want to come?"

"No, thanks. I'm going to say hello to Winter," I say, nodding at my friend who is sitting heavily pregnant on a chair by the window. Thorne smiles at me before I walk over, pulling up a chair and sitting down to rest my sore feet.

"Being pregnant sucks, doesn't it?" Winter protests, and I look down at my little bump, knowing I have a while to go yet.

"Yes, but at least the morning sickness is gone for now," I admit. I always thought that was the worst of the start of pregnancy issues.

"Though I will admit this pregnancy is much easier than the twins were," Winter says, and I follow her gaze over to her children who are a year older than Emery, and they are all extremely close. We all joke that Lucian is Emery's shadow, and we hope they date one day, linking our families. Lucian and Emery tell us we are all embarrassing them, which always makes us laugh as they have bright red cheeks when they tell us off. Alina and Emery are very close too, like sisters really, and hate when they can't spend the weekends with each other.

The supernatural school is opening next month in Dragca, mirroring the one open on Earth already. We have worked out a way to connect a portal between worlds that is in the schools, and Melody is starting a new class on all supernatural races. Bee and Nane helped with that. They have transformed the royal gardens into their homes, and now it is more beautiful there than it ever has been. They actually get along pretty well now, and after everyone got used to the fact Nane isn't all bad, it got better. Shaking myself out of my daydreams, I watch my daughter playing with her new puppy, all her friends around her, and how loved and happy she is. My mates are laughing with Winter's mates, and they have become good friends since the war.

"I think I'm carrying twins. Well, at least that is what Bee and Nane tell me," I quietly say, because I haven't told my mates what Melody told me this morning. She said she had a vison of the future and all our children together. They are going to be rulers to be proud of.

"At least you have a few mates to help with two newborns, Isola," she says, and we both laugh. "It's hard work, but worth it. Everything has been worth it."

"Do you think we will always have peace now?" I ask her, and she looks towards me.

"The fates gave us this life as a reward, and we will have peace. We fought our battles, and I'm glad we survived," she tells me, reaching over and holding my hand. I rest my head back on the chair as Emery waves at me before running to Eli, and he picks her up, making her laugh with whatever he said to her. I rest my other hand on my bump, feeling my babies kick, and smile.

We did more than survive, we won our wars, and we now live a life that could never be forgotten. We thrived and fulfilled our destiny. We fulfilled our fate.

The end.

132

EXCLUSIVE BONUS SCENE

"They don't make hot chocolate like this on Dragca, Win. I could drink this all day," I say after taking a long sip of from my cup and grinning up at my friend. Queen Winter winks at me before looking over at her mate Jaxson, and one of my mates, Elias as they both watch every person that walks past the small café we are sat in. I lean back in my seat, looking up at big ben in the distance, the old fashioned buildings that surround it.

"London is pretty amazing these days, huh?"

"I would prefer if you could have a craving for this café's hot chocolate any other time than when you're eight month's pregnant," Dagan says from his seat next to me, his arm wrapped around my chair.

"Craving is a craving," Winter says, sticking up for me, and she nods her head towards the counter where Atti is helping Korbin and Thorne que up to pay the bill. The café is full to the rim and we would never have gotten a table if Elias didn't demand some university student boys give their table up for a pregnant woman. Me. "Anyway, Atti is a witch and he can have you in front of the portal home in a second if anything happens." I smooth my hand over my bump as Dagan huffs in annoyance, knowing Winter is right. Winter needed some time away from her home just as much as I did. They have a tiny pair of twins at home, who are making them all exhausted, and a small day out to London is a perfect idea. I frown as Jaxson and Elias burst into the café, and Jaxson leans down as Elias waves for the others to come to the table.

"We should be leaving. There is still unrest in the city, and people are saying there are detectors out on the streets," Jaxson says. "I'm concerned they can sense Atti's magic and know we are here."

"What are detectors?" I ask, confused as I haven't heard that name before and seeing the worry on Winter's face.

"Human hunters with weapons. They have these machines that can sense magic called detectors. We have been monitoring their upgrades in technology recently, and it is quite frightening," Winter explains to me.

"We should leave then," I say, knowing there is no way anything is worth trouble while I'm pregnant and I cannot shift into my dragon. She is currently hibernating in a way, and I can just about shoot a strong of ice like I am. My body looks after the baby only, the way it should be. I stand up, only to cry out as a painful cramp slams into my stomach, making it feel tight like it could pop. It's too early for contractions, like a month too early.

"Issy," Thorne is the first one to grab me, holding me up.

"Was that a contraction?" Dagan asks, and it sounds like the whole café is silent as I nod, breathing out the next wave of pain. "The baby must be coming early."

"Outside. Now," Elias demands as Thorne and Korbin come back to my side in a hurry.

"Should we call an ambulance?" A human woman asks as Thorne picks up me up like a doll and carries me out. I hear one of the guys telling her they have a car outside before the door is opened and the cold air hits my face.

"Everyone hold on," Atti warns as we stop in a quiet alley by the café. I cry out as another contraction hits me, at the same time I feel Atti's magic move us away. Suddenly the world seems to spin, making nothing seem like it was and I feel Thorne let me go, sending the world into nothing but blurriness. Unexpectedly I fall onto a hard floor, pain reverting up my arm in the dark room. I cry out from the pain in my stomach, the water pouring out between my legs as my water breaks and how much my arm hurts.

"Isola? Jaxson? Anyone?" I hear Winter frantically shout and I pull my head up off the cold ground, looking around pointlessly in the dark for her.

"Win! I'm here, help me!" I shout back to her, my voice is nothing but desperate as I try to connect to where the hell we are.

"I didn't expect to see you here so soon, queen Isola," a familiar, old voice says before bright, warm light floods the room. I blink through the change in light as Winter gets to my side, and we both look at the hooded woman in a rocking chair. The ground in the room is all grass, and there is a strange bed of golden fluffy looking pillows in the middle.

"Who the hell are you and what do you want? If you think you are touching me or my friend, or her baby, then you have another thing coming. I will kill you first," Winter threatens, sliding in front of me and holding a hand out that glows blue.

"Niece, it is lovely to meet you and I mean neither of you any harm. Seems you have the same fire my sister always had," the fate says, and lowers her hood. Bright blue eyes, much like Winter's shine back at me and Winter drops her hand. I haven't seen the fate in a long time, not since I mated to Thorne and she helped us. I always felt safe around her, even if she has kidnapped me here.

"Why did you take us?" I ask her, my words ending on a cry as a contraction spirals through me.

"The child must be born with my supervision. I'm sorry for stealing you here, but I sensed the baby is coming. Some things must be," she replies. Oh, for the love of Dragca, she has to be kidding.

"Ahh!" I scream, holding onto my bump as Winter reaches for me, holding my hand as I lock my eyes with the fate. "I want my mates here right fucking now!" I shout at her.

"Do you want the child to be healthy and alive?" she smoothly replies, even laughing a little.

"Yes," I bite out.

"Then this is the way it must be. I promise once I have touched the child's hand, I will send you back to your castle and your mates. Both of you will be safe and that is all that is important," she responds, and I have trouble arguing with her when she is being so reasonable.

"Why did you let me come here?" Winter asks.

"This is the birth of a fate," she simply replies like that should answer everything.

"A fate?" I breathlessly ask, feeling the contraction building up as I struggle to talk. "My child is a dragon."

"There will be three new fates born, one to each important line. One of your future children, Winter, will be a fate. This child for you, Isola, is one. There will also be a fray child in the future. Each of these children are very special, and blessed in ways of the old magic and forever linked. I am linked to your child, Isola. I am her protector in a way. Please do not make my job difficult," she says, and crosses her arms. "All children used to be born with a fate and no mates in sight. I do not see why you need to complain."

"I don't have a choice," I bite out, my words ending on a long scream as sweat builds on my forehead. "But I love my mates and I would choose to have them here for this."

"Let's move you to that bed, Isola. I have had twins and I was there for two other births so I have an idea what to do. You are going to be okay," she whispers to me, trying to comfort me as best she can as I try not to cry. I need to be strong for my baby.

"Thank you," I say, crying out in pain as Winter helps me waddle to the pillow bed.

"I have delivered many babies as well," the fate adds and I glare at her.

"I don't trust you," I reply, a low growl filling my lips as my dragon stirs in my mind.

"That is a shame. I helped you many times," she resorts. "I am not bad."

"Bring my mates to me, and you have my trust," I reply. "Please."

"Not yet," she replies, rocking that damn chair of hers. I scream, feeling a building pressure and knowing I need to push. Winter finds a blanket and the fate clicks her fingers, making a bowl of water appear and towels. With Winter's help, we get my leggings and underwear off, and she helps me cover up with the blanket. I cry out for hours as I push, feeling like I am getting nowhere and Winter looks worried every time I rest, wanting to give up. I wipe my tears away, knowing I need my mates with me. I *never* planned to do this alone. All I want is them.

"I know you don't understand love, but I am begging you to get her mates. Isola *needs* them, and they will only bring love into this room for this baby. Fate's need love or they will not be what you need them to be. We both know this," Winter tells the fate, who stares at me as another contraction ripples through my body.

"Fine. It is not traditional, but love never is," the fate says and I smile for the first time since we got here as she clicks her fingers. All my men abruptly appear in the room and I don't know who to look at first. None of them ask questions as they run to me, wordlessly surrounding me and grabbing my hands. Korbin lifts my head up onto his chest, supporting me. Dagan speaks to Winter as he rests his hand on my leg. Elias and Thorne hold my hands tightly as I scream and push with every bit of strength I have.

"A girl," Winter tells me, and seconds later the sound of a

sweet baby cry fills the room and I cry in relief. Dagan helps Winter wrap our daughter as I cry into Korbin's chest and we all are so silent as we are overwhelmed with emotions as I can't wait to see her. Dagan lifts our baby, meeting my eyes with his tear filled ones as he hands me the tiny bundle.

"Hi," is all I can say to her as I take in her tiny little face, her sweet nose and pouty lips. She has my blonde hair, quite a lot of it and she is just perfect.

"How stunning," the fate says and I look up to see all my mates are frozen, and only Winter is left watching in silence as the fate comes to my side. She reaches a hand out, touching my babies little hand and there is a gold glow that shines for a moment. "She will be beautiful, brave and everything her destiny needs and more."

"I haven't forgotten my promise," I say, remembering how I promised to take her to the fate cave when she is older.

"I will train her there, and protect her for what is to come. When light is born, so very often the other side to the coin is as well," she apprehensively explains, and walks away to the other side of the cave as Winter reaches for my hand.

"What is her name?" the fate asks, not looking back as she speaks.

"Princess Emery of Dragca. The rightful queen and future fate," I say, knowing she will be so special in the future. I can see it in the fate's eyes, without even needing to look down at my daughter.

"We will see each other soon," the fate says, before the room rapidly fades away and I'm suddenly in my bed in my castle in Dragca. My mates all look around confused, and Winter just smiles at me from where she sat next to me on the bed.

"What the hell?" Thorne asks, rubbing his head as Winter and I can only laugh. Elias, Dagan and Korbin look just as confused.

"I think it's time I pop back home and tell my mates what happened. They might be a tad concerned," Winter says into the silence and I nod, wiping some tears away. "Congratulations, she really is beautiful like her mum."

"Thank you, dear friend," I say, reaching out and squeezing her hand before she climbs off the bed and walks to the door.

"Do we want to know what just happened?" Dagan asks, reaching over and stroking a finger down our babies face.

"Nope. Meet Emery, our daughter," I say, and I know we will discuss it more later. For now, we all hold our daughter, and watch as her beautiful blue eyes open to see the world.

133

EXCLUSIVE BONUS CONTENT

Remember the Wolf. (The Guardian Academy: Book One.)

My name is Em, short for...well I don't know. The social workers decided Emma was a good name for me.

See, I don't remember life before I was found naked on the streets of New York at only sixteen years old. That was two years ago, and I've been with my foster family ever since.

An accident filled, end of school trip leads me to find out my best friend isn't as human as she has been pretending to be, and it turns out neither am I.

At least humans don't shoot gold beams of light out of their hands as far as I know. I soon find myself at the gates to the Guardian Academy, a place for all young supernaturals to hide from humans and learn their powers safely.

If only I could remember my life...before it breaks my heart.

Based in the Her Guardians, Protected by Dragons and Her Fate world...

18+

EXCLUSIVE BONUS CONTENT

Prince Lucian

"For princess Emery to become who she needs to be- a fate. She must be forgotten. By you all," the old fate says, standing over me on my knees as I hold Emery as close as I can, feeling like I'm inches from fucking losing her after I just got her back. My mum said this fate is her aunt, and that she was there for Emery's birth. They are linked somehow. I can't even register what she just said until she repeats it once more.

"What the hell? Emery is the heir to Dragca, and so much more than that. No one could forget Emery," I growl out, feeling my wings itching to fly away with her. "You asked Isola to bring her to you early, and she did and only six months later you drop her outside your cave and tell me she has to be forgotten? I won't let you do this."

"Oh, you won't have a choice, prince. I'm sorry because things have changed that I did not see. Emery must pass the five choices of a fate to receive her power, and she must do this alone. I hoped to be with her, but my time as her guide is over. I sense your love for the princess, and if it is true, you will find each other once again, Prince Lucian," The fate finishes speaking before disappearing into nothing but silver dust on the ground. The dust raises into the air, spreading out like a blanket that stretches in every direction, before slowly lowering itself. I can sense the magic, and I know that I could never get Emery out of here in time to escape it. Reaching for Emery, I lean down, placing my hand on her pale cheek, pushing some of her long pale blonde hair out of the way and wishing she would open those beautiful blue eyes of hers. I've loved her since we were kids and I never told her. I was a stubborn idiot.

"Remember me, Emery. Find your home." I whisper to her, before kissing her lips as the silver dust washes over us, leaving nothing but dust in my hands that I can't remember how it got there. Or why I'm in Dragca to begin with.

Instagram
Facebook
Twitter
Pinterest

www.gbaileyauthor.com

Join Bailey's Pack

Join Bailey's Pack on Facebook to stay in touch with the author, find out what is coming out next and any news!

www.gbaileyauthor.com

ABOUT THE AUTHOR

G. Bailey is a USA Today bestselling author of books that are filled with everything from dragons to pirates. Plus, fantasy worlds and breath-taking adventures. Oh, and some swoon-worthy men that no girl could forget. G. Bailey is from the very rainy U.K. where she lives with her husband, two children and three cheeky dogs. And, of course, the characters in her head that never really leave her, even as she writes them down for the world to read!

Please feel free say hello on here or head over to Facebook to join G. Bailey's group, Bailey's Pack!
(Where you can find exclusive teasers, random giveaways and sneak peeks of new books on the way!)

Made in the USA
Columbia, SC
20 May 2024

35918785R00445